JACQUELINE BRISKIN

Jacqueline Briskin was born in London and grew
up in Beverly Hills, where she still lives. Her
bestselling novels include *Paloverde*, *Decade* (previously published as *California Generation*), *Rich Friends*,
and *The Onyx*.

By the same author

PALOVERDE
DECADE
RICH FRIENDS
THE ONYX

JACQUELINE BRISKIN

Everything and More

HarperCollins*Publishers*

HarperCollins*Publishers*
77–85 Fulham Palace Road,
Hammersmith, London W6 8JB

This paperback edition 1993
1 3 5 7 9 8 6 4 2

Previously published in paperback by Grafton 1985
Reprinted seven times

First published in Great Britain by
Granada Publishing 1984

Copyright © Jacqueline Briskin 1983

The Author asserts the moral right to
be identified as the author of this work

ISBN 0 586 06125 8

Set in Baskerville

Printed in Great Britain by
HarperCollinsManufacturing Glasgow

All rights reserved. No part of this publication may be
reproduced, stored in a retrieval system, or transmitted,
in any form or by any means, electronic, mechanical,
photocopying, recording or otherwise, without the prior
permission of the publishers.

This book is sold subject to the condition that it shall not,
by way of trade or otherwise, be lent, re-sold, hired out or
otherwise circulated without the publisher's prior consent
in any form of binding or cover other than that in which it
is published and without a similar condition including this
condition being imposed on the subsequent purchaser.

This is for
Bert and Lauren

Contents

Prologue

The gun was jarringly out of place.

This sunlit morning lacked the climate of violence. A breeze fragrant with citrus blossoms rippled through the small Beverly Hills back garden, while from beyond the tall redwood fencing came the peaceful racket of a suburban Sunday: a lawn mower's roar, toddlers' shrill cries, the masculine voices of Dodger warm-up coming from transistors – the home team was on a winning streak this June of 1970.

The two women facing each other across the handgun looked more as if they should be lunching together at the Bistro: both were in their early forties, handsome and obviously well-to-do. One wore slacks with a smartly cut taupe blazer, the other a Chanel blouse and skirt.

There was a small click as the safety catch was released.

'This is all crazy,' said the woman in slacks. Because she had known her attacker for so many years, she ventured a step closer.

'Stop!'

The intended victim halted. As she stared at the muzzle, her disbelieving expression hardened to horror. Her pupils contracted. Then, flexing her knees, she sprang, a clumsy, non-athletic leap, to grip the arm aiming the improbable weapon.

For a long moment that seemed an eternity, the pair remained locked in an outlandish wrestlers' hold.

The sharp sound rang out like a car backfiring.

One woman slumped to the ground. A heartbeat later, she died in the other's arms.

That gunshot would echo endlessly in print, on television, in people's hearts, for these two, together with another woman equally involved, led the sort of lives of which dreams are made. Between them they had vast wealth, beauty, acclaimed talent, triumphant careers, the adoration of famous men. The jealousies and loves, the friendships, the betrayals, the broken promises that formed a twisted path to this lethal moment would initiate hundreds of magazine and newspaper articles. A docu-drama mini-series starring Candice Bergen, Ann-Margret and Tuesday Weld would win an Emmy. There would be four critically acclaimed books written about the shooting, and Norman Mailer's *The Golden Girls* would become the runaway bestseller of the year.

In life and in death there was a heady glamour surrounding these three women who had everything – and more.

Book One
1941

Senator Robert La Follette often referred to Grover T. Coyne as the greatest criminal of the age. When Theodore Roosevelt spoke of 'the malefactors of great wealth', he aimed the remark at Grover T. Coyne. The name Coyne, in most people's minds, has always been synonymous with ruthlessness and staggering wealth.

– Grover Coyne, a Biography, *by Horace Soess*

GERMAN ARMY INVADES POLAND

– New York Times, *1 September 1939*

The casualties of last night's raid were dreadful. In almost every block, houses are gone. Yet today Londoners are defiantly gay, the women wearing their smartest spring hats, the men their brightest ties.

– *Edward R. Murrow's* This is London, *28 April 1941*

Early this morning Chilton Wace, an employee of Roth's Haberdashery, 20098 Long Beach Boulevard, Long Beach, was shot by an intruder. He is reported in grave condition at St Joseph's Hospital, Long Beach.

– Los Angeles Times, *19 May 1941*

1

Marylin Wace leaned towards a medicine-cabinet mirror with a triangle broken from the lower-left corner, the only decent-size mirror in the house. She plucked a stray eyebrow with old loose-screwed nail scissors, and her hand did not falter at the loud bangs that shook the thin door behind her.

'What are you doing, camping in there?' Roy shouted.

Not answering her younger sister, Marylin extracted a hair with her makeshift tweezers.

There was more banging. 'I'll be tardy! Oh, now you've done it!' Roy's panic was comedic exaggeration. 'I'm wetting my pants!'

'Won't be a sec, Roy,' said Marylin, peering at her reflection to ascertain she had a clear arch.

The pronounced widow's peak of soft, gleaming brown hair and the small cleft of chin gave the face in the mirror a piquant charm. The nose was delicate, the clear skin luminous. Four months short of her seventeenth birthday, Marylin Wace would have been exceptionally pretty if it weren't for her eyes. The greenish-blue eyes had a depth that stopped her from being china-doll pretty. Without resorting to hyperbole, Marylin was a memorably beautiful girl.

Passing her tongue over Tangee Rose coloured lips, she formed a smile that was surprisingly free of narcissism. Marylin lacked even the most timid vanities of adolescence. As far as she was concerned, her beauty was merely a

13

validated passport to enter into the life of each new school. Through the Depression, the Wace family had moved at least three times a year – they moved whenever Chilton Wace was energized by his wife's Georgia-accented insistence that he look for a job 'a mite more worthy of your talents'. A good-natured hypochondriac with a wide aristocratic forehead and neat features, he relied on his feisty little spouse to make his decisions.

The Waces had been living in Long Beach, California, for nearly five months. Marylin's looks and gentle, quiet charm had eased her into the right clique at Long Beach Jordan High School.

She licked her finger to smooth both eyebrows. Because she fretted over her lack of height – she was a scant five feet tall – she pulled herself as straight as she could as she emerged.

Roy made a mock bow. 'Lovelier than Garbo,' she said sourly, then grinned. 'It's nearly worth wetting your pants over.'

'Oh, you,' said Marylin, affectionately tousling her sister's vibrant brown hair.

Roy was twelve, and her redundancies (affectionately called 'Pudgy Pudge' by her father) had not yet blossomed or indented into the curves of puberty. Her wide smile, large round eyes, and tilted nose gave her the look of a pretty, eager teddy bear. She considered herself triply cursed by her weight, her freckles, and her wayward auburn-brown curls that no amount of brushing could subdue. 'Pa didn't get home,' she worried.

'I know.' Marylin's eyes showed similar concern. 'That inventory's sure taking a longer time than he figured.' Chilton Wace was currently employed in Roth's menswear shop on Long Beach Boulevard, and Mr Roth had assigned him – the only full-time employee – to take inventory in the dim, cramped stockroom with its unpainted shelves of dungarees and racks of vivid, big-shouldered sportswear favoured by the dockhands and oil crews who inhabited the port town.

'Slave labour, that's what it is. Pa's too darn good-natured,' Roy said. The bathroom door closed on her.

Marylin was in a board-enclosed porch. Strong morning sunlight came through the glazed door which was the makeshift bedroom's only window, and there was a pervasive odour of petroleum from the surrounding forest of oil rigs. She edged around, making her and Roy's sagging iron beds, humming in tune with her mother's loud, cheerfully off-key rendition of 'South of the Border'.

A single room at the front of the cottage served as dining room, parlour, master bedroom and kitchen.

NolaBee Fairburn Wace was flipping pancakes at the old high-legged stove. NolaBee's skin had the drab, pocked texture that is a leftover from bad acne. Her features weren't pretty enough to make up for this flaw, and she would have been classified as a homely woman – if it weren't for the snap and sparkle of her small brown eyes and the mobile expression that indicated curiosity, interest, life. NolaBee Wace's nomadic existence had worn down neither her girlhood enthusiasm nor her sense of fun.

Her thin brownish hair was coiled in many strips of newspaper, a dishcloth of flour sacking served her as an apron, protecting her worn blue kimono.

'Good morning, Mama,' Marylin said as she went to kiss her mother's drab cheek.

Without removing the cigarette that dangled from her mouth, NolaBee smiled at this gorgeous creature who had improbably sprung from her. 'That blouse is right becoming,' she said. 'I reckon it never looked so good on Aunt Lucie Fairburn.'

Marylin forced a smile. The one thing she did not admire about her optimistic, lively mother was the way that NolaBee took it for granted that the Waces should wear hand-me-downs. Chilton Wace's wanderings during the Depression had never taken the family back to Greenward, Georgia, so Marylin did not know firsthand the home-place of generations of Waces, Roys and Fairburns, but she had learned the town's convoluted genealogies by the ribbon-tied cartons of old clothes that arrived every Christmas. Back in Greenward this cousin overused mothballs, that niggardly aunt cut off every button, this in-law sweated corrosive acid into her clothing.

'Here,' her mother said, sliding three large brown pancakes onto a plate. (At the beginning of the month there would have been bacon.) The table was not set: NolaBee kept house casually, messily, cheerfully, and meals were eaten wherever, *chez* Wace.

This sunny April morning Marylin elected to breakfast perched on the window ledge, and as she ate, she gazed down the steep slope that levelled out near the harbour. Tall, oil-blackened rigs towered over shabby little houses set amid untended yards. Marylin tilted her head to see the grey frame shack where a jazzy piano sounded all night and men came and went. With tight lips NolaBee had warned both girls not to go near – or even to look at – the place, so Marylin understood this was a bad house. Naturally she was forever angling for a sight of the three vividly dressed women who dwelt there. Each time she succeeded in glimpsing one, she felt a pang of guilt. Her mother did not want her to, and Marylin, though she had not inherited her father's timidity, was a dutiful child. Obedience was her one means of repaying NolaBee's lavishly adoring love.

NolaBee asked, 'Going to the Drama Club again this afternoon?'

Marylin turned hastily, blushing. 'We're reading *The Male Animal*.'

'I reckon you're the best little actress there.'

'Not by a long shot, Mama.' Marylin sighed.

'You need more confidence,' said NolaBee with an amused chuckle. 'Else you're never going to make it in Hollywood.'

A prodigiously enthusiastic fan of everything and everyone connected to the screen, NolaBee read and reread her tattered pile of *Modern Screen*s and never missed the broadcasts of Hedda Hopper and Louella Parsons. She gossiped about Claudette, Joan, Clark, Tyrone and Errol as she would family members. Whenever there was any spare change, she treated the girls to double-bill Saturday matinees, and more than half-seriously twitted her gorgeous elder, her pet, about becoming a star.

'Drama Club's a good way to meet people, that's all,' Marylin said, dipping a slim wedge of pancake in syrup.

'You'll be able to use everything you've learned, I reckon, once you're signed.'

Marylin's dreams had nothing to do with movie fame, but were mundanely centred on falling in love, marrying, having babies. 'Oh, Mama, stop teasing. You know I'm not any good.'

'What are you saying! Last Christmas in San Pedro, who got more curtain calls than anyone?'

'Mama, a high-school play, and – '

'Mrs Wace?'

Both mother and daughter turned towards the voice.

At the rusty screen door stood a tall, gangly boy. Marylin recognized him as the part-time janitor who worked with her father at Roth's. His name was Jimmy Brockway, and like her he was a junior at Long Beach Jordan; when they passed in the hall, he sometimes stammered out a greeting.

'Yes, I'm Mrs Wace,' said NolaBee.

'My name's Jimmy Brockway, I work at Roth's Menswear . . .' His voice petered off in a miserable gasp as if he were clutched in a stranglehold.

'Yes?' encouraged NolaBee.

'I sweep before I go to school . . . This morning, when I got there . . .' His voice faded again.

NolaBee's curl papers tilted at an odd angle. 'I reckon you saw Mr Wace, then?'

'Uhh, maybe I'd better come inside.'

NolaBee, usually so swift and sure, did not move, so Marylin set down her plate and went to unhook the screen door.

The boy's Adam's apple bobbled as he looked at her; then he turned away. Fixing his attention on the double bed, which was rumpled only on one side, he mumbled,

'Uhh, there was a problem over there. Mr Roth sent me to tell you.'

NolaBee and Marylin continued staring at him.

'Mr Wace . . . he . . . uhh . . .'

'Go on,' Marylin whispered.

'He's in the hospital,' the boy blurted.

Marylin gasped. NolaBee gave one loud cry.

'What happened? What's wrong with him?' Marylin demanded hoarsely. Among her father's numerous complaints about his health were chest pains.

'I don't know. Mr Roth just told me to tell Mrs Wace to get on over to St Joe's – St Joseph's.'

'Yes, the hospital,' said NolaBee, her face pale and squeezed into piteous lines.

'I'll take you – I have a car.'

NolaBee, yanking off the dishcloth-apron and pulling on a sweater, the brown one that Cousin Thela Roy had sent with holes already in both elbows, rushed out into the too bright sunlight.

'My sister!' Marylin cried urgently. 'I have to get my sister!'

She ran through the boarded porch, banging on the bathroom door. 'Roy. *Roy*.'

'You took your own sweet time, now let – '

'Open up! It's Pa – he's in the hospital.'

The door burst open. Roy stood there, the Arm and Hammer baking soda that the Waces used as toothpaste caking her mouth, which was nearly as white. As Marylin was NolaBee's girl, so Roy was her father's favourite.

NolaBee and Marylin sat up front in the Onyx jalopy while Roy rode in the rumble seat. Aside from that, not one of the three could ever remember any other details of the brief ride to St Joe's.

2

The Onyx shuddered to a stop in front of the hospital's stucco Virgin. Roy clambered down from the rumble seat and raced up the steps ahead of her mother and Marylin.

In the empty lobby she halted a few feet from the reception desk. A wizened peroxide-blond nurse continued reading her *Saturday Evening Post*, ignoring the intruders.

NolaBee's face seemed shrunken inside the Medusa's nest of curlers. Garrulous in almost any situation, she approached the desk silently.

It was Marylin who said in her soft little voice, 'We're looking for Mr Wace, he was brought here this morning. Do you know what's wrong with him?'

'Weights?'

'W-a-c-e,' Roy spelled.

The nurse slowly bobbed the eraser end of a pencil down a page of names.

'W-a – ' Roy started.

'Little girl, I'm not deaf,' said the nurse.

NolaBee gave a small cough. 'Is it his heart?'

The nurse, opening her magazine, said, 'Go down the left corridor as far as you can go, then turn to the right. You'll come to doors with a sign on them.'

Marylin and NolaBee gripped hands while Roy darted ahead of them.

On each of the double doors was painted:

Emergency Ward
No Entry
Ring for Information

'Emergency,' NolaBee whispered. 'Emergency?' A chrome and leatherette couch was pushed against the wall, and she sank down on it as if her legs had given way. Hand at her mouth, she watched Marylin press the button. A metallic buzz sounded briefly.

The three Waces stared expectantly at the doors. The faraway sounds continued, voices, a rumbling as if wheeled carts were being moved.

Nobody came out.

Roy jammed her finger down on the button, keeping it there.

After what seemed an interminable length of time both doors banged open and a short, fat nurse bustled out. 'What do you think you're doing with that bell?' she demanded.

'We're the Waces,' Roy said.

'Family of Mr Chilton Wace,' Marylin added politely.

'There's no need for this sort of ruckus!' The nurse glared at Roy. 'As soon as there's anything to hear, you'll be told.'

'But we don't know what's wrong with my husband,' said NolaBee in a strange, humble voice. 'What's happened to him?'

The nurse stared at her, taking in the old kimono beneath the disreputable sweater, the paper curlers. Then her scornful gaze turned to Roy, who had not yet put on her shoes or socks, her glance rising disdainfully to the curly brown hair that had been blown into a tumbleweed during the ride in the rumble seat. Her glance slid over Marylin to her immaculately polished saddle shoes bought on sale for a dollar because they were scuffed. 'That's for the surgeon to tell you,' she said coldly.

'Surgeon?' asked Marylin. 'But I thought . . . Nurse, hasn't he had a heart attack?'

The nurse backed through the left door.

Before it swung shut, Roy caught glimpses of a corridor that was empty except for a stretcher. She opened her mouth and began to scream.

The nurse bobbed back. 'Quit that racket,' she hissed.

'What's wrong with my Pa?' Roy howled.

'You damned little Okie charity case, don't you know you're in a hospital?'

20

'Where is my Pa?' Roy shrieked.

'He's in the operating room,' snapped the nurse with a malevolent glare. 'He was shot in the chest. Doctor's trying to get out the bullet, and I shouldn't be surprised if all this caterwauling has jarred his hand.'

Roy's screams halted abruptly.

NolaBee said in a flat, questioning tone, 'A gunshot?'

They stared at one another.

'There must have been a robbery,' said Marylin dully. 'Don't you think so, Roy?'

Roy couldn't answer. She was biting her lower lip to prevent her sobs from welling up.

'He'll be all right, Mama, he'll be all right,' said Marylin, her cheeks streaked with tears.

All through the morning they sat on the hard, cold couch, NolaBee gripping Marylin's hand. They were in an isolated part of the hospital and nobody came by except an old black woman swishing a broad, Lysol-soaked mop. She obviously didn't know anything, but that didn't stop Roy from inquiring about Mr Chilton Wace.

Roy felt as if she were suspended too high in a swing so that her stomach was eternally dropping away from her. Pa, oh Pa, you must get well, you must. Horrible itches erupted on her freckled arms and legs.

NolaBee reproved in a strangely pitched voice, 'you're not a monkey, Roy.'

Roy stopped scratching herself. Another itch became excruciating: unconsciously, she flayed it with her nails.

The big clock over the door ticked with agonizing slowness to 11.48.

Then the same short, fat nurse emerged through the doors.

The Waces rose, facing her.

'Dr Winfield asked me to tell you that Mr Wace never regained consciousness,' she said without inflection. 'He expired a few minutes ago.'

The widow and two orphans burst into spasms of grief that are natural in moments of disaster. NolaBee sank into Marylin's arms.

Roy flung herself onto the chill, comfortless couch, her sobs quickly ceasing. She was shivering with a chill more intense than she had ever experienced. Pa, oh Pa, how could you leave me utterly alone forever?

Mr Roth came over that afternoon, bearing a large, almond-filled coffee ring. He wept real tears when he passed on the little information he possessed. He had quit work around midnight, leaving Chilton to finish counting the Levi coveralls – 'Our biggest-selling item, we stock every size,' he explained. This morning he had returned to find his shop ransacked and his employee bleeding and unconscious in a heap of denim. Until now, he apologized, he'd been stuck down at the police station. 'I'll find out for you about the workmen's comp,' he promised as he left.

That Friday he returned with the forms. The Wace family would get $500 in cash, and $50 a month – $25 for the widow and $12.50 each for children below the age of eighteen.

After Mr Roth left, NolaBee lit her last Camel with tremulous hands. 'Five hundred dollars – that's more money than I've ever seen. But I reckon it won't go much further than paying off what we owe at the hospital and the mortuary.' Her voice cracked on the final word, but she continued resolutely. 'That fifty a month is half what your pa made, and we weren't livin' right lavish on *that*.'

'What about Greenward?' asked Marylin. Tears turned her huge, beautiful eyes greener. 'Will we go back?'

'Back?' Roy burst out with the combativeness that even in her worst hours she was unable to quench. 'I've never been there. And neither have you.'

'Your people live there,' said NolaBee, puffing smoke.

'Swell,' Roy said. 'Let's go where we can personally kiss their pinkies when they donate their smelly old clothes.'

'Lord, Lord, how I hate those hand-me-downs.' NolaBee sighed.

Both daughters turned to her in surprise.

'Well, that's news,' Roy said.

'What would you have had me do, little Miss Smart Mouth?' said NolaBee, affectionately tousling the reddish-brown curls. Then she coughed. 'I couldn't let your pa know how much I hated those old things. He felt bad enough as it was, not bein' a millionaire financier.'

Roy sniffed back a sob.

NolaBee handed her a handkerchief. 'We're not going home until it's a triumph,' she said. As punctuation, she tapped the long ash into her empty coffee cup.

'Mama, we're poorer than ever,' Marylin sighed.

'I reckon we're never going to let the family think your pa didn't take real good care of us. I don't want to hear a one of 'em ever saying, "Poor Chilton, he left his family poorly fixed".'

'What'll we do?' Marylin asked.

'Maybe win the Irish Sweepstakes,' said Roy.

'I'll think on it,' said NolaBee.

Two mornings later the sisters woke to find their mother sitting on Marylin's bed. The air smelled smoky, as if she had been there a long time.

'You look right young, Marylin,' she said.

'Everybody says nineteen.' Marylin's soft voice held a rare hint of testiness.

'Like this, no more than fourteen,' NolaBee pronounced. 'That's what your age is now.'

'I'll be seventeen in August,' said Marylin.

'You'll be fifteen then. We're moving to Beverly Hills.'

'Beverly Hills!' Iron springs twanged as Roy jumped from the bed. 'On what? The big loot from workmen's comp?'

'I'll find work. We'll manage.'

'Why Beverly Hills?' asked Marylin apprehensively.

'The movie people all live there. They have children in the high school.'

'And the town's sent out an SOS to recruit impoverished students?'

'All right, Roy. I've had enough of your mouth.' NolaBee

23

spoke tartly, but her hand rested gently on Roy's pudgy waist. She understood how much the child was devastated by her father's death. 'When Beverly Hills High puts on a play, I reckon there's scads of important studio folk there.'

'Mama . . .' Marylin sank back into the mended pillow-case, her eyes glazed with horror.

'Every place we've been, you've had the lead.'

'I try hard, I don't mind memorizing, but – '

'You're *good*.'

'Not in a place like Beverly Hills. Anyway, I'm nearly a senior – '

'You're fourteen,' NolaBee said inexorably.

'No, Mama. Please – '

'You need a right long time to let those big producers see you. Two extra years.'

Marylin began to sob softly.

Roy stared at the lovely bent head. And like an electric light suddenly going on, she understood a fact that had hitherto eluded her. Marylin paid a high price for her closeness with their mother. NolaBee, for all her vivid energy, lived by and through her beautiful daughter, vicariously sharing Marylin's triumphs, accepting her accolades, weeping her tears, intruding into her soul. And Marylin was tender enough to permit the invasion.

Roy jerked away from her mother's grasp. 'Mama, the whole idea's dum-dum. That's what comes from reading too many fan magazines.'

'I reckon they do write a lot of hooey about how stars get discovered, but there's a lot of truth, too. Actresses have to come from somewhere.'

'You can't really mean me to pretend I'm two years younger and keep getting up in front of those big shots?' Marylin said, raising her tear-streaked face.

'You've always got the most applause,' NolaBee said, for once adamant with Marylin.

'And it's not exactly because she's Katharine Cornell,' Roy said.

'I reckon the studio talent scouts know where to find

Katharine Cornell, but they aren't looking. They don't want Broadway actresses, they want beautiful girls.'

'Mama, it's crazy, there's no chance,' wept Marylin.

'I reckon you're a Roy, a Wace, a Fairburn. You'll make a chance,' said NolaBee. Drawn and pale, she looked like a gambler placing his last chip.

Book Two
1943

This year, because of the war, the Board of Education has been busier than ever. Immediately after the entrance of the United States into the war, the Board ordered air-raid drills to be put into practice. In cooperation with the Civilian Defense, essential supplies were purchased.

– Beverly Hills High School Watchtower, *1942*

Beverly Hills High School presented its annual Shakespearean Festival on 23 and 24 April for students and for the PTA mothers' tea. The sensation of the festival was Marylin Wace in the role of Juliet from Romeo and Juliet.

– Ibid.

Fernauld, Joshua R.: Writer, director. B. Bronx, New York, 20 Jan. 1896: ed., New York public sch. m. Ann Lottman, two children, Barbara Jane and Lincoln. Newspaper writer, novels Victims *and* Journey. *Began assoc. with screen in 1921, writing* Victims (Columbia). *Other films include* Lava Flow, *1938, Academy Award. Directed* Vigilance (Paramount), *1939.*

Pictures include: That Lost Love, Princess Pat, Mr Kelbo Goes to Berlin, After the Fall, Spring Laughter.

– International Motion Picture Almanac, 1942-43

There is an unspeakable clamor as the planes warm up before attack. When the last planes have left the deck, the commander's specially marked plane appears suddenly on the flight deck, brought up by an incredibly fast elevator.

– Life *article about Navy pilots, 2 April 1943*

3

Marylin sat holding a script on her lap, part of the semi-circle on the dusty, shadowy stage of the Beverly Hills High School auditorium. Like the other girls, she wore a pleated skirt and a pastel sweater that matched her Bonnie Doone ankle socks – the uniform for any girl uninterested in courting a reputation as a freak. The boys onstage wore the de rigueur cords and white shirts with the two top buttons open, and the sleeves rolled to just above the elbow. None of them could afford to look different. As it was, they were already considered weirdos or exhibitionists for taking Radio Speech or working on the Shakespearean Festival or bounding around the stage like *cucarachas* in the Voice Choir's production of a home-grown musical, *Fiesta*. They were the Juniors talented and devoted enough to drama to stay after school for these preliminary rehearsals of the class play.

They fidgeted tolerantly while BJ Fernauld, an over-weight, round-faced girl with a large red bow pinned behind her teetering black pompadour, scribbled down the margin of a smudged mimeograph sheet. BJ's father was Joshua Fernauld, the famous Oscar-winning screenwriter, and doubtless Miss Nathans, the drama teacher, when selecting BJ's comedy as the class play, had fallen under the influence of what BJ – in vaguely boastful secrecy – had admitted to her classmates was her father's 'light polish job'.

'Egads, I'm a genius,' BJ chortled, then pitched her tone

29

a couple of decibels deeper into what she considered a stage voice, booming, 'I can't find any evidence in my grade book to give you a B, Vera.'

'But Miss Brighton . . .' Marylin, playing Vera, groaned winsomely. 'Without the B, I'll flunk out of school.'

BJ: Precisely what you deserve.

Marylin: But why?

BJ: For just one example, you slept through class while I read *Romeo and Juliet*.

Marylin: I always did wonder how it turned out.

Marylin read the last line with arch yet adorable innocence, and the little group's laughter rustled through the dusty wings.

'Every time you say that, it cracks me up,' chuckled Tommy Wolfe, who pulled his chair slightly forward, a ploy enabling him to gaze unobstructedly at Marylin.

'Perfect comic timing,' BJ said. Her messy pompadour bobbled as she nodded admiringly.

'Aw, shucks, thanks,' said Marylin, miming diffidence by scraping the toe of one saddle shoe on the dusty boards.

The next half-hour she submerged her being into that of a flirtatious scatterbrain.

Marylin was jarringly superior to her fellow players. Though she modestly accepted this, she had no real comprehension of her own talent. The truth was, she viewed herself as a rather wishy-washy type. So how come on the stage she could turn into a fiery sexpot, a gawky brain, a vulnerably grief-stricken older woman in her twenties, a coldly intelligent bitch, a wise-cracking flirt, an ignorant peasant girl? She empathized with people, of course, but a lot of kids had an ability to fit themselves into another's shoes. She worked indefatigably, but that wasn't the entire answer, either. The closest she had come to summing up her abilities was to visualize herself as a clear glass pitcher into which every coloration of a role could be poured.

The important thing was that in the past two years, acting had become her salvation.

Marylin, dutifully obeying her mother, had kept those

two deducted years a secret. She walked the broad corridors of Beverly High and sat in its well-lit classrooms feeling a fake, a phony, a liar. Each time a messenger brought a note for the teacher, fear clutched her. Had Mr Mitchell, the ascetic-faced principal, uncovered the truth? Was this a summons prior to public expulsion?

Yet could she honestly label her years here as unhappy?

How was unhappiness possible at Beverly High?

The citizens of Beverly Hills spared no expense in educating their young. Few parents, even the world-famous and the vastly wealthy, considered sending their offspring to private schools. Why should they? Beverly High was a lovingly constructed temple to the goddess of learning. Cream-painted wings welcomed the students. Each morning as they trooped up the rolling green lawns, they saw carved on the lintel above the main doorway the gracious Sanskrit quotation: 'Today well lived makes every yesterday a vision of loveliness, every tomorrow a vision of hope.' The campus was lavished with patios, vine-covered pergolas, a square bell tower, tennis courts, playing fields; the school had an elaborate auditorium, professionally equipped shops and sewing and cooking classrooms. Its unique feature was an indoor swimming pool over whose chlorinated surface an electrically controlled parquet floor rolled out for dances or CIF basketball games: the cost of this was defrayed by an oil rig that pumped steadily in a discreet corner of the football field. The teachers, selected with more care than most university professors, presided over a campus that pulsated and jumped with energetic, mostly affluent, beautifully dressed, decently polite kids.

Marylin would have welcomed their friendship. Before this, she had reached out helplessly, gregariously to her schoolmates, but the secret permeated her like a dread disease, and she feared letting anyone close to her. In the crowded halls boys shuffled along worshipfully at her side; they hovered around her lunch table; a few of the most courageous asked for dates. To succour NolaBee's belief that she was the belle of belles, Marylin accepted bids to

31

proms and hops. The other invitations she rejected: 'What a shame . . . I'm busy that night.' In the inescapable affinities of Drama and Radio Speech, she formed tenuous wisps of friendships that she cut the instant she crossed school boundaries. If anyone, male or female, with a car offered her a ride home, she had a standard excuse: 'Thanks, but I promised to pick up some things for Mother.'

The Waces lived on Charleville in an illegally converted apartment above a garage, and when Marylin got home she would stand on the rickety, paint-peeling steps, inhaling long, slow belly breaths until her shoulder and neck muscles unclenched. She could never let herself respond naturally – and told herself she should be glad of the challenge: she was immersed in a perpetual role, wasn't she?

'. . . and now where is that shovel?' asked Tommy Wolfe.

Marylin replied, 'In your hand, loverboy.'

'End of act one,' said BJ. 'Curtain to tumultuous applause.'

Suddenly from the shadow-lashed darkness under the balcony burst the enthusiastic clapping of one pair of hands. 'Bravo, bravo!' called a pleasantly timbred masculine voice. 'Is this tumultuous enough?'

The group squinted in astonishment towards their unseen audience.

'Linc?' BJ jumped to her feet, raising a hand over her eyes to peer. 'Ye gods, it can't be!'

'No, it's Douglas MacArthur, I have returned. BJ, old girl, that's a pretty fair play, even if I do detect Big Joshua's fine hand.'

'How long have you been here?'

'About twenty minutes.'

'I mean, in Beverly Hills.'

'About thirty minutes. Nobody was home but Coraleen. She suggested you might be here.'

'Oh, you creep, you rotten creep. Sitting up there and not letting me know! Mother and Daddy'll kill you for not writing that you've got a leave.' BJ ran down the steps and up the aisle towards a tall young man dressed in a pale blue sweater and grey slacks. They hugged, continuing to talk. From the stage their bantering insults weren't fully audible, only the ripe affection in their voices. Though the intruder wasn't in a Navy officer's uniform, it was obvious who he was. BJ's older brother. She bragged constantly about Lieutenant (junior grade) Lincoln Fernauld, Beverly High class of '37, a Navy pilot aboard the *Enterprise*.

Arms around each other's waists, brother and sister strolled in step through the gloom towards the stage, and Marylin, looking at Lincoln Fernauld defined obscurely against the shadows, could see that his was a slender basketball player's build with long legs and broad, graceful shoulders. As the duo moved up the steps to stage left, she saw the strong sibling resemblance: the same thick black hair (his was crew-cut) and heavy black eyebrows and craggy nose. It was strange, though, how much more agreeably the features translated onto his long masculine face. His mouth went down on the left side as he smiled at them.

'Everybody, my brother. Lieutenant Abraham Lincoln Fernauld, born on the twelfth of February. Stinkin' Lincoln – or Linc.'

She introduced them in turn. When she reached Marylin, Linc Fernauld's grin faded momentarily. 'Maybe I've been stuck away from civilization too long,' he said. 'But you were pretty fantastic, Mare.'

She winced. This abbreviation of her name always made her wince. 'Thank you,' she said, adding with a tinge of aggression, 'It's Marylin. M-a-r-y-l-i-n.'

He raised one eyebrow wryly. 'Interesting spelling. Should go over big on the marquee.'

'It's a family name,' she said.

'One thing. Unless you want 'em shuffling and coughing in the balcony, you'll have to project a bit more.' This last remark was said with a thoughtful frown, and she sensed he spoke not to put her in her teenage place but to give his impression of her performance.

'My *bête noire*, a small voice.'

Everyone was gathering up coats, sweaters, books. In a chattering tangle they clumped up the aisle to the door that was left unlocked for them.

Linc, Marylin and BJ lingered in the vestibule, where the late-afternoon sun filtered through the windows to cast a golden tarnish on Beverly High's cased silver trophies.

'Come on, Beej,' Linc said. 'Treat you to a hot-fudge sundae at Chapman's.'

'Chapman's?' BJ said hopefully, then groaned. 'I'm on a diet.'

'Still? Well, we have Marylin along. She can eat it for you.'

'I'm sorry, but . . .' Marylin's routine refusal faltered. Linc was watching her. His dark brown eyes held an eloquently complex message: awe, lust, admiration, and another quality, indecipherable and compelling. She tried to look away and failed.

'Omigawd!' BJ hit her head. 'I can't do anything. This is Tuesday. Mrs de Roche will be there in twenty minutes.'

'Still pounding away on the Steinway?'

'My lesson's at five.'

'I'll drop you off at home,' Linc said, still looking at Marylin. 'Somebody has to eat your sundae.'

Marylin nodded.

Simon's, the big round drive-in on Wilshire Boulevard, served as official hangout for the Beverly High élite and those desirous of emulating them. Chapman's, an ice-cream parlour on Santa Monica Boulevard about a half-mile from school, drew only youthful gourmets interested in rich and delicious ice cream. At five the place was empty except for an older woman waiting at the cash register for her pint of chocolate to be mashed down into a cardboard container.

Marylin and Linc sat in the rear booth, facing one another. His glass was empty except for a residue of fudge in that indented pit where the spoon cannot reach. She was still conveying tiny coffee-flavoured spoonfuls to her mouth. Ice cream, Marylin's favourite food, was a rare luxury in the impoverished Wace household, and her habitual method of savouring any treat was to string it out as long as possible.

'You're a remarkably slow eater,' he said.

'Things I enjoy I do slowly.'

'I'll have to remember that,' he said, his voice slightly rougher, as if it came from a different part of his throat.

The tone shivered a strange, dauntless pleasure throughout Marylin's body. She smiled at him, then looked down, twirling her spoon in the last, softened dregs of pale brown.

'Have a steady?' he asked.

'Nobody.'

'Are you a Senior?'

'A Junior.'

'BJ's play is the *junior* play – how could I forget?' he said, hitting the side of his head. 'So then you're sweet sixteen?'

She could feel the flush travel up her face. 'Not quite so sweet,' she murmured.

'None of those salacious innuendoes, Marylin Wace. They can drive a man ape, if he's been in the Pacific for six months.'

'Sorry.'

'I'm twenty-three. Think being here with you makes me a dirty old man or a cradle robber?'

'Neither.'

'Do your parents let you go out with servicemen?'

'My father is dead,' she said, swallowing sharply. No matter how many times she uttered the words, they hurt to say.

'The war?' he asked quietly.

She shook her head. 'He was working – in a haberdashery shop – and a burglar shot him.'

He nodded and touched her hand sympathetically. Under the light pressure of his fingertips, a wanton tingling blossomed, travelling up her arm, drawing a sigh from her lips. If only *this* could go on forever . . . Crazy, crazy Marylin, she thought.

He moved his hand. 'I've heard about you. BJ, bless her,

writes endless letters, and there's been much ink used on this exquisite, talented creature in her drama class – '

'She does have a tendency to exaggerate.'

'Not in this case. Has she mentioned me?'

'Often. She's very proud. You fly an Avenger, a torpedo plane, and you've won the Distinguished Flying Cross – '

'She talks too much.'

Marylin smiled. 'Before the war, you were going to . . . Stanford?'

'Right.'

'What were you going to be?'

'The same as I am now. A man.'

'I meant, what were you majoring in? Medicine? Law? Or do you want to be a screenwriter like your father?'

'Oh, yes. Sure. Absolutely.' His face darkened into an expression of bitter unhappiness; she had to control herself from reaching over to touch *his* hand. He said, 'All right, I'll 'fess up. There's something I've always wanted to emulate. Publish two good, meaningful novels then sell out to do Hollywood garbage.'

She knew many who professed to despise or disdain their parents as parents, but to dismiss Joshua Fernauld (about whom there hovered the aura of sinful glamour invariably tethered to high-living men of vast talent in show business) as a hack shocked her to the core. 'He's a fabulous writer! He's got an Oscar to prove it.'

'From a jury of his peers,' Linc said acidly.

'His dialogue jumps to life.'

'I can see that one semester in high-school drama has turned you into a fine critic.'

'This snobbishness about the movies really gets me!' Marylin cried. Her outspoken anger completely bewildered her. What had catapulted her, Marylin Wace who avoided every unpleasantness, into this brouhaha? 'Why must people assume it's slumming to write a fine movie script, while writing crummy books or a trashy play is something sacred?'

He jerked as if she had probed a raw nerve. 'Would you

36

admit,' he asked with heavy vitriol, 'that your lack of understanding might emanate from a certain . . . shall we call it immaturity? Oh, hell! I should know better than to talk seriously to a high-school kid!'

Marylin's heart was galloping, sending a wild charge through her body. 'Millions of people see his work,' she heard herself say. 'He has a chance to influence them, to make them better or kinder. I've gone to *After the Fall* and *Lava Flow* four times each, and they always leave a kind of glow.'

'Why not take Fleischmann's yeast? That gives the same results.' His sarcasm was loud, brutal.

The counter girl and soda jerk were staring at them.

Marylin knew she must stop. She could not stop. 'Whether you want to admit it or not, if Shakespeare were writing today, he would be under contract to MGM or Paramount.'

'Thank you for that surprising insight.'

'He'd be like your father, earning Oscars, and I don't think this idea is coming as any surprise to you.'

His tanned hands clenched into fists on the tabletop, and there were lines on either side of his mouth. 'Listen, you movie-struck bobby-soxer, don't try to psychoanalyse *me*. Don't think you can figure out what's in *my* mind. Just because you're a gorgeous, gorgeous eyeful with a fantastic little body doesn't mean you're Sigmund Freud. Stick to the stuff below the beltline, that's more in your line. All you know about me is that I'm hot to make you.'

To her horror, Marylin felt tears welling in her eyes. If she were an actress with the least modicum of talent or technique, wouldn't she be able to hide these idiotic tears? He's only out to make me – that is the hidden complexity in his eyes, she thought, and put her shaking hand over her forehead.

'Hey,' he said quietly.

She took out a handkerchief, bending her head, and under the pretext of blowing her nose, dabbed surreptitiously at her eyes. She glimpsed his tanned fingers clenching and unclenching, and guessed suddenly that shouting matches like this were as alien to him as to her.

'Allergy,' she mumbled.

Money clinked on the table. Marylin hurried outside ahead of him and saw that dusk was turning the sky purple.

Linc put the key in the ignition of the big Packard, but did not turn on the engine. After a minute he said, 'I've been away too long. Forgotten the polite art of male-female conversation.'

'It's okay,' she said listlessly.

'I didn't mean to crumple you with my rhetoric.'

'I egged you on.'

He gazed into the twilight. 'You're right, of course. I have always known that Dad's a tremendous talent. There's not much triumph in being a perpetual spindly sapling dwarfed by a tremendous oak.'

'You mean you write too?'

'It's the Fernauld family disease. I'm not like BJ. She can go to him for help. Not me. Never! All I can do is snarl and skulk like a wounded cub. Let's face it, the war came as a benison. On the *Enterprise* there's no need for me to peck at the old Remington and inform myself that Joshua Fernauld is pouring out Pablum for the masses whereas Lincoln Fernauld is writing erudite, lyrical prose, the great American novel.'

'Linc –'

'Will you let me finish? Marylin, when this war is over, I'll be a plumber, a ditchdigger, a bank robber, anything except a writer.'

'I shouldn't have argued. It's not like me. And I don't know anything about literature or screenwriting.'

'You're remarkably astute about both,' he said. 'And another thing. I'd be lying if I said I didn't want to make you, but that's not all there is.'

'It's not?'

'You're one of nature's masterpieces, Marylin Wace. Though I long to touch, I enjoy looking.' There was a huskiness in his voice. Something had crept into the big car, an electricity that made her quiver. She felt prized open, vulnerable, submissive, waiting.

You've known him all of one hour, she told herself.

'Friends?' he asked.

'Friends,' she murmured.

'My parents must be home by now, and they'll expect to see me,' he said. 'Marylin, where do you live?'

She gave him her address, and they drove through the mist-shrouded twilight.

The Waces' apartment had been added on, an afterthought that perched like an out-of-place mortarboard atop a detached two-car garage. This undistinguished part of Beverly Hills was R1, to rent out any part of the small bungalows constituted a zoning violation, but with the wartime housing shortage the city fathers bent their straight backs enough to turn slightly in the other direction, so no police came to question the apartment's legality.

The blackout blinds were pulled every which way, and light blazed unevenly at the bottoms and through the rips at the sides. Climbing rickety wooden stairs, Marylin recollected their brief stop on North Hillcrest Road to let BJ out of the car. The Fernaulds lived in a commodious mansion that crouched like a placid Tudor lion on rolling, lovingly watered, expensive green real estate. She felt a shame that Linc was a witness to her poverty.

The smell of frying increased and NolaBee's loud, cheerful rendition of 'Poinciana' grew louder at every step, and Linc, grasping Marylin's hand, took her books.

As Linc and Marylin reached the top of the steps, NolaBee's song halted abruptly. Linc peered down at Marylin, silently handing her back her books. Then, without a good-bye, he turned, loping down the steps. Marylin watched him go, the outline of a tall, lankily graceful man disappearing into the evening shadows.

4

The apartment was square except for the narrow bite given over to the bathroom, and was unobstructed by walls. Into this space the Waces had crowded their eccentric conglomeration of possessions: three dented metal folding chairs circled an heirloom mahogany gateleg table, two looming, overgarnished Victorian wardrobes jutted out from the walls, forming an alcove for NolaBee's box springs and mattress, which was covered not with a normal bedspread but with a worn rubicund oriental carpet.

None of the Waces had any conception how to keep house, and personal possessions were strewn over every available surface.

A metal screen, haphazardly collaged by NolaBee with covers from fan magazines, leaned against the wall near the makeshift kitchen where she tended a hissing skillet full of chicken. A flowered apron swathed her black slacks, and her hair was concealed by the jaunty red turban that she wore to work.

For nearly a year now, NolaBee had been employed at Hughes Aircraft. The war, having scooped up ten million men, ravenously demanded armaments, and America's Depression-racked industry had burst alive, revving up to three perpetual shifts, hiring workers of either sex, every age and colour. Hughes's employment office had taken on the inexperienced NolaBee without query or quibble. It tickled her funnybone to wonder what her Fairburn and Roy ancestors would think if they could see her riveting wings to B-19s between two Negro women – the younger one the gold of brown sugar, the other a regular black mammy – and being right friendly with them both, too. Her ancestors and Chilton's had owned slaves, and NolaBee, like the rest of the extended family, was without the least dreg of masochistic, retroactive guilt. Her people, she was positive, had been just in every dealing with their human possessions, had tenderly nursed each aged darkie – how could it be otherwise? Her people were Georgia gentlefolk.

Turning a drumstick, NolaBee flashed Marylin a welcoming smile. Roy raised her curly brown head from her homework – she sat on the floor between the wardrobes, an area designated as her room because her iron bed formed an angle with the cherrywood bookcase whose bottom shelf held her joy and consolation, a secondhand table-model Radiola. 'It's nearly six,' she said. 'What kept you?'

Marylin, who was the only one of them with any craving for order, smiled dazedly. Without thinking, she picked up her mother's old jacket and Roy's hand-me-down blue topper and hung them on the coatrack.

'Yes,' said NolaBee. 'I was getting a mite worried.'

'The rehearsal – '

NolaBee interrupted, cocking her head. 'Oh, that's right. I forgot. You're starting on the play the screenwriter's little girl wrote.'

'BJ Fernauld.' Marylin spoke the patronym, her lips softening as for a kiss. 'After we finished – ' Her voice faded. Always exceptionally close to her mother, Marylin had never been afflicted with an adolescent's stubborn secretiveness, yet as she started to explain her lateness, to tell Mama about Linc, her tongue went thick. She did not want to share any part of the last hour.

'It's the Junior-class play, isn't it?' NolaBee asked, not waiting for an answer. 'I reckon there'll be a lot of people come to see it.'

'Probably just the kids, Mama. Anyway, it's not until the end of next semester.'

'Well, I reckon he'll be there, the screenwriter,' said NolaBee. 'I'll help you learn your lines after supper.' Fat spattered as she flipped a chicken thigh. 'Honey, I do wish you'd call if you're walking home after dark.'

'Somebody drove her,' said Roy. 'I heard the car.'

'A beau?' NolaBee's cigarette waggled as she smiled.

41

'Oh, Mama . . .' Marylin blushed.

'What's his name?'

'Linc . . . Lincoln.'

'Look at you, red as a beet.' NolaBee chuckled as she fished out pieces of chicken. 'I reckon this ole bird is done clear through. Girls, let's get at him while he's good and hot.'

After they finished eating, NolaBee shuffled the slick mimeograph paper, cueing Marylin in her lines. Smoke drifted lazily around the red turban and the gold-gleaming pageboy.

Roy stretched on her bed, listening to *Amos 'n' Andy* with her head touching the cracked pink paint of her little radio. When Marylin was working on her roles, the volume had to be kept down. All pleasure and work revolved subserviently around that hoped-for, worked-for, yearned-for career of Marylin's.

It was problematic for a girl entering Horace Mann Grammar School as late as seventh grade to carve a social niche, and though Roy had made a few acquaintances to chatter with at recess and lunch period, she had never been invited to a classmate's home. She imagined all the other kids dwelling in aseptic households that were presided over by the bland, trimly garbed mothers whom she saw in shiny sedans outside the school and by fathers who departed in the morning and returned at night on a schedule as inviolable as a Swiss cuckoo clock. An existence so opposite from her own that she in turn had never invited anyone to the topsy-turvy apartment.

Roy was nothing if not constant, and in her loneliness she set her family on a high pedestal and clung closer to them: she revered her father as a slain god, she saw Marylin as an exquisite heroine faintly tinged by tragedy, and NolaBee as a fascinating, dashing woman of unequalled bravery.

During the commercial she surveyed her mother and sister.

Roy would not have been mortal if she weren't jealous of

her exquisite older sibling. She did not resent the carefully hoarded, crumpled bills that were taken from NolaBee's big fake alligator purse to pay for Marylin's singing lessons, dancing lessons, her brand new clothes from Yorkshire's and Nobby Knit. No, it was when her mother and sister sat engrossed like this, their heads close, their arms touching, that a hot, liquid mourning flooded through Roy and she felt unworthy, unloved and unlovable.

'*De fashion show was a financh success, Amos?*'

'*Oh yes, it was great, all right. Made close to a hundred dollars fo de lodge —* '

'Give me that line again, Mama.'

'Whatever's the matter with you, Marylin? I declare, I never saw you like this, not paying an ounce of attention. Seems like you don't care at all.'

The happiness suffusing Marylin's lovely features dimmed. 'I'm sorry, Mama,' she said placatingly.

NolaBee repeated the line. Marylin's face assumed her role's slightly foolish eagerness, and she read Vera's lines. NolaBee watched, her long upper lip quivering as if she, not her daughter, were speaking.

Then the phone rang.

They all stared at the instrument that many days crouched atop the bookcase in black, abeyant silence.

On the second ring Roy picked it up. 'Yes?'

A pleasant baritone drawled, 'May I speak to Marylin Wace?'

'Who may I say is calling?'

'Linc.'

Roy held the instrument towards Marylin. 'Must be a Neanderthal. The missing *link*.'

Marylin jumped to her feet and ran across the room. She dragged the phone as far from Roy's bed as the cord permitted, pressing the receiver to her ear.

'Hello,' she said in that soft tone that Roy thought of as angora. 'Yes . . . Me too . . . Fine . . . Tonight? . . . No – yes. Yes, I'd like that. See you.' She hung up, and for a split second her eyes were out of focus, a newborn, blue-green look. Then she ran to the wardrobe with the chipped walnut veneer, flinging open the door. 'Mama, I'm going out for a snack.'

'A good thing, too. You barely touched your chicken.'

NolaBee was beaming archly. With uncomplicated cheer she twitted Marylin about her admirers, and had no idea how much the two years she had snipped from her daughter's life had distorted the girl's relationships. Despite Marylin's total lack of interest in her callow swains, Nola-Bee persisted in viewing the masculine telephone calls and prom orchids in the tiny, leaking Frigidaire as proof that her beauty whirled in breathless excitement between enraptured, wealthy admirers. 'I reckon this must be the same Linc who drove you home. Tell me about him. Who is he?'

Marylin was snatching a handful of rayon underwear that she had ironed yesterday, her good high heels, the powder-blue date dress. 'Oh, somebody's brother.'

'A match made in heaven,' cracked Roy. 'You're somebody's sister.'

Marylin didn't hear her. She had shut the bathroom door.

'I reckon if Marylin's new beau is coming,' said NolaBee with a wink, 'we better stack the dishes.'

Marylin was still immersed in the rituals of the bathroom when the brisk masculine footsteps rang on the rickety staircase.

Roy opened the door anticipating the usual, a perspiration-glossed, nervous-tongued male wearing a dark blue letter sweater adorned with a big orange B.

Instead she confronted a tall naval officer whose butternut tan contrasted with his white uniform.

'Hi,' he said easily as he removed the cap with the gold insignia. 'I'm Linc Fernauld.' He looked around.

'Some of us are getting fixed up,' Roy said in her best Cagney voice.

'The kid sister?'

44

'Actually her mother. A sad case of arrested development.'

He grinned. His smile tipped downward on the left.

'Oh, you, Roy!' NolaBee called good-naturedly. Freshly lipsticked, she sat on the sagging easy chair with the latest *Modern Screen:* – 'Linda Darnell Confides Her Five Greatest Passions'. 'Come on in, Linc. I'm Mrs Wace, and this little pest is Roy. You'd never know it from the way she acts, but she'll be in high school next term.' NolaBee coquettishly bent her turbaned head. 'My, my, you Navy boys certainly have the handsomest uniforms.' She squinted at the wings affixed to the white dress jacket. 'A pilot, then? Would you like some coffee? Fruit? – we have apples.'

'Will she be *that* long?'

'No, no. Are you from around here, Lieutenant?'

'Right now, I have an APO number, but my parents live on Hillcrest. My sister's a friend of Marylin's.'

'I'm sorry, but I didn't quite catch your last name.' NolaBee was putting another cigarette in her mouth.

He extricated a book of matches to light it for her. 'Linc Fernauld. I'm BJ Fernauld's brother.'

'Oh, yes.' NolaBee inhaled. 'When you called, I was helping Marylin learn the lines of your sister's play. She's got a right clever sense of humour. The way she tucks in those jokes so slyly . . .'

NolaBee had always possessed the gift of the gab, and though she expended no additional effort on Linc for his famed sire, she had him chuckling.

Roy, silent, darted a look at him. If, during an English test, she were called upon to describe Linc Fernauld in one adjective, 'clean' would be the word. Not only that shining uniform and his gorgeous tan, but his reactions, his words, the way he sat, somehow summoned up the one-syllable description of physical and mental decency. Clean.

The bathroom door opened and closed, sending sweet drifts of Apple Blossom cologne and dusting powder through the chicken-scented air. Linc, rising slowly to his feet, stared at Marylin.

The pale blue crêpe dress clung to her delicately sensual curves. Her smooth, gleaming hair was pushed back to show small blue-enamel earrings (bought at a Woolworth's sale) dangling against her slender, luminous neck, her cheeks glowed, her huge sea-coloured eyes were bedazzled.

NolaBee had unfolded the fan-magazine screen around the kitchen mess, and the hidden faucet dripped loudly in the long moment while Marylin and Linc gazed at each other. Marylin drew a quick breath. 'Hello, Linc. I see you've met Mama and Roy.'

'Charmed them, I hope.'

'Absolutely,' said NolaBee. 'But anyway, you have to have her back here by 10.30.'

'You're a hard woman, Mrs Wace.'

He draped Marylin's coat over her shoulders.

After the door closed on them, NolaBee had a thoughtful look. 'They make a right handsome couple, don't they? Did you see the way he looked at her?'

'Mama, she's cuckoo about him, really cuckoo. He's the One.'

In a family of three females it is inevitable that a disproportionate amount of conversation centres on romance. The Waces speculated endlessly on characteristics of the One who would rescue each from her single state – even the widowed NolaBee came in for a good share of ribbing from her daughters.

'You're bein' right silly, Roy. She's just a child, she has her career. There'll be others, loads of others.'

'His father's a big screenwriter, the family's rich.'

'I reckon Marylin is as good as anyone, she's a Wace, she has Fairburn and Roy blood.' NolaBee rose, as if that settled that. 'Marylin'll go through a horde of beaux – and so will you, my little curlyhead.'

Roy held still under the affectionate, smoothing hand, praying it would continue forever.

But NolaBee swung over to the sink. 'Come on, Roy, hon, let's get those dishes done.'

5

Linc took Marylin to the Players on Sunset.

It was too early for a nightclub to swing, so most of the small round tables were empty. Pink lights sifted down on a trio of rum-guzzling Army officers and their dates, a sailor with an extravagantly made-up blonde, a few civilian couples. The quartet was playing 'Stardust' with a slow, inviting riff, yet nobody had ventured onto the floor. The red-jacketed waiter brought Linc his Southern Comfort, and with a flourish placed Marylin's ginger ale in front of her.

Linc took a long drink. 'Been here before?' he asked.

She shook her head.

'You're a funny girl.'

'Me?'

'For openers, the last thing you look like is a "Marylin Wace".'

'What should I be called?'

'Mmm . . . give me a moment. Something ethereal and beautiful, unusual but not pretentious.'

His eyes possessed a mysterious magnetic force and she could not turn away.

He snapped his fingers. 'Rain.'

'That's not a name,' she said.

'Rain, absolutely. Rain. And a plain yet aristocratic surname. Any ideas?'

'Fairburn,' she said.

'On the button.' He made a circle with his thumb and index finger. 'Fairburn – where'd you dig it up?'

'A family name. My mother's.'

Raising his glass, he said, 'Rain Fairburn. Gentle and pretty-sounding, yet a touch theatrical.'

'Not pretentious, though.'

'Boggles the mind, doesn't it, how right it is?'

'Right as rain,' she said.

They smiled across the little table.

'Linc, what is it like . . . out there?'

His mouth tensed. 'Long stretches of boredom interspersed with a few minutes of monstrous, degrading terror,' he said.

'How can you force yourself to go into danger?'

His thick black brows drew together. 'Baby, in case it's escaped your notice, this isn't a debriefing. It's happy hour.'

His capricious reversal to this afternoon's leaden sarcasm was like an icy wind, and she froze with the realization that he had probably determined that she was using the war as a conversational ploy. She gazed at the elegantly rhythmic black men on the bandstand.

After a few chords he said, 'Avoid the subject, okay?'

His eyes, dark brown with small gold flecks, were watching her apologetically – almost anxiously.

The anger's not part of him at all, she thought.

Again they smiled, and she felt immersed in a sumptuously delicious joy. It occurred to her that this euphoria went beyond its obvious romantic connotations: despite Linc's sudden fault lines of rage, for the first time in years she was at ease with someone other than Roy or her mother. Indeed, in their enveloping intimacy she felt as if she were floating several inches above her chair, rosy as the lights, graceful and airy as the sweet, rippling notes.

The musicians segued into 'These Foolish Things', Linc rose to his feet. 'Shall we?' he said.

They moved onto the empty, polished square, he took her in his arms, which were shaking a little, and she closed her eyes. They whirled and dipped slowly, as if they shared the same motor responses, they drifted in the slow cloudlike chords, they swayed in time to the poignant, rippling beat.

The winds of March that made my heart a dancer
A telephone that rings, but who's to answer?
Oh, how the ghost of you clings!
These foolish things
Remind me of you.

She wasn't sure if she sang aloud in her huskily musical little voice, or if, like the music and the trembling pressure of his hands and body, the words were part of her soul.

'Marylin, you know what they say about couples who dance well together, don't you?' he said against her ear.

'What?'

'Tell you later.'

The music stopped, and they pulled apart, still holding hands.

A tall, narrow-shouldered Army captain, obviously loaded to the gills, banged on his table. 'Encore, encore, for the Navy looie and the knockout little broad with him.'

The quartet reprised 'These Foolish Things', and Linc and Marylin again drifted across the floor.

The drummer blew into the mike. 'That's all for now, folks,' he announced. 'We're gonna take five.'

As Linc led her back to the table, he said, 'Would you have dark thoughts if I suggested we get out of here?'

'Should I?'

'Absolutely.' He glanced at the watch on his wrist. 'Nearly ten anyway. Is 10.30 a big deal to your mother?'

'It's a school night.'

'You afraid of her?'

'No. It's just she works so hard for us, and I don't like going against her.'

'You're a soft, gentle girl, Marylin. I fear for you.'

'Why?'

'Fernauld's Rule. The soft and gentle inherit the earth – by getting trampled into it.'

'Hah!' she said happily.

'It's a basic fact of life.'

'Didn't you say something about leaving?'

Outside, the mist was thicker, and along Sunset Boulevard the hazy, shimmering streetlights resembled enormous, other-worldly shasta daisies. As they curved west, she sat close to him and he held her hand. 'Another thing that's wrong about you,' he said as they passed Mocambo's with its stream of cars waiting at the entry for the parking attendants. 'You seem older.'

It was destined, it was fate, an irrevocable karma that she admit, 'I am.'

'An old soul, as the Russians say.'

'No. I'm eighteen.' Only the faintest flutter of her heart and voice marked the unlocking of the secret that for two years had incarcerated her in solitary confinement.

'Come again?'

'I was eighteen last August.'

His hand loosened on hers, and he gripped the gearshift. They halted at a boulevard stop sign. 'Were you sick as a kid or what?'

'No. After my father died, my mother got the idea that I ought to be in movies – I'd always been in the school plays. She decided if we moved to Beverly Hills, I'd be discovered – you know how many movie people's kids go to the high school.' As she remembered that Linc's father was the legendary Joshua Fernauld who not only wrote smash films, but had directed several, the blood rushed into her face and she blessed the darkness. 'I was seventeen then, nearly, but she figured I'd have the best chance if I entered as a freshman.'

He said nothing until they reached the next stop sign at Doheny Drive. 'Why didn't she go the usual route?' he asked. 'What about storming the studio gates?'

'Mama thinks that sort of thing is common.'

'Common. Yes.'

'Besides, it hardly ever works.'

'True, true.'

His tone attacked her, withered her, yet surprisingly she felt no darts of regret at telling him. 'Please don't be like this, Linc,' she entreated.

'I'm filled with admiration is all. The ingenuity of it. One fine day, Darryl Zanuck or Jesse Lasky – or is it Joshua Fernauld? – will be watching his darling perform, and right there, lighting up the Beverly Hills High School auditorium stage, will be our own little geriatric Marylin Wace.'

She clasped her trembling hands together. 'Please?'

'Any more confessions – are you, for instance, a part-time call girl?'

'Oh, Linc,' she sighed.

'Shame.' He gave a jarring laugh. 'It certainly would expedite matters if I could offer you a few bucks and not have to go through the gyrations.'

'I've never told anyone before,' she said.

'I don't blame you for that. Some of the kids – like BJ, for example – might feel they'd been had, taken advantage of, used.'

She shrank into the Packard's plush upholstery. 'I haven't hurt anyone,' she said.

'A simple case of gulling and deception, your Honour.'

He sped past the poinsettia field that, by clear December light, waved like a rippling blood-red flag on the eastern border of Beverly Hills. Turning down Arden, he zoomed by dimly visible big houses. Some animal, Marylin wasn't sure whether it was a cat or a dog, darted from the fog into the glaring headlights.

Swerving with an instantaneous reflex, Linc jammed down on the brake. The tyres squealed. They skidded in an arc. Marylin gave a little cry as her body jerked forward and her out-thrust hands hit the dashboard. Controlling the car, he pulled over under the big palms, turning off the motor.

'Marylin, all right?'

'Fine.' But she was gasping audibly, still in a physical terror.

With a swift movement he pulled her into his arms. This was no reassuring gesture of comfort, but a continuation of his mystifying out-of-proportion savagery. He was kissing her, a rough, bourbon-scented kiss that plunged his tongue

51

into her mouth, he was pushing aside her coat to grasp her breasts. She, still wrapped in shock, braced both hands on the white uniform, pushing him away.

'Linc, please – '

'Quit saying please,' he muttered, and bit a kiss onto the vein at the pulse of her throat.

We might have been killed, she thought, then realized that he must live with this sort of danger. A *few minutes of monstrous, degrading terror*, he had said. As his raging sarcasm had seemed grotesquely out of proportion a minute ago, so now did her own panic at a near-miss of a minor accident. This warm, living body had been exposed to racing bullets, would be exposed again.

She gave a breathy cry and began feverishly caressing the tendons of his neck above the uniform. Her mouth pressed around his in a wild fugue of kisses, her nerves quivered, alive, she was moist down there, perspiring, her heart pounded until she thought it would surely break out of her body – she could feel his heart equally fast. She shoved off her coat, he unzipped the side of her dress.

His touch slowed, expressing the tenderness that she was positive was the *real* him, and time seemed to halt, waiting, waiting, until the exquisite moment when his fingers traced her naked nipple. They were breathing each other's breath in an endless openmouthed kiss. Her habit of prolonging each pleasure remained: she wanted this sumptuous melting to last forever – yet at the same time her body trembled with the need for his caressing hands to move downward, she ached for her body to be part of his in the unknown act, the irreversible act, the awesome mystery. Nice girls don't, she thought. I just met him. Oh, I want, yes I want, darling . . . love . . . Please . . .

They were both shaking as if in the final stages of delirium tremens as he pressed her awkwardly against the door, moving his back to the steering wheel.

Light blazed into her eyes.

'Roll down your window, sir,' said a muted masculine voice from behind the glass and glare.

'Jesus Christ,' Linc whispered, moving from her to crank down the window.

Cold, she was frozen without him. Then mortification overtook her. The glare revealed that her good dress was rumpled up to her slender thighs, which gleamed white where the wartime rayon stockings did not reach, and the unzipped bodice was pushed awry to expose one very round pink-tipped breast that had slipped out of her bra. She yanked her coat over her, sarong style.

'May I see your licence and ID, sir.'

Linc extricated papers from his wallet.

'So you live around here, Lieutenant,' said the policeman. 'Listen, it would be better all round if you parked in your own driveway.'

'Listen, it would be better all round if you minded your own damn business!' Linc retorted. Lipstick smeared his furious mouth.

'I could give you a ticket for that.'

'You're scaring the hell out of me! Go ahead, write the damn ticket. Just quit shining that flashlight on my girl, okay?'

The glaring light was turned away. The policeman handed back the licence. 'All right. Move along,' he said, returning to his squad car, waiting while Linc started the big Packard.

As they turned on Carmelita, Linc said, 'So much for *amor*.' Reaching over for her shaking hand, he held it briefly to his recently shaved cheek. 'Marylin, stop me if I'm wrong, but offhand I'd say you're a virgin.'

She never had submitted to more than a good-night kiss from those hot-handed children. 'Yes, but I . . .' she stammered. 'Linc, I wanted . . .'

'Given luck, you'll have another chance to seduce me.'

The mention of her wild passion brought the heat of humiliation to her face, and she turned to refasten her bra.

'Marylin, I didn't mean to embarrass you,' he said. 'For a few hours, wouldn't you say we've had a stormy relationship?'

'Very.'

'It's not the real me,' he said. 'Prior to the war – except with Big Joshua, of course – I was the most phlegmatic oaf you could ever hope to meet.'

'Never an oaf.'

'More of a bookworm, actually. The quiet type who later retreats behind horn-rims and a pipe.' He slowed the car, kissing her cheek, then pointed to the dashboard clock. 'Fifteen minutes late already. I'd better get you home.'

The next morning, as she emerged from the apartment, she saw Linc across the street, sitting on the Packard's running board. He wore slacks and a sweater. 'What do you have first period?' he asked.

'Study hall.'

'The perfect class to ditch. Have you eaten breakfast?'

'Yes.'

'Then we'll go over to Simon's and you can watch me eat.'

She did not go to school that day.

Or the next.

Rehearsing BJ's play no longer seemed important. The important thing was to go down to the deserted iodine-scented beach and sit in front of Roadside Rest on the cold sand while gulls screeched endless circles over their heads.

They held hands, sometimes they kissed, gently, lingeringly, but mostly they exposed what they were.

She told Linc about the family in Greenward that she had never met, the Waces and the Roys and Fairburns who each Christmas sent red-ribbon-tied cartons of hand-me-downs; she told him of their constant moves, the failures the Depression forced on her father, his pitifully futile death. She told Linc of her closeness to her mother, her skills and deficits as an actress, her less-than-joyous two years at Beverly High.

Her life sounded a puny thing, drab and unimportant, when compared to Linc's.

His father, Joshua Fernauld, was a lapsed Catholic who at one time had belonged to the Communist party; his mother was Jewish, a niece of the fabled Lou, Maxie and Hesh Cotter, the flamboyant three who had founded Cotter Brothers Studio. The Fernaulds held traditional Sunday barbecues, where Linc had met most of the movie greats and some whose names lit up Broadway, people so famous that Marylin never thought of them as drawing human breath: Spencer Tracy, Gertrude Lawrence, George Gershwin, Maxwell Anderson. Linc extravagantly admired Anderson's work.

Looking at the huge, curling breakers, he declaimed: 'And if you seek forgiveness then pass it over in silence and consider it forgiven. Forget it utterly. It won't help to remember some fatal awkwardness.'

An insane joy quivered through Marylin that she could reply: 'But I have to say it and say it honestly, and then wait to hear a verdict from you.'

He hugged her shoulders. 'Hey, you know it.'

'*Key Largo.*'

'That's my girl.'

He talked about his great-uncles, now all dead, who had been part of the rough, scandalous early Hollywood, he talked about boyhood fears and saints, his ambivalences towards his father, his struggles to write.

Marylin was always conscious of his superiority, not only in age, family, schooling and sophistication but also in the depth and quality of his intellect.

There was a sweetness to him, a niceness that she could never reconcile with those sudden lapses into dark, bitter rage.

Once – he had been telling her about a short story he had worked on aboard the *Enterprise* – he fell abruptly silent, gazing with fierce, brooding dread at the grey, chill horizon of the Pacific.

'What is it, Linc?' she asked.

'Nothing.'

Hunched over like that, he looked so desolate that she

risked provoking him. Touching his shoulder, she said, 'It's bad out there, isn't it?'

He flung off her hand. 'Wonderful, just wonderful! Two times through high school and you can read minds. Listen, didn't I get it across to you? If you want your jollies about the war, listen to H. V. Kaltenborn or Gabriel Heatter. Or better yet, go see *Wings of Eagles!*' It was Joshua Fernauld's latest box-office triumph, a story of 'gallantry in the Army Air Corps'.

Tense, stiff-legged, he covered the long stretch of dry sand to where big breakers hurled their final shreds of foam. She watched him standing there with his back to her, hands thrust into his pockets. Why did I push him? she thought desolately. When he returned, his eyes were red. 'Buy you a hamburger,' he said quietly.

Those two days they talked about everything – except the war.

On Thursday, around five, she handed Linc her key, and he unlocked the door.

NolaBee sat facing them in the sagging armchair. A cigarette was clamped between her grimly narrowed lips, her thin shoulders held high, her expression robbed of its usual liveliness.

'Mama,' Marylin said, tugging nervously at her long shirt (a relic of her father), whose tails hung over her blue jeans, which she had rolled up above her slim, shapely calves. 'Linc brought me home.'

'You,' NolaBee said, jerking her head towards Roy, who was gazing curiously at them, 'go on outside.'

'It's Antarctica,' Roy protested.

'Go!'

Roy grabbed a library book and the sweater that this past Christmas she had inherited from Cousin Doris Fairburn. The door slammed on her and there was only the squeak of NolaBee's rocking chair.

'Mama . . .' Marylin started, and her voice broke. She coughed. 'Perhaps Linc ought to go too.'

NolaBee did not answer until Roy's footsteps on the

outside staircase had faded. 'He'll listen to what I have to say. It concerns him too. Where have you been Wednesday and today?'

Marylin blinked and stepped backwards.

'Well? I reckon if I ask a question, I deserve an answer. Some woman from the attendance office called an hour ago, asking about your absence. I had no answer, but I want one now.'

'She was with me, Mrs Wace,' Linc said quietly. 'Don't blame her, I talked her into it, explained it was a patriotic duty.'

'Duty. I reckon Marylin's got her own duty. Maybe she hasn't explained to you what a struggle it is for us to live here in Beverly Hills, where she can get the best education there is.' NolaBee crossed her arms. 'Marylin knows she can't fool around. She's not one of these spoiled Beverly Hills girls who has everything on a silver platter.' NolaBee stubbed out her cigarette. 'The thing that gets to me is how she could play hooky when she has her rehearsals.'

'The junior play,' Linc said, 'is not so crucifyingly important.'

'She's the star. The others depend on her. *I* depend on her.'

They were talking to one another, yet both were looking at Marylin. Her heart thumped slowly, and her chest ached as if she were being stretched apart by implacably hostile forces.

NolaBee rose from the chair, drawing a breath so that her meagre bust showed in her old red pullover. 'I reckon you better not come around here anymore, Lieutenant.'

'Mama . . .' Marylin murmured, a wretched sound more like a groan.

Linc reached for her hand, gripping it, pressing his large firm palm against her cold, trembling one. 'Mrs Wace, Marylin's old enough to decide that for herself.'

'A little girl. Sixteen.'

'Eighteen.'

NolaBee's mouth opened in a round O, and her eyes went

dull with confusion and betrayal. She crumpled back into the sagging springs of the chair, homely in cheap, garishly bright sweater and slacks. Marylin took a step forward. Linc gripped her hand, not letting her move away from him.

'Frankly, Mrs Wace,' he said, 'your plans for Marylin stink. Take it from me, Dad's in the industry, I know what goes on. All the odds are against her making it.'

NolaBee looked up. 'I reckon she's as pretty and talented as Teresa Wright or – '

'She's beautiful. She's luminous and special. And certainly she's a good-enough actress. But she's too gentle. She lacks the wolf-bitch instinct, she's got no bitch in her. She'll be mangled.'

'That's downright ridiculous talk,' NolaBee snapped. 'What all have you been telling him, Marylin? That I push you?'

'I *want* to act, Linc, you know that,' Marylin said reproachfully.

'For your mother,' Linc said. 'Not yourself. Think about it, and you'll realize I'm right.' He released her hand. 'I'll see you at seven tomorrow night.'

Marylin glanced at her mother, who was hunched over in the rocker. 'Linc, I can't disobey Mama,' she said with a long sigh.

Linc's expression was as unhappy as hers. 'Mrs Wace,' he said, 'I give you my word there'll be no more ditching school. Sunday night at twelve my leave is up. At twelve hundred hours I report back to the *Enterprise* – we're docked in San Diego for repairs. That's classified. Until we sail, there'll only be weekend leaves.'

A sad little whimper was wrested from Marylin.

NolaBee's forehead puckered. She turned from her beauteous child's desolation to Linc's dark, pleading eyes. Suddenly she gave a snort. 'Sailors!' she said. 'Don't reckon I could stop a Navy pilot, could I?'

'You're tough, Mrs Wace, but not that tough. Dinner, Marylin. See you at seven.' The door closed quietly behind him.

'Thank you, Mama.' Marylin went over to her mother and bent to kiss her.

'Cutting school,' NolaBee reproached.

'I'm sorry, so sorry. I know how hard you work for us – for me.' Tears were rolling in large drops from the lovely eyes.

'You've been right foolish. You might try thinking of Roy and me, always pulling for you.'

'I do, I do. But I'll die if I can't see him.'

'Looks like he knows it, too. Marylin, that sailor takes you for granted. You've let him think he's the be-all and end-all. It's puffed him up. Men! They're so vain! Imagine him believing that your acting's not your real life!' The snap had returned to NolaBee's eyes. 'I'm amazed at how little sense you've got, lettin' a man think he's so much to you.'

'He's *very* important, Mama.'

NolaBee gripped her wrist tightly. 'You haven't done anything really bad with him, have you?'

Marylin turned crimson, and shook her head.

NolaBee tightened her grip. 'I know what's best for you. Certainly a girl with your looks has scads of beaux. But you mustn't let any man get in the way of your career. You've got every single thing it takes to be a real star.'

'No I don't, Mama. Besides, all I've ever wanted is someone to love who loves me, to get married.'

'You're not some poky, ordinary little girl.'

'It's what matters to me.'

The ash of NolaBee's cigarette fell on her sweater, smouldering. She brushed at it, continuing to peer into her daughter's tear-streaked face. 'Honey, listen to me, I'm not denying he's a mighty attractive young man, and that Navy officer's uniform would turn any girl's head. Sooner or later, though, he's going to try to take advantage of you.'

'Oh, Mama.'

'Don't "Oh, Mama" me. I'm not so old I don't remember. Men're all out for one thing, and this war gives 'em their excuse. They're sweet-talkin' fools until a girl gives in, and after that they lose all respect.'

'It's not like that at all.'

NolaBee frowned. 'He hasn't tried anything, has he?'

'I've only been with him in the daytime,' Marylin whispered.

'They'll try in the daytime what they can't do at night,' said NolaBee.

'Mama, you're hurting my wrist,' Marylin said.

Peering at the beautiful red face, NolaBee let go. 'You're a good girl,' she said finally. 'But always remember, you have your career. That's first and foremost.'

'Mama, I want love, a husband . . . babies.'

'That'll come later.'

'I wish you didn't count on me to accomplish so much. I worry I'm going to let you down.'

'Sometimes you're right silly, Marylin. You're not going to let me down. When you're at the top, I reckon you'll thank me for bein' a believer.' She gave Marylin a gentle push. 'Now, go on down and call Roy. She must be freezing out there.'

6

The next day, Friday, in the break before last period, when she had Drama, Marylin stood pressed against the wall by the thunderous crush in the hallway. As she worked the combination of her locker, BJ Fernauld shoved through the crowd. 'My leading lady returneth,' she said.

Despite the full mouth caked with orange lipstick, the pudgily round face, the messy pompadour, there was so much of Linc in his sister – the Indian hair, the prominent nose – that Marylin felt huge waves of affection. 'Hi,' she said.

'Where have you *been*?' BJ demanded. 'Did you have a cold?'

So Linc hadn't mentioned being with her. Marylin

fumbled past the number. Composing herself, she turned two revolutions, starting the combination again. 'I'm all better,' she murmured.

'Praise Allah. You have no idea what it's like, rehearsing around you. Well, what happened at Chapman's?'

'We talked.' Briefly Marylin rested her cheek on the cool metal. 'He took me home.'

'Listen, he's a very unusual person, very talented in all sorts of ways.' BJ's voice rose. 'I hope you don't get the idea he's a creep, taking you out.'

'That,' Marylin said, 'is hardly my criterion for creephood.'

'I didn't mean it as a slap, but, well, you are a junior in high school, and he'll be twenty-four in February.' BJ sighed. 'He's sure been weird since he got home.'

'What do you mean, weird?'

'I mean *weird*. He really was a sweetie, even for a brother. Before the war, he was never mean. Oh, sometimes he battled Dad, but then again, Dad's not an easy man to live with – we're cursed with one of those fathers who tries to run a person's life entirely.'

'What about Linc now?' Marylin asked, pushing her biology book into the locker.

'He can be perfectly normal, then all at once, for no reason at all, he explodes like a bomb. He barges out of the house. Either that or he's going around touching everything, as if he's blind.'

Twisting the dial of her lock, Marylin asked, 'BJ, has he had a bad time out there?'

'No, he's been lolling around on paradisiacal Pacific islands,' BJ snapped. 'Of course it's been rough. He's a pilot and there's a war on, or haven't you heard?'

They began pushing their way through the noisy hall.

'What happened?'

On the crowded stairs, BJ said, 'I guess it's no big military secret. He flies a TBM, a torpedo plane. Torpedoes have to be dropped right on target. Which means he has to zoom right down onto the Jap ships. So not only are Zeroes

61

chasing him, but those Kongo battleships and Hayataka or Shokaku carriers are training their guns on him.' BJ's voice rounded magniloquently as she classified the Japanese ships. 'He was shot down.'

Marylin closed her eyes. She stumbled on a metal-edged step and bumped into a short, frizzy-haired boy. 'Shot down?' she whispered.

'In November. He floated around for nearly a day before he was picked up. He got the Distinguished Flying Cross – but he positively blows up if anybody mentions it. I mean, he keeps flying off the handle. Yesterday I heard my parents talking. They're worried sick.'

Marylin clutched her notebook to her breasts, dizzy with a sickening urgency to hold Linc, to interject herself between his body and Japanese flak.

'You sure you're better?' BJ asked. 'If you don't mind my saying so, you look punk.'

'It must be terrible, knowing every day you might have to face enemy fire.'

'He has the Air Medal and the Distinguished Flying Cross!' BJ barked. 'They don't give those medals to chickens.'

'I didn't mean that he was a coward, BJ. But I know I couldn't keep forcing myself to risk my life.'

Before BJ could retort, the warning bell sliced like a buzz saw through the other sounds. They bolted towards Room 217.

In class Marylin's discipline deserted her, and she could not concentrate on her lines . . . *a few minutes of monstrous, degrading terror* . . . how long had he floated in that warm, shark infested sea, uncertain whether these waters were his grave? All that kept her from crying aloud was BJ sitting in the next row of desks, BJ, who resembled him and who sat unscathed in this Beverly High drama classroom.

When the final bell of the day rang, she found herself leaving with BJ. The school's painted brick walls glowed like rich cream in the afternoon sun while on the street below, carloads of kids honked and waved with frenzied

Friday-afternoon excesses. Wasn't there an irreconcilable paradox between Beverly Hills and the flame-exploding maw of hell that was the war?

She started to walk towards Santa Monica Boulevard with BJ. BJ – proud to be seen with Marylin Wace, who though not one of the school's true élite, was certainly its most beautiful adornment, and well known, besides, by virtue of her acting – strutted along with her messy black pompadour high, bragging cheerfully about the numerous boys crazy about her, accomplished, adorable paragons who by some fortuitous chance attended other schools. Marylin nodded whenever it seemed obligatory. She did not turn at Charleville. Instead, she continued on with BJ, crossing the two Santa Monica Boulevards.

Here, separating two identically named thoroughfares, lay the Southern Pacific tracks – also used by the trolley line – which sociologically bisected Beverly Hills. To the south of the tracks lay the unhurried business district and quiet streets of apartments and less expensive homes. To the north, on larger lots, stood houses that regardless of size sold for considerably more, a geographical snobbery accepted by every shop keeper when he charged your bill.

BJ understood the class implications of stepping over cinder and steel, but Marylin moved across the few yards without so much as a thought. Not only was she too poor to catch on to the subtleties of class coloration, but her luminous blue-green eyes had a blind spot where such pretensions disappeared from view.

On the north side of the tracks, further buttressing the division, lay Beverly Gardens, twenty-three blocks long, eighty feet wide, a narrow manicured park of lawns, flowerbeds, pergolas, a cactus garden, a lily pond, rose gardens. As the two girls walked along the promenade, which was soft-dappled by the shade of weeping evergreen elms, BJ continued her monologue. A khaki truck bearing khaki-clothed soldiers lumbered along Santa Monica, trailing exhaust and wolf whistles.

Both girls waved.

'Listen,' BJ blurted. 'How about coming over to the house?'

Marylin hesitated. Her nerves ached for physical reassurance that Linc was not locked into watery depths; however, since for some reason he had kept their relationship a secret, she worried about his reactions if she showed up on North Hillcrest Road with BJ. 'What about the Gramophone Shop?'

'Hey, a great idea! I'm dying to get Frankie's "Night and Day".'

In the shop, the girls browsed over bins of records whose paper wrappers were cut out in a circle to display the credits.

BJ selected five. Marylin picked up only 'These Foolish Things' by Tommy Dorsey, wishing she could afford to buy it, though the purchase would have been idiotic. The Waces had no record player.

All four of the booths were occupied: beyond soundproofed glass, people listened raptly to inaudible music. BJ plopped onto the narrow waiting bench. 'You want me to talk about Linc, don't you?' Her dark eyes were shrewd.

'Oh, BJ.'

'I'm not exactly a moron, Marylin. My brother takes you for an ice cream and all at once we're buddy-buddy.'

Marylin stared down at her record, considering how sick she was of a life filled with lying. 'That's true, BJ, but I do think of you as a friend, too.' This was honest. BJ's braggadocio might irritate, yet she had brains and – more important to Marylin – a bounding warmth, like a big, ungainly St Bernard puppy. 'The truth is, I like you a lot. And admire you – your play's a wonder.'

BJ wriggled with pleasure. 'Hey, I do believe those two in there are leaving.' A grey-haired couple were replacing records in an album imprinted *Excerpts from Carmen*. 'Let's go wait there before some other classical creeps take over for another year.' As they shifted positions, she asked, 'You find Linc devastating, don't you?'

'I'm in love with him.' A common-enough confession

exchanged by Beverly High girls, but Marylin's voice quivered on a note of visceral sincerity.

BJ leaned against the glass wall. 'So it's like that. Listen, I don't blame you. He's a terrific guy and groovy-looking. If he weren't my brother . . . Oh, Hail Mary and preserve me from incestuous thoughts.'

'Does he have a lot of girls?'

'Some. The latest is Rosellen St Vincent – she's a Pi Phi at Berkeley. She came down to spend a weekend after he graduated from flight school. I'm positive she goes all the way.'

Marylin sighed, richly jealous of Rosellen St Vincent and her sexual activities with Linc.

'Would you rather not hear about her?' BJ asked.

'No. Yes. I don't know . . .'

'Well, anyway, it's probably cooled off. He hasn't talked about seeing her this time.'

'How long has he been in the Navy?'

'Since the day after Pearl Harbor. Dad was furious, I can tell you. It was his idea to get Linc into the quartermaster corps and keep him here in California. The funny part is, Dad's a gung-ho physical type and it's hard to imagine Linc in a war. I mean, he's very caring of life, if you know what I mean. I can't see him shooting at anyone, even a Jap in a Zero.'

The classical couple emerged and BJ and Marylin went into the booth.

'He seems very complicated,' Marylin murmured in a fishing expedition.

'Is he ever! Listen to this. He had this poem published in *Atlantic Monthly*, and he never told any of us. I mean, what's the point of getting something printed if you aren't going to let everybody know?' BJ paused. 'Look, that was a clunky remark I made about you worming into my good graces because of Linc. And I'm sorry.'

'You don't have to apologize, BJ.'

'Sure I do. Aren't we friends?' BJ grabbed her record. 'Let's put that on first.'

Oh, how the ghost of you clings!
These foolish things
Remind me of you.

7

Despite their awesome bulk, aircraft carriers are thin-skinned. When the *Enterprise* had limped into San Diego in early January it was after thousand-pound bombs had caused costly fires and a torpedo had wreaked hell on the steering mechanism. Work proceeded on the enormous craft night and day: the estimate of the time the repairs would take was, of course, strictly hush-hush.

'But how long will you be here?' Marylin asked.

They had just left the rambling, ugly barn of the Avalon Ballroom on the Ocean Park Pier. Linc did not answer. Instead, he tilted his head to catch the last of the cool, pulsating notes of Jimmy Dorsey's alto saxophone. They moved through the swirl of uniforms and bright dresses, the shrieks from the plummeting roller coaster, and the sweet smell of caramel corn. In the parking lot there was only the waves breaking far below the tarred boards with the incessant hollow roar that one hears listening to a shell.

'Linc, you must have some idea how the repairs are going. Isn't there any scuttlebutt?'

Again he said nothing, but when they reached the Packard he took her hand, gripping it. 'Lay off, Marylin, please lay off.' His long fingers crushed hers.

She got into the car, hating herself for rousing his demon – or whatever you wanted to call the war-hideousness that devoured his living entrails.

Yet she had to know, didn't she, how long those repairs would keep him safe and with her?

Chaotically consumed by love, Marylin had turned into

time's miser, endlessly counting and recounting each hour and minute she would spend with Linc. She could bear that he had never told her that he loved her, bear that he had never taken her the couple of miles to North Hillcrest Road to introduce her to that renegade Catholic/Communist father and exotic Jewish mother, from whom (Marylin was positive) he and BJ had inherited their black hair, dark eyes and strong noses, even bear that he never spoke of any degree of permanence or even temporary fidelity. What woke her shaking in the nights, what debased the glory of her time with him, was her total ignorance of how long they had before the *Enterprise* was returned to seaworthiness.

As they drove, her balloon of silence threatened to burst with a gush of inquiries.

Linc drew up at an enormous clump of syringa that hid a shabby bungalow court.

On the narrow cement walkway Marylin flushed with the sense of wrongdoing that this place always engendered, yet the scent of the small, wiry lemon tree that grew by the door of number 2B stirred the most profound spiritual emotions that she had ever experienced. The question of whether to enter never stirred her mind.

The small room's Spanish-plastered walls were covered with framed pictures of groups: Hawthorne Grammar school and Beverly High graduations, posings of clubs and athletic teams. The apartment's leaseholder, Linc's lifelong friend, was stationed in Lompoc and Linc had a key. He and Marylin had been coming here since that Friday night in early January, their second evening date.

He put his arms around her. Photographed Beverly Hills children watched from the ombré shadows while Linc and Marylin clung together as if reunited after a long, arduous separation.

Afterwards, she drowsed.

She was walking in some enchanted green place, a forest of great ferns growing to incalculable heights over her head, music drifting all around her, hauntingly familiar music that she could not quite place, a blending of classical and popular that might have been Freddy Martin. Though she could not see Linc, she knew he was someplace near, and so she was secure, happy. 'Linc,' she called out, 'where are you?' 'Here,' he answered, close by. She pressed through a feathery thicket towards his voice, finding herself in an empty dell where small yellow primroses grew in profusion. 'Where?' she cried. 'This way.' His voice, again near, drifted from the opposite direction. The music changed to a plaintive, mournful minor key, and a sense of doom settled over her. 'Linc!' she cried. 'Please tell me where you are!' There was no answer, only the sound of sobbing.

She awoke.

Linc sprawled facedown next to her, the thin blankets thrown off him, his long, well-knit body shuddering, the muscles of his shoulders and torso showing with each heaving gasp. By the dim light from the living room she saw that tears streamed from his closed eyes.

'Linc,' she said, kissing his shoulder, which was damp with sweat.

He jerked awake. For a moment he stared blankly at her, his dark, tormented eyes still seeing his nightmare; then he focused on her and buried his face between her breasts.

'Bad dream,' he muttered, rubbing his cheeks dry, leaving red marks on her sensitive skin. He kissed the small dark mole just above her navel.

'Nifty spot for a beauty mark,' he said in a normal voice. 'Not that you need one.' He lifted up on his elbow, staring at the small, exquisitely lush body.

'Linc, okay?'

'When I'm with you,' he said, 'all's right with the world.'

He embraced her with tenderness, adoration, yet these delicate qualities did not preclude the blazingly vital electricity between them that had, from that first fateful Friday, cancelled out any shame or guilt on her part. She had graduated since then from a carnal ignoramus to an eager acolyte and then to an equal partner. Together they moved with tremulous languor, and his breath against her ear

68

made her think of waves reverberating forever against the shore, receding and lapping, and all at once that involuntary, incomprehensible stillness preceding orgasm was upon her and she held her breath, attending the moment before she was borne away. 'Oh, Linc, Linc, Linc, I love you, love you . . .' And they both sped swiftly, artlessly into the great sea of life and love.

When their breathing quieted, he twisted off his ring. Heavy, hand-hammered silver formed his initials. 'You wear old ALF for a while.'

She looked into his eyes, trying to gauge his meaning. He had never hinted at going steady or being engaged. So why a ring? All at once, like an evil needle piercing her, she recalled her mother's words: *Men use the war as an excuse to take advantage of girls.* Linc was so very honourable. Was his conscience rubbing him, did he need to throw her a sop, payment for her virginity? Yet he surely knew that her body collaborated freely and joyously with his.

He fitted the warm silver on each of her fingers. It even slipped off her thumb. 'Guess you'll have to put it on a chain.' His throaty warmth belied his teasing tone. 'In *intime* moments, what a clangour with my dogtags.'

She kept looking at him.

'Oh, Marylin, those beautiful eyes, those beautiful sea-coloured eyes. Listen, I'm giving you something of mine. Is that so odd?'

'What does it mean?'

'That you're gentle, wonderful, soothing and so beautiful that it's not quite believable. That I'm out of my head about you. Marylin, what does a ring usually mean?'

She gripped the silver in her palm. Here, finally, was the admission of love, the symbol that she had longed for, and her soul should have been soaring on hosannas, yet a sadness that had to do with the brevity of time ached in her throat – *how much longer until he sails?* – and she had to cough before she said, 'I love you so much, Linc.'

'It's binding on my part,' he said. 'Not yours.'

'Always.'

'No, I mean it. You're free to look around for some equally devastating Beverly High graduate.'

'I'll love you forever,' she said. 'I belong to you.'

'For the time being, this is between us.'

Again that odd secrecy. Why? 'Yes.'

He smiled at her.

She began to cry. 'Darling, I can't bear not knowing how long we have.'

He pulled away. 'The general time frame is until death do us part, right?'

Death . . . She shivered. 'You know what I mean.'

'I always have trouble reconciling how tenacious you are with that gentleness.'

There was a shrill buzzing. It was the red Westclox alarm that they always set for 11.45 in case they fell asleep.

'There's your answer,' he said, pressing down the stem.

The following Tuesday, just as she and Roy (who had graduated from Horace Mann and would start at Beverly in January) came in from school, the telephone began to ring.

Marylin ran to it.

'I'd abandoned hope,' Linc said.

'We just came in the door.'

'This is classified, so I count on you not to tell any Japanese or Nazi spies.'

A knot twisted around her heart. 'The repairs?'

'Completed.'

Her knees went weak and she sat on Roy's bed. 'You mean . . .'

'Yep.'

'Oh, Linc . . . Not even this next weekend?'

'Nope.' There was a rustling as if buzzards had come to perch on the long-distance wires. His voice sounded faraway and thin. 'You have my APO address.'

'I'll write all the time. Is it tonight?'

'I think so.'

'Oh . . .'

Another flap of ghostly wings.

'Marylin.'

'What?'

'I may send some of my stuff from time to time.'

He's leaving, she thought, leaving ... An immense, crowding misery was upon her and she could scarcely move her lips to form words. 'Your writing?'

'It's just for you.'

'I'll keep it.'

'Wearing old ALF?'

She touched the ring, which hung around her neck on a silver-plated chain that had come in one of her Christmas cartons. 'Always.'

'Good.'

She could hear a distorted banging at the other end of their bad connection. Then: 'Oh, shut up! Give a guy a chance!' Linc's anger was muffled as if he were holding his hand over the mouthpiece. Then his voice came through the crackling. 'The barbarians are at the gates. Listen, don't take ALF off, okay?'

'Never, never.'

'That's my good-luck charm you're wearing.'

She was shaking and tears blinded her, but she used all the points of control she had learned in her acting lessons to say clearly, 'Linc, I love you.'

'Marylin – '

The phone went dead.

'Linc?' she cried. 'Linc?'

The connection was dead, but she did not hang up. Instead, she hunched over on Roy's bed, her tears falling onto the instrument.

Roy, who had been at the refrigerator studiously drinking from a milk bottle, came over to clumsily pat her shoulder. 'Is Linc shipping out?'

Marylin ran into the bathroom, the only place she could weep in privacy.

8

Every day from 11.20 to 12.10, the Beverly High student body descended on the cafeteria. The kitchen staff of six women and a man turned out a creditable full-course lunch in spite of rationing. There were also lines that dispensed triple-decker tuna or cheese sandwiches and thick malts, as well as exterior windows where a sweet tooth could be satisfied with ice cream and packaged cakes – Twinkies were the most popular. No soft drinks or candies were sold on any grounds belonging to the Beverly Hills school system.

In the environs of the cafeteria one could see the school's social strata, which bore no relationship to the hierarchies of the outside world. The scholarly, the acned and the humble beings who lacked any idea of status ate at the long tables inside. Those more in tune with the scheme of things sat on the patio.

Marylin was at a round table away from the visible storm of movement, the blue table umbrella keeping the bright April glare from the clipped-together sheaf of legal paper on which her attention was focused.

Opposite her, Roy and Althea Cunningham were sharing Althea's package of Hostess cupcakes.

Sunlight heightened the incongruity of heavy makeup on their childishly soft faces. Round little Roy's freckles were not quite obliterated by Max Factor's Pan-Cake, and her mouth was excessively maroon. Althea – tall and very thin – had smudged her topaz eyes with mascara and drastically enlarged her fine lips with great swoops of plummy lipstick.

Even in its ridiculous upsweep, Althea's hair was really something. Straight, silky and ash blond, with lambent streaks that varied from palest gold to gleaming silver.

The two freshmen had struck up an acquaintance at Orientation, in their first hour at Beverly, and since then had become inseparable. Almost every afternoon Althea walked with Roy and Marylin along Charleville to the apartment. There the two younger girls stationed themselves in the bathroom, experimenting with makeup, combing their hair into high pompadours over NolaBee's wadded rats, emerging to consume boxes of graham crackers and gallons of milk that the Wace household could ill afford.

NolaBee, though, chuckled indulgently, delighted that Roy at last had a friend.

There were certain strange aspects to the friendship. Althea never spoke about her parents and had never once invited Roy to her home. If either Marylin or NolaBee said a word, Roy loyally shouted them down. 'So what? We live closer to school. And who cares about families?'

Althea had gone to private school, so the Waces guessed she must come from one of those classy houses north of Santa Monica Boulevard – or possibly even a north-of-Sunset mansion. Rich she certainly was. There was no question about that. Every afternoon at five, a heavyset elderly coloured woman, obviously a servant, would honk the horn of a Chevy coupé with an A gas-ration sticker on the windshield. Althea would run down. After a few minutes the phone would ring, and Roy would pick it up and chatter away for another forty-five or fifty minutes. 'I declare, I don't know what all those two find to talk about,' NolaBee would say to Marylin, laughing.

Althea's clothes were peculiar. Finely tucked blouses made of creamy *crêpe de chine* rather than the usual white cotton; sweaters handknit in an out-of-date way with patterns; very long and narrow Oxford shoes. 'No snap,' was NolaBee's opinion. 'I reckon without Roy that Althea Cunningham's an unhappy little thing.' Another remark that Roy vehemently denied.

A nearby table crowded with freshman boys erupted into laughter, and a short boy stood, nodding his sandy crewcut towards Roy before departing with a self-conscious strut.

73

Althea said, 'Noticed by Mr Big Time himself!'

'Oh, hug me!' cried Roy.

'Not until we meet thereafter.'

'You can say that again.'

They talked about boys in a language of catch phrases all their own.

A brunette had come over to the table. 'Hi, Roy,' she said, her smile displaying elaborate braces. Squeezing her looseleaf to her breasts, she inquired, 'How did you do on the English quiz?'

Roy grinned cheerfully. 'Flunked, most likely. You?'

Althea stared down towards the gym buildings. Her joyous expression was replaced by remote hauteur. She sat next to Roy in the English class, and it was humiliating not to be greeted or questioned – but then it seemed to Althea that her classmates always either ignored her or tormented her. She wanted to viciously batter the intruder while at the same time she wished fervently that *she* had been asked about her quiz results.

'Roy, what about that Tri-Y meeting?' the girl was asking.

Idiot, jerk, Althea thought, her fingers clenching. Nobody.

Suddenly she was overwhelmed by the desire to be home at Belvedere, alone in her airy room that overlooked the Italian gardens. People drained her spirit and made her miserable. Had it always been like this? Or had she begun to feel an outcast only after *it* had happened? . . . Althea squeezed her eyes shut, banning the dreaded memory.

The girl left.

'Is it animal, vegetable or mineral?' Althea drawled.

'Oh, Betty's a good kid,' Roy said.

'The correct answer is all three – if you consider the salad caught in her braces,' Althea said. 'I for one wouldn't be caught dead with those Tri-Y drips!'

Marylin glanced up from the papers on her lap. Like NolaBee, she was glad that Roy had a friend, yet she had reservations: Althea seemed to have some sort of complex that made her belittle the other kids.

After a moment Roy said, 'If you don't want to go to the meeting, neither do I.'

At that moment a crowd of sophomore boys began an elaborate horseplay on the other side of the patio: the two friends watched, then leaned towards one another giggling and whispering.

Marylin reached for her thermos and poured cocoa into the cup. The flavoured milk seemed to have picked up a metallic taint.

But what did taste right to her now?

Though Marylin's ignorance of certain reproductive information was near total, a truth had been known to her subconscious for weeks now: the cause of this faint, omnipresent nausea.

She was pregnant.

She was utterly alone, terrified and certainly unable to confide this shame to anyone. Was it possible that until a few months ago her innermost thoughts and dreams had been innocent enough to expose to her mother? Twice she had started to write to Linc, only to have her fingers cramp perilously when she attempted to form the words 'I think I'm having a baby'. Prudery was appallingly inane at this point, yet she could not put her disgrace on V-Mail.

She had no idea of what to do, none.

Her one prayer, and she repeated it on a never-ending prayer wheel, was that the *Enterprise* would return to San Diego.

Sighing, she looked down at Linc's large spiky handwriting on yellow legal paper.

This was 'Island', the sheets with the story had arrived yesterday. At home in a box she had twenty or so other stories: some were only a single page, others were long – one had fifty pages. In these tales of different men aboard an aircraft carrier, the main character of one story might play a minor part in another, or an omnipotent *I* might insert a description – Linc had written that this narrator was a fictive device, yet she intuitively accepted *I* as Linc. Each character rang so utterly true to her that she wondered if he had crawled under his shipmates' skins.

A few stories were based on her and Linc. 'Island' was one of them.

Of course he knew quite well he could not block out the war, any more than he could stop time, yet it was a conceit of his that when he was with Rain, if they saw no family or friends, admitted no mention of the war, why, then the war did not exist. The hours he spent with her were an island, a place where peace and love existed, where there were no cream-coloured Zekes firing on him, no huge gun muzzles on Japanese ships blazing colourful death – green, yellow, black, blue-white, pink, purple – no crouching over his stick praying there was enough gas to get him and the two others back, no memories of floating alone and crying out for Hobbs and Cariu even though he had seen neither of their chutes open. He kept the island pristine of these things, and each time he came there he found it more difficult to leave.

Rain, of course, wondered about his furtiveness, and doubtless it, like his foul humour, hurt her. For the most part, though, loving him, she accepted him, and did not raise too much of a fuss that he kept their relationship in the present.

[I described Rain in the story about the pilot and the cop, didn't I? A small, delicately built girl with enormous sea-green eyes and a beauty mark near the shell of her navel.]

He did all he could to protect the island, and when it was threatened, he could get pretty brutal.

On this particular leave, he had determined to –

'Marylin.' Tommy Wolfe was leaning on their table.

'Hi, Tommy,' she replied.

'You have gym next, don't you?' He was red about the ears.

'Sure thing.'

'Me too. I'll walk you down. Uhh . . . I mean, it's a chance to go over our new lines.'

Roy and Althea were staring. They knew that Tommy, who was in the junior play and hung around at lunchtime, had a big fat case on Marylin.

'I already learned mine,' she said.

Tommy hung his big, carefully combed head in embarrassment. Roy and Althea tittered.

'It's a good idea to try the scene together, Tommy.' Marylin tucked 'Island' carefully into her notebook. 'That way we'll be ready in drama class.'

Miss Nathans, the drama teacher, a recent graduate of USC, a tall young woman with the full figure of a Viking boat prow, sat at her desk in the centre of the dais-cum-stage. Normally she called out cheerful greetings, but today her face was sombre as she watched her students stroll to their desks and start to chatter. Marylin, who sat in the front row, took out a blue V-Mail sheet and began to scribble her profuse, heartfelt admiration of 'Island' – contradictorily, when she was writing to Linc, her problem was most remote. The buzzer sounded.

Miss Nathans rose to her feet. Normally she took roll with perfunctory swiftness before getting down to the work she enjoyed, but today her modulated contralto reverberated lingeringly over each name. Thirty-one pairs of eyes gazed with expectant curiosity at her.

'As some of you may have noticed,' she said with the same intense depth that she had taken roll, 'the author of our class play, Barbara Jane Fernauld, is not with us this afternoon.'

There was a buzzing in the class, and everyone turned towards the empty desk-seat as though to ascertain the truth of this, although two minutes earlier BJ had not answered. Marylin alone held still, her frightened eyes fixed on Miss Nathans' high-coloured face.

'Barbara Jane was called home during third period. Her family received the sort of news dreaded by each of us who has a loved one serving her country. Her brother, Lincoln Fernauld, Beverly Hills High School, summer class of '37, is missing in action . . .' She paused.

She's a liar, a liar, a liar, Marylin thought, shivering. A rotten, lousy, hateful liar.

'At Beverly,' Miss Nathans intoned, 'Lincoln was on the Bee and Varsity basketball squad, he was a Squire, a Knight, a four-year Palladian, he was city editor on the *Highlights* and head editor on the *Watchtower*.' Miss Nathans paused again, a longer pause. 'Will the class join me in a minute of silent prayer for the safety of Lieutenant Lincoln Fernauld.' She bowed her head.

In the worst of revelations sometimes there is a moment of benumbed grace before horror takes over. Missing in action?

Linc?

It couldn't be. 'Island' had arrived in yesterday's mail.

Missing in action?

Then the truth encompassed Marylin with preternatural vividness. From one of the longer stories she knew in full, ineradicable detail what it was like to be shot down. In this ghastly, distorted instant the immolation was hers.

She cringed backwards in the burning cockpit, seeing the fire spread from the gasoline filler pipe, her ears heard the engine of the spinning plane shrill like a woman, her body felt the bone-consuming heat, flames seared her hands as she yanked off the heavy gloves, her fingers struggled helplessly with the recalcitrant buckle of the safety belt, her desperate lungs gasped in the asphyxiating smoke, she was standing up in her seat frantically attempting to force her way out of the burning plane while the solid wind wall of slipstream trapped her . . .

She did not realize that she was clutching her books and purse to her breasts, stumbling towards the glass-inset door.

'Marylin,' Miss Nathans called after her. 'You are not dismissed.'

Marylin pushed into the cool, empty hall. She was still trapped in the incendiary hell of the TBM cockpit.

'Marylin.' Miss Nathans had followed her. 'You know as well as I that it's against school rules for you to leave in the middle of class.'

Marylin gazed wildly at this apparition amidst her torment.

'Whatever is it? You're white as a sheet . . .' The drama teacher's voice, worried and no longer theatrical, came from far away.

Marylin's books and purse slipped from her grasp.

A great, hollow silence opened up.

9

Marylin swam back to consciousness.

She lay on something hard, a starched white cap atop a wrinkled visage hanging over her, while at a distance blurred the anxious faces of Miss Nathans and Tommy Wolfe.

I fainted . . . Why? As memory spoke, her body convulsed feebly.

'Wait a minute before you try to get up,' said the school nurse's New England twang.

Marylin became aware that something soakingly warm wrapped her lower body, and there was an ammoniac smell. Moaning, she closed her eyes.

'Don't be embarrassed, that happens,' said the nurse briskly. She glanced over her shoulder, and Tommy disappeared.

'Marylin, dear,' Miss Nathans said, 'I'll see how you are later.' She went back into the classroom.

After a minute or so the nurse helped Marylin to her feet: with one assisting arm around the slight waist, she led the girl slowly down the stairs and along the main corridor to the brightly sunlit first-aid room. NolaBee was on the day shift at Hughes, so there was no point in calling home.

'You live on Charleville,' said the nurse crisply. 'Miss Nathans goes in that direction. She'll give you a lift.'

'What about my sister?' Marylin's voice sounded odd and tinny to her. 'My sister will worry.'

'I'll send a note to her class.'

79

With impersonal competence the nurse helped Marylin off with her wet clothes, giving her a loose gown that tied with strings. Marylin stretched nauseated and light-headed on one of the beds that were separated by a curtain from the dispensary. She could hear the nurse's quick, expert typing, hear a fly buzzing nearer, then farther . . . nearer, then farther. That gruesome you-are-there clairvoyance was gone and her mind reiterated 'missing in action . . . missing in action . . . missing in action'.

Though shivering, she did not pull up the khaki blanket folded over the foot of the bed; though the curtain was phlegm green, ugly and menacing, she did not take her eyes from it. Like that poor trapped fly, her mind endlessly revolved around the three words.

Missing in action.

Missing . . . in . . . action . . .

It meant his plane had not returned, it meant he was somewhere, but not on the *Enterprise*.

It did not mean that he was dead.

He was shot down once before and he was okay, she thought, forlornly trying to comfort herself. Why doesn't the nurse open a window and let the fly out? Missing in action . . . missing in action . . .

The final bell buzzed. Feet thundered on cement hallways, lockers clanged, voices shrilled and roared.

Roy and Althea burst into the nurse's office, both demanding at once, 'Where's Marylin Wace? What's wrong with her?'

'Which one of you is Roy Wace?' asked the nurse.

She sent Althea packing before she would explain to Roy that Marylin had fainted.

'Fainted?' Roy asked. 'She's never fainted.'

'It happens a lot. No wonder, the way you girls diet nowadays. She had a little accident with her clothes. They're in this bag. And here's a note for your mother.'

Marylin borrowed Roy's hand-me-down blue coat.

The three of them squeezed into the front seat of Miss Nathans' rattly brown LaSalle coupé. When the car pulled up in the garage driveway, Marylin said: 'Thank you, Miss Nathans.' She had scarcely spoken to Roy in the nurse's office, and these were the first words she had uttered since they had left Beverly High.

Climbing the steps, Roy gripped her sister's fragile arm. She felt protective, flustered, sympathetic and inadequately young. As she used her doorkey, she asked, 'Marylin, what happened?

Marylin, without replying or taking off the saggy old coat, sat at the table.

'Anything I can do to help?'

Marylin gave her a blank look.

'What about something to eat?'

Marylin blinked as if somebody had shone a flashlight in her lovely blue-green eyes. 'Oh. Maybe a cup of tea.'

Waiting for the water to boil, Roy reached her own conclusions about the fainting spell. In movies and novels a swoon generally announced a baby was on the way. Roy knew only the vaguest outline of the process (oh sure she jabbered with sophisticatedly raised eyebrows to Althea, but that was only *talk*) so she imagined that passing out had been Marylin's first inkling of pregnancy. And Linc was thousands of miles away! No wonder the poor girl was in a state. How gruesome.

Roy carried a sloshing cup of liquid that was more milk than tea to the table and sat opposite her sister. 'Marylin, listen, I'm not a little kid anymore.' Her menarche had occurred in January, by clever chance the same month that she started Beverly.

Marylin looked up. 'What?'

'If something's . . . wrong . . . I'll do everything to help.'

Marylin shook her head.

'However bad it is,' Roy said. 'I promise I wouldn't tell anyone, not even Mama.'

Marylin stared at her with the wide-open, vague look of a strafed refugee.

Roy's natural loyalty and sympathy gushed, and she had

to fight back tears. 'I'm your sister,' she muttered, hugging Marylin's trembly shoulders. 'You can trust me.'

'I'm cold, so very cold.'

'Here, let's get you into bed.'

At a little after six the rickety outside stairs shuddered under footsteps, and Roy, thoroughly frightened by her sister's zombielike inertia, galloped to open the door for her mother. NolaBee, as usual, lugged a big brown bag of groceries. Seeing Marylin, salt white under a heap of faded old patchwork quilts, she thrust the bag at Roy and ran to her crumpled, beautiful child. Marylin sat up, holding out her arms, and when NolaBee clasped her, she buried her face in her mother's meagre bosom and began gasping in terrible deep sobs.

'Darlin', darlin'. What is it?'

'Linc . . . he's . . . missing in action . . .'

'Oh, my poor darlin'.'

'I'm so . . . cold.'

'Mama's home.'

'. . . and frightened.'

'Mama's with you.'

Roy, watching her mother rock her sister in her arms, crooning as if Marylin were a little baby, felt her own face and ears go hot. What a juvenile she'd been to leap to the melodramatically wrong conclusion. Then her eyes filled with tears. That dreamy dreamy guy, she thought. To atone for her evil misconception about her sister's purity, she put away groceries on the crowded, messy open shelves.

'Marylin.' She went to the bed. 'Want me to call BJ? She'll know what's going on.'

Marylin jerked from her mother's arms. 'That's a wonderful idea! Maybe he's been found. I'll do it.'

Her hands shook and she could not thumb through F's in the slim Beverly Hills phone directory, so Roy looked up the number and dialled, handing her the phone.

'May I speak to BJ?' Marylin asked.

Roy could hear a coloured maid's voice at the other end explaining that Lieutenant Fernauld was missing and the family was not taking calls. The febrile excitement drained from Marylin's face, and she stood holding the instrument as if she did not know what to do with it.

NolaBee hung up and led Marylin to her own bed.

During the night, Roy awakened to hear her mother's voice, intense and throaty: 'You can't, darling, it's just plain impossible.'

'And what about that operation? Mama, it's murder, *murder.*'

'Marylin, listen to me, listen. What's inside you now is nothing, a tiny nothing – '

'It's part of Linc.' Marylin's voice convulsed in ragged little sobs that to Roy were even more pitiable than her earlier tears of irreconcilable grief.

'Hush, hush,' NolaBee soothed.

'I won't kill Linc's baby.'

'You know what people will call it, I reckon. Darlin', we can't let our baby be a bastard.'

'Linc'll come home!'

'Course he will. But it won't be in time. After, you can be married right and proper, and have lots of other babies. This one, Marylin, it's not fair to the poor little innocent. Even if you do carry it, you'll have to give it away. A child needs a name, a father, a right proper life.'

Her mother's Southern voice spoke the common-sense truth, and Roy knew it – yet wasn't there another, more human truth of life and love?

The covers rustled as if somebody were turning over.

'I can't do that thing, it's illegal, and besides, I just can't. This is Linc's baby, part of him. Mama I'm so confused, so miserable, but don't try to make me do it. Because I won't.'

'Darlin', it's the only way. A mistake like this could ruin your life forever. I reckon you'd never get a chance at a career.'

'I hate acting!'

'You hate everything now.'

'I've always done what you've told me, Mama, you know that. But not this time.'

'It's only like, well, a scraping. Somebody I know on the wing assembly had it done last month, she had a right good doctor.' NolaBee's voice cracked and Roy knew her mother was crying. 'Oh, my sweet beautiful, as if I like it any more than you do! But there's no other answer.'

'Why don't we move?' Marylin said in a stronger voice. 'Pretend the baby's yours. Or that I'm married – '

'Marylin, you know as well as I do how close we are to the bone. Where would we get the money to take care of a baby?'

'I'll leave school and work,' Marylin said.

'And who would raise it?'

Marylin's awful, ragged little sobs started again. Roy's eyes were oozing in sympathy. 'Me,' she said, the syllable loud in the darkness.

'Roy. You shouldn't be eavesdropping,' accused NolaBee.

'I'd have to be stricken deaf not to.'

'You go back to sleep.'

But Roy got out of bed, stumbling around the big wardrobe to the double mattress that her parents had shared, crawling in next to Marylin, putting her arms around the fragile, shaking body. Even now, in her tears and unhappiness, Marylin had a tenderly sweet smell, not Apple Blossom cologne but her own unique bodily scent.

'Marylin, I'll leave school too. I'll look after the baby.'

'Roy,' NolaBee said, lifting up to reach over to pat her younger daughter, 'you're being right sweet, but you girls aren't talking sense. We can't ruin Marylin's life and the baby's too. There's just no way out except . . .' Her voice broke into a gasping sob.

The three Waces wound their arms around each other, rocking together as they wept.

Towards dawn, Roy and NolaBee drowsed.

Wedged between her mother and sister, Marylin lay with her aching eyes wide open, her fingers clenching the initialled silver ring, ALF.

Suddenly a plan came to her, a crazily simple plan.

She would go to Linc's father.

The famous Joshua Fernauld. Rich and powerful. A writer of noble novels and screenplays that celebrated the dignity of human life.

She would explain about Linc and her . . . No. She would give Mr Fernauld Linc's stories – Linc had written far more eloquently of what they meant to one another than any words she could utter.

Mr Fernauld would not let his grandchild be scraped away.

10

Trudging northward in her bobby socks and navy gabardine suit, a reconstructed hand-me-down that was the most sombre outfit she owned, Marylin cradled the box containing Linc's short stories.

A cold April wind had blown away the mist, revealing each architectural embellishment on North Hillcrest Road – a lavishly tiled Hispanic dome, the ornamental stonework on Norman crenellations, the elegant fanlight of a Colonial mansion. The impeccably pruned trees and shrubbery were rattling *money, money, money*.

Marylin added awe to her morbid churn of emotions.

This morning NolaBee had been determined to call Hughes that a family emergency was keeping her home, but Marylin had summoned her every tenuous acting skill to convince her mother that she was fine now, sound of mind and body, and could rest in bed alone.

After her mother and sister had left, she remained immobile, her eyes fixed on the long, twisting water stain on the ceiling, her mind filled with the horror in the burning cockpit. Though she no longer suffered the immediacy of that first horror-struck paroxysm, a bleakly miserable anxiety enveloped her, and she held tight to that thin shred of comfort: he was missing, not dead. Around nine she attempted to focus on her approaching face-to-face confrontation with Joshua Fernauld, but the incalculable importance of this meeting with the famous stranger paralysed her already dislocated mental processes. Finally she accepted that her sole chance of success lay in preparing as for a role. Tearing a sheet of three-holed paper from her notebook, she struggled with her dialogue: *Mr Fernauld, I'm so very sorry about Linc. I've been dating him – more than dating. I've brought along some stories he's sent me. The ones he wrote about us are on top. I need to ask your help about something. When you've finished reading, you'll understand.* She rehearsed in front of the bathroom mirror, after a while managing to say her lines without a sob.

At 10.20 – she had determined eleven the earliest acceptable hour to call – she had set out, mechanically repeating the speech as she covered the miles.

She crossed Elevado to the seven hundred block, where the Fernaulds lived. Big, gleaming cars lined both sides of the street, and Marylin absently determined a ladies' club meeting was in progress nearby. The only other time she had been to the Fernaulds' was when she and Linc had dropped off BJ, and then she had been too involved to fully take in how dismayingly impressive the large Tudor-style house was. She gazed up in dismay at the massive heap of crimson bricks traced with Virginia creeper.

The front door opened. A man in a natty blazer emerged, and during the moment that the door remained open, the roar of voices blasted out.

A *party*? Marylin reacted with confusion and fear.

Her preconceptions had staged this scene between two players, herself and Joshua Fernauld – Linc's anxious father.

Though she had always been forced to conquer her fears, she had never viewed herself as a bona fide coward, and now she asked herself how – in the midst of her flaying cares – *how* could she be in such a panic about entering Linc's house simply because for some crazy reason it was filled

86

with owners of Cadillacs, Chryslers and chauffeured Lincolns?

Think of what Mama wants to do, she told herself.

Racing up the path, she desperately clunked a polished brass door-knocker shaped like a mermaid.

The door was opened by a coloured woman with reddish processed hair and a fine figure beneath her grey silk uniform. Hadn't Linc – and BJ, too – spoken with warm affection of a black couple? Yes, Coraleen and Percy, who had been with the Fernaulds since BJ's birth.

'Yes?' Coraleen inquired pointedly.

The sound of convivial voices blew about them, and Marylin could not speak.

The servant's red-tinged eyes peered questioningly at her. 'You're a friend of BJ's?'

'No . . . yes. Marylin Wace.'

'Come on in, honey. I'll get her.'

The maid's kind tone soothed Marylin a trifle, and she stood in the cathedral-like entry, gazing around. Other than on a movie screen, she had never seen such pure swank. Each detail was perfection from the intricate spoolwork on the massive curving staircase to the sparkling, handsize drops on an enormous chandelier surely imported from Versailles.

Through the archway to the dining room, she saw a man moving around a long oval table helping himself from various silver bowls and platters whose contents were works of art. Food that appeared a gorgeously different substance from the haphazard if tasty brown meals that NolaBee served up. Flowers made of bright radishes and carrots adorned thinly sliced, radiant pink meats – you'd never guess there was rationing. A monstrous crystal bowl refracted the jewel-hued balls of out-of-season melon. Loaves of every ethnic variety stood sliced yet left in their twisted or rounded or oval shapes. Marylin could only guess the delicacies in the twin chafing dishes, but even the humble potato salad lay beneath a glinty blackness that she accepted must be the first caviar she had ever seen. On the sideboard, an elaborately chased silver tea service was flanked by a rich variety of frosted cakes and cream pastries. Queasily Marylin turned away.

Across the hall, in a living room filled with bright chintz and antiques, a pair of bald, grey-suited men gesticulated a conversation. The main orchestra of voices, however, came from behind the living room.

The general air of a large, jovial party, while unnerving to Marylin, roused a wacky hopefulness in her. The Fernaulds are celebrating, so that must mean Linc's been found, she thought with a fast-beating heart.

The voices blared louder.

BJ, wearing a draped black date dress and ankle straps with spiky heels, had opened a door behind the stairwell and was coming towards her. Her pompadour wisping in black strands, her lipstick worn off except at the well-defined corners of her mouth, she looked completely herself. 'How swell of you to come, Marylin,' she said warmly. 'Did you cut school?'

'I heard yesterday,' Marylin said. 'I tried to phone you.'

'We aren't taking calls.'

'Your maid told me . . . BJ, this party – does it mean Linc's been found?'

BJ's eyes closed. Marylin could see the lashline was red and puffy. 'He's dead,' she said in a small voice.

'No!' Marylin denied with unaccustomed vehemence. 'Missing in action.'

· 'At first it was only missing in action, so there was some hope. But Dad got on the horn, calling every top brass he knows in Washington, and we heard for sure last night. Linc was on a mission involving a big, well-armed Jap convoy – we don't know where, of course. But it was fierce. Linc's been credited with two direct hits. Evidently quite a few of our planes . . .' She made a spiral gesture downward. 'Linc made it through the attack and started back with the survivors, but his plane was damaged. He couldn't keep up. A whole group of Zeroes zoomed in, he couldn't manoeuvre . . . Three of our planes saw his go down.'

'No parachute?' Marylin whispered.

'The TBM has a three-man crew. There were no chutes . . . none . . . Linc's dead.'

Marylin's heart slowed, her head felt weird and hollow, and she felt exactly as she had in the school corridor yesterday. I can't faint again, she thought, clutching the box closer. She tensed her muscles, as if readying herself for physical combat, and with a tremendous effort thrust from her mind what BJ had just told her. She had the rest of her life to consider that ultimate obscenity, Linc's death, and only the next few minutes to rescue his child.

'Word is we wrecked their convoy,' said BJ, vainglory pitiable in her thin voice.

Marylin began to cry.

BJ, though unaware of Marylin's full relationship with Linc, had heard the confession of love coming from her friend's beautiful lips, and because Marylin Wace was a Somebody at Beverly High, this stamped the crush with a validity lacking in other schoolgirl pashes.

She held out her round, black-crêpe arms. The large-boned, plump girl and the delicately fragile small girl held each other in a mourners' embrace.

They wept several moments, then pulled apart.

'What makes you think this is a party?' BJ blew her nose. 'Behold a Class A Beverly Hills wake. The heads of three major studios have already passed this way. Come on in.'

Across the rear of the house stretched a panelled card room with four substantial, green-baize-topped tables surrounded by large velvet-upholstered armchairs. Behind an ornately carved bar, a maroon-jacketed coloured manservant (Percy?) dispensed drinks to a group of men already boisterously drunk. Beyond this room was a sunporch bright with wicker and big pots of daffodils, and beyond the sliding glass doors, an aqua oval swimming pool. In both rooms, suntanned, resplendently attired men and women held glasses and chatted – Marylin wondered if that really could be Edward G. Robinson, and was that redhead in half-profile actually Greer Garson, or somebody who looked and sounded exactly like her? Could that big, handsome naval officer possibly be Clark Gable? BJ led her around conversational groupings ('. . . I'm using Van for the part . . .' '. . . buying the handmade sterling flatware from Porter Blanchard . . .' '. . . stationed in London, thank God . . .') to a chair.

Here sat a diminutive woman whose dyed blond hair was carefully arranged around a face so thin that the small bones of her cheeks and jaw showed clearly.

'Mother,' BJ said, 'I'd like you to meet a really good friend of mine, Marylin Wace.'

'Mrs Fernauld,' Marylin said, swallowing, 'I'm so very, very sorry . . .'

'Thank you, dear,' Mrs Fernauld said hastily, as if fearing that overt sympathy might endanger her fleshless composure. 'How kind of you to come.'

'We're *very* good friends,' said BJ.

'People are being so nice,' said Mrs Fernauld. 'Why don't you get her something to drink, BJ, dear. A Coke? Ginger ale?'

A candle was burning in a glass with Jewish letters around it. Seeing Marylin's glance, BJ said with defiant truculence, 'For the half-Jewish side.'

Marylin had never wearied of hearing Linc talk of his colourful Jewish relations, but BJ never mentioned them.

'The *yarzheit* candle comforts Grandma, I'm sure Emma understands,' said Mrs Fernauld, her bony fingers twining with BJ's large, plump ones. 'BJ, dear, you remember Mrs Harper?'

BJ was drawn into Mrs Fernauld's group. Marylin sat down, holding the box awkwardly on her lap.

On the couch next to her, a tiny, very wrinkled lady, also with bright blond hair, had turned to stare. 'So, pretty little girl, you're a friend of BJ's?' she asked in a buoyant accent.

'Yes . . .'

'So you're the only one here who didn't know Lincoln, so that means you can make with a few honest tears?'

Marylin had not realized she was crying.

90

The old lady handed her a wadded, moist handkerchief. 'If you don't mind a used one?'

'Not at all. Thank you . . .'

'They grieve, you mustn't think they don't grieve. They show it different, that's all.'

'I understand . . .'

Tears welled into the old lady's eyes. 'You tell me what God means, letting a boy like that be killed. A Phi Beta Kappa, all the promise in the world. Such a decent, good boy, such a *mensch*.'

At the word, BJ broke away from her mother's group. 'Oh, you met Gramma. Mrs Lottman, Marylin Wace,' she said hastily. 'Come along, Marylin, let's get something to eat.'

'Eat?'

'It's lunchtime. There's tons of food.'

'I have to talk to your father.'

'Dad's pretty stinko.'

'I'd wanted to tell him . . . how sorry I am . . .' Marylin wiped at her eyes.

BJ accorded her friend Juliet-widow's rights. 'Come along,' she said, leading her back into the card room and towards the bar, where the drunken group was arguing with simultaneous obstreperousness about Roosevelt and the need for a second front.

BJ waited for a lull, then put her hand on the arm of the largest, loudest man.

Big-chested, he was dressed in a gaudy Hawaiian sports shirt and white duck pants. His fatherhood could never be in doubt. Here, below deeply tanned forehead ridges, were the thick brows and bony promontory of a nose inherited by both his children. His long onyx eyes, also a genetic imprint, were bloodshot and angry.

'How's my Beej?' he said. 'You guys all know her?'

'Know her?' said a red-faced man, teetering back and forth alarmingly. 'Jesus fucking Christ, Joshua! I'm her godfather.'

'Must be pretty far in my fucking cups to forget that,'

said Joshua Fernauld. 'Beej, what can I do for you?' His voice was unusual, reverberating deep and gravelly within that barrel chest.

'Can I talk to you a sec?'

'Sure thing.' He held up a hand to his friends. 'Gotta talk to my Beej,' he said, and put his arm around her, opening the door to the left of the bar. Marylin followed them.

They were in a medium-sized room that seemed larger because its sole furnishings were a maple captain's chair, a battered maple desk topped with a very old typewriter, and a sagging leather couch. The Spartan heart that pumped the lifeblood of cash through this exquisitely appointed Tudor mansion.

'Well?' said Mr Fernauld.

'Dad, this is a special friend of mine, Marylin Wace.'

'Hello, Marylin.' Mr Fernauld breathed liquor over her. 'Has anyone ever told you that you are, to coin a phrase, one gorgeous little *shiksa*?'

Marylin blinked.

BJ, with the floundering embarrassment that she had displayed about the candle and her grandmother's unknown word, said loudly, 'You're not Jewish, Daddy.'

'Shush, lower your voice, Beej. You wanta ruin my brilliant career?' He gave a braying laugh.

Marylin's mind had gone white with terror. When she had determined to come here, it had been with the idea of bearding a sensitive author, a dignified, thoughtful humanist alone in his grief. Certainly never in her worst terror could she have conjured up this awful, booming drunk in a flowered shirt. Linc was sensitive, fine, decent even in his edgy anger. How could *this* be his father? Well, he is, she thought.

'Mr Fernauld,' she said in low breathiness, editing her rehearsed speech, 'I have some things of Linc's, and I want you to have them . . .'

Before she could complete even this truncated preamble, the reddened eyes had gone blank.

She thrust the box towards him. Across the top she had

red-crayoned: 'For Joshua Fernauld. Please return to Marylin Wace, 8949 Charleville, Beverly Hills, Calif.'

As he squinted down at the box, his drunken features contorted. 'How dare you come here at a time like this, you nashty little cunt!'

Marylin, who did not know this word either, could not mistake the distillation of pure animal fury. She stepped back, the box still extended.

'Daddy!' BJ cried. 'Daddy!'

'You have some sweet friend, BJ, I have to inform you of that. Some sweet little friend. Push into the house at an hour like this, at thish particular hour, to try to get me to read her crap at thish hour, an hour like thish – '

'Daddy, Marylin's in my play, she's a friend, she's – '

'All right, Beej, all right.' He patted BJ. Then he turned to Marylin with a look of anguished, venomous hatred, snatching the box roughly from her hands, shoving it into the top drawer of the scarred maple desk. 'Don't hold your breath!'

He staggered back to his friends, and through the open door she heard him bawl. ''Nother damn shcript to look at. Jesus God almighty, now, even now they shove their fucking stupid shit at me. Oh God, God, my only begotten son dead . . . Even now . . .' He was sobbing. One of his group slammed a drink at him, and he gulped at it, spilling some down his Hawaiian shirt.

Marylin's insides crawled sourly up her throat.

BJ was staring at her with reproachful eyes. 'What made you do that? I didn't know you were trying to write. You should have come at Dad some other time.'

'Bathroom?' Marylin gasped.

BJ led her back into the hall. 'There's the powder room,' she said, pointing.

The door was locked.

'Can you wait?' BJ asked without warmth.

Marylin shook her head.

BJ gestured up the stairs. 'Mine's the first on the left.'

On sunlit tiles, Marylin knelt in front of the john,

vomiting in heaving, teary waves until only clear liquid came.

For a long time she remained in that attitude of prayer, and sometimes it happened that the windswept branches mercifully drowned out the party sounds.

Her body ached as if she had been whipped, the muscles quivering, the nerve endings raw. Never again in her life would Marylin so acutely experience the physical dimension of mental anguish.

She was seeing Linc as he lay naked with her in the double bed of apartment 2B, seeing the small chickenpox scar above his left eyebrow and the smile that went down on one side, seeing the tenderness in his eyes. Love, she thought. Oh, love . . .

Love was irrevocably dead somewhere in the depth of the Pacific.

Rising unsteadily to her feet, she went down the thickly carpeted stairs, clutching the banister. The dining room was now noisy with cheerfully chattering people filling bone-china plates with beautiful food. She let herself out the front door.

Fifteen minutes later, a Beverly Hills squad car found her wandering along Carmelita; the cops insisted on driving her home.

NolaBee was waiting. Later she told Marylin that when, telephoning home, she had got no answer, she had been terrified, and rather than climb aboard the waiting bus, she had by some miracle found a cruising cab. A ruinously expensive journey.

'He's dead,' Marylin said. 'Mama, he's dead.'

After that she said nothing. She let herself be undressed and put in bed, she let herself be fed bread and milk, she let NolaBee talk soothingly.

There was no fight left in Marylin Wace.

11

'It's a pretty day,' Marylin said. 'Why stick inside?'

'What a question to put to a registered nurse on duty,' Roy replied. NolaBee, working overtime on this soft, sunny Saturday, and other Saturdays, to pay back the money she had borrowed for the operation, had left Roy in charge of her sister. 'Mama said – '

'Mama's been coddling me,' Marylin interrupted. 'Call Althea.'

'We *had* been talking about a good browse,' said Roy wistfully.

'Then go on.'

'What about you?'

'I'm healthy as a horse.'

'A horse ready for the glue factory,' Roy replied, squinting at her sister.

It was past noon, and Marylin was not dressed yet.

In her long-sleeved flannel nightgown, she sat on her bed, bare feet tucked underneath her, her hair, unwashed since the operation, straggling around her shoulders. Her face was colourless except for the delicate lavender shadows that made her huge eyes seem more blue than green. (How, Roy asked herself, did her sister manage to summon up such heartrending beauty when anyone else would have looked an absolute witch?) The operation in a Culver City doctor's office – Roy had not been told a single other detail – had taken place two days after Marylin's visit to the Fernaulds' house. 24 April. A week ago. NolaBee admitted privately to Roy that she was worried: 'My friend was back at work after three days, but Marylin still looks and acts so darn peaky.'

Marylin had used hundreds of the off-brand pads that

NolaBee bought for the three of them. Though she denied having cramps and never complained, she would sit for hours blankly cuddling the hot-water bottle. She moved hesitantly. She shivered. She pushed her food around the plate and – though an ice cream addict – did not even finish the Chapman's coffee flavour that NolaBee had splurged on to tempt her. But (Roy inquired of herself) was this so weird? After all, the girl had a genuine gold star pinned to her heart, didn't she? From time to time, Marylin would dash in the john and the water would run for ages before she emerged, lovely skin blotchy, eyes reddened.

Marylin was watching her. 'You and Althea always have a fun time together on Saturdays.'

Roy looked away, torn. It was true that she and Althea revelled in these warm spring Saturdays. Mornings they strolled on Beverly Drive, parading their new hairdos and makeup, going in and out of Kress's and Woolworth's and the Gramophone Shop, lingering over the cosmetics at the cologne-scented counters of Owl and Thrifty. They spent hours in Taffy's, Yorkshire's, Nobby Knit, trying on summer clothes. Roy found a sensuous delight in the fresh, virgin smell, the crispness of unworn fabric. A becoming outfit held out infinite hope: if she could only afford to buy this, she would be a new Roy Elizabeth Wace, entitled to popularity and love.

She and Althea would fortify themselves with slabs of ice-cream cake drenched with hot fudge and mounded with whipped cream at Albert Sheetz or strawberry malteds so thick they had to be eaten with a spoon at Martha Smith's – Althea paid from her change purse. The afternoons they invariably passed in the wondrous darkness of the Fox Beverly or Warner's Beverly – again Althea's treat.

But, Roy thought. But. Mama left me in charge because there's not another soul for Marylin to turn to. Old Mr Hale, landlord of this illegal apartment, was visiting his son in San Diego, and the neighbouring burghers stuck up their noses at the gypsy Waces. What if something dire happened? A haemorrhage or something?

'Does it still hurt?' Roy asked.

Marylin raised her eyes to the ceiling. 'No.'

'Sez you.'

'Sez me. Roy, if you want to know, I'm dying to have the place to myself a bit.' Marylin's soft murmur held a plea.

After a pause Roy said, 'I'll toodle along.'

She dialled Althea to make the arrangements, then coated on her makeup.

'We might drop in at the library. Want any books?'

'Pick me a novel. Say hi to Althea.' Marylin mouthed a smile so actressy that Roy turned away.

After Roy had jogged noisily down the steps, Marylin stretched out on the patchwork quilt, which smelled of dust, letting the tears come.

What a luxury to be able to mourn in solitude.

Weekdays NolaBee worked graveyard shift so she could be home with Marylin while Roy was at school. Marylin was never alone. Waves of breathlessness would clamp over her, a symptom that she knew was not a sequel to the abortion but the result of her inability to express her grief. Yet when she wept, NolaBee looked drably crushed, Roy embarrassed. So Marylin, empathizing with them for having to live with such a sad sack, held herself in check. Like a polio victim drowning in his own lungs, she was drowning in her unshed, unsheddable tears.

Linc, forgive me, forgive me, she thought, hugging a pillow to that bleeding, empty part of her.

The door shook under a series of vigorous knocks.

She looked up, her wet face startled and guilty as if she had been caught in the midst of some unthinkable depravity.

'Who is it?' she wavered.

Another knock.

'Who's there?' she shouted.

'Me. Joshua Fernauld.'

The resonant, gravelly voice brought back that drunken annihilation in his writing room. Her stomach cringing, she sat up. 'Mr Fernauld,' she called, 'I'm not feeling well.'

'I have them.' His voice was muffled by the door, yet he sounded sober. 'The stories.'

Marylin rubbed her knuckles over her eyes. To regain Linc's writing had become an obsession with her. 'Oh, thank you,' she called. 'Would you please leave the box by the door.'

'We have to talk.'

Face that monster? Never! 'The flu's pretty bad. I'm very contagious.'

'You're giving me the runaround, Marylin.'

However awful a man he is, she thought, he's Linc's father, he must be grieving in his own hideous way. 'Be there in a sec,' she called, pulling on her ratty blue chenille robe, tightening the tie, blowing her nose, running a comb through her hair. She moved slowly to the door. With a deep breath, as if stepping onto a stage, she jerked at the cracked porcelain knob.

Joshua Fernauld held the box crayoned with her name under his left arm. He wore another of those loose flowered shirts over his thick torso, his tanned, creased face shone, and the heady sweetness of suntan lotion surrounded him. His eyes glinted like polished dark stones as he stared intently at her.

'I do appreciate this, Mr Fernauld.' She reached for the box.

He did not relinquish it. 'I thought I was coming in to talk,' he said.

'I really do feel pretty rotten.'

'Honey, I've been reading these since 3.30 this morning. I'm not about to be turned away.' The command in his tone and the confident vitality of his stance brooked no denials. Linc had said, *Big Joshua always gets his way.* He continued to stare at her, a physical impact emanating from those eyes. She held the door open for him. The contrast between his impeccable mansion and this messy apartment washed over her and she bent to retrieve Roy's nightgown and one of NolaBee's rayon stockings.

'Don't do that,' he said. The folding chair creaked under his weight. 'I despise fussing.'

A dish caked with eggs was set carelessly on the window ledge, and she carried it to the makeshift kitchen.

'For Christ's sake, sit down.' He stared at her until she obeyed. 'You're Rain, aren't you?'

Her throat clogged, and she looked down at her hands. 'Sort of, I guess.'

'Before we go any further, I was informed, informed good and loud by my Beej, that I was the epitome of obnoxiousness the other day. I was loaded, sodden, blind, but I do remember being damn primitive.' The gravelly voice emerged more quietly.

Marylin divined that Joshua Fernauld was apologizing. 'I understand,' she sighed. 'It's okay.'

He touched the box. 'Damn fine stories, marvellous work.'

'I think so too.'

'Only a fine and sensitive young man could have written them. He was that. A fine, decent young man, Rain – '

'Marylin.'

He fished out a crumpled handkerchief, blowing his prominent nose with vigour. 'This war – I can't disassociate myself from my anger at the waste – the barbaric, outrageous waste. Linc was a master of the language – Marylin, he was *good*.' For several minutes Joshua orated about Linc's stories and poetry, then blew his nose vigorously again. 'I haven't been able to talk about him before. Not to Ann – my wife – or BJ. Anyone.' He paused. 'You know that story, "Leave"?'

'"Home Leave".' It was a brief stream-of-consciousness piece about a pilot and his disastrous return to his calm and prosperous home.

'Yes. "Home Leave". He talks about his ambivalence towards me.' Tears welled in the big man's eyes. 'Christ, imagine him being ashamed to be jealous! The innocence and purity of it! Didn't he realize my goal was to have everybody including him worship at the shrine of the great *I am*?'

'Mr Fernauld – '

'Joshua.'

'I can't call you that!' she burst out in bald anger, then held her sodden handkerchief over her mouth. How could she be hollering at this overwhelmingly superior, older, famous *monster*? His cheeks momentarily quivered. She added in a consoling murmur, 'Envy's really a form of admiration. Linc admired you. He wasn't able to tell you. He felt too overpowered, I guess.'

'The conundrum of fatherhood, the endless, insoluble conundrum. Even when you don't intend to be casting a huge shadow, you do.' Joshua got up, going to a window, rapping his knuckles on a dusty pane. 'I was only twenty-three when he was born, a funny, pink, helpless creature with my mouth, my eyes, and later, my shnoz. Here was another Joshua, but one that would have the things *I* missed out on, a big house, clothes, riding lessons, tennis lessons, swimming lessons, a convertible. The works. I was the classically proud father, yet it cut deep into the vitals, when it became obvious that he didn't need anything from me to make him a finer man than I am. Sweeter, kinder.'

He spoke with such despair that again she found herself consoling. 'Maybe you were like that when you were young.'

'Me? Oh, that's rich, Marylin. You don't know how rich it is. You're looking at a gutter rat out of Hell's Kitchen. If I hadn't discovered writing, I'd've made one spectacular hood. Been head of the Mob by now – or in the electric chair. From the word go, a bastard, a driving, pushy bastard, greedy to grab the best life could offer, the finest liquor, the most beautiful women, the biggest houses, the flashiest cars, the warmest companionship of the richest and most famous, the goddamn hottest career. To you alone I confess that I joined the Party not because my heart bled

100

for capitalist enchained humanity, but because in those days you sold novels and earned hotshot reviews by being Red in tooth and claw.'

There was a pull and magnetism, a power in the deep, rough voice as it rolled out a confessional of what she would later learn were routine failings for a sizeable minority of the Beverly Hills population.

'Linc loved you, Mr Fernauld, he told me that.'

'He did?' Joshua turned. Tears wet his cheeks. 'Jesus, how I loved him.'

'He knew that.'

'How? We were exact opposites, he unassuming, honourable, aberrationally modest about his accomplishments . . . If you only knew how I was prodding him to blow his own horn! Trying to get him to be like his old man. As if the goddamn world needed two Joshua Fernaulds!' He rested his big, greyhaired head against the window. 'How do you go on living, how do you keep going through all the stupid, shitty motions?' He started to sob, a rusty, clumsy sound that he cut off with a loud blowing of his nose. 'Honey, would you happen to have some booze around?'

'I'm sorry, no.'

'Not so much as cooking sherry?'

Marylin shook her head: even in her misery the ludicrousness of NolaBee preparing meals with elegant wine sauces brought a faint curve of a smile to the beautifully scrolled lips.

'There is pain, such pain,' Joshua said.

'I know,' she sighed. 'Mr Fernauld, I could fix some tea.'

'Tea? God help me, tea! My mother was forever brewing pots, the same leaves two or three times, to ease her journey through this vale of tears.'

Taking this as acceptance, Marylin lit a match to the front burner, filled the kettle.

'When Linc came home,' said Joshua, who had followed her to the kitchen, 'that first leave after he was downed, he was jumpy as hell. All raw nerves. He certainly captured it in "Home Leave". Before the war, he'd argued back, but in

101

general he'd been a thoughtful kid. A hard-core reader. Yeah, an unregenerate bookworm. Once I caught him with my copy of *Ulysses*. I told him I wasn't about to let any son of mine lie about the house turning into a bookworm faggot, then gave him a good, swift kick in the ass – physically.'

'Yes, he told me. He said he was set to run away. Instead, he went out for the basketball team. He enjoyed playing, enjoyed it a lot. He said you were right.'

'He did?' Joshua shook his head. 'Anyway, that leave, when I saw how shot his nerves were, I wanted to hug him, to soothe him, but of course I shouted and argued at the drop of a hat. Even chewed him out for becoming a Navy pilot – I had in mind a safe desk job for him. I was worried as hell, and that made me even more scurrilous. Then he seemed to calm down, to unwind. That was your doing, wasn't it?'

'Maybe. I think so.'

'You made him very happy.'

'I loved him,' she said simply.

'It's damn obvious why he was nuts about you. You're a spectacularly fantastic-looking little dish, but it's more than that. You two belonged together. You're a gentle sort, and so was he.' Joshua paused. 'Why did you bring me the stories?'

Marylin could feel the heat travel up her throat to her face. To cover her confusion, she rinsed out two cups – every dish they owned was dirty and in the sink.

Joshua kept watching her. His eyes might be the same darkness and shape as Linc's, but the resemblance ended with flesh and pigmentation. Joshua Fernauld's eyes were alertly probing, twin instruments voracious for her soul's secrets. In a flash of insight she realized that Linc's characters were drawn from someplace within himself, just as his father's films emerged from acute powers of observation.

'Why?' he repeated.

'It doesn't matter,' she said.

He leaned forward, continuing to stare at her. The cup in

102

her hand slipped, and she fumbled, catching it maladroitly against her empty, cramping stomach.

He asked, 'A baby?'

After a brief hesitation she nodded.

He looked at the faded robe, her drawn, lovely face. 'And now?'

'Now it's too late,' she said, turning away.

'You had a D and C?' His voice was gruff with misery.

She dropped her face into her hands and gave way to the ragged sobs. He reached his arms around her, drawing her to a thick, hard body and the smells of aftershave and sweat. She made no attempt to stop weeping, but let Linc's weeping father hold her. Both were sobbing for the same reasons, for a sensitive, fine young man whom the war had first bitterly traumatized, then destroyed, and for his baby, who between them they had contrived to kill.

They were quietly drinking tea when NolaBee came in with her inevitable bulging grocery sack.

'Mama, this is Linc's father, Mr Fernauld.'

NolaBee's pitted cheeks blotched with redness. Marylin, between gasping sobs, had told her of her trip to the Fernaulds'. Setting the bag on the floor, she folded her arms. 'We thought the world of your son,' she said with rapid ungraciousness, then added, 'Mr Fernauld, I reckon you needn't have come visiting Marylin when she's ill.'

'I understand her illness, Mrs Wace.'

NolaBee pulled back her thin shoulders, a peppery, acne-scarred little woman facing down a man she certainly had a use for. 'You might reckon Marylin is a tramp, but that's not so. She made a mistake not because she's a bad girl but because she loved your son. She's a lady through and through. A Wace, a Fairburn, a Roy, and where we come from that means a lot. Her great-great-granddaddy was General Fairburn, on Lee's staff, and – '

Joshua raised a large paw-thick hand. 'Peace, Mrs Wace, peace. We stand at the bier, weeping together.'

She stared at him in confusion and then said, 'Marylin,

you look right peaky. You sure this man hasn't been upsetting you again?'

'Mama, he brought me back Linc's stories. We've been talking about them.'

'Humph.' NolaBee's snort meant she was unconvinced. She looked around. 'Where's Roy?'

'I asked her to go to the library for me.'

'Mrs Wace, won't you join us for some of your own tea?' Deliberate charm was in Joshua's invitation.

NolaBee plumped down in the chair, getting out a cigarette.

Joshua sat next to her. 'I was drunk and behaved despicably when Marylin came to the house. It was the worst day of my life, but I promise you, I'm not a lush or a bastard.' He fished a gold lighter from his shirt pocket.

The flame illuminated NolaBee's drab skin for a long moment. Then she bent to accept his light. 'I reckon you're a bit of one and a whole lot of the other, Mr Fernauld,' she said with a coquettish smile.

By the end of the following week, Marylin had recovered enough to return to school.

12

Though most of Beverly High's wide-flung breadth slept in obsidian dark, the far north windows – the auditorium's foyer – streamed yellow brightness. The school's triangular parking lot had long ago filled, and nearby streets crawled with cars squandering rationed gasoline in the search for a space.

It was 17 May, the night of *Vera*, the junior play.

The cast (including Marylin), the stage crew, BJ and a jittery Miss Nathans had been at the school since four this afternoon.

Night made the familiar steps exotic, strange, and Roy and Althea fell silent as they climbed. Roy wore a peculiar, knee-length crimson cape which had been in some long-ago trousseau, a nose-thumbing gesture at the sea of camel topcoats. Althea, too, defied convention with a chubby of some odd, ultra-soft grey fur.

A few steps below them were NolaBee and Joshua Fernauld. At the last minute, Mrs Fernauld had suffered a recurrence of some chronic, unnamed ailment that often confined her thin body to bed, so Joshua, alone and tardy, had picked them up. Althea was already in the apartment, sharing the scrambled-egg-sandwich dinner.

NolaBee was saying, '. . . that you're in for a big surprise tonight.' All keyed-up, she had been talking ceaselessly.

'Life is full of 'em,' retorted Joshua Fernauld. 'But my BJ, Lord bless her, has a mouth on her, and we've heard nothing but *Vera, Vera, Vera* for months. She's served us up every goddamn surprise there could be.'

NolaBee chuckled. 'Marylin – '

'I anticipate being bowled over by your lovely.'

'You aren't going to be even the teeniest bit sorry about . . .' NolaBee lowered her voice confidentially so that Roy could not hear the rest of her remark.

In the month since Mr Fernauld's visit, the two families had become quite close. The Fernaulds had invited the Waces to a barbecue supper in the garden of their palace, where Joshua had entranced them – especially NolaBee – with the inside dope about movies he had written and directed, the bickering, the foul-ups, the famous stars. The Fernaulds had taken the Waces to two screenings at the Academy, a shabby private theatre on Melrose, where Roy had been struck dumb at the sight of so many known faces in human size, and had even been introduced to a pair of genuine greats in the living flesh, Ronald Reagan and his wife, Jane Wyman.

The two girls pushed ahead into the vestibule, where, from the ceiling, was strung an enormous poster:

Vera
a play by Barbara Jane Fernauld
starring
Marylin Wace and Thomas Wolfe

Diagonally across the ticket window was slashed a streamer printed SOLD OUT, and lines waited at the two auditorium doors for girls with black sashes to take the tickets. Inside studying their programmes were many of the student body, Mr Mitchell, the principal, and other faculty members, as well as the doctors and lawyers, the star sports columnist, the famous composer, the movie people, plumbers, millionaires, shopkeepers and divorcees who made up the big and little fish parents of Beverly Hills High School.

As Roy and Althea moved to the front of the auditorium, several groups of girls smirked or raised eyebrows. Roy flushed. Althea gazed right back with her cool little smile. All cover-up. Though she had applied her cosmetics and worn her mother's chinchilla to attract attention, she shrank from the critical eyes. Althea was balanced on a tense plateau between superiority and inferiority, between shyness and hauteur. She would accept nothing less than the right crowd, agonizing to be noticed and accepted by them, yet she was too timid to make any move towards their company. And Roy, intensely loyal, knowing Althea's indifference was a pose, allowed herself to be locked into one of those symbiotic alliances so commonplace in early adolescence.

The girls jostled into the last available seats in the third row. Several rows behind them, NolaBee's old violet felt hat bobbed animatedly towards Joshua Fernauld's thick shock of prematurely grey hair.

The overhead lights dimmed in uncertain waves, and a spot wavered against the folds of crimson velvet. The left curtain pulled back and Miss Nathans stepped onto the proscenium. Her Viking figure was encased in tight purple rayon, and a huge corsage of red roses and silver ribbon bristled on her shoulder.

106

'I take great, yet sad pleasure,' she intoned in her most resonatingly theatrical voice, 'in announcing that the junior class has voted to dedicate their annual play to the memory of Lieutenant Abraham Lincoln Fernauld, Beverly High, summer of 1937. At intermission the Minute Maids will pass among you. They will be wearing the red-white-and-blue aprons that are familiar to students. We urge our parents and guests to dig down deep and buy war stamps and bonds in honour of Lieutenant Fernauld, who – like many another Beverly Hills High School graduate – has given the full measure of his devotion that we might continue to enjoy the fruits of freedom and democracy.' She paused. 'Would you please join me in a moment of tribute to a gallant young man.'

The spotlight shifted jerkily to the flag.

People rustled to their feet; the men – and two women – wearing uniforms snapped up their hands, holding their salutes. A backstage bugle sounded taps, slowly, truly. This was one of those moments that redeem warfare by permitting humans to emerge from their fixed, immutable loneliness. The Beverly High auditorium was welded into one being, the poignant notes universally shivering on the skin and bringing ubiquitous tears. Roy's eyes dampened solemnly not only for Linc but for all the immortal dead, for all the brave young heroes who rode eternally into the wild blue yonder.

At her side, Althea whispered derisively, 'How tacky can you get? Cashing in on BJ's brother to sell a few dollars' worth of stamps.'

That's Althea all over, Roy thought, blinking. She never gives in to mushy group emotions, she has a kind of hard honour. Maybe her family's royalty.

After a long minute's darkness to allow the audience to dissolve its sombre mood, the curtain edged apart on a living-room set.

Marylin was alone onstage. She wore a red sweater and pleated plaid skirt, saddle shoes. The lights picked up the gold glints in her hair as she hunched over a very large, thick book. Waiting until the scattered applause had faded, she ran a finger across the page, lifting her head to frown with her painted eyes.

Without saying a word, she had limned the dumb bobby-soxer. She *was* Vera the adorable dimwit. After a perfectly timed pause, she hurled the encyclopaedic tome to the boards, and while the audience roared with laughter, she turned on a prop radio. An instant too late the 'Hut Sut Song' blared. Marylin bounced around centre stage doing a gay little solo jitterbug as she sang the mindless words in her husky little voice.

In less than ninety seconds alone on the stage, she had stamped an evanescent lightness on the evening.

Poor Tommy Wolfe overturned a prop chair and drew hoots of laughter which demoralized him into going up in his lines. The inadvertent clangour of the air-raid alarm, a repetitive series of three blasts of the bells, jarred the others into going up in *their* lines. Nothing could dismantle the joyous, comic mood set by Marylin.

Among the shaky, made-up high-school kids, she played Vera with the authority of a star.

Roy found it impossible to believe that this ebullient dummy lighting up the stage was Marylin, Marylin who yesterday had wept her private tears, then crumpled on her bed as if her delicate bones had just been stretched on the rack, a silent misery that had caused NolaBee to dart continuous worried glances at her.

The first-act curtain brought thunderous applause. The bustling Minute Maids sold well over the two thousand dollars' worth of war stamps and bonds that had been set as the entire year's quota for the junior class.

The response to the final, second-act curtain was yet more electrifying, a hooting, stamping, whistling pandemonium. 'Vera, Vera, Vera,' the audience chanted when the cast stepped forward to take their group bows. Curtain call followed curtain call.

NolaBee, Joshua, Althea and Roy forced their way amid the congratulatory throng to the green room.

Backstage, there was an orgy of kissing, giggling, hugging by Miss Nathans, the stage hands and cast. Marylin, in her sweat-drenched costume, was the centre of weeping girls and swains with shy, adoring eyes. She radiated excitement, her heavy stage makeup glowed.

BJ had her partisans, too. Joshua shoved them aside to lift his plump, large-boned daughter from the dusty boards in a great bear hug.

'By God Almighty, Beej, I better look to my laurels!'

'Daddy, you know the lines that got the biggest laughs were yours.' BJ, having something to brag about, suddenly turned modest.

NolaBee was embracing Marylin. 'My baby. I was so proud.'

'A star was born right on our own Beverly High stage,' said Roy, her wisecracking tone sinking timorously downward. Marylin's performance had awed her: it was as if superhuman plasma had been injected to blaze within her sister's veins.

'The rest of the show was lousy,' said Althea. 'But you were something else, Marylin.'

Marylin turned her gaze on her sister's odd friend. 'Why, thank you, Althea. But all of us were super – until that darn air-raid alert went off.' Her vivid smile showed this was not intended as a reproof, but as a generous sharing of success with her fellow thespians.

Joshua draped his thick arm over Marylin's shoulders in a demi-hug. 'And as for you, star lady, I'm dumbstruck!'

'It was a great audience, Mr Fernauld.'

'Great audience, bull! You were magnificent, you quiet little thing, you! God knows why I'm so astonished – I've been around enough top actors to know it's basically an introvert's business.' He released her. 'Has your mother told you about my nefarious wheeling dealing?'

Marylin turned to NolaBee. 'Mama?'

The small brown eyes glinted with triumphant secrecy. 'Mr Fernauld's ruined the surprise.'

'But – ' Marylin started. She was interrupted by a surge

109

of the ecstatic crowd as a fresh wave of admirers fell on her.

'I reckon we'll have time to talk about it when we celebrate,' NolaBee called over the shrilling. 'Mr Fernauld is taking all of us to the Tropics.'

Sugie's Tropics on Rodeo Drive was one of the movie hangouts often mentioned in the columns of Hedda Hopper and Louella Parsons. To the open lanai and the famous Rain Room came Errol Flynn with his jailbait cuties, Tyrone Power, Robert Taylor, Johnny Weissmuller, Ida Lupino, Hedy Lamarr, Ingrid Bergman – all of them.

The restaurant was dimly lit, and though Roy craned her neck it was impossible to see if any stars were hidden in booths behind fake palms and ferns.

Joshua ordered enormous platters of crisp fried shrimp, richly meaty spareribs and rumaki. Roy, who had never eaten Chinese food, devoured most of the plump, bacon-wrapped chicken livers.

NolaBee, BJ, Roy and Althea (who was spending the night at the Waces) leaned over the table in a postmortem of *Vera*, their excited voices rising above the blare of the band's continuous reprises of 'Sweet Leilani' and 'The Hawaiian War Chant'.

Marylin was silent, swirling the ice in her ginger ale. Her extravagant vivacity had drained and her lovely features were tired and sorrowful.

A camera girl wearing a flowered sarong stood over their table. 'How about a picture?'

Joshua glared up morosely from his third bourbon.

But NolaBee said, 'It'd be a right nice memento of the night for the girls.'

So the four crowded together on one side of the curved booth. Roy and Althea wet their lips in a glamourpuss way, BJ pushed a heavy black strand of hair into her pompadour and Marylin formed her beautiful smile a shade mechanically.

The flash bulb flared, and the photographer inquired, 'How many copies?'

'Six,' Joshua said. 'One for everybody.'

When they were again spread out in the booth, NolaBee lit a cigarette, blowing a smoke ring. 'My, Marylin, aren't you the teeniest bit curious about the surprise?'

Marylin looked at Joshua. 'Mr Fernauld, you said you had been wheeling and dealing?'

'Of course you know who Art Garrison is, Marylin?' Joshua asked, and without waiting for a reply, continued. 'Art Garrison is founder and great white chieftain of Magnum Pictures.'

'Magnum!' BJ cried. 'That sausage factory!'

'Pardon me, Miss Beej Know-it-all! Okay, I grant you Magnum's not Metro or Fox or even mine own Paramount, but it rates about with Columbia and God knows it's miles above Republic. The point is that Art Garrison is my buddy, my poker buddy. Last week I let him win two pots in succession, then prevailed on him to set up a screen test.'

NolaBee gave her throaty chuckle, Roy gasped, and Althea and BJ stared admiringly at Marylin.

She clasped her empty glass with both small hands.

'No need to be nervous,' said Joshua, his booming voice strangely gentle. 'All it means is that Art'll arrange for some footage of you so he can see how you photograph.'

'Marylin, just what you've been longing for,' said Nola-Bee. 'Aren't you going to thank Mr Fernauld?'

'After what I saw tonight,' said Joshua, 'Magnum will be thanking me.'

'No,' Marylin whispered.

'What?' NolaBee's voice broke with surprise.

'I can't.'

Joshua said, 'Sure you can. I never saw anyone with more of the right stuff. Talent oozes from your pores. All you need is an agent with clout, somebody to speak up for you. Leland Hayward is like a brother to me.'

'I know why you're doing this,' Marylin said in a rising tone. 'You're paying me off, aren't you?'

'Marylin!' NolaBee cried. 'You apologize right this minute!'

111

Joshua downed his fresh drink in one gulp. Wiping a thick knuckle across his lips, he said, 'I owe you one, yes. I damn well owe you a big one.'

'What ... what happened wasn't anybody's fault but mine, Mr Fernauld. I'm not going to see Mr Garrison.'

'What are you saying?' Agitated, NolaBee pushed over the empty coconut shell in which her drink had been served. After years of dreams, plans, hard work and privation, she had arrived at the promised land, and her entry visa was being revoked by a few words. 'Joshua, you saw her. Tell her again. If anyone belongs on the screen, it's Marylin!'

'I said no, Mama!' The muscles below Marylin's cheeks were working. 'Roy, Althea, let me out. *Let me out!*'

The younger girls slid hastily from the booth, and Marylin ran towards the door. NolaBee trotted after her.

BJ, having read Linc's stories, by now understood that Marylin's love for Linc had been far from unrequited. 'Talk about rushing things, Daddy. Mother's right, you are beset by impatience. Why on earth didn't you give Marylin some time?'

'My generosity is terrible and swift,' he said sourly. 'Party's over, girls. Get a move on.'

A wind had come up, rattling the floodlit palms outside the Tropics. In the protection of the entry, NolaBee was talking with low vehemence to Marylin.

As the others emerged, NolaBee turned to Joshua. 'Marylin has something to say to you.'

'Mr Fernauld,' Marylin murmured, 'I'm sorry I jumped on you like that. You're giving me a wonderful opportunity and I'm very grateful.'

'Your first instinct to refuse was impeccable. The industry's a zoo. You have to be equipped to bull your way through the sh ... through the mire.'

'I'll work very hard,' Marylin said.

'I reckon the surprise was too much,' NolaBee said. 'What with the excitement of BJ's play and all.'

Marylin nodded, the antithesis of that bouncy, dumb little chick she had played. Her real self was a tenderly vulnerable Puccini heroine, and Joshua's penetrating eyes rested another moment on her.

The group drifted down the curved ramp, waiting quietly on the sidewalk. On this, the four hundred block of Rodeo Drive, empty lots gaped like missing teeth between exclusive specialty shops and old frame houses that had become business places. The Henry Lissauer Art Institute, one of the remaining houses across the street, showed a bluish light upstairs.

As Joshua's big Lincoln was driven around from the parking lot, the photographer rushed through the bamboo-covered door. 'Mr Fernauld, Mr Fernauld!' she called, brandishing a sheaf of palm-imprinted cardboard folders. 'Mr Fernauld, here's your photographs.'

13

Art Garrison, an energetic near dwarf, pretended omniscient knowledge of film but ran Magnum by playing his hunches. He watched the test of the girl Joshua had suggested (doubtless another of the big, talented bastard's on-the-side cuties) with a justifiably sour expression. A terrified, badly made-up amateur mugged and waved in grandiose gestures to an invisible audience. Even while the projector whirred, Garrison's minions were scabrously remarking that this bimbo couldn't act her way out of a paper bag. They winced silently when their liege lord ordered the test run again.

She doesn't photograph all that badly, decided Garrison. Nice bone structure. And those big, frightened eyes pull at your guts.

Leland Hayward, one of the most powerful men in Hollywood, had been coerced by his client – and friend – into becoming the novice's agent: under routine circumstances anyone represented by Hayward commanded the tops in salary. But he, too, had viewed the depressing screen test. The contract negotiations took less than five minutes. Hayward accepted, on Marylin's behalf, every studio-slanted clause of Magnum's boilerplate.

Two days after Beverly High closed for summer vacation, NolaBee signed her full name to her minor daughter's seven-year, six-month-option contract. It was the closest thing to slavery permitted in the United States.

As far as the Waces were concerned, Marylin had fallen into a fortune. Her first year's salary, a hundred and fifty a week, was exactly triple what NolaBee earned (without overtime) at Hughes, but before Marylin could cash her paycheque it was eviscerated by her agent's ten per cent, her Screen Actors' Guild dues, withholding taxes and enforced contributions to Community Chest and Red Cross, a weekly War Bond. She needed clothes – Magnum demanded that its starlets look glamorous at all public functions – and a used Chevy for the drive to Hollywood.

Those summer months of Marylin's grooming, NolaBee avidly followed each detail of her elder daughter's lessons on how to walk, talk, stand, sit, smile, comb hair, apply cosmetics, pose for stills and address members of the press.

That summer, Roy embarked on a life of her own. Since they had moved to Beverly Hills, she had whiled away the hot, languid days of the long vacations alone. (Marylin had had a summer job at Fran Pallay, the florist.)

That year there was Althea.

Mornings the coloured lady, M'liss, would drop her off at the apartment, and the two girls would sit cross-legged on the narrow strip of grass next to the garage, laying out their plans. Some days they elected to simply stay put in the empty apartment. They would pore over NolaBee's movie magazines for the beauty secrets of the stars: Roy squeezed lemons from the tree, lavishing the juice over her face, her arms, the area of her round little breasts that showed above her swimsuit. 'Olivia de Havilland says lemon juice worked miracles on *her* freckles!' Althea rubbed salt and oatmeal into her face, Claudette Colbert's prescription for abolition

114

of whiteheads. They washed their hair with the gluey melt of old soap ends in water that served the Waces as shampoo, and afterwards Roy brushed vinegar through her stubborn wet hair in an attempt to straighten the despised curls; they exchanged hour-long manicures, keeping the half-moons of their nails meticulously free of Marylin's Revlon polish. They helped themselves to her new makeup, they used her new calibrated tweezers, they shaved their legs with her razor.

Sometimes they shopped on Beverly Drive, driving the salesladies to near-insanity with their interminable deliberations. Many days they would buy nothing, or they might end up selecting earrings with pendant stars that made a tiny, tinny clatter, or big fabric flowers to adorn their pompadours. Though these items were paid for by Althea, they were common property, to be exchanged freely.

Other mornings they would clamber aboard the crowded Wilshire bus, lurching westward to the section of beach where the Beverly High kids all crowded, Roadside Rest – so named for the ramshackle hamburger stand on the boardwalk. Wearing one-piece white bathing suits similar to the sexy number that Betty Grable had made famous in her pin-up, they found space for their towels on the hot, jam-packed sand and perfected an all-round tan by rolling over at the precisely timed intervals when Frank Sinatra's records changed on the microphoned jukebox. The Beverly High crowd all went to Roadside, and after a cluster of boys dashed by, diving into the dangerous surf, they would ask one another, 'Did you see the way Li'l Abner looked at you?'

'He didn't!'

'He did, I swear he did.'

Their friendship was tight as a bowline knot, whose two ropes must be unravelled in order to come apart. Yet Roy had never visited Althea's house, had never met Althea's parents.

Althea spoke of home only in answer to a direct question,

115

and then unwillingly. When NolaBee asked what her father did, she turned away to stammer coldly that he bred collies. Collies! NolaBee also inquired about M'liss, the coloured woman. M'liss, Althea murmured, had been her nurse.

Althea's secrecy sometimes bruised Roy. Wasn't it the Big Two against the world? They were best friends, weren't they? Surely Althea could trust *her*. For the most part, though, Roy staunchly viewed her friend's mysteriousness as something tragically worthy of a royal Russian émigré.

'I reckon you two ought to play over at her house *sometime*,' NolaBee said.

'Why?'

'Stop frowning, Roy, it'll give you wrinkles. I'm not criticizing your friend, she's a right distinctive little girl, and I'm glad to have her here. But hasn't it struck you as mighty strange that she never invites you to visit?'

'I don't mind, Mama. Besides, what if there's . . . something she's ashamed of?' Roy floundered between steadfastness to her friend and wriggly pleasure in her mother's interest.

'Ashamed? She has that nice mammy and she went to Westlake School, so her family's well-fixed. What could she have at home to be ashamed of?'

'Maybe her father's a Nazi spy, maybe her mother's got some dread social disease, I don't know. We don't need to go to her place to have fun, so what's the dif?'

'I reckon it's a matter of principle,' said NolaBee. With a musing look she went back to straightening the hem of the new white strapless that Marylin was to wear at the Hollywood USO: Magnum sent groups of young actresses to entertain servicemen – and hopefully garner some publicity.

In the morning, Althea would phone to say she was on her way, then Roy would go downstairs and wait. One Tuesday in mid-August when a thin, opaline mist hazed the sky, Roy was settled on the kerb, a page of yesterday's *Herald* protecting her orange gym shorts, on whose white stripe 'R. Wace' straggled in black embroidery.

As the grey Chevy drove up, NolaBee who was on swing shift that month, trotted down from the apartment, her dragon kimono catching behind her on the splintered wooden steps. 'Hello, there,' she called to M'liss. 'I'm Mrs Wace, Roy's mother.' The small, lively brown eyes were snapping, the smile was infectious.

The dignified coloured woman beamed back. 'Good morning, ma'am. I'm Melisse Tobinson.'

'Would you mind, M'liss, if Roy spends the day at your place, and maybe has a little bite before you bring her home?'

'Mama!' Roy cried. She was conscious of Althea gazing off into space with her most aloofly miserable expression.

'Now, Roy, I can't be home for supper.' This was hardly unusual: NolaBee rotated on all three shifts. 'I reckon M'liss will see to it that you don't starve.'

'I surely will, Mrs Wace.'

'You from Georgia, M'liss?'

'Yes, ma'am. And you, too, from the sound of it.'

'Greenward.'

'That right? My aunt's from Lester.'

The two exchanged genealogies, uncovering the fact that a remote cousin of M'liss had cooked for a Fairburn.

'Mrs Wace, I'll have Roy back here by ten, if that's all right.'

'I sure do appreciate this.' NolaBee grinned and hurried up the staircase.

'Why don't you get your suit, Roy?' Althea said in a surly, inhospitable tone. 'We can swim in our pool.'

Roy changed into her good white shorts, shoving her swimsuit in a paper grocery sack. Anticipation pulsed through her, yet at the same time she felt a clamminess under her armpits. Had her mother cut the Gordian knot of the Big Two?

14

Althea was silent, sitting tense and pale between Roy and M'liss as the servant drove them swiftly northward. They crossed the tracks of Santa Monica Boulevard, passing into the territory of money, turning left on Sunset, where two women on horseback clipped along the bridle path. After a couple of blocks they drove north again, upward into the rolling estates of Beverly Hills, winding along an alley where the property was hidden behind high box hedges tangled with oleander. M'liss turned in at a smallish house that faced directly on the narrow street. Roy let out a sigh of relief. Not so snazzy after all, she thought. Ahead of them, barring their way, loomed ten-foot-tall filigreed iron gates. Centring each was an elaborate intaglio with the curlicued name 'Belvedere'. Dismay hollowing her stomach, Roy accepted that the Cunninghams had a gatehouse.

M'liss gave two loud honks. A thin old man came hurrying out. '*Buenos días*, M'leess, Mees Althea.' He saw Roy and broke into a grin that displayed three missing teeth. '*Una comadre*, ehh?'

M'liss winked. 'From the high school.'

He swung open the left gate, and without conversation they curled through a grove of enormous sycamores, emerging into celestial hillocks and meadows where triangular red flags fluttered above ovals so smooth that they appeared gigantic, buffed emeralds. Belvedere had its own golf course! They rounded a bend, passing a peacock imperiously spreading its vivid-eyed tail, coming upon two men sweeping a tennis court. In the distance glittered a swimming pool.

Then suddenly the house was visible.

Roy couldn't control her gasp. A vast, chastely imposing Georgian mansion whose bricks glowed with a rosy tinge, as if mellowed by slow centuries. Yet this was Beverly Hills, a town incorporated – as Roy had learned in Horace Mann Grammar School – on 14 November 1914. No house here could be as serenely, regally historic as Belvedere appeared. A flock of white pigeons wove through the creamy columns of the entry like a living scarf waved in welcome; then the birds nestled on the slate roof. Everything was still again. In the static moment it seemed to Roy that the entire estate could vanish with a wave of a star-tipped wand.

M'liss, following the gravel drive around the corner, parked near a side door. 'Have a fine time, Roy, hear,' she said, and went inside.

The two girls stood awkwardly outside the Chevy, not looking at each other.

After a minute, Althea said in a remote tone, 'Since swimming's on the agenda, shall we head down to the pool?'

The main room of the poolhouse was easily three times as big as the Waces' apartment; along the rear wall hung watercolours of various yachts in full sail. Roy wondered distractedly if they all belonged to the Cunninghams.

'You take that dressing room,' Althea said, disappearing.

Roy opened the door and was in a kind of boudoir with a white-painted vanity and a couch slipcovered in hunter green and white stripes. She ducked into the enormous green tiled bathroom. Her white swimsuit was still a little damp from yesterday, and as she pulled it over her plump hips, sand skittered across pristine tiles. Scrabbling on her knees, she mopped up the grains with dampened toilet paper. She could feel the blood heating her face, yet her hands and feet were icy.

In her outlandishly romantic imaginings of Althea's mysterious background, she had never conjured up anything remotely akin to this. She toyed dazedly with the idea that her friend was the child of a housekeeper or servant. But then would M'liss be her nurse? And why would the old Mexican gatekeeper call her 'Mees Althea'?

No.

Althea was rich.

Grotesquely rich.

How could you retain a normal friendship, call yourselves the Big Two, in the face of this kind of wealth?

Tugging down the white wool around her thighs, Roy emerged into the main room of the poolhouse.

Althea stood waiting in her white swimsuit, her long slender face set in the disdainful half-smile she showed to those whom she thought had slighted her.

'Hi,' Roy said sheepishly.

Althea nodded.

'Embarrassed silence in the palace of the Sun King,' Roy said.

Althea shrugged.

'You didn't think that was funny?' Roy's throat was dry. 'You're right. It wasn't funny.'

Althea said nothing.

'If you want to know the truth, I never even imagined there were mansions like this.'

'I hate this place,' Althea muttered.

'You do?'

'Belvedere,' Althea said venomously. 'Forty-three rooms in the main house. Tell me, are forty-three rooms necessary?'

'I guess somebody thought so.'

'A lot of rooms and in not a single one is anyone who cares about me, cares if I'm happy or not,' Althea said bitterly.

'I care.'

'You?' Althea turned on her in a kind of fury. 'Who are you trying to kid?' In Althea's anger was a bleat she had never let Roy hear before.

Roy's insecurities lessened, her natural warmth asserted itself, and she put her arm around her friend's tensed shoulder. 'If you'd like to know, I'm terrified you won't be the other half of the Big Two anymore.'

'Why?'

'I live in a dumpy illegal apartment over a garage, my

120

mother's Rosie the Riveter. I'm poor, you idiot, that's why. More people are loathed because they're poor than because they're rich.'

Althea sat on the edge of the pool and Roy perched next to her. Staring at the careful pedicure they had worked on yesterday, Roy cleared her throat. 'Have you always lived here?'

Nodding, Althea pushed that luscious streaky blond hair under a white rubber cap. 'You might as well know the worst. Mother's a Coyne.'

Coyne. A name commonly lumped with Rockefeller, du Pont and Vanderbilt.

'A real, genuine C-o-y-n-e?' asked Roy, swallowing.

'One of Grover's daughters.'

Grover T. Coyne. Roy had learned about him from Mr Hunt in American history this past semester. In the 1800s Grover T. Coyne had gathered together one-half of the railroad mileage in the United States, he had watered the stock (Roy had never quite encompassed the meaning of this), he had defrauded the freight shippers by overcharging whenever possible, he had put his competitors out of business by undercutting them, he was the archetype of a robber baron. Was it Commodore Vanderbilt or Grover Coyne who had said: 'The public be damned'?

Althea had taken American history the same period: she had listened to the liberal Mr Hunt's diatribes against old Grover T. while doodling on the canvas cover of her notebook, a perfect imposture of your average Beverly High frosh.

'Listen,' Roy said. 'It could be worse, she could come from Anaheim, Azusa or Cucamonga.' It was such a feeble joke that she added, 'Har de har har.'

'It's an article of faith among Coynes that Daddy married Mother for the money.'

Roy asked sympathetically, 'Do they neglect you, your parents?'

Althea blinked, and there was a wild expression, almost like fear on the smoothly tanned face. Then she laughed, an

121

ugly sound. 'Stop thinking in clichés, Roy. Why assume the rich neglect their children? Some do, some don't – not by a long shot.' She gave another peal of that discordant laughter and slipped into the water. Facedown, arms extended motionless over her head, she kicked viciously across the pool.

Roy watched the water bubbling and splashing. Her bewilderment at Althea's secrecy had disappeared. In a quick flash it had come to her that even in a rich community like Beverly Hills, wealth as vast as the Coynes' set you apart. Althea had experienced the same separation that had been dictated to Roy. As Roy had suffered in school for her crumpled brown lunch bags and cloddy hand-me-downs, so had Althea borne the brunt of reprisals for Belvedere.

Roy, though, had never blamed NolaBee for her situation. Althea seemed bitterly, unhappily resentful of her parents.

After a minute Roy jumped into the pool, swimming like a frog in her Y-WCA-learned breaststroke over to a red-and-blue inflatable ball. 'Catch,' she shouted, managing a feeble hurl at Althea.

The tension broke. The girls floundered in the heated water, sailing the beach ball back and forth.

The brown-and-white-striped pool towels were sheet size, indestructibly thick, and 'Belvedere' was woven into the selvage. They were sunning themselves on a lush terry when a tall, round-shouldered woman stepped down the terraces.

'The doyenne of the castle,' said Althea.

'Your mother, you mean?'

Althea, without replying, rolled onto her stomach and pressed her narrow, arched nose into her towel.

Mrs Cunningham wore no lipstick, and with her old-fashioned flat-waved hairstyle and her loose pinstriped shirtwaist, she looked, even for a mother, dowdy, without sparkle, plain. And yet somehow she was distinguished. Three times as distinguished as thin Mrs Fernauld for all her smart clothes and carefully coiffed dyed blonde hair.

But why? And would I think Althea's mother so impressive, Roy wondered, if I didn't know she was Grover T. Coyne's daughter?

Mrs Cunningham had reached the pool deck. Her height, shapeless bosom, body build and receding chin gave her a marked resemblance to Eleanor Roosevelt.

Althea did not budge from her prone position. Roy, though, forcibly instilled with Southern courtesy towards elders, had jumped to her feet.

'Mother, this is my friend, Roy Wace.' Althea used a cold, balky tone. 'Roy, my mother, Mrs Cunningham.'

'How nice to finally meet you,' said Mrs Cunningham, clasping her hands together. Her only jewellery was a broad gold wedding band.

Roy said, 'It's a real pleasure to be here, Mrs Cunningham. This house is . . . Belvedere is really a showplace.'

'How kind of you, dear.' Mrs Cunningham looked up at one of the enormous staghorn ferns that hung outside the poolhouse as she inquired, 'Will you girls be lunching with us?'

'No,' Althea said sharply.

'Your father and I would enjoy it,' Mrs Cunningham said.

'I told Luther we'd be eating down here,' Althea said.

Roy didn't have the foggiest notion who Luther was, but she knew Althea was lying. Althea had spoken to nobody but her since passing through the wrought-iron gates.

'I do hope you change your mind, then,' said Mrs Cunningham with a clipped, old-fashioned politeness. 'Roy, I am delighted to have met you.' She held out a large, soft hand to be shaken.

Roy watched the tall, dowdy figure cut across the grass terracing to a greenhouse with a domed roof. 'Why did you have to act like that?' she asked.

'Like how?' Althea retorted dangerously.

'Rude.'

'This'll come as a shock to you, but not everybody swarms all over her mother like a puppy begging for a little love.'

123

Roy's face burned, but she persisted. 'I was only suggesting you could have been a tetch nicer. She'll blame me because you're fresh.'

'We have a private war going, Roy, Mother and me. You're not any part of it.'

'What about your father?'

A shadow flickered in Althea's eyes. 'I do believe,' she said, 'that you'll have a chance to judge for yourself.'

It was about 11.30 when a tall man wearing a white shirt and grey trousers came down from the house. From him Althea had inherited her streaked light hair and oval, handsome face. Althea tanned a lush ochreous brown, though, and his face was ruddy in the manner of fair-pigmented sailors. He was not exactly handsome, yet he had a rapidity, an unconscious attractiveness that Roy did not generally connect with older men. Swoon, swoon, she thought, contrasting him with his round-shouldered, dowdy spouse. *It's an article of faith among Coynes that he married her for her money.* At his heels trotted a large collie with a plumy tail and very full ruff.

Althea sat up. 'Hello, Daddy.' Smiling guilelessly, she looked younger, a little girl almost.

'Well, here I am,' he said. 'Ready for presentation to the mysterious Miss Wace.'

Roy, who was already standing, giggled.

Althea made the introductions, adding, 'That's Bonnie Prince Charlie.'

'He's beautiful,' Roy said, holding out her hand. 'Shake, Bonnie Prince.'

The collie backed away.

'Don't take offence. He's like that with everyone but me,' said Mr Cunningham, pulling up his trouser knees as he sat on a wrought-iron chair. 'Roy. That's an unusual name for a girl.'

'My grandmother was a Roy, and we're from the South,' Roy explained shyly.

'Whereabouts?'

'Greenward, Georgia – actually, I've never been there

124

'. . . I was born in San Bernardino. The truth is, I've never been out of California.'

With flattering interest, he took off his dark glasses. His pale hazel eyes alert, he questioned her about herself, her mother and sister. Most of the time Althea answered for Roy. The Cunninghams were bouncing quips backwards and forwards as if they were contemporaries rather than father and daughter, yet at the same time Althea continued to smile with that juvenile joy.

Despite Mr Cunningham's easy charm, Roy found herself tongue-tied. She did not know if this shyness were caused by Belvedere or by Althea's bewildering, wholehearted affection towards her father, which was a complete about-face from her recent embittered anti-parent tirade.

'Tell me, Roy, what can Mrs Cunningham and I do to persuade you to join us for lunch?'

Althea's expression turned guarded and sullen. 'So Mother sent you?'

Mr Cunningham smiled whimsically at Roy. 'You see, do you, Roy, how my child respects me? She doesn't believe I have a single idea of my own.'

'Mother was down here an hour ago.'

'She wanted to meet Roy.' He raised his very light eyebrows. 'You have no idea, Roy, how cut off we parents feel when a child moves into a life of her own.'

'Alas for Althea, she's been with me, not living it up in a den of iniquity,' Roy said. In the brief ensuing silence, Mr Cunningham glanced away while Althea, who often made infinitely more risqué remarks, stared at the diving board. Roy felt like a coarse, crude peasant. 'We don't do anything much,' she finished lamely.

'We would be happy if you'd join us,' said Mr Cunningham, stroking Bonnie Prince Charlie's ruff.

'All right,' Althea said. 'But after this, Daddy, we'd appreciate a little privacy.'

'I understand,' he replied gravely. 'I'll explain how you feel to your mother.'

15

When Gertrude Coyne was born in 1895, her father, Grover T. Coyne, at sixty-four, was one of the two richest men in the United States, and her mother, his plumply vivacious, nineteen-year-old third wife, had already embarked on a career of fervid spending concomitant with her position, throwing herself into a rivalry of extravagance with her stepchildren, two of whom were several decades her senior.

Amid the unprecedented, unparalleled ostentation, Gertrude was a cowed, nervous wraith. A woefully plain little girl with her father's receding chin (hidden in his case by a bushy white beard), she attempted to disguise her height by slouching, a habit that nurses and governesses were ordered to break with a torturous iron-stayed jacket to be worn below the exquisitely stitched *jeune fille* clothing.

Her parents ceaselessly voyaged across the Atlantic in the *Lyonesse*, their steam yacht. Her two sets of adult half-siblings ignored her, as did her brace of lively full brothers. Clumsy and shy, Gertrude suffered insomnia and indigestion prior to the inexorably formal birthday parties given for the children of her mother's clique. A high fever of unknown origin necessitated the cancellation of her coming-out ball – after the half-million white roses were in place.

When her father died leaving her five million dollars outright and an inviolable twenty-five million trust fund whose capital she could not invade but from which she would receive an income of approximately eight hundred thousand a year, she said, 'Now I'm going to live simply.'

The summer of 1916, her younger brother was tutored by Harold Cunningham. Harry, the name he preferred, was a handsome young man with fair hair that flopped over his high forehead. Though Harry came from a respectable-enough Boston family, he was church-mouse poor – his widowed mother had sold her house, then her engagement ring and pearls to send him to St Mark's and Harvard. In 1917, when the United States entered the war, Harry enlisted: a sepia photograph of him in his high-collared officer's uniform sat next to Gertrude Coyne's gilded Empire bed.

Harry had been in a few drinking scrapes, and besides, he was too demonstrably impoverished and altogether too charming to be a fit consort for Gertrude's trust fund. Society gossiped endlessly, and the papers were full of 'The Heiress and the Tutor'. Had old Grover T. Coyne been alive, there would have been no marriage. But his widow, still plumply attractive, had her sights fixed on becoming the Duchess of Rochemont, and a lacklustre daughter in tow fitted in not at all with her plans.

She threw a squandrously splendid wedding.

The newlyweds debated where to set up housekeeping. Harry, caring only to be comfortable and adored, shrank from the Coynes and their exalted circle, who had him pegged as a fortune hunter. Therefore they counted out New York. Boston would forever reverberate to the scandal of their marriage. Gertrude believed the South to be sloppily decadent. Europe, too, they discarded, for neither was adventurous enough for expatriate life.

Then Gertrude recollected, 'When I was ten we wintered out West. California was lovely, the mountains, the sea, the sunshine.'

Beverly Hills delighted the Cunninghams. It was entirely lacking in social glue. The mansions strewn in the green landscaped hills north of Sunset Boulevard were inhabited by people that Gertrude considered the middle-class fringe: film stars, producers, retired Mid-west industrial magnates, oil millionaires – each household minding its own business.

'This is it,' the young couple agreed. They set about planning and building Belvedere.

It took a number of years for their union to be blessed. Over the drawing-room fireplace hung a Danilovna portrait of Gertrude, her homely face radiant as she gazed down on the pink-and-white infant in her arms. Her maternal delight proved short-term, for the genes were there. Early on, Althea showed the Coyne arrogance mingled with Gertrude's own lamentable timidity. Harry adored the child, who had an attenuated, feminine version of his fair good looks.

Gertrude blocked her jealousy as unflaggingly as she denied to herself the possible meaning of certain distant sounds that occurred during Harry's infrequent, drink-induced bouts of derangement. Her love had deepened to worship. And like many adoring wives, she formed a membrane of self-deception that thickened, thus permitting the marriage to flourish.

Because of this shadowy, hidden area, neither parent chose to gainsay Althea. They granted her a remarkable amount of freedom, acquiescing to her whims. They gave in to her about attending the public high school, they permitted her friendship with this impoverished little Wace girl.

The rear of Belvedere was banded with two levels of broad porch. The upper, Althea explained to Roy, was used only for dinner; lunch was served on the lower veranda, which was actually part of the gardens. The mist had totally burned away, and the sun blazed down, but here, under trellised vines, the murmurous green shade was pleasant. A manservant named Luther, who had strands of mouse-coloured hair combed across his bumpy head and wore a loose white linen jacket, manoeuvred in and out through the French doors with grapefruit halves followed by cold lamb, creamed peas and little new potatoes.

Mrs Cunningham sat at one end of the table, Mr Cunningham at the other. Althea and Roy, in their shorts, side by side, faced towards the golf course. 'It's only six holes,' deprecated Mr Cunningham. Mr and Mrs Cunningham recounted their mornings. He had been in the kennels. 'You'll have to let me take you through this afternoon, Roy,' he said with amiable warmth. 'Althea, did I tell you Silent Night had her litter?' Mrs Cunningham had worked with orchids in her greenhouse, which she did not offer to show.

Roy scarcely knew what she ate. She lifted heavy sterling cutlery, the nerves of her fingers tingling with her effort to avoid a hideous gaffe. Yet despite her heebie-jeebies, Belvedere touched her imagination and she could not control her surreptitious glances at its proprietors.

Mrs Cunningham, dowdy, timid of manner, monstrously rich – a Coyne! Mr Cunningham, charming and easy. If he had, indeed, married for money, it was not apparent. He smiled often at his wife, and when he spoke to her, there was affection in his voice. Conversing with him, she gazed into his dark glasses, her lipstickless mouth twisting with enthusiasm.

Althea spoke only to her father.

The Cunningham family, Roy reflected, was like three telephone poles, the two farthest apart – Mrs Cunningham and Althea – connected only through Mr Cunningham. Still, mothers and daughters go through brittle times, and this was a mild eccentricity.

Mr Cunningham said to his wife, 'Did these delicious peas come from your garden, Mutty?'

'Of course, Ducky.'

'Come on, Roy,' Althea said in a shaking voice.

The Cunninghams glanced at one another. Mr Cunningham said, 'Althea.'

'We're *finished*, Daddy.'

'But Mother and I aren't. I'm sure Roy is looking forward to dessert.'

At this lightly spoken paternal reproof, Althea looked desolate, ostracized, frightened.

Luther served them crystal bowls of sliced fresh peaches, fruit also nurtured in Belvedere soil. Althea watched impatiently as Roy spooned up the last sweet, juicy slice. 'May-we-be-excused?' she blurted.

Again the parents glanced at each other. Mr Cunningham said, 'Sure thing, Toots. Roy, you make sure you have a good time.'

129

Roy thanked her host and hostess, repeating 'scrumptious' several times, then barged inside the French windows, where Althea waited.

Althea walked several steps ahead, leading the way through a panelled hall as high and large as the lobby of the Fox Beverly, up a broad staircase, along a gallery-corridor whose aromatic odours of floor wax could not drown out the faint must from the tapestries of hunting scenes. She opened a door and when they were both inside pressed the bolt. In her whole life Roy had never locked the door of a room.

They were in the ultimate girl's bedroom. A fireplace, a big bay window with a curve of pillowed window seats, wallpaper of the same charming blue forget-me-not pattern as the chintz bedspread, curtains, and upholstery. A glass-fronted cabinet displayed a collection of demure china and crystal horses. A *chaise longue* waited temptingly in the alcove shelved with books and record albums.

Althea, who still had not spoken, took out the Firelli-conducted recording of the final movement of Tchaikovsky's Sixth, stacking the four records on the big Magnavox. The mournful chords added to Roy's uneasiness. When she was no longer able to bear the turgid atmosphere, she murmured below the music, 'They don't seem such monsters.'

'What did you expect?' Althea retorted. 'Fangs?'

'I mean, a lot of people fight with their mothers, I do myself at times. It's not exactly the collapse of the Allied armed forces.'

'Is that your considered opinion?' Althea asked.

'All I have to say is that for a parent hater, you're a real Daddy's girl.'

The next record dropped. 'You don't understand one single thing about us,' Althea said, expressionless.

'Most girls would die for a room like this.'

'That just proves what morons most girls are.' Althea blew her nose, a muffled, unhappy sound.

Sympathy clogged Roy's own sinuses. 'Althea,' she admitted, 'I *did* feel sort of eerie at lunch, but then again, I've never eaten a meal served by a butler. Is it really so infested around here? I mean, your parents seemed very close. They aren't getting a divorce, are they?'

'A divorce? Don't be such a child, Roy. What could be more *ordinary* than a divorce?'

NolaBee often stated with great pride that there had never been a broken marriage among any of her wide-flung connections. 'Don't blame me for not understanding the problems of the feelthy rich,' Roy said, 'but life here can't be any weirder than in my home, can it?'

Althea knew a few details of poor Marylin's romance, and though Roy had disclosed nothing about the abortion, maybe Althea guessed. 'Consider this,' Althea replied with odious acidity. 'If all were perfection at Belvedere, do you imagine I'd have my own way about going to a public school, spending my days every which way I want?'

'Never thought of that,' Roy said, her eyes round. 'Can't I help?'

'The perfect definition of solipsism. Roy Wace believing she can alter the inescapable.' Althea sat on the window seat gazing out.

When Althea was in this kind of a snit, any remark, however innocuous or placatory, was a flung gauntlet.

Without further conversation they listened to the dreary movement which, Althea told Roy, was composed in a presentiment of death.

Afterwards they went down to the tennis court. Roy had learned to play only last semester at Beverly, while Althea's years of private lessons had endowed her with a crushing forehand and a near-professional serve, both of which she used with calculated determination. It wasn't a game, it was a rout.

They ate dinner alone in the breakfast room.

To Roy it seemed weeks before M'liss came up to say she would drive her home. Althea elected not to accompany them. At the side door she said in a low, swift voice, 'It's been hideous, hasn't it?'

'Not really.' Roy's voice cracked. 'Oh, Althea, you were so *mean.*'

'It's this ghastly place, Roy, it's nothing to do with you.'

'Positively?'

'You're my best friend. You always will be.'

'Honestly?'

'All my life.'

Roy opened the door of the grey Chevy feeling happier than she had all day.

That night Roy lay awake a long time. NolaBee was still riveting wing assemblies at Hughes, but Marylin's quiet breathing sounded on the other side of the wardrobe. All at once she gave a muffled cry that seemed to hang in the stuffy air of the apartment.

'Marylin,' Roy whispered.

The bewildered sobbing continued. Since Linc's death, Marylin often cried in her sleep. Roy padded across the dark room to touch her sleeping sister's shoulder.

The piteous little sounds quieted, but Roy stood in the darkness, her hand poised compassionately for several minutes before she returned to bed.

Were there really morbid disorders behind Belvedere's oleander-tangled box-hedge? Wasn't it possible that Althea, embarrassed about hiding the truth, had heaped on insinuations of dark, dire secrets to cover up her lies?

Roy squeezed her eyes shut until she saw red dashes. She despised herself for thinking this way, yet she couldn't stop questioning the mysteries surrounding Althea's relationship to her parents.

She was still puzzling things through an hour later when NolaBee unlocked the door. She tiptoed around, undressing, washing, then came over to Roy's bed. Roy could smell the staleness of work, the cigarette smoke, on her mother.

'Roy, you 'wake?'

'Yes.' Roy held open the blanket. 'Come on in.'

NolaBee snuggled down on the bed, as she often did with Marylin, pulling the covers over her, whispering, 'Well, how was it at the Cunninghams'? What did you do over there? Did you meet them, Althea's parents? What time did M'liss bring you home? What did you have for dinner? Did you have a nice time?'

'They live north of Sunset in a huge, huge mansion that makes the Fernaulds' place look pipsqueak.'

'I reckoned they were very well-fixed. Go on, hon, tell me.'

Roy whispered enthusiastically about the forty-three rooms, the tennis court, the swimming pool with its own house, the six-hole golf course, the vast shady porch where they'd lunched – 'It wasn't truffles under glass or caviar, like you'd expect, just plain food.' She described Althea's perfect room, adding with enthralled awe, 'I guess you'd call it a *suite*.'

'Her folks sound right nice. Why do you figure Althea didn't want you to meet them?'

Roy's eyes closed. She had always yearned to have such a night-whispered conversation, the kind Marylin and her mother shared, but the price for such closeness was too steep. Talking about Althea's veiled hints regarding her parents – or her own reservations – would be exposing her friend.

'Oh, a lot of kids like to keep stuff to themselves. Mama, I'm dead tired.'

'Good night, curly-top, sleep tight,' NolaBee said, kissing her forehead, and climbing out of the bed.

16

Althea, too, was awake.

She lay on her back, the position in which she normally fell asleep, but her muscles were taut and her face hot as the events of the day whirled in her mind. This morning, when Mrs Wace had forced the issue that Roy visit Belvedere, Althea had fought off nausea. It was that old, bitter sickness. Would she always experience this furious helplessness with people?

As a small child at Belvedere, she had found life bearable, even happy sometimes. A governess and tutors had given her lessons until she was eleven; then she had started Westlake School for Girls. Sensitive and timid, entering school late, she was a natural patsy. When the other girls discovered she was part of the Coyne family, they immediately nicknamed her 'Your Highness'. Althea, on the surface of her mind, understood that they picked on her because her wealth made her different, yet behind conscious thought hovered the question: could her schoolmates see through her flesh to that unmentionable shame? Did they have some clue, undetectable by her, yet visible to their eyes, that she was a pariah?

She had battled until her parents reluctantly allowed her to transfer to Beverly High. She had made her first friend. The hours she spent with Roy at the Waces' funny little apartment were the happiest of her life. Losing Roy was more than she could bear, so she had never risked inviting her to Belvedere. Yet miraculously, Roy's brown eyes had still shone with affection even after seeing the place and hearing her mother's patronym. This fidelity, for some odd reason, made Althea think less of Roy. And possibly Althea's feelings of superiority over her friend had brought about that one dangerous moment during the Tchaikovsky album when she had been tempted to blurt out the deep, heinous truth about herself.

Althea shifted restlessly, opening her eyes to stare into the blackness. The chintz curtains were triple-lined, so no hint of light penetrated the room.

On the New Year's Eve of her tenth year it had been dark like this . . . She shivered as memory rose up to confront her.

The sound intruded above the rustle of branches and the tenacious throb of crickets, a spontaneous creaking within her room.

134

Althea's heart banged heavily as she jarred awake. Drawing on her deepest wellspring of courage, she opened her eyes.

There was no night-light!

In the terrifying blackness, her breath burst from her lungs in a gasp of terror.

A big girl of ten shouldn't be afraid of sleeping in a room without the bedside lamp, or so her mother often repeated with a warm hug. Her father had worked out a compromise – Daddy was a genius at smoothing things between them. He suggested placing a small night-light in Althea's dressing room, with the door left ajar so that a slim beam pointed towards the twin beds. How could she have forgotten to turn it on?

Then she heard another sound, this like the panting breath of an animal.

Althea's mind raced through her litany of terrors, the ghost stories she had heard from M'liss and the horror tales she had read about malevolent spirits who refused to die with their fleshly abodes, foul incubi, werewolves. But those dreads belonged either in the past or in some remote Teutonic mountains. This was the present, some moment between 31 December 1938, and 1 January 1939 – Daddy had brought a bottle of champagne to her room and he, Mother and she had gravely clinked each other's glasses, then her parents had gone off to their New Year's party. This wasn't a place where supernatural beings dwelt, it was Beverly Hills, California, USA.

'Who's . . . there?' The night blackness swallowed her quaver.

This time the creaking sounded closer. It was footsteps.

Once a cat had climbed up to her parakeet's cage, and that poor bird's frantic acceleration of wings was how her heart now felt.

'Go away.' Her whisper was shaky and thin. 'Please, please, go away . . .'

A body lurched onto her bed, shaking it. Gasping and hot, it enveloped her in the overwhelming stench of liquor.

With a jagged groan, it crushed her chest against something crisply stiff, mashing its scalding, moist face to hers.

The cheek prickled. The crispness was a dress shirt. It's not a ghoulish horror, Althea thought. It's a mere human mortal.

'My daddy keeps a gun,' she whispered, hoping she sounded brave, knowing she didn't. 'He'll come in and kill you.'

The man put his mouth over hers in something that she did not recognize as a kiss, for it was all slobber, smells of stale liquor, teeth and a huge, predatory tongue. She struggled, flailing her hands, kicking her bare feet. But she was a thin, terrified ten-year-old, her assailant a grown man.

His hands fumbled on her shoulders and down her flat, gasping chest in a caress more insidious than cruel, his fingers forming rough circles on her belly button. With a series of swift, rough yanks, he pulled off her pyjama bottoms. His hungry fingers burrowed in her butt and the most private place that nobody else touched. Even when she was little, M'liss had always handed her the sponge to wash the convoluted creases. She knew that these rubbing, pressing fingers were not only painful and terrifying, but also shameful.

She tried to squirm away, and, failing, clamped her thighs together. One swift, rough movement of his knee pried her legs apart.

Suddenly he released her. She could feel him fumble with his clothes before he crawled on top of her, crushing the breath from her. His heart pounded through the starched shirt, beating with the same wild rapidity as her own.

Again he fingered her private place – no, he was shoving a hard, pulsing thing there. Big, huge. What could he intend? He was pushing and battering until the pain was unendurable.

She screamed in terrified agony as the enormous thing somehow went inside her.

She was torn apart with pain. As the thing jerked back

and forth, she screamed again and again, but the gasping mouth over hers muffled the sounds.

The heavy body convulsed, and then the torso raised up and she could breathe.

Tears were streaming down her face, there was a hot, unpleasant smell, and the bed was wet.

The mattress springs shifted as he got up. Footsteps staggered away.

The bedroom door opened, admitting a faint light from the corridor.

Gripping the doorjamb, his evening clothes dishevelled, stood her father.

The door closed quickly and quietly.

Althea lay shuddering and shaking with convulsive sobs, hurt radiating in waves from the violated core of her.

Now she understood that abominable freaks of nature are not the real danger. You are destroyed by those close to you, those you love and trust.

She had no idea how long she lay there, but after a while she moved stiffly to turn on the bedside lamp. She was oozing blood and there was blood all over the sheet.

She dragged into the bathroom. She washed herself and pulled on underpants, stuffing them with hankies. Then she gathered up the soiled sheets and her pyjamas, shoving the wadded bundle into the back of her dressing-room closet. Tomorrow, she thought, I'll bury everything in those tall papyrus behind the Italian gardens. Nobody goes up there.

Her instinct to hide the evidence came from a shame that had penetrated the marrow of her not yet hardened bones. Her father was strong and brave, the most wonderful man alive, so she must be unspeakably wicked for such a thing to have happened.

The following day was very hot. Althea and Roy went to Roadside. They lay on their towels, giggling each time a boy charged over the blazing sand on his way to the surf.

Althea made no mention of Belvedere or the previous day. Roy avoided the subject too.

17

That fall there was no question of Marylin's returning to Beverly High. If she were under eighteen she would have had to attend classes in the clapboard bungalow that was the Magnum schoolhouse, but NolaBee produced her birth certificate and Marylin was absolved.

Once the edges were rubbed from her awe as a new-comer, Marylin realized that the studio was a factory mobilized for war – similar to Hughes, except that rather than building aircraft, Magnum employed a large group of highly nervous people to keep up the morale of civilians and the armed services by grinding out every budgetary level of film – and, not incidentally, making abnormally large profits.

To NolaBee's disappointed chagrin, the studio put no effort behind making anything of Marylin. Art Garrison had dismissed her from his mind as soon as she was turned over to the Magnum department that groomed 'talent', the generic term for 'actor'. Marylin Wace – the powers that be had not gone to the minor effort of changing her name – lined up as one more pretty young fledgling actress whose option could be dropped at the end of the year. Her publicity consisted of one glossy that displayed her lovely curves in a two-piece bathing suit, a shot that rather than making her appear cheesecake sexy showed her as lumi-nously vulnerable, plus a layout in *Modern Screen* with three other Magnum starlets.

Marylin, grieving and guilt-ridden, lacked that patholo-gical drive so indispensable for success. She had no plans for self-aggrandizement. In a town of voraciously ambitious beauties, she had come this far only because of her mother's prodding manoeuvres and Joshua Fernauld's apparent need for penitence. She was a dispensable cog in the factory

138

wheel. In November, the end of the first six-month period, her option was picked up. She could just as easily have been dropped.

Through the fall she played a variety of silent bits.

Just before Christmas, Roy brought home the news that BJ's mother had died.

The Waces had seen nothing of Ann or Joshua Fernauld since Marylin had signed her contract back in June, yet to the three of them her death seemed a monstrous unravelling at the top of the fabric of Beverly Hills. To them, Ann Fernauld's bony, smart presence epitomized that rarefied, exotic creature, an upper echelon Industry wife. Marylin wept for Linc's mother. NolaBee and Roy wore sombre faces for a few days.

Immediately following the private funeral, Joshua and BJ drove down to the Fernauld house in Palm Springs.

The Waces mailed their condolence notes to the desert resort.

In December Marylin was assigned to *Angels*, a quickie espionage film, and given two lines, her first speaking part.

Early on the morning of 3 January, the first workday in 1944, Marylin was on Stage 2, where *Angels* was shooting. Her minuscule role was that of a tough, collaborative French *demimondaine*, a prime case of miscasting. In her skintight print dress, with her hair coiled elaborately atop her head, wearing screen makeup – orange Pan-Cake, false eyelashes and nearly black lipstick – she looked a sad, sweet child forced by the most harrowing of circumstances into the streets. She sat on a folding chair well out of range of a brightly lit bustle of activity that surrounded a sleazy *brasserie* minus a ceiling and front wall. The property master was straightening the interior under the shrill-voiced scrupulousness of a buxom elderly script girl whose job was to ascertain that no prop had strayed from its position on the previous day's shooting.

Marylin's character was to wriggle her derriere across the

139

brasserie set-up, and she gazed at the marble tables, envisioning her undulations.

She retained her ability to lose herself in a role. Otherwise she was not getting over Linc's death at all. From the beginning she had dreamed of him, but the last few months the dreams had taken on a ruthlessly sexual dimension from which she would awaken hot and sweating, her breath coming fast, her thighs clenched together.

These joinings with Linc were not dreamlike. They did not fade or shift insubstantially in the manner of dreams. He encompassed her flesh with such fully contoured sensory verisimilitude that she had begun to entertain a furtive belief that the original missing-in-action report had been correct: either Lieutenant (jg) Abraham Lincoln Fernauld was alive on some remote atoll or else constant mourning had driven her around the bend. Who but a madwoman could share such an overpowering erotic passion with a man whose firm flesh had long since dissolved into warm Pacific currents? Her body, familiar friend who told her when it was time to eat and sleep, her body must possess knowledge that the Navy Department did not.

She gave a tremulous, unconscious sigh, unaware that Joshua Fernauld had emerged from behind a nearby backdrop and stood watching her.

'Happy New Year,' he said.

She blinked in disbelief. Roy had passed on the info that BJ and Joshua were planning to stay away a full month.

'Mr Fernauld. We heard you were in Palm Springs.' She paused, adding with delicate and sincere sympathy, 'We were so very sad about Mrs Fernauld. She was a fine person, a lovely, generous lady.'

'Yes, I got your notes. No need for sadness, Marylin. The last few months were monstrous for Ann. The big C is no delicate disease.'

'Cancer?' Marylin's low, soft voice wavered. The word was never printed in an obituary, seldom spoken aloud.

'Yes, cancer. She had a hysterectomy two years ago, then a breast removed last winter, but it had already spread

140

through her. If that merciful Jesus of my boyhood truly existed she would have gone before Linc.' The heavy, overtanned features sagged.

For the first time, Marylin found herself pitying Linc's overpowering father. 'You've had a terrible year, Mr Fernauld,' she said softly.

He shrugged and pulled a folding chair next to hers. 'Joshua. It's really not too difficult to master. Three syllables. Josh-yew-ah.'

'Joshua.'

'You're a quick study,' he said. 'Marylin, Random House wants to publish Linc's novel.'

Months ago – it must have been at the beginning of summer – Joshua had borrowed the stories for a week to copy.

'Publish?' she asked blankly. 'Novel?'

'A bit of stitchery with a few unifying paragraphs. Presto, a novel. I sent it directly to Bennett Cerf.'

Her enamelled fingernails pressed into the flowered print over her thighs. 'You shouldn't have.'

'Why? It's the finest, most sensitive work to come out of this war, and I am quoting Cerf.'

A balding young man had come over: he was Johnny Kaplan, the second assistant director. 'Hi, Marylin,' he said.

'Johnny.'

'Be another fifteen minutes.' Johnny Kaplan smiled.

When he had returned to the hollow, clattering activity, Marylin said, 'Those were Linc's personal observations about the men on the *Enterprise*.'

'That's why he fictionalized.'

'He never intended them to be published.'

'If there is one thing I am damn well certain of on this earth, Marylin, it is that every writer hungers for his words to see light of day, either in print or on a screen.'

'Not Linc.'

'How are you so positive, so richly positive? Tell me how you know what an extremely complicated young man with

141

an IQ of over 160 would want. I sure as hell don't, and,' Joshua added bleakly, 'I was his father for twenty-four years.'

Those stupid tears again. She inhaled deeply, as she did to calm herself before the cameras.

He rested his arm around the back of her chair. She could feel the faint emanation of his body heat, smell his cologne and sweat. 'You'll get the royalties,' he said.

'That means the book is mine?'

'Legally and morally, yes.'

'I won't sell it.'

'Oh, Christ! Those huge sea-coloured eyes accusing me as if I had horns and a pitchfork. Listen to me, Marylin, this is not an act of necrophiliac despoilment. This is a fine and beautiful book that Linc wrote with his heart's blood. His legacy to the world. He had no child . . .' Joshua halted abruptly, saying quietly, 'Erase that, forget I said it. Don't, Marylin.'

'I'm . . . all right.'

'Your eyelashes will come unglued, you'll run streaks in that mucky Pan-Cake.' His arm moved around her and he clasped her padded shoulder. 'No crying allowed on Magnum time – not until we make you a star.'

She managed the saddest little smile. 'That'll be the day,' she murmured, shifting from his grasp.

'We'll discuss it at lunch. Ever been to Lucey's across the street?'

'That's very kind, but – '

'Stop saying no, Marylin, I say goddamn stop saying no.'

'I promised to have lunch with Johnny Kaplan, you just met him.'

'OK, so then I'll drive you home, when shooting's over.'

'My car – '

'It can stay in the lot. I'll bring you in tomorrow morning.' He got to his feet. The intense desert tan somehow increased the dictatorial power of the large, thickset body.

142

'All right,' she sighed.

He smiled. 'See you at the main gate at five.'

She waited in the cold twilight, half-blinded by the head-lights of cars streaming out the Magnum gate, the damp January wind slashing against her legs in their wartime rayon stockings.

I may send some of my stuff from time to time. It's just for you.

Your writing?

It's just for you.

Expecting Joshua either in the big Packard that had belonged to Mrs Fernauld – Linc had used it – or his own Lincoln Continental, she did not focus on the odd, foreign-looking car that honked so insistently until the familiar gravelly voice boomed, 'Marylin!'

Joshua was pushing open the door of the low-slung two-seater.

As they roared forward, she said, 'I've never ridden in a sports car.'

'A handmade custom job. It's a Delahaye 135. Been working on Ronnie Colman for months to sell me this sweet hunk of perfection.'

His enthusiasm for the English racing car lulled Mary-lin's tense determination to keep Linc's last wishes.

At the apartment, Joshua walked her up the unlit wooden staircase.

'My mother is home, so we won't have a chance to talk,' Marylin said. 'But, Joshua, I want you to know I'm really serious about protecting Linc's privacy.'

'You sweet little Mary-linn you.' Joshua's teasing was gentle. 'I've been holding off until we got here. Your mama'll be on my side.'

Marylin halted, turning to him. Her soft brown hair, released from its upsweep, blew around her white face.

'Why the surprised outrage?' he asked. 'Linc told you I obtain my ends by fair means or foul, didn't he?'

'Those stories are mine, you said so.'

The large fingers clenched the rail. 'Look at it from my

143

point of view. I have a something, call it a gift, call it a goddamn albatross I carry on my back, but it's me, my identity – you're an actress, I don't have to explain to you what creative work means. Now. I have an only son. He inherits my nose, my eyes, as well as my accursed gift – my blessed curse. He goes off to fight, but he sends back part of his soul, part of him as real as his eyes or his nose, then he's goddamn killed. This book is a continuation of me, yet finer than anything I can conceive of doing. Now, I ask you, how can I allow that to be buried?'

Marylin sighed. 'Joshua, Linc would have said if he intended publishing those stories.'

'He was hedging – it's common enough with writers. He was afraid, Marylin, afraid that his work would be found wanting and rejected.'

The door was flung open. NolaBee stood outlined by the light behind her, turbaned head tilted to one side. 'Marylin, is that you? We've been waiting. I thought we'd drive on over to the Ranch House and eat hamburgers – who's that with you?'

'Me. Joshua Fernauld.'

'Joshua! My, what a time it's been! Why are you standing out there in the cold? Marylin, where're your manners?'

In the warm, messy apartment, NolaBee's condolences washed over Joshua with a certain widowly warmth, a sharing commiseration that said 'welcome to the ranks'. Roy, the makeup heavy on her freckled embarrassment, mumbled that she, too, was sorry about Mrs Fernauld.

'Why don't you come along with us to the Ranch House?' NolaBee asked.

'What about BJ?' Roy asked.

'She's still in Palm Springs with her grandmother,' retorted Marylin, who had already asked this of Joshua. 'Mr Fernauld must have dinner waiting for him at his house.'

'It so happens that I'm at loose ends.' Joshua paused, looking at NolaBee. 'Before we go, there's something Marylin and I have to finish hashing out.'

NolaBee's expression was alive with curiosity. 'About Marylin's work over at Magnum?'

'Indirectly,' he said.

'It's about publishing Linc's stories,' Marylin said in a beleaguered tone. Her head ached across the brow. 'Nothing to do with my acting.'

'But it *is*.' Joshua sat at the old round table where a nearly empty grape-jelly jar centred a scattering of crumbs. 'I hadn't told you the best part, Marylin. I've finished a script of the novel.'

'You mean Linc will have a movie credit?' cried NolaBee. 'Why, Joshua, I reckon you're giving him something much better than the medals.'

'Mama,' Marylin sighed. 'Those stories were never intended for publication.'

Joshua and NolaBee ignored her.

He said, 'I really had two scripts. The first I outlined to sell Paramount on the idea. Jesus, you should have heard me spinning the top dogs the story they wanted, every wartime cliché in the book. The second was the version I always intended. An honourable adaptation.'

'Aren't you the sly one?' admired NolaBee.

'In my business, seduction's a necessity. Paramount has plans to make it as a big-budget A. I'm counting on Leland to convince them to borrow Marylin for the part of Rain.'

NolaBee gasped. 'No!'

'Wowee!' cried Roy.

Marylin stared reproachfully at Joshua, and went to pour herself a glass of water, holding her wet fingers against her painful brow. 'The book belongs to me,' she said sharply. 'It's not going to be sold.'

NolaBee said, 'Marylin, you're being right silly. Linc would have wanted this movie – '

'No, NolaBee,' Joshua interrupted. 'The book yes, the movie no. But I've been working at Paramount long enough to know their publicity is tops. *Island* would be promoted in the grand style. Big drums banging all the time, à la *Gone with the Wind*. The hoopla would be the making of Marylin.'

'This is your chance, darlin',' cried NolaBee. 'If you don't grab it, you'll be playing tacky little bits forever.'

'Linc wouldn't want it,' Marylin said stubbornly.

'But this is what all I've worked and slaved for.' Nola-Bee's voice was heavy with blackmailing maternal reproach.

'I'm starved,' Roy put in. 'Can't we discuss this at the Ranch House?'

They sat at one of the Ranch House's barbecue tables eating oblong rare hamburgers, salad and crusty hash-browns. Marylin, whose headache had resurged violently, toyed with her food. Joshua watched her reflexively, his obsidian eyes unreadable.

When NolaBee, perky and bright-eyed next to him, brought up the matter of Linc's book, Joshua derailed the subject. When you were with Joshua Fernauld, he dominated. They did not speak of *Island* again that night.

The next few days, NolaBee worked ceaselessly on Marylin. Though desperately unhappy and prey to uncontrollable weeping fits, the girl nevertheless steeled herself to resist her mother, an unspeakably difficult task when being bombarded with veiled reminders of personal self-abnegation, of sacrifices and unending toil aimed towards this precise chance.

In the end it was Marylin's own clamouring memories that broke her. She would question herself over and over whether Linc's ambition had been to make it as a writer. The answer always came up the same. He had. If only to prove something to his father. It would be harshest inequity to doom his work to the eternal darkness of the drawer of her bedside table.

Angels came in on its twelve-day shooting schedule, and Joshua dropped by for the wrap party. It was a low-budget film, so the refreshments were simple: Coca-Cola, potato chips and cookies. Offering him a soft drink, Marylin told him in a low stammer, 'Go ahead with the publisher and the script, Joshua.'

He spiked his drink, gazing over the paper cup at her. There was an intensity in his look that caught her like a lasso, and she could do nothing but gaze back at him, wondering at the thoughts behind the craggy features. Suddenly she shivered.

—————— 18 ——————

Island, by Lincoln Fernauld, New York, Random House, 1944, 320 pp., $2.50.

Just one of the magnificent qualities that sets this book apart from all the other war stories that we are reading is the wealth of known colour that makes this, today's war, different from any other. *Island* is set aboard an unnamed aircraft carrier, and we enter into the hearts and minds of its men. We are staring with exhausted eyes as our fuel gauge sinks to empty, we are struggling with two heavily batteried fluorescent wands to signal in a crippled F6F whose nineteen-year-old pilot has never before made a night landing, we are a young lieutenant attempting to declare his love before sailing while a line of impatient men wait to use the single pay phone, we are perched on the flag bridge in a tall steel chair looking at the fleet entrusted to our care, we are adrift on a cruelly empty sea praying that somehow the Kingfishers – the OS2U rescue planes – will find us . . .

This, from *Saturday Review*, 7 April, like all other reviews, blessed *Island* for its gem-perfect detail, lyrical clarity, its understated war-time drama, and concluded with an elegiac paragraph for the loss of so great a talent as Lieutenant (jg) Lincoln Fernauld.

Random House advertised nationally, the Book of the Month Club selected *Island*, but it was the massive studio publicity campaign about the search for Rain Fairburn, the beautiful, tenderly young heroine, that put the novel across. For three months, *Island* fever swept the country.

John Garfield, borrowed from Warner's, was cast as Lieutenant Nesbitt. On 6 June 1944, D-Day (when Allied soldiers slogged through the surf, fought, bled and died on Normandy beaches re-christened with the un-Gallic names Omaha, Utah, Gold, Sword and Juno), shooting began on *Island*. As yet no Rain Fairburn had been found.

On 19 June, a joint Magnum-Paramount publicity release announced that the juicy plum had gone to a newcomer who had felicitously changed her name to Rain Fairburn.

Marylin, who heard the news only a few hours before the release, envisioned Leland Hayward conniving like a demon to get her this role. Her gratitude to her agent was tear-drenched and slightly overwrought.

She concluded with, 'I'll do everything I can to live up to your faith in me, Mr Hayward – I can't put into words how very much I appreciate your faith in me.'

'Don't thank me, honey, thank Joshua. He told Frank Freeman he wouldn't renew with Paramount if they didn't borrow you for the part. He told Freeman you *were* Rain, he ranted, he stormed. He bulldozed. A powerhouse, that's Joshua when he's hot after something. Thank him.'

'I guess he explained about me and Linc?' she said. 'He's doing it for Linc.'

Leland Hayward gave her an enigmatic smile and said nothing.

At the end of June, Marylin's option was again picked up, and she received the stipulated two hundred a week. (Paramount was paying Magnum twelve hundred a week for her services.) Though the *Island* royalty cheques had not yet started to flow, Marylin had received a substantial hunk of cash for the movie rights, enough for NolaBee to quit Hughes and to make a down payment on a small wrong-side-of-the-tracks Mediterranean-style house on Crescent Drive – the place was going for a bargain price because it was adjacent to the parking lot of Ralphs' Supermarket.

Marylin spent little time there. Her life had become an

unending cycle of rising in the dark, working with nervous intensity through the day, arriving home to choke down the soft eggs that a concerned NolaBee poached or boiled, then falling into her bed with muscles aching and brains ajangle to study her lines for the next day. A grimly isolated existence analogous to a jail sentence.

Her puerile inexperience, the demands of being in front of the camera almost continuously in a major high-budget feature, the never-ending fusillade of half-truths and outright fabrications about Rain Fairburn (her!) emanating from the columns and radio slots of the gossip queens worked to pathological effect: she moved in a daze of sheer animal terror.

The film's director, Bentley Hendrickson, a soft-spoken, moustached homosexual, not unreasonably resented a borrowed newcomer being foisted on him, resented that magazine writers and photographers were permitted on *his* set to interview this pretty, totally incompetent nonentity. He would drawl out a stinting word or two of directorial advice to the other actors, seasoned craftspeople all, then slouch in his canvas director's chair offering Marylin no palliative word of encouragement, no constructive criticism. He ordered retakes, up to fifty of them, for her scenes.

To Marylin these scenes were a nightmare parody of her times with Linc. She was too paralysingly close to her role. For once she could not bury herself in her work.

Every move she made was wooden.

Bentley Hendrickson's bitchily exaggerated ennui, the executive producer's iciness as he looked directly at her when he repeated how far behind schedule they lagged, the crew's hostile witness to her eternal inadequacy, were unbearable. At times she froze with humiliation and grief. Shivering uncontrollably, she would rush from the set to the converted trailer that was her dressing room.

By the end of the second week she was reduced to a terrified, near-catatonic wreck.

On the following Monday the first scene scheduled was Rain hearing by telephone that her lover is sailing. Lamentably evocative. Marylin huddled in the trailer-dressing room, ruining the makeup artist's labours with a torrent of tears.

The second assistant director knocked to tell her they were ready for her.

'Be right there,' she said in a muffled voice.

Fifteen minutes later, still in the trailer, she was repeating the identical words to the first assistant. This time her voice rose a hysterical half-octave.

A few minutes later, without a knock, the door opened. Joshua filled the metal door frame – he had to bend his shock of grey hair to enter. The trailer shook as he crossed the threshold.

She sat up, jerkily dabbing at her eyes. 'Joshua.'

He was producing a pint of Southern Comfort from a paper bag. 'You look in desperate need,' he said.

'Yech. Put that away. I've got the stomach flu.'

'Flu, bull! What you have is a massive, full-blown case of camera jitters.'

'I don't!' she burst out, then crumpled back on the daybed. 'Yes! Yes I do! All those people out there depending on me! Joshua, I'm no good, I never was. You'll have to get Mr Hayward to withdraw me from the film – I'm positive Paramount wants to replace me. Magnum won't pick up my option! And I'm glad, glad!' The words raced out, high-pitched, near-demented. 'I don't belong in movies, I shouldn't even be an extra. I don't have what it takes!'

He was pouring Southern Comfort into her water tumbler. '*Mea culpa*. What a horse's ass am I, not to have foreseen the difficulties involved for you in this part.'

'I'm not an actress.'

'You're an actress to the bone. Listen to me, Marylin. That scene you're meant to be playing is a close-up. A close-up shows mental processes.' He thrust the glass into her hand. 'Down the hatch.'

The smell was nauseating, like sweetly rancid straw. 'I'll throw up.'

'Marylin!' he commanded roughly.

150

She gulped. The cloying liquid went roughly down her throat, and fresh tears wet her eyes.

'Thinking,' Joshua said. 'Thinking. That's the long and short of your scene.'

'But – '

'But nothing. I should know, I wrote the damn script. A close-up. Listen to me, Marylin, I repeat what is graven in stone. A close-up is to show the audience a thought. You can think, I goddamn know you can think.'

'Think? I'm so stiff with fright that my mind's ready to shatter like glass. Ask Mr Hendrickson – ' She clutched at the glass. 'Joshua, he hates me.'

'That's his *shtick*, he stands aloof from his actors until they give a performance for him.' He poured a little more liquor in her glass. 'Let me pass on a trick that I used when I was a brash young writer pitching stories. I'd face those fat producers, my guts griping with anxiety, and imagine them in their big chairs, smoking their big cigars, wearing long johns.'

The Southern Comfort had ignited a comforting warmth behind Marylin's breastbone. 'Long johns?' She giggled.

'Red long johns. With flaps in back.' He gestured with a raise of his hand that she drink again. This time she sipped. 'Marylin,' he said, 'this is your picture, you *are* Rain, and we both know it. Hendrickson can go screw himself – I hear tell that is his true preference anyway. So think of him jerking off in his red long johns.'

At the lewd mental picture, she blushed and giggled again.

'Better?'

'Tight,' she said.

'Nothing wrong with being a little snookered on the set – not too much, but just enough to unwind.' He put his arm around her, drawing her down the trailer steps. She sat on a stool, letting the Southern Comfort's warmth spread through her as the makeup man did repairs. Drawing a breath deep into her abdomen, she moved onto the brilliantly lit circle.

A half-hundred highly skilled professionals stared at her. Bentley Hendrickson sighed and leaned back.

Panic leaped onto Marylin like a tiger.

Then she saw Linc's father, a massive figure of strength, winking at her as he tapped his thigh.

They're all wearing long johns, she thought. Itchy red ones. Her body relaxed. She murmured, 'Ready.'

A special-effects man started the telephone ringing. She reached for the instrument, thinking, thinking of the primal desolation of those minutes when Linc had informed her of the *Enterprise*'s sailing. Tears came into her eyes. She let them ooze down her cheeks.

She couldn't tell if she was projecting as much acting skill as a papier-mâché doll, but for the first time since she had started *Island*, she understood what she was doing.

'Cut. Print it,' Bentley Hendrickson said in a soft, drawly voice. He rose from his canvas chair, coming over to hand her a box of Kleenex. 'I seldom use a first take, but that was perfect, Miss Fairburn. Perfect.'

Joshua, lowering his *Hollywood Reporter*, winked again. Marylin flashed him a look of gratitude.

After that she was able to go onto the set every day and draw on her too-poignant memories. Joshua often came over from the Writers Building. She was too strung up to go to the commissary for lunch, so he would order the thick sandwiches for which Paramount was famous, sharing them with her in the trailer.

One evening when they were viewing the rushes, he said quietly, 'You're beautiful – but then, so are a lot of girls. *You* have that extra magnetism – God alone knows what it is, and no mortal's put a name to it. When you're in the frame, you draw the eye. That, little Marylin, is what makes a star.'

She stared up at the screen, unable for the life of her to comprehend what Joshua meant. All she saw was her own enormous image making crucial blunders in every movement.

* * *

152

At the end of shooting, Joshua sat next to her in the studio projection room while the Paramount executives watched a screening of the rough cut of *Island*. Marylin had not realized until now how much of herself the camera had captured. She saw a young girl dancing with her lover under flickering lights, saw her wild flight through empty streets to be with him one more time, saw her brave face shatter into grief as he went towards his ship. Around her she heard muted sobbing and the loud blowing of a nose.

'The End' appeared on the screen.

There was a moment of hideous silence; then applause burst out.

'A shoo-in for Best Picture of the Year!'

'We've got a smasheroo!'

'And what about Magnum? They've got some winner in that girl!'

'A sensational find, that little peach, luminous as Ingrid, more gorgeous than Lana. Magnum'll clean up with her. She'll put Garrison's half-ass outfit on the map.'

Bentley Hendrickson leaned over from the row behind to take her hand and kiss it. 'You blazed like a comet up there.' By now there had formed a thin sheen of professional friendship between them, yet even so she did not know how to respond to his softly respectful tones.

After a few minutes she whispered to Joshua, 'Can we leave?'

'Why not?'

'You're the writer, you work here at Paramount with these people.'

'So what?' he said. 'Come on.'

It was a cool, damp September night and the few lights on the studio street shone through the mist with rainbow haloes.

A couple were walking by: 'That little Fairburn girl can act rings around Vivien Leigh . . .'

That little Fairburn girl. Me, Marylin thought. They're talking about *me* in the same breath with Vivien Leigh and other stars. Elation warmed her briefly; then she discounted the remark as she had discounted the praise in the projection room. This was Marylin's first time to catch the brass ring, but tonight, as for the rest of her life, her humility about her craft made any compliment, however sincerely made, sound false in her ears.

'Hear that?' Joshua asked.

'People feel obliged to say something nice at studio screenings.'

'We'll have to do something about that ego,' he chuckled, taking her arm. 'You know what else they're talking about?'

'Linc's book. Your wonderful script.'

'They're talking about Joshua Fernauld making a horse's ass of himself mooning around the set with a girl nearly thirty years younger than he is.'

She eased from his grasp. Despite her staggering guilelessness, her youth, her inexperience with any man but Linc, she had sensed with a remote part of her mind that Linc's father had fallen for her. Now shame crept through her. Indefensible, disgraceful, that she had not attempted to avert his desire for her. She could not conceive of his emotions as being anything more than the hots. Everyone in the Industry knew of Joshua Fernauld's libidinous forays on young actresses. (Linc had been bitter on his mother's behalf and BJ, her friend, sometimes made vaguely embarrassed boasts about 'Daddy's little romances'.)

'Well?' Joshua drew her into the shadowy doorway of the Accounting Building.

Well? she thought. Briefly her mind filled with a not-quite-recapturable remembrance, the tremulous moment when Linc had kissed her outside apartment 2B, the scent of the wiry lemon tree . . . Her lips parted softly.

'He's dead,' Joshua said, his voice a harsh lament. 'There is no commingling between the quick and the dead. The movie should have been catharsis enough. You should be over him by now.'

'Are you?' she whispered.

His arms went around her, a tactile force pressing her against his tall, thick, warm body. Resting his cheek on her

154

hair, he touched her neck lightly, tenderly. 'Marylin, I loved my son, I still love him – would that I had died for him. But he's dead.' The words rumbled within his chest, reverberating against her body. 'I've wanted you since I brought back his stories and you were so broken and lovely in that rag of a bathrobe.'

She felt not the least desire for Joshua – indeed, with him 'it' seemed incestuous, ugly, wrong – yet she *had* clung to him during the filming. I owe him something, she thought. Another, lesser thought flashed: at least I don't have to explain about Linc and me.

When Joshua bent his mouth on hers, she kissed him back.

He drove her along Sunset to a nearby motel with a blinking green sign: The Lanai.

When he took her in his arms, she realized he was trembling all over. He kissed her with reverential tenderness, the kiss turning unequivocally lustful. He toppled with her onto the firm double bed, undressing her, exploring her innermost recess until she was physically ready.

He made love with an experience that lasted until she murmured that she had come enough – which was true, orgasm had followed orgasm, yet they were physical quivers, not the haunting, lingering seizures that now existed only in her dreams.

Moving swiftly, Joshua gave a cry that garbled her name, then collapsed.

Over his shoulder in the lustreless mirror Marylin could see an indistinct reflection: the back of a large, thickset, gasping man, his buttocks startlingly white in the middle of his tan, curled on top of a slight girl.

The image was no more real to her than the flickers on the screen earlier that night.

Numerous retakes were needed on *Island*. Marylin reported daily to the Paramount sound stage, where the excessive tension that had possessed actors and crew was dissipated, replaced by an easy jocular camaraderie as they wrapped

155

up a film everyone knew would be good. Joshua took her out to leisurely lunches. Unaware that these were the final days she would be able to appear unselfconscious in public, she enjoyed his bravura conversation. Joshua had an inexhaustible supply of industry anecdotes that he related with outrageous accents and masterful humour that cracked her up completely – once she lay down in the booth, actually lay down, in a helpless ravagement of laughter. His range of knowledge extended far beyond Hollywood. He read vastly and catholically, and he peppered his talk with literary references. He had a firm historical command of politics, the causes and implications of the war. He understood and explained the works of Einstein and Freud. Never a bore, he let her have her say. When she spoke, timidly, about the craft of acting, his tanned, deeply lined face was heavy with concentration.

She looked up to him as she would a brilliant professor. This non-erotic suggestion of being his student extended into the Lanai Motel. Never once did she feel as she had with Linc, an equal partner.

'I reckon you ought to start going out,' NolaBee said. Since quitting Hughes, she was constantly fussing around the kitchen concocting dishes to tempt the fugitive appetite of her beautiful child. At this moment she was stirring a great dollop of butter – bought with the last of the Waces' red ration stamps – into mashed potatoes.

'I have lunch with Joshua.'

'That's not what all I mean, and you know it. He's Linc's father.'

'Verdon Conant.' Marylin mentioned a young actor that Magnum publicity often teamed her with.

'He's one of *those*,' NolaBee said, letting her hand dangle from her wrist. She was peering worriedly at Marylin. 'Been over a year, darlin'. I won't have you moping around. You're going to be a star. Now it's time for you to have fun with beaux, maybe meet Mr Right.'

Book Three
1944

What famous screenwriter was seen tête-à-tête at the Hollywood Brown Derby with luscious oh-so-young Island star Rain Fairburn?
— Louella Parsons' column, Hearst Press, 3 November 1944

D-DAY

— New York Times *Extra*, 6 June 1944

Almighty God, our sons, pride of our nation, this day have set upon a mighty endeavor, a struggle to preserve our republic, our religion, and our civilization, and to set free a suffering humanity. Some will never return. Embrace these, Father, and receive them, thy heroic servants, into thy kingdom.
— Broadcast prayer of President Roosevelt, 6 June 1944

Of all the thunderous hits in the successful annals of Magnum Pictures, we're proudest of Northern Lights *with that wonderful new Magnum luminary, Rain Fairburn. When you play this great new box-office attraction, you will experience not only the biggest hit of the year, but you will enjoy an equally important success, the heartfelt gratitude of your patrons.*
— Ad in Motion Picture Herald, 9 April 1945

The 1944 Pulitzer Prize for fiction goes posthumously to Lincoln Fernauld for his wartime novel, Island.
— Time, 7 May 1945

Ingrid Bergman (Gaslight); *Claudette Colbert* (Since You Went Away); *Bette Davis* (Mr Skeffington); *Rain Fairburn* (Island); *Greer Garson* (Mrs Parkington); *Barbara Stanwyck* (Double Indemnity)
— Nominees for Best Actress, 1944, Motion Picture Academy

19

1944 was Roy and Althea's sixteenth year: on their birth-days they would be eligible for State of California drivers' licences. In spring, though, because Belvedere was clas-sified as a farm, Althea achieved an early licence and ownership of a car.

It was not, of course, a new model – no new cars had rolled off the line since the war began – and neither was it the convertible for which Althea had pleaded and raged. It was one of the cars used around Belvedere, an Oldsmobile station wagon, a utilitarian vehicle square of line and homely with its green hood and varnished wood body, not zooty at all. It possessed, however, one consummate virtue: Hydra-Matic transmission. There were no gears to strip, no clutch to burn out.

After a couple of days cruising around Belvedere's gravelled roadways with the chauffeur, both girls could drive. (This was by far the longest time Roy would ever spend at the estate.) Althea passed the driving test, and Roy, who had only a learner's permit, could drive when her friend was in the car.

Althea, with her casual generosity, designated the station wagon as joint property, and together they stencilled 'Big Two' with dark green paint on the wood of both front doors.

The previous summer Marylin had forever departed Beverly High. This June BJ had graduated. Roy adhered to Althea's unstated wish that they remain an inviolate duo.

With their standoffishness, their knowing, secret-code badinage, and their outré makeup, they had garnered reputations as 'cinches' or 'hot stuff' – though no Beverly High boys had dated them.

Althea and Roy gave rides to pairs of hitching servicemen. More often than not, these men asked them out. If the guys were young, reasonably c and c (couth and cute), the girls accepted. In their draped, shoulder-padded dresses, they descended with their dates on Hollywood, sitting in movie cathedrals or dancing at the Palladium.

These dates infused Roy with a tiny amount of self-esteem. Althea, though, gained no such confidence. What, she would ask Roy, did an evening with a GI or a gob signify? What triumph was there in jitterbugging to the razzmatazz beat of Gene Krupa when all around on the huge, crowded dance floor a thousand girls were likewise dancing with that most ubiquitous of commodities, an enlisted man? Privately, Roy considered Althea a little cold-blooded about it. Yet if they parked afterwards – and they often did – on one of the secluded ledges along Tower Road, she would hear slithering, shifting, groaning sounds on the front seat of the station wagon.

Roy herself didn't mind kissing, not even those saliva-exchanging French kisses, but when hot hands inevitably snaked towards her cotton brassiere or her pink rayon panties, desolation overcame her, for she understood that her date had lost his embryonic regard for her.

That summer NolaBee, once again a housewife, fixed Roy a late breakfast every morning, and Roy, joyous at securing her mother's total attention, ate her Shredded Wheat recounting a bowdlerized version of her previous night's date. That summer Marylin bought Roy two brand-new size-twelve dirndl dresses at Taffy's, and Roy had no hickeys on her freckled skin. That summer saw monstrous battles along the coastlines of Europe, blood drenched the circumference of the globe, yet the sun chose to confer its benevolent warmth on Roy Wace in the prosperous, peaceful little town of Beverly Hills, California.

That summer, the girls met Dwight Hunter.

They were driving home from the beach along Wilshire,

peasant blouses over their swimsuits, both a little groggy from too much sun. It was Roy's turn to drive. At the intersection of Santa Monica a clanging red streetcar held up traffic. Near the landmark fountain with its graceful kneeling statue stood a sturdily built young man. Wearing covert slacks with a white shirt, he had a sandy crewcut, and from this angle showed a profile somewhat like Van Johnson's.

He held out his thumb.

I'd pick him up in a snap if he were in uniform, Roy thought. (The girls had resolved a convoluted system of boy-girl mores; in the Big Two's books, if you gave a ride to a serviceman you were patriotic, to a civilian, just cheap.)

He turned, glancing into the open window directly at her. As they regarded one another across Wilshire Boulevard, Roy felt a strange quiver in her abdomen.

He gestured with his head at Santa Monica Boulevard in the direction of the ornate dome of the Beverly Hills City Hall, whose tiles – green, blue, gold – were brilliant in the late pink sunlight. Roy was continuing along Wilshire to her house. Yet with only a fractional hesitation she nodded. He jogged across the street.

Althea turned to her. 'Why are we picking *that* up?'

'He's sort of Van Johnsonish.'

'Yes, they're both masculine,' Althea retorted. 'Besides, dear heart, he's heading along Santa Monica. Which we are not.'

'So we'll zigzag a few blocks,' said Roy, leaning over to pull at the back-door handle, releasing the lock.

'Thanks, I was giving up hope,' the man said. 'Big Two . . . I don't get it.'

'A sobriquet,' Roy said. 'Which as you doubtless know means – '

'A nickname,' he finished. 'Yours?'

'Bright boy,' Roy said.

He and Roy chuckled. Althea was silent. The streetcar had passed. As the traffic moved, Roy cut a sharp left onto Santa Monica. 'How far are you going?' she asked.

'Crescent.'

Roy twisted around, taking her eyes off the traffic to gaze exultantly into his eyes. 'Coincidence of coincidences!' she cried. 'I live on Crescent too. The house next to Ralphs'.'

'I'm on the six-hundred block, north,' he said.

'The right side of the tracks,' Roy said. 'Do you go to Beverly?'

'UCLA.'

'Oh?' Althea drawled with a faintly deprecatory smile. 'Waiting to get caught in the draft?'

Roy, watching in the rearview mirror, saw him redden. She said hastily, 'I'm Roy Wace, and this is Althea Cunningham. We're seniors.'

'I'm Dwight Hunter. We moved here last April.'

Roy asked, 'From where?'

'Up north, Marin County,' he said. 'Hey, Roy, stop!'

They had reached the block-long Beverly Hills post office that by some architectural blunder faced grandiosely onto the tracks. Roy swerved to the kerb, jamming down the brake. Dwight jumped out, then leaned on the window. 'Thank you.'

'*De nada*,' Roy said.

'It won't be *nada* in one second,' Althea said. 'The police will be upon you.'

Roy gave Dwight her sparkle smile and pressed on the accelerator. They swerved around the corner.

'Yech,' Althea said.

'I thought he was c and c. Also intelligent.'

'*I* heard no sign of brilliance, only that he was 4-F.'

'He never said he was. Maybe he's a medical student or under age.'

'How about that limp?' Althea asked.

'What limp?'

'You didn't notice?'

'No.'

'You need glasses.'

'Who, me? Hawkeye? Listen, if *I* didn't see, it's nothing. Maybe he sprained his ankle playing football.'

'What are you suddenly? St Bernadette of the cripples?'

Roy didn't even try for a comeback. Althea had sunk into one of her unpredictable morose spells.

The air was not fully clear between them until they left Warner's chattering about the Bette Davis character in *Mr Skeffington*.

Without discussion, they drove to Simon's.

As usual, the brilliantly lit drive-in lot was jammed with cars full of young people, as were the two interior semicircles of counters and booths. From the counters at the centre constantly flowed laden trays, which were picked up by high-stepping, short-skirted carhops. Energetic ribbons of bebop twined from every car window.

Simon's was the ground zero of Beverly High's social life. On these summer evenings, everybody with the least pretension of being hep wound up here. Althea, who was driving, had to cruise around endlessly before a slot in the fourth row was vacated.

In their marked station wagon they were amply conspicuous targets for masculine innuendos while they waited the routine thirty-five minutes for pretty, blonde Kitty, the most popular carhop, to take their orders of club sandwiches and lemon Cokes.

'Hi, Roy . . . hi, Althea,' said a quiet masculine voice.

Dwight Hunter had one saddle shoe on the running board.

'Well, fancy meeting you here,' Althea said in a level cadence. 'Still hitching?'

'I walked over.'

'Then,' Althea said, 'you better trot on in. I see a free stool at the counter.'

Roy blurted, 'I'm stuffed from dinner. But idiot that I am, I ordered a club sandwich.'

'Want me to help you out?' Dwight asked.

'That's the idea,' Roy retorted happily.

He opened the back door, slamming it shut with a firm, satisfying thwack.

Wound up for disaster – any crude crack directed from a nearby car – yet intoxicated with pleasure, Roy perched on her knee, her arm braced on the back of the seat to face

163

Dwight, and asked questions. This summer he had graduated from Menlo, a prep school near Stanford, his father, a vice-president at Onyx Motor Company, had been promoted from their San Francisco plant to head up the assembly in Glendale, where they now spewed out tanks. Kitty returned with their trays, affixing them to the rolled-down windows.

Althea spoke for the first time since Dwight had entered the station wagon. 'What about your foot?'

'Leg, you mean,' he said in a subdued voice. 'I had polio when I was a little kid.'

'So you're 4-F?'

'My right leg is only a little shorter. I haven't taken the physical, but I've heard of cases like me being inducted. If I am, the Army's hardly gaining much in the way of a soldier.'

Roy watched him, her eyes round, her freckled, sun-reddened forehead creased with concentration. 'What do you mean?'

'To be honest, I've never understood the quirky thing inside us humans that makes us put on uniforms and march out to kill our own kind,' Dwight said.

Althea said, 'Sounds like conscientious-objector talk to me.'

'It must take a lot of courage to be one, a conchie,' Roy said softly.

'A lot of courage,' Dwight replied. His smallish features dissolved into a boyish uncertainty.

And Roy rushed in. 'Heard the new Tommy Dorsey, "No Love, No Nothin"?'

Then the carhop was smiling her blank, pretty smile into the car. 'Will that be all?'

Dwight reached for the bill.

Roy smiled her thanks at him. Then she heard herself say, 'We're the only Waces in the book.' Blood rushed to her sunburned face. Wrong, colossally, stupefyingly wrong! If Dwight wanted her number, he had a larynx.

As he moved around the thick-parked cars, Roy noted that he stepped with idiosyncratic force on his right foot.

'See?' Althea said. 'That conchie talk's cover-up, sheer cover-up.'

'He can't help having polio. And you didn't have to tell him he was yellow right to his face,' Roy snapped. She was furious at Althea – and at herself for making that excruciating gaffe. 'I like him.'

'There's no accounting for tastes.'

'Look, maybe we shouldn't go to the beach tomorrow. I'd like to stick around the house a bit.'

Althea's hand tightened on the gearshift until the knuckles went white, yet her voice retained that arch inflection. 'All alone by the telephone?'

'I don't want to go to the beach, all right?'

'As I live and breathe,' Althea said. She turned the ignition key, her face set in her superior-sad-frightened look.

For once Roy neither relented nor backed down.

20

I quarrelled with Althea, Roy thought when she awoke the next morning. Her lack of guilt or dread astounded her. I made a jerk of myself with Dwight Hunter. Even this distressing fact did not dampen her buoyant well-being.

Stretching, she conjured up Dwight Hunter, his grave, slow voice, his even features.

After a while she pulled on the long, old cardigan that had belonged to her father and now served her as a bathrobe, and went into the bright, disordered kitchen. NolaBee sat at the table, a saucerless cup of coffee on the *Los Angeles Examiner*, which was opened to the drama page. As Roy came in, she smiled. 'You slept mighty late. It's after eleven. After the picture show, did you girls go someplace?' She was at the refrigerator, taking out a half-filled tumbler. 'Here, hon, I squeezed too many oranges when I fixed Marylin's.'

165

'Thank you, Mama. We went to Simon's, and this interesting UCLA man I know was there.'

NolaBee took a fresh cigarette, her small, alert eyes twinkling on Roy. 'What about Althea? Was there a beau for Althea?'

Roy shook her head.

'I've been meaning to mention this, Roy. Seems like it's time for you to branch out a little on your own. Sometimes Althea can be standoffish, and men don't like that. You're bright and cheerful. Lots of men goin' to fall for my curlytop.'

'Mama, I did something awful.' Roy swallowed. 'I gave him my phone number.'

''Course you did.'

'It doesn't seem pushy to you?'

'Pushy? How else could he call? Roy, you're going to have to learn to have some confidence around men. Remember, you're a Fairburn and a Wace.' NolaBee tilted her head fondly, surveying her younger daughter's freckled, embarrassed face. 'And a right nice-looking girl.'

Roy, anxieties propitiated, sipped at the pith-laden orange juice with its not-just-squeezed flatness.

NolaBee ran her finger down the column. 'Listen to this, Roy, from Louella Parsons. "Word from Paramount is that *Island* will be *the* box-office smash of the year! And rumour hath it that its lovely new star, Rain Fairburn, is seeing *mucho* of Joshua Fernauld, who penned the script from his hero son's novel." That's real nice publicity, it's good for Marylin. Wouldn't the fans laugh if they knew the truth?'

'Mama ... ' Roy chewed at a bitter orange seed. 'Maybe she likes him.'

''Course she does. Mr Fernauld is Linc's father. And just look at how he's helped her. Why, she wouldn't be anyplace without him.'

'I mean, the way the newspaper says.'

'You're bein' silly, Roy. Why, he'd easier be *my* conquest – he's older than me.' Refilling her coffee cup, NolaBee frowned. 'She ought to have some proper beau by now.'

Roy nodded absently. Snips of music floated ethereally through her head.

At the ring of the telephone, she jumped up and ran.

It was Dwight. 'Are you busy this afternoon?' he asked.

'No,' she breathed solemnly.

'I have a class until three . . . okay if I come over right after?'

'That'd be groovy.'

At two she was ready in her new blue-and-white-check cotton sunsuit.

At 3.37 the doorbell buzzed. Before, she had been in the car with Dwight; now she realized he was shorter than she had imagined, only a couple of inches taller than she. She smiled at him, trying to think of some witty remark, but he was so deep-minded, a real brain.

'Uhh, can I get you something?' she stammered.

'I'm dying of thirst.'

'Water or lemonade?'

'Any beer in the house?'

'For that I have to see your ID,' she retorted.

He laughed. Elation jumped through her, and her nervousness vanished.

They carried their glasses to the backyard with its pungent, uncut grass – NolaBee ignored the lawn mower, concentrating on the victory garden along the wall. Facing each other on the glider, they rocked idly, easily, back and forth.

'Do you know my brother, Pete?' he asked. 'Peter Hunter. He's a junior at Beverly High.'

For a moment the motion of the swing nauseated her. School and that idiotic unearned reputation! 'No,' she mumbled, shaking her head.

Dwight moved his knee, touching her calf with his own.

Her flesh trembled and her forebodings evaporated. He leaned forward, lightly touching his lips to hers. Every part of her concentrated on that sensitive pressure, her very soul seemed connected to him through their joined lips.

The front door opened and NolaBee, singing 'Begin the Beguine' loudly, moved through the house to the kitchen. Opening the screen door, she stuck out the old blue turban

167

that she had enlivened with a large rhinestone Scottie. Well, you have company,' she said.

Roy introduced them. For the first time she felt an edginess that somebody might not fall for her lively, wonderful mother. But wasn't she the exact opposite of the carefully put-together north-of-Santa Monica ladies?

NolaBee chattered cordially a few minutes before remarking, 'I'm frying up a pair of chickens for dinner and that's way too much for us three women. I'd sure appreciate it, Dwight, if you'd help us out.'

'I don't want to put you to any trouble, Mrs Wace.'

'Trouble? We're just going to sit out here on the porch and have a picnic.'

'I'd love to stay, then.'

While he telephoned his mother, Roy whispered, 'Mama, doesn't he look exactly like Van Johnson?'

'Mmm, maybe a little, around the nose and chin. Yes, I think I see it.'

Marylin, gorgeous with only lipstick and her hair yanked back into a ponytail, got home around six, and a few minutes later Joshua Fernauld drove up in his enviable British car.

The patio lacked furniture, so the five of them sat on the low cement-block wall of the patio, eating hot, crispy chicken and biscuits dripping with honey. Roy noted that Mr Fernauld planted his large self next to Marylin, an unimportant observation that faded in the woozy delights of sitting so close to Dwight that their arms sometimes nudged.

After supper, Mr Fernauld offered Dwight a lift home.

Roy said, 'You don't have to leave yet, do you?'

'Now, Roy,' NolaBee admonished, 'have you forgotten? We're going on over to the Morgans'?'

Roy, who never willingly visited the Morgans, the elderly, fussy Christian Science couple next door, pierced her mother with a reproachful glance. After the pair had driven off in a triumphant roar of mufflers, she demanded, 'Mama, why did you do that?'

'Roy, first thing you have to learn is never let a boy

suppose you have nothing on your mind but him. Let him dangle a hit. That Dwight'll call soon, you'll see.'

NolaBee's prophecy came true. The next five days, which remained hot, Dwight visited every afternoon, remaining for supper at NolaBee's behest.

He had no car. Confined to the house and yard, they were forced to comport themselves sedately. A frustrating state of semi-derangement to Roy. She ached to have Dwight initiate the caresses she had fought off so adamantly in the middle seat of the station wagon.

Island's royalties had paid for a maroon brocade couch, which was deep, soft and perfect for necking purposes, but alas, those warm nights the living room became a highway along which NolaBee and Marylin travelled for endless glasses of ice tea and lemonade.

The only undisturbed body contact permitted them was a few minutes of groaningly ardent soul kisses outside the front door – NolaBee terminated these embraces by switching on the dim yellow porch light. 'Oh, Dwight, thought I heard you leave.'

When Dwight wasn't around, Roy would day dream of him, her delectable reveries occasionally shattered by a bleak thought that swooped down on her like a persistent bird of prey: I wonder what's with Althea?

The only other time since the inception of their friendship that the girls had been incommunicado for longer than a day was the previous Christmas, when the three Cunninghams had gone back East to the Archie Coyne's camp in the Adirondacks, a virgin tract of lakes and mountains that, Althea mentioned in passing, had its own ski lifts.

As the hot August days passed, the enforced separation took its toll on Roy. She felt lousy enough at having lost her confidante, at being unable to pour her wondrous new emotions into her friend's delicately moulded ear, but what felled her utterly was the guilt of knowing that Althea missed her far more. After all, *she* had Dwight.

I really have to give her a buzz, Roy would think. Each time she reached this decision, she would hear – actually hear – the bitchy note in Althea's cool voice as she called Dwight chicken. Like an unworshipped icon, the telephone remained in the ledge indented in the rough stucco of the hall.

On Thursday morning Althea phoned.

'Hi,' Roy mumbled. 'Long time no see.'

'Yes, a lot of water under the proverbial bridge,' Althea said, pausing. 'Firelli's at Belvedere.'

'Firelli!' Roy gasped. 'You can't mean *the* Firelli?'

'None other. He's a friend of my parents. They're in Washington – I told you Daddy's a dollar-a-year man for the State Department, didn't I? It's fallen on little me to entertain the maestro.' Althea's voice dropped to lecherous depths.

'Your parents *really* know Firelli?'

'Through my grandmother. Are you and Dwight an item?'

'We're seeing a lot of each other, yes,' Roy said guardedly.

'Then why don't the two of you drop by and spend an afternoon with him?'

'Sounds fabuloso, but I'll have to ask Dwight.' Then Roy burst out, 'Althea, without you it's been Lower Slobbovia.'

'Ditto,' Althea said.

'I mean, it's swell of you to call.'

'You'll adore Firelli. It's hard to believe he's so ancient.'

'We have one minor problem. No car.'

'Pick you up, natch.'

When Roy hung up, she leaned back in the folding chair by the phone, limp as if a great, crushing stone had been removed from her body.

21

It was hardly a secret that Carlo Firelli was English.

His life was an open book – a renowned open book. The thirteenth child of a poor greengrocer, he had been the youngest applicant to win a full scholarship to the Royal Academy of Music, had conducted his first triumphant concert before that black-clad dwarf, Queen Victoria, and had refused knighthoods from both George V and George VI.

Roy, however, knew Firelli only by the patronym splashed across the few classical albums that she enjoyed. So what surprised her most about the famous old conductor was his English accent — not hoity-toity, but a pungent, distinctive Birmingham.

She broached the subject of his misleading Italianate name.

'In my youth I had the idea that a bloke called Charlie Frye would never be seriously considered in the world of music. So I transcribed my name to Italian, and it pleased me mightily.' His sweet, deep bass wordlessly sang a triumphant theme unknown to Roy. 'Now when I look back on that boy, I rather approve his vanity, yes, I admire that brash lad.' The round old face broke into a gay cobweb of preordained wrinkles as he chuckled. 'Does that sound swollen-headed, little Roy?'

'No, honest.' She returned his smile. 'You seem to enjoy everything, Firelli.' (On being introduced, he had insisted that she and Dwight drop the prefix of 'Mr'.)

'Why not? Life is a gift, and to refuse a gift is churlish.' He glanced down ruefully at his stout belly. 'But I daresay I should be a good sight thinner if I didn't enjoy the nutritional oblations so much.'

The old Englishman's thick haunches and short, very wide legs were clad in dandified white flannels, a cravat circled his roly-poly neck, and he had rolled up his shirt sleeves because, he told Roy, the California sun blessed his arms. A jolly halo of white hairs stood out from his pink skull.

Roy had never met anyone like the British conductor. It wasn't his fame — lately through Joshua Fernauld she had met several famous people. None, however, possessed this gusto, this indefatigable delight. In his late seventies, Firelli fitted right in with the young people, so they felt none of the constraint that elders generally stamp on gatherings. He radiated good cheer and tolerance. His small raisin-dark eyes were innocently wise, nonjudgemental, accepting.

'I know what you mean.' Roy sighed. 'Me, I never pass up a meal or snack – as if you couldn't tell.'

'You? Tosh!' He tilted his large, haloed head admiringly at her new shorts and the hand-me-down blouse that bared the freckled upper curves of her breasts. 'Tosh, I say. Little Roy, if only you knew how perfect you are.'

They were reclining on chaises near the pool. The water churned with Dwight's methodical Australian crawl and Althea's swift butterfly. Roy, having the tag end of her period, couldn't go in.

'Firelli, why are you in Beverly Hills?'

'To raise filthy lucre. England needs the stuff, you Americans have it.'

Too late she remembered reading about the posh benefits he was doing: with Firelli, though, one felt no humiliation at ignorance. 'I'm mad for your records,' she said.

He leaned forward, unabashedly delighted at her compliment. 'Which is your very favourite?' he asked.

'The one that has "Full Moon and Empty Arms".'

'The Rachmaninov, yes. I think it's jolly good, too.'

'When's the next concert?'

'I conducted at the Bowl three nights ago. That's my coda. I stay for a few days at Belvedere. Then it's back across the pond.' He made a face. 'That convoy zigzagging brings on violent seasickness, it does.'

She wanted to ask how well he knew the Cunninghams, but didn't, not because of any reticence with Firelli but because Althea, squirrelly-secretive about her family, might construe this as prying, and Roy did not care to poke any holes in their rewoven friendship.

Firelli pushed heavily to his stubby feet, panting a little. 'I am going inside for a cuppa and a snooze. Tell the others I'll see them at dinner.'

Roy watched the stout little figure waddle up through terracing towards the gracious, rosy-bricked mansion. Imagine! Me talking to *Firelli*, buddy-buddy!

Dwight hauled himself from the deep end, chest heaving. The polio had slightly atrophied his left leg, and the thigh muscles were a shade less stocky than the right.

Althea, too, got out of the water, pulling off her rubber cap to shake her pale, lovely hair. 'The maestro gone up to the house?'

'Yes, he said he'd see us at dinner. He seemed tired.'

'He's been wearing himself out since the war began, and this tour's been a huge strain. Mrs Firelli used to make him rest, but she died last year. That's why Daddy insisted he stay at Belvedere for a few days.' Althea turned to where Dwight was drying himself off with one of Belvedere's luxurious pool towels. 'Dwight, how about a Blue Ribbon?'

'Is there one?'

'No. That's why I asked.' Smiling, Althea went through the open French doors.

Roy asked Dwight quietly, 'Enjoying yourself?'

'The living legend! Firelli! I can't believe it!'

'Who can? And what about Belvedere?'

'It's really incredible.' His eyes were fixed on the sha-dowed poolhouse, where Althea bent over the miniature refrigerator to get the beer. 'Althea's totally different than I thought.'

'Phooey on first impressions,' said Roy, forgetting she always trusted them.

After dinner – eaten by flickering candlelight on the upper veranda – the old Englishman disconcerted and delighted them by sitting down at the music-room grand piano and, with superb rhythmic swing, playing any popu-lar song they named.

After he hoisted his stout self upstairs, the party pooped out.

Dwight said, 'Listen, maybe we better get on home.'

'Here.' Althea slipped the car keys from her slacks pocket, draping the chain over her long, slender forefinger. 'You two take the wagon, bring it back when you come over tomorrow.'

Roy glanced at Dwight. The overhead lights caught his

eyes with an odd flatness, and as he gazed back at her, his broad lips drawn tightly over his large, square teeth, a vulpine smile that excited Roy so that she could scarcely breathe.

They drove up to a dark, narrow ledge overlooking Beverly Hills. Lights blinked below while the radio spread the cool, limpid notes of Benny Goodman's 'And the Angels Sing'.

'C'mon over here,' Dwight said, putting his arm around her, drawing her to him, kissing her. The skin of his face felt hot yet oddly dry, and he smelled clean, of chlorine from the pool. While they kissed, the hands Roy had longed to cup her breasts, did. Her pulses beating a staccato, she imagined she would swoon.

The radio ballad changed. His grasp roughened, foraying under the square cut neckline of her blouse, and his tongue thrusts pushed deeper into her throat. She felt a chill. 'Don't,' she murmured with the faintest reproval and gripped his thick broad wrist.

In this Oldsmobile station wagon she had necked with servicemen, pick-ups, yes, yet all seemed to recognize a code: they had gone as far as Roy had let them, sometimes persisting in a wordless tug of war, but when, by her actions, she let it be known that there was nothing doing, that she was a 'nice' girl, they desisted and either went back to kissing or sulkily removed themselves to the other side of the seat, adjusting uniform trousers.

Dwight, though, ignored her restraining grasp. His hands clamped like an iron pectoral on the bare flesh below her brassiere.

She squirmed. 'Stop it.'

'Want you so, baby.'

The endearment thrilled her, and for a moment she gave his hands autonomy. He made a swift sortie, pushing down the zipper of her shorts to invade below the waist of her pants. Horribly mortified – he surely must feel the elastic sanitary belt – she tried to tell him to stop, but his tongue trapped her voice. His fingers jabbed downward, grabbing crisp brown hair.

174

He pulled back, and his mouth wet against hers, he said, 'I have a safe.'

Safe? A word she had encountered before in this station wagon, and it baffled her. Though Roy talked sophisticatedly, she had only a muddled, unclear acquaintance with the physiological truths of sex. What, exactly, was a safe? It certainly had to do with the ultimate surrender. Was *that* what Dwight wanted of her?

'It'll be absolutely all right, I promise you,' he said, sprawling onto her, squashing her down flat on the seat, pushing at her shorts. Using both hands, she shoved him, but he was too strong for her. With a loud, vibrant sound, the shorts tore.

'No!' Summoning all her force, she squirmed from under him. In the wrestle, her knee must have caught him in some vital place, for he released her with an agonized groan.

Pulling back to the wheel, he hunched over.

'Don't be like this,' she whispered. 'I care so much.'

'Some way you show it. Jesus, you could've permanently damaged something.'

'I didn't mean to hurt you, Dwight.'

'Listen, I don't care you've got the curse.'

A subject so taboo that hearing it spoken aloud was like being doused with ice water. 'It's not that,' she mumbled.

'You put out for the others. Pete says you do, he says everybody at Beverly High knows about the Big Two.'

Roy began to cry, her hiccuping little sobs sounding hollow in the dark privacy for which she – in her romantic idiocy – had yearned.

Dwight turned up the radio. Under the cover of a station break, he asked, 'Is it because of my leg?'

'Oh, Dwight . . . how can you think that?' She blew her nose, and while Herb Jeffries sang of flamingoes, she mumbled, 'That stuff at school, it's all a horrible mistake . . . Althea and I, we act different from the others, so people invent the most horrendous lies about us. It's not true, not true at all. We aren't that kind of girls.' She blew her nose again, adding in a bleakly apologetic little voice, 'I'm a virgin.'

After an endless minute he said, 'It's okay.'

The next afternoon on the drive to Belvedere, neither referred to the previous night's contretemps.

Firelli and Roy played gin while Althea and Dwight floated close together on inflated blue rafts.

The following day was Firelli's last.

They celebrated his departure with a *bon voyage* supper in the poolhouse. The huge orange moon that magically lit Belvedere's domain was twinned in the oil-slick blackness of the pool.

After the lemon mousse, Althea said, 'Firelli, we really should play some of your records – a swan song.'

'Let's, let's!' cried Roy, who was slightly tiddly from her glass of champagne.

'For my young American friends I'll choose my best loves,' said the old Englishman.

'We'll have a Firelli concert in the music room,' Althea said. 'You go ahead and pick. I have to get these dishes together – Luther's already furious about serving us down here.'

'I'll help you straighten up,' said Dwight.

'Great,' Althea replied.

Firelli started up the brick steps.

Althea said, 'Roy, you go with him. Otherwise we'll be in for total heavy stuff.'

Roy's bubbly mood broke, and her throat clogged with a nasty tightness that she recognized as jealousy. 'It's not fair leaving you two with the mess,' she said thinly.

'We'll be up in jig time,' said Althea. 'Shoo! Scat!'

Roy stood in a moment of wretched indecision, unable to look at either Althea or Dwight. Blinking with shame at her disloyal jealousy, she ran after the maestro.

Firelli bounced up through the moonlit grounds, vigorous as a rubber ball. Other than his naps and early bedtime, he exuded boundless energy. Suddenly he said, 'She's very unhappy.'

'Althea?'

'Yes. I wish I knew the whys and wherefores.' His English voice was gruff with sadness. 'Poor child. However much she laughs and tries to hide her misery, it's always there, like a recurring theme. She can't escape it.'

'She does have moods.'

'I'd give anything to be able to help her,' said Firelli. 'But she'll have none of it – she equates kindness with pity.'

Roy sighed.

'Can you accept, Roy, that life is harder on her than on you?'

'I guess.'

'You won't let this business hurt your friendship?'

'Firelli, whatever are you talking about?'

'Althea and the boy.'

'You just don't understand American kids.' Roy gave a fraudulent little titter. 'We're all three on the same wavelength.'

He reached out and took her hand. 'That gallantry, that loyal courage, Roy – don't ever grow out of it.'

In the music room, Firelli browsed around the shelves, taking his time as he selected the heavy albums that he considered his triumphs – the first movement of Brahms's First Symphony, the final movement of Beethoven's Ninth, Selections from *St Matthew Passion*.

Dwight and Althea did not appear.

Roy's hands fumbled as she took out Ravel's *Bolero* and the popular movement of the Rachmaninov Piano Concerto Number 2, both albums slashed diagonally with FIRELLI in crimson.

'Maybe Althea meant us to bring them down to the poolhouse,' she said.

Firelli shook his big, sparsely haired head. 'The machine up here is truer by far.'

'I'm going back down to make sure,' Roy said.

'No,' he said with a force she hadn't heard from him before.

But Roy ran outside into the moon-drenched night.

The stout old man bounced after her.

When Roy came to the terrace above the pool, she saw the lights of the poolhouse were out.

Firelli, who had caught up with her, gripped her arm with surprisingly youthful strength. 'Don't go down there.'

For a moment she struggled; then he released her.

Reaching the deck, she stumbled over a soft mound. It was, she realized immediately, one of the thick towels. Yet her heart pounded as if she had trod on a corpse. The small, downy hairs on her arms standing up like multiple warning antennae, she moved, stealthy as an Indian brave, to the windows.

Peering inside, she could see nothing in the darkness. They're not here, she thought, her breath clouding the pane. Then her eyes caught a movement. She rubbed at the moist glass. She could make out the shadowy outline of a slim, upraised leg and bare foot moving in some rhythmic dance that touched not the earth.

Anaesthetized by unreality, Roy watched the foot hold absolutely still, clench into an arch, wave frantically and disappear, becoming part of the big, lumpy shadow that writhed in a violent tempo.

Firelli pulled her away from the window.

22

The chauffeur drove her home.

In her room, she opened the window, resting her cheek against the screen, which had an unpleasant, rusty aroma, thinking words like 'alone', 'forlorn', 'betrayed' without assigning meaning to them. She kept seeing the rolling shadow that was Althea and Dwight, the spasmodic jerk of the high-arched feminine foot. What had happened in the poolhouse no longer surprised or shocked her. The past few days, Althea and Dwight had drawn inexorably closer. Why should she be astounded that Althea had gone the limit? Althea has the courage to show Dwight that she loves him, Roy thought with the dull heaviness that stems from a feeling of inferiority.

That night she tossed, turned, and honestly believed she did not sleep. Yet there she was, jerking awake to bright morning light.

'Roy!' NolaBee stood over her bed. 'Wake up, Althea's here.'

Althea stood in her doorway. 'You left this,' she said, holding up Roy's white raffia purse.

'I'll be in the kitchen,' said NolaBee. 'Marylin's new sundress needs pressing for the USO show on Sunday.'

The door closed. Althea dropped the purse on the bed and sat at the vanity raising her chin in what NolaBee referred to as a Lady-Vere-de-Vere expression. 'Why don't you pin the scarlet letter on me? What else are friends for?'

'All right, so you did it,' Roy said listlessly.

'And not for the first time, dear heart.'

Roy, in a shocked reflex, sat up, staring at Althea. Althea, her reflection wretchedly disdainful, gazed back at her in the mirror.

'But you're really gone on Dwight, aren't you?'

'I haven't altered my opinion one iota.'

'You mean you do it with . . . anybody?' Aghast, Roy groped for words. '. . . in the station wagon?'

'You'd be surprised at how unimportant an act it is.'

Roy's stunned shock mingled with the dismay of being a gullible jerk. She blurted the first words that came into her mind. 'But don't you worry about, well, a baby?'

Althea gave a low, indulgent laugh. 'What do you think I am? A dumb hillbilly?'

Was this a dig at poor Marylin? Suddenly Roy remembered her sister's beautiful tormented white face, her protesting sobs.

Jumping from the bed, she raised her arm, putting full force behind her slap to Althea's smoothly tanned cheek. The blow resounded in the small, shabby bedroom.

'I don't want to be friends with you anymore!' Roy shouted.

179

Althea lifted her hand to the reddening mark. 'Because of *him*?' She used the same baiting humour, but there was an odd flicker, like fear, behind her eyes. 'All *he* wanted from either of us, I can assure you, was a quick lay.'

'You knew I really *liked* him.'

'Well, now you're cured,' Althea said.

Roy, panting and furious, glared at her, then slowly sat on the bed. 'It's not just Dwight,' she said after a long silence. 'It's us.'

'What's wrong with us?'

'Everything. The way we shut out the others. The way we sneer at people. The way everybody snickers at us – God, how I loathe our reputations!'

'What's the dif *what* those Beverly High clods think?'

'You care as much as I do,' Roy said.

'That's your opinion.'

'I'm going to change.'

'Do tell.'

'For one thing,' Roy said, 'I'm not going to spend an hour every morning plastering on makeup. For another, I'm not going to make sophisticated little asides about things I don't understand. I'm going to be like the other girls. I'm going to be ordinary.'

'Ordinary?'

'Average-ordinary.'

Althea blinked more rapidly. 'The reason we're friends is, you aren't.'

'I can sure try to be.' Roy's head had a funny hollow feeling, and her eyes were gritty from lack of sleep. 'I can sure try.'

'You need a little time to escape the green-eyed monster. Believe me, there's no reason to be jealous. I don't intend to see that 4-F gimp again.'

'Oh, you inhuman *creep*!'

Althea, with a narrow smile, ran from the room.

The Big Two patched it up. You don't cut off three intense years with one knock-down-drag-out fight. Yet everything was different. Roy could not define the change. The best

180

explanation was that an invisible curtain had rolled down, separating them.

Oh, Althea picked her up and drove her home from school, they chose adjacent desks in the two classes they took together, and they shared a table on the crowded patio. But at the beginning of the semester Roy joined SPQR and the Verse Choir, and more often than not she invited other girls to eat lunch with them. Althea responded to Roy's new friends with either silence or quick, nervous humour. She was often absent.

Neither saw Dwight again.

But every time Roy glimpsed a billboard with Van Johnson's face or heard a moony song, she would experience a seeping kind of hurt, as if an internal wound had reopened. She never considered blaming Dwight – or even Althea. The episode had reinforced her unshakable conviction that Roy Elizabeth Wace had been born with some freak genetic defect that made her impossible to love.

Yet once she got into the social swim, she became popular among the lesser lights of the senior class, kids who either did not know about her rep or were willing to overlook it.

One blowy Friday afternoon in November, as Althea drove Roy home, she announced, 'I'm getting a private tutor.'

'You? Althea G-for-Genius Cunningham?' Althea, unlike Roy, invariably had capital A's neatly printed down her report card. 'Why?'

Althea stared at the traffic light. 'I'm departing the hallowed halls of Beverly.'

'Leaving school? Are you allowed to?'

'If not, then Mother's arranged an illegality.'

'Althea, you only have a bit of your last semester left.'

'It's all decided.'

'We'll still see each other, won't we?'

'Why not?' said Althea.

After Roy got out of the car, she stood in front of her house, her skirt whipping around her as she watched the station wagon with 'Big Two' emblazoned on the front doors disappear up Crescent Drive. An inconsolable sadness overwhelmed her, a haunting sense of loss, as if some living thing – a plant, a kitten – entrusted to her care had died.

She had let their friendship die.

On an overcast December night, Marylin, BJ, Roy and NolaBee, wearing formals, drove with Joshua in a Paramount limousine to Grauman's Chinese Theater.

Police linked arms, struggling to hold back the excited fans who surged towards every arriving car. In the courtyard with cement impressions of famous hands and feet, Marylin was asked to speak a few words for the radio public. She whispered into the microphone, 'The story was everything. I wouldn't have been anything without Lincoln Fernauld's magnificent novel.'

The announcer for once was silent, a long valedictory pause while Marylin stood absolutely still in her shimmery white strapless, a gown that every reader of gossip columns would soon know had been made by Adrian from a parachute donated by a downed naval pilot.

Then she put her hand on Joshua's arm, and he escorted her into the lobby. Marylin Wace entered Grauman's Chinese a beautiful girl with an inordinate amount of newspaper coverage in a hard-eyed business where a hefty press push meant nothing – unless the customers laid down hard cash to see your image.

She emerged Rain Fairburn, a star of the same box-office magnitude as those other young luminaries, Lauren Bacall, Jennifer Jones, Jeanne Crain, June Allyson.

Three days after the première, on 18 December, it rained heavily. The north-south streets that centred at the Beverly Hills Hotel followed the ancient pattern of arroyos, and water sluiced along them, running knee-deep at intersections.

The downpour eased briefly as Roy left school, and she slogged through the drizzle with Heidi Ronoletti and Janet Schwarz. The discussion centred on graduation formals.

'Roy, you *have* to come with me,' wailed Heidi, a flat-chested math major with lovely brown eyes and dark curls that turned to frizz in this weather. 'When I shop with Mother, she insists on buying me the droopiest thing in sight. You have a real eye.'

'Yes, Roy,' Janet chimed in with her squeaky voice. 'You know right away what suits people.'

'Hey, flattery will get you someplace.' Roy grinned. 'Over the vacation, let's make the rounds together.'

When the other girls turned right at Bedford Drive, Roy's expression grew thoughtful. For a while now it had been apparent there was money enough for her to enroll at nearby UCLA. Roy's new clique had already decided between the usual feminine college majors, teaching and social work. Neither occupation drew her.

Now a career idea came to her full-blown.

She would be in fashion.

Roy was far from a clothes horse. Still, a brand-new outfit signified much more to her than to most girls – weren't new clothes a negation of those horrendous, smelly hand-me-downs? Clothes *spoke* to her.

I'm not artistic like Althea, she thought, so that lets out designing. She glanced to her right. In the watery gloom, the creamy façade of Saks glowed softly. Retail shops, Roy thought. I'm pretty good at maths. I could take a business-administration course. With that degree I could become a buyer, a manager even.

Her lungs expanded with rain-clean air as she thought: Whoopee! I have a major, I have a major!

She splashed through the gutter, kicking at the racing fingers of eucalyptus leaves, hurrying home to tell Nola-Bee.

Nearing the house, she thought of Dwight, and the excitement drained from her wet, freckled face. Dwight, Dwight, Dwight . . . Will I ever come first with anyone?

Roy was convalescing slowly. Though she had come around to accepting that on her part it had been puppy love, and on Dwight's merely the promise of sexual assuagement, it was not in her to remove herself easily from

183

any object of her affection, an organic stubbornness shared by the other two Wace women.

She opened the front door, which was never locked. From the absence of cheerfully garrulous greetings, she decided that her mother was out. Changing her sodden shoes, she went to fix herself a hot Ovaltine.

In the kitchen, NolaBee hunched at the table, which was bestrewn with clippings about *Island*. Arms folded, head down, she was shuddering convulsively.

Roy's body went icier than her slippered feet. All at once she was positive that the same type of tragedy that had killed her father had somehow destroyed her sister. 'Mama, is it Marylin?'

'She just called from Yuma.' NolaBee raised her head. Tears made her skin yet more piteously bad.

'Yuma? But that's where people go to – '

'She's eloped with that man,' sobbed NolaBee vehemently. 'She could have had a million beaux at her feet, she could have had her pick of young men, but she's married him!'

Roy's terror was alleviated. 'You mean Mr Fernauld? But, Mama, you *like* him.'

'I wanted the world for my beautiful baby,' NolaBee whimpered. 'Not an old man . . .'

'What a hideously rotten thing to do!' BJ cried.

'Beej, I know this is inconceivable to any child, but being a parent does not preclude one from having the emotional needs of the rest of humanity.'

'Oh, we knew *that*, Linc and me, we knew that well. And so did Mother and the entire world!'

'All right, you've spilled your bitterness, you have me cut down to size. But the fact remains – the solid, unalterable fact. Marylin and I are married.'

'BJ, I'd've given the world not to hurt you like this.' Marylin's soft voice shook. 'We should have told you first.'

It was early the following evening, the newlyweds had this minute returned from Arizona: the hall chandelier of the Fernauld home shone down on the exposed surfaces of three souls.

'And you!' BJ turned her rancorous, tear-streaked face on her friend. 'All that talk of loving Linc. What happened to that? As soon as you got his book to star in, did it evaporate?'

'Let it go, Beej,' commanded Joshua. 'Calm down.'

'Why? Does it hurt to hear that she'll hop in bed with any man able to help her big fat career!'

'You're talking to my wife.' Joshua's voice rumbled from his thick chest. 'And before you take that tone with her, you'd do well to remember that this is *my* house.'

'Oh, Joshua,' Marylin sighed.

'You tell me, then, why she marries a guy thirty years older. She got the role of a lifetime from Linc. What do you suppose she wants from *you* besides another leg up in the Industry?'

'Come on, Marylin!' Joshua shouted, grabbing their two mismatched overnight bags. The curving staircase shook under his angry footsteps. At the top, he turned, booming, 'Marylin!' And stamped in the direction of the room he had shared with his first wife.

Marylin did not move. Despite her fragility and seeming pliability, in the territory of the heart she invariably stood her ground. BJ was her friend. 'Listen,' she said quietly. 'It's not like that. Joshua's been good to me, and helpful, yes. But I care for him . . .'

'Care?' BJ's messy black pompadour wobbled angrily. 'Is that the new synonym for "love"?'

Marylin shook her head.

'So why?' BJ asked.

'Because,' Marylin said, 'he loves Linc too.'

'My father, Big Joshua, hotshot-about-town, marries a girl in love with somebody else?'

'He accepts that I'll never get over Linc.'

The outrage and hurt flickered less in BJ's teary eyes. After a pause, she spoke more calmly. 'My living here's not going to work.'

'Maybe later it will. Please, please try not to hate us.

Your father needs you – and so do I. You're the only real friend outside of my family that I've ever had.'

BJ said with the faintest hint of pride, 'You were my friend, too.'

'Were?'

'I'll *try* to adjust.'

'BJ, for me there was no other alternative. Joshua's the only man who can possibly understand what Linc will always mean to me.'

BJ sighed. After a moment she said, 'I'll be at the dorm. Tell Daddy, okay?'

Marylin poised on her toes to kiss her new stepdaughter's soft, moist cheek. Then she followed her bridegroom up the handsome curved staircase.

23

On 7 May 1945, in the cathedral city of Rheims, at a long, scarred table, Colonel General Alfred Jodl signed the documents of Germany's surrender.

VE Day!

The task of whipping the Japanese remained, but church bells chimed, factory whistles shrilled endlessly, car horns blared a joyous cacophony as the forty-eight states erupted into a gargantuan orgy of stranger-kissing, boozing, indiscriminate hugging, street conga lines and sex.

The following afternoon, Althea climbed the steps of a roomy old frame house opposite the Tropics on Rodeo Drive. Next to the front door was neatly gold-painted: THE HENRY LISSAUER ART INSTITUTE.

Althea had been a student for three months.

The institute had been at this location less than five years: for two decades previous to that, however, Henry Lissauer had conducted a prestigious atelier just off Unter den Linden in Berlin.

186

Numerous exiles from Hitler's Europe had converged on Beverly Hills, glossing the quiet, wealthy community with a sophistication previously lacking. The town now boasted several cosmopolitan art galleries, an elegant Viennese bakery, polyglot milliners and *modistes*, chic jewellers, as well as the Henry Lissauer Art Institute. For the most part, these refugees had a large red J inside their brown *Reisepass*. On leaving their native land, each had become *ein Staaten-loser* – a person without a country. Yet the United States considered them enemy aliens. Thus they were tethered to a ten-mile radius of their homes, ordered to carry at all times a pink book with their photograph and forced to observe an eight-o'clock curfew. But this was very mild stuff when contrasted with what they had escaped.

The main threat, and it struck queasy terror into each of the *Staatenlosers*, was that for any small infraction of the enemy alien regulations, or for any minor run-in with the law, he or she would forever lose the chance of becoming a United States citizen.

Henry Lissauer had escaped the greater horrors that were to befall European Jewry only because early in 1936 his rotund, bustling little wife had insisted they apply for immigration. It took nearly two years and most of their savings to procure the necessary papers. A few days before the permits stamped with an eagle-topped swastika arrived, there was a grim encounter with a gang of rowdy Nazi boys. The stout, jolly little wife had taken cyanide.

Now Henry Lissauer lived for two things: United States citizenship and the institute.

Lacking artistic creativity, he nurtured talent as tenderly as he would have the children denied him and the late Frau Lissauer. Each of his twenty-two students had met his rigid if elusive criteria. He insisted on a fresh eye. He had his own mysterious methods of divining this vernal vision, which had nothing to do with technique or formal training – he had turned away several applicants approaching professional stature. Once enrolled, a student could take part in any class from elementary drawing to advanced oil – or needn't show up at all. The sole obligation was to attend a weekly conference in the institute's slit of an office on the second floor of the old frame house. During this interview Lissauer would discuss the student's work and progress, his myopic brown eyes apologetic behind his bottle-bottom-thick spectacles.

Althea, reporting for this mandatory meeting, paced back and forth along the corridor that smelled of paint and chalk, her expression hardening like plaster before she knocked. 'It's me, Mr Lissauer, Althea Cunningham.'

There was no response. Henry Lissauer, who often ran a few minutes late, had invited his students to step inside and wait.

Along the beaverboard walls of the narrow office he had tacked a pastiche of sketches, watercolours and unstretched oils. Some of these student works were competent. Many, though, were monstrosities of clashing colours or awkward composition that grated on the eye, or of subject matter that was banally mawkish – a weirdly proportioned kitten playing with yarn raised Althea's gorge. Perplexity and envy burned ferociously within her.

No work of hers had ever received the accolade of being pinned up by Mr Lissauer. What qualities invisible to her ignorant (though fresh) eye did these horrors possess?

Althea's entire life had been passed, or so it seemed to her, in a frantic attempt to attain what others considered excellence. For her, every compartment of life – looks, grades, talent, success in love – was constructed like an Egyptian step pyramid: you were either at the squalid, crowded bottom, the mediocre centre, or atop the airy peak. Those above her she admired enviously, those below she ignored. Before she could climb the pyramid, she must first discern the order of the steps.

She squinted again at the other students' work. Dreary, dreary, she thought. Yet because these daubs were tacked up, they shone with enviable glamour.

Propping her gold-initialled portfolio against her chair, she closed her eyes.

In the months since she had left Beverly High, Althea's appearance had improved immeasurably. The ratted, high pompadour was gone. She wore her pale, streaked hair drawn back into a smooth coil at the nape of her long, slender neck.

At Westlake, her tall, thin body and narrow Modigliani face had been at violent odds with what the other pre-teen girls called pretty, so she had considered her appearance monstrous: at Beverly High the makeup she had caked on her adolescent face had been a mask without which she dared not appear. At the institute, though, she had been asked to sit. Henry Lissauer and the two artist-teachers on the Institute's staff had pointed out to the class her unique and unusual qualities. Thus emboldened, she had gone cold turkey, leaving off the pastes and cakes and goos, using not even lipstick – a stultifying departure in style for 1945.

Without Roy Wace, Althea's loneliness had been an actual illness at first. She had stuck to her room, shivering with a subnormal temperature, too disconsolate to read, playing the same records until they were malevolently scratched, emerging only to take her lessons from the whispery old Bostonian who had tutored Archie Coyne's children. Roy, whom she had trusted absolutely, Roy, her mainstay, Roy had deserted her – and because of that nonentity, that square, that *cripple*, Dwight Hunter! Those occasional Saturdays with Roy were torment. When they were over, Althea would succumb to fits of animal trembling. Finally, with surgical precision, she cut off all contact, refusing to take Roy's telephone calls.

The misery of those winter months proved to Althea what she had always known: people were her nemesis.

Since she had entered the institute, though, her life had begun to take on logic and meaning.

Not that the drawings she produced pleased her – Althea possessed the misfortunate faculty of overdiscriminatory self-criticism. Yet the end result did not alter the inexplicable, all-enveloping pleasure she experienced as she sat on her canvas stool holding her drawing board tilted against one knee. Drawing was not a new thing to her. She had enjoyed it as a small child, before she knew it was shameful to enjoy a solitary pastime.

She waited in Henry Lissauer's office nearly a half-hour before the door opened. 'I am sorry to keep you so,' he said in his halting Teutonic voice. 'A few countrymen were celebrating with me this great victory.' The curfew prevented evening gatherings, so other exiles sometimes dropped by the institute in midmorning or late afternoon to talk of intellectual matters while sipping strong, brandy-laced coffee from thin Meissen cups. 'Hnn, so on this occasion you forgive me?'

'Everybody's been going wild,' Althea said with a smile.

Though Lissauer's baffling artistic selectivity maddened her, he had somehow got through her armoury of defences and she trusted him. Possibly she was disarmed by his unprepossessing, near-comic appearance. With his small, thin body clothed in a neat, foreignly narrow dark suit and overbalanced by his massive head, he reminded Althea of a large balloon on a string.

Still smiling about the defeat of those Nazi scum, Henry Lissauer sat behind his desk inquiring about Althea's week of work.

Encouraged by the shy benevolence of the eyes behind thick spectacles, she volunteered how much she enjoyed drawing and sketching.

'Do you have perhaps some charcoals to show me, then?'

She unzipped her portfolio, hesitantly bringing out a single sheet. This week, stationing herself in Belvedere's fountain-centred French rose garden, she had turned out at least fifty sketches. Although this rosebush was far from the technical best, as she had worked she'd felt a spontaneous, urgent knowledge of the leaves, the blossoms, the thorny stem that grew from the yellow California adobe rather than the softer, older soil of France.

Henry Lissauer peered at the sketch, laying it above the clutter on his desk, pressing his bony fingers on either side as he bent down, scrutinizing. He raised his pale, large face. 'Hnnn. Hnnn. This you really *felt*. There is a quality here, a sense of being . . . How do you say it? Of not belonging.'

She blinked in surprise. 'That's it exactly.'

'This I should like to keep, if I may?'

'Of course, sure.' Althea leaned forward, not attempting to hide her pleasure as the oddly proportioned little German made space and tacked up her rosebush.

He stepped back, nodding.

Now, her goal attained, Althea felt a faint jolt of disappointment that intensified as she glanced around at the other work. The longed-for honour was tarnishing swiftly. In a few moments she was thinking: Oh, God, one more daub.

'Please take it down,' she said in a clogged voice.

He turned to her. 'Hnn?'

'If that's where you intend leaving my sketch, I want it back.'

He looked at her, his eyes seeming to radiate beams through his spectacles. 'You feel the other work is not good, and that makes yours not good also?'

He understood her.

Being understood presented dangers from which Althea could not protect herself. Her affection for the exile flickered like a light bulb during a power dim-out. Hunching her shoulders, she thought her old litany: there are enemies, only enemies.

'Each one of these,' said Henry Lissauer, gesturing, 'they represent the proof I am right. I select a student, but unless this student becomes one with the work, I am failed. Some of these works are inept, that is true. But believe me, each shows a breakthrough. The innocent eye. Not copying another artist, but having the courage to *see* reality.'

'May I have my sketch back?' she whispered with stiff lips.

Silently he untacked it, handing it to her.

She crushed the paper, throwing it in the office's big wire-mesh wastebasket.

'This you should not do,' he reproved with anxious mildness. 'You are my most promising student. This is strange to say of a great heiress like you, Miss Cunningham, but you are hungrier. You have more of the hunger for perfection than the others. I think therefore that you will succeed more.'

'Is this the psychoanalytical society in session?' Althea's smile was wide.

'You will succeed, hnn, but you will never believe that you have succeeded.'

She ran from the office, nausea churning. His kind eyes and perceptive remarks terrified her.

That evening the Cunninghams, as usual, ate in the dining room with its mural of flowers and birds painted *in situ* by Cecil Beaton. The conversation centred on the following morning, when Mr and Mrs Cunningham would return to Washington – off and on he performed hush-hush work for the State Department, work having to do with his fluency in Russian. At the German surrender, an urgent message recalled him immediately. Althea sat at the Sheraton table midway between her parents, discussing their trip with casual tolerant humour.

After the broiled sole was served, Mrs Cunningham asked, 'How is your painting?'

'I don't paint yet,' Althea retorted, her composure fading. How she loathed her mother's invading questions!

Mrs Cunningham drew in her receding chin anxiously. 'Mr Lissauer promised Daddy that you would learn to use oils and watercolours.'

'True, Toots, true,' said Mr Cunningham.

'Then he's a miracle worker. He can't even teach me how to sketch!' Althea gulped down a fragment of buttery fish, reminding herself that she was mature enough not to be scrubbed raw by each inquiry her mother aimed at her.

'I have every faith,' said Mr Cunningham.

'Did I tell you?' said Mrs Cunningham. 'Aunt Edna has heard of Mr Lissauer.'

'Should I fall on my knees and cry Hallelujah?'

'Now, now.' Mr Cunningham smiled. 'Your aunt's knowledgeable in the art field – after all, she has what's considered the best collection of moderns in the country.'

Mrs Cunningham said nervously, 'I only brought it up to reassure you.'

Althea dropped her fish fork loudly on her plate. 'Aunt

Edna,' she cried, 'is a fat, blind philistine who tosses her money around to give herself a big reputation! She doesn't know real art from a hole in the ground!'

Mr and Mrs Cunningham glanced at one another over the length of the table. Mr Cunningham refilled his wineglass.

The scene rattled Althea, keeping her awake: after turning restlessly for nearly an hour, she went onto her veranda. A sycamore grew so close to the house that one of its branches had attached itself to a point on the veranda rail. On impulse, she clambered onto the limb as she had done when very young – a forbidden daredevil trick – straddling it like a horse, feeling the roughness of the bark through her silk pyjamas.

All around, twigs and branches creaked, timpani to the deep croaking of the frogs and intermittent sawing of crickets. Her face hot, she kept going over her juvenile outburst.

The night sounds soothed her, and she began a mental thumb through of her life plan. She would retreat to a small grey wood house in the rugged, foggy crags of Big Sur, and have nothing to do with the rest of humanity, who inevitably hated or despised or betrayed her. She would waste no more of her yearning on people, but would train herself to paint the sunlight shafting through towering branches of the millennia-old sequoia trees, paint the fog lapping over majestic coastal rocks that had been sculptured by eternity. She would live an existence dedicated to art, she would be a pure artist like that divine lunatic Van Gogh, but *she* would not permit herself to be driven bonkers by human indifference. In her lifetime she would allow no showings, but after her death, the world would resound with praises for Althea Cunningham. She smiled as she composed yet another posthumous review redundant with words like genius and magnificent.

'Althea?' Her father's slurred, questioning voice came from inside her room.

Startled, she caught her breath. Her fingers and toes

went cold as a corpse's. Oh God, God, she thought, please not that.

'Where are you? I want to say good-bye to my Toots . . . Althea . . . ?' There was a coaxing tenderness in his drunken voice.

She clung to the sycamore branch as if pressing herself to become living wood. The sound of her own heart banged loudly in her ears.

'It's your daddy.' Raspily hoarse, yet wooing of tone.

She heard shambling footsteps retreating through the room.

The door opened. A final, 'Toots?'

She sprawled there like some boneless sea creature, not moving.

The door closed.

She waited a full minute; then her held-back breath burst out in a long, sobbing gasp. She swung her leg over the tree branch, climbing off shakily. Inside the dark bedroom she locked the window and ran to the door to press home the dead bolt.

It was then that the drunken laughter sounded.

She saw the big, weaving shadow. 'Fooled you, fooled you, Toots . . .'

She cowered against the door. 'Go away . . . Daddy, please don't. Please . . .' Her whisper shook.

But he was roughly jamming her to himself in the strong, inescapable embrace of a drink-demented man, shuffling with her towards the bed, his breath hot and boozy around her. This horror had occurred infrequently, maybe a dozen times at most since she was ten, yet it had blighted and coloured her every mortal response.

'Don't!' she cried hoarsely. 'No!'

Even as she struggled, she was remembering herself as a small child, ill in that bed and being soothed by these strong hands with fingers elegantly tapered like her own. The bedside chair crashed over. He shoved her backwards on the mattress.

She gave up.

When the crushing, thumping assault on her body had

194

ended and he had staggered from the room, she buried her face in the pillow, which smelled of liquor, of his sweat and hair lotion, and smothered her storm of childish sobs.

The following morning as she drank her orange juice her father came downstairs carrying a grey topcoat over the arm that held his briefcase. Her mother, shoulders rounder than usual, followed a step or two behind him.

Mrs Cunningham hugged her good-bye, and Althea searched the timid, homely face, wondering for the thousandth time if her mother could possibly be unaware of the indefensible, unbearable secret.

'Well, Toots, it's good-bye time again,' said her father, smiling with fresh-shaven pleasure.

To even mentally question what he recollected of the previous night brought a strangling tightness to her chest. 'Have a good trip, Daddy,' she said, smiling back with the same innocence.

'What would you like us to bring you back?' he asked.

'Oh, the National Gallery,' she said.

There were no spaces remaining behind the institute, so she parked on Brighton Way. She closed the front door of the wagon, her palm covering the ghostly remnant of the scraped paint: 'The Big Two'.

As she reached the institute's back steps, Henry Lissauer emerged to meet her. 'Miss Cunningham,' he said, the apologetic kindness in his eyes magnified by those thick spectacles. 'I have been thinking about our interview yesterday. This is important, that you must learn to see your work exhibited.'

Anger, inexplicable, sudden, and consuming, forced tears into her eyes. 'I don't like my sketches made fun of,' she said through clenched teeth. 'That's hardly the way to help a student, is it?'

'I assure you I had no intention of ridicule. Believe me, nothing . . . I have every respect for you.'

'It's a piece of cake for a famous teacher to poke fun at a novice. That's what makes it so rotten.'

195

His scrawny body seemed to shrink inside the dark suit. He swallowed rapidly.

Seeing him like this, cowed, she felt her abrupt anger fade. 'Then you really liked my rosebush, Mr Lissauer?'

'It was good work, excellent.'

'Truly?' she asked in a demure whisper.

'Again I say, you are my most promising student.'

'I believe you,' she said, resting her finger on his black serge sleeve.

His arm trembled.

She preceded him into the institute, feeling young, clean, inviolately strong.

24

The walls of three upstairs bedrooms at the institute had been knocked down to form a commodious U-shaped studio where windows of different sizes and shapes gave onto three exposures. On this cool May morning two weeks after VE Day, a fortyish nude lounged on harem pillows, a small electric heater casting a rosy glow on her pendulous breasts while the unwarmed flesh of her buttocks, thighs and arms resembled that of a pale plucked chicken.

Fifteen students had showed up for this live-model session. Twelve were female, a not unusual proportion for a wartime classroom; they wore engagement diamonds with or without wedding bands, and a smock to cover their sweater sets and sensible tweed skirts. Althea alone was ringless and had on a man's shirt over shorts.

One of the three male students had set up his easel to the right of Althea's. She did not know his name. He had joined the institute only that day. The morning session had nearly ended and his canvas remained untouched, pristine. He slumped on the stool in his Army fatigues, squinting at the model with his deep-set dark eyes while his broad, working-man's fingers played with his brushes.

At first his sullen self-preoccupation had irked Althea, and she had ignored him ostentatiously, but working in oil was new to her, and soon she was absorbed in plotting her composition with a thin wash of turpentine.

Henry Lissauer's voice broke her concentration. 'Yolanda,' said Herr Professor. 'Rest, hnn?'

The model pulled on a sleazy, too-short robe. The voices of the student painters rose in a shrill hubbub.

'Got a butt?' The man in fatigues was looking at Althea.

'I don't smoke,' she replied coolly.

He shrugged and slumped back on his stool, returning to his brooding examination of the empty dais. Althea glanced sideways at him. He had a broad Slavic face with belligerently high cheekbones, a short, blunt nose and coarse curly brown hair that grew low on his forehead. He was about twenty-five and common as dirt, she decided. But she had to admit to herself that he was attractive.

Henry Lissauer had come to examine her morning's work. 'Very good, Miss Cunningham,' he said. Since their run-in two weeks earlier, he approached her with bashful respect, as if he were the student, not she.

She smiled graciously. 'Doesn't that leg look a mite improbable?'

'May I show you?'

'Please,' she acquiesced.

He picked up one of her thick sable brushes, dipping it in the coffee tin that contained turpentine, and with a few strokes altered and humanized the limb. 'There,' he said with a humble smile.

'Thank you, Mr Lissauer,' she said, touching his arm.

He took little gulps of air, then moved to the next easel.

'Horak, you better commence.'

'What's the hot rush?'

'The model,' said Henry Lissauer. 'After lunch she will be here only one hour.'

The man in fatigues shrugged.

His canvas remained untouched at 12.30, when they broke for lunch.

The institute was across the street from the Tropics, but

that watering spot was reserved for expense accounts or leisurely seductions. Several of the students strolled over to Beverly Drive to eat at Nate and Lou's deli or Jones Health Food, but most brought sandwiches to eat in the big kitchen. Roxanne de Liso, who when not using her metal crutches was confined to a wheelchair, invariably sat at the head of the deal table. Her husband, Henri de Liso, was a set designer, and Roxanne, her face vivid with expression, led conversations about art and artists. At first Althea had been drawn to sit at the table. But one day Mrs de Liso talked about Joshua Fernauld: 'Yes, a baby! Of course he's absolutely nuts about that gorgeous child he's married to, but imagine starting a new family when you're fifty.'

So Mrs de Liso knew Marylin Wace Fernauld! Althea fled from the too painful reminders of her other life, making it her habit to lunch alone on the back porch.

The door behind her opened and she heard a jabbering rush of women's voices.

The new student, the common-looking guy in fatigues, emerged, sitting on the step below her to unwrap a pack of Camels.

'Why not join me?' Althea said caustically, and when he didn't react, she added, 'I'm Althea Cunningham.'

'Gerry Horak.' He slid a cigarette between his broad lips. 'What gives with you and the head honcho?'

'You mean Mr Lissauer?'

'You're pretty cosy with him.'

'Cosy?' She did not mitigate her disdain with a smile.

'He's eating out of your hand. "May I show you, Miss Cunningham?"' He mimicked Henry Lissauer's German accent. 'Not that I blame him. You're quite a dish.'

'Me and Herr Lissauer. There's an interesting thought.'

'Look, I'm not trying to insult you. He's a little old and not exactly handsome, but he's a decent sort.'

'Does your mind always take these adorable twists?'

'Then there's nothing between you?'

'Nothing but this mad little love nest up in Benedict Canyon,' she said.

He grinned. 'Listen, for a minute there I was positive you

two had something going, and I wanted things on the level before we get anything on the burner.'

'What makes you think I'm interested in your burners?' She bit into her sandwich.

Gerry reached over and took the other half. 'I can tell.' His grin was uneven and very white.

She surprised herself by grinning back. Though Gerry Horak's crude cockiness irritated her, she felt easy with him. Why? She shrugged. Who cared? It was simply true. She had no need to measure her words or throw him off with alternate aloofness and intimacy.

'Why didn't you paint?' she asked.

'Getting what I want in mind first.'

'You shouldn't let a blank canvas intimidate you.'

'Is that how you figure me? Chicken?'

'Yes. And while we're on the subject, are you in the service?'

'Yep,' he said, unbuttoning his shirt. A jagged, slick red line cut from his left shoulder, broadening into a bandaged area across his dark-haired, muscular chest, reappearing in a thin line to trickle into his khaki pants.

The mass of fresh scar tissue roused no revulsion, only a pang in her chest that she recognized as admiration. 'You *were* careless,' she said. 'How did it happen?'

'Going up a hill near Salerno.'

'What did you do before?'

'Bummed around,' he said.

'But never painted.'

He finished the sandwich and picked up his cigarette, which was balanced on the rail. 'It's that obvious?'

'The thing is not to let a blank canvas frighten you.' As the institute's newest student, she had been on the receiving end of advice for months now, and she enjoyed doling it out. 'After lunch, paint. Don't worry what you get down. The first few times, it's bound to be rotten.'

'Thanks for the tip.' He grinned, pushing to his feet.

She watched him go inside. She was positive her instincts were correct; Gerry Horak knew nothing of art. How could he? He's an assembly-line worker or a mechanic, she thought, he's a labourer through and through. Small tingles of excitement went through her as she visualized the hirsute, scarred chest. Were those battle wounds his admittance ticket to Henry Lissauer's carefully guarded institute?

She finished her lunch, absently watching a truck driver haul cartons through the back door of the adjacent silverware shop while she ruminated about Gerry Horak.

In the studio, the others were already intently working, except for Gerry, who was cracking his black-haired knuckles.

Taking her place, she glanced at his easel.

She heard her own gasp of surprise.

His canvas jumped with vehemently assertive squares of colour that had been slashed on with a palette knife. Though unfinished, the nude's lavender and blue skin tones showed a body flaccid with use, the head thrown back, the full thighs raised and slightly apart, a Levantine whore sprawled awaiting her next client.

An intimidatingly masterful painting. One that seemed impossible for the most talented professional to have done in less than twenty minutes.

Gerry was watching her, one thick, dark brow raised almost to his low hairline.

She felt the heat on her throat, then suddenly she laughed. 'And I was wondering whether Mr Lissauer was compromising his principles by letting you in! Do you always paint so quickly?'

'Takes me a long time before I start, and then, whammo!' He threw a glob of chrome yellow on the foreground. 'Where are we going after we get out of here?'

She drove him to Belvedere. For the first time in her life, she felt no embarrassment about bringing someone to her home. In fact, for some unfathomable reason she wanted Gerry Horak to view the imprint of her matrilineal wealth.

'Well?' she asked as Pedro opened the gates.

'Am I meant to be intimidated?'

'Aren't you?'

'Sure,' he said, glancing around at the grove of magnificent, fresh-leaved sycamores. 'The place gives me a hard-on, I want to throw you into the backseat and hump you. Sex and money have a lot in common, at least if you're a painter. No good painter is a eunuch, and to clear his mind he needs plenty of poontang. He also needs a sucker to buy his work. That's the two necessities for a painter, pussy and patrons.'

'And here I am, both,' she said. One of the peacocks preened by the tennis court's protective green fencing. 'If you're trying to shock me, you aren't.'

'Like hell I'm not. Nobody's ever talked to you like this, have they, you proper little rich debutante?'

'Let's get one thing straight. I am not a debutante, I never will be. I'm an artist.'

'Not yet you aren't, baby, not by a long shot,' he said. 'Maybe you could be if you set your mind to it. We're alike, you and me. Both hard-minded as nails.'

'I'm tougher than you.'

'Like hell.'

'Oh yes I am. Nails aren't hard, they bend. Me, I'm a diamond. You'll find out.' Althea, surging with vital energy, pressed on the accelerator, and the wagon skimmed over gravel. It seemed to her she had spoken the truth. At this minute it was beyond belief that she had ever in her life lacked confidence.

'What does your old man do?'

'Nothing.'

They were approaching the house, and he glanced expressively up at the massive expanse of rose-hued bricks for which a Georgian house in Kent had been torn down. 'In a pig's ass, nothing. Men cut off their left ball for a joint like this.'

'You really think the crude talk is adorable, don't you?' she said. 'He performed his life's labours in a single day. He married a Coyne.'

He jerked around to stare at her, his eyes goggling with surprise gratifyingly akin to hers when she'd first seen his painting. 'Your mother's a Coyne?'

'Grover T.'s daughter,' she said.

'Jesus! But didn't the old buzzard die in the 1800s?'

'Nineteen-eleven. Mother's out of his third wife.'

She led Gerry through the big, silent rooms, showing him the dining room's Beaton mural, the drawing room with its Danilovna portrait of Gertrude as dowdy Madonna, the study lined with da Vinci sketches taken from the Coyne Fifth Avenue mansion before it was razed. She took him upstairs to view the delectable Sargent of her voluptuous grandmother at twenty.

When they entered Althea's room, Gerry reached out for her, grasping her upper arms, pressing her against the wall, thrusting his leg between hers. He was her height, but stocky, broad-boned, resilient of flesh – and amazingly warm. His hard penis thrust against her pelvic bone, opening a wildly incandescent tingling in her moist vagina. A passion she had never before experienced enveloped her, and she put her arms around him, his mouth met hers, and she opened her lips, returning his kiss. Suddenly all her newfound confidence evaporated and she was a small, helpless animal, as trapped as she'd ever been with her drunken father. But this was infinitely worse, for at those times she retained a sense of integrity because the act was being done to her, against her will.

She jerked away, her breath coming fast.

He examined her with the same intense squint he had focused on the model this morning. 'What gives?'

'I just don't care for the caveman approach,' she said, pinning her cool, pale hair back in its knot, feeling a modicum of self-possession return to her.

'You wanted it as much as I did.'

'Of course. With Gerry Horak, what woman wouldn't?'

'I'll wait. You'll come begging for it.'

She laughed. 'Modest, aren't you?'

'Baby, that was *me* kissing you. The chemistry went clear off the scale.' He spoke without gloating, his dark-stubbled face impassive. 'Don't worry, I'm not about to push you. It's up to you to set the time.'

She took another composing breath and sat on the

202

window seat. 'What lies beneath this tough-he-man exterior? Tell me about yourself.'

'I'm not one for going into the personal past, or hearing anybody else do it, either.'

'Thank God. I meant your career.'

Before the war Gerry had been represented by Longman's on Madison Avenue, the most prestigious gallery in the country. He was their youngest artist and had been bought by important private collectors, including her Aunt Edna. When he talked about the sales, faint sweat glossed his face – he had not lied about equating sex with money. Yet this equation, she understood, came not from warping meretriciousness but from the quixotic innocence of a true artist: as he had told her, his two needs were women and the acceptance of his work that money proved.

She had guessed correctly about the labouring background.

'In case you're thinking I'm some kind of highfalutin' guy who puts on a tough act, my grandfather came from Bohemia as a contract labourer – that's a good deal lower than a slave – to Lackawanna Steel. He was killed in a routine accident.'

'My grandfather owned Lackawanna before it was absorbed into US Steel.'

'Probably some flunky of his refused to pay for the rail that would have saved my grandfather from falling into the blooming pit. What's one more Hunkie more or less?' He leaned back in the window seat, both amused and bitter. 'My brothers still work for the Lackawanna division.'

'There's a big block of US Steel shares in my trust.'

They both chuckled, as if this linked them.

'And what about the US Army?' she asked.

'No separation until the medicos release me. I'm an outpatient at Birmingham – that's the military hospital in the San Fernando Valley. Every Monday I hitch over there.'

'And the institute?'

'One of the doctors is a Kraut, and he told Lissauer about me. Lissauer's letting me use that room out back gratis, and also share the models. He's really okay. But nervous as hell about everything. Can you imagine? He checked with city hall to make sure it was legal, me sleeping in the garage room – his own damn property! Jesus, I never saw anybody shake in his boots like that.'

Gerry made no further passes, and at seven he refused her dinner invitation. He also refused a ride back to the institute. She stood at a drawing-room window watching him curve down Belvedere's broad, well-lit gravel drive in an infantryman's efficient slog.

Except for that one disintegrating moment in his arms, she was more at ease with him than she had been with anyone in her life, including Roy Wace. With him she felt in complete charge, mistress of her body and mind and emotions. A delicious sensation of power. She stretched her slim young arms above her head. I'll make him wild for me, she decided. Then I'll play it cool and watch him crawl. She felt no vindictiveness, only a sense of playing an exhilarating game.

25

To Althea, the amazing part was how easily she and Gerry Horak melted into a couple.

Their relationship, deeper than she had believed possible, was urgently, relentlessly erotic, the more so for the purposeful lack of physical contact. They were two warriors engaged in warfare. Gerry was intent on waiting for her signal – her surrender, as she thought of it – and she went through torments to control herself from reaching out and touching his dark-haired hand. Not to give way first had become the most significant battle of her life. Thus, in an atmosphere of overheated sexual craving, their relationship remained what was then called platonic.

At the institute, they worked side by side, sharing lunch – she had requested Belvedere's stolid, plain-cooking chef to give her extra sandwiches each day. When the second session ended, they would load their easels and large cherrywood paint boxes in the station wagon; these lengthening days of May and early June, as well as weekends, they painted Belvedere's shaded dells and sunlit vistas. Gerry never offered advice, yet she improved immeasurably by working at his side. She copied his use of large arm movements rather than delicate swerves of fingers and wrist, she learned to splash on colour with wholehearted confidence, and, like him, she worked in abandoned exhilaration. Once finished, though, her work brought actual tears of frustration to her hypercritical eyes. When stood against the poolhouse walls alongside Gerry's, her canvases were outlandishly amateurish. His paintings dazzled the eye, arrested the mind, haunted the soul – he was topnotch. Yet he destroyed most of them with furious strokes of a palette knife.

'Why do that?' she asked.

'It's total crap,' he said.

'What are you, fishing for compliments? It's terrific!'

'Yeah, terrific crap. Ahh, fuck, I'm no English gentleman. Romney or Gainsborough or one of those old dead guys, they could handle all this careful landscape. I'm not la-di-da enough to paint Belvedere.'

'You haven't liked anything you've done of the models at the institute, either.'

'How could I when you're the one subject that gets my nuts aching? Painting you, there'd be no problem.'

'How would you pose me?'

'Standing inside there.' They were working near Mrs Cunningham's greenhouse. 'I'd show you behind the glass, alive, aloof, trapped in your goddamn unattainable virtue. Well?'

'Well what?'

'Model for me.'

'Oh, I don't know. There's my own work.'

'The world'll survive without a week's production.'

'Thanks.'

'And what about us?' he asked roughly. His eyes glittered, his angrily set jaw was dark – he shaved every morning, but by afternoon his face showed five-o'clock shadow. 'Althea, what about us?'

Triumph bubbled warmly through her. I've won, she exulted.

He stood behind her, clasping her shoulders. His fingers caressed the musculature of her collarbone, dispatching excruciatingly sweet sensations through her breasts to centre in the nipples. She could smell the odour of his sweat mingling with paint, feel the hot emanations of vitality, and she leaned back against the solid flesh, craving with every nerve to feel him inside her. She was weak and trembly, she was mush. She hadn't won at all, but had again fallen into that disintegration where her free will no longer existed.

She managed to pull away from his caress. 'My parents are coming home at the end of the month,' she said, moving a few steps from him.

'Who gives a fart? I asked you a question.'

'Will I sit for you?' she asked, knowing her bitchiness added to her attraction for him.

'Oh, hell! Why play the snow maiden for so long? I'd swear you're not cherry?' It was a question.

'That,' she said, 'is for me to know and you to find out.' Her facetiousness rang phony in the afternoon shadows.

He lowered one thick eyebrow, squinting at her. 'I've never felt like this with any other broad. We'll be terrific together. You're going to love it – and me.'

'Think so?'

'Absolutely. And the portraits of you are going to be hot-damn masterpieces.'

That night for the first time he accepted her dinner invitation. She told Luther the table was not to be set in the hexagonal breakfast room where she routinely ate without her parents, but in the echoing formal dining room.

Cecil Beaton birds hovering around them, she and Gerry faced each other across yards of candlelit antique mahogany. A last-ditch effort on her part. She intended proving to herself that Gerry Horak was a nobody, a cipher, a crude Hunkie labourer. So what if he were warm, vital, outrageously talented and had sex appeal that could melt a marble block? In the Sheraton chair usually occupied by her tall, dinner-suited father, he sat wearing Army fatigues streaked with cerise paint, showing not the least anxiety about which fork to use for what course as he ate hungrily. Shouldn't his rotten table manners cure this tumultuous beating of her heart? Yet in the serene candlelight she accepted that Gerry Horak was made of incorruptible elements, the material of genius, which defies and renders meaningless the barriers set up by class and money.

Luther, a sneer on his lips, served them ice cream made from strawberries grown in the kitchen garden.

Gerry said, 'So this is how Coynes live.'

'The rest of the family look down on us for roughing it out in California.'

'Things are tough all over,' he said. 'Where's the brandy?' he asked. 'I always thought you rich bastards ended up meals with brandy.'

'It's not been put into law yet.'

Not smiling, he gazed at her in a way that made her breath catch. 'Althea,' he said, and came around the table, taking her hand, leading her into the hall, where the only light was taupe candleflame that flowed from the dining room. His eye sockets were darkly moist hollows compelling her. She leaned forward to kiss him.

When the kiss ended, they were both shaking.

'Where?' he said into her open mouth.

'My room,' she said in a low, unrecognizable murmur.

But when she snapped on the light of her blue-flowered bedroom, something happened. The erogenous frenzy drained from her, and she felt a sudden chill. She had returned to the place where the utmost betrayal had been forced on her. She stood unresponsive in Gerry's embrace.

'Lovely hard swan-haired broad – ' he muttered, kissing her forehead, her eyes, her throat. After a few moments he pulled back. 'What gives, Althea?'

'I can't,' she whispered.

'What the hell!'

'It's impossible, Gerry,' she said wearily. 'I'm sorry.'

He lifted her chin, peering at her. 'You're afraid, aren't you?' he asked with a gentleness she had never heard from him.

'No.'

'Baby, baby. What's got to you is this room.'

Without knowing her particular stigmata, he comprehended the truth.

'I'm sorry, Gerry,' she repeated helplessly.

'No sweat, my poor frightened baby.' He kissed her lightly on the forehead. 'I should be furious at you for being a prick tease, and here I am playing the tender lover.'

'I'd hardly classify that last remark as tender or loverlike,' she said.

'That's more like it.' He kissed her forehead. 'That sounds like my cold, hard rich bitch.' With another light kiss he turned and trotted down the staircase.

Watching his squarish shadow recede down the elegant stairwell, she longed to call him back, but that ancient shame trapped her.

The following day her father called from Washington. 'There's a storm of work, planning this international conference before it opens in San Francisco next month. We can't be back for a while.'

An exquisite relief drenched over her, though it was unaccountable why she, who had the perfect if never-voiced means of blackmail, should care whether or not her parents were in Beverly Hills to disapprove of Gerry Horak.

'. . . international conference,' her father was saying. 'It's called the United Nations. The papers have been full of it.'

Consumed by Gerry, she had been blind and deaf to news of the outside world, but she replied enthusiastically. 'So *that's* what you're working on in Washington.'

'Big doings, Toots, I have a part in big doings,' said Mr Cunningham happily.

She laughed. 'Love you, Daddy.' Which, God help her, she did.

* * *

The next afternoon Gerry began painting her. Or rather, posing her. Inside the greenhouse, he had her recline under baskets of yellow Comtesse de Breton orchids; he stood her against Mrs Cunningham's pride, a twenty-foot-tall piece of driftwood on which massed white Olga orchids glowed in a galaxy; he moved her from aisle to orchid-filled aisle, raising her arm, bending her knee, tilting her head: he examined her from every possible angle without opening his paint box.

It was Saturday morning before he got the effect he wanted.

She was posed inside the greenhouse while he worked outside. He stared through the glass at her so long that her muscles began to quiver; then he picked up a brush and lost himself. Two hours later, she emerged to see what he'd got on canvas.

Her image, surrounded by a flock of voracious, birdlike orchids, half-veiled by the iridescent sheen of glass, had the chimerical quality of a woman gazing out of that mythical garden in the golden age before humankind had learned pain or weakness, a woman eternally young, invincibly strong.

'My God. Gerry . . . it's staggering. Fantastic. Is that how you see me? Eve before the fatal apple?'

'Yeah, before Kotex or dirty diapers, when there was only endless musky fucking.'

She laughed, moving to view the vivid wet oils from a different angle. 'Be as vulgar as you want. Nothing can make this less terrific.'

'Yeah, it's good.' He gave an excited laugh. 'God, Althea, I'll paint you and paint you until the walls of every damn museum in the world are one gigantic Althea Cunningham orgasm.'

His words roused her, and as she gazed at the gleaming, magnificent portrait, undeniable proof of his love, passion suddenly overwhelmed her, dizzying her. She turned to him.

They clung, breast to breast, thighs quivering against thighs. 'Come into the greenhouse,' he muttered hoarsely.

'The gardeners – '

'The hell with gardeners.' He curved her hand over his erection. 'Do you feel that, Althea? I've had that hard-on for two months, since the morning I met you. The hell with the gardeners.'

Her blood was on fire, and there was no argument in her, only this out-of-control trembling. Arm around her waist, he half-dragged her, half-pulled her into the greenhouse, where they sprawled on the tanbark, neither of them aware of the roughness, both groping to push aside the separating cloth. He lowered himself between her legs, and gasping, she looked up into that broad Slavic face which was transformed by passion yet blurred with tenderness; then she abandoned rational thought entirely, closing her eyes as she was caught up in ecstasy. This loss of control was not frightening or humiliating, but a kind of hitherto unrealized miracle. Almost immediately she gave a series of birdlike, involuntary coital cries, and he began his swift thrusting.

They lay joined on the tanbark smiling at each other.

She touched the hard scar on his chest, saying, 'Gerry . . .'

He shook his head slightly. 'No sticky speeches, there's no point, we don't need words, not when we're the same goddamn animal. Just lie there looking like a beautiful, satisfied empress.'

26

After that first time, they went to Gerry's place, a cubicle off the institute's detached garage. A pair of thin olive-drab GI blankets covered the swaybacked iron bedstead, termite dust sifted perpetually onto the linoleum, plywood replaced a missing windowpane, and there was a constant drip of the shower into the yellowing tub. Gerry was indifferent to the flophouse surroundings. Althea found them relentlessly aphrodisiac. No sooner had she stepped through the warped door than she was embracing him. They would eat dinner at Belvedere, returning through the quiet dark streets of Beverly Hills to the institute, parking the station wagon in one of the empty spaces next door behind the silver shop, a nod towards discretion, though by night there was no traffic in the black shadowed alley and Henry Lissauer still obeyed the enemy-alien curfew to the point of never leaving the house proper after eight.

Gerry made love the way he painted. He would undress her leisurely, caressing and adoring her, an immense amount of joyful, sweet foreplay that inevitably plunged her into orgasm. Once he was inside her, though, his tender concern evaporated, and he drove swiftly and selfishly to his own climax while she responded with upheavals deep within her womb.

Mr and Mrs Cunningham went directly from Washington to San Francisco, where delegates from all over the globe were gathered. Althea scarcely read their long letters about the international furore – and neither did she pay attention to the news about the United Nations in papers or on the radio.

That month Gerry completed a half-dozen significant portraits of her. Then he determined to do something outsize, an eight-by-ten-foot canvas. He made studies in Belvedere's greenhouse, then nailed up his canvas on the institute's deep back porch. Lissauer and his students watched the progress. The narrow, tenderly curved girl's body in a chaste white summer dress transcended its surface, assuming a sensuality that was made explicit by Althea's intimate, anticipatory smile. Though Althea and Gerry's outward manner towards each other remained bristling – unromantic in the extreme – the vibrant eroticism of the portrait proclaimed their intimacy as surely as if they had fallen in the carnal embrace on the dusty floors of the institute.

Althea knew the others were talking. In her new security she would think: so what, so what?

One morning in July she parked on Rodeo, entering the front door, going through the kitchen to get a fresh look at her portrait.

211

It was not there.

Althea had never dared loose the proprieties: she could not go openly to Gerry's room. But when he failed to show up in the studio for the morning's model – a derelict sourly redolent of cheap wine – her alarm swelled like an abscess. Lissauer, circling the easels with his preliminary critiques, reached her.

'Mr Lissauer,' she asked, 'did Gerry Horak mention he was going someplace?'

Lissauer turned away. The Assyrian profile was impassive, but his scraggy neck flushed. Since Gerry had arrived the elderly teacher had behaved towards Althea with hurt dignity, as though she had jilted him, a quietly expressive jealousy that endeared him to her: 'Mr Horak will not be with the institute any longer, Miss Cunningham.' The halting voice was solemn with a trace of fear. 'He is leaving this morning.'

'Leaving?'

'It is possible he might already be gone.'

With a little smile, she wiped her brush absolutely free of paint on the rag before placing it in the can of turps. So, she thought. He's taken off without one word to me. In a few breaths her recent confidence had melted like sugar in water, and she was again an outsider, an unworthy creature who could not even command the lasting affections of a common labourer. Oh, how could she have forgotten this sense of frustrated despair? Gerry's been laughing at me all along, she thought, and so has Henry Lissauer – everybody at the institute is rolling in the aisles about me.

Lissauer was pointing to the canvas. 'Hnn, hnn. The figure . . . if you place the figure here on the left, Miss Cunningham, there will be a triangular composition . . .'

'Yes, Mr Lissauer, that's what we all want, isn't it? A nice obvious little painting.'

He stepped clumsily to the next easel.

Althea could scarcely breathe. I have to see if he's still there, she thought. Leaving squiggles of paint to harden on her palette, she raced down the empty stairs. Midmorning heat had softened the blacktop, and she felt the give as she

212

darted around the students' cars to bang on the warped door.

Althea let out a sigh of partial relief when Gerry called, 'It's open.'

Naked except for his GI khaki shorts, he was cramming olive-drab clothing into a duffel bag. His bare chest, no longer bandaged, showed the scar tissue an angrier maroon than usual, and he moved stiffly, as if the not-yet-healed wound pained him, which she knew it often did. He had not shaved, and the thick, dark stubble gave him a dangerous look.

'Ahh, so the rumour is true,' she said with potent vindictiveness. 'Our fine-feathered Hunkie is fleeing the luxury of Beverly Hills.'

'I was coming up to the studio to explain.'

'One of God's chosen people already did.'

'What a shitty way for you to find out,' Gerry said, apologetic.

Althea looked uncertainly at him. 'You really were going to tell me?'

'What do you think, I was running away?'

'You didn't mention a word last night.'

'Lissauer came out here about an hour after you left. The poor chickenshit Hebe, he had to slug down brandy to get up the nerve to tell me I couldn't use the premises anymore.'

'He knows we've been coming here?' Her voice rose. 'He's been spying?'

'It seems one of the students went to him. Said she doesn't like what's going on, a young girl being seduced.'

'It's that damn de Liso cripple!' Althea burst out. She had formed a near-hatred for Roxanne de Liso, who praised Gerry's work resoundingly, vivaciously, knowledgeably.

'I'm pretty sure she's not the one.'

'That jabbering bitch!' Below the surface of her vehemence, Althea was exulting: Gerry didn't betray me, she thought. 'So Herr Professor finally summoned up the nerve to tippie-toe out of his house in the dark?'

Gerry, who had finished packing his few possessions,

straightened with difficulty. 'Althea, Lissauer was doing me a favour, letting me stay. The plain damn truth is, I should never have brought you here. It was a shitty way to repay him. I've gotten to know him pretty well. He's red-hot to become an American. If there were any problem with morals, his chances at citizenship would be compromised.'

How dare Gerry defend their enemies? 'That's a long word for you, "compromised".'

He sighed. 'You're seventeen. The law says what we do here is rape. Statutory rape. Lissauer could be blamed too – the Beverly Hills cops are very tight assed. The poor bastard's a man without a country, a resident alien. You've read about what they found in the concentration camps, the hell it's been for Jews over there.'

She hadn't read about Hitler's death factories. The grisly revelations, the war still blazing in the Pacific, the formation of the United Nations had escaped her notice because of this stocky, near naked man.

'Will Mrs de Liso wheel herself into City Hall to tell the police?'

'Christ, Althea, quit laying it on her. More likely the blabbermouth was that prissy broad, Mrs – '

'Gerry!' Althea interrupted in alarm. 'If Mr Lissauer gets in trouble, *you* could go to jail!'

'Me?'

'Rape, you just said rape!'

'Nothing's going to happen to me,' he said, gripping her shoulders, conducting a modicum of physical reassurance. 'I'm going to move in with a buddy – he can use the rent money.'

'And what about us?'

'Business as usual. Afternoons and weekends I'll come over to Belvedere to work on the portrait.'

'If we make love, you'll be in danger!'

'What the hell gives, Althea? This isn't like you – you don't run scared.'

Until you came along I always ran scared, she thought. And did not even consider her next words. 'It'd be legal if we were married,' she said. Then her narrow hands clenched into fists, and she looked away. Girls didn't propose. The girl waited, forever if necessary, for the man to avow that he wanted her to have and to hold. How disastrously wide she had laid herself open!

The springs of the bed creaked as Gerry sat down. 'We belong together,' he said slowly. 'We're simple and right together in a way I never believed possible. For some reason we're lousy bastards apart, but together we're decent.'

She nodded at this truth she had not heretofore recognized.

'But there's the little matter of your family.'

'Them!' she said contemptuously.

'Face it, I'm a low-life slob who eats peas on a knife. Steelworkers' sons don't marry Coynes.'

'Gerry . . .' Her voice went very low. 'Are you putting me off?'

He shook his head. 'No. I'm a foot-loose guy involved in my work. I've never figured on the permanent thing. But you're not like the others. I meant it – we're good for each other . . . and I don't just mean in the sack. I want to be with you the rest of my life.'

'Then don't worry about my parents. I can handle that end.'

'I haven't met them, but take my word, when it comes to this sort of thing, the rich bastards have their own set of rules, rules that would've made the Gestapo blush. They'll see me in hell before they let me marry you.'

'You sound like you've been involved with some other nubile heiress.'

'I have,' he said tersely.

'Well, in the case of my parents, there's another little matter. I have a little something on them. A pretty horrendous skeleton to rattle.' As she spoke, she was overcome by aching, nostalgic grief for those days of innocence when noises in her room dredged up only old ghost stories. Hunching on the unpainted stool, she began to cry.

She had never wept in Gerry's presence, and as far as she was concerned, this gasping, hiccuping breakdown proved a greater intimacy between them than sex. He held her wet

215

face to his scarred chest, stroking her gleaming hair, not speaking.

After her regressive tears had ended, he cupped her wet face. 'I love you,' he said.

A few minutes later they were loading the duffel bag and canvases and the enormous, unwieldy wet portrait in the back of the station wagon. She drove him a few miles south and west to Sawtelle, an older section of Los Angeles that drowsed like a passed-over hamlet in its shabbiness. The paint had long ago peeled from his friend's rundown shack, and the weathered boards and shingle roof were quilted with Algerian ivy.

Althea was back at the institute for the last hour of the modelling session, her face arrogant and cold as she washed in the outlines of the derelict.

The following day was very hot, but it had cooled off slightly by five. She and Gerry were in the poolhouse, Gerry – shirtless – frowning as he swiftly plastered paint on a corner of the enormous canvas, she standing in her pose. She heard the purr of an engine coming up from the gate. The sound of the car continued to the front of the house.

'That's weird,' she said. 'Only my parents use the front door.'

Gerry frowned – he despised chitchat when he worked.

'I'm taking a break,' Althea said, clicking in her high-heeled white sandals along the pool deck to the diving board. From here she had a clear view of the house and front courtyard: raising a hand, she squinted into the long, hard rays of the lowering sun.

O'Rourke held the car door open and her mother stood waiting while her father, holding his briefcase, emerged from the custom Swallow limousine.

Althea clasped her arms across the bodice of the white batiste frock she wore for the portrait, her mind darting in alarm. Why were they home? They hadn't let her know. Had that terrified refugee telephoned them? The servants had mentioned nothing about their arrival.

Gerry, unaware of the catastrophe, continued to work.

'Well, what do you know,' she said in a loud, jocular voice. 'Surprise of surprises.'

He turned, blinking. 'What gives?'

'The Belvedere delegation to the UN has returned.'

'Your parents?' Still holding his paint-smeared palette knife, he walked over to the diving board.

'Rich bastards.' She used his term. 'See the horns and hoofs.'

'I'll put on my shirt.'

'That's right, play the ardent suitor.'

'Althea, they have to know about me sooner or later, so what's wrong with sooner? Besides, aren't you the girl who said she could handle them?' He was grinning, but he reached a comforting arm around her waist.

At that moment her father glanced down the terrace. She was too far away to read his expression, but she saw him pull his shoulders back as he continued to gaze down at them.

'You're getting paint on my dress,' she said, moving from Gerry.

Her father waved.

Why am I so afraid? Althea wondered as she waved back.

27

In the cool, austere hall, Luther eased forward, murmuring to Althea that the Cunninghams were awaiting them in the library. Althea's dread increased, and she drew apart from Gerry.

The mansion, while lacking the Belle Epoque excesses of earlier Coyne homesteads and in Mrs Cunningham's eyes a simple home, was hardly a cosy place, being furnished with excellent early-nineteenth-century English antiques of a decidedly formal nature. Nowhere was this formality more obtrusive than in the library. Occupying the entire downstairs portion of the east wing, the carved butternut panelling, the exceptionally high ceiling, and the shelves filled with thousands of books that ranked up to it emphasized the room's massive proportions. Next to the mammoth fireplace, the concert Steinway appeared a small ebony toy.

The late-afternoon light filtered through thick silk curtains onto a pair of Hepplewhite armchairs where Mr and Mrs Cunningham sat so still that they appeared to be sculptured red granite effigies. Then Mr Cunningham rose, holding out his arms.

'Toots,' he said.

'Althea, dear,' her mother said.

'Daddy, Mother, what a surprise.' Althea crossed the enormous carpet that had been woven for this room. Parental kisses did nothing to assuage the banging of her frightened heart. 'Why didn't you tell me you were coming?'

'We didn't decide until this morning. We took the train down,' said Mrs Cunningham.

Althea said, 'But what about the conference?'

Gerry had halted at the door.

Mr Cunningham, staring at him, said in a louder tone, 'Come on in. You must be Mr Horak.'

Althea said, 'Yes. I wrote to you about my friend.'

Mrs Cunningham, who had somehow transmuted her bovine shyness into a regal chill, remained seated while Mr Cunningham, who wore clothes easily and well, stood stiff in his summer-grey suit as if it were a general's full-dress regalia. Gerry came towards them in his paint-smeared, unironed fatigues, a peasant. Althea had a sudden vision of her lover touching his curly brown forelock.

She introduced him formally.

Gerry, of course, showed no subservience. He behaved with his usual surly ease, as if he belonged wherever he happened to find himself, as if he were innately equal to kings – and Coynes. 'Pleased to meet you, Mrs Cunningham,' he said.

'Ahhh, yes. Mr Horak,' Mrs Cunningham said.

'Sit down, Mr Horak, Althea.' Mr Cunningham waited until they took places at either end of a ten-foot black leather sofa. 'I won't beat around the bush,' he said. 'We left San Francisco for one reason. We've been having some disturbing reports – '

'Reports?' Althea interrupted sharply. 'What do you mean, reports?'

'Every week M'liss telephones me,' said Mrs Cunningham breathily.

'She *spies* on me?' Althea whispered.

Mr Cunningham replied, 'She telephones your mother to tell her about Belvedere. You know how close they are.' M'liss had been nurse to Gertrude Coyne as well as Althea. 'Of course the main topic of their conversations is you. We want to hear all about you.' Mr Cunningham's weak, handsomely amiable face retained its unaccustomed lines of sternness. 'We've been very disturbed to learn about the increasing intensity of your, uh, friendship. You seem to spend all your free time with Mr Horak. Afternoons, evenings, weekends.'

'Gerry's been painting me – '

'Althea,' Gerry interrupted, looking at her. 'Your father's right. They haven't left the United Nations to play word games.' He raised one thick eyebrow expressively.

Althea, furious and wretched that M'liss, her nurse, her friend, had been spying and tattling, told herself that Gerry was right, the betrayal made no difference. Sooner or later her parents would have to learn where her affections lay. She nodded at Gerry.

He said, 'I've been painting Althea, sure. But it's gotten pretty heavy between us.'

Mr Cunningham mopped his high, lightly lined forehead. 'Ahh, I see. Heavy,' he said. 'You realize, don't you, that Althea's only seventeen?'

Gerry nodded, saying quietly, 'She's not an ordinary girl.'

'But only seventeen. She's still a child. Whereas you are twenty-five.'

'How do you know that?' Althea asked. 'More counter-intelligence?'

'Try to understand, dear,' said Mrs Cunningham in her

219

nervous way. 'If we were in New York, we would know who all your friends were – or somebody in the family would know. But out here in Beverly Hills, nobody has any roots. There are people here from everywhere. Some of them are, well, meretricious. We don't live ostentatiously, but still they might want to . . . use . . . They might be interested in us for the wrong reasons.'

'Althea, you're so single-tracked in what you do,' said Mr Cunningham. 'We have to protect you.'

'Yes,' said Mrs Cunningham, her shoulders more rounded than ever. 'You're our little girl and we want only the best things in life for you.'

'Oh, Mother, must you be so corny!'

'We checked into Roy, too,' offered Mr Cunningham placatingly.

'Of course. Naturally,' Althea said. 'After all, everybody knows what a dangerous, swindling, avaricious fortune hunter your average fourteen-year-old is.'

'We don't need to apologize for loving and protecting you,' said Mr Cunningham. 'Or for thinking a teenage girl doesn't have all the sense in the world. You never invited Roy here and you were at her place all the time. Naturally we had to find out about her people.'

'They're poor,' said Mrs Cunningham. 'But they come from a fine old Southern family.'

'Then you know where I come from,' Gerry said. 'Nothing fine or old or Southern. Just dirty Pittsburgh steel mills.'

Mr Cunningham planted his English-made immaculately polished shoes slightly apart, as if bracing himself. 'There are things I must say to Mr Horak that aren't pleasant. You think you're very adult, Toots, and worldly in that art school. But to me you're still my little girl, and, well, if it were possible, I'd prefer to spare you . . .' He broke off, turning abruptly.

Not before Althea saw there were tears in his light hazel eyes, actual tears. 'There's nothing about Gerry,' she lied in a thin voice, 'that I don't already know.'

'Not by a long shot.' Gerry grinned at her, the first smile anyone had attempted since the onset of this confrontation.

Mr Cunningham shifted in his chair, reaching down for his attaché case, resting it on his grey-clad knees, opening it to extricate a manila folder. He took his glasses from their alligator case. His every movement seemed deliberately slow to Althea, as if he wanted to give Gerry time to feel the mortification.

Gerry's broad face gave the impression of calm, but Althea saw the flat anger in his eyes.

'Born in Pittsburgh in 1919,' Mr Cunningham read. 'Fourth child of Anton and Bella Zneckitch Horak. His father immigrated as the child of a contract labourer, his mother went to school until she was ten and then worked as a servant girl, marrying at thirteen. Their first child, a son, was born five months later – I'll skip most of this. In 1933, the father was sentenced to six months.'

'Yeah, time in the slammer for trying to organize a union, which was legal. The police work for you, not us. But jail wasn't the worst of his problems by a long shot. After he got out, he couldn't find a job anywhere. Not because of being in the slammer, not because of the Depression, he was top pourer. The mill owners had him blacklisted for being a union man. Christ! Did you ever see anyone die by inches in front of you? Between them, my older brothers managed to keep the house going. Dad stole the food money, *stole* he the most honest of men! He drank it up. He couldn't stand being a deadweight, so he drank like a fish. A couple of months before the war started he fell down the stairs and broke his neck, but he'd died years before.'

Althea winced. She did not want to hear about the rock-bottom torments of Gerry's poverty, she tried not to listen to the indignities of his youth – she needed him inviolably strong, without a crack or Achilles' heel.

'You left school at sixteen and worked in the CCC.' Mr Cunningham riffled pages. 'You won a poster-art competition and were awarded a scholarship to Pratt Art Institute.' Mr Cunningham ran a buffed fingernail down a fresh page. 'In 1940 a Penelope Wertenbaker sued you for child support – '

221

'She lost,' Gerry interjected. 'Mr Cunningham, Althea knows I'm not a plaster saint.'

'Later in the same year,' Mr Cunningham continued, 'a family called Gilfillan, well-to-do people from Kansas City, used the same agency that we did. They had you investigated because you wanted to marry their daughter – '

Gerry interrupted. 'Marriage was Dora's idea.'

'In any case, the family paid you off.'

'When the Gilfillans decided to become patrons of the arts and buy three of my paintings, I didn't follow her back to Kansas City.'

'They discovered the two of you had been . . . intimate. You refused to set things right.'

'Would your crowd,' Gerry asked with furious mock humility, 'think it the right thing to marry a girl whose parents had just loaded you with dough to steer clear of her?'

'Is this meant to horrify me, Daddy?' Althea asked.

'I want you to get the whole picture here, Toots. I won't deny Mr Horak's thought to be promising by his gallery, and he was decorated for bravery.'

'You were?' Althea turned to him.

'I kept firing an M1 at this farmhouse, later the brass decided it was glory humping, but me, I wasn't about to let the Krauts capture me – those Nazi bastards got their rocks off by working prisoners over.'

At the coarseness, both Cunninghams winced.

'I gather all of this is a heavy parental move prior to breaking us up,' Althea said.

'We've never been like that, have we?' reproached Mr Cunningham. 'We want you and Mr Horak to decide the matter for yourselves.'

'Yes, dear,' Mrs Cunningham said, her protuberant teeth bared anxiously. 'We've always let you make your own decisions.'

'But to do that properly, we had to give you the facts,' said Mr Cunningham, closing the folder.

'All right, now I have them,' Althea said.

Mrs Cunningham rose to her feet, turning to Gerry. 'Mr Horak, if you'll excuse me, I'm a little tired. The journey.'

Solicitously holding his wife's arm, Mr Cunningham left the library with her.

Althea turned to Gerry, asking quietly, 'Was that Penelope girl's baby yours?'

'Could be.'

'And that other girl, was she pregnant too?'

'She fixed it.'

'You're a stinker, aren't you?' Althea said without reproach. How strange it was that hearing the details of Gerry's impoverished background, of which she was already aware, had repelled her, yet hearing for the first time the details of his sexual transgressions, far from dismaying her, gave her a queer pleasurable sense of superiority.

'That's hardly what jolted you,' he said. 'You didn't enjoy hearing how rich bastards can grind a man down.'.

'Okay, that's true. But nothing they say can alter the way I feel.'

'Don't underestimate them.'

'Do I detect faint, faraway bugles calling retreat?'

'Baby, we'll be together always – if it's up to me.'

Her father returned to the door. 'Mr Horak, if you'll excuse us, my wife has a gift for Althea.'

Gerry nodded his good-byes. Althea listened to him echo across the black and white marble squares of the hall, her eardrums rawly sensitive to those fading heavy footsteps. After the side door had opened and closed, she asked with a truculence she rarely used with her father, 'What is this wonderful gift?'

'Come along up and see.'

Mrs Cunningham was in their upstairs sitting room, one of her plainly tailored Liberty-print robes pulled tight around her. Mr Cunningham went to close the door.

'Your grandmother gave me something for you,' said Mrs Cunningham. She reached for a flat leather jewel box, and lifted out a necklace: Thirty strands of tiny, impeccably matched luminous seed pearls were suspended from six flashing diamond bars – Althea had seen this choker riding high on her grandmother's carefully rejuvenated throat. It was part of the magnificent Coyne pearl collection.

She took the necklace, which was surprisingly heavy and had a metallic odour, moving to the mirror, fastening the diamond clasp with icy fingers. Her neck was far more slender than her grandmother's, so the masses of small, glowing pearls drooped between their diamond stays. 'It doesn't fit,' she said.

'We'll take it to the jeweller,' said Mrs Cunningham.

'Pearls are meant to be worn,' said Mr Cunningham. 'We'll have to entertain now.'

If her mother had made the remark, Althea would have hit back with poisonous daggers of sarcasm, but since her father had spoken, she tightened the priceless anachronism from an opulent age around her throat, wondering how her mother had convinced the old lady, whose name was hardly generosity, to part with this treasure.

Moving away from the mirror, she dropped the pearls in her mother's large, soft hand. 'Put it with the other loot in your safe.'

Althea went slowly along the tapestried corridor to her room. She accepted their strategy. They were going to woo her with her own wealth, they were going to try to get her to view Gerry as unworthy.

Well it won't work, she thought, clicking the bolt behind her. Without Gerry, she would return to being that weak, skeletonless creature forced by her natural enemies – people – to dwell in a carapace of pretended indifference.

Yet she could not stop thinking of Gerry's uneducated mother, married and pregnant at thirteen, his jailbird father drinking himself to death in a Pittsburgh tenement.

28

The next day at the institute, during the lunch break, she was called inside to the phone. It was Gerry.

'What gives?' he asked.

'We keep on with my portrait.'

'Won't they have something to say about that?'

'Business as usual,' she said, controlling her voice. 'I'll pick you up at the usual place at three.'

The following few afternoons, they spent in the poolhouse: colour and composition fused together.

Her parents said nothing to Althea about Gerry's continued presence, and neither did they discuss returning to San Francisco. Her mother worked in the greenhouse, where great whirling fans dispelled the excess heat; her father made up for lost time in the kennels. At dinner both spoke to her with the cautiously balanced politeness of strangers at a formal gathering. Sometimes her father would mention a Coyne connection who had given up his own concerns for the duration to serve his country in its hour of need, one as Undersecretary of the Army, another as ambassador to a recently renamed African land, a third in the State Department as personal adviser to Franklin. They were reminding her that these were her people. The ruling class.

Midmorning on that hot, ultraclear August day, her father for the first time visited the poolhouse.

Gerry, with his inhuman power of concentration, continued blocking in a troublesome shadow at the bottom of the canvas.

'So this is *la vie bohème*,' said Mr Cunningham, and put on his glasses to examine her larger-than-life, clothed yet nakedly erotic portrait.

Althea, still in her pose, watched her father's cheeks draw in so that his face went gaunt.

'I'm a bit too old-fashioned,' he said finally. 'I can't judge if it's good.'

'It's fabulous,' she said truculently.

Gerry glanced at her. 'Let's take a break, okay?' He set down his palette, rubbing at his chest – the severed, not yet knit muscles ached dully when he stood painting. 'Mr Cunningham, I'm glad you dropped by.'

'Oh?'

'You know exactly the kind of guy I am, so there's no

need for me to horse around politely, is there? So I'll get right to the point. I'm nuts about Althea, and she feels the same way. Whether it's now or in three months when she's eighteen is up to you, but we're getting married.'

Harry Cunningham's face drained under its ruddy surface. 'Married?'

'It's set between us,' Gerry replied.

'Yes,' Althea whispered.

Mr Cunningham sank into a bamboo chair.

'Daddy, are you all right?' Althea asked.

He didn't reply. After a long silence he repeated, 'Married?'

'Yeah,' Gerry said. 'The when is up to you.'

Mr Cunningham's hands were clasped so tightly that the knuckle bones showed like ivory knobs. 'I'm the last man alive to be put in this situation,' he said. 'Has Althea told you that I was her uncle's tutor when I met my wife? There was a huge amount of talk, and I've never outlived the charge of fortune hunting. But whatever our varying degrees of wealth, my wife and I had a great deal in common. A love of books, good music, a mutual way of looking at the world.' He turned to Althea. 'Those things are what's important in a marriage.'

'Gerry and I have painting – art. We're a lot alike.' Althea's voice was inflectionless. She kept it that way; otherwise she might rush to embrace her father, whose shrunken misery was touching her profoundly.

'Believe me, I've been there,' Mr Cunningham said. 'He wouldn't be half so attracted to you if you were a poor girl.'

'He's never hidden that,' Althea retorted.

'Jesus, the money!' Dark stains showed across Gerry's back and in deep circles under his arms. 'The money, the damn money!'

'Althea's kind of wealth has to make a difference.'

'Okay, so it did at first.'

'Are you telling me you're indifferent?'

'Screw your wife's billions!'

For a few long moments in the poolhouse there was only the sound of a faraway Belvedere lawn mower. Then Mr

226

Cunningham's chest expanded in a deep inhalation. He got to his feet. 'Horak,' he said, 'until Althea is eighteen and legally of age, I don't want you seeing or communicating with her.'

'Oh, how rotten!' Althea cried.

'I wouldn't be much of a father if I didn't use every advantage in my power,' he said, facing her. 'You think that backgrounds don't matter, Althea, but they do. Believe me, they do. Each partner brings to marriage a pattern imprinted by his own family. A deep-set pattern. When I read the detective's file, I skipped long parts. There were several reports on the police blotter about disturbances at the Horak household. Mr Horak beat his wife.'

'It began after life got so lousy for him,' Gerry said directly to Althea. There were tensed lines of hurt around his mouth.

'You have exactly thirty minutes to get off our property, Horak,' Mr Cunningham said. He walked across the pool deck with the stiff, slow pace of a much older man.

'He couldn't have laid it more on the line, could he?' Gerry asked.

'He'll change his mind.'

'Didn't sound like it.'

'They always give in to me, Gerry. They have to.' Her words rang sharply, like hailstones. 'Not to worry. They'll welcome you into the family with open arms.'

Once again she drove Gerry the few miles westward to shabby Sawtelle. He had left the enormous, near-completed canvas in the poolhouse, but the smaller portraits he had done of her were in the wagon. Many were not yet dry, and he unloaded them first, strewing them across the sidewalk, which was buckled by the roots of a sheltering pepper tree.

Althea didn't help. From the car she gazed at the shack whose roof sagged beneath its burden of Algerian ivy. The place had a bohemian rakishness that reminded her of the Waces' funny little apartment where she had been so happy.

I'll make them accept Gerry. *What if they don't?* Then I'll have to hit them between the eyes with the truth.

Gerry banged down the back of the wagon, coming to fold

his arms on her window. He leaned forward, kissing her cheek. 'Darling, darling,' he said quietly. He had never used this endearment before. 'I might be a low life, but I'd rather bow out than see you look ashamed and hurt like this. You're a miraculous, cold, wonderful creature, and I love you too much to see you broken.'

She drove slowly back to Belvedere.

All afternoon she crouched on her bed, steeling herself. Once I say the unsayable, she thought, Daddy and Mother will surrender unconditionally. It's axiomatic. Yet never had the future seemed more cruelly inimical.

She did not join her parents for dinner. When she heard them coming up the staircase, she went into her bathroom to dash cold water on her face. As she smoothed back her hair into its chignon, the face that gazed back at her from the mirror looked desperate.

From the Cunninghams' sitting room came the strains of a Mozart horn concerto. It was her father's favourite. Number 2 in E Flat Major, K 417.

She tapped on the door. 'It's me,' she called.

'Come on in, Toots,' her father retorted.

He put down the evening newspaper, her mother marked her place in a slender novel. The cool summer night air belled real lace curtains, the French horn bounced along. Althea stood in front of the unlit fireplace.

'Toots,' said Mr Cunningham gently. 'We know you're upset, and we don't blame you. But sometimes parents have to be firm. It's infinitely better to break off now, before anyone gets hurt. You'll meet a lot of eligible young men.'

'What sort will they be, Daddy?' she asked, sitting on the couch opposite the one where they both sat, her head tilted politely.

'Won't you try to be reasonable?' her father asked.

'Oh? Is it unreasonable to want to know the type of man you *would* welcome into the family?'

Mrs Cunningham said breathily, 'Mr Horak's background isn't really what we have against him, dear.'

'Yes, some of your best friends are steelworkers.'

Mrs Cunningham pressed her large soft hands together. 'It's a great many things added together.'

'For just one example, those unsavoury scrapes with women,' her father said.

Althea quivered with the old core misery of being alone against the world. 'I know he's not a Trappist monk!' she cried vehemently. 'He's an artist! A fabulous, terrific artist. Longman's represents him. He had a one-man show at the Phoenix Museum before he was drafted.'

'Drafted,' Mr Cunningham said. 'It's all there in that one word. Drafted. None of the men in our family waited. They volunteered.'

'Gerry was decorated for bravery, you told me that yourself.'

The last record ended, plunging them into silence.

Mr Cunningham rose to replay the stack. Bent over the large, elaborate Magnavox, he spoke with more irritation than he had hitherto permitted himself to show. 'What is the matter with you? You're not an infant. We're all speaking English. Why won't you at least try to understand our point of view?'

'Because it's all old-fashioned crap!'

'Althea.' Her mother murmured the reproof.

'He's coarsened you already,' Mr Cunningham said.

Mrs Cunningham sighed assent. 'Please, dear, this discussion is upsetting us all.'

'And it's pointless,' said Mr Cunningham. 'Our minds are made up. What I said this morning goes. You are not to communicate with Horak. If he persists in seeing you, there are methods of handling the situation, methods far from pleasant. You are under age. We don't want to be unfair, but you have to understand. We are fighting to protect your future.'

'Isn't it very clear that he's just not our type of person?' Mrs Cunningham asked.

As usual, it was her mother's anxious, breathy voice that detonated Althea's final fuse.

During the afternoon Althea had planned the words she would use if worse came to worst, an eventuality she had been unable to believe – hadn't her parents always given in to her? – but her emotions carried her in violently destructive waves and she forgot the phraseology.

'Yes, isn't it horrendous that Gerry's parents were such low peasants? I couldn't agree more. I wish he came from some fine, respected family where the father doesn't work for the money, but marries it.'

Mr Cunningham turned to grip the edge of the mantelpiece, his white summer dinner jacket stretched eloquently across his shoulders.

'You are not to talk like this!' Mrs Cunningham's cold, harsh whisper was one that Althea had never heard before – it was the exact intonation that old Grover T. Coyne had used so destructively in his killing rages.

Althea held her head higher. 'Gerry and I are getting married, it's decided.'

'You are not,' whispered Mrs Cunningham in the same terrifyingly malevolent tone. 'We love you too much to let that happen.'

Althea's fixed smile remained acidly cynical, but the eighteenth-century chords rattled inside her skull and her mind raced unbearably.

'I know how much Daddy loves me, Mother, but do you? When I was ten, on New Year's Eve, he came to my room.' As Althea spoke, the old, unquenchable shame burned like a fresh scald and her voice rose, high-pitched and childlike. 'When I was ten he showed me how much he loved me – '

Her mother slapped her across the face.

There was vicious power behind that seemingly soft hand. Althea, surprised, fell back, stumbling into a chair.

'You little slut, you filthy little slut, cohabiting with the dregs of the earth!' hissed Mrs Cunningham.

Althea's jaw began to tingle, her left eye to throb.

'You know . . . you must have guessed . . . about Daddy and me . . .?' Althea heard and loathed her beseeching note.

'You're a liar, a lying slut!'

'It only happens when he gets very drunk,' Althea whimpered as placation.

'*Liar!*' panted Mrs Cunningham, grabbing Althea's

230

upper arms, pulling the girl to her feet, shaking her so violently that the thick, streaky pale hair cascaded from its tether of bobby pins.

'Mommy . . . you must have heard – '

Mrs Cunningham slapped her again. '*I refuse to hear lies!*'

Mr Cunningham had leaned his forehead on the chastely carved marble fireplace, his tall, slender body racked by shudders.

Mrs Cunningham dragged Althea to the door. Opening, she hissed in that awful whisper, 'We don't want to see your lying face until you're ready to apologize!' She shoved her daughter into the hall, slamming the door after her.

Althea leaned against the jamb. The record ended, and during the interim before the next one dropped down, she could hear her father's gasping sobs, her mother's breathy consolation.

She ran to her own room, falling across her bed.

29

Althea's sobs were uncontrollable. 'I am wicked, so wicked' went repetitively through her mind in the bouncing rhythm of the Mozart horn concerto. She tried to remind herself that she was the victim here, but each time her weeping lessened she would recollect her father's animal shudders, and her tears would gush anew.

It was nearly midnight before she recovered from the crying jag. Throwing off her clothes, she crawled between the monogrammed sheets of her mother's trousseau. Her throat and chest ached from prolonged gasping, her jaw-bone throbbed from her mother's harsh slaps.

Heretofore, although irritated by her mother's timid stance and breathy platitudes, she had loved her. She found the transformation almost impossible to accept – it was as though a pet white rabbit had monstrously expanded into a devouring snow leopard. She knows, Althea thought. Of course she knows, but she'd send a squadron of B-52 bombers to raze Beverly Hills if it would protect Daddy.

Althea wept herself to sleep.

She awoke to the sound of the door opening.

The corridor was pitch black, as was the room with its interlined curtains, and in this impenetrable darkness the creaking of solid brass hinges wrapped itself around Althea's neck, choking her.

'Daddy?' she whimpered in a thin gasp.

There was no reply.

The door closed. Was the intruder in the room?

'Daddy?' she whispered again.

Silence.

After what seemed an hour, she gathered the courage to reach for the switch of the bedside lamp.

The large familiar room with its ell of bookcases and bay window was empty.

The next time it was sunshine that awoke her.

M'liss was opening the flowered chintz curtains.

'Miss Gertrude said you were feeling peaky, so I brought up your breakfast.' The pink tray with its wicker stand rested on the other bed.

'I'm fine,' Althea lied. She felt stiff and sore, as if her body had been beaten with ping-pong paddles.

M'liss came over to the bed. The yellow-tinged old eyes peered worriedly down at her. 'You sure don't look so fine.'

Wondering about bruises or puffy eyes, Althea said, 'I had a touch of insomnia, that's all.'

'Mmm,' M'liss said, nodding her grey hair with its smart navy straw hat.

She was dressed in her good summer outfit for services at the African Methodist Episcopal Church on Adams Boulevard: going to church with other black people was the sum total of Melisse Tobinson's social life. She was the only black servant in Belvedere, and the others never invited her to accompany them on their days off, not because they scorned her colour but because Negroes did not venture into the churches, stores, restaurants and movie theatres of

232

Beverly Hills. There was no law against such excursions, nor even overt pressure, only the strangling discomfort of being totally unwanted. Althea, in her own loneliness, had recognized symptoms of the same disease in M'liss. After a tormenting day at Westlake she would head for M'liss's warm downstairs room. Once Althea outgrew the need for a nurse, M'liss had taken over Belvedere's sewing. The wrinkled brown fingers sped a needle while Althea used her crayons, the two of them companionably listening to soap operas on the small domed radio.

M'liss puffed Althea's pillows against the headboard, then set the tray in front of her – the *Los Angeles Times* and *Examiner* funny papers were tucked in a side basket.

Althea sat up cautiously. 'Did Mother say anything else about me?'

For a moment Althea caught a flicker of some viable unhappiness in M'liss's high-cheekboned, coffee-coloured face. 'Like what?' She began picking up clothes.

'Dear heart,' Althea said, 'no coyness necessary. She told you about the ban on Gerry, didn't she?'

'He's not your kind of people.'

Suddenly Althea remembered who it was that had been telephoning her parents. 'You're a wonderful friend, aren't you!'

'He's trash.'

'Even the servants around here are too tony for words!' Althea's tears threatened again, and she turned her head on the pillow, drawing a deep, shuddery breath to get control of herself.

M'liss laid a cool hand across Althea's forehead and throbbing cheek. She went into the bathroom, returning with the thermometer.

When the glass was under her tongue, Althea lay back. Red squiggles darted through her head, and an odd lassitude made her aching body feel heavy. Maybe she *was* coming down with something.

'A hundred and one,' M'liss pronounced, briskly shaking down the thermometer, then unpinning her hat.

'You'll be late,' Althea said.

233

'The church'll be there next week. Come on, eat some breakfast.' She set the footed tray over Althea, removing the china covers.

Althea looked with distaste at the crustless triangles of buttered toast, the still-steaming poached eggs. She hadn't eaten lunch or dinner the previous day, and this meal, too, repelled her.

When M'liss carried off the untouched tray, Althea lay flat on the bed. That scene with her parents had used up her defiance. She was woefully in need of some proof of continued parental affection – a warmly spoken 'Good morning' would do. Normally, during her infrequent illnesses, her father spent hours in her room, and her mother dropped by often with small gifts. Today they ignored her. *We don't want to see your face until you're ready to apologize.*

She longed to hear Gerry's voice, but she had no number for his new place.

Monday morning, Dr McIver called. The deep-voiced old gentleman listened through his stethoscope, held her wrist and took her temperature. Exchanging glances with M'liss, he intoned that the patient must remain in bed.

She couldn't stay in bed. Yesterday's lethargic sense of having survived a beating was gone, and she crackled with nervous energy. In her white silk pyjamas she paced around the room inventing scenes in which her parents repented, recanted, lifted their anathema on Gerry and scourged themselves for causing her illness. She was determined that *she* would never apologize – the thought of grovelling made her cry again.

She was frantic to see Gerry.

When, on Wednesday morning, M'liss informed her that she still had a hundred and one, it struck Althea as strange that she did not feel the least trace of those migratory cranial twinges that accompany a fever. She had never learned to read a thermometer. As soon as her onetime nurse left, she held it under her tongue for three full minutes by her clock, then went to the bathroom window, shifting the glass tube this way and that. She could see the mercury: it stopped at the red normal line.

She let the thermometer drop, and it shattered on the tiles.

She was showered and dressed when M'liss returned with the breakfast tray.

'Well, if it isn't the great jailer-spy herself,' Althea said. 'I know all about the phony temperature, the great intrigues with the doctor.'

'Honey, your parents didn't want you making the mistake of a lifetime. The reason I went along with them is they're right.' M'liss, who was seventy-three, lowered herself segmentally to her arthritic knees to gather the tiny shards of glass. 'You're a Coyne. You can't mess around with trash.'

'Words of social wisdom from faithful old Mammy.' Althea's voice broke a little; then she said, 'One valuable lesson I learned from this. Trust nobody.'

'You learned that years ago,' M'liss said. On her knees, she regarded Althea with sadness and understanding, then pushed stiffly to her feet. 'I care about you, honey.'

'You're still my friend, M'liss.' Althea sighed. 'I'm going to see him. Will they take it out on you?'

'You know better than that. The family's always been wonderful to me.'

The station wagon was in the garage, and nobody was around to stop her from driving it. Pedro, without demur, opened the wrought-iron gates.

Althea exceeded the legal speed limit to Sawtelle, squealing to a halt in the shade of the pepper tree. She ran up the cracked cement path to rap on the door. The rustle of Algerian ivy was her only answer. Loud, repetitive banging brought the same lack of response. She sat on the splintery step to await Gerry's return.

Across the street in a vacant lot, thin brown children played war, crawling along their adobe-soil foxholes to aim wooden sticks. 'Ksh, ksh! You're dead!' The shrill, exuberant cries of their mock battles halted at noon. There was a nearby taco stand, but Althea did not move to buy lunch.

It was after five when the old Ford pulled up behind the station wagon and a blonde got out, hefting a big grocery sack against her hip. With a raised, questioning eyebrow she swayed on very high-heeled sandals towards Althea.

Althea stood. Her legs and backside were numb and prickly. 'Hi,' she said. 'I'm looking for Gerry Horak. Know when he'll be back?'

The woman used her free hand to push back her bleached hair, which she wore in a Veronica Lake swoop over her left eye. 'Gerry?' she said. 'Gerry left.'

'Left? Where?'

'Who knows? He just got together his junk and took off.'

'No address, no nothing?'

'Gerry's hardly the type who gives out itineraries.'

Althea pressed both hands against her thighs. 'You sound like an old friend.'

'Gerry leaves a swath of us old friends behind him, doesn't he?' The woman's fuchsia-painted lips twisted in a cynical smile of comradeship. 'Here, take this a sec, will you.' She thrust her heavy brown paper bag into Althea's arms and searched through her purse. 'Key, key, where is that damn key?' Finding a jangling chain, she said, 'Eureka!'

'Is this your house?'

'In all its palatial splendours, yes.'

'I thought it belonged to a man.'

'My husband. He's overseas, ETO. Hopefully stuck there for a good long time without enough points to be released. To be honest, Gerry's more my type. A terrific guy, Gerry, if you don't mind the unreliability . . . Listen, you aren't mad he stayed here, are you?'

'Not I.' With a cool little smile, Althea set the bag down on the veranda. 'With him, that's how it is.'

'You said it, sister!' The woman laughed. 'Listen, if he should show up, any message?'

'None.'

'Sure?'

'Positive.'

'Not even your name?'

'Not even my name.'

The blonde shrugged. She stood on the porch, lighting a cigarette. As Althea got into the station wagon, she waved.

Althea started the engine. She was trapped inside her mind, which was working in a curiously unselective way.

It's one thing to talk sophisticatedly of a lover's previous flings, quite another to be faced with a bleached blonde who reeks of cheap lilac perfume and who tells you in chummy tones that he's concurrently been sleeping with her. Althea stepped down on the accelerator, digging down the quiet street. Fool, fool, fool, fool! How long, O Lord, how long would it take her to learn never to trust anything human?

Sweat broke out on her face and body, and suddenly it was imperative that she let Gerry Horak know exactly how unimportant to her he was, how little she cared about his stupid affair with the peroxide kid.

As she sped through a boulevard stop sign, she wondered how she would avoid accidents on the way to the institute.

30

Althea got there just before six, the witching hour when Henry Lissauer invariably crossed Rodeo Drive to Mama Weiss's restaurant for his early dinner so he could be home in time for the curfew. She pounded the knocker until the door opened.

'Miss Cunningham.' His mouth opened and closed uncertainly before his large face jelled into that ceremonious dignity. 'I was informed of an illness.'

'Rumours, rumours.' She smiled glitteringly. 'I have to talk to you.'

In a nervous, barring gesture he stepped athwart the threshold. 'I am on the way out.'

Althea eased by him into the hall. 'This won't take a sec,' she said.

'We can talk when the institute is open – '

'Mr Lissauer,' she interrupted with another too-bright smile. 'Gerry Horak has a ton of things at my place – paints, brushes, canvases. It's cluttering up the poolhouse. My parents are at me to get it cleaned up. He's moved again. What's his new number?'

At Gerry's name, Henry Lissauer's chin had braced back. 'I have no information about Mr Horak.'

'But you were friends, he lived here. You must have *some* way to get in touch with him.'

'We have not talked since I . . . hnn . . . had to request that he leave. He gave me no forwarding address.'

'Don't you understand? I must get his stuff back to him!'

'Miss Cunningham, I apologize, but I cannot help. Hnn, hnn . . . now, if you will excuse me.'

The Mozart rollicked through her head. 'You won't tell me because you're jealous of him!'

Henry Lissauer flinched. 'Miss Cunningham, I beg of you,' he said, his supplication heavily accented. 'You are upset. Please, please go home to your parents, they will know how to take care of . . . of what Mr Horak has left in your house.' His rimless spectacles enlarged his weepy look of anxious pity.

Oh, God, God, here was Althea Coyne Cunningham raising a ruckus and exposing the ultimate shame of being yet another in the long line of idiot females taken in by Gerry Horak.

She fled down the institute's three front steps. The door closed swiftly and a chain rattled.

In the station wagon she sat hunched over the steering wheel. She could not return to that gracious jail presided over by her tormentors – God, they'd have a big, knowing laugh about Gerry's defection. But where else could she go?

'Roy,' she said aloud.

The Waces' house on Crescent had never become the refuge to her that the garage apartment had been, and the wounds inflicted by Roy still festered unhealed, yet without a demurring consideration Althea drove the few blocks to the small stucco bungalow.

The door was answered by Roy, wearing shorts and an off-the-shoulder blouse.

Her large brown eyes widened, her mouth opened in flabbergasted surprise before stretching into a joyous, welcoming smile. 'I don't believe it!' she cried, turning to shout through the empty house to an open window, 'Everybody! You'll never guess who's here, Althea!' She gripped both Althea's flaccid hands, drawing her inside. 'Joshua and Marylin and BJ are over.'

'I was passing by,' said Althea.

'Hey, are you okay? You look sort of beat.'

NolaBee called from the yard, 'Bring Althea right on out.'

A triangular red brick incinerator barbecue had recently been erected in the small, overgrown yard, and Joshua Fernauld, swathed in aromatic smoke, clad in a check sports shirt and Bermudas, presided with a long fork over ripely brown chicken. BJ was rising to her feet – she too wore shorts, displaying her massive thighs. Marylin lay on a new redwood chaise longue, her loose dress showing a gentle mound of pregnancy.

NolaBee stubbed out her cigarette before hugging her guest.

'Well, Althea, I reckon you've been a stranger around here too long.'

BJ patted her shoulder. 'Long time no see,' she said.

And Marylin, smiling her lovely, luminous smile, shifted, as if she, too, would rise to embrace Althea.

'Now, Marylin,' said NolaBee, her eyes anxious. 'You know what all the doctor told you.'

'Listen to your mother. Stay put,' Joshua commanded his young wife before holding out his big hand to Althea. 'You're a sight for sore eyes.'

Their welcoming smiles of uncomplicated friendship befuddled Althea: she felt like a soldier behind foreign lines. 'I just dropped by,' she said. 'I better be going.'

NolaBee said, 'That's right silly. Call your house and tell them you're having supper with us. My son here' – she smiled archly at big, paunchy, grey-haired Joshua Fernauld – 'makes the grandest barbecue, and I've got my beaten biscuits ready to pop in the oven – I reckon you remember my biscuits? And there's – '

'No need for commercials, Mama,' Roy interrupted. 'Althea, you're staying and that's that.'

'Tell us about the art school,' said NolaBee. 'Roy says this Mr Lissauer takes only the top artists, and . . .' For a couple of minutes NolaBee vivaciously passed on her third-hand knowledge of the institute.

Althea's cool, forced smile did not falter.

Joshua Fernauld, watching her from the barbecue, said, 'Althea, girl, you look in need of a pick-me-up. Roy, sneak around your lady mother and give our friend here a medicinal snort of that Haig and Haig I brought last week.'

'Now, Joshua,' NolaBee said. 'I reckon you know the girls are too young to drink.'

'Oh, Aunt NolaBee,' BJ groaned. 'When are you going to get over being such a Carrie Nation? Believe me, college is where a girl learns how to hold her liquor.'

'Beej,' Joshua said, 'for that *you* don't need college. It's in the blood.'

Laughter and that damn Mozart! Althea escaped into the kitchen.

Roy followed her. 'Something's wrong, isn't it, Althea?' she said gently. 'Let me help?'

'Dear me, I must have fallen into a snake pit of good Samaritans.'

'No, simply the other side of the Big Two,' Roy said, patting Althea's arm.

At her touch, Althea's tears began flowing, irrepressible as on the previous night.

'Hey, Althea, hey,' Roy mumbled awkwardly. 'Come on in my room.'

The pink-and-blue children's wallpaper had been replaced by trim lines of yellow roses. Roy scooped up skirts and blouses draped over the chair and vanity stool – despite her love affair with clothes, she had not yet learned to treat them with respect. She went to get a roll of toilet paper, 'reasonable facsimile', as the Waces called it, to use as Kleenex.

Althea dabbed at her streaming eyes.

'Roy, Althea,' BJ bawled outside the window. 'Daddy says the chicken's ready.'

'Don't wait for us,' Roy called back. 'We're catching up. We'll be out in a bit.'

Althea gasped out, 'I keep hearing this music. A Mozart horn concerto . . . I don't even *like* the revered Wolfgang Amadeus. Roy, if only the music would stop . . . if only . . .'

Though Roy considered herself an entirely different person from when she had been one of the Big Two (she had become so utterly normal that she had signed up for the fall sorority rush week at UCLA), the claims of friendship never died within her. She could not bear to see Althea, who hid every sign of emotional stress, break down. Near to sympathetic tears herself, Roy tore off fresh lengths of toilet paper as she murmured soothingly. Finally she went to pour Joshua's Haig and Haig into a tumbler.

'Here, drink this.' She handed Althea the glass, conscious of similar scenes in various movies.

Althea's hand shook. A few drops of Scotch spilled, but she downed the rest, coughing amid her tears. 'That horn concerto,' she gasped. 'God, I hate it!'

The wacko remarks combined with the out-of-character, unconsolable tears convinced Roy she could not handle this on her own.

Outside, in the cooling twilight, Joshua sat at the foot of Marylin's chaise while NolaBee and BJ occupied the new redwood love seat. After the wrenching sobs in the bedroom, there was something almost excruciatingly normal about four people finishing up a barbecue supper with coffee ice cream – Joshua invariably brought along Marylin's favourite flavour.

As Roy stepped onto the patio, NolaBee said, 'There's breasts and drumsticks on back of the barbecue and biscuits in the oven – I reckon you and Althea had loads to tell each other.'

'Where is she?' Marylin's soft voice asked.

'She's really shook up about something.' Feeling as though she were betraying a confidence, Roy scarcely moved her lips. 'She just keeps crying.'

'Crying?' said BJ. 'That's not the Althea Cunningham *I* knew.'

'She's been at it since we went inside.'

NolaBee's head tilted. 'That long?'

'She looked deep in the slough of despond, at the bottom of foggy hollow, when she got here,' Joshua said, touching his lips to Marylin's cheek before he stood. (Roy had noted he seemed utterly incapable of keeping his kisses or his hands off Marylin.) 'I'll go check.'

'Now, Joshua, you just stay put,' said NolaBee. 'I reckon after all these years, the poor child'll feel more comfy with me.'

'My specialty, NolaBee, my area of competence,' he said. 'Working with actors or writers, you either get a bead on hysterics – or you quit.'

Roy trailed him to her room, where Althea slumped on the bed weeping.

'Althea,' said Joshua, a deep-chested rumble. 'Stop this.'

'I . . . can't . . .'

He pulled her up from the bed, shaking her. Her head wobbled from side to side, but the sobs continued, mechanical as a cracked record, so he held her against him. Behind her back, he used both hands to mime the dialling of a telephone. 'Her parents,' he mouthed.

Roy shook her head, whispering, 'She doesn't get along with them, they're oddball.'

'*Get them!*' His lips puffed out imperiously.

In less than fifteen minutes, headlights halted outside the house. Before the chauffeur could emerge from the limousine, Mr and Mrs Cunningham were hurrying up the path.

NolaBee waited at the open door. 'Come right on in,' she said. 'I reckon you're the Cunninghams. I'm NolaBee Wace. Roy and Joshua – my son-in-law, Joshua Fernauld – are in with Althea. The room at the end of the corridor.'

'Before we go in, dear,' said Mrs Cunningham, gripping her husband's arm, 'shouldn't we find out from Mrs Wace what the problem is?'

'We don't rightly know,' NolaBee said. 'She started to cry after she got here, and she just keeps crying.'

Mrs Cunningham's right eye twitched. 'My poor little

girl, that's not like her at all. Thank you so much for your kindness to her.'

Althea was crouched on the bed like a sphinx, her head bent between her arms, while Joshua, behind her, massaged her quaking shoulders. As her father came in, she raised up, holding out her arms.

He half-knelt to clasp her. 'Toots, Toots, it's all right.'

Mrs Cunningham had halted at the door. 'What is it, dearest?' she asked. 'What happened?'

'I . . . went to the institute.' Her gasps increased.

'Hush,' said Mr Cunningham. 'You'll tell us later.'

Between them, the Cunninghams supported their hysterical child out of the house. Althea's sobs had ceased when they reached the car.

After she got into bed, she rested her splotched and puffy face against the pillows and received her parents.

Her father said, 'You were gone so long, nearly all day. We've been crazy, Toots.' He perched on the end of the bed – he had pulled over one of the prettily upholstered slipper chairs for his wife. 'Where were you?'

Within Althea's brain prowled the intense pain of the peroxide blonde's disclosure. Someone else had to share the torment. 'It's too horrendous.'

'You can tell Daddy and Mommy,' said Mrs Cunningham.

'I drove down to the beach and sat on the palisades thinking,' Althea said tonelessly. 'Then I went over to the institute.'

'Why there?' asked Mr Cunningham. The beruffled bedside lamp cast an odd, divisive shadow across his narrow hawk's nose.

'I wanted to talk to Mr Lissauer about this idea I had for a seascape. He pretended to be really interested. He invited me inside to talk. Everybody had left, we were all alone. And then . . .' She shuddered.

'Go on, dearest,' said Mrs Cunningham.

'He started kissing me. He doesn't look it, but he's strong, so strong. He pushed me down on the floor – '

243

'That filthy refugee bastard!' Mr Cunningham jumped to his feet. 'We should never have let any of them in!'

'Did he . . . harm . . . you?' asked Mrs Cunningham, moving to kiss Althea's cheek.

'Not the way you mean, but I trusted and respected him – he was my *teacher*. It was so cruddy . . . so ugly . . . having to fight him like that. Somehow I managed to push him off and run to the car.' She gave a shudder. 'I felt dirty, ashamed – Oh, I don't know what I felt. I wasn't thinking at all. The Waces lived close, so I drove there.'

'My poor precious,' sighed Mrs Cunningham. 'And nothing more happened?'

'Isn't that enough?' Althea's eyes closed. The Mozart was fading, fading into inaudibility. 'Mommy, Daddy, will you stay with me until I go to sleep? . . .'

The Cunninghams sat on either side of the bed until Althea slept, then they moved to the upholstered window seat, Mr Cunningham fiercely clutching his wife's hand. There was no need for subterfuge or hiding their innermost secrets. They had an enemy that they could face and destroy together.

The following morning, two Beverly Hills police officers spent less than five minutes in the upstairs office of the Henry Lissauer Art Institute with its founder. They were waiting for him downstairs in the dusty hall when the sharp retort rang out. Students burst from the ell-shaped studio, watching while the two policemen shouldered down the locked door. The office with its awkward paintings reeked with the acrid odour of gunpowder. Smoke still hung in the air above a World War I Mauser that lay next to the body.

That particular day, 6 August, a bomb weighing four hundred pounds was dropped on Hiroshima, exploding with a destructive power greater than twenty thousand tons of TNT, brazing the sky over Japan with the light of a hundred suns. It goes without saying that this miracle bomb crowded the story of the art teacher's death from the news.

Althea, with her parents on the *Super Chief* speeding eastward for a recuperative stay at her grandmother's Newport 'cottage', Eastwind, did not hear of Henry Lissauer's suicide until three years later.

Book Four
1949

Best Actress Nominees: Jeanne Crain (Pinky); *Olivia de Havilland* (The Heiress); *Rain Fairburn* (Lost Lady); *Susan Hayward* (My Foolish Heart); *Deborah Kerr* (Edward, My Son); *Loretta Young* (Come to the Stable)
— Motion Picture Academy Awards, 1949

Former GI's have bought homes at record pace.
— Caption under aerial photograph of Levittown, Life, *31 March 1949*

The volcano that bubbles continually on Stromboli, the tiny, northernmost of the Lipari Islands in the Tyrrhenian Sea, is nothing compared to the lava of endlessly flowing gossip surrounding Ingrid Bergman and Roberto Rossellini. The latest rumor has it that Miss Bergman is expecting.

— KNX News Broadcast, 5 August 1949

Ingrid Bergman, who has been admired and respected in this country, has saddened and disappointed her legions of fans by her infamous behaviour. Our hearts go forth to her suffering husband, Dr Petter Lindstrom, and to her innocent daughter. It would be the gravest injustice to the moral standards of this great nation to permit this foreign national to return.

— speech read into Congressional Record *on 23 August 1949*

31

Marylin's alarm buzzed and she squashed down the gold button without opening her eyes. Luminous green hands would only tell what she already knew, that the ungodly hour was 5.35. Shooting would begin on the *Versailles* set at nine, and Marylin, scheduled for the first scene, must be at Magnum by seven on the dot for her elaborate transformation into an *ancien régime* glamour girl. (If it weren't for the powdered wig she would be wearing today she would have had to arrive an hour earlier for a stint with the hairdresser.) Joshua clutched his arms around her, planting a sleepy kiss on her lips. 'Angelpuss,' he muttered.

'Have to get up . . .'

'Adore you.' Tightening his grasp, he bussed her again; then his arms loosened, and he gave a shuddering snore.

Marylin, yawning, padded to the bathroom. Joshua's three Oscars gleamed on their shelf above the toilet – the one on the left he had accepted this year, 1949, for Best Original Screenplay, *Thus Be It Ever*. Shucking her nightgown, she adjusted the gold-plated faucets of the outsize shower that her predecessor had planned with the finicky, exacting care that showed in every detail of the Tudor-style house. It had never occurred to Marylin, raised by NolaBee – an exuberantly uninterested housewife – and lacking any sense of rivalry with Ann Fernauld, to make changes in wife number one's *chef d'oeuvre*. The decor as well as the household arrangements continued as before, with a business manager paying the bills and Percy and Coraleen holding the domestic reins in their capable brown hands.

Cold water sluiced over Marylin. She shivered, her mind clearing.

In her dressing room she selected a sheer summer blouse with a pretty red striped dirndl, calf-length in the New Look, thrusting her bare damp feet into red Capezio ballerina slippers, combing her long brown hair back into a ponytail. The mirrored walls reflected her, diminutively exquisite, remarkably unchanged from the huge-eyed girl who had reluctantly entered Beverly High as a freshman.

Billy must have been on the ready for her door to open. In cowboy hat and seersucker cowboy-imprinted pyjamas, he burst from his room. She knelt, kissing the warmly pulsing milk-scented neck as she lifted him.

'Whew! You weigh a ton. Soon you'll have to pick me up.'

'That's what you always say,' he said.

'It's true.'

'Yeah, when?'

'Already I can't make it down the stairs with you, can I?' She carried her son into his toy-lined room, putting on his bathrobe.

Billy had inherited her changeable aquamarine eyes. His small button of a nose had a hint of a bump, a possible indication that it would beak out luxuriantly like his father's. Other than these genetic endowments, Billy was Billy. A thin, wiry little boy with a narrow, humorous face and thick, curly blondish hair that threatened to turn brown.

While Marylin ate half a pink grapefruit centred with a maraschino cherry, rye toast, and overmilked coffee, Billy bounced around the breakfast room regaling her with a monologue about the new hamster that he and Joshua had bought at the Beverly Hills Pet Store. 'A rat, that's what Ross calls it,' he said, raising his eyebrows in quick, humorous scorn at his young Scottish nurse's ignorance. 'Hah, I told her! Rat!'

Marylin's sparkling eyes followed her son. Billy was her joy and delight, her compensation for marriage to an older husband who elicited her affection, her admiration, even

250

her passion, but never her love. For Marylin Fernauld, love eternally drifted with warm currents in a barnacle-encrusted TBM.

'Come on up to my room, you can hold him,' offered Billy magnanimously.

'Tonight.' From the three-car garage came the smooth throb of a well-tuned engine. Reluctantly she set down her napkin. 'There's Percy.'

'So what time'll you be home?' Billy demanded.

'Mmm, around six.'

'So late? You need a new contract.'

She burst out laughing. Joshua, in this precise belligerent disgust, would decry the velvet-lined jail cell that was her seven-year contract with Magnum. Her salary had reached its maximum of three-fifty a week, and more often than not Art Garrison refused to loan her out to Fox, Metro, Paramount, Warner's for twenty times that. She was bankable, which meant those cold-eyed New York financiers would melt when it came to lending Magnum the wherewithal to shoot a Rain Fairburn film. (Marylin, who was far from the only star thus contractually trapped, didn't really care: Joshua earned big bucks and her salary more than adequately supported the small house on Crescent, as well as putting Roy through UCLA.)

She and Billy went into the hazy morning, where she smothered his squirming, protesting face with good-bye kisses. He was waving his black cowboy hat as the big postwar Chrysler pulled away.

While Percy steered smoothly along Sunset towards Hollywood, she sat in the backseat murmuring her lines, occasionally halting to thumb through a small worn leather notebook for a self-written character note. Though everyone else recognized in Marylin that inexplicable and undefinable phenomenon, star quality, she herself didn't believe in it. She worked endlessly and hard on every role.

At the intersection of Fairfax, she glanced around. A small dark blue coupé was keeping pace in the next lane. In the mist she was unable to see the make of the car.

She returned to her script.

As Percy eased the car below the arched iron letters MAGNUM PICTURES, a dark coupé halted on Gower Street outside the gate. Was it the same car? The question fluttered momentarily; then she forgot it.

On the north side of the private road loomed two enormous new sound stages: both had been constructed with profits from Rain Fairburn movies.

Her most recent Christmas gift from her grateful employer was a refurbishment of her dressing room in the Stars' Building. In this lavish concoction of white silks and curved lucite, she sat with her hair smoothed flat to her head, costume protected by an enveloping cape, while Tippi, the crinkle-faced Danish makeup *artiste*, striped different shades of Pan-Cake over her face and throat. On the dressing table lay a small stack of slit envelopes. Her sacks of fan mail, opened by secretaries in the front office, for the most part were answered with a black-and-white glossy imprinted with the autograph 'Rain Fairburn', but these few had been delivered because their message was in some degree personal.

Marylin began reading: a request to appear at a benefit for St John's Hospital from a Beverly High alumnus whom she had known slightly; a letter from a man who introduced himself as her father's oldest and dearest friend, announcing he was coming to Los Angeles, and would she take off a day to show him around Magnum studio; a remote cousin soliciting funds for the Greenward Genealogical Society.

Tippi consulted a chart, measuring a precise triangle from Marylin's mouth, hairline and left nostril, affixing a black velvet beauty mark.

The fourth envelope was different.

It must have been brought to the studio, for it was unstamped and addressed in large block letters to 'Mrs Joshua Fernauld'. Few fans called her this.

Tippi began gluing on a furry streamer of lashes. Marylin closed her eyes as she drew forth the letter. Shaking it open, she read: 'Marylin, if you want to see me, I will be hanging around the front gate.'

No signature.

The paper slid from her limp fingers. Who needs a signature when the large, spiky handwriting is engraved on the heart?

'Marylin? . . . what's wrong? Marylin, are you all right?' Tippi's voice was the remote buzzing of an anxious mosquito. 'Gott! Rudy, she's conking out. How should I know why? Hurry! Get that idiot doctor . . .'

Marylin came to, coughing feebly. Ammoniac, vinegary odours burned her nostrils.

Her brain felt like cottonwool. She imagined herself in her own bed, waking up to the buzz of her alarm clock, and was bewildered by the studio doctor's black-rimmed glasses above her . . . Behind him were Magnum's top executives, the most worried expression belonging to the big boss, Art Garrison.

They're all here, she thought. She was lying on the white dressing-room couch, her constrictive corset loosened.

Turning away from the insistent odours, closing her eyes on Magnum's top brass, she allowed her disjointed thoughts to float. I passed out. The only other time I did that was at Beverly, when I heard Linc was missing. Linc? The letter . . . Linc's writing. How could that be? Linc's dead. Killed in action. The war's been over four years. He's dead. But the letter was in his handwriting, delivered to the front gate this morning.

Staccato masculine voices hammered at her ears.

'I'll be fine,' she whispered. 'Just leave me alone a bit.'

'She needs to rest,' said the doctor.

'Get the hell back to the stage!' roared Art Garrison's voice. 'Shoot around her!'

They filed out. Garrison's choleric face bent over the couch. 'Rest as long as you need,' he said. 'Take the morning off.'

Only Tippi and the doctor remained.

He took her pulse. 'It's steady,' he said. 'Drink a big glass of orange juice for your blood sugar. And don't try to do anything for the time being.'

The door closed on him.

'I'll get the orange juice,' said Tippi.

'And do me a favour? There's somebody out by the front gate.'

Tippi's left eyebrow went up, a studied inquiry.

Marylin said, 'Sign him in.'

'If you promise not to move from the couch,' the makeup woman replied.

As soon as she left, Marylin got dizzily to her feet, holding on to white upholstery to reach the light-bulb-surrounded mirror, wincing at what she saw. Restorative sponging had smeared her heavy makeup; the one false lash made the other eye look crazily bald. Tiny rhinestone buttons down the front of her bodice were undone, and her loosened corset jabbed into the disarray of elaborately seamed satin. She pulled off the eyelash, then dragged up her heavy skirts, attempting to refasten the corset, a task always performed by the wardrobe mistress because the hooks were at the back.

A little rap sounded.

Linc?

Satin slithered, and Marylin stood immobile.

It seemed to her that a rhythmic drumstick was beating on the white silk walls of the dressing room before she realized the sound was her heart beating in dreadful hope.

32

The near-invisible hairs rising on her arms, she opened the door.

By the drab light of the wainscoted hallway she saw a tall black-haired man wearing a crewneck sweater. As they peered at each other, his mouth pulled rigidly down on the left side.

Linc . . .

Her mind jigged back to those vivid erotic dreams. So she hadn't been a nut case after all, the irrevocable bond of love *had* endowed her body with more certain knowledge than the Navy Department.

254

Her eyes were tearing, and he was an iridescent blur.

Her instinct was to clutch him, to reassure herself of his corporeal reality. As if sensing this, he moved swiftly inside, limping stiffly as he crossed the velvety white carpet to stand by the open window. It was a few minutes before nine, when studio limousines gathered at the Stars' Building to deliver illustrious passengers to remote sound stages, and the purr of motors idling filled the dressing room as she and Linc continued gazing at each other.

In Marylin's convulsion of disbelief and happiness, her first coherent impression was of youth. He's young, she thought, young. When she had first met him he had been an 'older' man, an officer, vastly superior to her in every way including the chronological. For the past six years, though, she had been surrounded by Joshua and industry big shots, by her producers and directors, men with pouched bullying eyes and important sagging jowls. Linc looked so seductively, decently *young*.

The deep tan had faded, and his cheeks were tinted with the apricot quality seen often in portraits of Spanish grandees.

He gazed back at her with the same bemused disbelief, then shook his head as if to clear it.

'In this act,' he said, 'I guess I play Oedipus.'

At this, a fraction of the intoxicated bliss drained from her. She was, indeed, his stepmother. 'They told us you were killed in action,' she whispered. 'I didn't marry him until a long time later.'

'Of course it *had* to be Dad,' Linc said. 'He's the only real man in the Southern California area.'

Memory has a sanctifying effect, and she had forgotten Linc's flares of temper. Swallowing sharply, she took a step backwards. 'He liked me and I . . . well, who else would have been able to understand what I felt for you? What I still feel?'

'Yes, who else?'

Wretched at the pain in his eyes, Marylin sought for proof of her enduring love. Going to the desk for her blue pocketbook, she fished out the ring that she always kept with her. She extended it towards him. 'Your good-luck charm . . . ALF.'

'I guess the right person was wearing it,' he said in the same caustic voice, walking in that stiff gait to the dressing table, picking up the lucite frame to examine the photographs of Billy on either side. 'My brother, eh? As a kid I always wanted one. Of course he's a mite young to share a chummy bull session, but – '

Her small fingers clamped around heavy silver initials as her own indignation exploded. Linc, in his pain, could make cracks at her for marrying Joshua, he could curse Joshua, mock God himself. But he could not say one nastily intoned word about her Billy! Snatching the frame from his hand, she clasped it to her elaborate satin bosom. 'We've all grieved for you, mourned you,' she said in a shaking voice. 'Where were you skulking? Why didn't you come home?'

For a moment the gold flecks in his irises glinted too brightly; then he sat on the couch, right leg outstretched, hand at his forehead to shelter his eyes. An abrupt crumpling that wrenched her heart intolerably.

With a fluid movement, she crossed the room to kneel in front of the sofa. 'Linc, I didn't mean to blow up at you. I can't help myself when it comes to Billy. I care so very much. With you and him, it's like my skin is inside out.'

'Still?' he asked, not looking at her.

'Yes, still. After I heard you were missing, I thought I would die. Can you imagine what it was like? I was pregnant – '

He raised his head. 'Billy?' he asked with lamentable eagerness.

'No,' she sighed.

He sighed too. 'The timing's all wrong, isn't it?'

'I wanted to keep our baby more than anything in my life. But we were poor . . . Oh, I can excuse myself for the rest of my life. The simple truth is, Mama thought it was best, and I was weak, so horribly, horribly . . . weak.'

'Marylin, you're not weak, you're gentle. Don't cry.'

She dabbed at her eyes, depositing a brownish residue of Pan-Cake on the Kleenex.

'I've been in Detroit,' he said.

'Detroit? But what happened? When your plane went down, they reported no chutes opened.'

'They didn't see mine open, that's all. After the attack, those of us who were left started back together. We were all nearly out of gas, bucking a fourteen-knot headwind. The Zekes seemed to come out of noplace. My first warning was a spurt of tracers. The plane was already on fire, including the central cockpit. The escape hatch must have stuck, because Buzz and Dawdell never got out.' Linc spoke levelly, but the apricot colour had drained from his cheeks. 'I figured if the Zekes saw my chute open, they'd strafe me, so I didn't pull my ripcord right away. I don't know how far I fell, but I was terrified it was too far when I did pull. The chute opened, jerking me up, and I felt as if God were swinging me on a gigantic pendulum. I hit the water badly and broke my leg.'

'Who picked you up?'

'One of their destroyers, a day and a half later. Their medic set the bones. There was infection but he managed to save the leg – and me. He was no taller than you, Marylin, with thick shoulders and the damnedest bowed legs. They put me in the hold. He used to come down and glare at my leg, sucking in his breath. He wasn't an officer, so he couldn't have been a doctor. Maybe he'd been a medical student. I never found out – I couldn't speak Japanese, and he, of course, had no English. He did his best with me. I've often thought of him, hoped he's alive. God knows he saved my leg – and probably my life, it turned out. Now it's over, I'd like to write to him, maybe he could use some kind of help . . .'

She gripped his hand. 'Go on, Linc.'

'A few days after they picked me up, they fished out another American guy floating in his life jacket. He had third-degree burns over most of his body, and was coughing like mad. I never did find out what happened to his ship, but he was Dean Harz, a gunner's mate. The squatty little medic sucked in his breath a lot, and swabbed the burns. But in a few hours Harz was dead. Gasoline in his lungs. A lot of Navy guys died that way. I took his dogtags, figuring I'd return them to his family. The Japanese medic was watching. He took away *my* dogtags. And the next day he brought Harz's tattered uniform, washed, and made me change.'

'But . . . why did he do that?'

'He knew where I was going in the Philippines.'

'A prison camp?'

'You could call it that, yes. The Japanese never signed the Geneva Convention. It was against their code to be taken prisoner. The commandant of our camp was of the school that all prisoners were scum. And any officer so debased as to let himself be captured alive deserved the big treatment.'

'Oh, Linc.'

'Anyway, the medic had known about the camp commandant and had demoted me to enlisted man. I was Dean Harz. So all I got was a visit to the hot box, an occasional whipping, starvation, nothing really bad.'

'Darling,' she murmured.

'The seventh level of hell in glorious Technicolor. Beheadings, torture, the works. I wanted to bow out of the whole affair. Marylin, you're all that kept me going. "Island", remember? I would spend a whole day recreating a minute or two with you. What you had worn, what you had said, the way your eyes would turn greener when you smiled, the luminosity of your skin, every too-damn-beautiful part of you. Nothing overtly sexual, though. A small bowl of wormy rice with an occasional fish head a day does not nourish the libido. You were my refuge, my shield against the obscenities inflicted on us, the obscenities we perpetrated on ourselves. Contrary to popular literature, a prison camp does not bring out the admirable qualities of humanity.'

'Linc,' she said quietly. 'It's not in you to behave badly.'

He formed a sad, dark smile.

'I know you,' she said.

'Well, so let's put it this way. At least I never stole anyone's rations. That was the most heinous – and most tempting – crime. Towards the end I contracted typhoid. When our guys marched into the camp, I was completely out of it. I woke up in a nice clean bunk on the *Brady*, a hospital ship. I was, of course, Dean Harz. Good old Dean has no family, unless you count a cousin in Gary, who ignored his letter. There were magazines on the ship. Dean read them and caught up on the news of the late Lieutenant Fernauld's near and dear. Life is full of surprises.'

'Linc, we were told you were *dead*.'

'Look, I'm sorry I blew up before – seeing you hurt more than I expected. I didn't mean to sound so accusatory.' He looked towards the window. 'Mother . . . Did she die of cancer?'

'So then you knew she had it?'

Closing his eyes, he shook his head. 'No, but I should have guessed. She'd had one operation, and on those last leaves she seemed, well, frightened. I had my own fears, though, and we never did connect.'

'Linc, she was a lovely, lovely lady. When we met her, she had lost you, and knew she was going, too. Yet she took the effort to be gracious to us.' Marylin fished through her mind for family tidbits of solacing cheer. 'Did you know BJ's married?'

'Little Beej? Married?'

'His name is Maury Morrison and he's really nice. He's at USC law school on the GI.'

BJ's husband was Jewish. She, who had always been slippery if not secretive about her mother's religion, had been married by a rabbi beneath a flowered *chupa* in the Fernauld back garden, and from then on had become open about her maternal heritage, not in a bragging or defensive way, but as if she had turned an interior knob to adjust. The young Morrisons belonged to Temple Israel in Hollywood, and BJ occasionally peppered her conversation with the Yiddish phrases that her lapsed Catholic father had used for decades. Marylin, always considering BJ her best friend, had moved yet closer to the stout, good-natured, loud-voiced young Jewish housewife.

Linc was smiling. 'Well, hubba-hubba. When?'

259

'Two years ago. She dropped out of school. They've got this adorable baby, Annie, she's six months old. Billy's ready to bust, being an uncle. Annie's called after your mother, and she looks exactly like her. Linc, wait until you see her!'

Linc's hands clenched on his stiffened leg. 'Full fathoms five, A. Lincoln Fernauld lies, his bones of coral, pearls his eyes.'

'Linc, are you telling me that you aren't going to see *anybody*?'

'This one visit is my quota,' he said.

'Not even BJ and Annie? Or Joshua?'

He sighed and shook his head.

'If you had any idea how he grieved for – '

'Marylin, I never should have come today.'

'If it's just this once, why did you?'

'The flame asks that of the moth?' He pushed to his feet, gazing down as if he were memorizing her exquisite, over-made-up features.

The lavish decor of the dressing room melted away as she stared back at Linc. In his eyes she found the answer to why he had stayed away for these long years. He had not wanted to wreck the life she and Joshua had glued together. Even when he was at his most vulnerable, a starveling racked with typhoid, he had elected not to imperil them. Instead he had picked up the scattered pieces of another man's past.

'Darling,' she murmured.

His eyes were wet, and so were hers.

There was a discreet rap on wood. 'Marylin,' Tippi called. 'I've brought you the orange juice.'

Linc, without a farewell, opened the door, edging out as the makeup woman entered.

Marylin paid no attention to whatever it was that the Danish accent said. Her sweetly *triste* tears were as one with her humming joy.

He's alive, she thought.

33

The scene scheduled for the morning was shot in the afternoon. Under hot klieg lights, France's absolute monarch by divine right, Louis XV, for the first time meets his domain's most beautiful woman, who subjugates him with a smile and a flicker of her false eyelashes. Marylin played up to Tyrone Power (Louis) with such tender joyousness that the director called it a take and moved on to the next set-up. At home, Billy introduced her to his hamster, now christened Rat, and she rested her glowing cheek against the smooth flat pelt. A French film that Joshua wanted to see was screening at the Academy theatre. Afterwards in the lobby the Fernaulds ran into friends, and Marylin's soft, husky little laugh rang.

At home, after they had looked in on Billy's sleep, Joshua said, 'What gives, Marylin? Has good Saint Nicholas arrived early?'

He embraced her.

Her exultant euphoria dropped away. This was her reality, a husband whose substantial flesh smelled of suntan lotion, Chivas Regal, and not-unpleasant sweat. Joshua, father of three children: her beloved, her best friend and her son, whose woolly blankets she had just pulled up. Normally, the vital authority of Joshua's advances aroused her willy-nilly, but tonight his purposeful kisses were as unerotic as a row of Xs on the bottom of a postcard. She pulled away, moving into their room. Following, he reached for her again. 'Mmm?'

'Not tonight, I, uhh . . . Joshua, I had a little dizzy spell this morning.'

He pulled back, scrutinizing her. 'Dammit, why didn't you tell me? I'd never have let you go out tonight. Dizzy spell? What do you mean, dizzy spell?'

He'd hear about the faint sooner or later. 'I . . . well, I blacked out.'

Joshua's heavy face went ashen below its surface tan. The slightest ailment of his gorgeous angelpuss terrified him – hadn't he already lost one wife to catastrophic cellular multiplication? 'Blacked out? Jesus frigging Christ!'

'It happened during makeup. Low blood sugar, Doc Green said.'

'That quack, that horse's ass!'

'Don't get excited, Joshua. It was nothing.'

'That money-grubbing, prick-face Garrison!' Joshua's voice shook. His poker friendship with Garrison had evaporated under the Magnum insistence that Marylin be tied to every fine-print clause in that skinflint original contract. 'Are you telling me that the bastard kept right on with the shooting schedule *after* you fainted?'

'Joshua, I rested all morning.' Actressy syrup. 'It was the ballroom sequence, and they had two hundred extras on the payroll.'

'Goddamit, Marylin! Isn't it enough Magnum's got you at a pippy assistant director's salary? Do they have to squeeze the life's blood out of you, too? I'm calling Garrison this minute!'

'All I need is a good night's sleep – '

Joshua was already dialling. While she brushed her teeth, she could hear the rumbling voice laying down the law to Magnum's top dog.

He slammed into the bathroom. 'You're sleeping late tomorrow.'

'But the extras – '

'You're always in a hot sweat about other people's problems, Marylin. You're too nice, too damn considerate. Let Art Garrison worry about his own frigging costs. I'm here to watch over you. And you're staying home!'

When the lights were out, his forceful bluster ended, he kissed her cheek tenderly and rolled onto his own side of the big bed rather than making his usual invasion of her space.

On her back with her arms taut at her sides, she listened until her husband's breathing changed to measured gusts.

Then, turning onto her stomach, she swam in this morning's happenings, buffeted by alternating waves of grief that she and Linc must exist forever separated and that incredible rapture – *he's alive, alive*.

The curtains were showing a faint light when Billy tiptoed noisily into the room, crawling between her and Joshua. She put her arms around her son, burying her nose in his petal-soft cheek. They both drowsed.

Joshua commanded breakfast in bed for her before going forth to the brutal internecine warfare that was a studio story conference. When Billy returned from his thrice-weekly nursery school, he stamped his Keds in fury at his father's absence. Joshua stayed home because of Billy. Having given up directing entirely, he refused to write at the studio unless, as today, there was an urgent battle over a first draft. Indeed, he would desert his often-renovated typewriter in favour of excursions with the kid. He held Billy on his lap and let him kibbitz poker games – several of the card players also had layered families, but none was quite so bananas about his autumnal offspring as Joshua. The amused cronies encouraged Billy to smart-mouth them all. Billy was, as his old man often remarked with a doting smile, the archetypal Beverly Hills movie brat.

To assuage her little boy's disappointment, Marylin suggested a mother-son outing.

'Where?' he asked.

Marylin honestly considered it random chance when she replied, 'The apartment where I used to live.'

'And then Wil Wright's?' Billy demanded.

'Of course.'

She steered along quiet Charleville, blinking behind her dark glasses. How was it possible that these small houses with their tiny strips of greenery had once seemed to her as out of reach as an enclave of royal palaces? Outside the garage with its rickety staircase leading to a flat-roofed, illegal apartment, she stopped, leaning over to unlock the other door for Billy, who scrabbled out from the backseat, tugging down on his cowboy hat.

Not until she herself got out of the car did she see Linc,

his hands thrust into the pockets of his grey flannel slacks, his black hair stirring in the breeze. An aeon ago he had thus gazed at her in the early-morning gloom, and now her mind obliterated the rush of a gardener's hose, the smell of just-mowed grass, Billy. Once again an impecunious, unhappy Beverly High bobby-soxer and a taut-nerved Navy pilot were being drawn together as if by gravitational force.

Then she heard Billy shouting, 'Mommy, come on! I'm going upstairs.'

The railings had broad interstices through which a small child might easily tumble. 'Wait for me!' she yelled.

'Billy?' Linc asked quietly.

Her face grew hot, as though she had manoeuvred her little boy to an assignation. 'Who else?' she snapped. 'What are you doing here?'

He rapped on the hood of a dark blue Chevy coupé. 'I rented this.'

'Oh.'

'I had no idea you'd come too, Marylin,' he said very quietly.

'You were right, we can't see each other,' she said, wishing she didn't sound both feisty and shaken.

A convertible swerved onto Charleville. Billy, bouncing up and down impatiently, was on the sidewalk, but his movements zigged with swift unpredictability. She swooped on him.

Holding the squirming child tightly, she said, 'Billy, this is Mr . . . Mr Herz.'

'Harz,' Linc said. 'Hello, Billy.'

Billy said, 'Howdee, pardner.'

Linc made a swift gesture from his belt to point his index finger at Billy. 'Draw!'

Still in his mother's grip, Billy, too, aimed an imaginary pistol.

Linc staggered backwards, clutching at his chest. 'You got me.'

Billy laughed excitedly. 'My dad does just like that!'

Colour blotched Marylin's cheeks. She set the child down.

'Mr Harz, we're going up to where my mommy lived. Come on.'

Linc climbed the creaking steps with them. Billy reached for his hand.

'This is far enough,' Marylin said. 'We don't want to disturb anyone.'

Billy said, 'Oh, who cares about a dumb apartment? We've been here a hundred hundred times. Anyway, Coraleen and Percy's is a million million times better!'

At this mention of the faithful Fernauld family retainers, Linc's expression grew purposefully blank.

Billy pulled at his hand. 'Come along. Now we're going to Wil Wright's.'

Marylin turned to Linc. However tormenting the itch of being with both half-brothers, the thought of Linc getting in his rented car and driving off shrivelled her heart. Briefly she lifted her dark glasses to look at him with her naked eyes. 'Do.'

He followed them in his rented car to Wil Wright's.

There were no other customers in the red-and-white striped ice-cream parlour. They sat near the counter at one of the plate-size marble tabletops, Billy ordering a sundae for the delight of spooning hot fudge from his own individual pitcher, Linc a chocolate soda, and she a scoop of coffee flavour. Wil Wright's ice cream, buttery rich, clung to the roof of the palate, and Marylin, an ice-cream addict from way back, was forced to ration her visits – the camera exacts outlandish retribution for every ounce on a small woman. This was a rare treat, but with Linc sitting so close that she could feel the warmth emanating from his thigh, she let most of her scoop melt thickly into the footed metal dish.

Billy, bored from sitting with his silent, moony elders, raced energetically around the little tables and spindly wire chairs while the two short, full-faced waitresses – they were alike enough to be sisters – beamed indulgently, having already secured Marylin's autograph on red-and-white-striped paper napkins.

'My mother and Roy are away,' Marylin said without

265

premeditation. 'They live at 114 North Crescent. Tomorrow afternoon, I'm dropping over to see about the mail.'

'One-one-four?'

'The house next to Ralphs,' she murmured. 'I'll be there around two.'

34

She got there just after one.

NolaBee and Roy had departed on Monday for an automobile trip to Yosemite, leaving the front room bestrewn with proof of their last-minute changes in packing. Marylin scooped up her mother's things, which smelled faintly of tobacco smoke, carrying them to the front bedroom. Blushing, she made the double bed, changing the linen; then she returned to put away Roy's pale blue cashmere sweater and raglan-sleeved coat.

Around the vanity mirror where Roy had once tucked crazily posed snapshots of herself and Althea Cunningham were arranged group photographs of the Kappa Zetas. Roy's wholehearted, eager smile and short, resiliently curly hair jumped out from the conventional shoulder-length pageboys and primly curved lips. The Kappa Zeta house was relentlessly mediocre, and Marylin could never sort out the sorority sisters, although she had attended several 'Relative Teas' (suffering the oblique, condemning glances of curiosity) and also thrown Sunday barbecues for Roy's closer friends.

As she straightened the photograph of Roy in her mortarboard and graduation robe, Marylin heard the rap on the front door.

Her head lifted and she was momentarily incapable of movement; then, flushing deeply, she ran to answer.

Wordless, she and Linc embraced in the dim living room, straining their bodies close, a fiercely shared urgency to annihilate the years of separation, to forget the shroud over their future, to exist in this one instant that was theirs alone. With an inarticulate whimper, Marylin drew him towards NolaBee's room.

Here, beside the recently made bed, they again clung together, his hands moving downward to clasp the peach-shaped outlines of what the Industry described as a 'small but very fine ass'. Marylin was shaking and breathing unevenly, not only with desire but also with a complex longing to return to a mythical island inhabited by love, youth, unfettered joy. The drawn curtains did not quite meet, and a finger of sunlight drew a narrow line across their clinch.

That incandescent line touched their naked joined bodies, the far-off bells of the Good Humor truck sounded against their unhearing ears, and they rediscovered each other.

'Mine?' Linc asked, tracing the small mole near the hollow of her navel.

'You made it famous.'

His hand, no longer demanding, curved over the luminous flesh. 'Famous!' he asked. 'You've lost me.'

'Remember? It's in *Island*.'

'Oh, that. Never read it.'

She smiled.

'Marylin, I dashed off those stories and mailed them.'

'And since you got back, you haven't been able to locate a copy?' The same soft, disbelieving smile curved her lovely mouth. 'After all, you're never in a library.'

Linc, as Dean Harz, had become a librarian at Detroit's pillared main branch.

'I've been petrified to look.'

'You're what you wanted to be. A fine writer.'

'Writer? I wanted to best Dad, that's all.' He raised up on his elbow. 'You're an actress – I saw that the afternoon I barged in on you treading the dusty boards of dear old Beverly. You not only have the magic, you have the dedication. I have neither. I am not a writer. I, am, not, a, writer.'

'You only won the Pulitzer.'

'It's not all that unique for inspired youth to bring forth one novel. You'll see. There'll be a half-dozen by guys who were in the war, followed up by a mountain of – '

The telephone rang.

They both jumped guiltily. It's Joshua, Marylin thought in sudden irrational terror, although this afternoon her husband had taken Billy to the San Fernando Valley Stable, where the little boy would jog circles on his stout Shetland pony until both mount and rider were exhausted. Her voice quavered as she said, 'Probably for Roy – she's the popularity kid.'

But the jangling had shoved Joshua into the bed with them, and he remained there after the unanswered phone ceased to ring.

'I wish,' she said with a tremulous sigh, 'I wish Billy were yours.'

Linc kissed her ear. 'Offhand, I'd have said you wouldn't have changed a hair on that tough little head.' He paused. 'We'll have to find a place.'

'I'll drive myself to work and use the car at lunch. There's a motel on Sunset, the Lanai, about six blocks from the studio ...' She halted, aware she must be blushing.

'Dad's place?' There was a well-practised anger in the question: Linc's jealousy was a sturdy weed growing amid his filial ambivalences.

'We went there – It was after your mother died, Linc. Let's find someplace else.'

After a moment he said, 'I'll scout around.'

In the immediate vicinity of Magnum, there were no other motels with the Lanai's prime virtue, a stucco wall that hid day-rate fornicators from keen-eyed drivers. So the Lanai it was.

It had always been Marylin's habit to lunch in her trailer on the set, so she fabricated an excuse about medical treatments. The two rumours promulgated at Magnum were that she was seeing a shrink or getting boffed, and since she was famed as – *mirabile dictu* – a faithful wife, the shrink won hands down.

The high-voltage impatience of the industry men who surrounded her was absent in Linc. The war and prison camp, he said, had beaten the rat-race hurry out of him. If a difficult take kept her, she would find him waiting in the room (they always got number five), absorbed in one of those small paperback books that he carried with him everywhere. She realized in his unruffled presence how much she shrank from those harried, voraciously ambitious bigwigs, all of them so driven.

Marylin felt less guilt about her fall from grace than she would have imagined. By some mental sleight, she disconnected the anonymous motel room from her work, her family, from Joshua and Billy. She had returned to a past where she was her truest self, a quiet, lovely girl who wanted only the man she loved to love her.

Another surprising revelation was that adultery intensified her affection for Joshua. She had to bite back effervescent confidences to her husband: after all, wouldn't Joshua, Linc's father, be overjoyed to know the truth?

'I've booked reservations,' Linc said. 'My train leaves Union Station on June twenty-ninth.'

'The twenty-ninth? Linc, that's tomorrow!' She had just showered and, naked, was combing back her hair. Snatching up her towel, she covered herself as if he had introduced a stranger into the room. Linc, already dressed, lay on the bed watching her.

'There's something to remember,' he said with forced whimsicality. 'When you blush, your breasts turn the palest pink.'

'Do you have to get back? Are you worried about your job?' He had told her that he'd telephoned his immediate superior about a particular tenacious California virus.

'Haven't you noticed? I'm way out of my depth, and not treading water anymore.'

'I want to be with you all the time.'

'That's it, in a nutshell.'

Bending, she drew on a nylon. 'Linc,' she said, 'we could tell Joshua. He would understand – '

'Marylin, Marylin, if you think old Dad would welcome home the prodigal and pronounce his blessings over us, you are crazy.'

'He would be delirious you're alive and – '

'Sure he would. Unfortunately, alive, I covet what he has. He'd pull out all stops. You'd be shoved into one of those messes that ruin a career. No more Rain Fairburn.'

'I can live without her.'

'And Billy?'

'Joshua would give me Billy,' she whispered.

'In your married life, have you ever seen him offer his congratulations as the graceful loser?'

Would her husband sink to using their beloved little kid? He might, she thought, it's possible. He never sounds retreat. She sighed unhappily.

'So then we're agreed about the potential here for wrecking your life.' Linc's lips were an alarming white. 'We've managed without each other for enough years to know it's feasible.'

As she tucked her blouse into her full cotton skirt, she began to cry. Crossing the room, he put his arms loosely around her, and they swayed together like two orphans at their parents' graveside.

'Marylin, my sweet, gentle, beautiful Marylin.'

'You *really* think he'd be vicious about Billy?'

'I'm not trying to paint Dad as the heavy, but he does fight with every available weapon, doesn't he?'

'Yes,' she sighed.

He led her along the exterior pathway and down the concrete steps to her Chrysler. 'Good-bye Marylin,' he said, leaning on the open window. 'Good-bye, love.'

She notified the studio that she was ill, and drove home with her handkerchief gripped to the steering wheel.

She went directly to bed. Joshua was out somewhere with Billy. When he returned, he called the internist.

The doctor, connecting her malaise with the fainting spell, diagnosed a virus.

She lay in bed the next three days, forcibly kept there by a worried Joshua, surrounded by a funereal trove of flowers – American Beauties from the *Versailles* crew, white cymbidium from Art Garrison, an enormous mixed basket from her agent Leland Hayward.

She was back on the set Friday, five pounds thinner (a fortune in period costumes had to be taken in), depressed and silent except when the cameras were on her.

Shooting ended in mid-July. Joshua rented a sprawling furnished house in Malibu and the Fernauld household moved there.

Marylin spent her days on the sand under the yellow-and-white umbrella, protected by a large-brimmed straw hat and a loose ankle-length beach coat – the sun's rays are anathema to a screen actress, whose pigmentation must retain the pristine pallor that embraces Max Factor Pan-Cake.

Joshua, sleek as a brown bull seal under his Coppertone, would sprawl on the hot sand beside her. Sometimes she caught him examining her with a curious, waiting expression that she could not fathom.

'What is it, Joshua?' she would ask, quelling her guilty tremor.

'I'm here with one of the most gorgeous broads in the long history of the planet earth, and being neither a fool nor blind, I enjoy looking at her, that's what. I'm goddamn happy, that's what.'

Other than his occasional piercing glances, her husband was himself. In his deep rumbling voice, he amused her, wooed her, bossed her, and protected her from intrusions of every sort. In the foamy white curls left by the breakers, he frolicked with Billy.

The hot, quiet days with her child soothed Marylin's wounds until she returned to that quiescent state of half-life that she had hitherto accepted as marriage. At night, between sheets that smelled of faint must and the sea, she succumbed to Joshua, her mind and body aching for a less-domineering lover.

* * *

271

In October *Versailles* was scored, edited. The studio fired its big guns of publicity, sending Tyrone Power and Marylin on separate but equal junkets. Detroit was the third city on the Rain Fairburn tour.

35

A threatened thunderstorm delayed take-offs in Chicago, and the flight with Marylin, her fifty-two overweight pounds of baggage, three fellow veterans of *Versailles* and Cabbie Frick, Magnum's head publicist, arrived in Detroit two hours late. As the plane taxied along the runway, a long dark Cadillac drove onto the field, and the stewardesses held back the other passengers until Marylin and Cabbie – he carrying her hatbox – had dashed through the gritty gale from the still-rotating propellers to the limousine. She arrived at a tall-towered radio station for the end of the six o'clock news. A dispatch about unrest along the Sino-Korean border was cancelled in order that Rain Fairburn might breathe a few words of delight about her latest film. She was sped to the Book-Cadillac Hotel, where in her eighth-floor suite the local Magnum man was affably hosting a press party. Marylin excused herself to the eight men and three women, going to the toilet before smiling for photographs and parrying unctuously personal questions about herself, her career, her husband, her child, until seven, when she had to dress for the local première.

There wasn't a moment to call Dean Harz.

Cabbie Frick carried along the near-empty plate of soggy hors d'oeuvres, feeding her the unappetizing morsels in the elevator – she couldn't risk getting grease on her elbow-length white kid gloves.

In the lobby a group of dignitaries headed by Mayor Smith welcomed her on behalf of the city and, stomach rumbling, she joined a motorcade for the few blocks to the

272

Fox Theatre on Woodward Avenue, where searchlights probed fingers into the cloudy black sky.

As the limousine pulled up, an excited blare rose from the crowd: '*Rain Fairburn, Rain Fairburn*'. Police linked arms to hold back the surging fans. '*Rain Fairburn!*'

Two rows of loges had been roped off for Detroit's top municipal officials and the Hollywood visiting fire-men.

During the newsreel, Marylin excused herself, climbing over knees and feet, leaving a trail of thrills at being touched by a real live Chanel-scented movie star. In the empty lobby she closed the door of a neo-Hindu phone booth, inserting her nickel with trembling fingers.

The phone was answered on the first ring. 'Jeanne de Pompadour, I presume?' Linc said.

Joy, sudden and sharp, filled her. 'I've been frantic you wouldn't be there.'

'Are you kidding?'

'Then you'll come to the Book-Cadillac?'

'Whenever you say.'

'About eleven. I told them at the reception desk I might have a visit from an old friend.'

'You will,' he said. 'See you then.'

'Linc, don't hang up!' she cried urgently. 'When you get to the suite, ring room service and order a salad, two lamb chops and a baked potato . . . and, oh, some ice cream. I've only had two stale hors d'oeuvres since breakfast – and breakfast was a tough old doughnut at a Chicago radio station.'

'Oh, for the glamorous life of a movie star.'

She returned, beaming, to her seat.

'Linc,' she murmured, 'are there any vacation places around here, you know, like up at Lake Arrowhead, where we could rent a cabin?'

He kissed her naked shoulder – they lay entwined in one of the double beds. 'Michigan's famed for its woods, and I know of the very cabin. But stop me if I'm wrong. Aren't you in the midst of a ballyhoo?'

'What about it?' In the darkness her soft voice rose, defensive.

'Since when have you been the kick-loose type?'

'Since right now,' she said.

Kissing her shoulder again, he made a sound of disbelief in his throat.

'It's the truth. Linc, if you only knew how sick to death I am of being responsible for things I personally don't give two hoots about!' Her words bubbled swiftly in concepts hitherto unvoiced, out of shame that she was spitting on what everyone considered the glittering prizes. 'My life's always belonged to other people. First Mama worked and slaved so I could have this career – and she still spends most of her time thinking about advancing me. I'm not complaining, Linc, but it's a burden, such a heavy burden, to carry another person's dream. Then there's Joshua. He pushes me ahead too.'

'That's something I've often wondered about. The Big Joshua I knew would never have allowed his wife a career.'

'I think in his mind, the busier I am, the more likely I am to be happy with him.'

'The devil finds work for idle hands, mmm?'

'I don't mean to sound rotten . . .'

'But there's a ring of truth in your theory.'

'At Magnum, you know what they call me? A thorough professional. By that they don't mean whether or not I can act. They mean I show up as ordered at the crack of dawn for makeup, that I bleach or dye my hair on request, lose or gain weight, go on crazy locations, accept every script, every director, and hop like a Mexican jumping bean across the country doing publicity. Well, for once I'm doing what pleases me.' She twined her arms around his neck, pressing her naked breasts against his chest. 'For three days out of a lifetime I'm going to forget what everybody wants of me and do exactly what I want.'

'And that's disappear?'

'Sink completely from sight.'

But in the end Marylin's aversion to inflicting hurt prevailed, and she dispatched a telegram to North Hillcrest

Road: 'AM AT THE END OF MY TETHER STOP TAKING OFF A COUPLE OF DAYS STOP LOVE MARYLIN.' She scribbled a note to the rangy publicist, Cabbie Frick, promising in hasty writing to catch up with the group in Baltimore.

She propped the hotel stationery on the desk. As she and Linc went out the door, the draught blew her message under the flounced skirt of the dressing table.

Sitting on the rustic bentwood chairs, sheltered by the narrow porch, Marylin and Linc watched the curtain of rain advance above the mottled purple waves on the lake.

She wore thick, fuzzy socks and a heavy red-and-black lumber jacket bought two mornings earlier when they had halted to stock up on food at an old-fashioned country store – the shrivelled septuagenarian shopkeeper called her 'missus' without a blink of recognition. This one-room log-cabin with the grey-stone chimney, the only structure in this inlet of virgin forest, belonged to Linc, who had bought it with Dean Harz's back pay.

The sky split in a dart of lightning. Marylin held her breath, and almost immediately the thunder roared. Huge drops slashed down so hard that the cove bubbled like a boiling cauldron.

'It's awesome, isn't it?' she said. 'Not exactly frightening, but . . .'

'But you come from the city, where nature's tame in tooth and claw.'

'Exactly.'

Another bolt of lightning struck yet closer, and she jumped. Linc reached for her mittened hand. They held hands on the porch until the thunder receded and the curtain of rain came down more softly; then they went inside.

Brick-and-board shelves were filled with books, and in the stone hearth, pine logs crackled. Linc held a spill of fire to the butane stove, scrambling eggs and frying bacon. Watching him go about his homely tasks, Marylin tried to recall the raw-nerved edgy young pilot she had fallen in love with, and though she found faint echoes of him each time

Linc's mouth formed the one-sided smile at her, that abrasiveness was gone. Linc was an exceedingly attractive, quietly literate, compassionate man – he was the one gift that her girlhood self had requested of life.

He tore off a corner of toast made over the fire. 'What beats me,' he said, 'is how we knew *then* that we were right together.'

She nodded thoughtfully.

By the time they had finished the dishes, the rain had let up. Arms circling each other's waists, they crunched through fallen leaves and wet pine needles, the great drops that gathered on twigs sometimes plopping onto their bare heads.

Marylin took a breath of clean-washed air. 'I'm going to tell Joshua,' she said.

Linc's arm tightened on her. 'Oh?'

'These couple of days have convinced me that the worst mistake we can make is not being together.'

'The ramifications still exist.'

'Linc, he'll be fair about Billy.'

'Why? Will the great echo chamber of God's voice convince him to be St Joshua the Just?'

'Must you always be clever when you talk about him?'

'It was a pretty sad attempt, wasn't it?' He released her, walking around a mossy fallen tree in silence. 'Marylin, listen, some things about me maybe you don't realize. First of all, I'm never going to be the great American novelist. I don't have the least desire to write. Working among books suits me to a tee. I like my job, even though it's unremunerative. I'm not in the least ambitious anymore – possibly the delightful vacation I spent in the Philippines stunted me. Or then again, maybe I was never red-hot fired-up except when it came to showing Dad. I could never make it big in the Beverly Hills fast-step.'

'It's never been important for me, either.'

'Face it, Marylin, you're a top-rank star.'

'I told you, Linc, always for somebody else, never me.'

'I have planned how the two of us would confront Dad,' he said quietly. 'And every time I do, I think of that mess with Ingrid Bergman.'

276

The affair of the Swedish star with Roberto Rossellini, her director in the film being shot on Stromboli, the remote, tiny, barren island in the Tyrrhenian Sea, had resounded throughout the western world. On the confirmation of Ingrid Bergman's adulterous pregnancy, censure was read into the *Congressional Record*. The actress's Hollywood career was completely kaput and her eleven-year-old daughter lost to her.

'Poor Ingrid,' Marylin sighed. Magnum had borrowed Bergman to play with Marylin in *Northern Lights*. 'Joshua won't let me go easily, I agree. But before he'd put me through *that*, he'd give me a divorce. And besides, Linc, he loves you. The ambivalences between the two of you are even worse for him than you – he thinks you're dead, he despises himself for every argument you and he ever had.'

Linc's logger's boots splashed through a mulchy swamp of fallen leaves. 'God, how I've missed him,' he said in a low, strangled voice.

'Then you'll come back to Beverly Hills with me?'

His words burst out loudly: 'I'm sick to my soul of always skulking with you.'

When she telephoned the junket in Cincinnati, Cabbie Frick, who was being held responsible for her leap from the publicity trail, informed her with obvious satisfaction that Magnum had put her on suspension.

'I wrote you a letter,' she said.

'With what? Invisible ink?' The words hissed venomously through the speaker. 'I never got any letter.'

36

After Linc paid the cabdriver, he hefted the Navy-issue duffel bag stencilled 'Dean Harz, Seaman First Class' on one shoulder and blinked fixedly at the house. Early-morning sunlight glinted on the open window of the powder room.

Marylin, bedraggled after a day and night in airports, in a wreck about the coming confrontation, understood that Linc, in this belated homecoming, must not only be caught up in this same web but also be assailed by dredgings from his earliest boyhood, memories of his dead mother, his living father. She took his free arm. She had no luggage – her new heavy clothing had been left in Linc's cabin, and the justifiably vengeful Cabbie Frick had abandoned her great mound of tour suitcases in Detroit.

'Funny,' Linc said bemusedly. 'The place seems bigger *and* smaller than I remember.'

With a sympathetic squeeze she let go of his arm to extricate her key chain. Just then the door burst open and Billy hurled himself at her.

Lifting her son, she kissed his cheeks and forehead.

Then she looked at the front door. Veiled in the hall's shadows stood Joshua, as strong and thick and as immobile as a Rodin bronze. Across the threshold it was impossible to make out his expression. The morning quiet was broken by the squabbling of two blue jays.

'Linc?' Joshua said hoarsely.

'Dad . . .'

Joshua took an unsteady step forward, halting to lean heavily on the hall table as if to prevent himself from falling.

The duffel thudded down. Linc moved swiftly up the steps.

Father and son embraced in a masculine bear hug.

Joshua pulled back, staring at his resurrected firstborn. 'Linc?'

Linc made an inarticulate noise. He was weeping.

'What's Mr Harz doing here?' Billy asked.

'Mr Harz is . . . Daddy's son. He's really Linc . . . you know Linc.' Photographs of Linc as a boy and in his officer's peaked cap smiled from silver frames on the living-room grand piano and on Joshua's writing desk.

Joshua, too, was weeping. Seeing them in this emotional embrace, Marylin was struck by the genetic affinities of father and son, the bumpy, dominant nose, the thick, black brows, the very dark, wet eyes. Their revealed emotions made Joshua look older, and Linc – dishevelled by travel – younger.

'This is the damnedest, the damnedest,' sputtered Joshua, for once at a loss for words. 'I don't believe it. They said you were dead.'

'The reports were only slightly exaggerated. I was in a Japanese camp.'

'A prisoner?'

'They picked me up and took me to the Philippines.'

'But the war ended years ago.'

'I was sick and then . . . well, reasons, reasons.'

Joshua blew his nose loudly. 'So where the hell have you been hiding?'

'Detroit.'

'Detroit?' Joshua turned to Marylin. For a few seconds his moist, piercing gaze settled on her. She summoned her craft, putting on an expression of noncommittal blandness. If only she weren't standing in the doorway with the morning sun full on her.

Joshua blinked, giving an infinitesimal nod as if a mental cog had slipped into place.

'What the hell are we doing standing here?' he boomed. 'Come on in, Linc, no, don't worry with that damn thing, Percy'll get it. *Percy! Coraleen!*' he bawled. 'Come out here prepared for the surprise of your frigging lives!'

There ensued a swirl of hugs, tears, blown noses, trills of joyous disbelief, a triumphant confusion that Joshua blusteringly led, and it wasn't until Ross, Billy's Scottish nurse, her pleasant smile firm, drove her charge off to nursery school that Joshua permitted the emotional volcano to cool off. The servants retired to fix a second breakfast.

Marylin went upstairs. A shower and change of clothing did nothing to alleviate her weariness – or her taut-nerved apprehension. Joshua's stumbling and tears of joy, his clutching embrace, had been instinctive, the real thing, unequivocal emotional honesty, but after that there had been a subtle shift. His joy at the miracle of Linc's return was balanced by her three days spent incommunicado, a

279

disappearance speculated about on the front page of every paper she had glimpsed at the airport news stands.

When she returned downstairs, father and son were in the breakfast room drinking Bloody Marys, engrossed in conversation. Quietly she took her place opposite Joshua.

'Billy's taken over your old room,' her husband was saying. 'The kid's the one big change around here. Linc, your mother did a job on this house, a damn good job, and Marylin liked it too. We've left things as they were.' He refilled his glass, adding a jolt more vodka to Linc's drink in spite of Linc's negative wave. 'But enough of us. Tell me about that goddamn limp. Not that it's a big deal, you could still beat me at tennis – '

'Did I ever?'

'Who remembers? Let's hear how you came by the fucker.'

Linc explained about his TBM being shot out from under him, his rescue and the Japanese medic. When talking to his father, Marylin noted, he fell into an atypical loud archness. And Joshua became a caricature of himself, benevolent yet boomingly profane. The masculine rivalry between the reunited pair tangled deep into the roots of their obvious love.

Percy set out platters of smoked salmon and whitefish, of crimson corned beef and warm pastrami – fatted calf, Beverly Hills style. Afterwards he lugged in Ann Fernauld's heavy Georgian tea set, which was removed from its place on the sideboard only on state occasions, while Coraleen bore in a richly fragrant offering from her own hands, small caramelized coffee cakes that had been kneaded and baked within the hour. 'I remembered how crazy you were about these, Linc.'

Joshua speared a pecan-rich pastry onto Linc's plate. 'Jesus H. Christ, can you believe it, can any of you believe it? It's as if all the mystic Catholic bullshit my mother believed in has come to pass – *Kyrie eleison, Gloria in excelsis deo!* My son returned unto me.' This was as close as he had come to mentioning Linc's prolonged absence. He had drunk and eaten heavily, as if fuelling his fevered pleasure.

(Marylin, like Linc, had eaten practically nothing.) 'And by God, you've beaten me at my own game, won yourself the Pulitzer.'

'How long do you figure it would take a roomful of monkeys to type *Hamlet*?'

'None of that modesty crap. Linc, work like *Island* is never accidental. Don't tell me, I know.' He faked a punch in the direction of Linc's jaw. The servants left, and Joshua continued in the same unrestrained, endlessly voluble strain.

The evasions boomed unbearable against Marylin's ears. 'Joshua, did you get my telegram?' she asked quietly. 'Let me explain – '

'Sure I got the wire,' Joshua interrupted with a stagy chortle. 'Believe you me, flying the coop like that was a stroke of genius! It's about time you showed a little temperament. Angelpuss, haven't I told you over and over that you let those bastards work your ass too hard? You're always too damn willing to please, so naturally they take you for granted. Well, this has set Art Garrison back on his heels. We aren't friends anymore, but I say this without spite or malice. The dwarf's a roaring little bully. It's time he had another think about you. Suspension, hell! The squeaky wheel gets greased. Shouldn't be surprised if Leland won't get him to tear up the old slave contract and write you a new one. Hell, you're a star. Let 'em pay you like one.'

'Last June,' Linc said, 'I went to see Marylin at the stu – '

Joshua jumped to his feet. 'Great God!' He slapped his forehead. 'We've forgotten Beej! She doesn't know! Linc, she'll kill me. Beej's married, Mrs Maury Morrison. Maury's the sweetest guy, in his last year of law school. Those two stinkers, they've made an old granddad out of me. Wait until you get a load of the infant – Annie's the spit of your mother.'

He crossed the hall to the den, from whence they could hear him announcing to BJ that her older brother was alive, yes, dammit, alive.

Linc pushed away his coffee cup. There was a new

vertical line between his eyebrows. 'I didn't think I'd feel so much, seeing Dad,' he said. 'Love and the whole bag.'

'We have to tell him when he gets back.'

'He knows, Marylin, he knows. Poor old Dad, he hasn't changed one iota. He's going to bull his way through.'

'*Linc!*' Joshua roared from the hall telephone. 'Come say hello to your sister. The brat's convinced I've slipped my tether.'

The house filled quickly. First came BJ and her husband, Maury, sandy-haired and tall, with Annie, who though teething and drooly, did remarkably resemble her maternal grandmother. A brace of Linc's wealthy Cotter cousins. BJ's in-laws. Y. Frank Freeman, big boss at Paramount. Leland Hayward, Humphrey Bogart and a swarm of Joshua's other friends.

Joshua forced celebratory drinks on everyone, and loud laughter spilled through the big den and sunroom onto the brightness of the pool deck. Trimly uniformed cateresses from Haenchen Haynes began passing hot hors d'oeuvres while the extended dining table was being set up as a buffet. Though Marylin had become accustomed to these lavish impromptu gatherings, her weary mind kept shifting back and forth between the present and that long-ago Beverly Hills wake. She forced herself into the role of hostess.

BJ, Maury and Joshua stayed close to Linc. Women fell on him, reddening his cheeks with lipstick, men clapped his shoulders. Marylin heard endless congratulations on the Pulitzer for *Island*. She heard eerily few probes into his delayed postwar return home – it was almost as if the force of Joshua's will were silencing such questions.

This was the first time Marylin had viewed Linc in the Beverly Hills surroundings that were his birthright. He was at the same time more charming and more brittle, his face showing tension and a light gloss of sweat.

Billy veered around the adults, constantly darting back to squander his supply of riddles on his newfound brother – not a mere kid like everybody else's brother, but a regular grown-up.

The crowd grew.

Finally, around five, right after Roy and NolaBee arrived, Marylin felt she would quite literally expire if she remained another minute in this high-decibel mob scene. Without excusing herself, she escaped up the curving staircase, kicking off her high-heeled pumps to stretch fully clothed on the elaborately quilted, raw-silk bedspread.

She slept heavily.

The sound of the door opening awoke her. It was dark outside, but otherwise she had no sense whatsoever of the time. The sounds of revelry continued unabated. Joshua fumbled for the light, closing the door, moving unsteadily towards their bed.

'Took a nap,' she murmured.

The bed springs bounced her as he sprawled heavily on the mattress next to her. He brought into the cool room the smell of expensive cigars, liquor, overspiced food.

'My angelpuss,' he muttered.

Reaching both arms around her, he roughly pressed one heavy leg between hers. Then he was pulling up her skirt, which sleep had rucked. For a moment she was too startled to realize his intention.

'No,' she said, sharp.

'Yes, I say goddamn Yes.' His words were slurred, but his movements were iron-strong. He yanked roughly at her silk panties.

'Stop!' she cried.

But she was a tiny woman and his muscles were thick and strong from tennis and swimming daily laps.

Marylin, struggling, could not believe in Joshua's metamorphosis. Never, even when totally swacko, had he forced himself on her. She hit at his face.

With a grunt, he rammed his knee upward into her crotch.

The agony blinded her.

For a moment she saw nothing but darting white lights; then his face came back into focus. The big features were loose, animal. He lurched his body onto hers.

'No,' she whimpered. 'No.'

But a hot, sweaty, implacable two hundred and fifty pounds crushed down.

As Joshua forced entry into that terrible ache he had just inflicted, she screamed, and her scream became part of the hubbub. I hate you, I hate you: the thought seared her brain with each thrust.

He fell away from her. 'You're mine.' His slurring voice came from deep within his barrel chest. 'Gonna stay mine.'

'I love Linc . . . you've known that always.'

He pushed from her, hoisting himself off the bed, staggering to the dresser. Small objects clinked and thudded as he emptied out her purse. He held up a gleaming object that through her teary blur she recognized as Linc's ring.

'See this? Take a last look, for we are about to bury it in the ocean deep, where it belongs.'

He stumbled into the bathroom. She heard a splash, and then the toilet flushed.

Returning to the room, he teetered over the bed. 'Mine,' he sobbed, and toppled down. Almost immediately, snores burst from him.

She sat on the edge of the bed gathering strength to move. She loathed Joshua with all her wounded, violated body, all her enfeebled, spinning brain. Her one thought was to escape her husband's house.

37

Roy sat on the stairs balancing a plate of beef Stroganoff and endive salad; on the step below her were the half-empty dishes that BJ and Maury had deposited a minute ago when Willie Wyler had called them to come have one of those new instant Polaroid snapshots taken with Linc.

Sitting like this, her full, cerise striped skirt draped around her, her soft pink wool blouse tucked into the cinched waistband, her makeup purposefully light, her brown curls cropped in a stylish new poodle cut, Roy was charming. If there had not been the inevitable comparisons with Marylin's ethereal loveliness, people would have called her a looker. As it was, she dwelt eternally in the shade. She considered herself plain, untalented and, God knows, no brain.

Years ago, when she had told Althea Cunningham that she wanted to be ordinary, she had meant it with her whole heart, and since then the ordinary had become her hazy, unattainable *fata morgana*. To Roy, her KayZee sorority sisters possessed the glamour of unflappable normality, so she had bent every effort towards becoming like the others. But she never could suppress herself. Enthusiasm, like her brown curls, burst out all over the place. This inability to fit into the pillared chapter house she attributed not to any lack of the sorority, but to her own unworthiness.

Unlike the majority of her House, she had not trapped herself a returned veteran, but on graduation last January, she had landed a good job. If one stretched it, one could call it a career. Mr and Mrs Fineman, who owned Patricia's, a tiny women's specialty shop on South Beverly Drive, had hired her to do the books and help out the secretary. Patricia's clientele were the wealthiest women in Beverly Hills, and they expected skilled advice about their fashion dilemmas. After two months, the Finemans had allowed Roy to wait on a few of these exacting ladies. She discovered a flair for putting together Dior's New Look on young second wives. The Finemans, who liked her, had rewarded her with two raises.

Slight reverberations warned Roy that somebody was descending the stairs, and she pushed BJ and Maury's plates out of the way before turning to see it was her sister.

'Oh, Marylin. So you're up,' Roy said cheerfully. Then she noted that the pale cream lounging pyjamas were buttoned wrong. Marylin always looked as if she had stepped from the proverbial bandbox, so this was no minor aberration.

Roy felt the weight of protective anxiety slip over her. 'Marylin, honey, what is it?' she asked, getting to her feet.

'Where's Linc?'

Roy, arriving just before Marylin had gone up for a rest, had seen her sister and Linc exchange a tender glance across the crowded den. The situation, in all its romantic glamour, was as explosive as an A-bomb. Roy nervously avoided it. 'You really do look wiped out,' she said. 'Why not rest upstairs a bit longer?'

Marylin darted a queer, terrified look up towards the bedrooms. 'No! Is he still in the den?'

'Mr Wyler was taking photographs there a few minutes ago.' As she spoke, NolaBee's raspy laughter sounded above the congenial chatter in the dining room. (NolaBee, with her energy, slapdash clothes and gregarious Southern loquacity, had made a big hit with the movie crowd.) 'Mama's playing hostess. You really should finish your nap.'

'I need Linc!' Marylin's huge blue-green eyes were shadowed, as if she were ready to cry.

Roy draped her arm around her sister's delicately proportioned shoulders. 'Honey, I can see you still have it bad for him, but let's not go around wearing the old heart on the sleeve.'

A tear trickled onto the sculptured pale cheek.

Roy said hastily, 'Hush, it's okay. I'll go find him for you.'

Just then a stout man and an excessively thin redhead came into the hall.

'Marylin, darling, isn't it the most about Linc?' rasped the redhead. 'We're absolutely thrilled for Joshua, for all of you.'

'Hello, Mr and Mrs Rimmerton,' Roy answered for her sister. As the couple moved into the dining room, she whispered, 'Marylin, better go wait someplace where you're not so available.'

Wordlessly Marylin headed towards the front door.

'It's freezing,' Roy said.

But Marylin was turning the bronze knob. As she slipped outside, Roy thought If that's love, I'm better off without it. This particular notion held a couple of sour grapes: her perennial worry was her regrettable virginity. Was she frigid? Did she have impossibly high standards for a mate? (She would never consider giving in to anyone who didn't have honourable intentions.)

She began her search for Linc in the living room, where Johnny Mercer was accompanying himself as he rasped out

'Skylark'. Linc was not in the crowd gathered around the grand piano. Neither was he part of any of the chattering groups eating at the permanent card tables. She went into the overheated kitchen, where Coraleen, Percy and the caterers bustled. None had seen Linc recently. Roy ran upstairs. The door to BJ's old room was ajar, and she could see Annie curled in sleep by the bars of the crib kept there for her.

A faint light shone around the closed door of Billy's room.

She heard Linc's voice. ' – I had the books in that case and the games and stuff in this one.'

'Linc, was this your room? I mean, really truly?'

'Use your noodle, brother. Where else would they put a guy and all his junk?'

The half-brothers were sitting on the floor with the lights out, and as Roy opened the door the tall candle between them flickered, casting wavery light, chiaroscuro, on the faces of child and man.

'Linc,' Roy switched on the light.

'Turn that out, Auntie Roy!' Billy shouted. 'This is us brothers' campfire!'

'Hey, Billy Boy, hey charming Billy,' Roy said. 'Linc, M-a-r-y-l-i-n wants you. She's a-l-l u-p-s-e-t – '

'You spelled my mommy's name!' Billy shouted. 'Get out, Auntie Roy!'

Linc was pinching out the flame with his fingers. 'Brother, old buddy, we'll continue the powwow after you put on your PJs.'

As he reached Roy in the doorway, he asked quietly, 'Where is she?'

'Outside, in front.'

The bad leg didn't impair his speed, Roy noted. He charged down the curving staircase, ignoring the plump, outstretched arms of a motherly woman to duck out the front door.

They were still wild about each other, that was only too obvious, and though Roy lacked knowledge of why Linc had chosen to return so tardily to Beverly Hills, she understood he had everything to do with Marylin's jumping off the publicity jaunt. They were like two comets racing in tandem. How could Joshua miss seeing the brilliance? What a murderous mess, she thought as she turned to soothe her outraged nephew.

When the door opened, Marylin flung herself, gasping and shuddering at Linc.

'Hey, hey. You're shivering all over.' Pulling off his sport coat, he wrapped her in wool warm from his body. 'Love, what're we doing out here?'

She pressed against him. She had calmed enough to think in somewhat linear coherence. Joshua's his father, she thought; he loves him, and there are enough stumbling blocks in the relationship already. How can I tell him?

'Nerves,' she said.

He took her chin between his fingers, staring down at her. The light from his mother's prized Georgian carriage lanterns cut his face into harsh planes and prominences. 'Dad went upstairs a while ago,' he said slowly.

'He passed out on the bed.'

'What did he say?'

'Nothing.'

'Marylin?'

Memory burst within her, the liquor smell, the heavy, scalding weight crushing her, the pain. She could not suppress her shudder.

'For God's sake, Marylin. Did he bat you around? Does he do that?'

'No . . .'

Linc continued to examine her. A dog barked up the block and other nearby dogs joined in.

'I didn't want him,' she whispered.

'He raped you?'

'I didn't want him,' she repeated.

Linc's eyes went flat as obsidian stones, and his body tensed. After a moment he said quietly, 'I'll get you out of here.'

* * *

Without any luggage, she wearing his jacket, they checked into a motel a mile or so south of the Fernaulds' summer rental in Malibu.

38

The following morning she discovered she was spotting. Her period wasn't due for two weeks.

'I better find a doctor,' Linc worried.

'No!' The rape had filled her with a victim's shame, and Joshua's kneeing was too poisonous to speak about, especially to his son. 'Linc, I'll be fine.'

Linc crossed Pacific Coast Highway to the general store, buying a box of twelve Modess, aspirin and a paperback by Faulkner, *Mosquitoes*.

Understanding her need for quiet, he sat reading. His presence and the grumbling of the sea soothed her and she was able to talk, with burning cheeks and guarded circumspection, about the few agonizing minutes in the bedroom.

'. . . he was very drunk. I guess that's why I can't keep on hating him . . . very much, anyway.'

'That's how it is with him. You want to despise him, then for some reason you find you can't. God, I'd forgotten the whole syndrome! When I was fourteen, I figured out about his girls. What took me so long, I can't tell you. Arrested development, maybe. God knows, he never kept them a secret – when he attached himself to a new one, he all but took out ads in the trades. On Mother's behalf I loathed him, yet on my own, I harboured admiration. At least my old man had the guts not to be a hypocrite like the others.'

'To my knowledge, he's never cheated on me.'

'Why would he? You're his goddess, it's written all over him. Now, *why* he fell for his son's girl, well, there's something only a good psychiatrist could figure out.'

It was after five when she felt up to navigating the hundred feet to the motel office with its exterior telephone booth. Linc produced a handful of silver, then strolled to the sandy ledge to look down at breakers, the kind of tactful consideration about personal privacy to which Joshua never succumbed.

Percy answered the phone.

After the greetings, Marylin said, 'Get Billy for me, will you, Percy?'

'I'm sorry, Mrs Fernauld,' Percy said embarrassedly. 'But Mr Fernauld, he say, well, he say anything regarding Billy must be cleared with him. He's been drinking heavy all night and day, drinking like he done when Linc died – when Linc was missing. If I put Billy on the phone, he'll fire us, sure. I feel awful about this, Mrs Fernauld.'

She closed her eyes. 'That's all right, Percy. Tell Mr Fernauld I'll be over in an hour or so.'

'He stepped out a while ago. And, well, you know how it is with him. Tonight he might get some sleep. Best to try in the morning.'

She hung up and rested her aching forehead against the sand-pitted glass of the booth.

Linc returned. 'That was quick.'

She explained Joshua's interdiction.

'What a shitty thing to do,' Linc muttered.

She sighed. 'Billy must be positive I've run out on him.'

'The poor little kid.'

'You warned me, Linc, I know, but it seemed impossible Joshua would act like this.'

'The ageing bull elephant defends his territory every dirty whichway he can.'

'I said we'd go there tomorrow morning. I'll explain it all to Billy then.'

Joshua opened the door. His thick grey stubble showed, and he had on the same slacks and Mexican wedding shirt, now rumpled and food-spotted, that he'd worn for the festivities of Linc's return.

'Well, if it isn't my beauteous helpmeet and my devoted offspring.' Joshua, a heavy drinker, held his liquor well, but when he was loaded, his tendency to hectoring elaboration grew more pronounced.

She pushed him into the hall. 'I came to see Billy,' she said.

'Billy, my lovely, is in the companionship of his peers. The young of Beverly Hills attend nursery school, my beauty, despite the adulterous storms raging behind the handsome facades of their homes.' He wove unsteadily to his writing room.

Marylin and Linc followed.

The desk was littered with bottles and dirty dishes, and the air smelled dead, a combination of sweat, stale food, liquor, stubbed-out cigarettes.

Marylin said, 'I'll pick him up.'

Joshua was pouring a tumbler of J&B. 'The fuck you will, beloved.'

'He's mine too.'

'A fact you seemed happy enough to ignore when you departed this roof two evenings past.'

'You know damn well why she left,' Linc said in a low, shaking voice. His face was suffused with passionate rage. 'I should have killed you.'

In reply, Joshua downed his drink.

'Can't you remember?' Linc demanded. 'Were you too blind drunk to remember what you did? Let me give you a hint – Marylin's still bleeding.'

Joshua sank into the worn seat of his captain's chair, the only chair in the room, momentarily permitting his un-shaven chin to rest against his soiled shirt, a position of either grief or irrevocable defeat; then he raised his head. 'I goddamn well remember doing to *my* wife what the law allows, a privilege you, my small-balled, long-lost scion, have to sneak,' he said savagely. 'Now, get out before I beat the living shit out of you.'

'You really think I'd leave her alone with you?'

'You knew from the beginning, Joshua,' Marylin said. 'You understood why I married you.'

A tiny muscle was working in the lid of Joshua's left eye. 'The pair of you! Puling children! What do you think, you're playing on the swings in Roxbury Park? This clawing, painful *vérité*. Marylin-Rain, you leave Joshua Fernauld for Abraham Lincoln Fernauld and his hotshit Pulitzer, and you'll find yourself smack in the middle of a big, juicy dog turd of a scandal.' He gestured at a heaped mass of newspapers on the floor. 'Have you been keeping up with the news? No? Well I have. The front sections carry a paragraph about the miracle raising of the dead Pugh-litzuh Prize-winning author of *Island* from his watery grave, and the entertainment pages are full of questions about Rain Fairburn's suspension. The star, in seclusion, could not be reached for comment, but her devoted husband avers she has been laid low with a dire, mysterious bronchial ailment ever since she wore herself out shooting *Versailles*.'

'Thank you Joshua,' Marylin murmured.

'Oh, I am the soul of Christian forgiveness.' The eye was ticking vehemently. 'I absolve you of every past trespass. In the future, alas . . .' Joshua poured himself another drink. 'If in the future you persist in trespassing, John Q Public will get to sniff those dogshitty tracks – Rain Fairburn disappears with stepson. Heartsick husband breaks down and admits Rain and son have long-term affair.'

'I don't care about acting.'

'Who's talking careers, my pocket-size Venus? Tell me, do you honestly believe any judge would give over a four-year-old innocent into a ménage that defines the word "motherfucker"?'

'Oh, Joshua . . .'

'Listen to me, and listen carefully. You persist in spreading your sweet movie-star twat for Prizewinning Novelist – '

'That Pulitzer really bugs you, doesn't it?' Linc broke in, his fists clenching.

' – and I hire the best frigging lawyers in town. They'll fix me up with custody and you won't get visiting privileges with Billy from 11.55 until midnight on 29 February.'

Linc said, 'We'll hire lawyers too.'

'Are you so flush from that big-time job in the Detroit Public Library?'

'Marylin has the royalties from *Island*.'

Joshua gave an ugly laugh. 'You just don't know the full generosity of our blessed Saint Marylin-Rain of the Motion Pictures. She has not only endowed numerous charities but also supported her family.'

'Lest you forget,' Linc said, forcing his fury into the channel of that regrettable archness, 'this is a community-property state.'

Joshua's tan was muddy. 'That Pulitzer and those As at Beverly and Stanford don't mean a rat's fart, do they? Why, you asshole half-kike, what do you know about life? You grew up in a big house with a Jewish mother to spoon-feed you caviar-matzoball soup whenever you sneezed. Whereas I – I had the real advantages. I learned to steal my daily bread before I was five. I know enough to always go direct for the jugular.' He drew a loud breath. 'Our joint accounts are closed out. The community property's buggered.'

'You bastard!' Linc's voice rose into a note that chilled Marylin's spine. And she realized that it was not only Linc's outrage on her behalf but a retroactive horror for his dead mother that caused him to reach across the desk and grip his father's collar. The chokehold pulled the drunken older man to his feet.

'Please stop it,' Marylin whispered. '*Please stop it.*' Her hands were clasped and she was actually wringing the small fingers.

She was at the end of her emotional tether, and some of this must have cut through Linc's fury, for he released his father, who slumped back in his chair.

'Joshua,' she said, 'why are you acting like this? We both love Billy, we want what's best for him. And you love Linc, too – you know you do.'

Joshua gulped his drink, hurling the glass at the brick fireplace, where it shattered in a noisy explosion. 'Yes,' he said bitterly. 'I love Linc.'

'Then why destroy us?'

'Jesus frigging Christ, listen to her. "Then why destroy us?"' Joshua mimicked Marylin's soft voice. 'After all these years, haven't you the least clue what I feel for you? Am I so fucking inscrutable? I can't help myself, I cannot help

293

myself!' He glared at Linc. 'Now, get your prizewinning Jew ass out of my house!'

'Let's go, Marylin,' Linc said in a level voice.

'Tell Billy I'll see him later.'

'What do I have to say to make you understand?' Joshua's face was darkly twisted as he stood to stare down at his wife. 'The choice is between my sons. You can pick one or the other. Not both.'

The telephone rang, but neither Joshua nor Marylin moved to pick it up. He swaying, she gripping the old desk, they continued to examine each other above the spindly old typewriter. On the third ring either the caller gave up or was answered on another extension.

Unequal adversary that she was, Marylin felt the dangerous power of those bloodshot, wilful eyes. Yet she was fighting for what she loved best, Linc and Billy. 'Judges give children to the mother,' she said.

Joshua blinked and his jaw sagged with surprise. 'You mean you're going through with a divorce?' he asked, his voice as full of disbelief as his expression.

She nodded.

'You're damn well telling me you're walking out on Billy?'

'I'll get him, Joshua.'

He swivelled to face the yard, where Percy was using a long-handled net to fish eucalyptus leaves from the pool. She stretched her hand as if to touch her husband's thick, quivering shoulders, but Linc pulled her from the Spartan room.

While Linc arranged in the motel office for them to stay through Sunday, she dialled Leland Hayward's number to see what her agent could do about her suspension – not that she desired armistice with Magnum; she would infinitely prefer returning to Detroit with Linc. But she needed money, money, money, in order to pay sharp lawyers to get Billy for her. Therefore, work she must.

The secretary put her on immediately and her agent greeted her with his most hearty tone, informing her he had been trying to reach her. Metro was hot to borrow her for a light comedy with Gene Kelly, and if she reported to Magnum Monday morning, all would be forgiven.

'Have you heard that I'm leaving Joshua?'

Rather than answering directly, her agent referred to Clause Fourteen in her contract. 'You agreed in writing, and I'm reading this, Marylin, "not to commit any act or become involved in any situation or occurrence or make any statement which will degrade her in society or bring her into public disrepute, contempt, scandal, or ridicule or which will shock, insult, or offend the community, or which will reflect unfavourably on the company".'

'A divorce isn't immoral.'

The four-times-married Hayward agreed heartily through the telephone. 'But let me throw it all on the rug, Marylin. Garrison says before you get through the Magnum gate, you have to promise no more fooling around with your stepson.'

The sky clouded, giving an ugly purplish cast to the sea. 'Do I have to give you ten per cent of my heart, too?'

'Marylin, I don't make the rules. This Bergman brouhaha has everybody running scared. The exhibitors won't touch her new film with a ten-foot pole.'

'Linc,' she murmured, 'is going back to Detroit.'

'Good. Now we're in business.'

'I need more money,' she said. 'A lot more.'

He said he'd try to hammer out a reasonable raise.

39

Magnum's head set designer had corrected for his employer's deficiency in height by providing a dais for the outsize desk. Marylin, her mind empty of everything except panic to earn a salary that would bring her salvation, stood on deep-piled carpet below this intimidating altar listening to Art Garrison roar out the riot act. There would be no more episodes like her disappearance, there would be no more of that incestuous crap. If there were, she would find herself in *serious trouble*.

Serious trouble spoken in this poisonous half-whisper meant only one thing. Blacklisting. Intangible and unprovable, the blacklist was the studio system's ultimate weapon against its alcoholic or homosexual or intractably scandal-prone luminaries. A more formidable anathema than a papal excommunication – the religious outcast, after all, can embrace another sect to worship God, but every one of the rivalously embattled studios bowed in obedience to the elusive interdict. A blacklisted actor, no matter how big a star, never again acted in front of a Hollywood camera.

I need the money, I need the money, thought that most valuable property, Rain Fairburn, whose shapely, dimpled knees were like water. She nodded agreement.

To ameliorate the harsh ultimatum, the voice that spoke from the depth of purple upholstery gave Marylin dispensation to separate from Joshua. But – a hairy finger waggled at her – none of that Oedipus shit. Again ritual balm eased the harshness. Out of the corporate goodness of Magnum's heart, she would henceforth receive a thousand a week. The raise was a pittance compared to Rain Fairburn's true worth, but Marylin, in her desperate need, babbled her gratitude. It was Garrison's ritual to personally hand the upper hierarchy of his vassals the first paycheque of a raise. Marylin ascended three shallow steps to take the yellow paper that normally was mailed to her agent's office. Without a glance, she thrust it into her purse.

She drove directly from the studio to Stanley Rosewood's offices on Wilshire Boulevard. The broad, slab-faced attorney shared honours with Greg Bautzer when it came to arm wrestling over stickly settlements and alimony, but Stanley Rosewood, everyone agreed, had the edge in custody messes.

In his sunny private ofice – far more *gemütlich* than Art Garrison's – Stanley Rosewood went through an obligatory attempt at dissuasion. Marylin firmly restated her intention to terminate her marriage.

The lawyer's facial planes relaxed. 'You know about my fees?' he inquired.

Joshua had taken charge of those personal negotiations not handled by the business manager; Leland Hayward hassled out the professional finances. Marylin had a sinking sense of her fiduciary ineptitude that she covered with a spirited smile. 'Refresh my memory,' she said.

'The initial retainer is twenty-five hundred.'

A sum so dismayingly beyond reach that her bright expression must have sagged.

Stanley Rosewood added smoothly, 'Under friendly conditions, that often covers it. Let's be frank, though. Joshua Fernauld is a powerful man in this town, used to throwing his weight around. You tell me he's opposed to this divorce. He's hardly going to toss in the towel about the minor child.'

'I'm Billy's mother.'

'It's true, custody is generally awarded the mother. But in one of my other cases, where my client has proved herself unfit, I can do nothing.' A discreet professional pause to let Marylin recall that Ingrid Bergman had retained Stanley Rosewood – she was beginning to feel herself harnessed in tandem with the misfortunately philoprogenitive Swedish actress. 'There the court will decide for the father.'

'But I'm a fit mother.'

'I'm only saying we'd better be prepared for a court battle. And your behaviour will have to be irreproachable. Your husband might use detectives.'

'Spy on me? Yes, he would.'

Stanley Rosewood nodded. 'Above reproach, then. You do understand that the preliminary payment is made in advance?'

Please, God, let Mama have that much to lend me, Marylin thought as she said, 'Of course.'

In her car, she took out her paycheque. The thousand dollars, less the diverse deductions, amounted to $715.23 out of which must come Leland Hayward's hundred-dollar agent's bite. With a worried frown she took out an envelope, scribbling numbers on the back. As she added the column her soft, beautiful mouth drew into a bleak curve.

Since the best part of her old salary was already pledged to supporting the house on Crescent Drive, the hoped-for maternal loan would take a long time to repay.

She had not yet discussed her divorce with NolaBee. The previous night when she had called home, her mother had been out, so she had broken the news to Roy that she would be moving into the house, explaining why. Roy had stead-fastly backed her decision, insisting Marylin take her bedroom: *The couch'll be fine for me, Marylin, I mean it.*

NolaBee, however, had not taken the dissolution of her beautiful older daughter's marriage with the same loyal equanimity. In a state of nerves, she had not slept. Though it was nearly noon, she answered the door in her old blue kimono with the dragon on it – no matter how many robes her daughters presented her with, NolaBee favoured this disgraceful garment.

She flung her arms around Marylin. 'Roy told me! Darlin', darlin', you can't mean it!'

'I do, Mama.' Marylin, battling to hold on to her precarious composure, released herself from her mother's clutch. 'And I need to borrow a huge amount of money. Twenty-five hundred dollars.'

'There's something like that, I reckon, in the savings, but –'

'I'll pay it back as quickly as possible.'

'Oh, Marylin, *you* gave me that money, it's yours. But a divorce? Why, nobody in our family ever, ever got one! And let me tell you, some of our women put up with an awful lot.'

'Mama, my mind's made up, so please don't make it any harder.'

NolaBee sat on the couch, taking a pack of Camels from her frayed sash. 'Darlin', listen to me. You know I never thought Joshua was The Man, he being so much older. But you did marry him. He's your husband. I'm not saying a word against Linc – my heart's just brimmin' over that he's alive. He's a right fine boy. And my guess is that he stayed away all those years for this very reason. He knew if he came back, your marriage would bust wide open. You were seein' him this summer, weren't you?'

Her mother's Southern voice divining the truth seemed to come from an echo chamber.

'How did you guess?'

'Mothers know a lot of things. Honey, the way you ran out on the tour, the way the two of you left the party the other night, that's not like you. You're my good, beautiful girl who never hurt a living soul.'

'Mama, without Linc there's no sense to anything.'

'They say a woman never gets over her first love. But nothing's the same, darlin', nothing's the same anymore. Think of Billy.'

'That's why I need the money. For Stanley Rosewood's fees. He's the best man in town. He'll get me custody of Billy. Then we can go to live with Linc.'

Swallowing smoke, NolaBee coughed violently. 'In Detroit?' Her small eyes peered in distress at Marylin.

'Yes, back East.'

'That's right ridiculous! How can you leave? You have your career, everything. Why, you're far bigger box office than that trampy Rita or that simpy Lana.'

'The minute the divorce is granted, I'm getting married. A normal life is all *I* ever wanted.' At her mother's wince, Marylin halted. 'Mama, Linc and I have always belonged together. He and Billy are what matter to me. And you're being a dear about the money, but you'll get every penny back.' Her voice shook.

NolaBee patted her arm. 'Darlin', you're in a state. I'll fix us some lunch, then we can talk.'

While NolaBee headed for the kitchen, Marylin went to use her mother's telephone, sprawling on the bed – once she and Linc had lain here, each holding a palm over the other's racing heart.

There was no answer at Linc's. Of course not, she reproached herself. He's working at the library.

He answered a few minutes after three, Pacific Coast time. She explained that Stanley Rosewood had agreed to take her case, and she had been reinstated at Magnum. 'I'm already on loan to Metro. A twelve-week shooting schedule.'

299

'I'll take a few days extra off at Christmas and fly out.'

'Linc . . . Art Garrison laid down the law about us. And Stanley Rosewood must know something's in the air. He says I must be very discreet, because of the custody.'

'You're saying we can't see each other?'

'I'm sorry, darling,' she said miserably.

'It's okay, Marylin, we can write or telephone every day.' His voice faded, and long-distance wires seemed to buzz louder. 'I wish I were hotter on the financial aid.'

'That's silly. Darling, I miss you so much already.'

'Me you.'

As Marylin hung up, slow, forlorn tears were seeping down her cheeks and onto the white wool of her suit collar. By some incredible savagery of fate – or Joshua – she was cut off from both Billy and Linc.

The following morning Marylin reported to Metro-Gold-wyn-Mayer's walled fortress in Culver City.

The comedy-mystery, tentatively entitled *Blazer*, was one of those hard luck films. Gene Kelly, her intended co-star, had been commandeered for a musical and his part in *Blazer* was given to Harvey Jameson, a mediocre actor from the Metro stable. When shooting began, the script was still undergoing major surgery, and each morning a small stack of coloured pages, dialogue changes, was handed out. The director, an old-timer with a light hand, fell prey to hepatitis; his replacement barked out commands that over-emphasized every comedic nuance.

Marylin, outfitted in forty-two bitingly chic costumes, was foil for the private eye, turgidly played by Harvey Jameson. An elegant clothes horse, a role without the least challenge.

So even under the camera she was easily distracted by her anguished problems, which were expanding like algae in a contaminated pond. Joshua's law firm frustrated every legal procedure aimed at peaceful dissolution of their marriage. Linc caught a bad case of flu and she worried about him alone in his apartment. Her vaginal discharge continued, and when she went to her gynaecologist, she shamefacedly whispered what had befallen her. Dr Dash, his face tense with outrage, performed stitchery in his examining room, then put her on an antibiotic that dragged her out.

Working, she longed to be at home, where she could drowse. Sleeping, she was harassed by anxiety nightmares.

Yet her purpose never wavered. She *was* going to spend the rest of her life with Linc.

Joshua, through friendship with a judge, had secured a court injunction that kept her from Billy. He had also deleted Roy and NolaBee from the child's visiting list. Marylin knew that her husband's cruelty was not gratuitous but the by-product of his love for her; however, in her lonely wretchedness she found herself visualizing him with longer teeth and a wild expression, a subhuman from a horror movie.

Ross, the kind young Scotswoman, Billy's nurse, risked unemployment by telephoning on her days off to report on her charge. Marylin read between the lines of the woman's cheerful burr. Billy, taking her prolonged absence badly, had become an unmanageable little monster.

Ten days before Christmas, Marylin splurged at Uncle Bernie's, and the toy shop delivered her purchases to North Hillcrest Road. On Christmas morning when she stepped outside for the paper, she found on the doorstep the lavish miniature station wagon, the Flexy, the cowboy outfit and the assortment of games, all were sloppily rewrapped in their bright paper. Nothing was missing, not even the lollipops attached to the crimson ribbons. Tidings of comfort and joy from her husband.

By the middle of January *Blazer* was almost in the can.

That last Wednesday of shooting, Marylin rode an electric horse while a projector electrically synchronized with the cameras threw rushing vistas of wintry woods through the blank screen behind her. Ticket buyers would see Rain Fairburn in a chic habit cantering her black Arabian steed towards – what else? – a deserted mansion.

301

As she dismounted from the wood-and-steel contraption, her dresser came over with a long-corded telephone. 'Marylin, a call for you.'

Marylin reached for the phone, assuming it was her mother. Worried about her, NolaBee drove her to and from Metro, either remaining on the set or calling four or five times to check on how she was managing.

'Marylin?' Joshua said.

As the hated, feared, familiar voice rumbled against her ear, she was struck dumb with foreboding.

'Dammit, I've been cut off.'

'I'm here,' she whispered. 'Is it Billy?'

'He's been in an accident.'

She was hurled into a nightmare where there was no warmth, no mercy, no hope, only one eternal moment of terror. 'Is he . . .?' She couldn't voice the final word, *dead*.

'He's in the examining room.'

'Where are you?'

'St John's.'

'I'll be right over. Oh, God! Mother drove me! God – '

'Marylin, you have to hold on tight.' The voice rumbled more deeply. 'What if Billy needs you?'

'But how will I get there?' Her question was a screech of agony.

'Tell them to send you in a limousine.'

40

The windowless waiting room – fraudulently bright, adorned with a crucifix and two small, unevenly hung religious prints – was empty except for Joshua hunched in a corner. As she came in, he stood.

His shirt and trousers were marked with rusty splotches. His tanned cheeks sagged heavily in a single plane, and the twin lines from the corners of his mouth were gouged so deeply that the chin appeared hinged in the manner of a ventriloquist's dummy. The emotions she felt on seeing him – hatred, anger, fear, pity – were like a few sparse snowflakes in comparison to the raging polar blizzard of her maternal anguish.

'Is Billy all right?' she demanded.

'No word yet. It's less than an hour since we got here.'

'An hour!' Into her mind came an ominous vision, Chilton Wace's death watch, she and her mother waiting with the docile humbleness of charity patients while chubby little Roy screamed her protests at a hostile nurse. 'And you haven't asked!'

'Damn right I've asked! If there's one thing I've done, it's *ask*. The hospital's a fucking octopus. No matter which tentacle I attack, the answer's always the same. No word.' He gave a loud sigh. 'Maybe it does take time when it's a head injury.'

'Head injury . . . ?'

'I'm not even sure of *that*. Maybe it's internal. But he was unconscious and the back of his head was bleeding.'

She could feel the blood drain from her own head.

'Marylin, for God's sake, sit down.'

She remained standing. 'Did he fall?'

'It was all my fault.' With his hands at his sides, his big shoulders sagging in the bloodied shirt, this was a Joshua she had never seen, a penitent, frightened man.

She sat down. 'What happened?'

He took the chair near her. 'We were on Beverly Drive. You know Billy, always in a hot sweat to look in the pet shop. Since you left, he's been more impatient than ever. And why not? Marylin, I told him that the reason you left was you didn't want to live with him anymore. You'd left him.'

'Oh, my God.'

'I'm a saintly figure, aren't I? A real prince.'

'No wonder he's been wild.'

'Yes, when it's not bed-wetting it's tantrums. So there the two of us were on Beverly Drive, Billy jumping up and down demanding to see the pet shop, Big Joshua determining now was the time to teach his kid the fine art of patience. I had something important to check out, I told him. In good time we'd go look at the puppies. Then I examined every single damn piece of equipment in the camera shop window . . .'

'He ran out in the street?'

The massive chest shook with an assenting sigh. 'The first thing I knew was brakes squealing. An old jalopy had swerved to avoid him, but he was thrown into the gutter. He lay there absolutely still, his head all bloodied. Crumpled, so small, so godawful small. The cops were there immediately – that's the Beverly Hills police force, always on hand *ex post facto*. They said something about an ambulance. But who could hang around waiting? I picked him up and drove him here, leaning on the horn all the way, keeping my foot down to the floorboard. As soon as they took him from me, I called Rehnquist – he's the neuro-surgeon William Randolph Hearst keeps on retainer. He was tied up with office hours, but I convinced him to come.'

'What does he say about Billy?'

'He hasn't gotten here yet.' Joshua's very dark eyes fixed on her. 'The cops said it would be a mistake to pick Billy up, but I did. Do you think I hurt him?'

Had she ever heard Joshua beg reassurance? 'I don't know, Joshua, I don't know.'

'There's a chapel down the hall,' he said.

His heavy steps faded. She was alone in the windowless waiting room, her mind circling like some crazed, rabid rat through the mazes of anguished fear.

She followed Joshua.

The chapel had a different odour from the disinfected hospital, a honeyed beeswax aroma that came from the votive candles flickering in their ruby-red glasses. In the front pew knelt Joshua, his massive greying head bent, his mutters disturbing the silence. 'Mary, Mother of God, blessed art thou among women, Holy Mother of God, pray for us now and in the hour of our death, Holy Mother of God . . .'

For an indeterminate time she watched her husband tell a nonexistent rosary, praying for intercession with a God in whom he did not believe; then she moved up the thick carpeted aisle.

He turned to her, burying his face in her natty jodhpurs. 'Marylin, I've screwed up in the worst way with my two sons.' His muffled voice rumbled against her. 'They were the joy and hope of my life, and I've lost them both. When Linc showed up, I was so delirious I could have written all over the sky, "He has risen, he has risen". But he wanted you, you wanted him. Those obscene things I shouted at him! Imagine calling your own son a kike? He's a brave, decent man, far better than I am, and I've always been proud of that – so why have I always been utterly incapable of telling him? With Billy it was like I was given a second chance, and what did I do? Oh, Jesus, what did I do?' His arms were clasped tightly around her waist and he swayed from side to side on his knees, rocking them both.

She touched the damp grey hair. 'Joshua, we have enough trouble without going into the past to borrow more.'

Releasing her, he sat on his heels, flinging out both arms. 'Behold and enjoy. Joshua Fernauld, the Great I Am, getting his comeuppance.' It was theatrical yet sincere.

'Mr Fernauld? Mrs Fernauld?' said a dry masculine voice.

They jerked around. A tall, narrow figure was outlined in the doorway of the chapel.

'I'm Dr Rehnquist,' he said, coming towards them.

Marylin was freezing in her Arctic dread, yet even so she felt a whisper of surprise. She had figured that Joshua must be well acquainted with the renowned neurosurgeon to lure him from his office – but obviously this assumption was false. With what domination of character had her husband, over the telephone, compelled a total stranger to leave his busy practice and come to the aid of their small son?

Joshua, standing, clasped her hand so tightly that the huge rhinestone ring – part of her costume – cut into her flesh.

'I've been examining Billy,' the doctor said.

'Well?' Joshua growled. 'No sugar-coated crap, no bull-shit. I want the truth.'

305

'There's a depressed fracture of the skull and, I believe, sub-arachnoid haemorrhaging – that means one of the veins on the surface of the brain has been torn. I'm on my way to scrub.'

'Must Billy have brain surgery?' Marylin's whisper shook.

'It's the only chance,' Rehnquist said.

Joshua was sweating heavily, and those deep-gouged lines of his jaw appeared yet more like polished wood.

It was Marylin who asked, 'If the operation is successful, will Billy . . . will he be all right?'

The neurosurgeon looked at her intently, recognition dawning in his eyes. 'I don't know the answer to that, Mrs Fernauld, I'm sorry.' The dry voice was gentle.

When they got back to the waiting room a party of sorts was straggling into being. NolaBee, Roy, BJ and Maury were there. One of Joshua's friends lugged in a silver ice bucket, two bottles of Johnnie Walker and some Dixie cups while his wife followed with a covered chafing dish that held hot garlic-and-cheese-scented hors d'oeuvres. More friends and family arrived. The purposefully *bon vivant* chatter skirted the subject of the emergency operation as well as the Fernaulds' separation.

Joshua sat next to her, grasping her hand and pressing it against his thick thigh. This is the man who raped me, she thought. Who defamed me to my four-year-old and returned my gifts with unseasonal cruelty, this the man who has done everything in his power to tear me from Linc. Do I hate him, pity him, what? She had no answer, but she did not pull her hand from the thick, familiar warmth.

'I can't take much more of this waiting crap,' he rumbled to her.

'What can they be doing for so long? He's got such a little head.'

'Why the hell don't they send out some word? They're a pack of sadists, surgeons, they have to be, it goes with the territory.'

After three long hours, Dr Rehnquist came to the noisy waiting room. He wore a blood-spattered green surgical suit, and a mask dangled from his fingers. His eyes were weary, his face grey and drained of expression. 'Mr and Mrs Fernauld,' he said in that calm, dry voice. 'Let's go someplace we can talk.'

The dinky office was crowded by a gurney. The doctor offered Marylin the one chair. As she sank into it, she thought: I am in this closet with two men wearing clothes splattered with Billy's blood. How much blood can a four-year-old lose and still live?

'We removed a splinter of bone and repaired the damage to the vein,' he said.

'Then he'll be all right?' Joshua growled.

'We'll know in time.'

'How long?' Marylin asked.

'Again, we can't say. Hopefully only days. But it could be weeks, months even.'

'What are the odds he'll pull out intact?' Joshua asked in a strangled voice.

'I don't like holding out false hope, any more than you want me to,' said Dr Rehnquist. 'The sooner he regains consciousness, the better the prognosis.'

'When can we see him?' Marylin asked.

'He's still in recovery. Tomorrow morning.'

At her mother's house, Marylin telephoned Linc to let him know what had happened. She would always draw a blank when it came to remembering his words, but she would never forget the comfort his voice brought her.

41

Billy was not in the children's wing but on the surgical floor. In the centre of the large, bright room, tended by a private nurse, amid a miraculous trellis of tubes and monitors, his body formed a flat, pathetically truncated line down the centre of the full-size hospital bed. Against the turban of white bandages, his face showed a jaundiced pinky-yellow. His respiration was slow and machine regular, his thick brown lashes never quivered. Even in sleep, Billy was a restless child, turning erratically and mumbling small, incoherent sounds.

Marylin stepped into the room while Joshua hung back in the doorway. She bent over the bed, her mouth dry, nausea caught in a hard spasm at the base of her throat. This was her first glimpse of her son in more than three months, and if it weren't for that slow rise and fall of his chest, he could be a wax effigy.

To reassure herself, she touched his cheek: below warm, petal-smooth epidermal surface, the flesh had a loose, vanquished plasticity.

'It's all right, Miss Fairburn, nothing will disturb our little patient.' The nurse fiddled with the bleached mercilessly taut blanket cover, her narrow wedge of a face fixed avidly on Marylin – Rain Fairburn.

Joshua muttered, 'He'd be better off dead than like this.'

'Never . . .' Marylin replied.

'When my mother finally died, the priest called death her final healing.' Joshua spoke in a low, angered rumble. He backed towards the door. 'If you need me, I'll be in the waiting room.'

Marylin nodded. She had learned from her craft that each character must react with a different obsessiveness to life-and-death anxieties. Just as it was unbearable for Joshua to look upon their insentient child, so she herself had been plunged into a superstitious dread that without her to stand watch, Billy might slip away.

She sat down in a chair by the window.

That morning the offerings began to flow in, creamy roses cunningly woven into a Pooh bear, a blue-and-yellow rocking horse formed of daisies, a chrysanthemum football, plush animals of various species.

Nurses adjusted Billy's tubes and bottles, doctors prodded him for reflexes, drawing up his eyelids to blaze flashlights into his unresponsive blue-green irises.

Joshua ordered lunch and dinner sent in for her: constitutionally incapable of apology, he was using every means of making amends for his brutish behaviour as well as having permitted this evil to befall their small son. Two shifts of private nurses relished meals from expensive restaurants.

That evening NolaBee, Roy, BJ and Joshua joined forces in an attempt to lure Marylin from her vigil.

She remained in her chair all night.

The nurse on the third shift was a plain, thick-ankled war widow who explained that she worked graveyard in order to be near her small daughter during the day. With a sweetly mournful smile, she spoke to Marylin as another mother rather than a source of gossip. In the night nurse's quietly undemanding presence, Marylin relaxed a little.

Around three in the morning, a light rain began to fall over the lit, somnolent hospital. Marylin, merged in that infinitesimal movement of Billy's chest, did not drowse, but her thoughts moved in a random, spacious manner. She heard an old song:

> Now that you've come, all my griefs are removed,
> Let me forget that so long you have roved,
> Let me believe that you love as you loved,
> Long, long ago,
> Long ago . . .

Then she recalled a line of poetry: 'The mills of the gods grind exceedingly slow, but they grind exceedingly fine.'

She herself did not need to search for a universal mechanism that meted out justice. An inexorable sequence of events had brought Billy to this hospital bed: she had left her child for her lover. (With vivid clarity Marylin remembered the pitch black Michigan cabin and its odour of sawed pinewood, the cries of a night hawk, and her rushing joy at wakening in Linc's arms.) Billy had reacted to losing her with belligerent misery. He had become an uncontrollable brat and run into the Beverly Drive traffic.

She stared at the small, expressionless, turbaned face.

My fault, she thought, my fault. She pressed two fingers against her throbbing temple.

In order for Billy to recover, she must relinquish her love.

309

There was, she knew, no logic to this decision. Surgical successes bore no connection to renunciation. Yet in her odd, half-hypnotized state of mind she also knew that in the small hours of the morning there prevails something beyond logic or sense, the reason known to the unarmoured heart.

Give up Linc?

The thought of being banished once again to that drab, loveless land filled her lungs, and she could scarcely breathe.

The next four days, Billy remained unmolestable in his remote cocoon. On the fifth morning, Dr Rehnquist ordered more X-rays for his patient. A bad sign. The possibility of further surgery was being considered.

After that first night, Marylin had been returning to her mother's house for a few hours of pill-induced sleep – in order to avoid the battalion of reporters, she had to sneak down to the basement loading dock, where Roy met her with the Waces' used Chevy.

Just after twelve on that fifth night, the war-widow nurse, Marylin's friend, telephoned. Maybe this was pure imagination, but when she changed Billy's I.V. she thought that she had seen the corner of his mouth twitch. Dr Rehnquist was on his way over.

Marylin called Joshua, who picked her up within ten minutes. They arrived in Billy's room to find the surgeon, dressed in old slacks, aiming a medical flashlight at their child's eyes.

For an interminable minute, Billy's face remained still.

Then the lashes trembled.

Joshua's large, damp hand engulfed Marylin's.

The eyelids drew up.

Those first heartbeats, the sea-coloured eyes were the terrifying blank blue of a newborn infant's. Then another flicker. The green intensified.

'Billy?' Rehnquist's arid voice rang in the night-still hospital. 'Billy!'

The child blinked.

'You had an accident. I'm your doctor.'

'Billy . . .' Marylin whispered

'Your – Mom – and – Dad – are – both – here,' Dr Rehnquist was booming oratorically.

Billy's pupils swelled. Doctor, nurse, parents, the dark and sleeping world beyond this room maintained a reverential stillness as the small face seemed to ripple.

Marylin could feel the shuddering of Joshua's thick body.

Then Billy's gaze turned to Marylin. His lips formed an infinitely faint smile.

With a soft cry, Marylin bent to embrace him.

After Joshua dropped her off, Marylin stood on the doorstep a few moments. Dawn pinkened the western sky, yet above the dark outline of the Santa Monicas the full moon still dangled like a pale, lost balloon. Her face set with mournful determination, she went inside. She'd had an extension installed in Roy's room, and she called the long-distance operator.

Sunday, Linc was home.

In a hectic rush of words, she explained about Billy.

'Marylin, love, I'm crying.'

'So am I.'

'He's a terrific little kid, my brother. Tough, too. Made of iron.'

She gripped the receiver tighter. How many of the crucial exchanges of their lives had been carried on through this unsatisfactory, unfleshed instrument? 'Linc, darling, I've been doing a lot of thinking the past few days.'

'Same here. This business, we have to settle it with the least hurt to Dad. Yesterday, when I talked to him, he sounded so old, drained.' The crises had cut through Linc's outrage: he had called his father the last three evenings. 'I'm pretty sure he's given up fighting the divorce. The way I see it, we'll live out there so he can see Billy as often as possible.'

'Dr Rehnquist said that the recovery will be slow, very slow, and uneven. There's a chance that he . . . he won't ever be really himself.'

'He will be.' Linc's reassurances never came adventitiously, but were always spoken from the heart, giving the words of solidity that comforted.

'Even if he gets back to normal, Linc, I can't take him from Joshua.'

During the ensuing pause, a bird outside the window began its early-morning chirps.

She said, 'I'm going back.'

'That's a decision made under the worst kind of emotional stress.'

'Linc, I love you, I always will.'

'I'm coming out.'

'Billy needs both of us. Ever since I left, he's been an emotional basket case.'

'You'll stay at the house until he's perfect. That'll give him time to adjust.'

'If I'd been home, this never would have happened.'

'We're going round in circles. Marylin, there's no reason for you to crumble with guilt now that he's getting better. He was hit by a car. An accident. Accidents happen.'

'Please don't make it more difficult.' Her voice shook.

There was another long silence, while her mind resounded with memories of that long-ago telephone call when he had told her the *Enterprise* was sailing. Finally he said, 'What's wrong with taking more time to consider?'

'Linc, darling, I can consider until the world ends. But how can I take my happiness at the expense of a four-year-old?'

'And you think this is the answer? Kids're aware what's going on with their parents. Believe me, I know.'

'Live your own life, darling,' she whispered. 'Be happy.'

'Happy?' A momentary bitterness tempered the word. Then he said crisply, 'When Billy's older, we'll have another chance.'

'I can't let you waste your life waiting.'

'You have no choice, love.'

'I won't write to you, Linc. I won't phone you.'

'You will, someday,' he said, and hung up.

Marylin collapsed on Roy's bed, gasping with loud, primitive sobs.

NolaBee, awakening, ran in terrified that her grandson had died. Marylin gasped out that it was the reverse, Billy was – as Dr Rehnquist had cautiously pronounced – on the road. Her mother crouched over her, trying to render some comfort for this mysterious sorrow at a time of joy.

Let me believe that you love as you loved,
Long, long ago,
Long ago . . .

Book Five

1954

Debbie Reynolds and Rain Fairburn are each buying dozens of the new, expensive Italian sweaters at Patricia's.
– Louella Parsons, Hearst Press, 21 January 1954

Today the joint services exploded a hydrogen bomb which is far more powerful than an A-bomb.
– President Dwight D. Eisenhower, television speech, 2 February 1954

Make no mistake, the motion-picture industry has itself an inescapable problem. With more than 20,000,000 television sets in the country, the box-office gross has slipped a drastic 23%, and Hollywood is in upheaval. Studio shake-ups are announced daily. High-cost contracts are being scrutinized for escape clauses. Most studios are eyeing the small screen as a possible source of revenue.
– Forbes, 9 May 1954

Plate XLV: Seine Embankment. *1954. Oil, 76 × 104 in. Los Angeles County Art Museum.*
This is the largest painting Horak executed in Paris. The style may be called Neo-Plasticism. The lines, surfaces and colours are units with which the artist has created an organizational force: the composition forms a whole to which nothing may be added or subtracted.

– Horak, published by Marlboro Books, 1965

42

Late one afternoon in August of 1954, Roy Wace dawdled along Wilshire Boulevard looking into the plate-glass windows of Patricia's. The shop's advantageous new location on Wilshire in the Beverly Hills high-fashion zone near Saks and Magnin's had come about through Roy. She had heard from the previous owner, a friend of Joshua's, that he intended to sell this large two-storey corner building. Roy's employers, the Finemans, a shrewd, childless couple, had been searching for larger, more visible premises for their class women's specialty shop. When Roy told them the property would be on the market, they had snapped it up before a broker entered the picture.

Roy moved back towards the kerb, halting, wriggling with sheer pleasure as she surveyed the entire row of windows. The shop mannequins were posed in versions of the coming autumn's styles, some sporting day dresses with smart little Peter Pan collars, others draped in modishly full-skirted suits or sophisticated beaded formals. Every outfit was red. Since the end of May, Patricia's windows had been decorated in a single, unified colour scheme. The idea was Roy's. (Well, she had picked it up on the Rue St Honoré during her buying trip to Paris.)

It goes without saying that both Finemans were not only very fond of Roy but delighted with her. Indeed, with her enthusiasm, her talent for imitation – a talent superior to creativity in their pricey trade – and her loyalty to Patricia's, they had come to view her as a surrogate

317

daughter. In her five years they had doubled her salary and given her the title 'Assistant Manager'.

Without thinking, Roy raised both arms as if gathering the line of elegant monochromatic mannequins to herself. Behind her, the men trapped in the hot rush-hour traffic smiled out their open car windows at the gesturing, fresh-looking young woman in the yellow dress with appliquéd daisies scattered down the flared skirt.

With one final glance at the crimson sweaters displayed in the side windows, Roy crossed to Patricia's parking lot, waving at the young black attendant, who waved back as she got into her car. Sitting gingerly on the hot leather of her Chevy, she smiled. A soft, dreamy smile. She was on her way home.

Home meant Gerry Horak.

She and Gerry – oh, scandal of scandals – were not married but lived together on one of the rustic ledges of Beverly Glen. They had known each other less than four months.

She had met him last May on that fateful trip to Paris, at a party on the Île St Louis given by Roxanne and Henri de Liso.

The de Lisos were friends of Joshua and Marylin's. He had been a top-notch set designer before being fired for his leftist leanings. (The Communist witch hunt, oddly enough, had never touched Joshua, a card carrier in the twenties, because long before it was politically expedient he had recanted, booming public anathemas on Trotskyites and Stalinists alike.)

Roxanne de Liso, who was confined in a wheelchair, had steered herself through her place of exile, a bewitchingly cluttered, wonderful old apartment, introducing Roy to various guests, most of whom were well-known Hollywood names. The conversation had centred in knowledgeably vituperative tones on Senator Joseph McCarthy. Roy, feeling like a hopelessly inadequate, ignorant reactionary, had shrunk with her glass of Beaujolais onto the little balcony with its smart row of potted geraniums.

A stocky, broad-shouldered man wearing a check sports

jacket leaned on the iron rail. Roy, too, looked out at the ivory moon sailing above the peaked rooftops with their charmingly askew ancient chimneys.

'*C'est plus belle, Paris, n'est-ce pas?*' she said in her careful Beverly High French.

Turning to look her up and down, he flashed her a grin. 'If you say so, baby,' he retorted.

'You're American!' she cried.

'Whatever the fat-cat parlour pinkos inside tell you, it's no crime,' he said, still grinning. In the dim light of the balcony, his teeth gleamed uneven and very white. He was in his mid-thirties, she guessed. The right age.

She introduced herself and he told her his name was Gerry Horak.

'It's just too much,' Roy sighed in enchantment. 'It looks just like a set from *La Bohème* – ' She stopped, wondering if this attractive, proletarian-looking he-man would get the allusion – and if he did, would he consider her a phony for using it? She added, 'This is my first time in Paris.'

'You're wasting your time in this dump. You might as well be back in – let me guess. Beverly Hills, California.'

'You have me down pat.'

'There's a place called Chien Noir in Montmartre where you can see real Frenchmen. Game to try it?'

Gerry Horak's truculent air challenged her, and she liked what she could see of his broad, strong-cheekboned Slavic face. An excitement surged through her. 'I have to get my coat and thank the de Lisos,' she said.

Going down in the wrought-iron elevator that held only two people, he put his arm around her shoulder and she felt a crescendo in her stomach, as if they were rising rather than descending.

He paid her way through a Métro turnstile, her very first time.

At Chien Noir, boisterously singing, wine-imbibing working-class Parisians crowded the long wooden tables, and Gerry's muscular calf pressed tight against her leg. Never in her life had she felt an electricity like this. She drank glasses of sour red wine from Burgundy, and it seemed the most natural thing in the world to walk up the Rue le Pic, turn on a street that was actually a long flight of steps, winding yet higher along a narrow alley. Gerry lived in a tall grey house with crumbling plaster angels nestled into its eaves. She linked her arm in his to climb the four flights of steep, dimly lit, garlic-scented stairs, pausing for endless open-mouth kisses with this man she had just met. She did not even know he was a painter until he unlocked the door of a large attic and she was overpowered by smells of paint and turpentine: enormous unframed canvases were racked against every wall. Undressing in the bathroom that doubled as a kitchen, she grew less tipsy. What are you doing, Wace, you bad girl? she asked herself. Yet her fingers continued unsnapping and unhooking. At the last minute, in a flash of sobriety, she pulled back on her slip.

Emerging, she said shakily, 'I'm a beginner at this.'

Gerry was already in bed, leaning against the brass headboard: a band of white scar like a ribboned order slanted across the thick brown hair of his chest. 'With that nice round ass?' he said. 'Baby, what a waste. You must have had a ton of offers. Why me?'

'Something crazy's come over me,' she murmured.

'Come to Poppa,' he said.

She ran on bare feet across the paint-spattered boards, climbing into the high brass bed. Trembling, she clung to his firm flesh.

For a long time he kissed and caressed her in a way that made her forget any embarrassment or regret, made her feel beautiful, desirable, wanted – or maybe she was still blotto. When she was embarrassingly wet down there, he moved onto her. From intimate talks with her KayZee sisters, she accepted that the first time would be uncomfortable, maybe painful. Surprisingly, though, it went swiftly and scarcely hurt. Afterwards she felt irrevocably bound to Gerry Horak.

The Finemans, who as a bonus had given Roy the trip that they normally took, had instructed her to take in *all* the showings as part of her education. For once Patricia's was remote and hazy in Roy's mind. She sat on spindly gilt chairs for the major collections – Chanel, Fath, Givenchy and Dior – thrusting the creamy embossed cards of lesser houses into the desk of her room at the Scribe, where she no longer slept.

With Gerry she strolled around the Place du Tertre, where a few of his buddies, in order to pay for their serious work, set up easels to paint Utrillo-style street scenes for the occasional tourist.

Together she and Gerry shopped on the Rue des Abbesses and the Rue le Pic for the meals that she fixed in the bathroom-kitchen. They played a silly, happy game, dividing their purchases by gender. There were boy-Gerry-foods, the meats in Au Couchon Rose, the oysters in Lepic sur Mer. The girl-Roy-foods were selected in Pâtisserie Babette and Crémerie des Abbesses. They made love in the afternoon with dusty shadows of pigeons coming through the attic skylight.

Considering she was crazy in love with Gerry Horak, she knew amazingly little about him.

When she inquired about his life in America, he put her off truculently. 'I'm not much at shooting the bull.' The meanings behind his vivid, huge abstracts eluded her, and she would have thought him a failure at his profession had she not discovered a slickly handsome four-colour brochure put out by his New York gallery: the first page listed the museums where he'd been exhibited, an impressive number of first-rankers that included the Tate and the Museum of Modern Art. From Roxanne de Liso she learned that he had spent a year in the psychiatric ward at the Birmingham military hospital in the San Fernando Valley. 'I don't mean to be a gossip,' said Roxanne, 'but I knew him back at poor Henry Lissauer's, and well, you seem to have fallen under the Horak spell. So you ought to know he does have a spotty history. Personally I've never seen a sign of mental instability, but he *was* in psychiatric confinement.'

Though Gerry never discussed his family, he definitely was not what her mother would call a gentleman-though-poor. His manners left something to be desired. He could be truculent. He invariably cut off her attempts to share her past with him. But so what? What difference did any of this make? At her advanced age when every single girl in her KayZee pledge group was married and had a minimum of two babies, she had finally found love.

Two days before she was to return home on the twenty-four-hour polar flight, she accepted that the most important part of her would die – literally cease to exist – if she were torn from Gerry Horak.

'Gerry,' she asked, her face burning, 'what about coming back to California?'

'California,' he said with a brooding look. 'Why?'

'You've been talking about trying seascapes in all different lights. I seem to recall that Los Angeles lies on the coast – I forget the name of the ocean.' She reached for his broad hand. 'Gerry, I have a good job, we could share expenses.'

'Look, babe, we get along just swell in the hay, and you're great to be with, too. And I'd probably join up with you if I hadn't been badly stung once. But now I stay clear of entanglements.'

'One rotten apple,' she said. 'All women aren't bitches.'

'It soured me. Eventually you'd be getting a raw deal, holding the bag.'

'I'll take my chances.'

They were resting on a sunlit bench in the slanting, cobbled little park near the Rue Ravignon. Shading his eyes, he squinted at her with a funny, wistful expression she had never seen on him.

'I'm self-centred about my work,' he said. 'I can be a mean bastard when I'm disturbed.'

'You need somebody to do everything for you so you *can* paint.'

'And it's not in my books to get married.'

'I respect that.'

'Later on you won't.'

'Hey, you're talking to a career gal.'

'That's what you say now.'

'Marriage isn't on my agenda either,' she lied. Once they were together, Gerry would see the manifold advantages of marriage to a woman with a full and loving heart.

Gerry continued to squint at her with that peculiar pensiveness.

She held her breath, waiting, waiting. A woman lugged two string bags into a house with fringed lace curtains.

'What the hell,' he said finally. 'I've been gone damn near four years, that's plenty.'

Returning to Beverly Hills, Roy did the unthinkable. She moved out of her mother's house to set up housekeeping with a man.

NolaBee poured out a stream of Southern-accented, smoke-punctuated pleadings, warnings, reproaches. Waces, Roys and Fairburns, she implied, were turning in their Greenward graves. When Roy carried out her cartons, NolaBee hurled her final invective: 'I reckon you're making your own bed, Roy, and my feelings just don't enter into it.' Roy invited her mother for dinner, to Sunday brunch; NolaBee refused, and with each refusal Roy felt that ancient, futile jealousy: her mother had forgiven Marylin *her* trespasses.

It wasn't that Roy wanted to alienate her mother or horrify her KayZee alumnae group. She couldn't help herself. Gerry Horak was in her blood. It was as if in surrendering her body to him, she had also committed her soul. He owned her. Yet, paradoxically, for the first time in her life she felt absolutely in the centre of herself. Adoring, loving, sexy. (She was uncertain whether or not she had reached the ultimate peak, but she found physical joy and a ravishing satisfaction in giving her guy what he needed.) I'm a real woman, she would think. Gerry's woman.

He never mentioned marriage.

Roy thought about it all the time. Panic, sweaty panic, overcame her when she thought they might not eventually be married.

She stopped to market, then drove up Beverly Glen. Here, in this steep canyon wilderness where mule deer mated and opossums went their solitary way, artists, musicians, writers and other oddballs avoided the bourgeois straights of the Eisenhower era.

She parked in a stone-paved notch, lugging her heavy

grocery bag up the fifty-three steps that led through a sylvan grove of spicy-scented eucalyptus.

Moisture curled the tendrils of her short poodle cut and she was panting by the time she reached the narrow grassy ledge fronting the redwood cottage. In the ruddy late-afternoon sunlight, Gerry – naked except for his faded cut-off jeans – stood slashing paint onto a huge canvas stretched against the wood shingle wall.

Totally absorbed, he did not notice her arrival, so she watched him a few moments. Sweat sparkled on the golden pink on his broad shoulders where the tan had peeled. Virile brown hairs sprang from his strongly muscled thighs and calves. Biceps swelling massive as a peasant's, he thwacked on a gob of paint.

The work itself, she ignored. All greens and browns, its meaning was inexplicable to her.

He could get pretty brutal when she watched him, so she proceeded into the inconvenient old kitchen. Before she put away the groceries, she took off her flower appliquéd yellow Adele Simpson – if she wore anything good around the kitchen, she invariably spattered herself. Barefoot, wearing old black toreador pants and a halter, she started the coals in the round portable barbecue outside the kitchen door, then peeled the potatoes, slicing them thinly to fry in butter.

She was washing the salad when she heard the shower.

These hot nights, they ate outside. She lit the hurricane lamps.

'Pretty swank,' Gerry said. The first words he had spoken to her in the hour and a half since she had arrived home.

Roy's freckled face crinkled eagerly. 'I aim to please,' she said. 'Have a good day?'

'Worked,' he said tersely. 'What about you?'

If she nattered when he was preoccupied, he would blow up, but once he had directed a question at her, she knew it was all right to talk. Between mouthfuls of rare porterhouse, crisp potatoes, and salad, she told him about a good customer who had returned a Galanos original with makeup stains around the collar, about the well-corseted young Brazilian matron who – hallelujah! – had bought

324

fifteen pairs of shoes with matching purses, a shipment of fall sweaters arriving in the wrong colours. Beyond the glass-enclosed candle flames, Gerry nodded. He was sympathetic to her, though not to Patricia's. He scorned the idle females who made a cult object of their ageing flesh. Roy was baffled by the impressive resentment that he nursed against these rich women whose elegant *modus vivendi* she admired without envy.

While she did the dishes, Gerry sat at the living-room table frowning over some sketches he had done last Sunday on the beach at Santa Monica.

The night air had cooled off the small cottage, and she sank onto the bulbous couch with its cretonne slipcovers, listening to the owl that lived in the live oak, to the crickets, the faraway cars. The hay-sweet scent of the grass that she had just watered drifted through the open windows to mingle with the smell of Jergen's lotion on her hands. For a few minutes she floated in the rustic pleasures.

She reached for *Time*.

Marylin's new movie, *Providence Valley*, was panned with bitchery and insufferable wit. A final ameliorative paragraph read: 'Rain Fairburn gives a luminous performance which so captures the innocence of first love that it is impossible to believe this lovely creature has two children. The crumbling studio system should recognize her qualities and not cast her in wells of mediocrity like *Providence Valley*.'

If they'd had a telephone she would have called Marylin to congratulate her on the paragraph. Resting the magazine on her halter, Roy considered the paradox of Marylin, who was universally viewed by the press as having the best of all possible worlds, a tip-top career as well as a long-lasting marriage, a child brought back from the dead to perfect normality. (Marylin's travail over Billy's hospital bed, gushily rehashed by the avid-eyed day nurse, had taken up nearly an entire issue of *Ladies' Home Journal*.) But the outside world was not privy to Marylin's heartrending stillness and pallor during Billy's slow recovery. Marylin once again had been suffering the unassuageable pain that follows amputation of love. Neither Marylin nor Joshua ever spoke of Linc, but BJ corresponded with her brother. He had moved to Rome. Marylin had patched her life together as best she could, tied to an ageing, domineering husband and a career that she had not sought, solaced by two adorable children. (Roy's fey little niece, Sari, had been born nearly a year to the day after Billy's accident.)

Gerry put down his sketchbook.

'There's a review of *Providence Valley* in here.' She held up the magazine. 'Hated the film, loved Marylin.'

'She was damn good,' Gerry said. With Roy he had attended the sneak at the Bruin. They occasionally went to the Fernaulds' Sunday barbecues, and as far as Roy could tell, he and Joshua hit it off at these hectic and lavish affairs – he certainly warmed to Marylin, but what mortal man wouldn't react favourably to that exquisite, luminous glow? NolaBee's continued failure to show up when they were at the Fernaulds' made it obvious that she was avoiding them. Gerry had laughed about it. But when Roy had wept, he comforted her.

Stretching vigorously, he came over, grasping her hand, pulling her to her feet. As they hugged, a delicate flush covered her freckled face. She could feel his rising erection.

'Love you so, Gerry,' she murmured.

She went into the bathroom to insert her diaphragm. No matter how hot and heavy they got, she always took it from its round blue metal box. Marylin's long-ago contretemps had indelibly marked her. Often, though, as Roy squatted with the rubber circle, a thought would come to her: Maybe being preg will do the trick. Yet she always pressed home the jelly-slathered disc. Bad enough that she was concealing from Gerry her unquenchable need for matrimony. She rebelled with all her warm and open mind at further subterfuge or devious trickery. In bed, she kissed down his scarred chest to his hard penis: he expected intimacies of her that once had shocked her to the core but that she now accepted as part of being his woman. He himself spent ages on what marriage manuals called foreplay. She was wet everywhere before he threw off the sheet to kneel behind her crouching body. This was the position he preferred, so she accepted it, though she longed to be face to face so they could kiss. (In those bleakest moments of pain when she wondered if he would ever marry her, she had decided that he preferred the anonymity of an abstract vessel.) His sweating body rushed swiftly over her, and then he collapsed gasping.

Had *it* happened to her? In all the heavy breathing, his or her own, she never could be positive.

43

At Patricia's, each customer had her own saleslady, and if that saleslady was busy, the customer waited, browsing in the little boutique that carried handsome belts, a few carefully selected glimmers of antique jewellery, Hermès scarves and crazily expensive sweaters. Generally by five o'clock most of the customers had completed their shopping.

Roy, in addition to her managerial tasks, had her own clientele. The following day at a little after five she was returning a richly coloured armload of fall evening gowns to the stockroom. Her feet hurt, and pain splintered behind her eyes. She had spent the entire afternoon waiting on the fortyish, sleekly attractive, alcoholic wife of a prominent surgeon; the woman, having tried on Patricia's extensive stock of size sixes, had just walked out sans apology or purchase.

The saleslady designated to watch over the boutique was nowhere in sight, and a tall, slender woman with a loose, streaked blond chignon stood picking through the unattended sweaters. From the back, Roy could recognize the easily cut beige silk as part of the Paris Fath collection. And there was something familiar about the hair.

'Do you have a saleslady, madam?' Roy asked. 'If you'll give me her name, I'll get her right away.'

The blonde turned. The long, handsomely patrician face relaxed into surprise. 'Roy?'

'Althea!' Roy dropped the formals on one of the velvet poufs.

Their embrace was a brief feminine hug, the sort in which bodies do not enter into configurations and kisses are pressed in the air near the cheek, yet for all the stereotyped awkwardness their eyes grew moist as inevitable memories assailed them: the Big Two . . . lunches in proud isolation on the Beverly High cafeteria patio . . . hours spent plastering on odalisque makeup . . . slow, croony Frank Sinatra records and the hypnotic seduction of Ravel's *Bolero* . . .

They drew apart.

Althea gave a little cough. 'So you work here?' she asked.

'Yes. I'm the assistant manager,' Roy replied proudly.

She didn't need to inquire about Althea's life. In the intervening decade Althea's doings had been duly noted by the press. She was twice married. At seventeen to Firelli – that wonderful old man, as Roy mentally called the English maestro. Invariably, though, Roy shuddered at the repellent image of her erstwhile friend's slim youthfulness locked in the marital embrace with that rotund little old man, an image far more loathsome than Joshua with Marylin because of the far greater age span. Althea had a son by Firelli. After their divorce, she had picked off another Englishman, Aubrey Wimborne. The lovely Mrs Carlo Firelli, the lovely Mrs Aubrey Wimborne, was photographed at the parties of Coynes, Guggenheims, Rockefellers, Mellons, at the Côte d'Azur estate of the Duchess of Alba and the châteaux of various Rothschilds, at the Paris Opera house between Firelli and Horowitz, in Bermuda with the Duke and Duchess of Windsor, at Princess Margaret's wedding to Anthony Armstrong Jones.

Althea said, 'Cheating and clawing your way to the topmost *haute couture?*'

Roy laughed. Yet suddenly she felt more than the four inches shorter that she was to Althea. What a stupefying chasm between their lives.

Mrs Fineman had come to stand outside the boutique area, a squarish, carefully coiffed and jewelled presence. As she stared at the heaped, rich-coloured designer garments, her fleshy face took on a disapproval that was both proprietary and maternal.

'I'm in the market for some evening things,' Althea drawled loudly. 'Like those little frocks you have there.'

'Yes, Mrs Wimborne.' Roy scooped up the armful of luxurious silks. 'If you'll follow me, Mrs Wimborne.'

She led Althea to the largest of the fitting rooms. Their reflections receded endlessly in the angled mirrors, and neither woman looked directly at the other. How strange to be confronted by an infinity of their paired images after so long . . . Roy could not help attempting to reconcile this serene and worldly Althea (who wore no smidge of makeup on her smooth, exquisitely tanned skin, not even lipstick on her narrow, well-delineated mouth) with the aloof, secretive, unhappy, overpainted schoolgirl Althea. Into Roy's mind popped a memory of those crazy, unending sobs reverberating through her messy bedroom. Her awe of her old friend vanished.

Roy asked, 'Are you living back here?'

'I'm at Belvedere while I get a divorce. A two-time loser. Hopeless, aren't I? What about you? Are you married? Divorced?'

'Neither. I'm in love,' Roy replied, not even attempting to disguise the radiance of her smile.

'In love?' Althea spoke in a questioning tone as if it were an expression she had never heard.

'You know – a mad, passionate involvement. He's the only thing in the world that matters to me.'

'Oh, Roy,' Althea smiled, shaking her head. 'You haven't changed – not one iota.'

'That may be true, but this is the first time I've ever really fallen. I'd all but abandoned hope. It's like a religious experience. It's like somebody's switched on all the lights. Do I sound corny? Well, love's done it to me.'

'I'm joyous for you,' Althea said with a superior little half-smile. This was her old way of dousing Roy's enthusiasms. After a brief silence, though, Althea was inquiring warmly, 'How is your family? I read about Marylin, of course, but tell me the news about your mother.'

Roy sat on the velvet bench. 'We're on the outs,' she sighed. 'Gerry and I live together without benefit of clergy.'

'You don't! But hadn't you become so veddy, veddy proper? Sorority life and all that jazz. Openly?'

'I *was* Miss Middle-Class Propriety for a few years. But now I live in sin.'

'Wonders will never cease.'

'He's the most important thing that ever happened to me.' Roy glimpsed a hundred repetitions in her cherry-red, sappily smiling face. She said crisply, 'I read you have a little boy. He's a bit older than Billy.'

'Carlo's almost ten – oh, drat! I keep forgetting he calls himself Charles now. That's Firelli's real name.'

'Yes, I know. I still remember nearly dropping in my tracks when I heard the English accent. He told me the whole deal about changing his name. Originally he was Charlie Frye.'

'Exactly. *My* Charles is gorgeous. The strong, take-command type – he treats me like a bit of fluff. At the moment he's keen for his grandpa's collies.'

'How are they, your parents?'

'The same. Mother tends her flowers and worships Daddy. He strides gracefully around, lord of the manor,' Althea said levelly. 'They defy time.'

It was closing hour, and outside the fitting room, soprano voices rippled.

Impulsively Roy said, 'If you don't have any plans, we could finish catching up at my place.'

'Your love nest? Wonderful!'

Althea insisted on buying one of the expensive Italian sweaters on their way out.

They left her maroon Cadillac convertible parked in the lot. In Roy's fender-dented Chevy they joined the slow-moving rush-hour traffic that edged along Wilshire. Each corner drew forth bantering reminiscences, Simon's Drive-in where they had followed the public antics of Big Timers, Armstrong Schroeder's, where they had sometimes gorged on plate-size apple pancakes, Beverly High's square clock tower in the distance. The conversation lapsed at the fountain where they had first met Dwight Hunter. They remained silent until they were passing between the two manicured green golf courses of the Los Angeles Country Club.

Then Althea inquired, 'What sort of man is he, your guy?'

'Gerry? He's completely different from everybody. There's nobody like him.'

'Let's be a trifle more explicit, Wace.'

'He has high cheekbones and narrow sort of eyes, not Oriental but Slavic. He's not exactly what you'd call handsome, I guess. He has a broody, interesting face. And a terrific build. Muscular, well-proportioned – he's not tall, about five-eight. I'm wild for him, but he's on another wavelength. I have such ordinary, middle-class values, and he's an artist, a real artist, a very talented painter – '

'What's his other name?' Althea interrupted.

'Horak.'

Althea made a choking sound.

Roy glanced away from the traffic. Althea was staring ahead, her slender neck held so rigidly that the tendons stood out.

'So you *have* heard of him?' Roy said. 'He's really quite famous.'

'I know him,' Althea said in that odd, strangled voice. 'We were both at Henry Lissauer's.'

'Lissauer? The German artist who killed himself?'

'Right.' Althea's voice dipped on the word. She drew a breath, asking in a worldly drawl, 'Is he aware we were girlhood chums, you and I?'

Roy thought a moment before admitting, 'I don't remember ever mentioning you. Gerry's not much on talking about old times or that kind of thing.'

'Well, well. Gerry Horak, of all people. Small world and will wonders never cease. Or coincidences do happen.'

'So you were friends?'

'One might call us that if one stretched the point.' Althea's tone was humorous, yet for a moment Roy felt something sinister, dangerous even, enter the car.

She gripped the hot steering wheel. This idea of hers was typically half-baked. What had possessed her to invite Althea home? Gerry scorned rich people, and Althea Coyne Cunningham Firelli Wimborne was the richest of the rich. Besides, it was clear that they had tangled somehow at that poor dead man's art school. God, he'll blow a gasket when the two of us stroll in.

Althea said, 'Possibly, Roy, your love nest isn't the spot for us to catch up on our shady past.'

Roy said with a surge of relief, 'Let's go to Westwood. Crumpler's makes terrific malts and hamburgers.'

At Crumpler's they sat wedged between noisy tables of UCLA kids. Althea talked in a high, staccato way about Gloria Vanderbilt, Grace and Rainier, Princess Margaret and Tony, the Windsors: undeniably there was a heady pleasure in getting the real dirt about these inhabitants of the celestial spheres, yet at the same time the gossip (and perhaps this was its purpose) demeaned Roy, showing her up as a gauche, insignificant nobody. She found herself compulsively serving up the Fernaulds' better-known peers and acquaintances – Greer, Cary, Marylin, Ava, Bing, Liz. The arch, phony ring of her tattling voice disgusted her and she barely touched her nutburger.

They drove back to Beverly Hills.

As Althea opened the door of her maroon Cadillac, she had a cool look that Roy found utterly enviable – she herself felt sweaty and dishevelled.

It was completely old times' sake that obligated her to say, 'Althea, what about lunch? I'm available on Saturdays.'

'Wonderful,' Althea said.

'I'll call you at the end of the week.'

Althea gave a high shivery laugh. 'Oh, and by the way, your Gerry and I had rather a falling-out. So it might be best for you if you didn't mention my name.'

Roy shook her head and raised her shoulders, an exaggeration of bewilderment.

Althea smiled. 'Doesn't he still have moods?'

At this slur, Roy's loyalties rushed to Gerry's side. 'He was in awful pain then! He was badly wounded in Italy.'

Yet as Althea started her engine, the defensive anger drained from Roy. 'I really meant it about lunch,' she yelled.

Althea did not seem to hear. The long wine-coloured car eased from the parking lot.

44

She had no clear idea of how she got to Belvedere. She was in her room, her body and face blazing hot, her reason decimated by great, turbulent emotions. She could hear Charles's clear contralto voice somewhere in the house, a faraway sound that made no more sense than anything else. Gerry Horak, the bastard, she thought over and over. Will I ever be quit of that mess?

Gerry Horak.

By a mad twist of fate's kaleidoscope, Gerry Horak had latched on to curly-haired, eager little Roy Wace, once dirt-poor, now a shopgirl.

Gerry . . .

He deserted me years ago, so why should I care that he's taken up with Roy?

Yet she was surging with helpless despair.

In the past decade she had trained herself like an Olympic athlete, controlling every weakness, subduing her obstreperous demons, and quieting her baleful insecurities. It had been years since she had felt this way, crushed, immobilized and at the mercy of another – or rather, at the mercy of her own torturous emotions about another.

When she looked at the clock it was 8.20. She had been in this room for nearly an hour. She tore off every garment she had worn with Roy Wace as if the pale silks were Heracles' cloak burning into her flesh. Glimpsing her pale, twisting reflection in the pier mirror, she went over to stand in front of it.

She gazed at the long, tanned body with its stripes of

milky white flesh where her bikini swimsuits covered as if she were confronted by a revelation. This yellow triangle, these full, firm breasts with wide-aureoled apricot nipples comprised her adulthood's victorious battlefield. When this was a hairless, breastless snake of a girl-child's body it had endured the ultimate, bloody defeat. This was the body that had carried her through her sentence of childhood, this was the body that she and her friend Roy had clothed in motley. This the body Gerry Horak had awakened and briefly eased of its guilts, this the body that he had impregnated, then casually abandoned. (Rancorous, festering memories of waiting eternal hours outside a shack covered with Algerian ivy, then hearing from a cheesy blonde that he had walked out on both of them.) The body that husbands and lovers had worshipped and roused to climax, yet ultimately had left unsatisfied. She cupped her large, resilient breasts, slipping her hands down her sides. How strange that none of her triumphs and torments had left a mark on this body.

After Gerry's desertion, she had attempted to destroy the baby – and herself, too – by swallowing a great number of pills. But she and the child within her had survived. During that first month of world peace, she had married Firelli – she continued to address her first husband as he was known to the public – in an Episcopal rite performed by a British Army chaplain under the broad, dangling crystals of a Zurich hotel chandelier. Closing her eyes, she could quite clearly see her bridegroom's wrinkled fingers trembling as they caressed this body, which he was incapable of taking. She had trusted Firelli then, she trusted him still. A luxurious sensation. He had given her son his name – that self-chosen, exuberantly Italian nomenclature. He had given her freedom. *It's clear as houses that you must get on with a real life and a real husband, Althea, little love, and I seem to be lasting forever.* After the divorce he still imparted his doting, prideful affection on the boy, and on her. If Charles had inherited Gerry's creative talent, such a gift surely would have been ascribed to the octogenarian English maestro, but Charles, thank God, might have been parthenogenetically conceived, so like her side was he.

She went into the dressing room, reaching for a robe.

It's been over for ten years, she thought, mentally articulating each word. It should be nothing to me what Gerry Horak does, or where he is. It's a crazy, fantastic chance, nothing more, that he, of all men, is attached to Roy Wace. Why should I care?

I'm no longer that miserable, endlessly weeping, suicidal idiot that he left without a good-bye, and in the oldest of lurches.

Yet she was so distracted by the fierce tangle of love, pain, loathing, outraged pride and unrelinquishable, punitive jealousy that she kept envisioning her hands cutting off the air in Roy's rounded, freckled throat. It was torment for her to know she was in the same city with the pair.

Why should I stay in Beverly Hills?

There's no need.

Nevada is the capital of divorce.

Tightening the sash of her tailored white silk robe, she walked along the corridor with its musty tapestries to inform her son of her decision to head for Nevada.

One of the guest suites had been refurbished in Black Watch plaid for Charles's visits, and a faint, permanent hint of boyish sweat hung in the warm air. He had surrounded himself with the sports paraphernalia of his international boyhood: foils, fencing masks, tennis and squash rackets hung on the walls; a large old sea chest held every type of ball; baseball and cricket bats ranged along the wall where the doting Cunninghams had ordered a hi-fi built in for him.

On the carpet below the turntable, Charles sat with his rather long chin resting on his scabby knees as he listened to his 'father's' latest LP: Beethoven's Fifth.

Smiling, he raised a hand, a greeting that indicated conversation should wait until the record ended. Althea, surrounded by the triumphant theme, sank into a plaid chair. To constrain her impatient, relentless turmoil, she focused her attention on her son.

Charles had tow hair (hers had been this identical near-white until puberty) of straight, fine-spun texture that,

335

despite recent combing, flopped over a high forehead. He had her refined bone structure. In the French khaki shorts and white shirt that was the summer uniform of the Lexford English School in Geneva, his height seemed precariously fragile, yet he managed to convey an impression of lean power, not the obtrusive strength with which Grover T. Coyne had amassed his incalculable wealth, but a more subtle quality, the self-possession that universally hardens the ruling élite.

As the boy nodded in time to the Firelli interpretation of Beethoven, his well-shaped, narrow lips were folded in the calm line that she, as a frantically self-conscious girl, had unsuccessfully attempted to form with her own mouth. His eyes were closed. Open, their hazel would show keen intelligence and a hint of remote wariness that was utterly lacking in fear. Though bound with the strongest of silver cords to her son, Althea freely confessed to herself that her tie was not milky pale, tender maternal love, but proud, admiring respect.

Charles knew how to rule. He controlled others at Lexford School not with his revered patronym nor with the huge fortune that would be fed to him through a complex root system of trusts, but by an innate, rational ability to subdue his few inherent failings and call upon his numerous strengths.

Althea saw her son as the vindicatory reverse of her own fabric: the chromosomal weaving had endowed him with the desirable qualities that she lacked — ordered self-assurance and the ability to govern the ominous world of people. She did not realize, because it had been years since Charles had succumbed to an unfettered display of affection, that the seamless wall he had erected around himself was weakest in her direction. He loved her.

The final resounding drum notes of the coda rolled, and the needle automatically raised from the record.

'Where were you for dinner?' Charles was not whining, not reproaching, simply inquiring. His clear rather deep contralto lengthened the A's, American style; yet he somehow gave the impression of conversing in the purest Oxford accent. He spoke his various languages in the most cultivated tones – Florentine Italian, Parisian French, Castilian Spanish.

'I met an old friend, Roy Wace. Remember, I've mentioned her. We had a hamburger and a malt.'

'Our native food,' he said. It was a small joke for the boy held three citizenships: the Swiss of his birth, the British of Firelli, and American, by virtue of having been registered at the consulate in Zurich.

She smiled. After a moment she said, 'I'm going to Nevada for my divorce.'

'Why?'

'It only takes six weeks there. I could be back in Geneva with you a little bit after your term begins.'

'Sounds a good idea,' he said. 'You know, Aubrey isn't such a rotten sort.'

'We're still friends.'

'Without him, though, I feel closer to Father.'

'Me too,' she said.

The uncomplicated ease of their exchange soothed Althea. The single resemblance between her son and his natural father was this ability to communicate directly with her. This inheritance she seldom dwelt on. She had no desire to entangle the creating emotions she bore Charles with the snare of love, hatred and bitter desolation surrounding her few months with Gerry.

Going to the shelves, she selected another Firelli album. 'Brahms' First Symphony?'

'Good,' he said.

'Would you like to go with me?' She fitted the record on the spindle. 'I'll be at Archie Coyne's ranch near Reno. It must be deathly hot there now, but if you come, we could get in a few early-morning rides.'

'I've always wanted to try a western saddle,' Charles said. Then his face lit in a seldom-used, ultimately disarming boyish smile. 'Cowboys and Indians.'

She ruffled the fine, near-white hair, the only show of maternal warmth tolerable to either. 'After the Brahms, it's bedtime,' she said.

* * *

337

Two mornings later, when Roy called Belvedere to confirm their lunch date, Luther, the old butler, told her Mrs Wimborne and Master Firelli had left town.

45

Roy, following Althea's chary advice, did not tell Gerry about running into her old friend.

That first week of September, a heat wave clamped down on Southern California. Light shivered above the softened asphalt streets of Beverly Hills, gardens wilted despite the constant whir of sprinklers and blazing sunlight assaulted the eyes. Few of Patricia's customers ventured from their poolsides.

Roy was like a medieval taster about her work: as an additional courtesy to her customers she had always taken the time to try on the various designers, ascertaining for herself how each garment fitted and hung. Now, in the empty, air-conditioned shop, she critically donned the autumn line, unable to prevent herself from eyeing all of the pale-hued size twelves that – with her employee's discount – she could afford. Would this be an appropriate informal wedding gown? Checking invoices at her desk outside Mr Fineman's office, she found herself scribbling *Mrs Gerrold K. Horak* and *Roy Horak* on her scratch pad then shamefacedly tearing up the sheets.

On Thursday evening, Mr Fineman said in his New York intonations, 'The way business is, Roy, you might as well take off Friday and Saturday.'

Gerry was in one of those hiatuses devoted to brooding that, though regenerative to an artist's creativity, are more demanding than work itself. He was primed for a little fun. That weekend they lolled by the ocean's crowded edge in Santa Monica and Roy turned crimson, popping out in freckles. They lugged a picnic basket to the Hollywood

Bowl for a Peggy Lee concert, they finished a quart of 31 Flavours Ripple Fudge ice cream, they made love outdoors in the dappling shade of the pepper tree.

Sunday cooled off a little, and in the evening she barbecued ribs, which they ate while lolling on the hay-scented ledge. Darkness was falling.

'I've never been happy quite like this,' she said.

'Damn right,' he said, grinning.

'Gerry,' she blurted, not really considering her words, only her primal mating urge, 'it'd be even more perfect, married.'

He pulled away, sitting up. In the dusk, his wide-planed face seemed thoughtful rather than angry.

Encouraged, she said, 'We get along so perfectly.'

'Babe,' he said, his voice softer than usual, 'we had this out in Paris. No permanent entanglements.'

'It's been good for you, too.'

'Yes, but I've had in mind to take off and travel. Maybe Kenya. The colours and light there are meant to be a knockout.'

'I wouldn't tie you down. You could come and go.'

'Promises are just hot air, Roy.'

'I mean them.'

'Sure you do. Now. But later they won't mean a good goddamn.'

'Darling, I wouldn't get in your way for the world.'

He held her wrist, his thumb moving gently on the inner veins. 'Say, you aren't knocked up, are you?'

She knew she ought to lie. But she was the world's most rotten liar. 'No,' she whispered.

'Well, then what's wrong with the way we are now? Free. We have all the good parts.'

'I'd be so sweet to you.'

'Christ, Roy! Big deal if somebody mumbles a few words over us and we sign a certificate. How will that make you any sweeter, or our life any better?'

'It's how people live,' she said. She might never get up the nerve again. 'Didn't we have to lie to the landlord here and tell him we were married before he'd rent to us? I can't

339

tell them at work that I live with you, or the Finemans would fire me.'

'You should have picked yourself a junior executive.' Gerry's voice rang more loudly in the hot, barbecue-scented darkness.

'The minute you want out, you're free to go.'

'I know you mean that, Roy,' he said, quieter again. 'And every damn argument I put up makes me a bastard – but what about Paris? There you swore you wanted a hotshot fashion career. What happened to that idea? What happened to the talk of me just sharing expenses?'

'It's worked out, hasn't it?'

'Sure, swell, but – '

'You told me yourself you've done some good work here.'

'You're a terrific kid, a real straightshooter, and if I were in the market, you'd be the one, but – '

'Gerry, I love you so much.' Her excruciating anxiety to convince him of the advantages of matrimony was an actual physical pressure crushing down on her. Arguments skittered through her brain, and she reached for his hand. 'I want to tell everybody about us.' Her voice was high. 'I told my old friend Althea Wimborne about us – she used to be Althea Cunningham when you knew her.'

Gerry pulled his hand out of her fervid grasp. There was a long silence. In the darkness she could see his hunched, bulky immobility, and somehow she knew he was tensely coiled.

As the silence stretched the pressure increased. Althea had warned her not to mention their meeting. *Why? Have I wrecked everything?*

An owl hooted, some creature rustled in the ivy. Roy knew she should wait, let Gerry speak first. Yet she blurted out, 'She said you met at the art school.'

'When were you such hot buddies?' Gerry's voice was a low, vindictive growl.

'At Beverly High we were inseparable.' Roy could hear the shrillness of desperation in her voice. 'I haven't seen her in ages.'

'Ages.' In a falsetto, he mimicked her. 'Didn't you just say you told her about *us.*'

'I ran into her a couple of weeks ago. She was shopping at Patricia's and – '

'You blabber and blabber about every assy thing that happens to you there, every rich cunt who walks in. Why clam up about this?'

'I invited her up here. When she heard about you, she didn't want to come. She made it pretty clear you two hadn't hit it off.'

He gave an unpleasant chuckle. 'It was worse for poor old Henry Lissauer. He really got it between the eyes.'

'Althea? I don't understand – '

Gerry was on his feet.

A moment later the light went on in the kitchen. She followed him inside. He had dumped the contents of her straw bag on the table. As he fingered through her things, his skin seemed flattened across his face, and his eyes were narrow. He looked terrifying – and alive. She realized that until now she had seen a comatose, etiolated version of Gerry Horak. 'Where the hell are the car keys?'

'On the nightstand – Gerry, where are you going?' She rested her shaking hand on his arm.

He jerked out of her hold. 'Get the fuck out of my way!' he raged.

She backed away, frightened.

He charged into their room, and returning stuffing money into the back pocket of his Levis.

She followed him outside. 'Gerry, please tell me where you're going.'

'Can't you ever the fuck quit blabbing?'

She stood on the step hugging her arms around herself while, below, the door of her Chevy slammed and the engine roared. At the wheel, Gerry often would brood about his work, forgetting the odometer, speeding recklessly. The sound of the Chevy faded into other traffic. With a shuddering sigh Roy moved across the grassy ledge to gather the supper dishes and leftover ribs.

As the hot, sweat-sodden dark hours passed, her anxiety

swelled to near-lunatic proportions. She prayed conti-nuously: Let him come back, let him come back. She had to have a chance to plead with him on her knees – no, plead with him while stretched prone next to his leather sandals. If only he would return, she would abide by whatever conditions he imposed.

Love had dwindled her into a beggar.

By 3 A.M. she was telephoning the police in a panic about accidents.

The bored voice reported that no 1949 Chevrolet, Cali-fornia licence number 2D9863, had been involved in a collision.

Roy lay back down on the bed, her hands clenched as tight as her jaw. Wedged between her fears were questions of Gerry and Althea's relationship. From their equally vehement responses, it was clear that they had loathed each other, and though Roy tended to view the passions of those near to her loyally, without parlour psychoanalysis, she could not block out the unthinkable plausibility that this vituperative hatred had once been its opposite, happier emotion, love.

Althea Cunningham and Gerry Horak?

Could two members of the human race be more dissimi-lar? The contrast went deeper than Gerry's abysmally poor background which made Roy's own impoverished, peri-patetic early childhood seem the rearing of an Infanta. Gerry's manners were rotten and Althea's aristocratic, he was totally unconcerned by the reactions of others while Althea forever hid her thin skin – and avenged herself for any wounds inflicted. They were even wrong physically – Althea was way too tall for him.

The many-paned window grew light. Roy forced herself from the bed, standing dully under the shower, then applying powder base to tone down her lobster sunburn.

Hoping against hope he would return, she waited until the last minute to call a cab and arrived at Patricia's late.

The cooling of temperatures had continued. Customers in sleeveless sheaths pushed their way through the glass doors.

Roy, with a set little smile, carried out fall wools and tweeds. *Why force him into marriage? Why couldn't I be content with my usual crumbs?*

Unable to deal with anything so immense as losing Gerry, she fastened her anxieties on how to get home. In a shrill voice she discussed her transport problem with the other employees, and Mrs Thomas, the well-corseted blonde saleslady who lived in Van Nuys, offered her a ride. Roy sat with the car window open, stifling her screams as la Thomas endlessly, mercilessly nattered on. Was this how Gerry heard her cheery tales of Patricia's? She was too weary, too miserable to pursue the wretched thought.

The old Chevy was not in its niche. Though she had not expected it would be, she felt an oozing in her chest, as if her heart's blood were draining. She dragged slowly up the fifty-three wooden steps.

The door was open. Her heart caught, her legs shook as she raced across the narrow, grassy ledge.

Gerry sat on the slipcovered sofa, his head buried in his hands. A ripe odour of liquor reached Roy's nostrils.

'Hi,' she said quietly.

He looked up. The skin was stretched over his broad cheekbones, and his mouth was tight. 'I wrecked your car,' he said in a subdued voice.

'Are you all right?' She, too, spoke quietly.

'Good shape,' he said. 'But your car's about totalled. I had it towed into the shop.'

'You look like you could use some coffee.'

'Sounds good.'

She went into the kitchen. When she brought in the steaming mug, he was still hunched on the sofa.

He took a long gulp of the black coffee. 'Listen,' he said. 'Barging out like that was a stinking thing to do, and I'm sorry as hell. I've been dead set against marriage for so long that I couldn't separate it from how I feel about you. Roy, I need you, babe. And if you'll still have me, I'm all for us being hitched.'

She should have been dancing in the clouds, but she sat opposite him in the stifling cottage, wanting to cry. Gerry's

343

eyes were sunk into deep, coal-dust marks. Slumped there with an abject, pleading expression, he reminded her of a tamed bear they had seen one day in the Place du Tertre, a poor bedraggled animal forced to perform acts unnatural to its kind.

Sympathy flooded through her, and briefly she thought that she should set him free. Then the imperious forces that had drawn her to him in the first place – love, the need to become part of him permanently, to bear his children – took over. I belong to him, she thought.

'Oh, darling,' she said. 'I've been so miserable without you . . .'

46

A good night's sleep cured Roy's depression and Gerry's hangover. Fixing his breakfast, she whistled 'Where or When'; he cheerfully devoured four scrambled eggs, sausages, a huge pile of toast encrusted with Hero plum jam. When her taxi honked below, he gave her an exuberant hug, smearing her lipstick.

That day he spent the proceeds from his big triptych – his first important sale in nearly a year – to buy her the car of her dreams, a powder-blue, brand new Thunderbird. (The old Chevy, engine rebuilt and body hammered out, would be his.)

Wednesday after work, Roy drove her snazzy new sports car the few blocks to her mother's house on Crescent.

NolaBee opened the door, her sallow face working. She was incapable of bestowing the same endlessly preoccupied love on her younger daughter that she gave her exquisite masterpiece, but her maternal devotion ran deep. She had not cut Roy off out of brassbound moral compunctions but as a realistic method of bringing the child to her senses: marriage was every female's desired goal, and Roy, with this one irrevocable blunder, was forever blighting her chances.

'Mama?'

NolaBee pulled her daughter into a cigarette-fumed embrace, a reconciliatory hug that dampened both pairs of eyes.

'Well, stranger, come on in,' she said, shifting a scrapbook and a large heap of red-pencilled papers from Burrelle's Press Clipping Bureau to clear a place on the couch for them.

She blew her nose on a rumpled Kleenex. 'Tell me about that smart-lookin' car.'

'Gerry gave it to me instead of a ring. Mama, we're getting married.'

NolaBee gaped, dumbfounded. She had been utterly convinced 'that man', as she called Gerry, would never do the right thing by Roy.

Despite NolaBee's near-visceral relief, mean, dark doubts were fraying her, unruly apprehensions that had nothing to do with artists' well-known inability to earn a living – hadn't she chosen dear, dead Chilton Wace over her other, more likely prospect? – but were wholly concerned with the personal. Gerry Horak came from poor trash and proved his lack of breeding by his brusque, sometimes downright coarse manners. The narrow-eyed, carnal way that he looked at Roy proved he had no respect for womankind. He would retreat into long silences, the sure sign of a loner. Gerry Horak was the worst possible choice for a husband.

Yet her Roy, pink-cheeked, was smiling a soft, joyous smile.

'Married?' NolaBee's exclamation was loud. 'My baby married? Both my girls – I declare, this makes me a success in life!'

'We're doing it next week.'

NolaBee couldn't repress a glance at Roy's nicely indented waist.

'Oh, Mama, nothing like *that*. We just want everything simple. We thought maybe at the Beverly Hills City Hall.'

'Waces and Roys and Fairburns don't get married in a poky old courthouse!' NolaBee cried. 'Honey, listen, I was right upset about the sordid way you two set up housekeep-

345

ing like that. What mother wouldn't be? But that doesn't mean I don't love my little freckle-face. 'Course I'll give you two a right nice send-off.'

'I'll have to ask Gerry. I don't know how he'll feel.'

'The wedding's up to the girl. I'll arrange for a minister –'

'Gerry said he preferred a judge.'

'A judge, then.' NolaBee blew out cigarette smoke. 'Darlin', we'll ask your old friends – what a shame Althea isn't here. The girls in the sorority you were friendly with, the people at your work. And there's Joshua's family, and BJ. and her in-laws. I reckon we could ask a few of my closest friends, too . . .' The pitted skin of NolaBee's face took on colour as her lively Southern voice planned on and on.

That night in bed, Roy timidly broached the idea of a wedding. Since the binge, Gerry had gone out of his way to be agreeable, while she, on her part, had been stepping on eggs to be what she considered his ideal woman, caring, tender, submissive, subservient to her man's wants. An after-you-my-dear-Alphonse situation. She concluded, 'Of course if you don't want a fuss . . .'

'Why not?' he asked, patting her naked backside. 'Why the hell not?'

They set the date for 19 September, ten days thence.

There was no time to have invitations engraved, so NolaBee and Roy asked people whenever they saw them, and the guest list and wedding plans mushroomed haphazardly. The day before the wedding, NolaBee baked two hams, and her quartet of best friends – one of them the wife of a studio head – came in to help her fix washtubs of potato salad, chicken salad and fruit salad with marshmallows in it. NolaBee had sent to Greenward for the recipe of her grandmother's punch, but Joshua boomed, 'Punch! This isn't a finger-sandwich tea for Southern ladies, Nola-Bee, it's a grand and glorious hymeneal party, a celebration of the eternal mating instincts in mankind. I'm handling the booze.'

Marylin promised to see to the flowers.

So the wedding ended up half-Wace, half-Beverly Hills. Two thin, nervous men perched tall, festively elegant arrangements of white chrysanthemums in every available cranny of the small house, then set about concealing the weedy carelessness of the backyard with a truckload of clay pots that overflowed with white blossoms – shasta daisies, margueritas, azaleas. Three bartenders in red jackets lined up rented glasses on the quilted leather bar that Abbey Rents had deposited on the patio. NolaBee, in her careless, vital way, crowded the sideboard and old round table that had come from down home with a conglomeration of dimestore bowls and cracked Haviland platters. By 2.30 the living room, dining room and garden were jammed with guests holding drinks.

Among the KayZee alums were all eleven of Roy's pledge group with husbands and small children. BJ and Maury Morrison disgorged a station wagon full of their children and his parents: it turned out that the senior Morrisons knew the Finemans from some kind of Jewish organization. Montgomery Clift, who was in Marylin's new movie, appeared briefly, sending ripples of excitement through the gathering, as did Susan Hayward. Roy was a favourite at Patricia's, and the staff showed up *en masse*, the black father and son who worked in the stockroom wearing handsomely tailored dinner jackets. Old chums from Beverly High like Janet Schwarz Fetterman, Heidi Ronoletti Hanks, and Bitsy Bennet Kelly brought their spouses. A sculptor friend of Gerry's lounged on the patio wall in his blue jeans. A gang of children led by Billy (hyperactive as if he had never hovered near the Great Divide) made constant forays on the buffet table.

The string trio that Joshua had commandeered from Paramount wove the disparate groups together with the sweet, tender ripples of 'Ich Liebe Dich' and 'Träumerei'.

Most eyes followed Marylin – Rain Fairburn – as she bent her lovely, luminous face to reassure her little daughter, Sari.

The honorary flower girl, Sari clutched her basket of white rosebuds as if for salvation. The mass of people terrified her. Except for her enormous, expressive brown eyes, Sari was a funny-looking little kid, all bones, sharp angles, and clouds of curly dark hair.

Sari's emotional responses lay naked on the nerves of her skin. She was incapable of learning the evasions that even children her age, four, have inevitably taken on as protection against the painful pricks of life. This day, she clung too adoringly to her immediate family, bucking off in frightened confusion from the other guests' greetings and alcohol-scented kisses.

At this non-traditional wedding, the bride and groom circulated among the guests before the ceremony. Roy, her eyes incandescent below her smartly feathered little cocktail hat, her curves encased by pale turquoise *peau de soie* designed by Mollie Parnis that was the Finemans' wedding gift – introduced Gerry to the mob. He had on the same check sports jacket that he had worn when Roy met him on the Île St Louis – NolaBee had failed to convince him to buy a suit. Despite this lack of groomly modishness, he was going out of his way to be amenable, teasing NolaBee – he would, he insisted, have picked her over either of her girls if she'd given him a tumble – laughing at Billy's bathroom humour, discussing art with the studio wives.

Roy kept patting his sleeve and gazing into his wide, smiling, satyr's face. For the rest of our lives, she would think, catching her breath. For the rest of our lives. She loved every one of the guests – and felt immense pity for them. Not a person here – not a person on earth – could have experienced this exaltation.

At 4.30 Judge Dezanter showed up. Tall, round-shouldered and seventy, he immediately stood Gerry and Roy in front of him.

Guests crowded around, and a fat, perspiring Paramount still photographer climbed on the low wall for a clear view. There was a chorus of shush, shush.

Judge Dezanter, displaying such white, straight teeth that they must be dentures, inquired of Gerry, 'Do you, Gerrold, take Roy Elizabeth as your wife?'

'I do,' Gerry replied in a clear, quiet tone.

The big white smile turned on Roy. 'Do you, Roy Elizabeth, agree to take Gerrold as your husband?'

The bodies surrounding Roy seemed to press inward, the faces were wiped blank of features – she could not recognize her mother or sister. I should let him off the hook, she thought in her sudden claustrophobic panic. Let him free.

The judge's pale lips closed over his teeth. He gave her a questioning look.

'I do!' she cried. It was not her voice but a loud, frightened gabble. Gerry had to hold her spastic hand in order to slide on the narrow gold band.

By the power vested in him by the state of California, Judge Dezanter pronounced them man and wife.

Billy Fernauld applauded.

The newlyweds shared a glass of Mumm's, the studio photographer recorded it, then snapped Roy Horak cutting the first slice of the many-tiered cake from Hansen's.

It was time for Roy to get her short, matching jacket. Marylin, holding Sari, went with her sister into the bedroom. The quiet, cool air retained a faint hint of the Shalimar that Roy had spread on herself before the party.

Marylin set Sari down, and the child grasped her mother's slender, shapely thigh through cream-coloured silk. 'Mommy, it's nice in here. Can't we just stay?'

'For a while, Sari.' Marylin opened her little beaded purse to take out a cheque. 'Here's another present.'

'Marylin,' Roy protested, 'you already gave us the sterling.' Chantilly by Gorham, service for twelve, including shrimp forks and iced-tea spoons.

'The silver's from the Fernaulds. Joshua, Billy and . . .'

'Me,' whispered Sari.

'That's right,' Marylin said, bending to kiss her daughter. 'This is just from me.'

Roy picked up Sari, pressing her cheek against the fine-spun dark hair to control her tears. 'I don't deserve a sister like you,' she mumbled.

'Money's the easiest thing to give,' Marylin said, continuing to extend the cheque.

349

'I mean, how did I ever get into a family with someone like you, sweet and gentle? I'm such a monster.'

'What sort of nutty talk is that?'

'I've always been jealous of you.'

'Oh, Roy, how *dumb*. You're way cleverer than I am – look at how well you've done at Patricia's. You know everything there is to know about business. Everybody likes you.'

'Sure, I'm a great kid. Just not very . . .' Roy's voice cracked. '. . . lovable.'

Sari's thin little arms tightened around Roy's neck. 'I love you, Auntie Roy,' she said in her small, whispery voice, which was like Marylin's. 'I love you a million times.'

'And I love you so much I could eat you up,' Roy growled in the child's smooth neck, then she took the cheque. It was made out for $5,000. Five, thousand, dollars! Her income for a year. 'Marylin, I can't take this.'

'I want you to have a nest egg, something to fall back on.'

Roy set Sari down. 'Then this isn't for Gerry?'

Colouring, Marylin said, 'You.'

'It's just not fair!' Roy said hotly. 'The way you and Mama hold it against Gerry that his family are blue-collar workers.'

'My feelings have nothing to do with his family.' Thick lashes veiled Marylin's incomparable eyes. 'But you're so wild about him, and sometimes he's . . . sort of nasty to you.'

Voices, laughter, and the string trio's convoluted arrangement of 'September Song' sounded through the windows.

'I didn't mean that the way it sounds,' Marylin's beautiful mouth curved pleadingly. 'But, well, you're my little sister, and I thought if maybe you had something of your own, you wouldn't be such a doormat.'

'Doormat? That's how it is for us ordinary girls. We have to work at keeping a man happy because we're not the most beautiful woman alive, not the object of millions of men's desire, not an old man's darling – '

Marylin gave Roy a stricken glance.

350

'I'm sorry,' Roy said huskily. 'That was a nasty dig, really nasty.' She injected humour into her voice. 'See what I mean? Unlovable. Marylin, I do appreciate the cheque, it's wonderfully generous. But I have to put it in a joint account.'

Marylin started to speak, but the door opened and above the party roar BJ said loudly, 'So this is where you are!'

Never a sylph, BJ had gained a good twenty-five pounds since Beverly High, and below her royal-blue taffeta the Merry Widow corset that constrained her bulk through the waistline, thrust her breasts upward and her ample hips outward. Otherwise she was the same BJ, with messy black hair and her too-orange lipstick eroding on her big warm smile. On the shelf of her bosom rested a large diamond-paved Star of David.

BJ stroked the dark hair of her spidery little stepsister. 'Hello, Sari, babes,' she said, and put an arm around her beautiful young stepmother.

Each still considered the other her best friend. While Marylin had never confessed that her love for Linc remained the wellspring of her being – BJ, after all, *was* Joshua's daughter – BJ accepted this love as a constant. She lent Marylin her mail with Italian postmarks.

BJ, glancing from Marylin's pallor to Roy's reddened face, asked, 'Hey, have I barged in on something private?'

Marylin, the actress, recovered first. 'Private? What sort of question is that from one of the family?'

'To tell the truth, BJ,' Roy blurted out, 'I came for my things, and Marylin followed me with some sisterly words about the holy estate of matreemonee.'

'You want *my* advice?' BJ asked. 'Whip him into shape quickly. That Gerry Horak's been a bachelor ages too long. They get spoiled and mean.'

Roy glanced around at the opened packages. 'Maybe somebody's given me a cat-o'-nine-tails.'

'You're a real character, Roy,' BJ hooted. 'Who knows, maybe there is one in the loot.' She added in a rueful brag, 'Lucky you, you didn't get thirteen percolators like we did.'

When they emerged, the party was breaking up and

Gerry and Joshua were standing arm in arm near the living-room fireplace. Joshua had taken off his sports jacket, and his shirt was pulling out at the back of his ample-waisted trousers. His hair was greyer now, and the grooves in his tanned face deeper, extending his look of dominance. He was pouring Scotch into the highball glasses they both held.

'How,' Gerry asked, 'did I ever get a hotshot movie writer-dash-director for a brother?'

'And how did I ever get a hunky painter?'

'The main question is, how did two slobs from the bottom drawer get hooked up to these two classy little Southern belles?'

NolaBee came over, blowing her customary cloud of smoke. 'It's time for the bride and groom to be leavin'.'

'Now you're talking,' Gerry retorted, with a wink.

NolaBee chuckled. 'Don't you get smutty with me around, else I'll have to paddle you.'

'Yes, Mama,' Gerry laughed.

It was amazing to Roy how her mother had drawn this son-in-law she had so recently rejected into the whirling orbit of her personality.

Gerry wrapped an arm around Roy's waist, and they went out the front door, ducking through the hail of rice that BJ had just distributed from an Uncle Ben's box. Somebody had knotted a traditional string of cans to the Thunderbird's rear bumper.

A few blocks away Gerry braked to untie their clattering train. When he returned to his bucket seat, Roy leaned over to kiss his cheek. 'It was a lovely wedding, wasn't it?' she murmured.

'Terrific, terrific.'

There was a harsh note in his voice that Roy tried not to let herself question. Marylin was right. She had to stop noticing her new husband's every arrant mood and worrying about it. He started the car again, and she sat back in the bucket seat, looking up at the one star in the soft Beverly Hills twilight.

Starlight, star bright, grant the wish I make tonight. Let me be a good wife, let me make him happy . . .

Book Six

1958

Death came to world-famed conductor Carlo Firelli in the midst of a recording session on 20 March in Milan, Italy. Born Charles Frye in Birmingham, England, 1872, he changed his name but kept close to his working-class origins by refusing a knighthood. Considered by many to be the greatest conductor of his age, he conducted the world premières of works by Verdi, Puccini, Mahler, Ravel, Rachmaninov, Stravinsky, Richard Strauss. He is survived by a son, Carlo Firelli II, fourteen (by his second wife, Althea Coyne Cunningham, granddaughter of Grover T. Coyne).

– Time, *23 March 1958*

Today we are taking you to the secluded Mandeville Canyon estate of Mr and Mrs Joshua Fernauld. He is an Oscar-winning director and writer; she is known to her fans all over the world as Rain Fairburn. They have lived here eight years, since the birth of their second child, Sara – known as Sari to the family. Hello, Joshua, Rain, Billy and Sari . . .

– Edward R. Murrow, Person to Person, *May 1958*

This Nina Ricci, all in shocking pink, has the full blouson top with a wonderfully slender gored skirt. Ladies, this is the look we'll be watching for this spring.

– Roy Horak at a Patricia's fashion show for the City of Hope
luncheon at the Beverly Wilshire, *10 November 1958*

. . . Horak and his huge, enigmatic paintings at Langley Gallery.

– 'People Are Talking About', Vogue, *November 1958*

47

Late one morning in November of 1958, Althea stood at her bedroom window deciding what to wear. Those cirrus clouds were ominously dark, yet in Central Park far below her she could see the last russet leaves scudding from branches, so what should it be, raincoat or fur?

Her warm bedroom with its glowing fire was a charming mélange of colour and furniture styles. The gilded Louis XIV bed was saved from overmagnificence by a diagonal placement, boxy contemporary armchairs stood in a close conversational grouping, the curtains were made of the white linen that had been used during long-ago summers to shroud her late grandmother's Fifth Avenue palace, an ultra-modern lucite desk chair suggested the same graceful form as the eighteenth-century lacquered desk.

Charles was at Groton now, so there was no need to keep the Geneva house open, and Althea considered this ten-room Manhattan apartment, furnished without the aid of an interior decorator, her home.

She desperately needed a home – a truce place.

Her two anchor relationships had been her son and Firelli. Then, last March, as the Maestro was recording Stravinsky's *Firebird* in Milan, his spherical head had suddenly turned crimson and he had crumpled on the podium, his dead fingers still gripping his baton. Althea began to suffer intermittent periods of depression. She recognized that the old man with his undeviating adoration had kept at bay her fiercest panics. (Aubrey Wimborne, a cultivated Londoner, had never seemed quite a human being to her, but rather one of the chic, clever accoutrements of an enviably handsome life that she had constructed.) Without the old maestro's platonic, unquestioning devotion, she was once again prey to that ineradicable sense of wrongness, that self-loathing, that terrifying lack of power.

In order to give a sort of spine to her racked, lonely spirit, she entertained relentlessly, using her grandmother's heavy Georgian sterling and priceless, soft-glinting, Napoleonic Baccarat crystal. She sallied forth to big bashes where the men wore white tie and tails and *soignée* women's jewels shone flawlessly. In this exquisitely panelled, signed antique bed she sated her passion with men of unquestionable social background.

Now, though, standing in her delightful bedroom, for no reason at all Althea thought of her old dream: the sea-swept boulders of Big Sur, a weathered cabin whose unplastered log walls blazed with the work of Althea Cunningham, artist. She hadn't picked up a brush since leaving the Henry Lissauer Art Institute. What a queer, lonely child I was, she thought, and turned brusquely from the window.

Wearing Russian sable, she emerged onto Fifth Avenue, striding into the wind. In less than ten minutes she had reached the General Motors Building.

'Althea?' a man's voice called behind her. '*Althea!*'

Believing the shout had come from the building's huge sunken plaza, she wheeled around, peering down at the men in topcoats emerging for the lunch hour along with clusters of laughing, bundled-up secretaries.

'Althea.'

A few feet away, panting as if he had been running, stood Gerry Horak.

In that first moment, as she looked into the broad, attractively coarse face glowing with the wind, an instinctive, purifying calm swept through her, and she felt as she once had in his arms. Utterly, irrefutably secure in herself. Then remembrance took over. And she burned with fury.

Assuming an expression of puzzled hauteur that she would give an accosting stranger, she then permitted slow recognition to dawn. 'Larry!' she exclaimed. 'It *is* Larry Horak, isn't it?'

His eyes narrowed, the flesh over his broad, high cheeks went taut with anger. 'Bull, Althea, bull,' he said. 'You damn well knew me right off the bat.'

They were jostled by the stream of hurrying pedestrians.

'Hardly,' she said, forming a patronizing smile. 'It's been years.'

'Cut it out, baby.' It was that old truculent, challenging tone. 'I'm the one who ought to be swinging at you, not the reverse.'

Remembering the brown children playing war in a vacant lot, the endless rustle of Algerian ivy, that crummy blonde, Althea spoke with drawling coolness. 'I'm sorry if the truth hurts, but I really didn't remember. And I can hardly stand here arguing about it. I should be at Lutèce – Senator André Ward is waiting for me.' A deeper inflection as she said the name indicated that André was her current paramour. She had, however, misjudged her reaction to Gerry's uninhibiting presence. 'Anyway, what makes you so positive no woman could forget you?' she heard herself demanding. 'You always were too damn sure of yourself, you lousy bastard.'

He grinned. 'It's good to see you're still the same tough, hard bitch.'

How strange that she, ultrasensitive to insult, should be excited by this unpleasantry. Gerry was still grinning. She gave him a springtime smile.

He took her arm. 'You look great,' he said. 'The classiest broad in New York City.'

Without further discussion, they made their way along the crowded pavement to the traffic light. She then said what was on her mind. 'The last I heard of you, you were involved with Roy Wace. Did you skip out on her too?'

'What's that supposed to mean, skip out *too?*'

They were crossing Fifth Avenue. Outside the park, carriages were lined up, their docile, blanketed horses breathing clouds of steam. 'You ran out on me,' she said.

'The hell I did,' he retorted, adding bitterly, 'I should have known they wouldn't level with you.'

'They? Level with me about what?'

'The MPs were waiting when I got home. Statutory rape. Me. You. I hadn't been discharged. It was the perfect set-up for your parents. The Japanese hadn't signed the surrender papers yet, and the press isn't admitted to wartime courts-martial. So as far as they were concerned, I could be filed away without a trace. I'd have done my twenty years to life in the stockade if it hadn't been for Captain Waldheim. A damn fine lawyer, Waldheim. He got me off on grounds of insanity due to combat fatigue. All that happened to me was that I spent one swell year in the military nut dish.'

His embittered grimace touched seldom-used nerves in Althea, and she winced in sympathy for the injustice done to Gerry Horak. Yet, walking with him into the park, she thought exultantly: He didn't leave me, he didn't desert me.

'Not that I should complain,' Gerry said. 'I don't know the kind of chokehold they had on poor old Henry, but it must have been hell.'

For a moment her footsteps slowed with the guilt of memory. Henry Lissauer was at her door. But how, as a distraught child of seventeen, could she have known that the German refugee was suicidal?

Ahead of them an old woman in a man's topcoat tended a brazier emitting a small, whirling tornado of smoke. Gerry bought a bagful of roasted chestnuts, peeled one and blew on it before he popped it into Althea's mouth.

They walked along hunched into the icy, buffeting wind, eating chestnuts, not talking.

Gerry crushed the empty bag into a wire-mesh trash barrel. 'How come,' he asked, 'you were so positive I'd done you the dirty?'

'I went to your place and waited and waited. Finally a blonde drove up. She told me you'd left town.'

'What blonde?'

'You weren't staying with a friend's wife?'

'Burt was away for a week, and he never had a wife. How could you figure me for screwing around? Althea, I was so nuts about you I wouldn't have looked at Rita Hayworth if she'd taken her clothes off and done the slow grinds in front of me.'

'But the woman walked right up onto the porch with her groceries.'

'I can't help that. She didn't live there.'

'She certainly seemed at home. Besides, how could she know all about you?'

'Beats me.' He dodged a red-checked, snowsuited child furiously pedalling a tricycle. 'Think your parents hired some Hollywood type?'

'An actress to throw me off the scent?'

'There's no other way to figure it.'

'. . . They might have done something along those lines,' she said, nodding.

'When I was released, you were married to Toscanini – '

'Firelli.'

Althea's correction was absentminded. Forcibly struck by the reason for her April-December marriage – this man's child embedded in her womb – she drew a little apart from him. An undefinable menace lay in anyone – even Gerry – learning Charles's paternity. Charles was sacrosanct unto her. Her child alone.

I won't tell Gerry, ever, she thought.

A gust of wind rippled her warm fur, giving a chill, unalterable inflexibility to the decision.

'Ahh, what's the use of hashing all this over?' Gerry asked. 'What's past is past.'

He put his arm around her, a shortish, muscular man in a black leather jacket and faded jeans, hugging a slender, elegantly shod woman wearing a fortune in Russian fur. Althea leaned towards him, and the wind lashed strands of her perfumed hair against his face. Linking his arm in hers, Gerry strode more swiftly.

Althea matched her step to his.

They came to a fork and she took the narrower right path. 'This is the way to my place,' she said.

'Jesus, it's a relief to be with you. You're the only woman I ever knew who doesn't yakkety-yak everything to death,' he said. 'You're living in New York?'

'I have an apartment. You?'

'LA. I'm here because Langley Gallery's putting on a one-man show of my stuff.'

'Langley's?' She pulled a knowing face. 'Impressive.'

As they entered the lobby, the warm air stung Althea's cheeks. Glancing in the oval mirror to see her unusual high colour, she remembered Roy's shy, flushed reflections in Patricia's as she talked about Gerry.

'You never told me what happened with you and Roy Wace,' she said. 'Do you still see her?'

'We're married,' he said.

An inferno ignited inside her skull. 'That's one for the books,' she said lightly. 'You and Roy.'

The doorman was buzzing for the elevator.

'Althea,' Gerry said quietly, 'there's been quite a few extracurriculars.'

'No need for confessions. I'm not your priest.'

'So my being hitched to Roy does make a difference,' he said.

She'd slept with many married men, experiencing no envy towards or guilt about the deceived wives. So what if she and Roy had shared a few inextricable years at Beverly High? Why should she feel this rush of hot jealousy, this panicky shame, this hurt?

The bronze-and-Lalique-crystal elevator doors slid open.

As they ascended swiftly, noiselessly, she put her arms around Gerry's waist, pressing her wind-flushed cheek to his stubbled cheek. 'Yes, it matters,' she whispered. 'But there's not a damn thing I can do about it.'

On the other side of the drawn white linen curtains, wind drummed hailstones on glass, but the room was warm, and a log fire sent its rosy glow across the dimness. Althea moved closer to Gerry, curling her naked leg over his. It was six o'clock, and they had been in the gilded bed for five hours.

Gerry stubbed out his cigarette, turning to put both arms around her. 'Would you think I was laying it on too thick if I said nothing in my life has been as right as being with you this afternoon?'

'I believe you,' she said. The boundless confidence he had always given her allowed her to admit: 'I'm glad it's not as good for you with Roy.'

'Want me to tell you about her?'

'We should get it over with, yes.'

'It was a mistake, marrying her.' He sighed. 'She's a good kid, decent, loyal as they come, and I'm a complete shit to her. I can't help it. She's always so damn humble, know what I mean? Looking at me in this simpy, adoring way, asking my opinion about her work, her clothes. "You're so much smarter than me," she keeps saying. "You have such a wonderful eye".'

'That sort of inferiority thing drives me up a wall.'

'Yeah, right. And then there's the house – we bought one in a tract just south of Beverly Hills.'

'You? A tract? You mean like Levittown?'

'That's it. Really Roy bought it. She used her own dough. Tracts have sprung up all over the city. This one has pretensions. Not Beverly Hills, but trying to be. Beverlywood it's called. She picked the model with the attached garage, and before we moved in she hired some joker to fix it up with a skylight and windows. A studio for me. The only damn problem is, I can't work there. I can't breathe in there.'

Althea stroked his naked shoulder. 'Poor Gerry,' she said with abstract sympathy.

'Christ!' he said. 'Me, on a street where every fifth dump is the same as ours! Ahh, what the hell am I complaining about? If the house pleases her, I'm glad. Christ knows, nothing else about the marriage has been any good for her. Since we've been hitched, I can only work in fits and starts – I junk most of the stuff. She never complains, ever. She calls me a genius and thinks everything I do is a masterpiece – and I should sell it to buy a new car, a new sofa, a new this or that. Shit. Every word I say about her sounds rotten. And Roy's the best. It's me. I'm a prick of a guy to live with.'

'Is she unhappy too?'

'That's the crazy part. I'd swear she's not. *I'm* the

miserable one. She works her tail off at Patricia's and then comes home singing. God, the ways she thinks she's pleasing me. Maple furniture with a fake cobbler's bench, recipes from some women's magazine. All for me. I try to say the right things, compliment her until I can't stand my phoniness anymore.'

'And then you hit out below the belt,' Althea said.

'Hit hard. You understand this, don't you?'

'I lived it with Aubrey Wimborne for three years.'

'After I explode, she goes in the other bedroom and bawls all night, then drags around looking like a whipped pup for a few days. It tears me apart, but when I try to apologize, I can't. You haven't any idea what a shit it makes me feel.'

'Aubrey was always laying himself out for me. At first I thought he was trying to please me, but then I realized his efforts were really a psychological probe. He was testing how far I would go. He *needed* me to play sadist to his masochist. Finally, when I couldn't bear myself any more, I left him.'

'I feel sorrier for Roy than I ever felt for anyone, but I can't change myself. Or her.' He sighed again. 'And then there's this business about having a kid.'

Althea shifted her long, smooth leg from his hairy one. 'You have a child?'

'No. Another thing to feel rotten about. Something's wrong, the doctors don't know which one of us it is. Before the war, when I didn't want 'em, I could have kids.' He paused. 'Maybe something happened to me when I was wounded at Salerno.'

Althea held her breath and said nothing.

'We've gone to three different specialists. The last one sat us down in his office – it was filled with off-tone Van Gogh prints. Folding his fat hands over his fat belly, he doled out advice. He told Roy her work at Patricia's was too much for her. "You should act like a woman. That generally does the trick," the fat turd said. Roy stared at me with this horrible, pleading, hopeful little smile. And I said, "I'm not about to get a job at some asshole cookie factory, so we damn well need your paycheque!" She began to cry in front of that fat doctor, dabbing her eyes with a Kleenex. I felt so sorry for her that I was ready to puke. There was nothing to do but get the hell out of that damn office with fake Van Goghs. I didn't go home for a week. Most of the time I was drunk and getting laid to forget how much I hated myself.'

'What about a divorce?'

The hail had momentarily stopped, and a hush surrounded the question.

'The one time I suggested it, she went off the deep end. She's not much of a drinker, but she got totally soused. She lay on the floor trying to kiss my shoes.' A shudder passed through Gerry's naked body. 'I think she would've killed herself if I hadn't backed down.'

'Aubrey hinted at guns and pills. Instead, he remarried.'

'There's no ditching out of this one, ever. Roy and me are stuck together. Once she dragged me to this play, *No Exit* –'

'Sartre.'

'Yeah. The exit-entialist play.'

Althea, laughing at his pun, kissed his neck. 'You're not such a Neanderthal as you pretend.'

'Hell is three people trapped forever in one room and not one of the poor sons of bitches getting what they want. Well, except for there being only two of us, that's Mr and Mrs Gerry Horak. I don't want to talk about it anymore.'

She clasped him tighter and they kissed a long, tender minute.

The rat-tat of hail began again, and there were only whispers and murmurs of their delight. She rose up, her pale, loosened hair trailing down his scarred chest. As he caressed her body, for some reason she determined to hold back her orgasm until he came. An exquisite torment. When, finally, he began to ride her, she collapsed against the mattress, shrieking at the top of her lungs because every cell of her body was bursting to form another more perfect entity in some far-off, fantastic land of sheer joy.

48

They had agreed to meet at Langley's at eleven. The gallery was on Madison Avenue a few blocks from her apartment, so she walked. The previous night's storm had passed, the only reminder of it a slush of papers in gutters. It was very cold, and the sky a brilliant blue. Clean-washed windows of shops displayed tempting luxuries, and pots of brilliant chrysanthemums spilled into sidewalks from florists' stores.

New York smiled on Althea, and she smiled back.

She turned into a flawlessly tended old brick house. Affixed to the ebony-painted front door was a brass plate:

LANGLEY GALLERIES
MODERN AND CONTEMPORARY ART

Her heels clicked over the parquet foyer and she glanced into the exhibition rooms: Gerry wasn't here yet. She signed the large leather guest book: the receptionist, a burly man who probably doubled as guard, handed her a slick, handsomely printed catalogue with 'HORAK' on the cover in Gerry's bold, black signature.

The thick carpeting hushed the footsteps of the pairs of affluent women who whispered as they solemnly examined the enormous, near-monochromatic paintings. Althea folded her arms, standing at a canvas with more square footage than many a room. On the fawn background, a huge, featureless umber globe was bisected by a brown line. A minuscule crimson dot in the lower-right corner signified that this work was sold.

A salesman limped over to her. 'Horak has grown nicely since his last showing,' he said in a middle-European accent that she could not quite place. 'Nowadays he's considered an excellent investment, in the same class as Pollock or de Kooning, but more accessibly priced.'

'Just browsing,' she said.

'If I may be of service,' he said, backing away courteously.

She had reached the rear room when Gerry came in. Here, among the reverential matrons and earnest salesmen, in his faded Levis and black leather jacket, he was a cocky aberration. Raising his hand in greeting, he strode towards her.

'What's the verdict?' he asked, disturbing the chapel stillness. A nearby couple turned reproachfully.

'I don't understand what you're trying to say.' She tilted her head at a vast painting. 'Life is flat and colourless?'

'Beats me,' he said. 'After I got out of the ward, I avoided anything representational.'

'What happened to the portraits of me, Gerry?'

'Burt had kept 'em for me, but they hurt to look at, so I slashed 'em. How about sitting for me again?'

'If you'll let me try my hand at you.'

'Have you been working?' he asked.

'No, but I'd like to start.'

'Yeah, what the hell! Why not? We'll be a whole damn portrait movement.' He laughed again.

The salesman reappeared. 'Ahh, madam, I see you've met our artist.'

'Yes, he's convincing me to take this one.'

'You're off your nut if you do,' Gerry said.

The salesman's jaw quivered as he managed a half-smile. 'I must say that an artist is the last person to judge the value of his own work.'

While the purchase was transacted, Gerry kept up a running repartee to the effect that if she had all her marbles she'd never pay this kind of dough for a gigantic brown blob that made no sense to her.

The salesman sniffed anxiously until she signed the cheque.

She and Gerry emerged from the gallery laughing, like naughty children. The place Gerry was staying was a long distance off, but they decided to walk. After a half-hour out in the chill, they were ravenous, so they ducked into a long, narrow delicatessen where conversation blared and fat waitresses squeezed around tightly packed Formica tables balancing plates on their arms. Althea and Gerry wolfed down thick sandwiches of fragrant, juicy pastrami on fresh, yellow-crusted rye.

If anybody saw me here they wouldn't believe their eyes, she thought. Althea Coyne Cunningham Firelli Wimborne, who comported herself with remote dignity, sitting in a noisy deli wedged between two pairs of gesticulating merchants, laughing as she mopped a water-sogged paper napkin at the long dribble of mustard on her silk blouse.

With Gerry she felt miraculously freed of striving and etiquette. She could be possessed by pleasure, laugh as loudly as an overexcited child, indulge her salivary glands and her impulses. She could be her own true self. Leaning across the narrow strip of Formica, she pressed a pickle-scented kiss on his cheek.

Replete, they resumed their walk, laughing and holding hands all the way to South Houston Street. A friend, currently painting in North Africa, had left him the keys to his loft. Most of the building was rented to rag-trade small-timers, and open doors revealed steamy workshops where Puerto Rican women sweated over their sewing machines or ironing boards while radios blared a cacophonous variety of Latin beats.

The loft smelled of gesso, turpentine, jute canvas, oil paints, acrylic paints, dust. Gerry closed the door. Taking her hand, he held it flat against his chest. His heart was pounding erratically.

'That's what happens when old fogies climb stairs,' she said, but her teasing voice faded to a whisper. 'Ahh, Gerry . . .'

They fell onto the mattress.

The loft became their meeting place.

Althea would have Gordon, her butler-chauffeur, drop her off around ten. She would find Gerry already at work in a faded khaki Army shirt that was splotched with paint. They didn't talk much. He painted her, she drew him, her

366

charcoals scratching away. Her renderings of Gerry, though lacking in technical skill, possessed a force, a significance that pleased her. My dream wasn't so idiotic after all, she would think.

He was painting a series of three-by-fives of her, working with almost photographic realism, a spacious style reminiscent of Hopper that marvellously conveyed both her high-voltage, irrepressible sexuality and the haunting aura of solitude that surrounded her.

Around four he knocked off work. They would eat in one of the nearby cheap, ethnic cafés, then return to the loft to make love.

They seldom went to her apartment. This had nothing to do with discretion: her cook and maid had rooms on the second floor, and Gordon went home every night to Harlem. But the whimsically elegant, priceless arrangements of the flat had been intended as mute testimony that Althea Wimborne was the best of the best. Now she had no need to prove anything.

Those weeks she cancelled the minutiae: nine dinner invitations, numerous lunch dates and cocktail parties, a meeting of the board of a children's home, two charity dances, a fund-raiser for André – she had kissed the senator off – a dog show and a big private bash for the opening of the Coyne Archaeological Museum, endowed by the Coyne Foundation.

Let people gossip about her absences. If voyeurs desired to find out about her affair with Gerry Horak, son of a drunken factory hand, let them. The rules of her world, recently so crucial to her, had become meaningless.

Althea also found that in her new, simpler way, her feelings about Roy had altered. After that initial mangling of jealousy and shame, she found herself seeing Roy not as a rival but simply as an old friend confined in the prison of an unhappy marriage. Someone once close but now unconnected to her.

By the fifteenth of December, Althea decided she could no longer put off her Christmas shopping. After the stores closed, she met Gerry at the Russian Tea Room. It was too late for the dinner mob and too early for the post-concert cadre, so the long, narrow restaurant was fairly empty. They had a large booth. Gerry, who usually sat close to her, stationed himself at a distance, ordering three bourbons in rapid succession. In her other life, Althea would have inwardly cringed at his rejection while outwardly manifesting an upper-crust indifference. Tonight, though, she ate her dinner, accepting that Gerry was upset and would presently tell her about it.

'Today I got two letters,' he said finally. 'One from Roy.'

Althea looked up from her blinis. 'I thought she wrote often.'

'Yeah, she does, but this one's different.'

'Different? How?'

He raised his body, fishing two envelopes from his trouser pocket, handing her the pale blue one, which held the warmth and curve of his body.

She scanned the once-familiar writing:

Darling,
    You have to forgive me for writing like this, but you have been gone for an eternity. I do understand how important it is for you to be around during the showing – but you said it would only be two weeks. And now it is over six weeks. Darling, I am not complaining. You and your career have always come first with me, you know that. But the house is so terribly empty without you, and at night all kinds of tormenting thoughts run through my mind.
    Have you found a girl?
    You know I've always understood that a man like you, a magnificent artist, can't be expected to be strictly monogamous. If you're having a fling, I can handle it. Darling, whatever it is keeping you in New York, I will understand. *But I have to know.*
    I am positive there is another woman – a wife can always tell, so you don't have to keep it a secret.
    The one thing I cannot bear is feeling cut off from you.
    I went to Dr Dash again, and he suggested a specialist who has a new kind of treatment. I'm going tomorrow. Darling, how I long to give you a child! Always remember, you are my everything, I

am nothing without you, I worship you with my whole heart, and I ache to have you home.

> If only you were inside me,
> I adore you.
> Roy

Althea felt a wave of queasiness. If this were anybody but Gerry Horak, she would be retreating from the misery in his face, from the sad, horrible love letter, from the dark underside of so disastrous a relationship. But this *was* Gerry, Gerry, whose clenched knuckles rapped on the white tablecloth.

She returned to letter. 'It's sick, Gerry.'

He raised his shoulders. 'She only throws emotional bazookas about one thing. Me.'

'She used to be cheerful, unsubservient. Maybe she was sozzled when she wrote it. You said she drank.'

'Only that one time when I suggested we split. I'm a bastard to let you see it, but when she acts like this, it gets to me.'

'God, no wonder. From my experience with Aubrey, I'd say it's a typical masochist's game.'

'No, it's the real thing.' Sighing, he pulled the paper from the other envelope, handing it to her.

Dear Gerry,

I reckon I am butting in, but poor Roy's been looking ill and dreadful for weeks now and I am sick with worry. She drags around and never says one word of complaint, but she's been seeing all kinds of doctors.

She would have a fit if she knew I was writing to you, but I reckon you have a right to know when your wife needs you. No art showing is as important as that. Remember how Marylin got herself released from *The Lost Sabrina* when Joshua had his heart attack?

Call me an interfering old mother-in-law, Gerry, dear, but you belong right here, making sure that Roy takes care of herself.

> Love,
> Mother Wace

Althea looked across the booth at Gerry. 'Then you're going back to California?'

'I'm staying put.'

'Because of me?' It amazed Althea how secure she felt as she asked the question.

He shook his head.

And even more amazing was that this negation did not destroy her. She dipped a bite of blini in sour cream. 'Why, then?'

'When she puts the emotional screws on me, I can't give in. I want to, but I can't. It'd be one hell of a lot easier to mouth a few nice, sympathetic words, give her the reassuring pat that she wants. But something always stops me. A black, mean mulishness.'

'I'd call it a sense of decency,' Althea said. 'They whine, and your guilts gush. It's Pavlov's dog pure and simple. Well, who likes to be reduced to a bundle of animal reflexes?'

That night they returned to her apartment.

They were drinking in the library when the telephone rang. It was Charles.

'Mother, I was hoping to get you,' he said, his adolescent voice briefly cantilevering into a bass. 'Have you made any plans for Christmas vacation?'

'Not yet,' she said.

'Naismith' – his roommate – 'has invited me. His people have a place in Maine with skiing.'

'I hear the powder's been perfect there.'

'Before I accepted, I wanted to talk it over with you.'

'Charles, we can see each other the weekend before.'

'I don't want you to have a lonely time. It's the first Christmas since Father died.'

Neither had to remind the other that she had been divorced from Firelli for many years. But except for those three hectically busy Christmases that she had been tied to Aubrey Wimborne, she had made it a point to spend the holidays in Eastbourne with her son and the stout, jolly old maestro.

'I have a million things I can do,' Althea said.

'You're sure you won't be alone?'

'Charles, I'm delighted that you're getting along so well. I want you to go.'

As she replaced the phone, Gerry's eyebrow went up, and she found herself flushing. *Charles's father*, she thought. 'My son,' she explained.

'It's great, the way you talk to him. Straight out. No browbeating or phoniness.'

'That's how we are.'

'I gather the kid's busy over Christmas. What about coming to Oaxaca with me?'

'Oaxaca?'

'I was planning to do a Mexican series.'

'Will you stop off in Los Angeles on the way?'

Gerry shrugged ruefully. 'I guess. That's how it goes. In the end, I always play it her way, but as rottenly as possible.'

She walked across the room to kiss his creased forehead. 'I haven't been to Mexico in ages,' she said.

49

Their suite in Hotel de los Reyes had a narrow balcony overlooking Oaxaca's main square – the Zócalo. With its bird flocks rising and dipping amid shade trees, its splashes of hibiscus and salmon-coloured bougainvillea, the Zócalo entertained an unending parade. All day black figures came and went from Oaxaca Cathedral. In the early-morning coolness, the beshawled old Indian tortilla vendors shuffled under the colonial arcades with the covered baskets that held their steaming wares. When the wooden cathedral clock (a gift from the Spanish king in 1735) was chiming 9 A.M. the tourists were already sitting at sidewalk cafés while itinerant pedlars displayed their gaudy heaps of serapes, rugs and shawls. Around noon rambunctious marimbas serenaded, and musical groups began alternating in the spoolwork bandstand. When early evening fell, young men with patent-leather hair stalked arrogantly around the square in one direction while clusters of girls sauntered giggling in the other. At all hours there circled ancient cars and grandiosely finned new cars, ramshackle trucks, ox carts, bicycles and *burros* – a cacophonous blaring of horns and ringing of bells.

Althea arrived in Oaxaca on 23 December, the Fiesta of the Radishes, when enormous radishes were carved into saints' likenesses. She arranged for demi-pension at Hotel de los Reyes. Gerry flew in five days later, on the day of the Breaking of the Plates, when *buñuelos* were eaten from earthenware plates that were then enthusiastically hurled into churchyards. He said nothing about his Christmas with Roy, but Althea surmised without recrimination that he had slept with his wife, showed up with her at holiday gatherings, and growled a justification for this trip – a new series of paintings, dammit.

Althea and Gerry's days slipped into an unassuming pattern of contentment.

They slept until 8.30, when a little maid with a pure Mayan face brought them thick-crusted *bolillas*, strawberry jam and a spouted pot of steaming chocolate whose foamy richness she gravely poured into huge, green pottery cups.

Gerry would drive off in their rented Studebaker to stare at Monte Alban, the hilltop city that millennia before the Spanish conquest had housed a population of forty thousand. He hadn't yet decided which of the mighty ruined pyramid temples, bizarre palaces, ball courts and ceremonial squares to tackle.

Some mornings Althea might browse through Oaxaca's vast *mercado*, protected from the sun's glare by strips of wood or canvas overhead. She bought Gerry pleated shirts and herself a collection of the local brilliantly embroidered cotton shifts. Saturdays, the Mixtec and Zapotec Indians from crazily named nearby villages brought their wares, and she picked out inappropriate gifts for her friends: naively brilliant wool serapes from Tlacolula, embroidered Mitla belts, a huge leather toy *burro* from Otzompa to make Charles laugh. She even selected a handsomely glazed black pottery urn from Ocotlán for Gerry to send Roy.

Most mornings, though, she would take her pastels or

watercolours onto the narrow balcony, attempting to capture one moment of the perennially changing Zócalo. Compared to the vivid reality, her renderings seemed pallid and awkward. Yet they gave her a sense of owning the square.

Around one Gerry would return to the hotel. They would lunch at a sidewalk café on the Zócalo, generally ordering tamales Oaxaqueño – banana leaves wrapped the rich *masa* which enfolded a delectable concoction of meat and the peppery *mole* sauce that left an aftertaste of chocolate on the palate.

During the siesta, they made love and slept heavily in each other's arms.

In late afternoon they drove, exploring the surrounding honey-toned hills and flatlands. Oaxaca's pre-Columbian inhabitants had raised innumerable tombs, and despite the ecclesiastical efforts to extirpate these marks of the ancient Mixtec and Zapotec religion, many remained. Althea and Gerry returned again and again to 'their' tomb. Over its entry lintel stood paired busts of a heavy-jowled man and a delicate-featured woman, obviously man and wife, a couple dead for long centuries yet joined in their cosy five-room eternal resting place. 'When the time comes, I'd a hell of a lot rather be here with you than planted in Forest Lawn,' Gerry said.

In the swift maroon twilight, they slowly sipped margaritas, tapping their salt-rimmed glasses in time to the Zócalo's strolling marimbas. At ten they would go inside to the candlelit, tapestried hotel dining room to eat a four-course dinner. Long before midnight they were asleep in their big soft bed.

One exceptionally hot morning in mid-January, Althea took her pastels to the ravishing green gardens of Oaxaca Courts, a hotel maybe two miles north of the centre of town. By noon even the shady trees and her big straw hat no longer protected her, and she started back. Within five minutes she regretted not having taken one of the cabs lined outside the hotel. Sweat dripped between her breasts and down her sides and she filled her mind with visions of the rewards at journey's end – a cool bath, a big glass of icy Dos Équises beer.

Dots were moving in front of her eyes by the time she reached the Zócalo.

'Althea,' a woman called. 'Althea!'

Althea jumped. Though some tourists had attempted conversation in the hotel or at the cafés, she and Gerry had remained aloof. Baffled, she stared in the direction of the call.

A young woman wearing a sundress that bared freckled shoulders was waving vigorously from an umbrella at the Café Manuela.

It was Roy.

Seeing Gerry's wife – her onetime friend – Althea first felt a hard clutch of fear.

She shifted the basket with her art supplies, wishing she could rush to the hotel, shuck off this moist, stupid native dress, bathe, and coolly armour herself in one of her cruise silks.

Roy waved again.

Althea drew a deep breath and avoided traffic to cross to the Café Manuela.

Roy hugged her with that remembered warmth. 'This is absolutely wild! Here less than an hour, and I run into an old friend. I can't believe it's really you.'

'It's me, but I won't be around to tell the tale if I don't get something cold to drink.' She raised her hand and the stout waiter with the wispy Charlie Chan moustache sped towards them. Althea ordered rapidly in Spanish.

When the waiter left, Roy said, '*Mucho* impressive. You didn't learn *that* at Beverly High.' She beamed at Althea. 'This is so fabulous. Gerry – my husband – is painting here. Remember, the last time I saw you, we were living in sin.'

Heat had swollen Althea's hands, and the chunky jade ring that Gerry had bought her cut into her finger. Roy was so ebulliently certain of herself that it was impossible to believe that Gerry was unwarned of her visit. Why didn't he tell me? Althea thought, wrenching off the ring. Why the secrecy?

'. . . all go to dinner,' Roy was saying. 'I'm dying for you to meet him. Oh, that's right. You know him. Have you bumped into him?'

'The place simply swarms with Americans.'

The happiness faded from Roy's face, and she looked down at her glass. 'I remember . . .' she said uncertainly. 'You and he didn't get along, did you?'

'Dear heart, that was in my infancy.'

The waiter brought Althea's beer, and she drank half of it swiftly.

'I love that dress.' Roy had recovered her bounce. 'The embroidery's fabulous. Where did you find it?'

'At one of the stalls in the *mercado* – it's owned by a cross-eyed Indian woman.' Althea, too, spoke convivially. She sipped the remainder of her beer, describing the shrewd widow who sold junk to American rubes, treasures to the cognoscenti. A bitter skill of hers, this, mining small talk out of her darkest anxieties.

Roy was laughing. 'I'm too dumpy for loose things, but I adore that. Lead on, McDuff, to the wall-eyed lady.'

'Where's your loyalty? I thought you only shopped at Patricia's.'

Roy was not listening. She was staring over Althea's shoulder, an expression of rapt adoration transfixing her face. 'There he is,' she murmured. 'Gerry. In that car.'

Gerry was pulling into one of the slanted parking spaces in front of the Hotel de los Reyes.

'So he is,' Althea said, drawing in a breath.

'Maybe, well . . .' The umbrella shaded them, but Roy's face was red, as if from heat stroke. 'Maybe it would be easiest if you . . . uhh . . . let us be alone for a few minutes. I'm surprising him.'

So Gerry did not know of Roy's visit!

Althea felt strength flow into her, and a measure of kindness. To preserve Roy from humiliation, she said quietly, 'You're silly to have come.'

'Don't I know it. Gerry's not like other people, he's an artist, he needs his individuality. That's why he's here – he's beginning a new series of paintings, and he wanted to get away from all the distractions.' Rising, she reached for her big straw purse. 'Better get it over with.'

'Wait.' Althea curved a restraining hand on Roy's wrist. 'We need to talk.'

'Later.'

'Before Gerry sees us together.'

The flush had faded from Roy's face and her makeup base showed like a film over her freckles. 'What are you trying to say?'

'I knew Gerry years before he met you,' Althea said rapidly. 'He was still in the Army, an outpatient at Birmingham Military Hospital in the Valley – '

'Yes, you told me. You and he were both at the art school.'

'We fell for each other.'

'You what?'

'We had a big thing going.'

'He hated you,' Roy refuted flatly. 'He called you Miss Rich Bitch.'

'My parents broke us up, they did it in a rotten way – I didn't know about it, but he blamed the mess on me. I blamed him. We pretended we hated each other – you can see the logic, can't you? When we met again this last November – '

'So *you're* what kept him in New York.'

'Yes. It started all over again, and we arranged to come down here.'

Roy was clasping her straw purse to the bosom of her sundress. A drop of perspiration showed on the side of her cheek. 'He's had other women. You aren't the first. You won't be the last.'

'Roy, I'm not trying to harm you.'

'How could you? You're just another tramp to him!'

'Hardly.'

'I've made a home for him, a place where he can work.'

'Roy, will you stop acting like this is the fall of the Holy Roman Empire – '

'You're such a cold fish!' Roy's pupils glinted, and in this fleeting instant there was something unfamiliar about her, a gross intensity, a wildness. The ringing of the cathedral's ancient wooden clock set up a deafening reverberation. 'You took Dwight Hunter away from me by sleeping with him.' Despite the tintinnabulation Roy's low voice somehow managed to be clearly audible. 'Well, this time it's different. You aren't getting Gerry. He's my husband.'

Gerry slammed the Studebaker door, moving towards the hotel's shadowy, deep-set entry arch.

'Gerry!' Roy's cry shrilled over the antiphonal church bells and the clatter of traffic. '*Gerry!*'

He turned, raising a hand to shelter his eyes, looking towards the Café Manuela. He froze momentarily in that position; then his hand fell to his side, his shoulders slumped. In this attitude of defeat his stocky body seemed thicker. For a moment Althea was positive he would cross to them. But he wheeled about, barrelling into the dark hotel entry.

Roy darted into the street. A pedlar's bicycle laden with tourist machetes swerved to avoid her, the wheels flapping as the rider steered frantically out of the way of a large truck. The bike fell towards the dusty pavement, the noisy bells covering the crash.

Roy had disappeared behind the thick, nail-studded doors of the Hotel de los Reyes.

Althea stared up at the windows of the rooms she shared with Gerry. The shutters had been closed against midday heat. She could see nothing.

50

Gripped by the violence of her need to confront Gerry, Roy was scarcely aware of demanding that the grey-haired desk clerk give her Señor Horak's room number. In the creaking elevator she held a hand over her heart. Calm down, calm down, she ordered herself. Calm down.

Though Gerry's other flings had driven her wild, she had

recognized them as casual alliances, no proper threat to her marriage. But this – whatever denials she had hurled at Althea – she accepted as catastrophe. Pure catastrophe. For her mind had sped back through the years to when she had first mentioned Althea's name to Gerry: he had reacted as if to live electricity.

The elevator decelerated, stopping a foot or so above the third floor; then the young operator jerked them down a few inches too far. Roy stumbled over the rise. Fleeing the boy's rapid Spanish apologies, she searched through the dim, cool corridor for the door affixed with the brass number 334.

She dabbed Kleenex at her brow and upper lip before rapping tentatively.

'Yeah?' Gerry asked. 'What is it?'

At his voice, a mawkishly grateful relief swept through Roy. She felt as if she had been rescued from oblivion.

The door was unlocked, and she let herself in. The exterior shutters of the high-ceilinged sitting room had been closed, and her first impression was of a dim cave where animals hibernated – animals that immediately became massive, old-fashioned pieces of upholstery.

Silhouetted in the archway to the bedroom stood Gerry. It was not light enough to see his expression, but his sandalled feet were apart and his arms bent at the elbows, a defensive stance. She had to fight that old painful need to figuratively kneel in humbleness and plead with him to love her.

'Okay, so you've discovered I'm not baching it in Oaxaca.' His truculence sounded forced. 'No law says I have to eat shit about it.'

'I didn't come here to spy.'

'Then what the fuck are you doing down here?'

'I wanted to surprise you,' she said quietly. 'But I'm the one who got the surprise.'

His head cocked as if her dignity astonished him. Did she usually rant like a fishwife when faced with his infidelities? Yes, she thought, oh God, yes.

'It's a shame you had to find out this way,' he said in a less surly voice.

'Althea explained,' Roy said in the same calm tone. 'She's always been the one for you, hasn't she?'

Her eyes had adjusted and she could see that trapped misery on his broad face. Nodding, he said, 'That's about the size of it.'

For a moment a pain, sharp and physical, stabbed her chest. 'And what about me? Didn't you ever feel the least little something for *me?*' There it was, that involuntary, degrading shrillness.

He grew wary again. 'You wanted in, baby. If you recall, marriage was *your* idea.'

'Gerry, can't you see you're killing me?' She began to cry. Why must she forever hunger for what he (or anyone else) was incapable of bestowing on her? Love.

Gerry's expression remained stony. 'Right on cue, the waterworks.'

'I can't help it,' she wept. '. . . the way I feel about you is worse than having Parkinson's or diabetes or . . . some other incurable disease . . .'

Her gasped-back sobs sounded over the shutter-muted clamour of the Zócalo.

'Ahh, what's the use? It always ends up the same. You the bawling, wronged, saintly wife, and me the bastard.' Gerry stamped through the darkened bedroom.

She heard a door close, a shower running. She sat on the couch, whose prickly blood-coloured plush gave off a faint peppery aroma. After a minute her tears lessened. Gripping her wadded Kleenex, she went to the other room. Far smaller than the sitting room, it was dominated by the high bed with ornately carved head- and foot-boards.

As she stared at the bed where her husband made love to another woman, Roy's mind worked with sudden incongruous lucidity. She had heard veterans say that in the heart of fray there comes a moment when the fear and the battle hype both recede and you comprehend without emotion whether or not you're going to make it. So it was with her.

I've lost him, she thought with a clarity unconnected to her passionate grief. Lost him . . .

379

She stood for a long time in the doorway.

The shower ceased. Gerry emerged from the bathroom, a towel wrapped around his waist, his wet hair hanging in his eyes.

'Wasn't the message clear enough?' he said. 'I've had it up to here.'

'We have to talk,' she said.

'Talk? Talk means first you pry everything out of me, then you shriek and wail about it!'

'Gerry, I promise to behave.'

He gave her a wary glance, then padded over to the bureau, leaving wet footmarks on the polished floor, scattering socks as he fished out jockey shorts. Facing away from her, he stepped into them.

'You and Althea are having an affair. See, I said it quite rationally.'

He moved to a big wardrobe for a clean shirt and clean Levis.

Roy said, 'It's not a fly-by-night thing, you and Althea, not a one-night stand. I accept that.'

He tilted his head to her. 'You're really on the level, aren't you? You really do want to hash it out reasonably?'

'We have to.'

He did up a shirt button, not looking at her. 'The truth is, Roy, it's never worked, you and me. It's my fault. I've felt trapped, so I've made life shitty for you. The best thing for both of us is to split up. Get a divorce.'

A divorce.

The word echoed and re-echoed through Roy's head, and she saw the dimness of the room as black. *Divorce*. Stifling an impulse to throw herself screaming on the flowered carpeting at his feet, she gripped the doorjamb.

Gerry was watching her with a peculiar begging expression.

All at once she understood that just as her soul and body were being stretched on the rack of love, so were Gerry's. For years he had been crazy in love with Althea, just as she, Roy, had been in love with him.

This fellowship with Gerry's torment elicited from Roy a

bewildering flood of emotions: barren hopelessness, a vindictive jealousy towards her rival, and – most heavily – an inanely adoring loyalty that made her yearn to help Gerry, to be his ally in winning a victory. Win a victory even though she was his unhappy opponent.

'A divorce . . .' she said weakly. 'Gerry, I just don't know . . . I don't think I'll ever get over how I feel about you.'

'You can't be enjoying this fouled-up marriage any more than I am.'

She sighed miserably. 'Not now . . .'

Gerry asked, 'Then at least you'll think about splitting?'

'I care so much, darling.'

'But you just said you were at rocky bottom.'

That pleading hope in his eyes wrenched her. '. . . maybe I could handle it if I went for some sort of professional help.'

'You'd do that? Try a shrink?'

'I think I need one.'

His blazing, grateful smile sent icy needles into her skin. 'You're a terrific kid, Roy, you always were.'

'But you have to give me time.'

'No sweat. Take as long as you need.'

She tottered down the long, cool corridor, and when she came to a door marked '*Baño*', she went inside. Here the shutters were not drawn, and the blazing subtropical sunlight slanted across the tub. She sat on the hot porcelain ledge, the sun glaring onto her, unable to control her shivers.

What have I promised?

A divorce?

Oh, God, God.

51

Althea shifted around to face the hotel, an empty glass in front of her. The Café Manuela waiters, who knew the handsome blonde American señora always lunched with her *esposo*, left her politely alone. The sweat-drenched mariachis gave way to the band that rattled out waltzes, the well-barbered businessmen drove home for their large, slow midday meals, while shabby workers came to sprawl with their tortillas in the dark shade cast by the Zócalo's trees. Brightly clad tourists crowded under every available café umbrella.

Althea's oval face was harmoniously composed, her hands clasped easily on the check tablecloth; she gave no sign of the maximum effort she was using to control her alarms. But as the slow minutes stretched she thought that if Gerry didn't come out soon, she might let out a scream.

Had Gerry and Roy reconciled? Or was reconciliation necessary? Had urbane Althea Wimborne fallen for the oldest line of all, the man in need of tenderness because his wife doesn't understand him? Was she – as Roy had hissed at her – simply one in a high-kicking chorus line of lays to Gerry Horak? Had he, the Pittsburgh slum kid, taken malicious pleasure in bedding a woman with her classy list of patronyms? The questions churned in her guts.

The waiter with the wispy moustache came over to remove her glass. Would the señora care to order?

She hated the waiter for his silly little moustache, she hated him for his smell of oily sweat and garlic, most of all she hated him for his soft brown eyes which spied on her interminable waiting. 'I'm not ready,' she said. 'Of course, if you *must* have the table?'

'No, señora, of course not. The señora knows she is always most welcome at the Café Manuela.'

He backed between crowded tables to the service window.

Her fingers began tapping on the tabletop, not keeping the beat of the bandstand waltz, *'Mi Corazón'*. How could she have permitted herself to slide right back into the insignificant hole from whence she had so painfully raised herself? How could she have left her son – her adolescent knight nonpareil – and her carefully selected coterie of friends and admirers? Why had she prised herself open like a vulnerable oyster? She was the world's idiot!

At that moment Gerry emerged from the hotel.

Relief jolted her, and she surveyed him as she would a stranger, noticing the curving breadth of his shoulders, his skin tanned the deep, reddish brown of Oaxaca's roof tiles, the thick, curly mop which grew low on his forehead and was in need of a trim. With the deep lines cut between his nose and the corners of his grimacing mouth, he resembled an ageing, unhappy Pan – or a weary labourer leaving the factory.

He sank into the chair next to hers.

'I'd just about given up,' she said with a wide smile.

'A drink for me, that's all,' he said. Heavy brown bristles shadowed his jaw: he had not followed his custom of shaving when he took his pre-lunch shower.

'Me, I'm ravenous.'

When the waiter came over, she smiled again, waving away the familiar gold-tasselled, food-spotted menu, turning to Gerry, listing her choices to him – an avocado salad, the tamales, tortillas, a Dos Équises.

Gerry did not repeat her order. After the waiter had ambulated in his heavy, duckfooted way to hand over the order to the kitchen, she said, 'What a ferocious day! It makes Marrakesh seem absolutely polar. Being a *gringa*, though – can you imagine this? – I walked all the way home from Oaxaca Courts.'

He reached for her hand, and there was something almost frantic in the tightness of his grip. 'Cut it out, Althea, just cut it out.'

'What are you talking about?'

'I can take everything but you playing with me.'

'Playing?'

He looked at her intently, a tiny muscle jumping in the lid of his left eye. 'Quit pretending she's not here.'

'Ahh, yes. Your wife.' Althea's irony was light; none of her imperilment sounded in her voice. 'Where is she?'

'Didn't she come out?'

'No.'

'She left the room a long time ago.'

'Possibly she's arranging for quarters next to ours. She

seemed quite crackers enough to poke holes in the wall and spy.'

'I told you. She goes off the deep end when she thinks there's another woman.' He raised his palms helplessly. 'The funny thing is that this time, when it's for real, she wasn't so bad. After a while she became almost herself, sane and level.'

A shrill bubble of voices burst as the three middle-aged American women rose from the next table.

'Wouldn't it solve matters,' Althea asked with carefully flat tones, 'if you simply told her to bug off?'

'She said she'd think about a divorce.'

'What married woman hasn't?'

'She's going to find a shrink.'

'Oh? In my circle, we seek an attorney to dissolve our marriages.'

'Althea, cut out the bitchiness. She needs help with this.'

'How long is the average term of a psychoanalysis? Five years? Ten?'

'I'd rather take my chances at Salerno all over again than be back in Ward Four.' He looked down at his hands, which were tattooed with Grumbacher paints. 'How can I condemn her to that?'

'So every time it looks like you might walk out, she goes into her Ophelia act – ' Althea broke off as the waiter came, remaining silent while a starch-scented darned white linen square was unfolded over the check tablecloth and large, heavy silverplate arranged. Gerry's bourbon and soda chaser was set down with a flourish. When the waiter left, Althea leaned forward. 'She knows how to play you.'

Gerry jerked down his drink, the muscles convulsing in his strong throat. He wiped his mouth with his knuckles. 'You know Roy's not like that.'

'About this one little item, she's obviously pretty shrewd.'

'I'm giving it to you straight, Althea. You're the only woman I care about, the only woman for me, but I couldn't stand it if Roy went nuts.'

Althea picked up a fork, staring at him. 'How will you avoid that?'

'What I have in mind is to give her time to work it through.'

'Sounds lovely. But what's in it for her? The minute she "works it through", as you put it, she loses you.'

'*She's* the one who brought up seeing the shrink.'

The cathedral's wooden clock chimed the quarter-hour.

'And where do you see me in all this?' Althea inquired.

'I know this is a hell of a lot to ask, but could you come back to Beverly Hills, live there? She'll be my wife in name only.'

'What a quaint expression.'

The waiter served her meal. Gerry ordered two more drinks while she toyed with tamales which, she said, had been revoltingly overspiced today, and sliced avocados, which today were absolutely tasteless. She punctuated her complaints with maliciously witty comments about the other patrons of the Café Manuela. The shade of the umbrella had shifted and half of Gerry's face was in the sun. The hard light showed his sweat-glossed unhappiness.

'You're a bitch,' he said finally.

'Do tell.' Her tone was as icy as the Dos Equises.

'That's part of your charm, the hardness. With the others I always felt I was putting up with a lot of menstrual cramps and whining because it was part of the bargain when I needed a piece of tail.'

'Delicately put.'

'Did I ever pretend to be anything but a foul-mouthed Hunkie bastard?'

She set down her fork. 'You're not a bastard at all,' she said slowly.

His eyebrows raised evocatively, and she felt a respite from the hurt that he was putting Roy's needs above hers.

'The truth is,' she went on, 'you've always been too buried in your painting to understand what's what. You've never learned the techniques and arts people use to prey on one another.'

He grinned. 'Is that a fancy way of telling me we're okay?'

She bit her lip. From now on his concern for Roy would

always cast a blight on their relationship. She would never again have that complete, uncomplicated spontaneity with him. Even in their most profound intimacies there would always be a trace of wariness.

Yet she had no choice. She loved Gerry Horak – worse, she needed him.

'I can't come to Beverly Hills,' she said, thinking of Charles's long, handsome face, the features growing and edging towards manhood. 'I need to be near my son. But what about coming back to New York?'

In an atypical, loverlike gesture, he kissed the palm of her hand. 'You're on,' he said.

'What about Roy?' she asked.

'She's meant to be washing me out of her hair,' he said, avoiding Althea's eyes.

52

Roy peeled another Kleenex from the box, blowing her nose – she had just stopped crying. 'He's not staying in her apartment.'

'You've mentioned that four times in this session,' said Dr Buchmann.

'Well, it's important, isn't it?'

'What do you think?'

She shifted in her easy chair. Dr Buchmann sat facing her in its twin. At her first appointment he had explained that he did not go in for the couch routine but preferred to talk in the comfortable atmosphere of a living room. The psychiatrist was in his fifties, a slow-moving, lanky Jungian with thinning brown hair and a minor speech impediment with R's, a trifling problem that roused Roy's (Woy's) easy sympathies, lowering her guard. His office was on Bedford Drive a few blocks from Patricia's, in the same white-painted brick building as the gynaecologist that she and Marylin used – indeed, Dr Dash had recommended Dr Buchmann.

Two months earlier in Oaxaca, on that sickeningly hot January day with the faraway band insinuating waltzes into the dark bedroom, it had been Gerry's misery that had elicited Roy's promise to seek professional help. Now she clung with desperation to her three hours a week. She budgeted herself strictly to pay Dr Buchmann's fees and left Patricia's an hour early, at five, on Monday, Wednesday and Friday to walk over. How could she survive without Dr Buchmann? To whom else could she confess the nights she lay in her bed kept awake by the frightful scratching (she knew it was hallucinatory) that emanated from Gerry's empty garage studio? Who else could she tell that she had no memory of what foods she shoved into her mouth at mealtimes, or of the blank-minded choking sensation that overtook her when it was time to connect the names that went with her customers' faces? She had once screwed up her courage to blurt out that she was drinking alone in the evenings. The nonjudgemental sympathy on Dr Buchmann's fine-skinned face had ameliorated his cautionary warnings.

'Of course it's important whether he moves in with her!' Roy leaned forward impatiently. 'How can you even ask? I'm the only woman he's ever lived with.'

'He's told you he wants to marry Mrs Wimborne, Roy.'

'That bitch is tremendously attractive! But she tires of her men – two divorces already. Dr Buchmann, remember, I told you about Oaxaca, when I felt so sorry for him that I said I'd think about a divorce. Well, now I see it wasn't so dumb. Eventually she'll throw him out. I'll ride out the separation. I'll wait however long I must to have a chance to get him back – I'll do anything to get him back.'

'Roy, listen to what you're saying.'

'I know I'm crawling after a man who wants out. But I can't help it. Never, not once in my life, have I come first with anyone!'

'You're a fine, attractive person. You're generous, loyal, bright, you've made yourself an excellent career. Your employers like you and trust you. Your family is devoted. You have a great many friends. To function properly, you have to learn to see yourself in perspective. That's why you're here.'

Roy sat back. 'Talking to you has saved my life, but if Gerry called tomorrow and told me to quit, I would.'

'I'd hoped we had come further than this,' said the psychiatrist quietly.

'Dr Buchmann, learning about myself has no connection with how I *feel* about Gerry.' Roy's throat ached as if a silk cord were tightening around her neck. 'I love him totally. He's my whole life.'

'Roy, Roy.'

'She's always stolen my guys! Maybe it's connected to some kind of lesbian tendencies she has, who knows.'

'That high-school story you told me is another situation entirely. This is an adult problem that you have to resolve.'

'What does resolution have to do with wanting somebody until every nerve in your body is frantic? Weren't you ever in love? Can't you understand? Without him, I'm nothing. I don't exist!' Roy raised her hands to her face, and the sound of hopeless sobs filled the beige office.

Later, Roy drove the long blocks southward. It was misty and the oncoming headlights frayed at her vision. Across Pico Boulevard, streetlamps glowed on neatly spaced, uniform little bungalows, this one gussied up with French Provincial shutters, that one with modern flanks of timber. Windows were lit in every house, and where the curtains were not drawn, Roy would see a man, a woman, children around a table or in front of a television set. Homes, families, she thought, the loneliness twisting within her.

She turned into her driveway, braking at the *porte-cochère* which had been added on with the conversion of the garage into Gerry's studio. In better times, homecoming had inevitably brought her a volatile quiver of pride for her wisdom at using Marylin's wedding present as a down payment on this house. Now, though, the house was a bleak, traitorous reminder that Gerry, uncaring of his abode, had itchy feet.

In the prim yellow kitchen she went straight to the

cabinet where the liquor was stored, pouring herself a stiff, neat Gilbey's. Numbing her dark, dark wretchedness with booze was a new thing to Roy: until January she had been drunk only once in her life – and that was after a fight with Gerry. With these gaping wounds, though, she could not make it through the long, aching nights without some kind of anaesthesia. Downing the gin, she poured another and went into the living room. She was still paying for the chintz sofa and chairs, the maple television, the cobbler's-bench coffee table, the dining ell's Early American suite. The somewhat gorged cosiness was undermined by three immense featureless oils from Gerry's Paris period – to Roy they resembled massive blue scars rather than abstractions of the Seine in its embankment.

The small house had no hint of Wace messiness. Roy rose every morning at six, cleaning compulsively, her mind cranking out idiotic thoughts that this might be the day that Althea and Gerry broke up, this might be the day he came home, therefore this table must be dustless, this sink scoured.

Carrying her drink to the bedroom, she changed into a velour robe. Later, she shoved a Swanson's TV dinner in the oven, continuing to drink while she ate in front of her maple 'entertainment centre' on whose screen small figures mimed to bursts of laughter.

When the telephone rang, she thought: *Gerry!* and dived across the room to answer.

'Hello, hon,' NolaBee said.

Roy sighed. Of course it wasn't Gerry. He never phoned. This was 8.30, time for her mother's routine call. She carried the long-corded instrument back to the couch. In a subdued voice she replied to her mother's questions. Yes, she was fine, yes, she had eaten supper, a proper one – she stared down at the divided foil platter with its congealing, scarcely tasted food. Chicken, peas, mashed potatoes and gravy.

'You have to take care of yourself, dear,' cajoled NolaBee. 'You can't let yourself get all down in the mouth because that man's gone off.'

'Why can't you understand?' Defence of her husband burst from Roy. 'Gerry's not an accountant, he's an artist! Artists must go where inspiration strikes them. He has to be free! Right now New York's the place for him.'

'Hon, I only meant he ought to consider you.'

'He does. He *wants* me there, but I have a job, remember?'

'I worry about you, Roy, all the time.'

After a few thumping heartbeats, Roy said, 'I'm sorry, Mama. I didn't mean to fly off the handle.'

A few minutes later the telephone rang again. It was Marylin. She, too, called every night, but instead of questions and intolerable maternal anxiety, she served up herself, the soft, husky little voice relating show-biz anecdotes of her latest film, which also starred Louis Jourdan.

Marylin was no longer contracted to Magnum – in this television age with the motion-picture grosses way down, no studio could afford to keep a stable of stars – so each of her film roles had to be negotiated for in the hurly-burly. Though Rain Fairburn currently had as much work as she could handle, she was fast zoning in on that certain age, too old to be the unlined, virginal love interest so obligatory to those increasingly peckish moneymen.

Sari got on the line.

Roy rested her head back on the couch, raising one foot and waggling it luxuriously. Being around Marylin's children eased an actual physical twinge in the area which, from the prodding of the medical profession in search of reasons for her infertility, she understood was the location of her womb.

'What about Sunday?' Sari asked. 'Auntie Roy, is it on for Disneyland?'

In so public a pleasure spot Marylin would be hounded after by autograph seekers, and Joshua's recent heart attack had temporarily grounded him, so Roy had taken on the enjoyable task of shepherding the outings of her brash, breaking-voiced nephew and her dark-haired wisp of a niece. 'It's engraved in red ink on my calendar. A red-letter day. Sari, luv, heaven forbid I'd mish – miss it.'

When Roy hung up, she squinted at the glass-enclosed pendulum clock on the mantel. Her eyes refused to focus on the Roman numerals, and she rose, walking over to peer. Ten to nine, which was ten to twelve Eastern Standard Time. She poured another drink before calling long distance.

The number that she requested did not answer.

She stretched on the couch, dialling long distance every few minutes. The number did not answer until the eleven o'clock news came on. It was two o'clock in the morning in New York.

'Yes?' Gerry's voice said roughly,

She held her breath.

'Who is it?'

She let the telephone rest on her breast.

'Roy?' came a ridiculous mouse squeak.

You're only a faraway voice, Roy thought, gazing at the ten-inch screen, where a row of Austrian Fräuleins kicked up their dirndls at a newsworthy festival. You'll come home to me.

'Dammit, you're hitting the bottle again.'

Sometimes she could not control her maudlin tears, but she always made the call: the only bright spot in the hopeless clouds was that Gerry still slept in Walter Kanzuki's loft and had not moved in with Althea.

'That shrink's making you worse, not better. You're going to cut this out, Roy, no more sloshing it down, no more breathing telephone calls.' His diminished voice rose half a decibel. 'I can't take much more!'

She hung up and went to bed.

Her sleep was dream-filled, unrestful, and she jerked wide-awake around two, her muscles taut, her mind fibrillating with self-loathing. No wonder he hates me. No wonder he prefers that icicle. How can I endure this living death without him?

'I can't make it tomorrow,' Althea said.

'What gives?' Gerry replied.

'It's April Fool's Day, so I'm flying home.'

'How long will you be out there?'

Expressively she spread her slender manicured hands. Taking off her leopard coat, she crossed the loft. On her easel was a creditable watercolour of tulips that she had done the previous afternoon. She tilted her head critically at it. 'The composition's not bad, but the colour's washy, don't you agree?'

'Come off it, Althea.'

'My father's having an operation – it's come up suddenly. He called this morning. So what else could a loving daughter do but rush to his side?' She lifted her chin arrogantly.

Gerry put his arm around her waist. 'Bad operation?' His tone was gentle.

She pulled away. 'Know what a colostomy is?'

'Oh, Christ.'

'The crab, the crab,' she said. 'The crab doth make dinner of us all.'

'Listen, I've never figured the screwy relationship you have with your parents, but why pretend you're not shook?'

'Because I *am* shook.' She closed her eyes. Delicate greenish veins lay on her translucent lids. 'Poor Daddy. While we were talking, he came apart – I've only heard him like this one other time . . .' her voice was muffled.

'I'll go with you,' Gerry said.

She touched her fingers lightly to his cheek, a gesture of tenderness. 'That's very dear of you,' she said. 'But appraising the situation logically, we won't be together much.'

'Yeah, I wouldn't brighten up his hospital room, would I?' he said. 'Still, I can be around when you need me.'

'Will you stay at your place?' Althea asked too easily.

'Jesus, who needs to start that crap all over again?'

'Again? Does that mean she's stopped her nightly beddy-bye call?'

'Nope. I'm not going to tell her I'm in LA . . .'

'Then how will you explain not being in New York?'

'Who knows? The usual. I need to go someplace for the scenery, the light.'

She touched his cheek again. 'We'll have to reserve you a hotel room.'

'You know me. I always manage to find a place to sack down.'

'My cousin's lending me his jet.'

'Another miracle?' Gerry gave a brief smile. He always grinned at the limousines, the well-furnished airport suites in which they rested and showered, the occasional private planes, the ease and efficiency that surrounded her shortest or longest journey.

'It's not me, love, it's my Aladdin's lamp.' She pulled the watercolour from its securing tacks on the board, tearing the paper in two.

'You rich have it easy.'

'True. All the goodies, including cancer of the colon.'

53

'His face was so terribly drained,' Mrs Cunningham repeated with an anxious shudder. 'Like putty.'

'Mother, after major surgery one cannot expect rosy cheeks.' As Althea spoke, she regretted her impatient flipness. But she was raw-nerved from waiting out the five-hour surgery and from the pain of her deeply troubled filial love. Besides, her mother's breathy voice had always irritated the hell out of her.

It was not quite three in the afternoon and rain slashed down with tropical intensity as they returned from the hospital. Beyond the glass panel, Ossie, Belvedere's new black chauffeur, held his greying head rigorously forward as he negotiated the water racing through the gutters that at every crossing balked the Silver Cloud.

Mrs Cunningham's jaw worked. 'Your father always had such marvellous colour.'

'Let us not use the past tense.'

'He looked so awful . . . Do you think we ought to call Charles out?'

'No need for that, Mother.' Althea's fingers itched to give

a reassuring pat to the large, soft hand, but the eternal trauma marred even this time of shared anxiety. Muddy water spattered the windows, and she said, 'And let's not borrow trouble. I, for one, believe the learned surgeons when they told us they had gotten all of the malignancy.'

The next few days Mr Cunningham lay morbidly listless, bleached of colour and spirit, recuperating at an insidiously slow pace. He had always viewed himself as all of a piece, a gentleman in heart, mind, intellect, body. From now on he would evacuate through a bag taped to his abdomen, a scarred, maimed pensioner to the Coyne millions: that his wife remained at his bedside, solicitously performing every small task for him before either of the private nurses could move, inexplicably added to his horror of himself.

Even more telling was his daughter's presence.

In normal health, he was able to consider their bond as purely that of father and beloved only child, but now, in his drugged weakness, her face and body blurred, forcing him to peer through a grim, dark veil beyond which wavered the shadowy outline of his anguish.

He would thrash to another position.

Five evenings after the surgery, as mother and daughter were being driven home to Belvedere, Mrs Cunningham said, 'Your father's worse when you're in the room.'

Althea went hot with mortification. 'You don't say.'

'Althea.' Mrs Cunningham gripped the leather armrest. 'We both want what's best for him, dear. I'm only pointing out he will recover more quickly with less company.'

'Far be it from me to impede his progress. I'll stay clear of the hospital premises. Or should I be banished from the city, too?'

'Your father enjoys seeing you.'

'You just said he didn't.'

'Why must you take on like this?'

'Daddy wants me, is that it, but you'd rather not have me around?'

Mrs Cunningham turned her large, homely face. She was

a Coyne, with the Coyne tenacious strength, she worshipped her husband, she rejected the daughter who was her rival, and in this one instant it all showed. 'It's best if you're not there quite so much.'

Althea drew a trembling breath. How, she asked herself, her mind prancing painfully, could this buck-toothed, unimpressive woman change her back into a helpless child, a victim?

'Quite so, then, Mother. As you say. One peek in the door, one bright, loving, daughterly smile, and then I'll fold my tent and silently steal away.'

'I want to go to Blum's,' she repeated.

'I heard you the first two times,' Gerry said. 'But we agreed not to hit any of the Beverly Hills places.'

'When I made that agreement, I wasn't dying for a coffee-crunch sundae.'

'Why are you being such a cunt?'

'I wasn't aware that eating a coffee-crunch sundae indicated anatomy.'

'Blum's is only a couple of blocks from Patricia's – '

'I grew up in Beverly Hills, dear heart, I don't need road maps.'

'A lot of the broads who work with Roy eat there,' he said wearily. 'She thinks I'm in Bermuda. She couldn't take knowing I'm here and not in touch.'

'Aren't you the protective husband.'

They were parked in Althea's Jaguar just north of Sunset Boulevard, where they could see the lights of rush-hour cars moving in rhythmic waves with the traffic signals.

'Althea, did he have a setback, your father? I thought he was getting better.'

'He is.'

'Then what's bugging you?' he asked, gently passing his hand over the sleeked-back skeins of bright hair.

'Ahh, Gerry, Gerry.' The streetlight cast a desperate glint on her large hazel eyes as she turned to kiss him full on the mouth, pressing her tongue between his lips, insinuating her body against his. He groaned, pulling her closer, and she reached down, feeling his erection. She unzipped his fly, slipping down onto the floorboards to take his hot, straining flesh in her mouth.

It was the first time since Oaxaca that she had initiated a blow-job.

'The red of the stripe in the Galanos is the perfect match for this Originala coat,' Roy said, hanging the two garments on a rack. 'There's several large scarves with the red, black and white, if the customer asks. And black patent pumps – I prefer the Ferragamos.'

'Matching shoes are what everyone wants for summer,' said Margot Lanskoy. 'What about having them dyed?'

'There's a red patent Delman sling pump that should be good,' contributed Mrs Sanderson, a trim older woman.

'The dyed-to-matches are *peau de soie*, and that's too dressy. The same goes for the Delman, with that diamante buckle.' Roy's warm smile showed she was not rebuking either of the suggestions.

'Now, Roy,' said Mrs Fineman from near the door. 'Don't be such a purist. Let's at least take a look at the Delmans.'

It was 9.15 on a Thursday morning, and in Patricia's cavernous, rack-filled dress stockroom, eighteen smartly dressed saleswomen were seated on folding chairs around Roy and her display of outrageously expensive summer clothing. On a rolling cart were a large aluminium coffee urn, a quart carton of half-and-half, used cups, and the richly scented remains of a big platter of Bailey's schnecken.

These Thursday breakfast meetings had been inaugurated by Roy a couple of years ago. At first there had been much grumbling at having to come in an hour early. Roy's formerly undeviating popularity had wavered briefly, but the sales staff received a one per cent commission: now the women entered enthusiastically into these seminars on assembling and accessorizing – a profitable and demanded aesthetic service that the rigidly departmentalized larger stores like Saks, Magnin's or Bullock's Wilshire were unable to perform.

A store clerk brought out a shoe box.

Roy placed the buckled, gleaming red pumps under the Galanos. 'Far too dressy,' she said decisively.

Everyone, including Mrs Fineman, nodded. Roy had developed an unusual fillip in her assemblages, and the Patricia's staff respected her opinion. 'Let me ask Mrs Horak what she thinks' resounded commonly in the airy, elegant fitting rooms.

The meeting was over, and only Roy and Margot Lanskoy remained in the stockroom, Roy writing up the numbers for each completed outfit on three-by-five cards, Margot finishing a third cup of coffee.

'You never mentioned your husband was back,' said Margot, smoothing grey silk pleats over her narrow flanks.

'Gerry?' Puzzled, Roy turned to the older woman. 'He's in Bermuda, painting.'

'Then he must have a double,' said Margot. Everyone in the store had accepted that Roy's husband had walked out on her and, liking her, had designated this 'Don't-Bug-Roy-Horak Month', but Margot, a fiftyish recent divorcée pressed for the first time into the Beverly Hills labour force, had a limited capacity for sympathy. She added, 'I saw a man but exactly the image of him at Blum's.'

A hot, formless fear swept over Roy. 'Was he in a booth near yours?'

'Not really close, no.'

'Then it could have been anyone.'

'You know me, farsighted as an eagle. This guy was an absolute dead ringer for your husband.' Margot's darkly painted mouth formed a smile. 'I must say I'm delighted he's in Bermuda, absolutely delighted.'

'What are you trying to say, Margot?'

'If I don't tell you, somebody else will. A tableful of us saw them.'

'Them?'

'A week ago, it was 17 April, this man, whoever he is, was there with a good-looking blonde wearing custom Chanel. Fortia thinks she knows her from *Vogue*.'

Endless anticipation does not lessen the extremity of horror a condemned prisoner feels as the gallows trap is sprung underfoot. Jagged pain encompassed Roy's mind.

He's here with Althea.

I promised him I'd try to work it through, and he's lied to me. He's not in Bermuda. He's here and never even phoned me.

Until now Roy had managed a clean split in her life. She had separated the weepy night-time drunk from the self-assured daytime assistant manager of Patricia's. But now her every nerve was screaming, and she thought: If I don't have a drink I'll die.

Leaving the stockroom and Margot Lanskoy, she found herself at her desk reaching inside the top drawer for her purse. She mumbled an excuse about the onset of the twenty-four-hour flu to Mr Fineman. Normally she never left the parking lot before six, and the attendant had to juggle cars so she could back out the old Thunderbird, her engagement present.

She had never got sozzled to the point of passing out. But when she got home, she did. Score another first for Roy Horak.

When she came to, her neat Early American parlour was plunged into darkness and a nasty, persistently repetitive sound vibrated. It took several jangles before she realized the phone was ringing.

She fumbled for the light switch. Gerry's big, smooth paintings whirled around her and everything in the room seemed out of whack, as if she wore distorting lenses. Holding on to the backs of chairs, she shuffled her way to the noisy black instrument.

'So you *are* there, hon,' NolaBee said. 'I'd just about given up. I let it ring and ring, and then reckoned that you'd gone out for a bite of supper with one of the girls at Patricia's.'

'No, I was washing my hair.' Roy's dishonest tongue felt swollen. A horrible sourness pressed behind her uvula. I'll barf if I don't lie down, she thought, carrying the phone back to the couch.

'You sound so funny. You all right?'

'I came home early with a splitting headache,' said Roy, stretching out.

'Taken aspirin?'

Lying flat, rather than alleviating the whirl of nausea, intensified it. 'Mama, I'll call you back.'

She staggered to the bathroom just in time. When she had finish vomiting, she sat trembling on the cold linoleum.

Gerry's here in Beverly Hills.

He invented that lie about Bermuda and the Winslow Homer light.

He's cut me out of his life forever.

The sharp pain that guillotined her at eye level had become intolerable.

Shoeless, in her white lace-and-nylon slip, she returned to the living room. A tumbler and fifth of Gilbey's sat on the floor next to the couch. The gin was gone.

On the kitchen shelf remained only some ornately bottled liqueurs.

She gulped at the maroonish liquid, which smelled like Syrup of Figs, then bore the bottle back to the couch, setting it down by the Gilbey's. *Lost Weekend* time, she thought. Next I'll be hiding the empties in the chandelier, except I don't have a chandelier.

Her titter ended with a sob.

The liqueur, instead of bringing a blessed nirvana, stoked up her mental processes until her panic at Gerry's ultimate rejection became a physical need for action, any action.

She picked up the phone, setting it on her chest over the nylon lace of her slip.

The numerical sequence of thousands of teenage calls came automatically to her index finger.

'Althea?' she asked thickly.

'Mrs Wimborne is not home,' said the remembered chilling accent of the butler – what was his name?

Roy shivered before she said, 'Then I'll speak to Mr or Mrs Cunningham.'

A pause. Then: 'Who may I say is calling?'

'Roy Hor – Roy Wace.'

'Ahh, yes. A moment, please.'

She could smell the sourness on her, a depraved, ugly odour.

Mrs Cunningham's voice greeted her; but Roy did not hear the words. Into her drunken, bereft anguish had come a petulant dart of resentment towards the dowdy multi-millionairess who was Althea's mother.

Words, like her recent vomit, flowed in a racking spasm.

'Your daughter's a bitch. A bitch, bitch, bitch!' she cried. 'A fucking, stealing, conniving bitch. She's got her sharp hooks into my husband. He's an artist, Gerry Horak . . .'

'*Who?*'

'Gerry Horak, he's famous and a genius, a real genius. What does a rich society bitch like her know about genius? He's absolute Greek to her, she doesn't understand a thing about him. What does she know about anybody? She only uses people to prove she's better than they are. All she wants with Gerry is the proof she can take him away from me. Well, she can't! Not with all your Coyne millions. Gerry's not interested in money, he's a real artist – '

'Roy, this is no time to talk.' The voice at the other end was hushed, anxious, almost pleading.

'So she's trapped him with her body. Well, you tell her from me, she's not going to get away with it!'

'I'm going to hang up.' There was a click.

'He's married to me, I'm Mrs Gerrold Horak! You tell her that I've changed my mind about working out a divorce, tell her that I'll never let him go! Never, never, never.'

Roy was weeping in the unnumbable pain of bitter loss, she was weeping in agonized, drunken self-loathing. What had she said? She couldn't remember.

How could I have screamed like that at Mrs Cunningham? Mother raised me to be a Fairburn, a Roy, a Wace, she raised me to have nice manners.

She dropped the receiver and her half-clad, grief-convulsed body staggered like an unprogrammed robot into the bedroom. She fell across the quilted chintz spread. Once she had shared this bed with Gerry, once she had awakened in the night to feel the scalding warmth of his naked body next to her.

Once . . . once . . .

54

It was nearly midnight when Althea arrived home, yet her mother awaited her outside the open library doors. The hall's overhead chandelier was not lit, and the blaze coming from the vast book-lined room cast an eerie elongated shadow of Mrs Cunningham's tall, full-bosomed, shapeless figure.

'What is it?' Althea burst out. 'Is Daddy all right?'

'That's what I must talk to you about,' said Mrs Cunningham. 'Come in here.'

Quelling her uneasiness, Althea obeyed.

Mrs Cunningham glanced around the shadowed hall as if to ensure an absence of snoops before closing the doors after them. She crossed the length of the brilliantly lit library to the massive butternut fireplace. Her thick, soft arms clasped to her sides, she stood erect as if behind a lectern.

'While your father is ill, Althea, I will not have any scandal.' She spoke without raising her normally breathy voice, yet managed a forensic command.

'Scandal?'

'You are seeing that Gerry Horak person. Now he has a wife.'

Althea's surprise was undetectable, but her thoughts bounced like a rubber ball. How does Mother know? Why should I feel ashamed? Gerry was banished from my life the first time in this library – is that why Mother's brought me here? In this light Mother's eyes are the flat, grainy grey of marble. Normally she never looks directly at me like this. Is her averted gaze the reason I've always feared her, even though on the surface she's such a big, timid cow?

401

'A lot of men have wives, Mother,' Althea said.

'In New York and Europe you may conduct yourself as you choose, but here, under my roof, and at this time, you will behave decently.'

'Mother, this may come as a surprise, but sleeping with a man is no longer the crime of the century.'

'I am warning you. *No scandal.*'

'Mother, let's not fly off the handle about everyday occurrences. Your daughter, a thirtyish double divorcée, is dating a soon-to-be-single man. Big deal.'

'Your old friend Roy Wace was foul-mouthed and hysterical about it.'

To Althea's distress was added a little shiver between her shoulderblades. Yet why the revelation that Roy was onto Gerry being in Beverly Hills should jar her, she did not know. After all, hadn't she herself vigorously contrived that Roy find out? 'Roy called you?'

'She wanted to speak to you. When she couldn't, she asked for me. Unfortunately, Luther transferred the call to the sickroom. She was most obviously inebriated. The entire time, I was trembling that your father would hear. I pressed the instrument to my ear as tightly as possible. It took all my willpower to hide my distress. I can't tell you the shock it was to find out Roy had married *him.* Of all the people in the world! And my heart sank when I heard you were seeing him again.'

'When did she call?'

'Around nine. She was absolutely deranged by drink. Shouting wild, lunatic threats. I remember her as an affectionate, well-mannered child. In a way, I pitied her. But, Althea, he's turned her into the kind of person who makes trouble.'

'Trouble, trouble!' Althea was suddenly trembling. 'What do you mean, trouble?'

'If your father had taken the call, think how awfully it would have set him back.'

'Always him! Always protecting him!' The old wounds, ripped open, bled profusely. Althea stalked over to the fireplace, thrusting her face close to her mother's. 'But what about me?' she asked in a whisper. 'I was a child, ten years old at first. You knew all along what was going on, yet you let it continue. Why? Were you so afraid of losing him that you couldn't dare risk mentioning it? Did you think he'd walk out on you if you tried to stop it? For God's sake, you're my mother! I know how a mother feels. How *could* you have let it go on?'

Mrs Cunningham moved to the Georgian library ladder, which rested against the shelves to the left of the fireplace. 'Sometimes I don't understand you, Althea. You were the sweetest little girl, loving and good. Never sarcastic, never off on these wild tangents. You never ran around with unsuitable people – '

'I had no friends, but you never noticed.'

'And now you've picked up that coarse, common nobody – have you no respect for Charles?'

'You know damn well whose child Charles is!' Althea cried out.

Charles's true paternity had never been voiced aloud. At the time of Althea's marriage to Firelli, however, the Cunninghams' ardent welcome to a groom of his advanced years had been tacit admission of the bride's pregnancy.

Mrs Cunningham paled. 'Keep your voice down,' she hissed.

'You know how you screwed up my life!' Althea screamed. She had a peculiar sensation that the moulded ceiling had risen higher and that the brass-fretted shelves loomed larger, as if she had dwindled to the size of a child.

Control, she importuned herself. Control is of the utmost importance.

Biting the inside of her cheek so she tasted the salt of blood, she moved from Mrs Cunningham. 'A shame that this mess happened, Mother, dear,' she said levelly. 'I apologize for losing my temper. It's been a trying time for all of us. I'll see to it that there are no more telephone calls.'

For a moment Mrs Cunningham's eyes piercingly catechized Althea; then her gaze slid away. Her expression returned to its usual anxious timidity. 'You understand, then?'

'You have every right to be upset,' Althea said. 'While Daddy's recuperating, he needs complete peace of mind.'

'I knew you'd feel exactly as I do.' Mrs Cunningham crossed the shadowy length of the library. 'Good night, dear. See you in the morning.'

She left the doors open.

While her mother's steps echoed heavily up the stairs, Althea poised immobile, then she began prowling the book-lined room.

I'm in for it, she thought.

Mother's right. Roy certainly is ready to go off the deep end and make endless trouble. Then everybody will be talking. Strangers, my friends, everybody.

The weight of malicious tattle and curdling laughter would crush Althea Wimborne, a creation as carefully and exquisitely manufactured as one of the Fabergé Easter eggs that her Coyne grandmother had collected.

I must get away from this mess, she thought.

She had no subliminal or peripheral thoughts. She could dredge up no rancour against or sympathy for Roy, who obviously had been driven to the brink.

There's no choice.

.I can't keep on with Gerry.

She halted by the piano, opening it, striking middle C. As the note sounded, she visualized Gerry's broad face, the tension lines around his lips and eyes. He had once appeared to her redeemed from humanity's psychological delirium by his art, but now she knew his weaknesses, the cardinal of which was loving her.

She loved him.

But what did it matter?

She could not brave a world bombarded with proof of her flaws and imperfections.

The grandfather clock gave a protracted bong, then another and another.

It was midnight. The witching hour.

She purposefully walked to the phone and dialled. When

Gerry answered, she invited him to the Cunninghams' Ojai ranch to go riding.

Stern mountains protect the wide, level floor of the Ojai valley, which aeons ago was the bottom of the sea, home to minute saltwater creatures and plants that, crushed by the weight of the ocean, became rich oil deposits. Now wells pump the oil and incredibly fertile topsoil nourishes every type of crop and fruit tree. The broad swale is a peaceful and lovely place. When the producers of the original *Lost Horizon* needed a location for mythical Shangri-La, they came to Ojai. The Cunninghams had purchased the 265-acre ranch between the little town of Ojai and the foothills specifically for the few days a year during Charles's visits that he and his grandfather – in Mrs Cunningham's terms – wanted to rough it.

Last night, when Althea had decided to cut off the affair, she had determined that the ranch was the place to do the deed. Gerry had never ridden and it was imperative that she see him at a disadvantage. There was no other way she could go through with it.

Mounted on her father's spirited Arabian, wearing old tan jodhpurs and a grey sweatshirt, she led the way up the mountainside along the Cunninghams' flinty, rocky private trail to a ridge called Brave's Nose for its long, aquiline shape. It had been a wet season, so poppies painted the steep, sunlit slopes with liquid gold. Vivid blue lupine clumped everywhere while in the dusky shade of the live oaks maidenhair grew profusely. At their approach, quail rustled heavily from the chaparral.

Althea turned to look back at Gerry. Gripping onto his pommel, he squinted intently up at the cerulean sky in the direction of the grey, nose-shaped summit that gave the mountain its name. 'What's that? It's too big to be an eagle.'

She raised a sheltering hand. 'A condor,' she said. 'You're lucky to see one. They're very rare.'

'So naturally they nest on land belonging to the rich bastards,' Gerry said, grinning. The sun had reddened the bridge of his nose and the skin above his high cheekbones.

Althea's spirited Arabian stallion pawed as she reined him so she and Gerry could ride side by side. Gerry's mount, a tall, mahogany-coloured Tennessee walking horse, the most gentle of animals, edged sideways without any pressure from him.

'I think,' Althea said, 'that you ought to go back to Roy.'

Gerry jumped as if hit with buckshot. His placid mount stumbled on the shale.

'What are you talking about?' he demanded.

'We've run the course, you and I.'

His eyes fixed on her, he growled, 'The hell you say.' He reached for her upper arm, squeezing through the flesh to the bone.

Excitement burned inside Althea's vagina, yet her resolve remained. 'You're her husband.'

'I'm leaving her and marrying you, remember?'

'She won't let you go. Not that I blame her.' It surprised Althea how devoid she was of recrimination or resentful anger. This was how she had always longed to be in a crisis. Benignly uninvolved. Removed from the sweaty, hormonal heat. Presenting her side of the argument from an unendangered parapet where she could not be stabbed or bludgeoned into blurting out ineptitudes. 'She'll fight.'

'What are you, a mind reader?'

'None of this is anybody's fault, Gerry, but she called yesterday evening when I was with you – '

Gerry interrupted. 'She knows I'm out here in California?'

'That's my fault,' said Althea, who usually bucked against admitting culpability. 'I just didn't realize she had such a drinking problem. When she talked to Mother, evidently she was loaded to the gills.'

Insects buzzed above the dry bushes.

Gerry sighed. 'The poor kid.'

'Yes,' Althea agreed. 'So you see, don't you, that she'd turn a divorce into the sort of circus newspapers thrive on. People like me are always in the centre ring. Gerry, I just couldn't take it. I'm a very private person.'

'I know what you are!' Gerry's hand had remained on her arm and he yanked her roughly towards him.

406

Her horse reared violently. She calmed the frightened animal, murmuring wordlessly, patting the straining neck. When the Arabian was stilled, she said, 'For God's sake, Gerry, one of us is going to get thrown.'

'Not you,' he said bitterly. 'Never you.'

'And what about you? You try to play tough guy, but you aren't. You're going to feel responsible and guilty about Roy.'

'Worse than that,' he admitted. 'But I learned the hard way that everything has a price tag.'

'It's not only me. There's my parents. Charles.'

'Are you telling me in this calm, rational voice that we're through?' He reached out again.

She reined her horse apart from his. 'Listen, any more caveman tactics and we'll both be thrown.'

She turned back down the trail, trotting easily, gracefully. He followed, jouncing in the western saddle yet somehow giving the impression of belonging on his large, broad-backed mount.

The Mexican groom took the horses, leading them to the commodious stables.

Gerry spraddled an awkward circle as if his thigh muscles hurt – as they probably did.

He moved to Althea. 'Now, are you going to tell me what this is all about?'

Althea leaned against the white-painted fence of the paddock, where two quarter-horses stood with her colts. She could feel the sun's heat on her skin, but below the epidermal surface was an unpleasant chill. That earlier dumbfounding calm had abandoned her. She was trapped in a riptide of love, pity, sorrow. How could she dismiss Gerry like an insolent servant when he was part of her pulsebeat?

Yet she heard her unimpassioned voice. 'I'm flying back to New York tomorrow, Gerry. And I don't want you to follow me.'

'You damn rotten rich bitch, you love me. And I love you.'

At the bitter anguish in his voice, her resolve wavered briefly; then she responded with a patrician smile.

He stared at her, his eyes narrowed in the abstracted

concentration that was his before he began to paint, then pulled her to him in a kiss that was all tongue and savage teeth.

For a fraction of time she kissed him back, a surrender crueller than an immediate rebuff, before jerking from his grasp.

Raising his arm, he slapped her full force across the cheek. The blow stunned her.

She staggered backwards, falling sideways on the soft earth. Stars. You do see stars, she thought. Involuntary tears welled into her eyes. She was trembling all over.

He did not offer a hand to help her rise. Staring down at her with beaten rage, he turned to jog back down the eucalyptus-lined road to the house. Althea pushed to her feet, brushing the seat of her jodhpurs.

A couple of minutes later she heard the angry squeal of his borrowed Buick convertible careening along the curves of the private road that led to the highway.

One of the mares had come to nuzzle Althea, but she paid no attention. She rested her forehead on the painted rail. She was not crying. Her tears of pain had dried and her eyes had become hot and gritty, as if the very fluid of life were gone from her.

55

Around four that same afternoon, Roy stood in the largest fitting room behind Crystal Klingbeil, who had flown in from Houston for the day to let Roy coordinate her summer wardrobe. Mrs Klingbeil was beaming entranced at the reflection of the white-beaded Norell sheath, while Roy, who had ordered the designer original with this specific customer in mind, had a doubtful glint in her eye. She was having second thoughts whether she could in good faith sell the roly-poly oil millionairess a gown that strained this way across her buttocks.

There was a tap at the louvred door and Mrs Fineman's powdered face popped in. 'Do you mind if I assist you, Mrs Klingbeil? There's somebody here to speak to Mrs Horak.'

Knowing that only the utmost emergency had brought her employer to interrupt this lucrative selling session, Roy was swept by a sense of foreboding. With a blank smile and a polite 'Excuse me,' at Crystal Klingbeil, she hurried to her office, which consisted of a desk and filing cabinet outside the Finemans' office. Mr Fineman stood tapping a yellow pencil.

'Two police officers,' he whispered tersely, nodding towards the closed door of his office. 'They insisted on talking to you.'

'Did they say what it's about?' Roy faltered.

'They showed me their badges and asked us to get you, that's all I know.' He touched her arm – it was rare for Mr Fineman to make an impromptu gesture of concord. 'Roy, I told them you had worked here as our most trusted employee for nearly ten years.'

'Thank you, Mr Fineman,' she said faintly.

The inner office also lacked the sumptuousness of the customer side of Patricia's. More filing cabinets, a pair of desks with unmatched reproduction chairs, an old horsehair sofa on which Mr Fineman took his postprandial snooze. By the streaked windows that looked out on the alley stood a pair of tall, bulky men. Despite their sports jackets – tweed and bright blue check – there was something about them that screamed 'cop'. They've stepped directly from a *Badge 714* set, Roy thought numbly.

The older of the pair was totally bald. 'Mrs Gerrold Horak?' he asked. 'Of 9621 Erica Drive?'

'Yes.'

'I'm Sergeant Wills, this is Officer Monroe.'

'What's it about?' she asked. Her mouth was dry.

'Before we get to that, you'd better sit down, Mrs Horak.'

His dispensation of professional concern made Roy's heart beat yet more erratically. 'I'm all right like this.'

'There's been an automobile accident near Ventura. Mr Horak – '

'Gerry? An automobile accident?'

'Yes.'

'Then you've made a mistake,' she said loudly. 'It's some other Gerrold Horak. Ventura – that's on the way to Santa Barbara. He never goes there. Never.'

'His driver's licence showed the same address as yours.'

'But his car's at the house!'

'He was at the wheel of a fifty-six Buick convertible belonging to Arthur Vought – '

'Artie?'

'The car was observed speeding erratically on Highway One. A highway patrolman tried to halt the vehicle. It skidded out of control, hitting the embankment. Mr Horak was thrown clear. He was dead by the time the highway patrolman reached him.'

Dead?

Gerry was *leaving* her, not dying.

Gerry was thirty-nine years old, and men of thirty-nine don't die. Gerry was passionately alive. Why would he be in Ventura?

An alien roar resounded in her head, which suddenly felt pumped with helium. As her head became lighter her body weight increased until her black suede Delman pumps were too insubstantial to support her body's gravitational pull.

'Mrs Horak? Mrs Horak, here. Rest here . . .'

She sank inexorably down, a small object trapped in a monstrous, whirling vortex. Hands helped her onto the rough horsehair, placing her head on the folded afghan.

Mr Fineman's outline blurred and then became etched on her vision with unnerving precision – she could see that one of his eyelashes grew from a minuscule wart. The two plainclothesmen had moved to flank him.

'Rest there a minute,' said Mr Fineman in the gooey tones used to encourage ailing small children to swallow their medicine.

'But Mrs Klingbeil . . . the beaded Norell . . . bought it for her . . .'

'If we lose a sale, we'll lose it. We're your friends, Roy, you're a daughter to us.'

'I better go home . . .' She struggled to stand.

He pressed her shoulders. 'Rest a few minutes. You've had a terrible shock.'

An awful, hollow, arthritic kind of ache afflicted Roy's rib and shoulder bones, making breathing difficult. She drew in shallow breaths, exhaling through her mouth. Opposite her hung the bulletin board covered with the Patricia's summer-season ads from *Vogue* and *Harper's Bazaar*. Roy stared blankly at models posed in ludicrously expensive outfits.

Dead?

The cops must have said goodbye. They were gone and Mr Fineman was excusing himself. Mrs Fineman came in immediately. 'My poor Roy,' she said, her fleshy face askew. 'Mr Fineman's calling your brother-in-law.'

Joshua took charge.

He drove to Ventura, identified the body, and arranged for it to be brought home. He set the funeral for 2 P.M. Thursday at Forest Lawn, he selected and paid for the ornate bronze coffin with gold-plated handles, he decided on the type of service, he ordered a messenger service to deliver to Pierce Brothers' Mortuary a brand-new dark suit – Gerry didn't own one. He telephoned Gerry's gallery in New York and his brothers in Pittsburgh, he sent out a press release, he saw to it that there was food, liquor, a bartender and caterer in the small tract house.

Joshua played the role of host to the many people who visited before the funeral. The Fernauld clan came, and BJ's in-laws, Roy's sorority alumnae group, her numerous friends and every one of Patricia's employees. Everyone attempted to distract her from her grief. Possibly they succeeded, because of those prefuneral days, she would recall only one conversation.

It was with Marylin.

NolaBee and Marylin were staying in the house with her. On the night before the funeral, NolaBee retired early and the sisters went into the compact yellow kitchen, Roy sitting in the breakfast alcove, Marylin using a padded mitt to take from the oven the savoury-smelling casserole that was

Coraleen's funeral offering – the Fernaulds' elderly couple doted on Roy.

'Coraleen's chicken Marco Polo, your favourite,' Marylin said.

'You go ahead. None for me.'

Marylin spooned out the cheese-covered chicken and broccoli. 'We both need a late-night snack in our stomachs after our drinks.' Marylin's use of the plural was kindness: she, as always, had been abstemious, while Roy had never been without a glass in her hand. 'This'll slide down easily.' She set the plates on the table.

Roy was soused enough to be obedient. She picked up her fork.

Since Gerry's death, though, the taste of meat had become abhorrent to Roy, and with difficulty, she swallowed the cheese-oozing bite of chicken. Gulping at her drink, she said, 'This thing's turned me into a vegetarian.'

'Then I'll fix you some milk bread.' An old Wace cure-all.

Roy shook her head. 'Nothing.'

Marylin reached her small, slender hand across the yellow tabletop to clasp Roy's cold fingers. 'I know what you're going through.'

'You can't . . .'

'When they said Linc was dead, I thought I would die, too.'

Roy got up. Before leaving, the bartender had arranged a kitchen counter with clean glasses, the vacuum ice bucket, soft drinks, liquor. Roy reached for the Johnnie Walker bottle.

Marylin's fork toyed with broccoli. 'Do you think that's a good idea?' she murmured.

'A teensy nightcap,' Roy said, switching to brandy. *How come with all I've drunk, I can feel this much pain?* 'It's really not the same. At least you knew Linc *had* loved you.'

'Oh, Roy, Gerry loved you, of course he did. Didn't he marry you?'

'It wasn't his idea. I talked him into living with me. Then after we had a big blow-up, he was sorry and agreed on the wedding.'

'The smartest thing he ever did. You gave him stability, you made him a real home.'

Roy sighed deeply. That arthritic pain through her chest remained. 'He didn't really care where he lived. A borrowed attic, a sleeping bag – any dump was the same to him. All he wanted was a place to work . . . and . . .' Roy's voice wavered. 'Marylin, I've been feeling guilty, so lousy, rotten guilty. I made his last months hell for him. Phoning him at all hours, fouling up his Oaxaca series. No wonder he preferred Althea.'

Marylin's lovely eyes darkened to a stormy, greyish green. '*Her.*'

'I'm so ashamed. The night before he . . . was killed, I called Belvedere to talk to her. She wasn't home. I'd had a few too many, and I made this big scene with Mrs Cunningham.'

'He was *your* husband, Roy.'

'He and Althea had an affair ages ago, long before I met him.' Roy's eyes filled.

'You're being right silly.' To cheer her sister, Marylin rendered a near-perfect mimicry of NolaBee's Southern tones. 'I reckon Mr Man chose you, hon.'

'They loved each other.'

'She doesn't know the meaning of the word!' Marylin's soft voice was relentless. 'Wherever she is, there's trouble!'

'That's not fair.'

'Everybody says she was the one behind Henry Lissauer's suicide.'

Gossip was so unlike Marylin that Roy's bloodshot eyes fixed questioningly on her sister.

'Roxanne de Liso was at his art school when he killed himself,' Marylin said. 'Roxanne said Althea was always making eyes at him. Mr Lissauer was Jewish but German, an enemy alien. Roxanne swore that the Cunninghams set Immigration on him. He shot himself the day the atom bomb dropped on Hiroshima. Althea had come over to the house and had hysterics the night before, remember?'

'That's old garbage, Marylin.'

The exquisite, gentle mouth was tensed. 'All the years

413

you two were so close, you had no other friends, but the minute you broke away, people swarmed around you.'

'We went through a difficult phase together, that's all.' Roy wondered why, when hatred surged dizzily through her, she was defending Althea.

'You're always so loyal, but this is pushing it too far.' Marylin stood as if to emphasize her words. 'Althea Cunningham is one of those people who should be avoided.'

'Oh, Marylin.'

'She's like a snake. It's her nature to spit venom.'

Though it was not yet May, ovenlike heat blew from the inland deserts, and the following day the temperature soared to the nineties. Fortunately, the funeral limousines were air-conditioned.

Roy, in the first car with her mother and Marylin, was battling nausea – she had drunk her breakfast. Despite her grief and physical discomfort, a small ripple of excitement ran through her. Gerry was waiting for her at Forest Lawn. She was on her way to him. Continually she reminded herself that he was dead, dead, dead, yet she could not quell this crazy idea that she was gliding towards a date with him.

NolaBee had suggested the rector from All Saints Episcopal where she was a communicant. He conducted the funeral service in the grey stone church. Afterwards six mortuary employees directed the congregation to their cars.

A long, slow procession followed the hearse through the rolling lawns of the necropolis to a deep gash in the lavish grass. Here, a dozen wooden chairs were sheltered by a marquee. The chief mourners sat while others gathered beneath elms and sycamores mopping their brows.

'I am the resurrection and the life, saith the Lord: he that believeth in me, though he were dead, yet shall he live, and whosoever liveth and believeth in me shall never die . . .' The rector had a fine bass delivery, but a treeful of sparrows drowned him out.

The casket began its slow descent into the grave, and as the creaking mechanism lowered the massive coffin, Roy was plunged into the brutal knowledge that Gerry, wearing a brand-new navy striped worsted suit, was being set down with jolting movements into the clayey yellow soil.

Until resurrection . . .

Forever.

This was our date, Roy thought. He below, me above . . .

Her body shook in uncontrollable spasms.

NolaBee and Marylin put consoling arms around her, BJ leaned forward with a loud, warm-voiced whisper of courage, and Joshua pressed a clean handkerchief into Roy's shaking grasp. Billy, his craggy adolescent face for once drawn into sober lines – no wise-ass stuff today – said, 'Aunt Roy, hey, Gerry's not really dead. People will look at his work in museums, and that's being alive.' Sari's tenderly loving pats fell on her hip.

Roy, encapsulated by her family, Roy utterly alone, Roy gasping out her torturous grief for her estranged husband.

People would have approached her, but the mortuary men formed a protective phalanx around the family, so there was a general dispersal to the cars.

After a few minutes Roy's outburst subsided. She blew her nose on a fresh handkerchief from Joshua's apparently inexhaustible supply.

A tall, slender woman in black was moving uphill through the sunlight and shade towards them. Her shoulders were curved inward and her large-brimmed hat was bent low.

The woebegone posture was so unlike Althea's arrogant carriage that she had nearly reached the open grave before anyone in the family recognized her.

'Takes a whole lot of nerve, her comin' here.' NolaBee's aside, spoken to nobody in particular, was surely audible to Althea.

'Come along, old dear,' Joshua said, taking Roy's arm.

Roy peered through narrowed lids at the suppliant figure edging towards the grave. Hot possessiveness swept through her, and in a burst of jealousy she understood she could not permit this final encroachment. Eluding Joshua's grasp, she took a few tottery steps, her narrow high heels sinking into immaculately mowed grass.

The two women halted on either side of the open pit.

Tears oozed down Althea's rigid face, making red blotches on the fine-pored skin. 'I know I shouldn't be here,' she murmured, slightly raising the hand that held the crumpled scrap of handkerchief, a gesture that managed to convey contrition and a fragile hope of forgiveness.

Roy's incoherent determination to guard her dead husband wavered: what must it have cost proud, aloof Althea to humbly beg permission to share in Gerry's final rites? The ties of friendship, so indestructible in Roy, tugged at her, and tears again welled in her eyes. She took a stumbling step around the heaped-up earth, opening her arms.

Althea moved towards her. 'Oh, Roy, you understand? I kept thinking he was meeting me here.'

'Yes, yes,' Roy sobbed. 'That's exactly what I felt . . .'

The widow and mistress shared a desolate embrace.

56

For I am persuaded that neither death nor life nor angels, nor principalities, nor powers, nor things present, nor things to come,

Nor height, nor depth, nor any other creature shall be able to separate us from the love of God, which is in Christ Jesus our Lord.

The red edging of tissue-fine pages had worn to a trace of pink, the black leather binding was separating from its caramel-coloured linen. Roy's paternal grandmother's Bible.

Reaching for her tumbler, Roy sipped, letting time bear her like a slow-turning torture wheel. Thus I would revolve – resolve? – for all eternity.

She had promised the Finemans to return to work after a week, but those seven days following Gerry's death had passed in a blur of visitors and NolaBee's cigarette smoke; thus she had no time to resolve things present, nor things to come. Both Mr and Mrs Fineman had sympathetically urged her to take off as much time as necessary. A month, two even. More difficult by far to convince her mother to let her alone: NolaBee, in the clutch of unrelenting maternal instinct, had to be shoved from the house.

But what was so pernicious about nipping in solitude? Why shouldn't she weep alone in her tedious grief?

The door knocker tapped.

Roy's head tilted. A neighbour? Friend? Her mother? The restless tapping continued, punctuated by the buzzer.

Setting down the Bible and glass, she went unsteadily to the front door.

Althea stood there. Pale hair slicked back. Pale, elegant cream sweater and matching skirt. Pale jacquard silk blouse.

Roy drew backward in the dim foyer. She couldn't bear close proximity to this tall, slender, immaculate body that Gerry had cherished and caressed. (In retrospect, the hysterical, graveside embrace seemed an impossibility, and several times during the last days Roy had caught herself boozily pondering the course of events had she been holding a gun.)

'May I come inside?'

Roy was loaded enough to forget manners. 'Why?' she asked truculently.

'My father's much better and I'm on my way home. I came over on the off-chance you'd have dinner tonight.'

Dinner? Roy realized it was dusk.

'Are you free?' Althea asked.

In the gloom behind Althea, a mourning dove preened atop one of the triad of spindly, silver birches. Funny name, mourning dove. What do you mourn, you slim grey bird? Death? Loss of love?

'Roy, is anything wrong?'

'Oh, God, oh, shit, shit, shit. What could be right?'

Althea stepped over the threshold, switching on the living-room light. She stared at Gerry's huge, smoothly executed paintings, blinked, then took in the couch with its Bible, bottle and sad, solitary glass.

'It looks,' she said quietly, 'as if you're in as bad shape as I am.'

'You?' Roy gave a discordant titter. 'You look like you stepped off the Rue de la Paix.' Balancing herself against the couch, she poured all that remained of the fifth of Scotch into the glass, drinking, shuddering as the line of heat travelled down behind her ribs.

'Roy, listen, you shouldn't.'

'Are you implying I'm a lush? Isn't it enough for you to steal my husband? Do you have to defame me, too?' 'Defame' came out oddly: 'de-vein'.

'I have enough on my conscience without you turning into an alcoholic.'

'Is that what you call having a little drinkee before dinner?'

Althea's long, delicate jaw tensed and her hazel eyes focused on a faraway point, as if she were hearing an interior monologue. Then she moved with swift intent through the living room to the kitchen.

Roy careened after her.

The liquor cabinet was open. Althea reached for the first bottle, wrenching off the top, letting the amber bourbon gurgle into the stainless-steel sink.

'That's my property!' Roy cried, grabbing a Haig and Haig pinchbeck to her midriff.

Althea reached up again. Roy, attempting to force Althea from her stash of liquor, dropped the Haig and Haig. It shattered loudly. Althea continued tearing gold foil from the neck of an unopened bourbon bottle.

'Stop it,' Roy whimpered, striking out at Althea. A faraway sector of her brain informed her she might slip on the broken glass, so she flailed like a mechanical toy boxer, but she was not close enough to impede Althea. After a minute, she ceased her efforts, snorting her tears as Althea spilled out every bottle. Finishing this task, Althea wadded and dampened quantities of paper towels to pick up the shards. She deposited the full yellow plastic weave wastebasket outside the back door.

'Where's your spare room?' she asked, her first words since she had come into the kitchen.

'I don't want you in my house!' sobbed Roy.

'I'm going home for a few things. I'll be back in a half-hour.'

'Didn't you hear me? *Get out*! I can't stand being near you.'

'That I know, dear heart. But if I'm not here, how will I make sure you aren't backsliding?'

'*I am not an alcoholic*!'Roy screamed, weeping.

'Not yet.' Althea's voice was steely quiet. 'Not quite yet. But keep on like this and you'll take the prize. We're going to get you through a week without benefit of the bottle.'

'Stay out of my life!'

'Things have gotten too dire for you, Roy. And as for me, I can't stand any more guilt.'

For the first three days of Althea's watchful presence, Roy either stayed in her own bedroom or went out alone into the backyard. The weather was drizzly, as it often is during a Southern California May. Roy hugged her moulting college camelhair around herself, trudging the perimeters of the small square of wet dichondra, around and around like a poor, blinded mill donkey.

She missed the liquor less than she had anticipated.

Though booze had hazed her anguish, Roy, forthright by nature, found it preferable to come directly at the truth, however cruel and raw. He is dead, she would think, circling her wet garden. He is buried in Forest Lawn. Low, keening noises escaped her lips.

Those first days she avoided her surveillant – no easy matter when you are trapped together within the confines of a twelve-hundred-square-foot house.

Those three long nights when Roy saw every motion of the phosphorescent green clock hands, a mournful acceptance began to seep through her. He is dead, she would think. Dead. The need to howl her misery subsided to a dull, resolute ache. She began to accept that Althea shared honours with her as chief mourner. Gerry's death, which had forever lessened them both, had forged a fresh bond between them.

On the fourth morning, when she heard Althea moving

around, she went into the kitchen. Althea was sipping coffee and eating a slice of apple-custard cake – the freezer was stuffed with funerary offerings.

Roy, giving a sheepish smile, spooned out some instant coffee.

'There's no cream left,' Althea said.

'I have some powdered junk for emergencies,' Roy said, reaching into the storage cabinet for the brown-glass jar before she slid into the booth opposite Althea. At the sight of the uncomplicated friendship in Althea's face, the remains of Roy's resentment faded entirely. 'Hey, jailer, good morrow to you.'

'How's it going?' Althea smiled.

'No pink elephants or crawly spiders, which must be proof positive I'm not about to hit skid row.'

'That's good news.'

Roy stirred white granules into her coffee. 'I do sort of miss Dr Buchmann, though. He's my shrink.'

'I'll drive you over.'

'So I'm not a trusty yet?'

'In a couple of days the parole board will discuss your case.'

Roy cut herself a wedge of the cake. 'Althea, did Gerry ever say anything about us not having kids?'

'We hardly ever talked about you. Once, though, he mentioned you guys had tried.' Althea stared out the window at the gloomy morning. 'He *did* care for you, Roy, he really did.'

Roy had not intended a purgative confessional, God knows not with Gerry's erstwhile beloved, yet she found that she had to continue. 'I feel so terrible about not giving him children.'

Althea, looking down, fingered a crumb. 'Don't feel guilty, Roy.'

'It's not exactly guilt. I just feel awful he didn't leave anybody to come after him. God knows we tried. We went to battalions of doctors – Beverly Hills is wall to wall with specialists. They asked every sort of personal question, they put us through the most embarrassing tests – one time we had to do it in the doctor's office. I had my tubes blown, they measured the motility of Gerry's sperm. They told us when to, and when not to.' Roy frowned. 'Listen, Althea, well, this idea keeps bugging me . . . He always thrilled me, and I was crazy for it, but well, I'm not positive I ever came. I mean, if I had, wouldn't it have done the trick?'

'Oh, Wace! How cretinous can you get?' Althea's exasperation was an emergence of their old two-against-the-world friendship.

'Well, a climax might have pushed the sperm up or something.'

'If conception relied on female orgasm, the world would be an empty place.'

Roy gave a pleased, embarrassed smile. 'I guess you're right,' she said.

This conversation in the breakfast booth broke a crucial dam within Roy. She began spilling out things she had not even voiced in Dr Buchmann's chair. The next days she talked until her throat had a raw edge. Often it seemed to Roy she must still be stinko drunk to blab the most humiliating and ecstatic moments of her marriage to a confidante who, after all, was the woman Gerry had really loved. Yet this same confidante was Althea, her oldest friend.

With all the flooding verbiage, however, she could not bring herself to take Althea into the locked garage studio. She didn't understand herself at all.

On the seventh evening of Roy's sobriety, the two women celebrated with a steak dinner, then took a walk.

Their heels clicked in the darkness.

Althea said very little until they crossed Beverwil Drive, then she stopped and took Roy's arm. 'There's something I have to tell you,' she said quietly. 'Gerry's accident was all my fault.'

This was the first time Althea had brought forth any details of her relationship with Gerry. 'His accident?' Roy faltered. 'What do you mean?'

'My parents have a ranch in Ojai.' Althea took Roy's arm, forcing her to walk again. They passed a house from which the aroma of lamb stew and the sound of television emanated. 'We went there to ride.'

'So *that's* what he was doing in Ventura. But Gerry had never ridden a horse – or had he?'

'Never,' Althea said. 'I wanted him in the position inferior.'

Roy stared at her, baffled. 'I don't understand.'

They were passing under a streetlamp, and Althea's face was bleached of all colour. 'Your call threw Mother, and she laid into me. She didn't know I was seeing Gerry again, and when she found out – Pow. Mother looks so timid and meek, but underneath she's all Coyne steel. I loved Gerry, but she threw me into a tizzy about it. So I decided I had to do without him. Does that make sense?'

'I reacted just the opposite. I clung on for dear life.' Roy sighed. 'What happened at the ranch?'

'I took him riding and told him we were through. I even told him to go back to you.'

'Thanks,' Roy said bitterly.

'Roy, the point of this isn't to whitewash myself but to explain what happened. When I ran into him in New York, it was as if the intervening time didn't exist – or you. Even when you showed up in Oaxaca, I never thought of you as Gerry's wife. It took Mother to point out that he was *your* husband and you might not take a divorce lying down. There would be a huge amount of talk. Pure and simple, I couldn't take the nasty gossip. Does that sound rotten? Well, that's me.'

Roy shivered in the night, recollecting Marylin's words about the nature of poisonous snakes. But that was talk, and she was in the dark, lonely night listening to her oldest friend desolately blowing her nose – Althea, who was helping her through *her* period of mourning. 'Althea, I blame *myself* for keeping him trapped.'

'But I was the one who sent him off in a mad swivet.'

'It was an accident,' Roy said firmly. 'A highway wreck.'

They turned homeward. Nearing the house, they saw light through the glass inset of the front door.

'Did we leave those on?' Roy asked.

'I'm positive not. Does your mother have a key?'

'She and Marylin both do. But their cars would be here.'

Exchanging apprehensive glances, they tiptoed in their walking shoes up the three brick steps to the front door. Roy pressed the button.

'Who is it?' called a young, masculine voice.

'Oh, Billy!' Roy cried. 'You terrified us!'

The door opened; beyond the vestibule rang the sounds of televised violence. An adolescent boy with a few scattered pimples on his beaky, clever face stood grinning at them. 'Behold, the housebreaker.'

Roy hugged him. 'What're you doing here?'

'Grandma hasn't seen you all week.' Billy had a jagged, humorous delivery. 'She infected Mom with her acute anxiety spasm. So I'm here to spy. Grandma drove me over – we almost hit a parked car on Olympic. I say it's pure *merde* giving a rotten freak driver like her a licence and denying a Le Mans knockout like myself on the arbitrary grounds of my age. Hey, hey. Aren't you going to introduce me to your cute lady friend?'

Roy said, 'Althea, may I present my nephew, Billy Fernauld. Billy, this is Mrs Wimborne.'

'Mrs Wimborne . . . let me think.' He snapped his fingers. 'Althea Cunningham of the world-renowned Beverly High Big Two.'

'How did you know that?' Roy asked, astonished.

'A gigantic intellect, astounding powers of intuition – also I saw her at the funeral.' To soften this reminder, he put his arm around Roy's waist, looking at Althea. 'Am I impressing you with my scintillating brilliance, Althea?'

Charles would never have called any friend of hers by a first name, but Billy's fast-spoken freshness made Althea smile. 'Tremendously,' she said. 'So you're Marylin's son.'

'Out of Rain Fairburn by Joshua Fernauld, or anyway that's what my *Racing Form* tells me.'

Roy aimed a mock punch at the belt of his Levis. 'Someday you'll go too far,' she said. 'Did you find food?'

'I made good headway in the chocolate torte, and finished off the roast beef in the refrigerator. Is that okay?'

'I'm glad you ate it for me.' Roy said. 'I was just going to take Mrs Wimborne in to see Gerry's studio.'

What?

Roy's mouth remained open in surprise at her own words. Shouldn't Althea's confession have roused hatred, not this immeasurable sympathy?

'I've been longing to see more of his work,' Althea said.

And at the same moment, Billy said, 'The sanctum sanctorum. Well, you two go ahead. I return to my homework and the ineluctable problems of Elliott Ness.' He winked at Althea. 'You really *are* a pretty lady. Come back next year when I get my driver's licence and I'll show you where Simon's used to be.'

The boy returned to the sofa, which was surrounded by plates and books.

'He's terrific,' Althea whispered. Her cheeks were pink.

'Very bright, too. In the genius level,' Roy said.

'He obviously dotes on his auntie.'

'And vice versa. I adore him and Sari. She's one big, tender heart, all feelings. Completely vulnerable, the poor baby. This way, Althea. Mind the step.'

The stucco, exposed beams and terrazzo floor – carefully covered with sheets of plastic – seemed to exude the mausoleum dankness of unused places, lacking the familiar aroma of paint, fixative, turpentine. The pair of enormous skylights were dark, blind eyes staring down on stacks of vivid canvases that were ranged at precise intervals around the walls. Against a steel easel was propped a brilliantly rufous canvas that Althea recognized as an abstraction of a sketch Gerry had made in Houston Street. On the cabinet counter, brushes were segregated according to size, and the paints (nowhere in view) must be neatly stored in the narrow drawers below. An atmosphere of tidy stiffness exactly the opposite of Gerry's usual work habitat.

'These are mine,' Roy said, smiling softly as she glanced around. 'I'm not sending any to the gallery.'

'Horaks are quite valuable. And now Gerry's gone, even more so.'

'I know. But I'm donating these to UCLA – I want them to name a gallery in his honour.'

'Have you approached anyone there?'

'Not yet.'

'Roy, endowing museums and universities isn't all that cinchy. First they have to agree, and then you have to hand over enough cash to provide an income for permanent upkeep.'

Roy's face fell. 'You mean I can't do it? I wanted so much to perpetuate Gerry's name . . . You know, to make up for his not having children.'

Althea, surrounded by Gerry's big smooth abstracts, with her oldest friend, said quietly, 'That's not true.'

'What?'

'He left a child.'

'No. He had some affairs before the war, and the girls got pregnant, but – '

'Charles is his son.'

The words sank into Roy's consciousness like a sharp-edged knife, and she retreated across the studio to stand over the cabinet. Her face was working wildly. Those years of uncertainty as to who could not parent a child! How absurd! She should have known Roy Wace Horak was the one with the lack.

For a moment of swirling violence, Roy felt she could pick up a palette knife and kill Althea for offering this ultimate proof of who was more of a woman – Gerry's woman.

Then her emotions swerved to the antithesis of violence and outrage. So Gerry's generations aren't buried below that improbably green grass, she thought, and turned back to Althea.

'Is that why he wanted to marry you?'

'He never knew. I never told him. I wanted to keep my son to myself. Chalk up another little item against me.'

They stood silent amid Gerry's inscrutable works.

'I appreciate you telling me,' Roy said quietly. 'It makes it easier knowing that a part of him is still alive.'

'It's not for publication,' Althea said, her voice cold. She already regretted the haphazard spilling of her secret. 'You understand that?'

'Of course I do.'

'That's easy to say now.' Althea had her girlhood expression of mulish, unhappy pride.

'You have my promise, Althea.'

Suddenly, with an odd little cry, Althea reached out and gripped Roy's hand. 'Why am I doubting Old Faithful?'

They left the chilly studio.

Althea packed. Billy and Roy helped her carry the assortment of Vuitton bags to her Jaguar.

'Thank you, Althea,' Roy said softly. 'Thank you for everything.'

'We're friends, aren't we?'

'To the ends.' Roy softly voiced the old catch phrase from Beverly High days.

Roy and Billy stood on the sidewalk, waving as the Jaguar drove off.

Billy said, 'The Coyne heiress is quite a dish, know that?'

Roy ruffled her nephew's hair, which was curly like her own. 'Kid, Althea's got a son older than you.' Then she drew a quick breath. Charles was Gerry's child. 'It's cold out here,' she said. 'Come on back inside.'

'If you'll drive me to school tomorrow, I'll spend the night.'

'Sold,' Roy said.

As she stripped the spare-room daybed of sheets scented with Althea's nonfloral perfume, she was thinking: Althea has Gerry's son.

And what do I have?

Her face rigid with the efforts of keeping back tears, Roy reflected on what she had. Her sobriety, the crumbs of love from her family, her niece and nephew, her work. And if these formed but a fragile bark to bear her across life's desolate and cold seas, well, she'd never gone first class.

57

That spring and summer Roy would fall asleep thinking of Gerry and awaken thinking of him with tears oozing from her closed eyes. Memories of him intruded on her at Patricia's. She read five or six thrillers a week, but even during the zippiest action his unhappy face would come between her and the print. She developed a case of hives. She was involved in three minor car accidents. Though she had lost the compulsive need for alcohol – the boozy haze through which she had just passed terrified her – she found herself addicted to sweets. As a girl she'd had a sweet tooth, but at Patricia's, wearing clothes well was part of her job, so she had to discipline herself to take a single chocolate, a bite of somebody else's dessert. Now she couldn't stop herself. She would devour a pound of See's chocolates, a carton of gingersnaps, a Sara Lee cheesecake. The sweetness always tasted slightly stale. She gained eight pounds, and her stylishly loose chemise hugged her hips and stomach. In desperation she took up smoking.

One morning in early September as she was combing her hair for work she found a few greys at the temple. Her throat ached with an ambivalently pleasurable melancholy that her life, like Gerry's, was over. The lugubrious curve of her freshly lipsticked mouth in the mirror struck her as humorous. 'Cut it out, Wace!' she said aloud as she yanked out the offending hairs. 'You're not on the widow's funeral pyre yet.'

By the time the autumn heat faded, she had lost four pounds, her hives had disappeared and the repainted car had no fresh dents. Her natural enthusiasm was winning out.

'As soon as you're finished with your customer, Roy, come on back to the office. Mr Fineman and I're having coffee,' said Mrs Fineman at the entry of the stockroom.

This invitation, offered on the opening afternoon of the January sale, struck Roy as portentous.

She edged into the office, her smile numb.

As soon as Mrs Fineman had poured coffee for her, Mr Fineman set down his cup. In his New York accent he said matter-of-factly, 'Roy, at the end of the month you're to mark down the entire stock. We intend to keep on with the sale until everything is gone.'

'But, Mr Fineman – '

'After that the fixtures will go,' he continued in the same arid tone. 'We're leasing the building.'

'You mean – is Patricia's closing?' Roy asked in a thin, high wail.

He nodded. 'We spent the morning with our lawyer and accountant. We didn't want you to hear our plans from anybody else.'

Roy was sitting on the sofa, the sofa on which she had slumped in the aftershock of hearing about Gerry's death. Another part of my life ending, she thought. Her fingers tightened on the cup handle.

But death alone is irreversible.

I can prevent this from happening, she thought. How? I'll take over the shop. You idiot, what with? Thirty-four hundred and thirty-eight hard-saved dollars in a Bank of America savings account, a mortgaged house, half-paid-for furniture? (Gerry's works were pledged to UCLA, with Althea underwriting the upkeep of the Gerrold Horak Gallery.)

Male and female voices were alternating. 'Whatever we can . . . highest recommendations to everyone we know . . . severance pay . . . speak to people in New York, if you want . . .'

Roy eased her throat by swallowing. 'Patricia's is the only place I've ever worked.'

The couple exchanged glances, and Mrs Fineman said unhappily, 'Roy, we know exactly how you feel. The accountant pointed out that we'd be far better off financially to sell. We could get a decent price for the goodwill, and the fixtures would bring much more in a going concern.

But this is our creation. We can't bear a stranger coming in, maybe lowering the standards, maybe turning Patricia's into a schlock shop.'

'I can't imagine working anyplace else.'

Affection, grief and worry showed behind the skilfully applied cosmetics on Mrs Fineman's heavy face. 'We haven't told anyone else,' she said, 'but, Mr Fineman's been having chemotherapy for some time now.'

Tears welled in Roy's eyes. She reached out her hand, letting it hover tentatively near Mr Fineman's. He seldom touched anyone. His hard, dry fingers grasped hers briefly.

'This takes a lot of gall, but – ' Roy drew a breath. 'Maybe *I* could buy Patricia's. I'd keep it absolutely top-drawer, you know that.'

In the ensuing quiet, her stomach lurched.

'Your brother-in-law would help you?' Mrs Fineman asked.

'I wouldn't ask him. But Mrs Fineman, you just said you're closing the doors. I'd pay you a hundred cents on the dollar for the fixtures, give whatever rent you ask.'

'It's not a question of money,' said Mrs Fineman. 'I meant, who would take over the financial aspects of the business.'

'I would,' Roy said.

'Roy, you're a fine manageress.' Mr Fineman rose, moving behind his desk. 'Believe me, though, being your own boss is another game entirely. First of all, you'd be undercapitalized. A business without enough cash is always on the thin edge. One bad season.' He snapped his fingers. 'It's over.'

'What if the economy goes into a slump and sales go sour? Or a sharp competitor sets out to take away the clientele?' asked Mrs Fineman.

'Woman's luxury trade is very chancy. There's no margin for error. Buy badly for one season and – ' A second snap of Mr Fineman's fingers. 'I've seen capable, competent managers take over businesses and go under in less than a year.'

'And once you're a Chapter Eleven, you're bad news,'

said Mrs Fineman. 'People don't want to be associated with you. Getting a job is nearly impossible.'

'You're too young for the responsibility.'

'With your verve and sense of style,' Mrs Fineman said, 'you have a real future ahead of you as a buyer for the biggest chains.'

'For your own good, forget the idea. It's too big a gamble.'

'Roy, dear, we're far too fond of you to let you risk it.' Mrs Fineman set down her cup to add weight to the refusal.

Under the Finemans' double barrage Roy's impulse had dwindled and turned ludicrous. Back keeping watch on the crowded floor, though, rebuttals bubbled to her mind. *She* had found this building. Hardly any of the marked-down mistakes were *her* buying selections. The salesladies writing up put-together outfits instead of a single reduced blouse were trained by *her*. Patricia's is my baby as well, she thought. As the week passed, her desire to buy Patricia's strengthened into a resolve. She tried to analyse her ambition, and found not logic but a complicated blend of emotions. The lure of a challenge, the need to fill the void in her life, and – possibly most important – that old, old inability to let go.

When the Finemans did not carry through their original intent to mark down the entire stock, Roy understood that they were seriously considering her offer. And in March, they acquiesced. They sold her the stock as well as the store fittings at a price set by their accountant (to be paid over three years), giving her a twenty-year lease. It was only at the insistence of their attorney that Joshua scrawled his name on both documents as co-signer.

The first months proved even rougher than the Finemans had prophesied. Some of the older – and wealthier – clients began shopping at Amelia Gray or I. Magnin's. The suppliers liked her, but that didn't prevent them from putting Patricia's on hold so that most of her merchandise was shipped COD. Roy, having refused to borrow from the Fernaulds, arranged a loan from the Bank of America, taking a second mortgage on her house. She scrimped mercilessly on herself, she worked sixteen hours a day.

When it came time for her fall buying trip, she flew on a charter, reserving a room without bath in the Rue des Abbesses not far from the tall grey building with the crumbling plaster angels where Gerry had borrowed a studio. The hotel might be cheap and clean, but it was a mistake for her to return to Montmartre. At night sorrow gnawed into her very gut. By day, though, she concentrated on the runways, jotting down every new trend, buying carefully yet not too carefully.

After Paris she moved on to Milan for the Italian showings.

The last day before her charter left, she travelled with a second-class train ticket to Rome. She wanted to visit a new designer. Francesca. Francesca used romantic, luxurious fabrics. Her spring line was perfectly proportioned for the so-called American figure, and her models posed in clever improvisations on the hot-selling Jackie Kennedy look. Considering this, her prices were excellent. Roy spent eight hectic hours, placing a far larger order than she had intended.

Back at her *pensione* above the flower-bordered Spanish Steps, Roy sprawled on the squashy mattress, buyer's remorse overwhelming her. Now I've done it! What Patricia's customer will plunk down money for an unknown designer? She didn't realize she had dozed until the persistent tapping awakened her. 'Signora 'Orak. Signora, the telephone.'

Roy knew nobody in Rome. In her blue funk, she decided that this was a long-distance call informing her of disaster at home.

'Yes,' she gasped into the wall phone.

'Roy,' said a male American. 'This is Linc Fernauld.'

She sank into the chair. 'A voice from the past,' she managed to squeak. 'How did you know I was here?'

'Francesca's a friend. She just spent a half-hour exulting about her tremendous sale to the most important Beverly Hills fashion personage there is. A young woman of brilliance and great warmth.'

'I really snowed her, didn't I?'

'Listen, I know it's last minute, but how about dinner?'

'Oh, Linc, if you only knew I've been dreading eating in this dining room.'

He came for her at 8.30.

Except for that one time at the Fernaulds' old house in Hillcrest, Roy hadn't seen Linc since his Navy days, and in her memory he had a deep tan and wore a resplendent officer's uniform. This Linc was paler and gaunter of face, which made him infinitely more human – doubtless this was a reflection of her own maturity, too – however after a couple of minutes with him she saw no reason to change her original adjective for him: clean.

He took her to the elegant Hostaria dell'Orso. They were led around tables of chattering, smartly dressed diners to a smaller room dominated by a massive, blackened stone fireplace.

As their waiter pared thin, rosy slices of prosciutto, from a ham with a hairy bone, Roy said, 'I've heard of this place, but I never expected anything so wondrous old.'

'It's a thirteenth-century inn. People, especially those related to the proprietor, swear that Dante slept in this room, and Leonardo, too. I've never seen any verification, but I've come across proof that Rabelais and Montaigne came here.'

'BJ's told me you're the *only* researcher in Europe.'

'That's my sister all over.' There was rueful fondness in his smile. 'Touchingly modest about her near and dear.'

They ate delicate threads of basil-scented fettuccine, followed by rich osso bucco, finishing with zuppa inglese.

'The perfect way for an endomorph to spend her only night in Rome, gaining ten pounds.' Blissfully Roy spooned creamy custard from the bottom of her plate. 'Linc, this meal is worthy of a month's dieting.'

Linc held his lighter to her Tareyton, then lit his own pipe, gazing through the coils of smoke at her, an expression in his very dark eyes that was somehow waiting. For what? Surely he didn't expect *her* to bring up the subject of Marylin.

He gave her the abbreviated Rome by Night tour,

steering his Fiat down Via Empero from the Brescian marble garishness of the Victor Emanuel Monument past the ancient, floodlit stones of Trajan's Forum to the massive Colosseum. Each time he turned to her, she saw – or imagined she saw – that anticipatory gleam. At her *pensione* they parked, strolling to the top of Spanish Steps so she could see the city below with its floodlit domes, spires, ancient monuments.

'Roy,' Linc said slowly, 'I want you to hear this from me. At Christmas I'm getting married.'

Roy turned, clutching his arm. BJ had authoritatively reiterated that Linc remained a bachelor because he was still mad for Marylin. (Roy often wondered in a wistful cloud of envy how it would be to have two males so wild for you that they lost their reason.) 'Married? A winter wedding,' she said, sounding inane in her surprise.

'I'm over forty.'

'Now there's a wildly romantic reason.'

'Gudrun is with the Norwegian embassy,' he said crisply. 'She's a redhead. A terrific skier, very intelligent, loves Beethoven and Tolstoy. We have everything in common.'

Roy hesitated, staring down at the flow of a familiar-looking dome. 'It's none of my business, Linc, but are you sure? Really sure? I've been through a marriage with a guy who still cared about another woman and take it from me, bliss didn't exactly reign on any side of the triangle.'

'All evening I've been wondering if, well, if seeing somebody from Beverly Hills would alter my feelings about Gudrun. It hasn't.'

'She's still a swell kid, right?' Roy said bitterly.

'In Italy, people have more sensible ideas about marriage.'

'You,' she said, 'are an American.'

'Roy!' he barked. 'Let it drop.'

She had forgotten Linc's brief, hot temper.

Bells began chiming from a hundred steeples below them.

'What time is that?' she asked.

He held his wrist up to a streetlamp. 'Three.'

'Three! God! I have a train to catch at seven.'

433

As they hurried down the cobbled street to her *pensione*, she noticed for the first time that he still limped slightly. By the drab, chill light in the foyer she saw lines were carved around his dark brown eyes.

'Linc, listen, we widows can wax very bitter about beginnings.'

'It's okay, Roy. I didn't mean to bark at you.'

'I was talking out of turn.'

'Come on, Roy. No big deal.'

'If you've chosen Gudrun, she must be a fabulous lady.'

'She is.' He took her hand in farewell. 'Roy, I'm sorry it worked out badly for you.'

'I really do wish you and Gudrun all good things, Linc,' she said, kissing him lightly on his cheek, which smelled of pipe tobacco and – faintly – of Roger & Gallet soap.

She had undressed and was folding her shocking pink wool shift into her suitcase before she realized that though Marylin had been omnipresent in her mind all evening, and inevitably in Linc's, too, neither had spoken her name.

And Roy vowed that when she saw Marylin, Linc would not be mentioned either.

Book Seven
1970

RAIN FAIRBURN SHOW SNAGS LOCAL EMMY
                          – Variety, *2 March 1970*

RAIN FAIRBURN schedule: Penny Crate, exercise expert; Jim Henson of the Muppets; Jacqueline Briskin, author of California Genera-tion.
                          – TV Guide, *1 April 1970*

FOUR STUDENTS SHOT BY NATIONAL GUARD AT KENT STATE
  President Nixon Calls College Protesters Bums.
                          – Seattle Post Intelligencer, *5 April 1970*

For those Winter Palace evenings of high romance, Patricia's sees you in Ungaro's black chiffon.
 – *Copy for full-page advertisement in* Vogue, Harper's Bazaar, Town and Country, *August 1970*

The Coyne New York Bank has prospered under the presidency of Archibald Coyne, grandson of its founder, Grover T. Coyne, but financial circles speculate whether or not the millionaire sportsman, now 57, will keep to his expressed wish to retire at 60. The bank has always been headed by a member of the Coyne family.
                          – Fortune, *August 1970*

58

Marylin, in her Channel 5 dressing room, leaned back against the leather padding of the swivel chair. Sharply aromatic odours escaped from the makeup man's vial as he carefully applied adhesive behind her left earlobe, then affixed a narrow flesh-coloured rubberized string. He followed the same procedure on the right side, securing the strings an inch behind Marylin's well-defined widow's peak, erasing that near-invisible hint of relaxation below her jawline.

'There you go, gorgeous,' he said. 'Thirty, I swear, not a day more.'

'Yesterday you said twenty-five.' At the moment her luminous smile felt comfortable, but if the strapping remained more than an hour her skin would be plagued by tautness.

Marylin shrank in dismay from the knife of youth – that cruel look to the mouth, that taut skin, those subsequent wrinkles aligning in unnatural directions – yet she was also cognizant that each slight droop or fine line is magnified by the cruel eye of the television camera.

This month, March of 1970, marked the eighth anniversary of *The Rain Fairburn Show,* now syndicated in forty-three markets and aired in Los Angeles from eleven to twelve noon. Monday through Friday. Marylin conducted interviews with actors and actresses hustling new films, writers hustling their latest books, wide-smiling politicians hustling for re-election, sad-eyed, overwrought comedians hustling for a job in Vegas – whoever lolled on the beige-upholstered chairs and couch of *The Rain Fairburn Show*'s set was selling himself or herself. The mercenary fact was so softened by the hostess's ravishing smile and angora-voiced questions that the women into whose homes her image was beamed considered Rain Fairburn a friend, a beautiful, gentle close friend who was introducing *her* friends. The show's consistently high Neilsen ratings were bolstered by Marylin's dazzling array of dressy sportswear: the credits flashed 'Miss Fairburn's clothes courtesy of Patricia's', a form of free advertising for Roy. (The shop had become far less staid under her ownership.)

When Marylin weighed her two careers, the scales tilted deeply in favour of acting. She missed bringing life to a role, she missed her craft's total immersion. For her, though, emoting on the big screen was an irrevocably departed luxury. Film actresses, unlike their masculine counterparts, are seldom permitted mature love. Her age aside, though, there was the financial aspect. TV sets had multiplied, begetting colour, threatening extinction to the neighbourhood movie theatre. Studios had become torpid dinosaurs ailing in their individual swamps. To make a film involved months, even years, spent in a slushy, unpaid quagmire of deals and counterdeals.

No money coming in.

And the Fernaulds were in dire need of a huge secure income.

In 1962 Paramount had not renegotiated Joshua's contract. Like many another forcibly retired bigshot, he called himself an independent producer, entering into the search for a hot property that (he repeatedly boomed at Marylin) would make very big bucks. In the meantime he brought in nothing. Always a big-handed giver, he overcompensated with ferocious generosity. No matter how the business manager cajoled, Joshua *would* buy Porsches for Billy and Sari and BJ's children, Van Cleef jewellery for Marylin, book passage for the entire family on the *Lurline* to Hawaii. He continued to keep extravagant court in the big Mandeville Canyon place that they had purchased many years earlier. He was forever putting option money down on plays or novels.

When the concept of *The Rain Fairburn Show* had come along, there had been no choice for Marylin. She had signed the contract.

The hairdresser stepped forward to cover the rubberized strings with a crimson velvet ribbon, recombing her gleaming pageboy, which was longer at the sides, around the headband – a much-copied style that had become known as 'a Rain Fairburn'.

Marylin stepped behind the louvred screen, slipping off her nylon makeup smock to don Roy's wardrobe contribution, a soft crimson blouse and matching midiskirt.

The door burst open.

'Boss lady, hey hey. I see you back there,' Billy called, grinning.

Her son was one of *The Rain Fairburn Show*'s three writers, but nobody whispered the word nepotism. Billy, when he was eighteen, had started out at the top, working the Carson show. After a couple of years, seemingly without rhyme or reason, he had quit – but then, Billy's swift moves were always inexplicable. On his return to Los Angeles, Marylin's producers exultantly snagged him.

Billy lacked his father's (and half brother's) height. He was a scant five-ten of wiry, nervous motion, forever fidgeting, gesturing, readjusting his glasses on his hereditary beak. He had grown from a movie brat into a witty, highly intelligent, neurotic, somehow endearing man. Other than the nose, he had nothing of his father about him – he did, however, bear a passing resemblance to Woody Allen, whom he knew and idolized.

Marylin stepped from behind the screen. Still buttoning her blouse, she tiptoed to press a fond kiss on Billy's cheek, wondering not for the first time what a psychiatrist would make of her trinity of men, married to the father, still in love with the son, a doting mother to another son.

'You smell adorable and look delicious,' Billy said. 'Too good for today's crowd.'

'You've already been in the green room, then?'

'Does it show?' He clapped his hand to his T-shirted shoulder. 'Has the tension in there caused a giveaway attack of dandruff? Hey, think terminal dandruff changes your status to 4-F?'

For a moment, Marylin's throat caught so she could scarcely breathe. Like the other mothers in America, she worried about her son's draft status. Billy had no college deferment, his long-ago concussion appeared to have left no damage. All that kept him out of Vietnam was a mercifully high draft number.

Billy was saying, 'I met your anti-porn lady and I've hacked out one remark for you to work in with her. When she goes into her number that humanity is being debased by the repetition of four-letter words, ask her which ones she means.'

'Billy, be serious.'

He scratched the back of his neck. 'Would *The Rain Fairburn Show* write me a major paycheque if I were?'

The hairdresser and makeup man were laughing, and so was Marylin as she did up the final button.

'Now you're decent,' Billy said. 'I'd like you to meet a new buddy.'

She pretended dismay. '*Another* comedy writer?'

'No. Carlo Firelli – the living one, not the legend. He calls himself plain, regal Charles.'

Marylin shivered as if her hand had unexpectedly contacted something damp and cold.

Althea's son . . .

She had never been able to accept Roy's renewed friendship with Althea Cunningham Firelli Wimborne Stoltz. How could Roy bear to be near the woman who had without conscience wrecked her marriage and then destroyed her husband? Yet Roy – incorrigibly steadfast Roy! – saw Althea whenever geographically plausible and the pair talked by telephone almost every Sunday. Althea had

440

endowed the Gerrold Horak Gallery at UCLA. And, tit for tat, when Althea's third marriage, to Nicholas Stoltz, had gone on the rocks, Roy had taken off, her first vacation since buying Patricia's, spending a month bolstering the new divorcée's spirits in the lavish confines of a borrowed Coyne château near Aizy-le-Rideau.

Billy opened the dressing room door wider. 'Hey, Charles, it's okay. Come on in.'

Charles Firelli had inherited his mother's height and attenuated elegance. The length of his lean, hard legs was not disguised by his grey slacks; his wide shoulders were bony beneath a rather shabby, magnificently tailored navy blazer. He had Althea's ash-blonde hair – though without the pellucid streaking – her long, handsome face. His broader, higher cheekbones gave him masculine strength.

He moved towards Marylin with inflexible dignity, seeming to anticipate respect. Ice water in his veins, just like his mother, Marylin thought as Billy introduced them.

'Mrs Fernauld, it's wonderful to meet you in person,' Charles said with courteous ease. 'I've admired your films, especially *Island*.'

'Charles, buddy, it doesn't take discrimination to admire a classic. Now let's hear it for her performance in *Lost Lovers of Tahiti*.'

'That bomb,' Marylin said, smiling at her son. 'Are you out here to visit your grandparents, Charles?'

Charles's eyes went flat, as if he preferred not to share his emotions. 'In an unfortunate way, yes,' he said. 'Mother and I are here because my grandfather is having surgery tomorrow morning.'

'I am sorry to hear that,' Marylin said. 'Is it . . . serious?'

'He's had four other operations,' Charles said in a remote tone. 'Our doctors don't hold much hope. This is all that's left.'

'Will you give your mother and grandparents my best?' said Marylin, ticking herself off for hating Althea while Althea was beset by tragedy.

441

'I certainly will, Mrs Fernauld. And I hope I see you again, soon.'

'Tonight,' Billy said. 'I'm bringing you to dinner.'

Briefly Marylin put her hand on her son's arm, an involuntary cautioning gesture, then asked herself why her dislike and fear of Althea should spill over onto this tall, good-looking, unemotional young man.

Billy pulled a disreputably crumpled sheet of paper from the pocket of his cords. 'Here you go, Rain Fairburn,' he said. 'The latest from the salt mines.'

'Thank you, dear.'

'Come on, Charles, let me guide you through more of the glamour of televisionland.' Billy did a soft-shoe routine to the door. Contrasted with the self-possessed Charles, he seemed more frenetic – and adorable.

After the two young men left, Marylin rehearsed the lines that Billy had patterned to fit her mild, nonmalicious humour, little jokes that she could feed to the day's guests.

The programme was shot live in front of an audience of about fifty people on wooden bleachers. Marylin skilfully guided her sweating visitors through their hustles.

By one o'clock she was in her car, driving herself home – Percy and Coraleen had retired, replaced by Elena and Juan from El Salvador, and Juan was a rotten driver.

Depleted by her performance, Marylin often succumbed, as she did now on this forty minutes along Sunset from the studio to Mandeville Canyon, to thoughts of Linc. She had neither seen nor communicated with him since she had made her long-distance renunciatory speech so many years ago, but from BJ she knew a good deal about him, including his marriage to 'that Norwegian girl', and his subsequent divorce from her.

He lived in Rome in a book-jammed flat on the third floor of an amber-coloured building. His services were respected by producers and authors in search of authentic and accurate historical detail – 'Research! What a criminal waste of a Pulitzer Prize!' BJ would cry. He skied in Arosa and Davos. He had kept his shape and his thick, greying hair. BJ would show Marylin snapshots, bragging with a tinge of envy, 'Come on, wouldn't you guess he's my younger brother? It's because he's kept away from the Beverly Hills rat race, the sweetie.'

BJ and Maury had gone to Rome for Linc's wedding at the Norwegian embassy, they had seen Gudrun several times during the two years and three months' span of the marriage, as a couple they obviously felt warm towards Linc's wife, yet BJ seldom spoke about her to Marylin. (To Joshua, they never mentioned Linc at all: whenever his firstborn's name came up, Joshua either charged from the room or diverted the conversation.)

BJ's atypical tact had earned Marylin's wholehearted gratitude.

Hearing about Mrs A. Lincoln Fernauld made her head throb with a sense of fullness behind her eyes. Indeed, during the entire time of Linc's marriage, she had been in a mild depression. She had caught cold easily, she had begun suffering from these darn sinus headaches. The physical dimensions of her jealousy – for she had come to realize that jealousy was at the base of her problems – shamed and repelled her. *She* had a life of her own, a husband, children, she cherished Linc, so why couldn't she rejoice in his marriage? In her reasonable mind, she *did* wish him well, yet her subconscious remained an intractable dog in the manger, grudging him his Scandinavian wife.

When BJ had broken the news that the couple had split amicably, nasty little quivers of exultation had passed through Marylin's entire body, and her hands had begun to tremble. Even though she felt pangs of guilt – after all, Linc must be going through a rough time – she could not dim her happiness.

He's single again, she would think. Billy and Sari are grown, so why have I never made an overture towards him? The answers to that were twofold. First, how could she desert Joshua, that ageing lion? She did not kid herself that it was simple duty that had kept her with her marriage but a complex array of feelings that ranged from pity to irate exasperation to warm, sharing affection.

Furthermore, over the years she had begun to doubt that the capacity for romantic love still existed with her. What was love, anyway? The sentimental inclinations and heightened hormonal secretions of youth. Love was for the young, not the mother of two grown children.

Sighing, Marylin turned right on Sunset, steering along the rustic folds of Mandeville Canyon, after a couple of miles turning right again at a shrub-secluded private driveway. She pressed the small remote-control box on the car seat. Wrought-iron gates swung open, closing behind her. She echoed across the wooden bridge that spanned an effervescent stream. During the rainy season the stream-bed filled naturally; otherwise a pump kept water rushing over the boulders. Live oaks spread luxuriantly, as did chemiso and manzanita, shrubbery that was for the most part native chaparral, yet nevertheless the Fernaulds' acreage required the full-time services of three gardeners. Up the hill to her left she glimpsed the rustic cottage that Joshua used as his office. Ahead of her, surmounting a long, grassy slope, lay the house.

Built more than forty years ago by Tessa Van Vliet, widow of the silent-movie star Kingdon Vance, the long, comfortable building was designed in the Californio style, with appurtenances once more coming into fashion – balconies, ornamental iron window grates, tile roof, massive exposed beams, rough white stucco.

Exuberant masculine voices resounded in the rear patio. Joshua and his elderly buddies were playing pinochle amid a scattering of large-currency bills, drinks, lavish platters of cold cuts.

She said hello, smiling at their admiringly scurrilous gallantries, then plodded upstairs to stretch out on the bed.

When she awoke the light was waning.

Joshua stood over her.

An unmotivated shiver passed through her. Although Joshua had never been physically violent since that brutal

444

rape, when he surprised her like this she was unable to quell her initial fear.

He went to press the door bolt, then sat on the bed undoing the pearl buttons of Marylin's robe, staring down at the small sensual body, which had changed remarkably little, the breasts as high and round, no dimming of the pearl lustre that caught the light so incredibly. Joshua, though, bore the stigmata of age on his body: the tanned, white-haired barrel chest and imposing belly had gone lax, blue veins knotted the thin shanks. Time's wounds humiliated him, so he unzipped and unbuttoned but left on his clothes as he lay down next to her.

He caressed her with all of the technical skill of his earlier years – and none of the spirit. Now his carnal transactions had an almost frantic quality, as if he were racing from failure. Like the creative demon that had ridden his youth, Joshua's concupiscence had waned. Still, after a few minutes he moved onto her, and she arched up for his entry.

Then . . .

Nothing.

He groaned, moving off her. She held him tenderly while her pulses slowed to normality. Joshua was her husband and if she did not love him, she felt much for him, and his mortification hurt her, too.

'I'll make an appointment with Webber,' Joshua growled. 'Jesus Christ! Isn't that the almighty shits, having to go to a quack urologist for a shot before making love to my wife?'

She cradled his head against her still-taut breasts. Any remark would provoke him to call her a ball-crushing startype. He resented her financial support, he resented her youth, he loved her desperately.

Below was the sound of a car driving up: Tuesday was inviolably family night.

'I better get dressed,' Marylin said, kissing Joshua's sweat-and-pomade-scented white hair. Despite her hapless condition, married to an often impotent, vindictively jealous husband, she had never considered infidelity. The man she yearned for dwelt on another continent, belonged to another life.

Eucalyptus logs crackled, throwing waves of spicy warmth from the dining room's massive fireplace.

Joshua bulked at the head of the oval Georgian table that Ann Fernauld had bought at auction, Marylin graced the other end; between them were ranged Sari, NolaBee, Roy, Billy and Charles Firelli. The table leaves had not been put in, for BJ's contingent was absent. BJ, Maury and their two younger daughters had flown to Israel two weeks earlier: Annie, married to a kibbutznik, had just given birth to her first child. Joshua viewed his ascendancy to the role of great-grandfather with a mingling of patriarchal pride and sheer terror at further proof of time's inexorable passage.

The gathering had just attacked enormous slabs of pink rib roast, over-sized baked potatoes, emerald-flecked spinach soufflé.

Joshua beamed down the table. 'Is everybody happy?'

'The beef is perfect,' said Charles, turning towards Marylin.

Marylin's lovely smile was a shade fixed. Since Charles had entered the house, she had been experiencing flurries of vague distrust that boomeranged back as an abrasive question. Why couldn't she see Charles as the handsome, assured heir of a vast fortune rather than as Althea's son?

Charles slit his potato skin. Steam burst out.

'Here, Charles,' Sari said, her dark eyes fixed on the cut-glass bowl of thick sour cream that she was pushing towards him.

Sari looked like a thin, shy waif in her faded jeans and a loose madras blouse. She neither plucked her brows nor straightened her cloud of soft black hair, and at nearly twenty she could have passed for thirteen. She had dropped out of her junior year at Mills College to 'get my head straight', a fairly typical move for Sari. She was forever attempting to reconcile her considerable intellect with her extraordinarily vivid emotional range. She would disappear for hours, sometimes hiking through the canyon, sometimes leaning against the trunk of an oak tree staring dreamily at the stream. Behaviour, Marylin and Joshua had decided jointly, befitting an incipient poet. But Sari, alone of Joshua's offspring, had never had any literary aspirations.

'Thank you, Sari,' Charles said in his grave basso.

Sari darted him a smile.

'The way you girls today let your hair hang, it's right unglamorous No style at all,' NolaBee pronounced, tossing her own ratted coiffure, which was now dyed a dashing shade of marmalade.

'Not everybody can be a sexpot like you, Grandma,' said Billy.

'Oh, you!' NolaBee cried, fluttering her eyelashes flirtatiously. She adored both her grandchildren; however, her Marylin remained the one person on this earth for whom she would willingly lay down her own life. 'But I reckon us Fairburn and Roy women always did have the knack of being belles.'

'You tell 'em, NolaBee,' said Joshua.

Everybody laughed.

Roy, choking a bit, took a sip of her Perrier. The others had Beaujolais, but Roy, since her siege with the bottle, had come to dislike the taste of wine. Besides, a glassful had nearly a hundred calories and, as usual, she considered herself five pounds overweight – that other bane of her existence, the curl in her brown hair, had been tamed into a sleek, straight curve by a Vidal Sassoon blow dryer. Her face had a pleasant certainty, a by-product of her success with Patricia's. 'Well, Charles, what do you make of my family? Aren't they exactly like I told you?' On her buying trips East, she had made it a habit to visit Gerry's secret son at Groton, then at Harvard. 'Did I exaggerate?'

447

'Yes, Charles,' Billy said. 'Let's hear your opinion of the humble peasantry of Beverly Hills and Mandeville Canyon.'

Charles, though one sensed humour was alien to him, retorted in the same vein as Billy. 'Your women are spectacular, your men talk either too much or too loudly.'

'Amazing, isn't it,' Billy said, 'how engaging us humble folk can be?'

'I fear for you, Billy, if this is your opinion of humble.' Charles glanced around the well-appointed, beamed dining room.

'Touché,' boomed Joshua. 'Touché!'

'Charles, what was he like, your father?' Sari asked. The mysterious, often unjust laws of genetics had denied the girl her mother's beauty while endowing her with the gentle, husky little voice. On the telephone the two were often confused. 'I've heard a million stories.'

'He was everything people said. A true musical genius. A magnificent human being.' The praise emerged in the rhythm of a much recited line of poetry.

Sari reacted like litmus paper to emotional chemistry. 'You must have been asked that ten million times. I'm sorry.'

For the first time, Charles levelled more than a cursory glance at the girl opposite him, looking into Sari's eyes, eyes that Joshua had once fancifully described as having the soulful darkness of an Italian saint. 'My father was old when I knew him, in his eighties. People told me he was a perfectionist on the podium, they said his orchestras stayed on pins and needles. For my part, I can't ever remember him shouting.'

'He had so much life,' Roy said. 'I must have told you this a thousand times, Charles. When I met him I was seventeen, and he bowled me over – I'd never met an older person who truly got such a kick out of everything.'

'The last time I saw him,' Charles said reflectively, 'he was on holiday in England. We have a house in Eastbourne – we have places in Geneva and London, too, but this he

448

considered his home. Anyway, it was an Arctic winter, and old people stayed indoors. Not Father. There are three levels to the front in Eastbourne, and we would walk along the one nearest the sea. I've tried to remember what we talked about, but I can't. All I can remember is my lungs hurt from so much laughing in the cold wind.' Charles stopped abruptly, as if the remembrances were too intimate to share.

After the dessert, Billy said, 'Charles, how's about joining me? The Ahhs are playing the Troubador.'

'This has to be an early night.'

'That's a helluva note when I've lined up a couple of the foxiest ladies in Beverly Hills.'

'Another time,' Charles said. 'Tomorrow is my grand-father's operation, and Mother's expecting me home around nine.'

'Althea's boy has right nice manners,' NolaBee repeated.

It was a half-hour later, the three young people were gone, and the others were settled in the deep upholstery of the den.

'So you said five times already,' Marylin retorted with a cantankerous annoyance so out of character that Joshua and Roy turned to her in surprise.

'I reckon it's true,' NolaBee retorted. Her chatter had taken on a repetitiveness, but other than that she showed remarkably few signs of the ageing process. 'Good looking as all get-out, and rich as sin. I reckon he has the girls swooning over him.'

'Nowhere near as many as Billy,' said Roy. Though fond of Charles, her heart of hearts found him too impervious.

'Our Sari was smitten,' NolaBee said archly.

'Sari?' Marylin and Joshua chorused.

NolaBee nodded vivaciously. 'Didn't you notice how she kept peekin' in his direction?'

'She did not utter two consecutive sentences to him,' Joshua barked.

And at the same moment, Marylin said, 'Mama, you know Sari's never been silly about boys.'

'I reckon this one isn't a boy,' NolaBee said. 'He's a man.'

'Wipe that matchmaking gleam from your eyes,' Joshua snapped. Sari was the delight of his old age, and his mother-in-law's implications annoyed him. 'Thank the blessed Virgin, as my sainted mother used to say, Sari's not the sort to fall for an international playboy. Which, by the same sacred oath, is just as well. Charles Firelli isn't in town for romance.'

Roy's face went sombre. 'Althea tells me Mr Cunningham's in very bad shape.'

The following morning Mr Cunningham underwent major surgery, his fifth time in that many years. He nearly died on the table – the team of surgeons were positive they had lost him, yet somehow the wasted, cancer-devoured body summoned the strength to survive and he was wheeled from the operating room aided by the most sophisticated life-support systems that money can buy. His doctors didn't expect him to make it through the day, but he did, a comatose skeleton regulated by machinery. Mrs Cunningham sat by her husband, her jaw quivering as she bulldogged the private nurses, reminding them when it was time to change an IV, to take the pulse or blood pressure. She fought death on death's own turf, armed with the power of desperate love and every ounce of Coyne proprietorship – a true Coyne *never* lets go of belongings.

The days stretched into a week.

As always, Althea's emotions about her father were a rat's nest. After a few minutes in the enormous flower-filled hospital room she would dash out, walking for hours through the surrounding quiet, shabby streets.

Charles often accompanied her on these forays.

'Darling,' she said, 'you're being wonderful to me. I don't know what I'd do without you.'

'It's hard on everybody,' he sighed. (Though Charles's emotions were tight-reined, he loved his grandfather, and the humiliations of sojourning Death disturbed him profoundly.) 'What you need is to forget for a bit. Why don't I make reservations at a restaurant tonight? I'll round up some people. Maybe Mrs Horak?'

'Darling, I hate to sound a drag, but I simply am incapable of conversation with old friends.'

'What about Billy Fernauld?' Charles asked.

'Is that Marylin's son?'

'Yes. With him no effort's needed. He's a charge. A terrific, unpredictable sense of humour.'

Althea came out of her convoluted absorption to look up at her son. His face was drawn so that the cheekbones seemed more pronounced than ever. She patted his hand. 'That's more like it. A young crowd.'

'He has a sister, a quiet little girl. She can round out the foursome.'

Charles made the reservations at L'Auberge on Beverly Drive, a spot not chichi enough for them to bump into any of his mother's friends yet serving food that was a reasonable approximation of Provençal cuisine.

Billy and Sari were waiting for them in a cushioned walnut booth.

Billy half-rose. 'Well, pretty lady, we meet again. Now I have my driver's licence.'

Althea realized she had already met this cheeky youth, who wore, of all things, a T-shirt under his tweed jacket. Yes, of course, at Roy's house. But it had been right after Gerry's accident, when random stretches of time had eluded her memory banks.

She found herself responding to the engaging grin. 'Good. Now you can keep your promise to show me where Simon's used to be.'

'Hey hey. You remembered.'

'Do you know Sari?' Charles asked.

The little red table lamp cast an odd shadow upward on the girl's thin, irregular features. How could Marylin have such a plain daughter? Althea wondered. 'No, I'm positive not,' she said.

Under the categorizing gaze, Sari looked away. 'I'm very pleased to meet you, Mrs Stoltz,' she murmured.

'You don't look a bit like either of your parents.'

'Not so,' Billy said. 'She has the Fernauld proboscis.'

'BJ and Linc both *did* have that nose,' Althea said. 'I met your half-brother during the war and thought him the most devastatingly handsome older man I'd ever seen.'

There was an uncomfortable silence. Billy had never seen Linc again, and Sari had never met him. A family rift, unexplained, buried under the snows of silence. Secrets, secrets. Then Billy said, 'And what about me? A devastatingly handsome younger man?'

'Not even in this atrociously bad light.' Althea laughed.

During dinner Althea found herself responding with outright laughter to Billy's masterful, wildly accented repartee about possible scenarios for every kind of film. The two of them carried the conversation until after they'd finished the main course.

While they waited for the dessert soufflé, Charles asked Sari, 'Where do you go to school?'

'I don't.'

'Oh?' Charles said, tilting his head with courteous inquiry.

'I'm taking a kind of sabbatical from Mills – that's a campus up in Northern California. I started pretty young, and this would be my senior year.'

'Good Lord, a college senior!' Charles said. 'I'm embarrassed to say I had you pegged for twelve.'

She looked across the table at him.

And Billy said, 'Come on, Charles, you're not so old that you don't know when a girl's prepubescent.'

'I *do* sound stuffy, don't I?' Charles said, looking at Sari. 'Next I'll be asking what you want to be when you grow up.'

'That's why I stayed out – I needed to find out where I'm heading. And what about you, Charles?'

'I'm going into the Coyne New York Bank.'

'Banking?' Sari asked, her doubts of the capitalist system near-palpable in the single word.

'Now, Sari,' drawled Althea. 'Charles didn't say he was signing a pact with the devil, he said he was going into our family's most respectable enterprise.'

'Althea,' Billy interjected, 'I'm with Sari. It shakes the mind, hearing what Charles's got in mind. Bankers are staid, fat-bellied conformists, which, in case you haven't noticed, Charles isn't.'

'I'm not going into Coyne New York to increase the family's net worth – we have more than we can possibly ever need. My intent is to use the bank's assets in a progressive way.' Charles's voice was low and compelling.

'You'll do it,' Sari said softly. 'You inspire trust.'

'Just the same, Charles,' – Althea smiled – 'better not let your cousin Archie hear you voicing those sentiments.'

Silence settled over the table. As if to sweeten the minor tension, their waiter descended with the steaming, puffed, sinful chocolate soufflé.

When they finished their coffee, Billy suggested a stroll. Turning left on Wilshire, the foursome split into couples. Billy and Althea walked ahead, Sari and Charles strolled at a more leisurely pace behind.

These few blocks on Wilshire were the only part of Beverly Hills that pedestrians used at night. Smartly jacketed groups browsed in front of window displays at Bonwit Teller, Sloane's, Saks, Magnin's, Patricia's.

Billy said, 'You're too high-bred and elegant to have sprung from these haut-bourgeois surroundings.'

'I was born in Beverly Hills.'

'Impossible. There's no hospital.'

'A delivery room was set up in Belvedere.'

'For the royal birth – I should have known. How many salvos did they fire from the top of City Hall?'

'Twenty-one, at least.'

They both laughed.

'You *are* my type,' Billy said. 'So tell me, are you enjoying yourself *avec moi?*'

'More than I anticipated.'

'Does it disturb you I'm younger?'

'I'm not sure what you mean.'

'That tone says you know exactly what I mean.' Billy took her arm possessively.

'Yes, the intent *was* to put you in your place.'

'What if I won't stay put?'

She couldn't repress her smile. 'We'll see,' she said. 'We'll see.'

'You've given hope to a drowning man,' Billy said, tucking his hand in tighter between her vicuña coat and its sleeve.

The other two caught up, Charles in his well-worn impeccably tailored grey suit, Sari in a long skirt and a muskrat jacket from another era. As Althea turned, Charles quickly released Sari's hand.

60

When Sari was a black-haired infant, incongruously plain in her lace-looped bassinet, Marylin had formed a late-night habit of checking her daughter's nursery. The ritual still prevailed, a time of pensive, uncomplicated mother-daughter intimacy.

Sari had chosen the only third-floor room (a dormered attic originally intended for a sewing room) because of its unimpeded view of the stream. Marylin was commanding herself to hide her distress while finding out about her children's encounter with Althea and Charles as she climbed the staircase.

The lights were out, and in the darkness the radio dial glowed an unearthly green: Joni Mitchell's pure voice soared like the clouds she sang of. Sari stood at the window, the spare outline of her body showing through a cotton nightgown turned to chiffon by moonlight.

'Did you ever see such a night, Mother? Look . . . the moon's nearly golden.'

'Beautiful,' Marylin said, closing the door behind her, feeling her way to the very old, crudely made rush-bottomed chair that Sari had found in the stable, a leftover from Tessa Van Vliet's time.

'Have you ever seen a moon this colour?'

'It's beautiful,' Marylin repeated.

'This must be how the sun looks from Mars, or maybe Jupiter.'

'Have a good time tonight?'

'Fantastic,' Sari said dreamily.

'I heard you come in, but not Billy.' Billy, who moved in and out of the house on whim, was temporarily ensconced in his rooms downstairs. 'Did he drop you off and go on someplace?'

'He drove Mrs Stoltz — Althea — home. Charles brought me.'

'Oh? That seems a lot of extra driving.' There was an edge to Marylin's voice.

Sari moved through the darkness to the bedside table, turning off the radio. The room was alive with the mournful chittering crickets and the faint rush of the stream.

'Mother,' she asked slowly, 'why're you so uptight?'

Marylin had always practised zealous honesty with both her children, avoiding parental hypocrisies, platitudes and phony circumlocutions. Tonight, though, she found herself equivocating. 'I meant . . . well, for Charles to come all the way out here while Billy takes Mrs Stoltz home seems wasteful.'

'You sent up sparks when I told you Charles had invited us both to dinner.' The soft, unhappy voice — so like Marylin's own — became near-inaudible. 'Don't you like him?'

'It's not Charles,' Marylin said, adding with regrettable savagery, 'it's Althea!' She drew a calming breath. 'Something she did a hundred years ago, but I can't ever get it out of my mind. She wrecked Auntie Roy.'

'But now they're so close.'

'That's your aunt all over. Once her friend, always her friend.'

'What was it Mrs Stoltz did?'

'Can you remember that before Uncle Gerry's accident he was away for a long time?'

'Yes, sure. Auntie Roy was so sad and unglued. You mean, Mrs Stoltz – ?'

'Yes. Gerry was with *her*. Those months were hideous for Roy. She worshipped Gerry. She changed from an eager, bright girl while we watched. There was nothing we could do to help – or to stop the life draining from her. When I say it, it sounds so corny, like the plot of that last tearjerker I was in – but, Sari, it's true. Althea took the living heart out of Roy, and after it was over, Roy kept right on being her friend.'

Sari padded cross the moon-silvered darkness to sit on the rug near Marylin's chair. 'Mrs Stoltz . . . I felt sorry for her because of her father. But . . . she has the weirdest eyes. The way she looked at me made me feel like a virus on a microscope slide. Do you think it has to do with that old junk, poor Uncle Gerry, or because she bugs out at the least hint of Charles looking at a female?' Her voice was tremulous as she said 'Charles'.

Marylin breathed deeply, then resorted to an actress's tone of neutrality. 'Offhand I'd say she doesn't have a thing to worry about.'

'What does that mean?'

'I don't know Charles very well, of course, but it seems to me he's the last one to do anything rash.'

'Oh, Mother.'

'I didn't mean that as criticism. But he, well, he's very sure of himself.'

'That's only how he *seems*. He's great-looking, terrifically intelligent, he has a famous name and a family mentioned in every history textbook. But underneath it all, he's . . . I don't know. Vulnerable. He can't express his feelings, so he pretends he doesn't have them.'

Marylin's maternal instincts jangled. Sari had dated two

boys, and both of them, the stammerer and the tall one with the terminal acne, had fitted like two pieces of a jigsaw puzzle with the girl's boundlessly loving tendencies towards nurturing. This insufferably stuck-up, poker-faced son of Althea's has somehow roused her sympathies. He'll break her heart. I'll kill anyone who hurts her. Reaching out in the darkness, she encountered her daughter's soft hair.

'Mother . . . won't you try to like him? For me?'

'Then there is . . . something?'

'It seems wild, doesn't it?' The soft voice shook with joy and uncertainty. 'He's so far above me.'

Marylin was remembering back through the years, to a deeply tanned young naval officer who in his whites was surely a deity descended, an impoverished girl who lived above a garage . . . that awful bleak doctor's office with the stirrups . . . the ignoble demise of part of her soul . . . Nobody had set out to hurt or maim.

'It's not a matter of who is too good for whom,' Marylin said. 'It's just that Charles is different. He has to be. His kind of wealth is living behind a thick wall. It sets you apart from other people, and life. It can make some men, well, exploitive.'

'Charles isn't stuck behind some "thick wall", he's not different.'

'I just can't bear for you to be hurt,' Marylin cried. 'That's the worst part of being a mother. You can feel all of your child's pain whether the child is grown or not.'

'Then try to see Charles as a person, not a stereotype.'

Chagrined and taken aback by her daughter's hostility, Marylin was silent for a moment. 'You're right. I *have* been connecting him with that mess with Gerry.' She paused. 'It'd be so easy for anyone with his name, his family, to be a phony, but Charles certainly seems sincere.'

Marylin spoke her lines skilfully, but Sari, of course, caught the placatory note.

She sighed and said nothing.

Marylin asked, 'Have you heard Billy's car?'

457

'No – maybe he's still with Mrs Stoltz. *Him* she likes. He cracked her up all through dinner.'

'He did?'

'I think he made her forget her father,' Sari said, rising to hug her mother, a dismissal that was firm yet not uncharitable. 'Good night.'

At the top of the stairwell, Marylin gripped the hand-carved banister. Under normal circumstances, she brooded about her too-sensitive daughter and seldom gave a concerned thought to Billy – other than his draft status. Billy had emerged unscathed from a near-fatal head injury not to mention lesser broken bones and a ruptured appendix. Billy was a tough, wise-cracking survivor.

Billy's only twenty-four, and Althea has a son his age, Marylin told herself. It was a kind of gesture for him to drive her home. Now, stop being ridiculous.

With stoic effort Marylin blocked these worries from her mind and slowly descended the stairs.

Althea had just broken down in a storm of tears.

She and Billy were in Belvedere's music room, surrounded by stereo components that had been installed by Firelli's top sound engineer. She had set a recording on the balanced turntable, and as the bouncy, perfectly recaptured notes had filled the room, she had recalled – too late – that this Dennis Brain recording of Mozart's horn concertos included Number Two in E Flat Major, the piece that had accompanied that monstrous, losing battle with her parents.

As tears poured from her eyes, she snatched up her purse for a handkerchief.

'Hey, Althea, hey there.' Billy's voice, lacking its aggressive humour, sounded oddly subdued.

She yanked the stylus from the revolving disc. 'It's my father . . .'

'I know, I know.'

'His favourite . . . record . . .'

'Listen, it's okay to cry. I do it myself sometimes.'

The devastating complexities of Althea's love-hatred for her father had always tormented and baffled her, and the only way she could bring herself under control was to count backward from a hundred. By the time she reached the fifties, her sobs subsided.

'Better?' Billy asked gently.

'I keep expecting the phone to ring,' she said.

'Your father's that bad?'

'He's just lying there, a corpse already.'

'The usual medical heroics?'

'To the hilt.'

Billy was sitting at the far end of a couch, his loafers resting on the low tray table. 'It's ugly,' he said sympathetically.

'Why in God's name can't people just die anymore?'

'In my opinion the answer has something to do with our medical fraternity's profound respect for life,' Billy retorted. 'How can you rack up a profoundly respectable Beverly Hills lifestyle if your patients conk out pronto?'

Althea smiled faintly, then began to weep again.

'In Dad's movies,' Billy said, raising his hornrims, 'when this situation came up, the male lead usually put his manly arm around his tear-stricken co-star. Critics of the time wrote that his scripts showed a deep knowledge of human behaviour. Do you think that analysis holds up?'

She wiped her eyes. 'Possibly.'

He shifted across the couch, resting his arm around her. He was bony, thin, and she could smell his deodorant and sweat, the comforting odours of masculine youth. She leaned her head on his T-shirt.

'You have sort of an outré relationship with your father, don't you?'

'Did Charles tell you that?'

'You mustn't keep underrating me, Althea. True, I write jokes for the idiots to snicker over, but that doesn't mean my mental processes are deficient.' His fingers rubbed her shoulder soothingly. 'Your father's been ill for years, and you should have adjusted, but you're still on the rocky edge. Want to dump on me – or do you save that for your shrink?'

459

'I don't have one. Sometimes I think I need one. But the thought of having somebody's dirty little eyes prying into me is – ' She shuddered.

'My sentiments exactly.'

'Billy, get out of here. When I'm shook, I do things I'm sorry about later.'

'I'll take my chances. Since I was fourteen and a half you've been the heroine of my wet dreams.'

'I bet you tell that to all the girls,' she said.

'Yeah, but with you it's true.' He nuzzled her ear.

Althea's affairs were carried out with mannered discretion and absolute secrecy. The minute any relationship threatened to go public, she ended it. Her innate and demanding instinct for privacy had been strengthened as if with a steel spine by her admiring love for Charles. It was deep necessity that she appear pristine and untouched – save by her legally wedded spouses – to her son. She could not risk seeing disgust in those clear hazel eyes.

She said carefully, 'I'm a good deal older.'

'Venus must be at least four thousand and sixty if she's a day. And if she materialized, I'd have a hard-on too.' Billy pulled away so he could look at her.

Dismayed to even briefly lose the warm comfort, she admitted that she was diverted by and attracted to this thin, humorously clever young man.

'Nothing like coming right to the point,' she said.

'Well?' he asked with a faint tremor. 'Are you going to order me forth?'

'The castle keep's no place to conduct an amour,' she said.

He put his arm around her shoulder again. 'You wouldn't want Charles to catch on, is that it?'

'Precisely.'

'He won't, I promise you.' He nuzzled her ear again. 'Mmm. Nice.'

Althea, responding instantaneously to the flick of his tongue in her ear, caressed the tendons of Billy's neck. They stretched embracing on the long couch.

Suddenly the side door, which led onto the *porte-cochère*, slammed. She jerked swiftly to her feet, going into the hall. 'Charles,' she called. 'We're in here.'

The hall chandelier shone on Charles's pale hair, which for once was not smoothly combed, and in the bright light she could see his expression clearly. He looked dazed, as if he had just been aroused from sleep – or reverie.

'Oh, Mother, hello.' Recovering, he strode swiftly across gleaming marble to her.

With an intense surge of denial, she told herself that there had been nothing out of the ordinary in his manner.

She could not bear any additional losses.

The Del Monte, a two-storey pink stucco apartment complex on Wilshire Boulevard with lush tropical foliage surrounding a kidney-shaped pool, offered daily maid service and catered to out-of-towners who paid a minimum of attention to their neighbours. A few days later Billy moved out of his parents' house and rented a one-bedroom unit in the Del Monte.

61

At the beginning of April, two weeks later, thick grey clouds from the north clamped over the Los Angeles basin. Although the air was chill and heavy with moisture, Charles and Sari remained sitting on the bare, tamped earth by the stream. Charles sat with his back spear straight, Sari angled towards him with upthrust knees so that her poncho fell around her, forming a grey tepee from which her hair emerged like soft black smoke.

Marylin could see them from her window.

As she had promised Sari two weeks earlier, she now saw Charles with a clear vision, simply for what he was. And what sane mother could pick fault with a tall, intelligent,

461

superrich, internationally well-educated paragon who voiced his opinions with a confidence that inspired absolute faith? Yet Marylin could not silence the small, naggingly disloyal question: what did this flawless gem see in her unspectacular though dear child? And each time she came up with only one answer: in this time of trouble, Charles needed some of Sari's boundless loving kindness. Beyond this understandable larceny, there was nothing to rouse the least maternal distrust. His treatment of Sari was a mixture of comradeship and *sang froid* politeness. Wouldn't he display a hint of shamefacedness if he were 'taking advantage' – whatever *that* meant nowadays –her daughter?

Marylin and Joshua had been forced to accept that Charles approached Sari as a genuine swain, Billy having with characteristic restlessness decamped into a service apartment on Wilshire. Charles dropped by the house every day, often joining them for lunch, dinner – a couple of times even for breakfast. He hiked with Sari, he listened to her records. An old-fashioned kind of romance that, as NolaBee put it, was right cute.

Charles picked up a pebble and skimmed it over the stream; a live oak branch hid the small stone's trajectory, but from the window Marylin could see Sari lean closer to touch the white cable stitch of Charles's sleeve. He nodded, pushing to his feet, extending his hand to help her rise before he brushed off his slacks. They started along the shell-lined path that led up the canyon to where a derelict adobe, Sari's old hideaway, marked the end of the property line.

Marylin's breath clouded the windowpane as they disappeared from view.

The next morning, Saturday, BJ came to visit. Maury and their two younger daughters had returned nine days after the baby's birth, but BJ (mother of three girls) had been unable to tear herself from the miracle of a grandson. She had stayed on, arriving back in Beverly Hills on Thursday, and used the next two days to recover a bit from jet lag and have her photographs developed. With Joshua, Marylin and Sari she sat in the den, opening package after package of colour prints. 'Will you look at this one,' she kept saying in her loud, cheerful voice, boasting about every inch of her grandson, about Annie's immediate recovery from the birth ('Remember, Marylin, we stayed in the hospital a full week and then came home in an ambulance?'), and about the enormous party on the kibbutz for the baby's circumcision.

The door chimes sounded.

Sari ran to answer, after a minute returning to introduce Charles to her half-sister.

'Hello, Charles,' BJ said, adding archly, 'come take a look at Sari's great-nephew.'

Charles bent his head attentively over three-by-fives of the infant. 'Very healthy-looking.'

'He's an absolute beaut,' said BJ, shuffling packages. 'Here's one of me holding him – oh, that bald gentleman is Maury, Sari's brother-in-law, the grandfather.'

'Come on, Charles,' Sari said in a choking voice. 'Let's get Elena to fix us a picnic.'

'Well, well,' teased BJ, raising one black eyebrow. 'Your antique sister putting a crimp in your style, Sari, babes?'

Sari, blushing furiously, pulled Charles in the direction of the restaurant-sized kitchen.

'So that's Althea's son, our own American Prince Charles,' said BJ *sotto voce*. 'Obviously he has a big thing going with Sari.'

'Mind your dirty mouth, Beej,' ordered Joshua, his anger scarcely veiled.

'Now, Daddy, you aren't living in the forties anymore. Different daughter, different time.'

'It's not like that,' Marylin said.

'Listen, I might be a grandmother, but my sight's not failing. I *saw* those starry eyes.'

'You might be a grandmother, Beej,' Joshua rumbled, 'but I can still turn you over my knee.'

BJ gave her loud, good-natured laugh. 'Plenty of padding now, Daddy.' She reached for a snapshot. 'Take a look at this one and tell me that baby isn't all Fernauld.'

The weather had warmed: Joshua, BJ and Marylin lunched on the patio that opened from the breakfast room.

Elena was bringing out the coffee when the phone rang. It was the author of a bestseller that Joshua was attempting to option, and he disappeared into the house for a long-distance conference.

BJ opened her big, worn Gucci purse. 'I didn't want to show this pack when Daddy was around,' she said. 'Linc flew in from Rome for the *bris*.'

Marylin fumbled as she opened a folder of slick prints. From the top one, Linc smiled at her. Her foolish, romantic heart beat faster, and a soft answering smile curved her own lips.

'He never changes . . .'

'Sure he does, but he stays the same shape,' said BJ, complacently patting her large, grandmotherly hips.

'How is he?' Marylin asked. She invariably put this same half-embarrassed question to BJ when BJ (after all, her stepdaughter) returned from Europe.

'All the jobs he wants. But how on earth can he be content to dig up the details for other people's books? Where's his ambition?'

'That Japanese prison camp cut his life in two,' Marylin said softly. 'What else?'

'He broke up with that Marjorie I told you about, the nice English one who looked a bit like Gudrun.'

'Was it rough on him?'

'Who knows. He *seems* happy.'

'Oh, BJ.' Marylin shook her head, smiling. 'That's the tone you always use about single people.'

'Well, what kind of life is it, divorced, no children – nothing.'

Marylin's small hand was fanning the stack. All the photographs included Linc. In this one he held the infant, in the next he stood with rolled-up shirt sleeves in front of a cabin. Here he was posed between BJ and Maury, here he draped an arm around the new mother, his niece. 'Did he . . . mention me?'

'He knows all about you.'

'How? BJ, were you telling him about me – ?'

'Stop sounding so indignant, Marylin. I didn't say a word. But you're not exactly the Nobody Kid, you know.' BJ spooned sugar into her coffee. 'Now, if you're asking whether he still cares, of course he does.'

'Has he told you?'

'No.'

'Then it's a sheer guess.'

'Why do you think he's divorced? Why else has he never come home?'

'Don't say that, BJ.'

'It's true.'

'I can't bear to think of him exiling himself because of me.'

'You don't need to sound so guilty, Marylin. Honestly you're too good to be true. Who else would put up with Daddy's *meshugas*, all that bluster and spending? I always say to Maury that Mother got the better of the deal. I really mean it. He might have cheated constantly on her, but at least she didn't have to work her tail off to support him.' The caring expression on BJ's full face showed that this speech was not one of daughterly disdain, but rather evidence of affectionate compassion for her best friend's plight. 'He hasn't been drinking since I left?'

Joshua had always been a heavyweight in his vices, and drinking was no exception. BJ exaggerated the importance of his occasional benders, while Marylin, in hopeless wifely pity, defended them. 'A couple of Scotches now and then,' Marylin said. 'How long was Linc in Israel?'

'A long weekend. Those kibbutzniks can be prickly with outsiders. It was nothing short of miraculous how they fell for him.'

BJ boasted nonstop about her brother's conquest of the kibbutz until Joshua's distant conversation ceased; then she grabbed the photographs from Marylin's hand, shoving them pell-mell into her purse.

After BJ drove off, Joshua went up to his cottage to rework the option while Marylin prepared for Monday's show, when John Fowles would be the prime guest: she was thoroughly enjoying her homework of reading *The French Lieutenant's Woman*.

The phone rang again. After a minute, Elena came in to announce it was for Señor Charles.

Marylin took the brief call.

She hung up carefully, then went into the stone-floored room originally intended for flower arranging, now used to store the old raincoats and shoes that the family used on the grounds. Changing her high-heeled sandals for Adidas, she hurried up the canyon towards the old adobe shack. At the footbridge she met Sari and Charles.

'I was coming to get you, Charles,' she said, her beautiful sea-coloured eyes moist with sympathy. 'They just called from the hospital.'

'Grandfather?'

Marylin put her hand on his forearm. 'I'm terribly sorry, Charles,' she said, and her voice broke.

For one moment Charles's posture stiffened with fathomless, grief-stricken guilt. Recovering, he said, 'I'd better get over to the hospital. They'll need me.'

62

The Coynes had a special permit to bury their dead in the family's upper New York country place, now Coyne State Park. Atop a gently rolling hill stood a replica of the Athenian Erechtheum, a perfect copy in every detail save one: above the shapely marble caryatids was incised: 'GROVER TIBAULT COYNE'. On slightly lower ground were the nearly as outrageous tombs of his three wives – the death dates of the first and third Mrs Coyne were nearly seven decades apart. Scattered in widening circles down the hill were the Carrara marble obelisks, onyx domes, roseate *Winged Victorys*, and Moorish cupolas that marked the burial sites of his sons and daughters (all lay here, with the exception of Mrs Cunningham), his in-laws, five of his grandchildren, and three great-grandchildren. The cemetery, tended by a task force of gardeners, enclosed from park visitors by a high and seemingly endless white stone wall, was jokingly called Mount Olympus by the family.

Though Harry Cunningham had passed most of his years in Beverly Hills, though he had never fitted in with his terrifyingly self-assured in-laws, Mrs Cunningham determined to lay him to his final rest here.

With the ease that wealth facilitates, Charles made the arrangements.

The morning following death, the baggage compartment of Grover T. Coyne III's DC-10 had awaited Harry Cunningham's massive pewter coffin. The widow had retired to one of the perfectly appointed bedroom cabins – her maid in attendance – and thus far on the trip eastward had wept continuously.

Althea and Charles sat in the stateroom.

Althea gazed down at the brilliant, endless cloud field. A dull ache throbbed across her forehead, and there was a rawness behind her eyeballs. She felt as if tears alone could alleviate her physical distress, yet her emotional responses were horribly awry. She could summon up neither honest sorrow nor a flicker of indecent glee that he was dead, her enemy, her lover.

She rapped her emerald on the inner glass.

All at once her teeth began to chatter, and her hands could not hold still. She was trapped by a phenomenon that transcended memory. She could actually feel the silky Egyptian cotton of her pyjamas, see the pitch-darkness, experience the heart-stopping horror of something unknown in the dark room with her, and as *it* moved closer, terror choked her so once again she could not breathe or cry out. She could smell the liquor, feel the hands pawing

467

at her hairless body, again she experienced her thrashing struggles to escape.

A whimpering groan escaped her.

Charles came over, resting his hands on either arm of her chair, looking down at her, his reddened eyes filled with concern. 'What is it, Mother?'

She leaned back, shaking, unable to speak.

'Shall I get you a drink?'

She nodded. When he returned with the highball her hands shook too much to take it. Placing the glass on the small table, Charles sat on the chair arm, bending down to cradle her shoulders with his arm. Her son's gesture was balm for her ravaged state.

He's a wonder, my Charles, she thought.

And into her mind popped a corollary: I'm not about to let him throw himself away on that plain, cheap little movie girl.

She ignored the fact that her lover was Sari's brother and that this weekend Billy was coming to New York to console her. In her pain she recognized only that Charles was the one person alive not her natural enemy, and she must see that he had the best of the best.

The jet passed smoothly above a break in the clouds. After a minute or two, her hands were steady enough to hold the glass. She took a long drink. 'Exactly what I needed,' she said. 'Thank you, dear.'

The family, or those of them that were in the country, felt it an incumbent duty to show up at the funeral on that rainy, chill afternoon. Immediately following burial they rushed back to the 'cottage'.

With the death of the third Mrs Grover T. Coyne, the immense country place, with its high gilt-and-crimson ceilings, oppressive dark marble and priceless *quattrocento* Italian furnishings, had been donated as a museum to the state of New York. The Coyne family, however, had retained the largest guest house, which they used only on these mournful gatherings. Around the sitting room's immense Gothic fireplace, fifteen black-clad people drank cocktails and chatted with imperturbable smiles. Gertrude, unnerved by her family at the best of times, retired immediately to her bedroom – she had the one with the famed Cardinal Mazarin bed. Althea, in her black St Laurent orphan's weeds, played chief mourner.

Her inferiorities surfaced when she had to face the Coyne tribe *en masse*, and besides, since the episode on the DC-10 she had been plagued by that imbalance, as if every floor tilted at a minuscule degree.

She therefore buckled Charles to her arm as her shield. He had mercifully inherited the damnable Coyne certainty. (She had never connected this assured aspect of her son with Gerry's strength.) Even with Charles, tall and bone hard at her side, she found herself fighting desperately to prove her worth, talking knowingly of Vietnam, David Hockney and the Paris showings – it would have been unseemly in a Coyne to mention the deceased.

At five, excuses were made and custom-built European cars departed crunching over the wet gravel.

The funeral rites had officially ended: the mortal parts of Harry Cunningham were considered laid to rest.

Charles asked, 'Will you go to New York tomorrow?'

The thought of staying at this gloomy place longer than necessary sent a shudder through her. 'Yes, of course.'

'I'm flying back to California with Grandmother.' Charles sank into a chair, his long legs stretched out in front of him, his expression drained. After Firelli's death, his grandfather had been the adult male of his life. 'Tomorrow.'

The room tilted more ominously. 'Charles,' she said, 'don't leave yet.'

'But you're doing so fabulously,' he said. 'You outshone everybody.'

'All front.'

Rain drummed against ancient French ecclesiastical stained glass, the logs in the fireplace jumped and crackled.

After a long hesitation Charles said, 'I promised Grandmother to stay with her the month before I start work.' He

469

would enter the Coyne New York Bank, which was fully controlled by the Coyne Foundation, at the beginning of May. 'She was pathetic when she heard I'd be at Belvedere.'

'I . . . well, I'm sure Grandmother needs you, but she can express her grief. With me . . . it's all bottled up and comes out so oddly . . .' Her eyes filmed with unsought tears.

After a long moment Charles's sleek head bent. 'I promised Sari, too.'

A dagger of hatred directed itself from Althea to Sari. Why can't she call herself decently Sara. I must keep him away from her. 'If you promised, then you must go to California . . .'

Charles blew his nose. 'Would it help if I stay until next Friday?'

'I'd really appreciate that, Charles.' Rising, she moved to touch his shoulder. 'I should be through the worst by then.'

He rose stiffly. 'See you at dinner.'

Alone, she leaned back into the opulent tapestry that had been woven for a fifteenth-century pope, and finally began to cry. Her smothered little sobs had nothing to do with the deceased – or rather, everything. It was her father's death that had upturned and unbalanced her.

She rested her wet cheek on the must-scented silken brocade of the chair arm, and suddenly recalled that Billy would be in New York this coming weekend.

Yes, she thought. That's good. I've been so incredibly sexy these last horrible weeks. I need his hard cock all the time. What's happened to me? I never panted for it, I never was crude.

Then she thought: Charles'll be with me at the flat, so Billy can't stay.

'You don't mind putting up at the Plaza, do you, Billy?'

'I had in mind your bed.'

'I can't have you at my place. Charles's staying on – this has been hell on him.'

470

'Let me sack down in the servants' quarters. I'll emerge only when summoned to service you.'

'Billy, no snideness, I can't bear it today.'

'Would it be headline news if Charles caught on you're not a virgin?'

To ensure the privacy of this call, she had taken 'a little drive' in the wet night, and now she perched in the phone booth of a Texaco station. 'We'll be together more in the Plaza – '

'Hasn't it sunk in, Althea? Don't you realize I'm flying to New York to be with you for exactly twenty-three hours? Don't you understand? I'm so crazy about you my eyes are bugging and I'm so horny for you it's become an embarrassment.'

'Mmm . . . I can't wait until Saturday,' she said, and replaced the receiver.

On Saturday, after Billy opened the door of his room at the Plaza, he returned to slump in one of the green armchairs morosely scratching his skinny bare feet while he watched television without the sound. The picture showed a sea of banners, then a close-up of a young, furious-mouthed man shaking a placard.

'More demonstrations outside the White House?' she asked.

'Right on. Amazing how the youth of the country has turned against patriotism, isn't it?'

'In World War Two, men lined up for blocks outside the Pacific Electric Building to enlist – it was Los Angeles's Army recruiting centre.'

'Just Nixon's luck, becoming president in these degenerate times. I should be in Washington marching with 'em,' Billy said, going to the television set. The picture dwindled, fading.

'Aren't you going to kiss me?'

'I've been considering playing it platonic, you know, like a school pal of Charles's.' He pecked at her cheek. 'That sort of thing, Mrs Stoltz.'

'You've never been petulant.'

'My God, doctor!' He grasped his chest. 'Tell me quick. Is it fatal?'

She sat on the edge of the bed, carefully.

'What is it, Althea? You look strung out.'

'We agreed when we started that we'd be discreet around Charles.'

All at once he went to a window, gripping the ledge. His back was curved and the vertebrae showed vulnerably through his T-shirt. 'I know this is a rough time for you, and I don't mean to heckle, but I've been sitting here thinking about us for hours. The relationship's got certain very depressing angles. In case you haven't noticed, I'm really hung up on you.'

'I care a lot too,' she said, not thinking, but needing him to hold her. She moved to the window next to him.

It was raining again, and below them the new leaves on trees in Central Park glistened.

'Then why don't we do something about it?'

'Oh, Billy.'

'That tone of voice. You sound as if I just inquired whether you'd go into the park with me and set up a mugging operation. Not marriage.'

'Marriage?'

'So why not? God knows there was a minor age gap between you and husband number one, maybe sixty or seventy years. What's so wrong with a virile young man separated by a mere fifteen years?'

'Eighteen,' she said. 'You're twenty-four.'

'Twenty-four. Is that one of the cardinal sins?'

'Billy, can't we stop this?' Her voice was amazingly cool and controlled. She reached her arms around him.

He gave a groan, hugging her so tightly that she thought he'd crack one of her ribs, kissing her, thrusting his tongue deep into her wide-open mouth while he groped at her breasts and buttocks. Without thought, she began yanking at the zipper of her black wool frock, letting it slide onto the carpet while she fumbled swiftly with her black lace bra to loose her large, erect-nippled breasts. As she tugged down her cobwebby black silk panty hose, her frantic fingernails started a run.

Under the hotel sheets, she clung to him conscious only of where their bodies were joined, that wet, dark tunnel where all her impulses towards love – even with Gerry Horak – had ultimately been doomed to defeat.

Alternately she used her muscles and he moved. I am myself again, she thought.

She stayed with Billy for hours. Until after eleven.

Despite the lateness of the hour, she used one of the lobby booths to telephone Archie Coyne, who as chairman of the Coyne Foundation controlled all the family-owned Coyne enterprises including the Coyne New York Bank. Again it was of utmost importance that Charles not have the least chance of overhearing. She explained the reasons behind her request to Archie, and he agreed to it.

63

Late Monday afternoon Charles let himself into the apartment. Althea was having a drink in the living room. She had recently remodelled the co-op with luxurious simplicity, and to the left of the windows, carefully planned shelves had been inset. Her grandmother's collection of Greek vases cast their shadows on the walls, graceful shapes of amphora, hydria, krater, rhyton and alabastron that made a refreshing departure from the routine blare of contemporary art.

'Charles?' she called.

He had been, she knew, at a meeting with the Coyne hirelings, those circumspect grey bankers who would be his immediate superiors. His fair, straight hair was ruffled by the wind and he moved wearily.

'Don't tell me you walked home from Wall Street?' she said.

'I needed time to think.' He sank into a chair near hers.

Crystal rang as she tapped her glass. 'Want one?'

'No, thanks,' he replied. 'Ogden told me a situation's come up in Stockholm – the second man's been transferred. I have to fly over there right away.'

She feigned surprise. 'I didn't know Coyne New York *had* an office in Sweden.'

'Since 1959. It's small. A good place for me to learn the foreign side.' He looked down at his fingernails. 'The thing is, I'm not so positive I want to go into Coyne New York.'

A tremor ran through Althea. I'm doing the right thing, she thought. Given any more time, that hippie slut would take him in completely. 'We talked about it often enough,' she said. 'You always told me you felt an obligation. Are you disappointed they want to start you at a minor office?'

'It's not that. For a time now I've been thinking I'd like to be in something, well, more human. I do seem to have an ability to lead people. What could be more depressingly crass than leading the rich into making bigger fortunes?'

'Oh, Lord! Charles, do you realize that sounds direct from the sandals-and-commune set? We both know that financial institutions have done more to eliminate poverty in this century than all the bearded gurus put together.'

'Yes. I know. Without an accumulation of capital there wouldn't have been any of the industrial advances. All I'm saying is, I'm not sure that *I* belong in the bank. Most people are forced to spend their lives earning a living. That's not true for me. I can choose what I want to do.'

'Archie will retire in a few years. I don't have to explain what it means, being the bank's president. Whoever has the job is chairman of the foundation.'

'I'm not the only cousin,' he said.

'Three's over fifty,' she said. Three was Grover T. Coyne III, the next in the line of succession. 'And after Three, who else would you suggest?' She listed the other third- and fourth-generation cousins. 'Dennis flitting with his pretty boys? Ridge and his gambling? Tinny with his divorces? That nincompoop Wallace?'

Charles sighed. 'You make me sound preordained.'

'You're the natural one to head the family, Charles.' She leaned towards her son. 'Tell me what the problem is about Sweden.'

'I'd planned on spending the rest of this month in California.'

She raised a delicate eyebrow, as if to say, Ahhh, so it's frivolous.

He drew in his cheeks so that the bones were more prominent. A cold, forbidding Coyne expression.

She clasped her drink in both hands. Her voice low, pleading, she spoke the truth. 'Charles, maybe I am pushing you, but that's because I've always been so filled with pride. You're everything I always wanted to be.'

Tuesday evening's SAS flight from John F. Kennedy to Arlanda Airport outside Stockholm was delayed.

Charles and Althea waited in the VIP lounge. Dark shadows showed beneath Charles's eyes as he slumped in his armchair.

Although her son was leaving tonight because of her purposeful manoeuvres, the last thing on earth Althea desired was for Charles to go. She needed him desperately. That peculiar sense of not quite being on level ground sometimes still hit her, or she would hear ghostly strands of music. She awakened at night sobbing, and found herself trapped in paranoid fits, when she feared everyone but her son.

A disembodied Scandinavian bass voice announced that the plane was now boarding. At the gate she flung her arms around Charles, hugging him tightly – she who had always maintained a cool balance between them in public.

'You'll phone and write often?' she asked.

'You're still in rotten shape – it's out of the question for me to be leaving.'

'Can't a mother get sticky once in a while?' She drew away, patting his cheek. 'Have a good flight, Charles.'

With the small group of other first-class passengers, he

moved reluctantly down the portable entryway, turnirg at the bend to look at her. She raised her hand, grateful he was far away – had he been closer, he would have made out the hollowness of her smile.

At home, she rushed into her room with its sleek new furnishings and corner planted with bromeliads. Leaving her clothes strewn on the dressing-room floor for Gerda to get the following morning, she gulped down two Nembutals.

She dreamed of her father coming towards her with his charming smile. The dream then changed him into a sinuous leopard with dangerous black markings. She dreamed of Charles in a furious rage beating her with his fists – or was Gerry the man mercilessly assaulting her? She dreamed of Roy screaming from behind a monstrous Greek mask. She awoke shivering.

The phosphorescent digits on her clock read 12.03.

She had slept less than an hour.

She stretched out on her back, ordering herself to let the soporifics take hold again. But the more she tried to relax, the tighter strung she felt. Her molars clenched, her blood pounded, her sexual organs itched with desire.

After a half-hour she turned on the light, putting the phone on her pillow to dial California. A voice answered after one ring.

'Billy?' she said.

'Me.'

She rested her cheek against the monogrammed pillow-slip. 'I didn't think you'd be in.'

'That's your sensual mind.'

'Sensual?'

'You were imagining me in the arms of your routine lusciously titted nympho starlet. That's Monday, Wednesday and Friday. This being Tuesday, I'm eating take-out sushi in front of the telly.'

'What are you watching?'

'Switchies.'

'What?'

'Switching the dial gives a surreal intelligence to the boob tube. This is pretty late Eastern Standard Time. Just get in?'

'Charles's flight was hours late and I stayed at the airport with him.'

'Yeah, yeah, that's right. Today's the day. So our Charles has taken off into the dizzy world of international high finance. Poor Sari, she's been dragging around. She'd figured on seeing him next weekend. Aunt Roy's taking her down to Laguna – not much of a consolation prize, but so it goes.'

Althea's eyes were stony. 'Sari? But she's just a baby.'

'Nearly twenty.'

'She can't be!'

'She told you the night we had dinner at L'Auberge.'

'It must've slid by me. Here I've been imagining her as twelve or thirteen . . .' Althea let her voice fade. 'Billy, you're totally on the wrong track about her and Charles.'

'He clocked in plenty of hours at the house.'

'To see your father – he admires his films.' She paused. 'If he led the poor child on, he certainly didn't mean to.'

'It's a Fernauld family failing, letting ourselves be led on.'

'That's what I called about. With Charles gone, the guest room is free,' Althea said. 'Can you be in New York this weekend?' She had intended to sound lightly amorous, but the question ended in a shrilly plaintive bleat.

'Hey, Althea,' he said. 'Hey.'

'Mrs Stoltz,' Gerda's Swiss-German accent was calling softly. A supportive throb of muted raps on the door. 'Mrs Stoltz?'

Althea rose from the depths of drugged sleep, her thoughts swimming torpidly around death and irreconcilable loss.

She glanced at her clock – 9.15. Though she often rose before this hour, the ironclad household rule was that should she choose to remain in bed, she be left undisturbed. 'What is it?'

'There's a gentleman who insists on seeing you – '

'No gentleman,' said Billy's voice. 'Me.'

477

Althea's annoyance dissolved. Thank God he's here, she thought. Though rigidly observant of proprieties in front of her servants, she called, 'Come on in.'

She had a blurred glimpse of Gerda's horror-struck face, then Billy shut the door behind him.

'Where did she train for guard duty?' he asked. 'Buchenwald?'

'She's Swiss.'

'That's what the *Übermenschen* all say.'

Althea's lips twitched in a smile. 'You got here fast.'

'Aboard United's red-eye. All these plants – baby, where's the jungle drums?' He slapped both palms on his T-shirt. 'Me Tarzan. Eeeyeehahh!'

'Shut up, you fool! You'll have Gerda calling the police.' She patted his arm fondly – he had seated himself on the monogrammed blanket cover.

'That's a terrific nightgown. Did I ever mention what cream silk does to my libido?'

'This is Wednesday. What about your job?'

'*The Rain Fairburn Show* will survive a week or so without me. Frankly, my humour's too urban for Mother.'

'I didn't mean to lead you astray.'

'No?' Behind the horn-rims, the quick, clever eyes remained fixed on her. 'Let's face it, that call last night was a *cri de coeur.*'

She turned away, admitting, 'It's been bad, very bad.'

He touched her shoulder sympathetically. 'Vith Doctor Fernauld, you don't have to avoid zee crucial oedipal area.' He affected the Viennese accent with infinite tenderness.

'Did they give you breakfast on the plane? Shall I have Gerda bring us some?'

'Later,' he said. 'Like they say in the novels, dot, dot, dot, a long time later.' He folded his glasses on the nightstand.

Encircling him with her arms, she drew him down to the warm, sleep-scented bed. There was a faint, faraway bounce of a Mozart horn concerto, then only Billy's urgent breathing against her ear.

478

64

One evening in early June, Roy came home with a load of groceries – Sari was coming to dinner. Kicking off her stack-heeled patent pumps, she set the heavy brown bags on the kitchen counter and began putting things away.

Patricia's had made Roy more than comfortable financially. She could well afford larger, more opulent quarters and a competent full-time maid-cook rather than a once-a-week cleaning man, but with her energies focused on the shop, she seldom gave a thought to raising her standard of living – a Mercedes was her one personal status symbol.

Picking up her shoes, she went into the living room. Long rectangles of darker beige showed where Gerry's oversize canvases normally hung. The paintings were on loan to the Gerrold Horak Gallery. A comprehensive retrospective would open at UCLA on 23 July with a huge cocktail bash to which everyone who was anyone in the business, political, entertainment and aesthetic life of the state had been invited. As Roy considered the retrospective, her eyes filmed with a sensual glow, and her lips curved in a softly amorous smile.

She took off her beige-brown-and-red-striped Missoni, looking hastily away from the mirrored reflection of a pleasantly curved body in panty hose and bra. Fat as a hog, she thought.

This flesh was hidden under a flowing silk caftan when the doorbell rang.

Sari extended a huge, artless bouquet of roses. 'I picked these a few minutes ago.'

'Oh, you beautiful things,' Roy said, burying her nose in fragrant petals. 'Sari, you're a darling. Come on in while I put on the lamb chops.'

Sari volunteered for salad duty. As she washed and

sliced, she drooped unconsciously. These eight weeks that Charles had been in Stockholm, Sari had wilted like an unwatered fern, reviving a little when her parents offered her a European vacation. In common with many a childless aunt, Roy had spilled her maternal instincts over her niece and nephew, exaggerating the importance of her role in their corporeal and mental well-being. She cursed herself endlessly for introducing Althea's son to Billy. 'What's the latest on your trip?' she asked. 'Made your airline reservations?'

Sari, peeling an avocado, stared down at her green-stained fingers. 'I don't think I'm going.'

'But it's your birthday present! And what about Lucie?' BJ's middle daughter had been given the vacation by Marylin and Joshua, ostensibly as a gift for graduating from UCLA, but in truth so she could accompany Sari. 'I thought you two had it all set to spend a week in Sweden.'

Avocado cubes slipped between Sari's thin fingers.

'Honey, I'm interested,' Roy said. 'But if you don't want to talk about it, I understand.'

Sari rinsed off her hands, sighing. 'Charles called last night. He says he's not positive he'll be in Stockholm when we're there. The bank's moving him around.'

Roy busied herself with slicing sourdough bread. 'That's how apprenticeships are, honey. You're sent from pillar to post learning the job.'

'Oh, Auntie Roy, why can't I be happy that for a little time we had a really good relationship going?' The spattering sounds of broiling lamb chops nearly covered Sari's soft murmur.

'Honeybunch, don't talk like that. It's not in the past. He calls and writes, doesn't he?'

'Yes, but . . . well, Charles is good at everything except feelings – the one thing I *am* good at. His letters are sort of formal. And you know how transatlantic lines are, they either rumble or echo every word you say. I just don't know anymore, I just don't know.'

It hurt Roy to look at her niece's woebegone face. 'What's so wrong with going to Stockholm to find out?'

480

'He's so polite he'll imagine he *has* to be there when I am, even if it's difficult for him . . . even if he doesn't want to be . . . Oh, let's leave it alone, okay?'

Roy, her eyes pitying, set the breakfast table with the roses and festive red-and-white place mats. 'I heard from Billy the other night,' she said, arranging the silverware. 'He hardly said a word about himself. He's sure closemouthed about what he's doing in New York. Should I be cherchezing for la femme?'

Sari, who had brought the salad bowl to the table, sat down.

'There's a pregnant pause if I ever heard one,' Roy said. 'So he does have somebody new?'

'. . . Auntie Roy, promise not to tell Mother? She was really shook when he took off like that. And this isn't anything sure.'

Fat sizzled loudly as Roy opened the broiler, forking the two larger lamb chops onto Sari's plate. 'I'm all discretion and ears,' she said.

'The night we went out to dinner, Billy was totally wrapped up with Mrs Stoltz.'

'Althea!' Roy cried. The plate tilted. Chops would have slid onto the linoleum but for the raised rim. 'You're saying, *she's* the woman?'

'Just vibes.'

'I have never heard anything so outlandish!'

'She's in New York.'

'So are four million other women! Althea? She's *my* age! Why, *Charles* is older than Billy!' It was not disbelief but furious outrage that made Roy bark out her words like a marine top sergeant. 'How did you ever dream this up?'

Sari shrank into the yellow booth. 'Nothing, nothing,' she murmured. 'Forget it.'

'I didn't mean to scream at you,' Roy said, patting her niece's thin arm. 'But it's too far-out to consider.'

'Billy's always gone for older women – that Nella, remember her?'

Nella, with whom Billy had lived for a few months when

481

he was twenty, was a model who worked the Patricia's fashion shows. 'An aged crone, twenty-eight,' Roy said ruefully.

'There's nothing definite that I can tell you, really. Except Billy was really on with Mrs Stoltz that night. And she kept smiling at him – yet Charles told me she was really in a mess about her father.'

Sari ate practically nothing. Roy, utterly forgetful of her current diet, downed both her lamb chops with all the fat, buttered slabs of sourdough bread, ravenously consumed the abundant contents of the salad bowl. All metabolic messages were cancelled and the meal churned in her stomach without assuaging her hunger. Sari's intuition replayed two of her worst recollections: the darkness of the poolhouse and Althea's long, slim, white foot arching in passion ... the hot Oaxaca hotel room and Gerry's shamefaced admission of an incurable love for Althea.

After Sari left, she found herself pacing up and down the living room as if she had been shot with massive jolts of Benzedrine. She no longer saw Sari's divination as an impossibility – in fact, the longer she considered Billy's abrupt departure and secretiveness, the longer she mulled over that damn Althea's lecherous propensities, the more feasible the two as a couple became.

She halted abruptly, her caftan swirling around her. All right, she thought. Either Sari's right about this, or she's wrong. Marylin and I will have to find out.

The following morning, before eight, Roy telephoned her sister. 'How about lunch?' she asked.

'Today?' Marylin's feathery voice was anxious. 'Roy, are you all right? Is it Mama? Have you run into problems with my wardrobe?'

'Nothing like that. I need to talk to you, that's all. If you're booked solid, we can make it after I finish work.'

'No, no. I'll be there as soon after one as I can.'

The sisters always lunched incommunicado at Patricia's: though Beverly Hills was reasonably sophisticated about well-known faces, Marylin dreaded the inevitable oblique stares in restaurants, the occasionally overheard whisper: *Don't look now, but there, in that booth, it's Rain Fairburn.*

Roy had ordered two Cobb salads to be sent over from the Brown Derby, and at 1.15 the two wooden bowls of chopped, crisp raw vegetables topped with chopped pink ham, turkey and bacon, as well as the pitchers of rich, lumpy Roquefort dressing, were set neatly on a tablecloth that covered the same scarred old desk that had served Mrs Fineman.

When Marylin came in, fragrant with a recent spraying of Diorissima, her clean-washed face aglow, Roy examined her sister as a young man might, accepting that the faint lines of brow and forehead, the minuscule softening of luminous flesh enhanced her beauty by rendering it accessible.

'Do I have a smudge on my face?' Marylin asked with her breathy little laugh.

'Sorry. I was thinking of something else. Marylin, sit down. Tea or coffee?'

'Tea, please.'

Roy sent the secretary to boil the kettle – she had taken space from an upstairs stockroom to build a large, pleasant employees' lounge with a stove and refrigerator.

'Now, what's this all about?' Marylin asked. 'It's not like you to make mysteries. Did Sari tell you something last night? My poor baby. Roy, I *knew* no good would come from that Charles.'

'She was pretty shaken. I'm fairly positive Europe is off.'

'It is.' Marylin sighed. 'When she told us, Joshua blew his stack – and you know he never does with her. He's decided that the moment she hits Sweden she'll get that Charles out of her system.'

'Charles isn't sure he'll be in Stockholm.'

'So he *is* bowing out! My poor, poor Sari. She takes everything so hard.'

Roy ladled a teaspoon of dressing on her Cobb salad. 'I

was really disturbed by something, well, she said about Billy.'

Marylin looked down, and the incomparable eyes were veiled. She took Billy's sudden departure without giving *The Rain Fairburn Show* any kind of notice as a complete rejection of her and her career. For the past two months she had felt herself locked into a dark tunnel. Her rejector, after all, was the child for whom she had sacrificed love. She would find herself brooding about Linc, wondering what their lives would have been had she not made that long-ago decision in favour of maternal duty. Though Linc had not remarried, he had also never once asked BJ about her. No man waits for decades. Linc was enjoying himself as a divorced man. To him she was doubtless immensely less important than that Gudrun, another memory among the rainbow of exotic, foreign girlfriends. And what did she have to show for her renunciation? A son who rejected her. Nothing, she had nothing.

Incapable of looking at Roy, she speared a small, glistening cube of ham. 'Billy? Last night he called us.'

Roy sat up straighter. 'What's new?' she asked.

'Joshua talked. I didn't. Something about making a picture – '

Roy interjected, 'Now, *there's* a different angle.'

'I know, I know. Like father, like son. The two of them always talking and planning the big box-office smash. But Billy's actually come up with financing.'

Roy set down her fork. 'Financing?' she asked slowly. 'Did he say who would give him the money? A bank?'

'No, private sources. Joshua said he was cagey, yet sounded positive it'll come off.'

'What about his social life?'

'I really don't know.' Marylin's smile was frayed. 'Roy, to tell you the truth, he hasn't given us his phone number, even.'

'Sari's decided he's fallen into some woman's fell clutches.' Roy spoke lightly, but her jaw was set.

'That's Billy. Always in and out of an affair.'

'Maybe,' Roy said slowly, 'it's Althea.'

'Althea?' Marylin asked, mystified. 'You think she had something to do with Charles leaving Sari?'

'I'm talking about Billy. Althea and Billy.'

Clutching her napkin, Marylin jumped to her feet. 'Are you crazy? What a hideous thing to say!'

'It's what Sari thinks, and she's Miss Sensitive about relationships and things. It does make a kind of ghastly sense, Marylin. And this movie financing fits right in. Althea could put up a cool fortune and never miss a penny of it.'

A truck was noisily backing along the narrow alley, and while the grating sounds poured through the office windows, Marylin's colour drained until the exquisite features seemed powdered with white flour.

Roy worried that she'd been too blunt. 'You okay, Marylin, hon?' she asked, leaning across the desk.

'We'll find out if it's true,' Marylin said in a normal voice.

'How?'

'I'll call Althea and ask her.'

The idea was so simple that Roy, a direct, to-the-point woman, felt idiotic for having fretted all these hours without considering it.

Marylin asked, 'Do you have her number?'

'My book's at home.'

Marylin reached for the telephone: A. Stoltz was listed in the Manhattan directory.

'Let me talk – I'm her friend,' Roy said. 'It'll be easier for me.'

'I'm the actress, or meant to be,' Marylin retorted, gripping the telephone firmly.

Roy held her breath. Her sister pressed the receiver to her ear; then a muscle jumped near the beautiful mouth, raising the upper lip for a vulnerable instant.

She jammed her finger on the button.

'Why are you hanging up?' Roy demanded. 'Did you chicken out? You should have asked for Althea.'

Marylin's sea-coloured eyes glittered in her stark white face. 'I didn't need to,' she said. 'Billy answered the phone.'

65

That same Thursday afternoon Marylin booked an early-morning flight to New York for Saturday, reserved a hotel suite and mailed Althea a special-delivery note: she would be in New York this weekend, and would Althea join her for drinks Saturday evening. *I'm staying at the Regency, and for me it's easier if we meet privately in the suite – I hope you understand. It'll be just the two of us.*

Marylin kept mum about the *folie à deux* of Billy and Althea, not mentioning it even to Joshua. Neither did she disclose her New York journey. Instead, she told her family that she needed to invigorate her flagging body with exercise and massage at the Golden Door Spa.

She spent the final two days of *The Rain Fairburn Show*'s work week bottled up inside herself, a preoccupation reminiscent of her studio days. Once assigned a role, she had withdrawn, not talking out her interpretive thrust even with the director, reasoning superstitiously that her emotional impact would poop out before reaching the camera's unerring eye.

She no longer felt rejected by Billy. In her mind, Althea was a blend of Judith Anderson's Medea, Lucrezia Borgia and the Wicked Witch of the North. How could she blame her boy for being spirited away on Althea's broomstick? In her mood of heightened maternal outrage, she was determined to wield all her talents to rescue him.

She was flying on one of those new jumbo jets. As soon as she buckled up in her first-class seat, she opened an undersize looseleaf whose spine was gone. She had used this notebook during the filming of *Island*, and had kept it – another superstition – for every film, putting in a fresh supply of lined paper on which to jot down notes to herself. Even for the simpy comedies, she had filled page after page with each particular woman's family background, transgressions, pet peeves, affections, aversions, gestures, sexual idiosyncrasies, musical and literary preferences, medical history. Inevitably, from this plenitude of detail she had uncovered the core of the character. This time, however, she was not moulding a fictional persona. She was ransacking her memory cells for images of Althea.

She was still writing when the plane landed.

On the drive into Manhattan she concentrated on her notes, not looking up until the limo passed above the East River. Her eyes were slightly bloodshot from working in the pressurized cabin. 'Althea never could bear people laughing at her,' she said aloud.

Having secured the key to Althea, she flipped back through pages of neatly written observations. At the Regency, the desk clerk handed her a message slip: 'See you at 5.45, Althea.' Marylin let out a relieved sigh. It goes without saying that she had fretted about her course of action if Althea did not show. (Would she need to camp outside of Althea's apartment building, or what?)

Miniature liquor bottles stocked the mini-fridge under the bathroom counter, but she ordered fifths of Scotch and vodka to be sent up at 5.15 along with an hors d'oeuvres tray. The next two hours she absorbedly prepared herself as she would for the camera, shampooing under the shower, blow-drying her brown hair, applying cosmetics in her magnifying travel mirror, donning a black silk jersey exactingly selected to dignify rather than glamorize her small body.

At precisely a quarter to six, the door buzzer sounded.

Marylin took a deep-breathing-exercise breath before answering.

Althea stood there in a honey-toned midi-suit with matching boots.

It had been years since Marylin had seen Althea, and she stared across the threshold at her sister's friend. She, too, was prey to that indefatigable arch devil, Time. Lines were pressed at the corners of Althea's eyes, and a fine wrinkle showed near the base of the still-firm throat.

Althea stared back, her head raised haughtily.

In this moment of empathy, however, Marylin recollected that Althea had always hidden awkwardness behind a facade of snooty reserve.

'Come in,' Marylin said with a surprising note of affection. 'Althea, I was so very sorry about your father.'

'Yes, I got your condolence note.'

'Won't you sit down? Let me fix you a drink. Vodka? Scotch – there's everything else in the refrigerator.'

'Why should we clutter the occasion with social amenities?' Althea inquired in an abrasive drawl. 'Let's get on with it, shall we?'

Marylin's misplaced generosity faded. 'I want to talk about Billy.'

Althea's mouth formed a quizzical smile. She said nothing.

'He told us he was going to make a movie and had arranged financing. He made a big mystery about who was putting up the money. Sari thinks you were pretty darn interested in him.'

'And clever little you put two and two together.'

'Then it's true, isn't it?'

Althea shrugged her shoulders. 'Marylin, maybe in Hollywood people play this sort of game with each other, but I find confrontations vulgar and distressing.'

Althea's disdain might be a front, but it chilled regardless. Althea had her claws in Billy. Marylin's mouth had gone dry, and dread swirled through her, but she managed to abdicate her inner ravages in favour of her particular discipline. Deciding that her diminutive stature was against her – she had played a similar scene with Barbara Stanwyck in *Recaptured Past* – she sat in a wing chair, her spine erect. 'Distressing?' she asked. 'How about the smirks when people see you with a boy younger than your son?'

'I couldn't care less what's in their nasty little minds,' Althea retorted.

'I'm not throwing myself on your better nature, Althea. Whatever Roy says, I'm not sure you have one. I'm only pointing out that you and Billy as an item aren't likely to escape being in the trash newspapers.'

Althea smiled as though she were thinking of a wickedly risqué jest. '*I* don't set out to be in them, dear heart.'

'Yes, but if there were some sort of scandal . . .'

'As I live and breathe, a threat. You'll set the *paparazzi* on me, is that it?'

'I won't have to. You're a Coyne, and they know it. As soon as they figure out Billy's my son, they'll swarm.'

'So I'd be wise to drop him, is that your gist?'

'It's the only sensible thing.'

'How do you think *he'll* feel?'

'It has to end eventually.'

'*I* haven't let myself think about *that*, Marylin, but Billy has. Oh, hasn't he just. He's talking marriage.'

Marylin could not control her tremors: she clasped her hands tightly to hide the shaking. 'Wouldn't that make a headline? "Billionairess Bags Baby as Fourth Husband".'

'Ouch,' Althea said. 'But, Marylin, dear, there's no point in discussing this with me. Your dear Billy is the one who's pushing for wedding bells.'

'He doesn't understand what he's getting into.'

'He's a full-grown man, a terrific, immensely talented man.'

'I'm his mother. I know that.'

Althea raised her chin. 'Joshua helped your career, and it seems to me there was a minor age discrepancy – aren't I right? I do seem to recall you mooning after his son.'

You bitch, you unutterable bitch, Marylin thought. '*My* marriage,' she said with all the dignity she could muster, 'is not what we're discussing.'

Althea shrugged again. 'I only imagined that Billy might remark on it, he might say something.'

'Believe me, Althea, I know the media. They'll have

489

catch-phrase jokes on the six-o'clock news. They'll print your very worst photographs. You'll be sold at the checkout lines. The public eats up this kind of story the way they do candy bars. Oh, how they love to feel superior to the rich.'

'Dear heart, I've already caught your point.'

'You and Billy as a couple is the next best thing to a juicy society murder.'

'There's no need to hammer away. I'm really quite subtle.'

'Wait until they're hounding you.'

'Marylin, you have a one-track mind. Let's not prolong this discussion.'

'It'll get a hundred times more coverage than your marriage to Firelli. In those days, news of the men coming home from war kept everybody occupied.'

Althea rose and glided to the door. 'Byeee,' she said almost gaily.

And with that, she let herself out.

A draught swept the room.

Marylin's slight body shuddered. Some fight I put up, she thought. Less than ten minutes. She didn't crack one iota. I've probably shoved her into marrying Billy. She destroys everything she touches, especially talented men. That poor German refugee killed himself, probably Gerry did too.

A nauseating odour like decaying flesh filled the air-conditioned air. Marylin realized that the smell came from the uneaten canapés, whose aroma she had considered appetizing a few minutes ago. Grabbing up the silver tray, she started for the door to put it in the hallway; then, fearing she might see Althea, she veered to the bathroom, gagging as she flushed the creamy pink morsels down the toilet.

Down the corridor, the floor was tilting like a slant board, and Althea had to hold on to the wall. Her breathing was harshly audible. She couldn't have been in Marylin's suite much more than five minutes, yet she was a defeated and broken shambles.

She had come to the Regency filled with memories of Roy's sister – ethereally beautiful and soft-voiced – anticipating some sort of gentle maternal concern that she could handle. This Marylin, though, had been an avenging deity out of myth, an implacable earth goddess who was dressed in smart black jersey and endowed with the super-human power to obliterate any who offended her. She transformed and transcended herself – like Mother, Althea thought with a tortured little gasp.

Faint music drifted through the corridor, and Althea made her way along the tilting floor to the elevator. A couple dressed for the evening emerged from a nearby room. With a delicate sneer, she rode down with them.

As the taxi wove through the Saturday-quiet streets, she let her head rest on the torn plastic seat cover and closed her eyes. Her mind jumped tormentedly along the well-worn steps from that old impotent rage to utter helplessness.

Oh, God, now I've done it. Now I've done it!

Made a public spectacle of myself.

Her fears touched on Charles. If he hears about me and Billy, he'll see me as a sex-crazed, pathetic old bag. Oh, I'll die. What is that noise? Is the driver playing a classical tape? Calm down, think it through. This is a civilized, quiet affair, discreet. I can ditch out before that hillbilly Hollywood slut spills any beans, before she strips me naked to my enemies.

The taxi halted. Calling to the doorman to pay the fare, she entered the foyer unsteadily. Inside the building, a metamorphosis occurred in her mind. From her previous frenetic free association, her thoughts began moving with unnatural slowness and intensity.

I will not be a mass laughingstock, she thought over and over.

She stepped into the elevator.

I will never risk losing Charles's esteem.

Billy was stretched on one of the living-room couches, a large yellow legal pad propped on his knees: from both Marylin and Joshua he had picked up the note-making habit, and since he'd been assured of the financial feasibility of his movie, his quick, fertile brain swarmed with comedy routines.

Setting down the pad, he puckered up in a harsh wolf whistle. 'Hey, hey, pretty lady, that's some nifty outfit.'

'I aim to please,' she said. Did she sound lightly pleasant? Was this a normal kind of remark? 'You haven't moved a millimetre since I left.'

'I thought of an ending. It burst over me like Fourth of July fireworks. Interested?'

'Speak on,' she said, sitting near him, gazing at him a little too devoutly.

Billy's mouth opened and closed, he gesticulated and gestured, and she knew he was drolly recounting an antic finale, but his words were meaningless.

She had never been quite clear up to now what she felt for Billy. He rejuvenated and revived her. He slept curled in a foetal position. He spoke exuberantly with – what was that throat-clearing word everyone was using now? *Chutzpah*. His blue-green eyes adored her. His cock was endlessly hard – why do I need it so much the last couple of months? *You're a supah lady,* he would say. In his arms, she felt like a normal person.

Billy was staring at her. 'Well?' he asked.

'Fabulous.'

'You're hiding that enthusiasm well.'

She stretched her lips in what maybe was a smile.

He regarded her soberly, then came over, bending to kiss her, a long, tender kiss, stroking her hair. 'The mean blues got you again?'

'I'm tired, that's all. Last night – ' she tried a leer, ' – left me a *peu* weary.'

'Listen, don't try to kid old Doc Fernauld. He's a specialist in you. Tell me what's wrong, and I'll kiss it again and make it better.'

'I just saw your mother.' She stopped abruptly. Was this a wrong thing to say?

'My mother? Marylin Fernauld, the beauteous Rain Fairburn?'

'Yes.'

'When I talked to Dad last night, he said she's secluded at a fat farm.'

'She's at the Regency. Suite 1803.'

Billy sat down slowly on the ottoman, his hands bracing his bony knees. After a moment or two he said, 'Let me guess. She's come incognito to the Big Apple to plead that you throw me back into the sea of amorous girls through which I routinely swim.'

Music played far away.

'And?' Billy flexed his fingers. 'You said to her?'

'I was so blind angry, who can remember.' Althea flicked her head. 'Billy, is the radio on in your room?'

'No. What did she say?'

'That's strange. It sounds like Mozart.'

'Can you remember mentioning I'm quote serious, un-quote?'

'When I did, she retorted: "Get thee hence, crone".'

'God, what gall! Here she marries a guy older than my grandmother, and then kicks up because I fall for a lady a few years my senior.'

'There's always a slight advantage being on the younger side of the situation.'

'Did Great-Grandpa Firelli tell you that?'

The music was louder, absolutely that dread Mozart horn concerto. 'I'm positive there's a radio on, or a stereo.'

'Will you quit changing the subject?' Billy jumped up. 'If you want to know, sometimes it crosses my mind you've offered me financing for *Capers* as a consolation prize.'

'Whatever happens, you have backing for your movie.'

'That's reassuring,' he said snidely, but his face had a look of anguish.

'Billy, please go and turn it off?' She could not control the quaver.

'There *is* no goddamn radio on!' Suddenly he darted across the room, pulling her roughly to her feet, wrapping his arms around her, pressing himself close to her.

She went wet and shaky with desire.

Suddenly she resented everything about her responses, resented the way the ground now seemed level, resented her lips kissing his mouth, resented her wanton hands as they caressed inside his jeans, resented the quivers in her pelvis.

Yet, surrounded by a fortune in ancient Greek vases, she clung to Marylin Wace's son.

'The bedroom,' he muttered, picking her up, and the wiry strength of his thin body as usual astounded her. She groaned with frantic delight as he forced her to kneel at the side of the bed. He yanked down her panty hose as far as her boots permitted, thrusting himself into her. She cried out again, this time an ecstatic wail that rose, then fell uncontrollable octaves.

As twilight darkened the lavender stripes between the slats of the shutters, they undressed and shifted onto the bed, twining their bodies in a variety of positions, and she utterly lost herself in the plunges from orgasm to orgasm — her rampaging descent into the pit of carnal oblivion was marked with uninhibited coital moans and cries.

It was dark when they finally lay spent side by side.

He switched on the light, peering at her, his eyes naked without his glasses. 'You love me,' he said as if stating an axiom.

'Yes, darling, I know it,' she said. Had he not calmed her crazy imbalance, silenced the baleful chords? Yet she could not have the world laughing at her, could she?

She could not risk losing Charles's respect.

The next morning, when Billy went off for his regular Sunday tennis date, she had coffee in bed. Leaning against the pillows, she telephoned all her friends whom she knew were in town. The question that popped up over and over again was: *But where have you been, darling?* She would give a ritualized trill of laughter and reply that she hadn't felt much like circulating since her poor father died, and then on the other end would be murmurs of condolence followed immediately by a brightly spoken invitation or a suggestion of lunch? A weekend on the boat perhaps? A few days at

494

'our place by the shore – we're having some interesting people'.

Invitations.

Dozens and dozens of invitations.

When Billy arrived back at the flat, she was showered and dressed in beige slacks and a creamy striped Giorgio Armani shirt. Over brunch she informed him she had quite a few engagements this week.

'Engagements?'

'You know, lunch and dinner dates.'

He gazed across the omelet and brioche. 'So,' he said, 'the Rain Fairburn school of acting got to you.'

'Time I went out again.' Was it a shade off-key, her voice?

'Am I included?'

'You'd be bored. My friends aren't exactly the *jeunesse dorée*.' There. That was better.

'Jesus Christ! I'll dye my hair grey and walk with a cane, how about that?'

His caustic outburst was accompanied by a pleadingly intense glance that, magnified by his glasses, struck her as inordinately funny. Her laughter bubbled out.

'God, Althea, it wasn't that excruciating,' he said. 'Okay, so we'll see each other when you aren't on the social seesaw.'

'Maybe I'll go over to Sweden for a few days.'

'You destroying bitch! How can you take off when you just told me you're too busy to pee!' His shout was more like a wail.

'Don't pout, dear heart.'

Colourful Italian pottery and crystal clattered as he jumped up from the table. He barged from the elegant dining room, his shoulders slumping as if he'd been lashed with a wet whip.

And she heard that music again.

495

66

When Marylin arrived home on Sunday evening, Joshua was out. He always slept until after ten, so they had not had a chance to talk in the morning, either. As she drove back from Channel 5, he awaited her on the front patio.

With a flourish, he opened her car door. 'Welcome home, angelpuss.' He kissed her. 'Eaten yet? Or did they put you on a fast at that cockamamie spa?'

She took his arm. 'I wasn't at the Golden Door.'

She felt his thick bicep tense.

'So where the hell were you?' he barked furiously. His jealousy had increased in direct ratio to his inability to avail himself of his conjugal rights.

'New York.'

'Who's there?'

'Billy.'

'Billy?' Joshua's muscles relaxed. 'So how goes it with our boy?'

'He's living with a woman – '

'So what else is new?' Joshua interrupted, winking. 'How is he? What's with him?'

She explained tersely that she had not seen their son, and that the woman involved was Althea Cunningham Firelli Wimborne Stoltz.

'So that's how our stud comedian's getting his financing.' Joshua chuckled lewdly. 'For services rendered.'

'He wants to *marry* her.'

'No need to look like the apocalypse is descending on us, Marylin.'

'Didn't you hear me? He's begging to be the fourth Mr Althea Coyne Cunningham.'

'Put your sweet mind to rest, little mother, he's merely spinning her the oldest line. Stop worrying about our Billy, he's grown, and endowed with more than enough moxie to take care of himself.' Joshua glanced back at the massive ironbound front door, which he'd left ajar, then spoke in a lower tone. 'Sari's the one we should be fretting over.'

'That family! They're fatal to our children.'

Joshua crossed himself, grinning to inform her he did not subscribe to such superstitious methods of averting the evil eye. She knew, though, that after a lifetime of flamboyantly outspoken atheism, he had lately been sneaking over for early Mass at the Church of the Good Shepherd on Santa Monica Boulevard in Beverly Hills. His overtanned, dark-spotted face settled back into elephantine creases of worry. 'Angelpuss, I don't like to think this, but our Sari might be, as my dear, departed sainted mother used to put it, in trouble.'

Marylin sucked in her breath. Remembrances of her illicit abortion jumped ruthlessly into her mind. A swallow rustled noisily from the nearest oak, and leaves swayed above them.

'Has she told you anything?'

'It's not her words, it's her sad, wan look.' He raised his palms, an unhappy admission of masculine helplessness. 'I don't know what's up. Time for you to have one of those mother-daughter talks.'

'Where is she?'

Joshua drew Marylin inside the entry hall, which was floored with the same handmade tiles as those outside. 'Have your lunch first. You've got to take care. You've been looking somewhat dragged out – beautiful, haunted, in need of creature care. I worry about you, angelpuss. Kids I've got plenty of, but I have only one wife.' His thick arm encircled her possessively, and he bent to touch a kiss on her forehead. 'Such as she is.'

He ate a large platter of cheese enchiladas, one of Elena's specialities, drinking cups of the strong, chicory-rich coffee whose beans he ordered air-freighted from Fauchon on the Place de Madeleine in Paris. Marylin barely tasted her cottage cheese and fresh peach. Setting her napkin on the breakfast table, she said, 'I'll go find Sari now.'

'If she's not in her room, she's probably mooning around at that old shack. As far as I'm concerned, she's up that damn hill too often.'

Sari wasn't in her snug eyrie, so Marylin put on her tennis shoes and started up the path.

As she crossed the footbridge, her motherly anxieties were briefly diverted by the sound of rushing water. Her business manager paid the bills, so she was ignorant of the sum that went to the Department of Water and Power to pay for this stream, but she guessed it to be exorbitant. Each month her outrageous paycheque disappeared, swallowed up by expenses and she sometimes awoke in the night, shivering at the thought that *The Rain Fairburn Show* might be cancelled. She had never felt comfortable in this lordly style of living but Joshua – once among Hollywood's tribal leaders, now left behind by the glitzy pack – needed conspicuous consumption as he needed air to breathe.

Across the bridge, the path was no longer defined by bricks. The Fernaulds' acreage was gerrymandered into an odd shape like a clenched fist with one pointed finger that climbed the canyon wall. Marylin started the long, steep hike up to Sari's hideout.

A flat white cloud passed across the sun and momentarily the breeze faded. In the odd light and unstirring stillness, she had the eerie sensation of being an intruder in the distant, vermeil world of photographs made in the previous century. Sari's world, she thought, asking herself what right she had to encroach?

She climbed more swiftly and her forehead had a delicate sheen by the time she reached the ledge.

In the shade of a clump of live oaks stood a derelict cottage. Crumbling adobe bricks showed veins of whitewash. Many of the roof tiles were gone. Nobody knew when the place had been built, but it probably wasn't as ancient as it appeared – adobe crumbles quickly back into the earth from whence it comes.

This was Sari's retreat, her refuge from the inevitable hurts of childhood and adolescence. She had never shared the place with anyone until Charles.

The sun had come out again, and at first Marylin did not see her daughter, whose dark blouse and jeans were camouflaged by a pool of black shade cast by a live oak.

Then Sari raised her arm.

'Oh, there you are,' Marylin said, wiping a finger across her moist forehead. She sat on the cool, mulchy earth next to Sari. 'Whew, I'd forgotten what a hike this is.'

Sari gave a smile and said nothing.

Ordinarily Marylin relaxed in her child's quiet, but this afternoon she found Sari's unquestioning acceptance of her appearance as frightening, if not downright uncanny.

Gazing up at the sky, she said, 'Sari, I wanted to talk to you. We haven't really talked about Charles since he left.'

Sari shifted away a few inches.

At this faint though pointed antagonism, Marylin tried to focus on her daughter's face: after staring up at the sun, at first she could distinguish only a pale blur surrounded by dark curly hair. 'I thought talking might help.'

'He's gone, it's over. You never liked him anyway.' There was a tense misery in the accusation.

'I . . . I changed my mind about him '

'Oh, Mother, what's the use?'

As their similar husky little voices intertwined, Marylin shivered. This conversation, in its own way, was starting off as disastrously as the one at the Regency.

Now, able to focus clearly, she saw that the irregular features were drawn and pinched, that greenish shadows lay under the girl's eyes. Joshua could be right, Marylin thought, ashamed that she had not previously noticed the physical dimensions of her daughter's unhappiness.

'Darling, it's not Charles. I *do* like him. It's Althea – Mrs Stoltz.'

'Did you come up here to make things worse for me?' Sari put her head down on her knees.

Marylin's lips tingled with inadequacy and she blundered into a confession. 'I once had an abortion. It was years ago.'

Sari's head raised questioningly. 'But why did *you* do that?' she asked softly. 'Mother, were you on a big movie?'

Do I seem so monomaniacally absorbed in my career? Have I immersed my ghostly passion for a man I haven't seen since before this daughter was born so thoroughly that she, who is all feeling and intuition, sees me as a nun wed to the holy camera? Marylin drew a tremulous sigh. 'I was in love with somebody else. Of course, it was before I met Daddy . . .' Again her voice wavered.

'Why didn't you marry him?'

'The war. That's not the point. I've always regretted the operation, felt a huge burden of guilt and shame that I didn't have the courage to keep the baby.'

'Things were so proper then. How could you?'

'That's what Grandma said. But in my heart I've always felt I could have managed something if I'd been stronger and braver. Sari, darling, if you *are* pregnant, we'll figure something.'

Sari bent her head again, and her hair hid her face. 'Is that what you've been so uptight about? You're worried I'm having a baby?'

'Daddy thought, well . . . maybe.'

In the ensuing silence the wind soughed, a warbler cried shrilly and a galaxy of gnats buzzed.

'Are you?' Marylin whispered.

Sari gazed at a distant point above the ridge of the canyon.

'Sari?'

'My period was sort of funny, not much. And I've been feeling rotten.'

'We'll see a doctor,' Marylin said decisively.

Sari turned. Those strange, greenish shadows made her eyes hypnotic. 'I'll go on my own,' she said.

'Sari, I . . . Your father and I want to help.'

'Help me to an abortion?'

'I thought I explained that.' Marylin closed her eyes. '18

April 1943, that's the date. I've never been able to forget it, it's haunted me all these years.'

Sari considered, her face showing its bone structure. In this moment she resembled Linc. My God, what a tangle, Marylin thought. What a monstrous, unbelievable tangle my entire life has been.

'Daddy'll kick up a fuss. You know how he is about me.' Sari's voice was choked and wavery.

Marylin heard her daughter's words as a lament for lost love, as a dirge of hopelessness for the future . . . and as a surrender to parental aid. She touched the girl's slumped shoulder. 'Darling, haven't you noticed that he's been going to Mass? He won't push you.'

Another cloud had passed over the sun, and Sari shifted, leaning forward, kissing Marylin's cheek.

'What's that for?' Marylin asked.

'Not saying that we could make Charles marry me.'

Marylin had not considered marriage: it was punishing enough, wasn't it, that the unborn child's other grandmother was Althea?

67

That same afternoon, mother and daughter drove into Beverly Hills. The offices of Dr Dash, Marylin's gynaecologist – still considered the town's best and classiest – remained in a white-painted brick medical building on Bedford Drive. (In this same building Roy still occasionally consulted with her psychiatrist, Dr Buchmann.)

Women in all stages of pregnancy crowded Dr Dash's prettily furnished waiting room. Though Sari lacked an appointment, the reception nurse – who was on the Fernaulds' endless Christmas-card list – slipped her into an examining room.

Seated between two heavily pregnant women, Marylin

hid behind a *Cosmopolitan*, not reading, assaulted by unremitting waves of primitive hatred. Her small fingers clenched the slick cover, and she thought: I could strangle both of them, Althea and Charles, with my bare hands.

'Miss Fairburn?' The nurse with the thick legs was beckoning her. 'Miss Fairburn, Doctor would like to see you.'

Dr Dash faced Marylin and Sari across his desk, reading them the results from rushed lab work, adding with a stern glance that though he was against terminating pregnancies except for health reasons, Sari *was* anaemic and underweight. He was offering them an easy out.

At twenty past five mother and daughter emerged onto Bedford Drive. Neither spoke. In the brilliant late-afternoon sunlight, Sari's pallor was more extreme. Marylin, too, had a dazed expression, but her eyes were hidden by dark glasses. Incognito in her trim white slacks, the famous Rain Fairburn hairdo concealed by a scarf, she could have passed as another of the *sportif* Westside matrons shepherding their generally bulkier female offspring between the boutiques.

The two were silent until they reached the parking structure; at the ticket taker's booth, Sari halted. 'I'm going over to Patricia's,' she said.

A diesel pickup emerged, spreading fumes and noise. Marylin blinked, positive she had heard incorrectly. 'Patricia's?'

'I figured I'd spend the night with Aunt Roy,' Sari said.

'*Now*? Darling, didn't you understand what Dr Dash said?'

'I'm pregnant.'

'Yes, but he seemed to think, well . . . maybe . . . you aren't in very good shape . . .' Marylin's voice trailed away. I sound like Mama, she thought, wanting to throw her arms around her pale child, then kneel on the pavement to beg forgiveness.

'I told you. No abortion.'

'That's not what I meant . . . not really. But we should talk the situation over with Daddy.'

'I have to get my head together,' Sari said.

A taste of bitterness was in Marylin's mouth. My other child deserting me, she thought. But Sari looked so exhausted and haggard that Marylin could not argue. 'Go on, darling.'

'It's nothing against you, Mom. You're being wonderful. I just need time, that's all.' She hugged Marylin.

Marylin's bitterness faded, but not the obdurate pressure of her maternal anxiety. Pushing back the soft black hair, she said, 'I'll call you later, Sari, darling. Say hi to Auntie Roy.'

Roy had only one lamp on in her pictureless living room and in this tea coloured gloom she watched a moth batter itself against the window. Not since Gerry died had she been swept by such self-remorse. On the cobbler's-bench coffee table was a near-empty plastic Oreo carton: the oversweet chocolate cookies were a poor substitute for the good stiff drink for which Roy's body, after all these years, cried out.

The den-guestroom opened onto the living room, and the door was ajar. Sari slept.

On the short drive home from Patricia's, the girl had briefed Roy on the situation. When Roy had attempted to show her sympathy, Sari had murmured in a wispy, shredded voice, 'Please don't say anything, Aunt Roy. I just can't hack talking about it yet.' At the house she had eaten a carton of peach yogurt, then gone silently into the den to make up the convertible sofa. Roy, leaving the dishes on the breakfast table, had stationed herself like a guard dog outside the room, keeping her ears pricked for any sound – there had been none.

Without thinking, Roy munched the last cookie, then clasped her arms around herself. Her self-indictments had reached unbearable proportions and she must either go clear, screaming out of her mind or seek solace – of any kind.

She ran into the kitchen, where her voice would not disturb Sari, dialling a number she knew by heart: the exchange told her Dr Buchmann was unavailable tonight. Roy barged back into the living room, going to the hutch that served as her home desk, opening the top drawer for her pink scratchpad. The psychiatrist had suggested when the overpowering blues hit her she should jot down her thoughts as a cathartic measure to rid herself of her worst self-indictments.

Althea, she wrote, then chewed on the end of the ball-point.

Until now she had always accepted that she kept up the friendship out of her innate sentimental attachment to the past – loyalty, if you will. Now, though, listening for the least sound from Sari, Roy came around to Marylin and NolaBee's contention that she possessed the best of reasons to avoid Althea for all eternity.

So why did I have to renew the friendship?

The answer twisted into a question: *Was this another way to tie Gerry to me?*

Did it somehow keep him closer to be around his mistress and his son – the son he never knew about?

Gerry never loved me, we were separated when he died, so why have I dragged my widowhood everywhere, like a security blanket? Men have asked me out from time to time – why didn't I accept? Why immure myself? I'm not Queen Victoria. I built a monument for him, The Gerrold Horak Gallery, wasn't that enough?

Roy's eyes moistened.

For years I've known that Althea was, as Marylin put it, a snake, so why did I bring both Billy and Sari within striking range of her venom?

She stared down at her round, legible questions, biting her lip.

Why do I assume Althea broke it off between Charles and Sari? For all I know, Charles was delighted to dump the poor, loving baby and begin anew in Stockholm with some gorgeous Scandinavian blonde. Oh, so what? He's Althea's son, and without good old Roy, Sari never would have met him. Without my good offices, Althea never would have gotten her nympho hooks into Billy –

There was a rustling within the den. Swiftly Roy moved to the door, opening it a wedge wider.

Her niece slept facedown, both thin arms hugging the pillow. In the colour-drained shadows, the hair on the pillow was a dark stain. Like blood, Roy thought with a shudder.

Sari, in her brief explanation, had made it clear that she had no intention of an abortion.

An illegitimate baby?

A great roaring sound filled Roy's mind.

Gazing at the dark splotch on the pillow, she felt her throat tighten in a convulsion of pitying love.

She peered at the sleeping girl, her expression changing until she wore her workaday look of competence and decision. Returning to the couch, she picked up the scratch-pad, this time not for easement of her soul but to draft a letter. 'Dear Charles,' she wrote; then her hand stilled. Roy's correspondence, mostly business letters, was dictated concisely to her secretary. Now she composed a meandering paragraph, then crumpled the paper. She floundered through the procedure four times before getting out her box of monogrammed stationery.

She wrote one sentence.

Signing her name, she folded the paper into an envelope, addressing it to *Charles Firelli/Sveavagen 56/Stockholm/Sweden* — she knew the address by heart, having already sent Charles several letters that purposefully mentioned Sari. (He had replied in his impeccable hand, never mentioning Sari.) Pulling on her coat, she again peered in at her sleeping niece before going out into the misty night, hurrying in long strides to the corner of South Beverly Drive, where the mailbox stood.

Swiftly she pushed the envelope inside, and the slot clinked shut.

At this moment Roy's second thoughts rushed out. Maybe Sari's right, maybe Charles *has* dumped her. How do I know whether he's a love-'em-and-leave-'em type? If he is, better she get over him now. Being trapped in a marriage with one-sided affection is a hell I wouldn't inflict on my worst enemy much less this vulnerable-hearted girl whom I adore. Between us, the family could give the baby

505

enough love to make up for lacking a father. What have I done?

She raised the slot, reaching her hand inside to encounter cold, rough metal.

Her letter had been swallowed by the hump-topped inviolable United States mailbox.

Charles would read her words.

The faint haze in the air sent chills of premonition travelling down Roy's back. *I never should have left Sari alone.* Her front door lamp shone iridescent ahead of her, and she ran gasping up the steps.

Sari had not stirred.

At breakfast Sari asked whether she could stay a few days. Roy, with a very human elation that she was needed more than Marylin, waited until she got to work to call her sister at the television station.

'But she'll be alone all day,' said Marylin's gentle, worried voice.

'That's what she said she wants. To crash someplace until she can get it together.'

'She told you . . .'

'Yes.'

'Roy, Dr Dash said she's run-down and needs to put on weight.'

'She had two eggs, English muffins, orange juice and a glass of whole milk for breakfast,' Roy said. 'I gained a pound watching her.'

'Be right with you, Jack,' Marylin's voice said from far away. Then she spoke into the instrument. 'Roy, you wouldn't believe the scene going on here. A guest didn't show. I'll get back to you – oh, my God, all I can think of is Billy and Sari. How am I going to manage today?'

'The show must go on, hon,' Roy said. 'It's the same for all of us working girls.'

Sari was still at Roy's house four days later when the letter came from Billy.

68

Normally Joshua's morning walk from his cottage-office to the mailbox by the electric gate was the highlight of his morning. He would climb back up to his little house with the letters, not showing them to Marylin, purposely imputing importance to their contents. On this particular hot, smoggy Wednesday he was attending the funeral of Pearlie Lubold, former chief of production at Magnum, a form of final obligation to his industry friends that was becoming onerously frequent.

Therefore a neat pile of letters, magazines and junk mail (the bills were mailed directly to the business manager's office) awaited Marylin on the hall table.

The smog and lack of sleep bothered her eyes, and she squeezed her lids shut before she shuffled through the envelopes.

When she came to a thick letter addressed to them in Billy's handwriting, the heap thudded onto the uneven handmade floor tiles. Billy never wrote to them, he always telephoned – and since she had made that calamitous New York trip, he had not called anyone in the family.

She picked up her son's letter. Tears filled her eyes – Sari's troubles and Billy's desertion had made Marylin weep easily.

After a long hesitation, she slit the envelope's edge. In the shadowy silence, the tearing noise sounded very loud.

5 June 1970

Hey Dad,

After scrutinizing the envelope to reassure herself that she had indeed been included on the address, she did not even try to tell herself that this omission in the body of the letter was unintentional. Obviously her son was paying her back for the disastrous *tête à tête* in the Regency Hotel; when hurt, Billy took on Joshua's clever vengefulness, a heavy streak of malice that her milder nature found incomprehensible.

Let's rap awhile about what's going on in the land of the free and the home of the brave.

I don't know about you, but sometimes I get the feeling this war is an enormous put-on, all done with mirrors and dress extras for the telly. A gigantic scam to sell advertising on prime-time news, not to mention bumper stickers.

Is there really such a country as Vietnam? Or are the battle scenes shot in the Philippines? Is Premier Ky a little-known off-off-Broadway actor with his eyes taped? Is Saigon really on the back lot? You made enough flicks to understand my question. Reality versus sleight-of-camera? And what about the My Lai massacre – was it a cleverly concocted script?

And how about this protective incursion Nixon has ordered on the alleged country 'Cambodia'?

I mean, is that or is it not far-out humour?

Could there, in reality, be such black comedy as daily body counts? I for one cannot believe it.

The question I am aiming at is: has our beloved St Richard the Nixon figured out a means of aiding the flagging economy of ours by inventing Southeast Asia?

Wars give a jab in the arm to industry, so why wouldn't a dedicatedly patriotic president appoint a clever bunch of showbiz types to invent one?

You can understand my frame of mind? Good. Then you'll also dig why I went into a recruiting office.

Marylin sank onto one of the paired hall chairs. Her hands were too shaky to hold the letter, so she smoothed the pages on her lap.

The sergeant on duty, a bluff old party, a ringer for Satchel Paige, embraced me. 'Welcome, son, welcome,' he wept. 'We don't get you college-type honkies often.' I received similar heartwarming unctuousness from everyone.

Imagine my shock, Dad, to hear I am physically deficient. Me, William Roger Fernauld, bred in clear Beverly Hills air, raised on Wheaties and fresh orange juice, *me* unwanted by my ever-loving Uncle Sam.

Marylin was mouthing the words, for the writing here fitted Billy's sharply overwrought jibing. T's remained uncrossed, O's unclosed.

This was my first concrete proof that the so-called battle for democracy in SE Asia is pure government bullshit. I ask you, if there really were a war, would they discard a volunteer able to count the bodies even into the hundreds simply because he once had a skull injury?

Marylin breathed a great sigh, retroactively blessing the driver of the car that had hit Billy.

By now my curiosity is thoroughly aroused. I have, therefore, used my friendship with the guys at *Rolling Stone*, and am on the payroll as a correspondent to bring home the real dirt on the situation. What ho, a foreign correspondent just like Bogey played so often. (Yes, Dad, I remember that you were his drinking buddy, I remember meeting him and wondering why he had hair in his movies.) I've had my shots and I am booked on a flight to 'Saigon'.
As soon as I find out the straight dope, I'll clue you in.
Give my love to Sari.

Marylin clasped the pages against her abdomen.
Billy in Vietnam. This was the bitter fruit of her weekend in New York.
Slowly she climbed the stairs to the large bedroom she shared with Joshua, to await his return from Pearlie Lubold's funeral.

'I do not believe this letter. That half ass, overintelligent clown of ours enlist? Sweet loving Jesus, he's more against this fucking, stupefying crusade than anyone in this torn-apart country!' Joshua's flamboyant bluster was all front.

In his own demanding, overpowering manner he deeply loved all four of his children, but Billy, son of his old age, was his illusionary self projected into the future to conquer this gadget-ridden second half of the twentieth century.

'The letter's not him – his humour's never overworked or cute.'

Joshua slammed a hand on his bureau, and his silver-topped military brushes bounced. 'He sounds like he's been experimenting with LSD, dropping acid or whatever they call their mind meddling.'

'It's my fault. I never should have gone to New York. Joshua, I've never interfered with him before. Why did I have to now?'

'Where in the letter, tell me, does it say he's been thwarted in love?'

'Althea, she must have done exactly what I wanted her to. Told Billy they were through.' Marylin's voice shook piteously.

'Angelpuss, quit blaming yourself.'

'That's easy to say.'

Joshua sat abruptly on the edge of the bed. The bluster had evaporated. 'First poor little Sari, now this,' he sighed. 'Sweet Jesus, what's happened to our kids?'

'The Coyne family,' Marylin responded bitterly.

'Billy's a comedy writer, not a war correspondent. Even those fuck-ups at *Rolling Stone* must have enough unscrambled brains to see that.' He slumped, arms dangling between his knees.

When Joshua had suffered his heart attack in the spring of 1956, he had refused to stay in his hospital bed for the medically prescribed six weeks of rest, leaving Cedars of Lebanon without his doctor's permission after twelve days to polish his current script: Joshua Fernauld had put his heart on probation. The doughty muscles had obeyed him all these years.

But now fierce anxiety pierced Marylin. 'Joshua, it isn't the end of the world,' she said in a tone of purposeful cheer. 'After all, he's not a soldier, he's a reporter.'

Joshua didn't reply. There was no reason for him to. Billy was courting danger, and they both knew it.

After a minute he said, 'It's time to talk some sense into him.'

'Joshua, we don't have a phone number. There's no return address on the letter.'

'Your sister's friend.'

'Hahh!'

'I'll soften her with reminders of how, lo these many years ago, I offered her comfort when she came to your mother's house in search of it.'

Althea's servant informed Joshua that Mrs Stoltz was out of town and would remain away for several weeks. Joshua then dialled *Rolling Stone*'s offices in Greenwich Village. Marylin's concern about his bum ticker faded. This was the Joshua Fernauld of old, ranting, booming, bellowing in the roar that had shaken the film hierarchy above and below him. Evidently the people on the other end were unimpressed. He did not find out William Fernauld's whereabouts.

He took out his three Gucci telephone books, thumbing through the alphabet for the most influential people, General Omar Bradley, US Army, Ret., Buffie Chandler, Henry Kissinger, Pat Kennedy Lawford, Governor Reagan.

BJ and Maury came over, and then NolaBee. The pinochle crowd. Roy. Among them they knew yet more heavyweights. The Fernauld phone lines stayed busy until long after midnight.

It was Secretary of State Kissinger who called back to inform them that Billy was already in Saigon, an accredited member of the press, and that the death rate for newsmen was pretty low.

69

Just before eleven on the following Sunday, Roy – smart in her new navy slacks with matching blouse and a taupe blazer – stood in her backyard cutting zinnias to take to the Fernaulds' where they were having brunch. Later, Sari would return here with her. Joshua and Marylin flinched from inflicting their daughter with their hyped-up anxieties about Billy.

The cheerful orchestration of a Beverlywood Sunday bubbled around Roy – the masculine voices broadcasting Dodger warm-up, the racket of a neighbour's car starting up, the gleeful shrills of toddlers as they splashed in their wading pool. Roy paid no attention to the sabbath choir.

The full sunlight did bad things to her freckles and small lines around her eyes and mouth. The family's dual crises had invaded her nights, yet at the same time her nurturing side got a real kick out of being needed by Sari. She knelt to clip an especially fine bloom.

'Auntie Roy,' Sari was holding open the kitchen screen door.

'Be with you in a sec, Sari. There's a couple more really luscious ones.'

'You have company.'

'Oh, nuts. Hon, tell whoever it is we're leaving right now.'

Sari moved onto the cement patio. 'It's Mrs Stoltz,' she said in a low voice.

'Althea?' Roy's grip on the flower stems tightened. Every trace of her perennial loyalty had been washed away on that night earlier in the week when she had accepted Althea as the instrument of her niece and nephew's downfall. But how could Althea be here? During the week's interweaving long-distance calls, Joshua had learned that she was in Sweden. 'Are you sure?'

'Oh, Auntie Roy!'

Roy peered at the house. In this glare the living-room windows were inscrutable blanks. It took her a few seconds to make out a tall, narrow shape that was – unmistakably – Althea.

Roy's first impulse was to step protectively between the pregnant girl and Althea. In the next instant she determined to get her niece away. Draping an arm around Sari's shoulders, she whispered, 'You go pick up Grandma.' (Joshua had driven Sari's Pinto to Beverlywood.) 'I'll spend a few minutes with her.'

'The way she looked at me, it was wild. Do you think she's angry because of Charles?'

'Sari, anyone ever tell you you're too darn sensitive?' Roy asked, improvising. 'Sometimes she has migraines.'

'I mean really weird. I'll wait for you, then you'll have a better excuse not to hang around with her too long.'

Althea had moved to the window. Though Roy could discern only the pure oval face, Althea surely must see the two of them in sharp, sunlit detail. Goose bumps formed below Roy's silk blouse. 'Grandma's waiting for us!' Her whisper was hoarse.

'I don't like leaving. She's – '

'She's upset because her father just died.'

'Auntie Roy, listen, she's really giving off bad vibes. If you're trying to get rid of me so you can have it out with her about Billy – '

'Don't be crazy. Now, will you please go pick up Grandma?'

'Okay, okay.' Sari moved towards the kitchen door.

Roy hissed, 'Go out the gate.'

'My purse is inside with the keys. Auntie Roy, what is with you?'

Althea opened the glass door that led from the living room.

'Althea!' Roy cried, setting the garden shears on the low brick wall of the patio. 'What a fabulous surprise! Sari said you were here, and I didn't believe her. When did you get into town?'

Frowning delicately, as if Roy had presented an insoluble problem, Althea stepped onto the cement patio.

Roy gave Sari a little push. 'Bye, dear – you guys start eating without me.'

'It was nice seeing you, Mrs Stoltz,' Sari said.

Althea's chin lowered a fraction, a minuscule movement that might, if generously construed, be labelled a nod.

Sari went into the kitchen; then the front door opened and shut. Roy expelled a breath of relief.

Althea said, 'The paintings are gone.'

'On loan. Gerry's having a retrospective.'

'Oh, yes, now it comes back to me.' Althea's voice was rushed. 'UCLA sent me an invitation.'

Sari's right, Roy decided. Something's badly out of sync. Her gaze darted covertly over Althea. The exquisitely pleated cream silk blouse and gored leaf-green Chanel skirt were heavily creased, as if slept in, and a few strands of pale hair straggled from the chignon. Even in their earliest adolescence Althea had always groomed herself meticulously. She was gripping her large, soft kid purse with such tension that the flesh had whitened around her brutally short nails. Had Althea ever been a nail-biter? Yes, that last grim semester she had attended Beverly High.

'Let's sit down,' Roy said, keeping her voice even, shifting one of the redwood patio chairs invitingly.

Althea did not stir from her listener's pose until the roar of the Pinto's engine faded into the Sunday sounds.

'What about something to drink?' Roy asked. 'There's nothing hard – not since you dried me out. But I do have Snap E Tom? Orange juice? Coffee?'

'Is she gone?'

'Sari? Sure. That was her car.'

'I don't suppose there's anybody else inside?'

'Of course not. Althea, you really look like you could use a little pick-me-up. Come on in the kitchen.'

'We'll stay out here.' Althea's imperious tone trailed off in a plaintive quiver.

'Sure, why not? Isn't this a perfect day? But first let me fix us some coffee.'

'I hardly flew all the way to Los Angeles to be entertained with instant coffee,' Althea said.

A lawn mower had started in the yard behind, and the sound rasped on Roy's uneasiness. 'Althea, what is it?'

'I want to know why you wrote that to Charles.'

'Wrote what?' Roy asked, bewildered.

'The letter.'

'Althea, you know he and I've always kept in touch.'

Althea opened the purse, taking out Roy's stationery. 'This.' She extended linen paper.

Roy could read her own writing. *Charles, there is something of absolute urgency to you that we must discuss in privacy immediately, so please telephone me at Patricia's (not the house) as soon as you receive this.*

The note she had composed with such effort on the night she'd heard about Sari's pregnancy. With her fears about Billy, she had completely forgotten writing and mailing it.

'Oh, that,' she said. 'It's nothing.'

Althea placed the folded, heavy linen sheet carefully on the redwood barbecue table. Her face and posture had the brittle, mannered look of an eighteenth-century porcelain fashion doll. 'What a distasteful way you've chosen to pay me back,' she said.

'Althea, what in heaven's name are you talking about?'

'For Gerry.'

It was the first time in years either of them had mentioned the unfair triangle. Despite their friendship, Roy had never completely left behind the pain and jealousy that surrounded being an also-ran with her own husband. Her throat ached as she asked, 'Anyway, how did you come by this?'

'I flew over to Stockholm for a few days.'

'So? Does Charles share his mail with you?'

'Hardly.' Althea prowled across the patio onto the grass. 'I saw the envelope with your writing, so I opened it.'

Revulsion choked Roy. From earliest memory, she had

515

embraced every dictum of her generation's ideals. She behaved with absolute rectitude. Never in her life had she opened even a catalogue addressed to another person. And now it flashed through her mind that Althea had never possessed this same code of honour. What a snap it must have been for her, arranging that the Coyne New York Bank dispatch Charles to Europe.

The lawn mower ceased. In the abrupt quiet, the chirp of a bird, the babies' shouts, the radios seemed sweetly, innocently bucolic.

Althea was staring at her fixedly. 'Well?'

'That's a rotten thing to do, snoop.'

'You don't have a child.' Althea plucked a camellia leaf. 'Want to know my deepest regret?' This question was confided, jarringly, in the significant tones of their girlhood confessionals. 'My . . . deepest . . . regret . . .' – Althea drew out the words on a long, plangent chord – 'is . . . telling Roy . . . Wace . . . about . . . Charles . . . and . . . Gerry . . . Horak.'

Roy jumped to her feet. 'You think *that's* why I wanted him to phone?' she cried, aghast.

'What else? You and he can't share any other urgent interests, can you?'

'Althea, listen to me. I would never in a million years betray a confidence, certainly never one this important. You know me better than that.'

Althea arched a pale, delicate eyebrow knowingly.

And into Roy's mind came a picture of her nephew – her dear, fidgety comic who used to drop by her house to devour her cakes and make her laugh until the back of her throat ached. Billy the peacenik trying to enlist, Billy in Saigon, Billy being helicoptered into some remote, godforsaken, Cong-infested jungle – Billy. 'But I suppose that it's only natural *you* would see it that way. My God, what happened with Billy? How did you manage to mess him up that much?'

'Billy?'

'Yes, Billy.'

'Where does this concern *him*?'

'You don't know he tried to enlist?' Roy wailed.

For a moment Althea's narrow, shapely lips twisted, as if in pain; then she said, 'I fail to see that a young man serving his country is such a lamentable thing.'

Roy's heart lurched, then raced furiously. 'It turns out he's 4-F – so he's gone into Cambodia as a press observer.'

'He's supposed to be a writer, isn't he?'

'You fishblood!' Roy shouted, her fingers curving as if to rake the length of that hatefully arrogant face until the blood flowed. '*Your* son's safe in Stockholm counting the family's money, while my nephew's being defoliated! He's always loathed this stupid Vietnam mess, he's done everything he could to stop it!'

'Let's not knock warfare. Through the ages it's worked miracles for immature boys.'

At this supercilious contempt for Billy's plight, rage swept through Roy until her whole body trembled.

'I can't believe we were ever friends!' she exploded. 'You're right! I ought to pay you back! If Charles discovered he's not Firelli's son but *my* husband's bastard, you wouldn't be the saintly, high-toned mother figure, would you? No. He'd see you for what you are! A cheap, lying whore!'

The long, oval face had jelled into impassivity.

And all at once Roy realized that Althea was bathed with sweat. When had this drenching begun? Surely only in the last minute or so; otherwise she would have noticed the soaked crescents under the armholes, the drops on Althea's forehead and cheeks.

Roy's rage subsided in a rush of appalled pity.

'I didn't mean that,' she said quietly, moving a step towards Althea. 'God, not at all. Listen, I've always been so grateful that you told me. It's meant a tremendous amount, knowing that Gerry wasn't cut off from the future. I swear I'd never tell. Never. Althea, that promise I made, it holds. It'll hold forever.'

'Charles's respect is everything to me,' Althea pronounced, twirling the camellia leaf so it reflected the sun whitely.

517

'I had something personal to explain,' Roy mumbied. 'That's why I asked him to phone.'

'I'll do anything I must. Anything. I don't suppose I can buy your silence?'

'Stop talking like this! Okay, so I blew my stack just now. But my God, Althea, surely you can't believe I'd go back on my word?'

Althea's drenched face did not shift from its graven, accusatory stillness.

Roy added, 'To tell him – to tell anyone – would be ugly, dishonourable. A really nasty thing to do.' Roy halted. *A really nasty thing to do.* God, how dumb it sounded. Roy Wace Horak, Miss Priss.

'Charles wouldn't believe you. Still, you might give him a doubt or two about me. I couldn't bear him doubting me.'

'Althea, I didn't *mean* that. It was my temper talking.'

'All his life, Charles's been special, a unique person. So far above the clods of the world that even they recognize it. He's exceptionally strong, he's brave. He's always in absolute control . . .'

Althea was listing her son's virtues in that queer, abstract tone while rivulets of sweat dripped down her cheeks and jaw onto her sodden collar.

Symptoms that Roy's commonsensical mind refused to file in the correct slot.

Crazy.

But she had known Althea too many years to accept that her friend had strayed around the bend.

Maybe she's having an early menopause, Roy thought, embarrassed. Maybe it's a hot flush. Waiting until Althea fell silent, she said, 'Come on, let's go inside. I'll fix some iced coffee.'

'I have to protect him, you do understand?'

'Oh, absolutely,' Roy said soothingly. 'Come on in the kitchen.'

'*My* mother never protected me.'

'It won't take a moment. I don't boil the water.'

518

Althea snapped open her envelope purse, reaching inside. Her hand emerged holding a gun.

Roy gaped at the small pearl-handled pistol.

She could not relate to the reality of the smooth, elegantly designed object. Oh, her optic nerves passed on the concept, *handgun,* but her occipital lobe refused to accept the message. She was as incapable of mentally registering this object as a lethal weapon as she was of accepting Althea's derangement. How could she?

This was a pleasant Sunday morning in a tract built by Dillon Webber in Beverlywood, this was a small back yard in which the bi-weekly gardener had planted two flats of zinnias. This woman was her oldest friend from Beverly High days, and an old Beverly High chum wearing Chanel *prête-à-porter* does not stand in the middle of your dichondra pointing a handgun at your chest.

Handguns belonged on television series. Handguns were worn by Brink's men picking up the cash deposit. In James Bond and other thrillers, Roy's preferred reading, handguns were invariably mentioned by make and calibre.

Lay that pistol down, babe, lay that pistol down, Roy thought idiotically.

Then, as if a dam had broken, actuality burst over her.

Althea intended to kill her.

Vital strength flooded to every cell of Roy's body. The mental capacity endowed by massive bursts of adrenaline informed her: *She's obviously clinical, so go easy, go very easy.*

'Althea,' she lulled in the syrupy tone with which she adjudicated the bickerings of her high-strung sales force, 'where did you get that?'

'It was my father's. Mother, the great custodian, stands guard over the care of his sacred possessions. Collies fed, bred and exercised, clocks and watches wound, books dusted, guns oiled.'

'Where does she keep it?'

'Where it belongs. The left-hand corner of the drawer of his bedstand.'

'You should put it back there,' Roy said.

'You'd adore that, wouldn't you? But you and she are the only ones who know about Charles, and Mother I don't have to worry about.' As Althea wiped her left hand across her forehead, sunlight dazzled on scattering droplets. 'Mrs Harry Cunningham isn't about to smear mud on the dear departed's grandson, his sole male heir.'

'Neither am I. Althea, you know me, exactly the same as your mother. I've never forgotten Gerry for a minute. He's still my everything. My big moments come when he has these retrospectives. You know I'd never harm his son.'

A small click.

Roy, despite her abysmal ignorance of weaponry, was aware that something called the safety catch had been released.

Panic reddened her vision.

Then her mind emptied of all its usual furnishing. She paid no attention to her frenzied fear, the subliminal borders of sounds, the smells, the brightness.

She was conscious only of a single command.

Get the gun away from Althea.

She edged forward, not hearing the lawn mower as it roared on again. Her little, mincing, Chinese-footbound-lady steps were the same as she had used to circle rattle-snakes when she and Althea had hiked in the Santa Monica Mountains.

Her total terror held an element of exuberance. In this instant she was her truest self, a primaeval creature whose mind and body are fused indivisibly, she was vibrantly alive as she had never been before. Her ankle hit a sprinkler head, yet such was her concentration that her body continued its glide and her eyes did not blink from Althea's oozing face.

They were less than five feet apart.

'Stop!' Althea ordered.

Go! Roy's command was not a thought but an all-enveloping instinct.

Crouching momentarily in her navy patent mid heels, she felt the stress of flexed power in her thighs. She felt blood fill the muscles of her arms. Her pupils were pinpoints and the retina held one brightly sunlit image. The buffed, jaggedly bitten nail of a forefinger pressed to the smooth steel trigger.

Now.

Roy lunged forward. An off-balance yet feline spring with her fingers curved like a jaguar's claws. Her right hand clamped convulsively on Althea's narrow, slippery right wrist.

Roy pulled, jerking.

Althea held firm to the gun.

Crooking one knee below Roy's trousered knee, she grappled Roy's capturing arm with her own left hand.

Thus for a prolonged instant they strained, adversaries stalemated in a clumsy wrestler's hold. Neither had ever fought physically, neither had ever attempted a contact sport. Althea, the taller, was stronger, Roy plumper and more desperate.

Roy's muscles strained. Sobbing, she butted with her shoulders.

Althea, with one foot raised, was caught off balance. Her eyes distended. Her mouth opened, white and frantic, as she staggered.

Galvanized, Roy increased her pressure on the slippery wrist, forcing the gun away from herself.

There was a dull, dry roar.

70

Althea heard the gun go off and felt its vibrating kick.

At that instant her body became unbearably cumbersome. Immense heaviness permeated her head and torso, the implacable force of gravity sucked at her legs.

What's happening? Althea thought wildly at the threshold of her consciousness.

With profound slowness, her body sagged.

And then the eternity of pain began, different from any pain she had ever experienced before, icy and torpid, crushing her chest, creeping interminably and inexorably outward to her extremities.

An endless echo resounded in her ears: 'Alllltheeeeaaa . . . Ohhhhhh . . . Go-o-o-o-d . . .'

Through the immeasurable agony, she felt the resistance, soft yet strong, to the engulfing inertia.

Roy's holding me up.

I was going to shoot Roy. But why . . . ? Roy's my friend . . . my only friend, ever . . .

She tried to say, *I didn't mean it, Roy, friend, other of the Big Two. I'd never hurt you.* But the immense pressure on her throat distorted the words into a gasp.

Then the vast, freezing pain drew her eyelids shut and she saw white bolts and flashes.

It might have been centuries later that she heard the infinitely distant rolled out thunderclaps. 'Altheeeeaaa, ohhhh, pleeeease hang on. Pleeeease? Altheeeeeaaa . . .'

Something rested on her chest, an intolerably endless pressure. The torment released her sphincter muscles and she opened her mouth in an eternal shriek of agony that came out as the faintest sigh.

I'm dying, she thought without surprise or sorrow or regret.

And by some merciful dispensation, she was released from the human time frame.

Althea is in her bed, surrounded by the darkness, the terrifying darkness, the creaking darkness. Something in her room has jerked her awake. In her breathless jitters, she tells herself to be brave. Daddy will protect me – there's no evil he can't vanquish.

Another creak.

'Who is it?' she quavers, paralysed.

The horrible thickness of a heartbeat crowds through her.

The lights burst on.

Not the tepid glow of ordinary electricity, but a shadowless brilliance that illuminates more radiantly than a hundred suns,

*enabling her to see with wondrous clarity each shading of the
rainbow blues in her pretty chintz curtains, the dappling of the
sycamore bark outside her windows, the graceful miniature horses in
her collection.*

*Her father's idolized face, so handsomely ruddy in this unearthly
glow, bends over her bed. 'I heard you call, Toots. What is it?'*

'I was scared, so scared. Somebody was in the corner by the door.'

*'It was us, dear,' says Althea's mother. She bends over the other
side of the bed, her eyes warmly loving.*

'But you're meant to be at a party.'

'We came home early to be with you at midnight, dear.'

*Champagne-scented kisses press warm on both of Althea's cheeks.
'Happy New Year, Happy New Year,' her parents chorus, repeating
an old litany from her babyhood. 'Our Althea is so happy and good.'*

*The sweetness of this alternative existence enveloped Althea, and in
her last blink in mortality's embrace, she thought with uncomplicated
spontaneity: Yes, that's really truly true. I am happy and good.*

71

The arching fingers unclenched and lay limp on the wet
grass.

Roy, gasping from the struggle, her heart racing wildly,
knelt beside Althea. There was a small hole in the tucked
silk blouse above the left breast, a thin circle of oozing
redness.

Althea lay starkly motionless.

Just a minute earlier it had been an impossibility for
Roy's mind to accept the handgun, so now her thoughts
refused to articulate the word 'dead'.

Althea's hurt badly.

She jumped to her feet. Halfway to the kitchen, where
emergency numbers were Scotch-taped inside a cabinet, she
thought of Dave Corwin, the young paediatrician who lived
across the street. She was trapped in a paralysis of indeci-

sion (the phone? the neighbour?); then she swerved, barging out the back door, sprinting down the side of the house and across the street, banging both fists on the black paint of the Corwins' front door.

Dave answered, barefoot, wearing blue checked Bermudas.

'Accident! A bad accident,' she gasped out. Frantic about deserting Althea, she raced back across the narrow, trafficless street to her house.

At the side gate she halted, staring at the body sprawled on the dichondra. Now she was unable to deny the stonelike rigidity. Althea looks so small, she thought, edging towards the still form. In this short time, the flesh of the serenely vacant flesh had fallen back from the delicate aquiline nose, the refined, narrow lips had assumed an odd, tilted curve.

The shot must have killed her instantly. Maybe she was dead before she hit the ground.

Dead . . .

Roy's knees buckled and she sank over her friend. All of their later ruinous jealousies and divisions were purged from her heart and she was drenched by excruciatingly poignant memories of those distant days when they had formed a united front against the other adolescents at Beverly High. Their secret jargon . . . the station-wagon door blazoned 'The Big Two' . . . the long happy dithering over a lipstick shade at Newberry's or Thrifty Drugs, the dark enchanted hours shared at the Fox Beverly . . . club sandwiches at Simon's . . . the hot sands of summer, interminable hours talking on the phone – about what?

Roy bent, pressing a tender kiss on the still-warm forehead.

She was kneeling there, rocking back and forth, when Dave Corwin, barefoot, carrying his bag, rushed through the gate.

The pleasant sounds of Sabbath leisure and chores were drowned by sirens. Motorcycle police arrived, then black-and-white squad cars, an ambulance, a hook and ladder.

The immediate neighbours already milled on the sidewalk in front of Roy's picket fence. Two members of the LAPD, one black, one Mexican-American, barred further encroaching. At the front door a thickset sergeant tapped his billy club into his palm. The doctor's wife, feeding her baby his bottle, was surrounded by eddying groups as she repeated over and over what she knew of the dire goings-on at Mrs Horak's. 'She banged on the door and my husband rushed over – he's still inside.'

Revolving lights pulsated atop squad cars, police calls barked in a constant staccato.

The sense of high drama peaked with the arrival of a genuine star, Rain Fairburn.

Joshua, his sagging, furrowed face grimly set, double-parked and wrapped a thick arm around Marylin, propelling them through knots of onlookers and reporters – a CBS station wagon had pulled up just ahead of them.

In Roy's living room, Marylin's steps faltered. She stared out the window. Roy's tidy little backyard seemed jammed to overflowing. Jauntily short-sleeved cops, plainclothes-men, photographers flashing vivid lights, a couple of medical types in white jackets lounging in the patio chairs drinking Tabs, neighbours gawking from their sides of the six-foot redwood fence.

One of the conferring plainclothesmen moved.

Marylin had a sudden clear view of green grass marked with a drawing, a white figure of a woman that might have been drawn by a child. Inside this outline lay Althea. It was difficult to believe she was dead. She wore a blouse that seemed to be embroidered by peasant hands, a reminder of the adolescent Althea who (with Roy) had outfitted herself in odd costumes.

Then Marylin realized her mistake. The blouse's rusty pattern was not embroidery but life's blood.

'Don't look at it,' Joshua said, pulling her away from the window.

The den was filled with cigarette smoke. A slight, narrow-jawed man, a Tareyton dangling from the corner of his mouth, leaned against the wall as he interrogated Roy. A youngish, balding man clad only in blue check Bermudas sat on the couch next to her.

With her pallor and the streak of blood marking her tan blazer, Roy looked a shaken wreck. As Marylin and Joshua came in, she clutched the hand of the man in shorts as if to introduce him. 'This is . . .' Her voice dwindled.

'Dr David Corwin,' he said.

'God, Dave, I've only known you ten years!' Roy said.

The doctor said to Joshua, 'I'm the neighbour who phoned you.'

Roy released his hand. 'Thank you for hanging on here until they came, Dave,' she said.

'Don't be silly,' he said, getting to his feet. 'If you need me for anything, no matter what, holler across the street. I'll be there.'

Marylin took his place next to Roy, gripping her sister's shaking hand in her own trembling one.

Joshua stood over the couch, blocking the two women from the narrow-jawed detective. 'You shouldn't be answering questions, Roy,' he said, the deep, rumbling voice concerned. 'I've called Sidney Sutherland. Don't say another word until he gets here.'

The detective nervously took the cigarette from his mouth. 'I read Mrs Horak her rights before she gave her statement.'

'I've got nothing to hide,' Roy said mechanically as if repeating the words for the umpteenth time. 'Althea came here all upset. She had a gun, but I'm positive she didn't really intend using it – you know how long we've been friends. I tried to take it away. She struggled. There was only one shot. An accident, I've told Sergeant Torby all about it. An accident, a horrible, unbelievable accident . . .'

Marylin put her arm around Roy's tensely held shoulders, and Roy, crumpling towards her sister, began to cry softly.

A cop in uniform came in and whispered to the narrow jawed plainclothesman, who nodded.

'The gun registration checks with Mrs Horak's statement.'

'So?' Joshua asked bellicosely.

'It belonged to the father of the deceased.'

'Then there's no further need, dammit, to badger Mrs Horak.'

The ruffle curtain windows let onto the backyard, and masculine voices drifted into the smoky den. The detective glanced outside. 'I have to talk it over with the captain,' he said. 'This is a bigger number than I can handle.'

'In other words,' Joshua rumbled, 'if the incident hadn't happened to a member of the puissant Coynes but to one of us peasants, then Mrs Horak would be free and clear?'

'You and Mrs Fernauld are hardly in the peasant class, Mr Fernauld, but that's just about it.' The plainclothes cop stubbed out his cigarette. 'Christ, a Coyne! Why couldn't this have been my Sunday off?'

The violent death of Althea Coyne Cunningham Firelli Wimborne Stoltz crowded both the Vietnam war and the domestic struggles against it from the evening news. Old photographs of Althea were flashed onto the screen. Only CBS News could boast jerky, handheld-camera shots of her covered body being wheeled from the garden of a tract house to the waiting ambulance. On radio and television, in the late editions, Althea was tagged in many ways: widow of the famed conductor, heiress to the largest family fortune on the globe, granddaughter of Grover T. Coyne, divorced wife of a distant cousin of the Queen of England, a socialite, a jet-setter, a close friend of Jackie Onassis.

CBS also showed a shot of Rain Fairburn being rushed into the house by Joshua and another clip of Roy and Marylin, hiding their faces, as they got into Joshua's Rolls-Royce Silver Cloud.

'Miss Fairburn's sister, Roy Horak, owner of an exclusive Beverly Hills women's shop, reportedly fired the death weapon. She was released on her own cognizance. Her sister, actress Rain Fairburn, hurried her from the scene.

Police are evaluating whether criminal charges will be filed. This is Terry Drinkwater reporting from Erica Drive, West Los Angeles.'

72

There was no question of Roy staying in her own house: she slept at NolaBee's.

Joshua arranged a press conference – 'It's easiest to satisfy the fourth-estate bastards in one fell swoop,' he said. On the following morning, Monday, he arrived before nine to make sure that coffee, Danish and plenty of name-brand booze were set out. At ten he sat next to Roy in NolaBee's dining room, once more the joke-slinging, gregarious pro from Hollywood's Good Old Days when the press was treated to extravagant weekend junkets.

Minicams and Nikons were aimed, tape recorders adjusted, notepads taken out.

'Have you any explanation for Mrs Stoltz coming to your house with a gun?' asked a frizzy-haired woman.

'Yeah, why would anybody want to shoot anybody?' interjected a stout television man. 'You, Rain and Mrs Stoltz were three lucky kids.'

'You had everything,' added George Christy from the *Hollywood Reporter*.

There was the sound of pencils and ball-points scribbling.

'Did she have any motive?' persisted the frizzy-haired newshen.

'None,' Joshua replied for Roy. 'But Mrs Stoltz had been under a great deal of strain since her father's death.'

Joshua expertly fielded most of the questions.

After exactly an hour, he pushed to his feet. 'That just

about wraps it up. Mrs Horak looks all in – this has been a tremendous strain on her. But we all agree she's been more than candid and very generous with her time.'

There was a scattering of applause, and everybody, including Joshua, departed.

Roy sank panting onto the living-room couch. But Nola-Bee's loquacious concern threatened to smother her. The only escape was to get out of the house.

Roy zigzagged aimlessly along the quiet Beverly Hills streets between Wilshire and Santa Monica Boulevard. Her body ached from the intensity of that struggle for the gun and her strained efforts to ease Althea's floppy slide to the ground. Her right ankle ached dully from hitting against the sprinkler head. She couldn't shake off an overpowering sense of guilt. Why had she mailed that dumb, mysterious letter to Charles? Why, when Althea showed up obviously deranged, had she not attempted calming measures, then slipped away to dial Dr Buch-mann for professional advice on how to handle things? Surely there had been a smoother way of getting the gun than trying to wrest it from Althea. *All my fault, my fault*, repeated her silent words.

Sunk into herself, Roy ignored the discomfort of the new patent shoes she'd put on for the press conference until a jagged tenderness in her left heel and right big toe informed her she had blisters. She limped homeward.

In front of NolaBee's house a nondescript grey coupé was parked. *Another* reporter? she thought. Maybe it's a sympathy caller. Whoever, I don't need 'em. She would have kept walking, but with each step the stiff patent dug into the raw flesh, so she hobbled up the narrow cement path.

NolaBee sat in the furniture-crowded living room with Charles.

For a moment of sheer masochistic relief, Roy imagined that Charles had come as an accuser to press charges. Charles's red-streaked eyes and controlled greeting, however, showed no trace of condemnation.

'I just got in,' he said.

She embraced him. 'I'm so sorry, Charles. I can't tell you how torn apart I am.' Tears ran from her eyes.

'You mustn't blame yourself, Roy.' A trite platitude that many had uttered, yet Charles said it firmly.

They pulled apart.

NolaBee's gossipy voice was already flowing. 'Charles says he wants to have a little private talk with you, Roy,' she said. 'I'm going in the other room directly. Charles, you will remember, won't you, to tell your dear grandmother that I'll drop over to express my sympathies the minute she feels up to it. Your mother was a right fine girl, Charles. What a terrible accident – it just doesn't seem possible. I cannot believe she's gone . . .'

NolaBee embroidered on this theme of personal incredulity until Roy said raggedly, 'If you'll wait a minute while I change my shoes, Charles, we can take a walk.'

She striped Band-Aids over her blistered feet, then went into the back bedroom. Here, NolaBee, a pack rat, stored boxes and cartons of her children's past. Roy found a pair of loafers from her college days.

Outside, in the smoggy sunlight, Charles took her arm. 'About an hour ago I talked to a Captain Sullivan,' he said. 'The police aren't filing any criminal charges.'

Roy sighed with relief. During the long, wakeful night, she had conjured up scenes from the hundreds of detective novels she had read, movies, TV shows, envisioning herself as unjustly sent to trial, maybe even sentenced to life. 'You're sure, Charles? There was some talk of referring the case to the district attorney's office.'

'Who told you that?'

'One of the reporters today.'

'Reporters,' Charles said coldly. 'We've had to post guards outside Belvedere to keep them out.'

'Was it the gun being registered in your grandfather's name that convinced the police?'

'Actually, when the detective took your statement, he had it evaluated an accident. But because of who Mother is . . .

530

was, he didn't want to seem negligent, so he referred the case to Captain Sullivan.'

'Charles, I could have handled it better. She was so shook-up, so obviously not herself.'

'She took Grandfather's death very hard,' he said, then paused. 'Since he died, she's been behaving oddly. The family said those weeks I was in Sweden she stayed holed up in her apartment, not taking any calls. Then suddenly she made scores of dates. I can't understand why. She was flying over to see me.' He paused again. 'At Belvedere, she didn't even say hello to Grandmother.'

'She only wanted the gun, I guess,' Roy said, wincing. She could still see that round circle of blood spreading on white French silk.

'That's what I wanted to ask. Why should she want to hurt you?'

Roy's steps faltered.

Here was her chance at a full and blessed confession. He wants to know Althea's motive, and what's so wrong with telling him?

Is it so monstrous that he's the son of my husband?

Okay, it might jolt him at first. Charles isn't the type to be thrown, though. Later, maybe he'll even accept me as a kind of surrogate mother.

His reddened eyes were fixed on her, calm with command.

Blinking confusedly, she looked down. She still felt that enduring, endearing schoolgirl loyalty as strongly as she had decades ago.

'Roy?' Charles prompted. 'What did she say?'

'She was all upset.'

'She must have made *some* coherent remark.'

'Let me think,' said Roy, who since yesterday had traversed this mine-infested territory a hundred times. 'First I offered her coffee. She refused. Then she rambled a bit about coming over to see me, although it was nothing so special. Whenever she came to town, we got together.'

'That doesn't sound too distraught.'

'It really was. Her clothes were creased – all her life your mother was impeccable. I'd never seen her like this. Sari said she looked strange, too.'

'Sari?' Charles turned away, but not before Roy saw a muscle jump in his eyelid.

'She was staying over. We planned to have brunch at my sister's, and she left right away. Althea asked whether she was gone or not. That's how she was. A little off centre, as if she couldn't keep track of what was happening.'

'She seemed fine in Stockholm, but she was only there two days, workdays, so I didn't have much time with her. We planned to go to Lake Siljan for the weekend. I've rented a place there. Then . . . she just left. No message to the servants or anything. *That* wasn't like her, but I invented an excuse – she had met friends and would contact me any minute. I should have tried to find her.'

They walked half a block in silence.

'It's so senseless!' Charles burst out.

'She was under a lot of stress.'

'I know, but why pick up a gun before she came to see you? She must have intended to use it all along?'

Roy ducked her head. 'Stop trying to find anything rational in this, Charles. A death in the family is a terrible trauma. Anybody can crack. Believe me, I know. She was out of it, she didn't have any idea what she was doing, or why.'

Althea, old buddy, old enemy, other of the Big Two, even beyond the grave you can place your trust in Roy Wace Horak, also known as Miss Priss Trueheart, who keeps all secrets. Then, to Roy's shamed chagrin, her knees went weak. She clutched at the hard, lean masculine arm. 'When's the funeral?'

'We're flying her back East to the family burial ground,' Charles said. 'As soon as I get back to Belvedere, we're leaving.'

'Have you talked to Sari?'

'I called. She was out,' he retorted in a detached tone.

Roy held on to his arm more tightly, halting them. A jacaranda tree bowed over the sidewalk and fallen purple blossoms strewed the pavement blocks. 'Probably she was up at the old adobe. She'll be terribly disappointed not to . . . not to be able to express her sympathies.'

'To be honest, I don't care to trade on this kind of situation.'

'I thought you two had quite a thing going.'

'Unilateral, I'm afraid,' Charles said brusquely. 'She cancelled her plans for Stockholm.'

'She told me she thought you wouldn't be around.'

'My work does shift me from place to place – but she certainly realized I'd have made every effort to be with her and her cousin.'

'Niece,' Roy corrected without thinking, stifling an off-kilter inner laugh. *She* thinks he doesn't want her, *he* thinks she doesn't want him. What masters we all are when it comes to screwing up our lives!

'Charles, she thinks you're evading her.'

'She told you that?'

'I tried to argue her out of it, but does she ever listen to common sense?'

'She *is* pretty much all feelings,' Charles replied noncommittally.

'Charles, listen, I'm going to talk out of turn, and if you're angry, blame it on a buttinsky aunt. Sari's so wild for you that she's positive it's unfair pressure on you to tell you that she's pregnant.'

For a moment Charles's tear-reddened eyes stared blankly at her.

'She's pregnant,' Roy repeated.

'And never told me?'

'Something about not wanting to tie you down.'

'She hasn't done anything?'

'Oh, Charles, you know Sari.'

'No, she wouldn't, would she? Roy, she really *believed* I didn't want to see her?' he asked, his voice sounding softer, younger.

'What's so odd? You thought the same thing.'

His lips pressed together, an expression of relentless

concentration. Roy smiled, her eyes misting. This was how Gerry had looked when he painted.

'Let's get back,' he said, taking her arm and abruptly turning around.

He forgot his manners enough not to see her to the door. He did not say good-bye. He got into the nondescript coupé – it must be one that the Belvedere servants drove.

Roy shifted her weight on her blistered feet, watching him speed northward on Crescent Drive. She smiled as the car swerved west on Santa Monica Boulevard in the direction of Mandeville Canyon and Sari.

Book Eight
1972

Granddaughter of Grover T. Coyne, Althea Stoltz, slain under mysterious circumstances.

– Reuter's bulletin, 21 June 1970

COYNE HEIRESS SHOT TO DEATH – Chicago Sun Times, 22 June 1970

The question on everyone's lips is why American police have hushed up the murder aspects of the recent death of Althea Stoltz? Londoners remember her kindly as the ever- so-young Mrs Carlo Firelli and then as Mrs Aubrey Wimborne, a member of the small, closed royal circle. (Sources close to Princess Margaret report that she is greatly saddened by her friend's death.)

The rumours surrounding this mysterious death were increased by the sudden marriage of Carlo Firelli II, son of the heiress by her first husband, to Sara Fernauld, daughter of Rain Fairburn – and niece of Roy Horak, who wielded the murder gun! Conjectures have been made that the victim's vastly wealthy family has squashed the case to avoid scandal.

There has been no news from California about reopening the investigations.

– Women's News, London Daily Telegraph, 3 August 1970

The case has all the glamour and mystery of a best-selling novel. A beautiful, youngish, much-married heiress to incalculable wealth, a famous and beautiful longtime star of the movies and television, a

successful businesswoman, whose lives were intertwined from early
youth in the glamour capital of Beverly Hills.
— Mike Wallace, Sixty Minutes, *6 December 1970*

RAIN FAIRBURN SHOW EMMIES IT FOURTH TIME
— Hollywood Reporter *14 April 1972*

One of the decade's biggest news stories broke in a quiet West Los
Angeles neighborhood on Sunday, 21 June 1970. During a struggle,
a bullet fired by Roy Horak, widow of the artist, Gerrold Horak, and
sister of Rain Fairburn, killed Coyne heiress Althea Stoltz. The
mysteries of the case, not to mention the glimpses into the lives of jet-
setters, kept the Golden Girl's slaying in the news for months.
— Voice-over accompanied by clips of Roy Horak, Rain Fairburn,
Althea Stoltz and Jacqueline Onassis, from The Decade In
Review, *NBC, 31 December 1979*

73

On a drizzly January day in 1972, the planning conference for the following day's *Rain Fairburn Show* was cancelled, so Marylin started home a good hour earlier than usual.

A hundred feet before her driveway she slowed nearly to a standstill to peer apprehensively at the dripping shrubbery that concealed chain-link fencing. After Althea's death, reporters, photographers, thrill seekers, ardent fans had lurked in these bushes ready to sprint when the automatic gates swung open. Joshua, to ward off trespassers, had hired a guard service: for nearly a year, shifts of two armed men had sat here in a parked car. Marylin, despondent over the absence of both children, had found a wan ray of sunshine that Sari (with Thea, the baby, and Charles) was escaping the harassment by living in London. Finally the ferrets and groupies had given up, sparing the Fernaulds a monumental expense.

Though it had been months since Marylin had spied an interloper in the bushes, her finger shook on the remote control, and she had to press the button twice before the gates swung open.

On the patio she halted as she saw Joshua coming down the path from his cottage-office. She hadn't honked, so he was unaware of her early arrival. His head was hunched like a turtle's and his umbrella bobbled whenever he lurchingly descended one of the shallow steps. His slowness was due to the agony that wet weather kicked up in his arthritic left hip joint. An old, crippled warrior, Marylin thought, her chest aching with pity – pity that had Joshua suspected would have spurred him into furious revilements of her.

He raised his head towards the parking area and saw the car – not her. (If he'd spotted her, he would have waved.) Folding the umbrella, he swung it jauntily as he moved more rapidly – his old stride almost.

When he reached the spot where the path had been curved to save a clump of big live oaks, he stopped and staggered. The umbrella fell from his grasp. With both hands he clutched his big belly.

It was as if he were caught by a slow-motion camera as he sank. He sprawled onto his back, his head lolling over the edge of the path.

Marylin, already racing towards her husband, screamed, 'Joshua! Joshua!'

Reaching him, she fell to her knees, lifting his head. His perpetual tan was bleached to the yellowish shade of adobe bricks, and his flesh was beaded with globules of mingled sweat and rain. His struggles for breath came in great, raspy sighs. Marylin's body reverberated with each of his fleshy convulsions. Her heart thumped, echoing his heart's efforts.

'Hold on, Joshua, darling,' she cried urgently. 'I'll get help.'

'No . . .' The rumbling depth of voice was a thread of itself. 'My hour . . . has come . . .'

'The paramedics, Joshua – they'll get here right away. They've got equipment.'

'Don't want to be . . . old man . . .'

'Joshua, I'll only be gone a minute.' She was taking off her jacket to use as a pillow.

'No paramedics . . . no doctors . . .' The gasped whisper was a command. The corners of Joshua's dark, pain-filled eyes tightened as he gazed up at her. 'Stay.'

He had always, by means fair or foul, forced her submission to his will, and at this penultimate moment she found herself obedient to him. She would not go down to their

539

house to summon howling fire department ambulances, she would not attempt to further imprison Joshua Fernauld within his old man's infirmities.

Sitting on the wet bricks, she struggled to lift the heaving, slippery weight of his head onto her lap. Tenderly she stroked a wet oak leaf from his chin.

His face contorted yet more agonizedly, the barrel chest arched, the big, veined hands clawed the air.

Abruptly he relaxed, blinking up at her as if she were a double rainbow. '. . . Angelpuss, love you . . .' he whispered. '. . . blessed are you among women . . .'

His breathing rattled into the hush of the drizzle.

In this solemn minute while death robbed her of a husband, Marylin pondered the meaning of Joshua's final words. The dark eyes staring into the heart of the ultimate mystery gave her no clue.

There was only the sound of light rain.

Her cashmere pullover was drenched through, her hair streamed with rainwater, yet she did not move. Blinded by tears, she stroked back the grey hair of this oversize, infuriating, often cruel, always generous bull of a man, her husband, who had fathered all that she held most dear on this earth. *Ecce homo,* she thought. She was not positive of the exact meaning, yet somehow the Latin phrase explained all the contradictions that had bound her, recalcitrant and balky, to him for these long decades.

Ecce homo.

In the bedroom wall safe, Joshua had stashed the complete arrangements for his final ceremonies and rites – an act of egotism, perhaps, but one that made life easier for those who were not quite sure how things lay between Big Joshua and God.

A requiem Mass was conducted at the Church of the Good Shepherd. He was given sanctified burial.

The next Monday evening, every seat in the Academy theatre was taken for the Joshua Fernauld Memorial – planned, of course, by the deceased. The old Hollywood and the new alike showed up, some dressed in grotty jeans and gold chains, others in dark suits; Loretta Young, Fred Astaire, Greer Garson, Jane Fonda and Henry Fonda; Art Garrison, Darryl Zanuck; Groucho and Joan Crawford, Warren Beatty, Governor and Mrs Reagan.

For thirty minutes that seemed less than five, the screen flashed with clips of Joshua's brainchildren that he had spliced from prints of his favourite films – three of them had won Oscars. Then, according to the deceased's directions, the children that he had sired stepped onto the stage. Billy, who had flown in from New York, where he was working for Coyne New York Bank, read a section of his father's first novel. BJ, her loud voice faltering through the PA system, essayed the closing paragraphs of his second novel. Sari gave a speech from *Eternal Vigilance*, which Joshua considered his finest film. Her words were often halted by tears.

Joshua had planned that his oldest child would conclude the memorial with Lieutenant Nesbitt's farewell from his screenplay for *Island*. The family questioned how he had been so positive that Linc, after all these years of separation, would come to the memorial. It turned out to be by sheerest chance that Linc was not there. Researching the life of Kemal Atatürk, he was driving a jeep through the wild northern Turkish countryside, and despite BJ and Maury Morrison's urgent cables, couldn't be located.

Thus it was Marylin's huskily soft, skilled voice that came over the microphone. The Academy theatre echoed with snorted back tears and heavily blown noses when she came to Lieutenant Nesbitt's final words, which were the only words spoken on this Monday night not written by Joshua Fernauld: 'Though I speak with the tongues of men and of angels and have not charity, I am become as a sounding brass or a tinkling cymbal. And though I have the gift of prophecy and understand all mysteries, and all knowledge, and though I have all faith that I could remove mountains and have not charity, I am nothing . . .'

* * *

When Linc finally returned to civilization, he sent off long letters to his three siblings. His condolence to Marylin was brief: 'I mourn him. Whatever my father's faults, he knew them, and never denied them. There won't be another like him.'

Though Linc echoed her own innermost thoughts, Marylin found cold comfort in the note. Why was it so short? Had Linc felt forced by the dictates of good manners to communicate with her? Did he assume that she did not mourn his father?

Marylin had always worked too hard to be much of a brooder.

But widowhood had shattered her in a way that she had never anticipated. How could she have imagined that Joshua's death would so utterly fell her? After all, he had never possessed her whole heart, they hadn't shared a bed for over a year, she had her career. Shouldn't she have been able to cope? Yet Joshua had extricated the centre of her being as neatly as if it were an apricot pit, taking it with him.

The Spanish Colonial on Mandeville Canyon had always been a crushing financial burden. She put the property on the market. In 1972, though, Southern California real estate was suffering one of its recurrent slumps and no qualified buyers appeared. She rattled around in the labyrinth of rooms whose spaciousness seemed yet more hollow without her late husband's booming voice, his heavy step, his massive body, the comings and goings of the bouncy, chipper old men who were his gambling buddies. She no longer pumped the stream. Without its expensive chatter, the trees of her canyon soughed with loneliness.

When the spate of sympathy calls had dwindled away, she began taking her meals on a tray by her bedroom fireplace, emerging from her room only to drive to the television studio. *The Rain Fairburn Show,* too, seemed an exercise in futility without Joshua's extravagances to support. She kept working only out of resigned inertia.

NolaBee, whose weakening eyesight had forced her to give up night driving, would come over in the afternoons to fret endlessly around the perimeters of her gorgeous daughter's lethargy. Roy used the telephone in an attempt to haul the widow out of her depression – the same ploy Marylin herself had used on her sister after Gerry's death.

Sari spoke on the transatlantic telephone every few days: her sensitivity helped Marylin's depression – briefly.

BJ dropped by the house often. 'You mustn't let it get you down, Marylin,' she would say, shaking her head. 'You've got to push yourself and get out.'

At the beginning of April, BJ suggested that she and Marylin take a couple of weeks' vacation in England.

'It's the perfect time for me. Maury's all wrapped up in a very complicated case.' A flush showed on the big, caring face.

'What about my show?' asked Marylin.

'No problem getting fill-in hosts for a couple of weeks,' BJ asserted. 'We'll stay with Sari and Charles in London. We'll sneak Thea away and I'll give you lessons on how to spoil a grandchild rotten.'

'I can't just take off.'

'If you were sick you wouldn't be doing the show, would you?'

'I'm not sick.'

'Marylin, we all miss Big Joshua, but face it, the last thing Daddy would have wanted was for you to go into a nose-dive decline like this.'

'You make me sound like a Victorian lady. Still . . . it *would* be fun to see the baby.'

'We'll take her to Eastbourne.' Again there was a hint of fraudulence in BJ's enthusiasm. 'I've never been to East-bourne.'

Marylin agreed to go. She accepted that this holiday had come about through BJ's machinations, and she was grateful: for the first time since Joshua died, she was roused from her dull lassitude.

In the week before they left she was busy making her

arrangements and buying gifts, so she did not stop to consider that BJ, whose propensity for minding other people's business had grown with the years, might have something else up her sleeve.

— 74 —

Eastbourne is a seaside resort sixty-odd miles southeast of London, where the chalk cliffs of the South Downs dip into the coastal plain. Three levels of terraced promenades face the Channel: the salubrious invigoration of these walkways was the major reason that Firelli had made his home in the staid beach town.

Marylin and BJ spent the first ten days of their vacation at Charles and Sari's big, casually run house near Hyde Park in London. The company of her happily married daughter and son-in-law (Marylin and BJ privately agreed that marriage had done wonders for Charles) delighted Marylin, but what restored her spirit most was her black-haired granddaughter, Thea. She and BJ wrapped the toddler in the lacquered perambulator, wheeling her on jaunts to Hyde Park, to Kensington Gardens, to Richoux for an ice cream. The plan was for the two friends to take Thea to Eastbourne for the weekend, but on Thursday the child's tiny (but definitely Fernauld) nose was clogged.
'We'll have to cancel,' Marylin said.
'That's ridiculous,' snapped BJ with a querulous note of alarm.
'How can we take her with a cold?'
'So we'll leave her for one night. Marylin, I'm warning you, I'm not going to miss my chance to tell everybody about staying at the Firelli museum.'
Weekends, Charles opened the downstairs rooms of the Eastbourne house to Firelli buffs and serious music scholars.

544

The library, music room, lounge and drawing room were chockablock with memorabilia. Literally hundreds of gold plaques, silver presentation trays, fancifully shaped precious mementos engraved in nearly every language of the globe. A library of catalogued scores marked by the Maestro's hand. Photographs of the rotund beaming little conductor next to long-dead European royalty as well as the pantheon of composing immortals from Verdi, Puccini, Rachmaninov, Mahler to Stravinsky. Above the drawing room's oak mantel hung a portrait of the conductor with his short, stout arm holding aloft his baton: the artist had captured in the round, alive eyes a hint of that cheeky young Charley Frye whose musical genius had wowed Queen Victoria. Facing Firelli across the dadoed room – and the decades – hung a somewhat cloyingly roseate portrait of Althea.

The caretaking couple, thrilled at entertaining a real celebrity like young Mrs Firelli's mother, Rain Fairburn, served the two women a midday banquet which included a joint of beef with savoury roast potatoes and a rich treacle tart drizzled with double cream. The afternoon was miscrable – cold, windy, with lowering skies that threatened rain. Marylin would have been content to nap. BJ, though, insisted that they walk off the caloric overkill. Swollen by the sweaters and California-weight suits under their overcoats, they buffeted their way along the windswept promenade closest to the sea.

The tide was high. Choppy breakers charged up the narrow, shingled beach, each seventh wave flexing in a crash against the sea wall. Salt dampness added to the chill. Marylin's gloved fingers were icy, her cheeks stung. She kept reminding herself that when in England one must accept such weather – but she couldn't help noticing that very few people were about. BJ, clearly, was having a wonderful time as she commented on the infrequent 'real English' types who passed. She fell silent, however, when one man approached them.

He was tall. The wind pressed his Burberry trenchcoat

against his lean frame and tangled his dark, greying hair. He walked with the least suggestion of a limp.

He looks just like Linc, Marylin thought.

That's too wild. I haven't seen Linc for years – decades . . . But from those snapshots of BJ's, he hasn't altered that much. Crazy, crazy, Marylin. How big are the odds of bumping into him at an out-of-season English seaside resort? A billion to one?

'Well, well,' BJ's loud voice chortled. 'Of all people, my brother!'

There are no odds, Marylin thought vehemently. 'You set me up!' she cried.

And with a dramatic gesture quite outside the range of her non-professional life, she turned, charging up a gravel path that led in zigzags through the wind-tossed shrubbery to the middle promenade. The outrage pumping through her was the strongest emotion she'd experienced since her husband had died.

She could not face Linc.

Since Joshua's death she had squirmed, flushing each time she remembered those poignant, what-might-have-been reveries. That terse, uncondoling condolence note! What a romantic idiot she'd been!

'Marylin!' BJ was puffing up the path. 'Are you crazy? Look, okay, I *did* plan it. But even if you've suddenly got a mad-on, Linc is my brother, you owe it to me to be polite to him.' Her hair, now dyed its original black, escaped to whip around her indignant face.

'Why can't you ever mind your own business?' Marylin shouted. She took a deep breath of salty air, realizing how ludicrously out of proportion her fury was. Lifting her gaze to the elephant-coloured horizon, she took a calming breath. 'BJ,' she said quietly, 'you've simply made an awkward situation for both of us.'

'Linc came of his own free will from Rome.'

'You've been cooking up this little scheme since before you got me to come to England!'

'Is that such a crime?'

'Does he think that I *agreed* to meet him?'

'So what?' BJ said defensively. 'And while we're on the subject, as far as I'm concerned, it took plenty of guts for him to show.'

'What does that mean?'

'That idiotic modesty!' BJ's retaliatory indignation was diffused by a brown-eyed sparkle. 'Honeybunch, I don't believe you've ever once stopped to consider that you aren't like the rest of us. It hasn't seeped in that you're not only unfairly gorgeous and young-looking, but you're also famous. The goddess of screen and tube gives Linc one look and runs like he's Frankenstein's monster – how do you think he feels?

Marylin knew exactly how. As abashed and miserable as she felt on reading that note. With an apologetic glance at BJ, she raced down the path to the front.

Linc's figure was dwindling in the direction of the Downs, whose summit, Beachy Head, was hidden by a low-hanging, nearly black cloud. She ran after him. By the time she caught up, her face was glowing with exertion.

'Hi,' she said.

For a moment he studied her, then, blinking, thrust his hands into his raincoat pockets. 'Hi,' he said gruffly.

Age, rather than increasing his likeness to Joshua, had lessened it, and now there was only the distinctive Fernauld nose and the darkness of the eyes. Linc's own character had moulded an air of thoughtful, quiet masculinity, which was other side of the coin to Joshua's flamboyant I-am-leader-of-the-pack personality.

'You caught me by surprise,' she said.

'I'd never have guessed!' For a moment it flared, that touchy edginess – how well she remembered the taut nerves of a quietly brave young Navy pilot pushed beyond his endurance. Then he said, 'So BJ didn't tell you I'd be here?'

'No. But I can't blame her. The past few months, I've been in the dumps. Negative about everything.'

A sudden gust of wind fountained spume up onto the

cement where they stood. To escape a dousing, they both instinctively ducked towards the bench. The mutuality of their movement drew laughter from them both. Probably it was this laughter that relaxed the tight-wound spring in Marylin's stomach.

'I'm sorry I bolted like that,' she said.

They started walking towards the Downs. Here there was less of a beach, and seawater puddled the edge of the promenade. They gave wide berth to the scallops of wetness.

Linc said, 'Not making the funeral threw me for a loop.'

'I got your note,' she replied. How could the words come so easily?

'God, *that*. I must have rewritten it thirty times.'

'You really did?'

They were talking with that old intimacy.

'I knew too much about your relationship with Dad. Over heavy on the sympathy seemed phony. Everything else was condescending to your marriage. Then there were my own feeling. About us. About you and him. A very rough letter to write. After I sent it, I decided I'd been brusque.'

'A little,' she admitted, smiling. 'A little. But why didn't I figure how difficult it was for you?'

BJ caught up to them. 'Well, you two, how's it going?' she puffed. With a glance at Marylin, she raised her big, round arms and ducked comically, as if warding off blows.

Marylin laughed, a soft, husky sound that was blown on the wind. 'You're forgiven,' she said.

'Beej, you're okay,' Linc said.

'Will you look at that sky?' BJ said. 'Come on, you guys, let's get a move on! It's about to pour!'

That evening the three of them stayed up talking until nearly two; rain drummed on the windows, but they were lost in the warmer climate of their youth.

The following morning BJ insisted on returning to her half-sister's Knightsbridge house by the 10.18 train. 'No, I absolutely won't stay. You guys need a chance to catch up without me and my big mouth,' she said, kissing them both.

The rain clouds had given way to blue skies with a few small, benign woolly puffs: though the temperature was only in the high forties, the sunshine made the day seem warmer. Marylin and Linc took a hike on the Downs. The thick, low grasses were sodden, and they hewed single-file to the gouged, narrow path whose underlying chalk gleamed whitely with yesterday's rain.

When the steep angle of ascent levelled out and the path widened so they could walk side by side, Marylin asked, 'Whereabouts do you live?'

'In Parioli, near the Borghese Gardens. Do you know Rome?'

'I've never been to Italy,' she said. 'They offered me *Roman Holiday,* but I – well I couldn't be there and not see you.'

'So it was Audrey Hepburn who won the Oscar.'

'Oscars . . .' Marylin looked at a blackberry bramble. 'I guess we're both thinking the same thing,' she said.

'Dad.' Linc paused. 'BJ told me he was pretty impossible at the end.'

'Getting old was very hard on him.'

'It must have been.'

'I cared a lot, Linc. Not love maybe, but real caring. Even when I didn't want to, I couldn't help myself. Joshua was like that. He put his mark on people.'

'Don't I know it!' The remark burst out of Linc with amusement and perplexity.

They began talking about Joshua, his openhandedness, his vigour, the way he had of taking over every situation, his rumbling voice, his ruthless tennis serve, the incredible talent that had propelled him, a very young man, to the topmost rungs of a fiercely competitive industry and kept him there. By the time they reached Beachy Head and gazed down at the sea ('It matches your eyes,' Linc said), they had not exactly laid Joshua's ghost to rest but had placed it in a comfortable position of repose.

Linc told her about Gudrun. 'Afterwards I realized how unfair it was to her, the marriage. When I saw Roy in Rome –'

'She never told me. When was it?'

'Before I got married – she'd just bought the store. Anyway, she warned me. But I cared for Gudrun, so . . .'

'BJ said she was a terrific lady. She remarried, didn't she?'

'Yes. She has a five-year-old, a boy. I get a big kick out of buying him Christmas gifts.'

They walked slowly back to the house in time for high tea. The caretaking couple put on a spread – rashers of gammon, soft-boiled eggs, toast, sponge cake, hothouse strawberries and rich clotted cream. Marylin served herself another dollop of cream, lingeringly savouring its textured richness.

'That's how you ate ice cream,' Linc said, smiling. 'You're the only person I ever knew who could enjoy a small scoop for a half-hour.'

It was dark long before they finished the meal. They went into the drawing room, which was the house's least draughty place, sitting on the well-worn Oriental rug to get full benefit of the electric logs.

'What I don't understand,' he said, 'is how you're even more beautiful.'

'Flattery,' she said.

'Truth,' he retorted, tracing the curve between her thumb and index finger, lightly, as if he were touching an iridescent soap bubble.

They had not touched before, and the headlong violence of her reaction to this slightest of tactile pressures frightened Marylin. Her heart raced, she trembled. An electric awakening that was fraught with peril. These past difficult years, the carnal side of her had been extinguished by work, worry, and by Joshua's repeated failures. Sex had become a defeated battleground, and even now she cringed from it. (This did not alter the fact that she was crazy in love.)

'Linc,' she asked, her soft voice shaky, 'do you know the

poem that ends, "I only know that summer sang in me/ A little while, that in me sings no more"?'

He moved his hand from hers. 'Edna St Vincent Millay,' he said. 'One of her best sonnets, and the saddest, I think.'

The caretaking couple tramped through the hall, calling out, 'Good night, Mrs Fernauld, Mr Fernauld.' They made their home in the carriage house. The side door slammed shut, loud, cheerful English voices momentarily mingled with the rustle of big old rhododendron bushes in the garden, there was the bang of a more distant door. Then Marylin heard only the final couplet of the Millay poem inside her own mind.

Linc, too, seemed preoccupied with morbid thoughts. 'Let's face it, my wife was caring, generous, bright, and so were Margaret and Jannie. I should've been happy with any one of them – except I never got over you.'

'Linc . . .'

'Just because I feel exactly the same about you as I did when I was twenty-three, that doesn't mean I'm going to jump on you the minute we're alone.'

The redness of the electric logs shone on her face. 'I wasn't worrying about that,' she said. 'It's me, Linc. I'm not . . . I'm not the same as I was. About . . . you know, about sex.'

There was a long pause. 'But you do still feel we belong together?'

'Of course I do.'

'Dad's old age was really rough on you, wasn't it?' Linc's expression was twisted with sadness. 'The Fernauld children left you to support his boozing and extravagances, didn't we?'

'I was his wife,' Marylin said. 'And there's been that sad mess with Billy.'

'Billy?'

'He was involved with Althea.' Marylin sighed.

'So it *was* true. I read it in the headlines and figured it was just more of their usual trash – the case made a huge stir in Italy. Were they together long?'

551

'Only a few months. I know I shouldn't speak ill of the dead – but Linc, she destroyed Roy's husband and a German art teacher. Naturally I was worried sick about Billy. I went to New York, talked to her. Somehow I managed to break it up. A couple of weeks later she went to Roy's house with that gun.'

'Do you know why?'

Marylin shook her head. 'Roy says she was sort of deranged about her father. Billy blames *me*. When he got back from Vietnam, he asked Charles to get him into Coyne New York Bank. He lives in Manhattan.' Marylin's lips quivered and she gazed up at Firelli's portrait. 'Since Joshua died, Sari's been a doll about the telephone calls. Billy's never once called. He's married – a cousin of Charles's, actually. I've never met his wife.'

'Ahh, Marylin.' Linc lifted his hand, as if to touch her shoulder, then splayed his fingers on the rug.

Marylin's flesh tingled painfully where he would have touched her, and she was very close to tears. Was she doomed to be fragile bric-à-brac, a useless ornament that could not be touched? But I love him, I love him, she thought.

It took all her courage to lean forward until the darkness of Linc's eyes filled her vision. She touched her lips to his.

His hand curved tenderly around her head, holding her mouth there. The trembling began again, and she twisted around so her breasts rested against his chest. Drawing her closer until the pressure of her double-strand pearls dug into her flesh, he covered her cheeks and eyelids with small kisses. Her nipples were as tender as they'd been when she was eighteen, her body felt as if it were melting, yet even now, caught in a riptide of physical pleasure, she could not repress her unhappy thought: This'll be another defeat.

To drown out the misery of it, she pulled at Linc's shoulders and waist, easing him down so that they could cling together on the rug.

'My love, my love,' he said, hoarsely, tenderly. 'Let's go upstairs.'

'No,' said Marylin. 'Here.' She pulled him closer, not recognizing her own voice because of the blood drumming in her ears.

When he went into her, she gasped, thinking: It's still summer. Then she thought no more. On a dusty rug woven in Shiraz, warmed by love and fake logs, Marylin Fernauld cancelled out the years.

A week later Marylin and Linc were married in this same old-fashioned, memento-packed room, a ceremony witnessed by Sari, Charles, the baby, BJ and the caretakers.

BJ, the matchmaker, was first to hug the bride. 'You're the two nicest people I've ever known,' she chortled happily. 'How can it possibly work?'

Epilogue

Family and friends converged on 25 September 1983, to celebrate NolaBee's eighty-fifth birthday. From Georgia came white-haired, shrunken cousins, from London Sari and Charles and their three children, Billy and his wife from Manhattan, Marylin and Linc from Rome.

Roy and Marylin threw the party, giving *carte blanche* to Per Hennecken, the feloniously expensive 'in' Beverly Hills caterer. He tented the entire back garden, decorating his clear plastic bubble with rented crystal chandeliers, tubs of European blooms. Gilt chairs and small round tables draped in matching emerald cloths circled a dance floor. As always with any Wace party, though, an irrepressible note intruded, a sloppiness that couldn't be blamed on the caterer – or the hostesses. After all, Marylin and Roy could hardly *not* serve the big, honey-cured Georgia ham brought by a Greenward kissing cousin, and neither could they ignore the cheesecakes and chocolate-mousse pies presented at the door by NolaBee's friends, so the ham found a place of honour on a folding card table and the desserts were displayed on the hastily dragged-in barbecue table.

After the buffet, most of the adults sat talking while the children – led by the Firellis and BJ's troop – gyrated in joyful, unpartnered confusion across the waxed boards. Sari and Charles shared a table with Billy and his slow-voiced wife.

Sari retained that look of leftover flower child, with the untrammelled cloud of dark hair and Frye boots showing

554

below the anachronistic ruffles of a lace skirt that she had discovered at a Knightsbridge antiques shop. Billy, though, had suffered a sea change. The curly brown hair had receded, and an additional thirty pounds were held in by his staidly tailored dinner jacket, the only formal masculine attire at the party. Billy had never forgiven Marylin. His magic gift of humour had disappeared someplace in Vietnam's blood-dyed rice paddies – or maybe in Althea's Fifth Avenue co-op. Charles had made the initial arrangements for him to enter the Coyne New York Bank, but after that Billy had skyrocketed on his own power. Within a year of his entry into banking, he had courted and wed Grover T. Coyne III's sweetly stupid daughter – and her prodigious trust fund. When Three had succeeded Archie Coyne as ruler of the Holy Coyne Empire, William Fernauld wore the purple shoes of heir to the imperial throne – the goal Althea had envisioned for Charles.

Billy's wife, wearing black enlivened by a strand of magnificent pearls, sat close to Charles.

Like Sari, Charles showed remarkably few changes: he still possessed the build, the lean command that goes with an immense fortune, but his old expression of aloofness was gone, replaced by a near-visible aura of contentment. His career of disbursing funds for Coyne International Relief and his marriage to this slight, love-filled woman had lifted him from his old stiffness.

At a nearby table, Marylin and Linc held hands under the green tablecloth, laughing with Róy and a pewter-haired lawyer named Cary Armistead. Roy had finally reconciled herself to her curly hair, and the greying fluff formed a nice halo to a freckly, pleasant face that was quite youthful – when not adjacent to her older sister's flowing loveliness.

Per Hennecken approached the co-hostesses, whispering that his staff was primed for the cake cutting. Rising, the sisters wound around the tables, bending over chairs of kith and kin. 'It's time, it's time,' they chorused, moving through the flower-swagged French windows into the dining room.

In the quiet living room a few of NolaBee's circle chatted,

while Mrs Cunningham, her recessive chin drawn down, nodded in agreement. These now were her friends, too. An unlikely friendship had grown between the raffish, still-juicy NolaBee, who had not a cent beyond the support of her daughters, and Gertrude Cunningham, a timid browser on the edge of her immense fortune. Several times a week the Belvedere chauffeur delivered NolaBee for lunch or dinner, happy visits when each widow elevated her dear departed to saint-hood and NolaBee repetitively embellished enjoyable anecdotes about 'the dear children' – as they called their mutual great-grandchildren.

Marylin, smiling to the elderly group, rested a hand on the rounded shoulders. 'Aunt Gertrude,' she said loudly, for Mrs Cunningham had grown hard of hearing, 'Mama's going to cut the cake.'

Mrs Cunningham, as best friend, led the teetering ladies to the plastic tent.

Marylin paused to examine a framed painting, Thea's birthday gift to her great-grandmother, a watercolour picnic scene that for all its joyous, ebullient primary colours was far from naive, a remarkable accomplishment for a twelve-year-old.

'Where on earth does Thea get it? I can't even draw a stick figure.' Marylin spoke ruefully to cover her pride. 'Nobody on either side of the family that I know of ever painted.'

'Althea did when she was young.' Roy spoke too loudly. 'And don't they say all the arts are one? You're an actress –'

'Was,' Marylin interjected.

'And look at Joshua's Oscars.'

'Let's not forget Firelli,' said Marylin. 'Firelli was the genius among us.'

Roy's cheeks and earlobes went yet pinker, and she hastily changed the subject. 'That Valentino is fabulous on you, Marylin. Everybody's saying you're more gorgeous than ever. A walking ad for matrimony.'

Marylin winked. 'Now, if only I could cook.'

In the Parioli flat, the moustached Giulietta managed

magnificent pastas and veal dishes while her daughter handled the laundry and cleaning. Marylin Wace Fernauld Fernauld for the first time in her adult life did not work: in the nearly ten years there had been one cameo appearance in a Costa Gravas film. *The Rain Fairburn Show* residuals and the lease money from the estate on Mandeville Canyon brought in far more than enough for her obligations to NolaBee. Marylin indulged herself with reading or pottering in the mornings while Linc researched. Afternoons, the couple would stroll hand in hand like children through Rome's ancient, narrow streets, either shopping or browsing or visiting the antiquities for Linc's work – he took photographs on request of his clients.

'And what about you?' Marylin asked. 'I really like that Cary. Mmm?'

'I *told* you, Marylin, he owns the unit next to mine, and that's all.' Roy was blushing again.

After Althea's death, the journalists and writers had stormed her house with their insinuating questions about the gunshot, a persistent harassment that had distorted and fed her own doubts. She had needed five hours a week with Dr Buchmann. The psychiatrist had suggested that in her fragile state the reporters were too much for her. Selling the tract house, she had bought an opulent condo in a Beverly Hills full-security building. Recently the next unit had changed hands and the new owner, a well-to-do middle-aged widower, had become a frequent guest in Roy's bay-windowed dining ell. He gave her red roses and suspense novels, he took her out to movies. Roy, whose masculine friendships consisted of expense-account lunches with hearty-smiling designers or manufacturers' reps, didn't know what to make of Cary Armistead's undemanding affection – or her emotions towards him. She knew only that for the first time in many years she looked forward to going home at night. 'Just a neighbour.'

'I reckon he figures he's a mite more.' Rain Fairburn was not entirely dead – Marylin's fond, arch mimicry proved that.

'Well, who knows what evil lurks in the hearts of men,' said Roy.

BJ poked her head into the room. 'So here you guys are,' she said. 'I've been looking all over. What a fabulous party! I've been having such a ball I forgot to show you the valuable heirloom.'

'Heirloom?' Roy said, laughing. 'We're all heirlooms.'

'This one has to do with my first triumph – and yours, Marylin.' BJ slowly, portentously opened her purse to draw forth a yellowed photograph folder imprinted with a palm tree and the words 'Sugie's Tropics.'

'Ye Gods!' Roy cried. 'Where did you dig that up? There hasn't been a Tropics for thirty years.'

Marylin reached for the folder. The sharply black-and-white glossy showed four smiling girls crowded into one side of a booth. Their shoulders were padded, their lips darkened. Roy and Althea had flowers tucked into their tall pompadours. 'The night of the junior-class play . . .' she murmured.

Roy took the photograph. Althea's proud, happy young face smiled up at her. Fifteen years old . . . or were we fourteen? The irreconcilable grief for the dead came to squat like a toad on Roy's heart. Oh, Althea, best friend, worst enemy, rival, I would give everything I possess to have you here tonight.

Those charming, radiant young faces . . . How come we were so positive we were dogs? We were all really quite pretty. Marylin, of course, was spectacular. What's that clunky pendant she's wearing? Of course, Linc's ring. Poor thing, that's why her smile is so heart-breakingly sad. She thinks he's dead.

Roy held the photograph to a lamp, scrutinizing it in an attempt to recapture what had occupied the hearts and minds behind those callow, unlined faces.

Love, she thought.

We wanted to love and be loved. Love's what we talked about endlessly, conjectured about, yearned for.

Maybe it was a flicker in the electricity, but Althea's

plucked, arched brows seemed to rise, sardonic and knowing.

Am I being sentimental? Roy asked herself.

No, she answered herself firmly. No. Love's what we wanted then, and love's what we've searched for ever since. Materially, we've had everything – and more. But our careers, our worldly successes, have always played second fiddle to the search for love. Old-fashioned, maybe, cornball, yes, but true. BJ appeared to have found the warmth early on. Marylin took most of her life to find real happiness – but now, oh how the joy shines from her. Althea's inscrutable wounds denied her love. And I . . . I got to the centre of the mystery, only to have love devour me alive.

She touched the slick paper. These four girls smiling with dark-lipsticked mouths would intermingle their dreams, their frustrations, their hopes, their lives, their blood. And in the end, all that would remain of them was this chemical imprint – and the mortal products of their love.

In the tent, the band struck up a fanfare.

Roy closed the folder, handing it back to BJ. The three women hurried to the tented bubble.

The cake had been wheeled in on a linen draped cart to where NolaBee waited. Holding out her low-tar cigarette, she rested her other hand on the hip of her loose, short silk dress – a shrunken Southern-belle flapper. 'Come on, you all, cake time,' she was calling to the few guests who still sat at their tables. Waitresses edged through the crowd, proffering trays. Everyone, even the teetotallers and children, took a glass of Mumm's.

It was prearranged that Linc make the toast.

'I've known this delightful Southern lady since 1943, soon after she moved to Beverly Hills, a town she has enriched by her lively presence. She's related to me in a great many ways that are too confusing to go into, but even if she weren't, I'd have fallen utterly for her. She charms everyone who comes in contact with her. I give you our most beloved birthday lady. NolaBee Wace. Mama.'

The assembly raised their tulip-shaped glasses, toasting.

'Now Linc,' said NolaBee coquettishly. 'I reckon that was a nice-enough speech, but you mustn't go around mentioning all those dates. Don't want the folks here to figure out my age, do we?'

Laughter.

As NolaBee plunged the beribboned knife into rich chocolate cake, the band played. 'Happy birthday ... happy birthday dear NolaBee [Mama, Grandma, Great-Grandma, Aunt, Cousin] . . .'

The munificent shared warmth surrounded Roy, and her singing wavered.

Charles – Gerry's son – gripped her hand, and Linc, who was holding Marylin's shoulders, put his free arm around her. The sisters turned to each other: their eyes were wet as their lips curved in smiles.